D1222707

THE WAY
TO THE
LANTERN

BOOKS BY AUDREY ERSKINE LINDOP

THE WAY TO THE LANTERN

NICOLA

MIST OVER TALLA

THE SINGER NOT THE SONG

FORTUNE MY FOE

SOLDIER'S DAUGHTERS NEVER CRY

THE TALL HEADLINES

OUT OF THE WHIRLWIND

THE OUTER RING

THE JUDAS FIGURES

The WAY To
The LANTERN

BY AUDREY ERSKINE LINDOP

DOUBLEDAY & COMPANY, INC., GARDEN CITY, NEW YORK

1961

With the exception of actual historical personages, the characters are entirely the product of the author's imagination and have no relation to any person in real life.

For Eve, With Love.

My grateful thanks are due to Cyril Hughes Hartmann for his invaluable help in checking the historical details of this book.

THE WAY
TO THE
LANTERN

Chapter 1.

To LIVE under the threat of death ennobles some people. Unfortunately it does nothing of the sort for me. I seem to have none of the resources my fellow prisoners are able to draw upon. They appear to have hidden reserves of endurance and resignation and some of them even achieve what seems to be a genuine gaiety.

Certainly there are a few on whom despair has written a very readable message — a certain grey look about the cheeks — but even they keep themselves quietly apart, and while they don't join in the grisly games that add daily to my nightmares, they make no objection to them.

The strain of maintaining an outward nonchalance has completely destroyed whatever modicum of humour I may have possessed. The thought of death and a mass grave has never moved me to gales of laughter. Nor have I ever acquired sufficient strength of character to clout a loved one happily on the back and give him a cheery, "My turn next."

They brought me here in the usual hackney carriage.

I was an object of a certain amount of interest to my escort; in the year 1793 the French authorities were not used to persons walking into the offices of the Committee of General Security in the early hours of the morning and giving themselves up! Much less could they understand my heated insistence on my correct identity. They felt, I imagine, that as I was going to die as a matter of course, the name in which I was despatched was hardly important.

When our carriage rolled into the Cour du Mai, it looked as if the world's least charming women were holding a convention. I understood it was their usual afternoon entertainment. They came to put the fear of God into the new arrivals and gloat over the condemned. The place was packed with them. They had taken up their positions as if the courtyard were a circus ring. Some of the abuse they shrieked even I wouldn't care to commit to paper. A gentle-looking girl with pretty eyes and not much older than my Puce called out to me that they were welcome to my head but that she would give a lot for the lower part of me! The others clapped, stamped their feet, and pelted me. I hadn't far to walk before I got under cover, but my face and clothes were spattered with filth.

Everything from rotting fruit to fish heads had been shied at me. One beauty emptied the contents of her chamber pot from the top of the perron just as I ducked inside.

In the Registrar's office I argued again, "I am *not* — I am *not* who you think I am. I can prove it. I have witnesses. All I need is the time to persuade them to speak in my favour. Surely you can give me a little time?"

The Registrar gave me a disinterested look and continued to record me incorrectly in his ledger. "You're putting down the wrong name!" I shouted at him.

The Registrar swung himself round in his armchair. Behind him a tall window had been screened halfway up, so that the light fell over the top of it. The Registrar stretched a hand to the racks behind him. With his pen in his mouth he pulled out my dossier marked "L."

"I don't come under 'L,' " I bellowed at him. "I should be under 'R' if I'm there at all."

"You are here," he informed me mildly, "under 'L,' 'B,' and 'R.' Today we are concerned with 'L.' Yes?" he said, looking up at a man who had just pushed past me. The man handed over a slip of paper. It was an execution-er's assistant submitting his receipt for the poor devils just delivered to him. He stared at the floor whilst the Registrar filed the receipt. "Very well," said the Registrar and jerked a thumb over his shoulder, "you can get on with that lot."

My stomach turned when I glanced in the direction of his thumb. There was a wooden-railed glass partition behind him. Sitting on a bench were three men and a boy. They looked as if they had spent the night there. The boy had his eyes closed and was gently whistling, and one of the men was solemnly ploughing through a bowl of stew. Their necks had already been prepared! I turned away. I felt giddy. It wasn't the last time I was to feel giddy in that little partitioned-off space. It was there that the final hours were spent between sentences being passed and carried out.

The executioner's assistant gave up his floor survey and nodded at me in passing. "Hot today," he observed as if he felt some pleasantry were required of him. Then he went off to join his colleagues, who were checking their batches in the bedlam outside.

The Registrar opened my dossier. He looked me up and down, his tongue between his teeth. "Height six feet and two inches. Yes," he agreed and put a tick beside it. "Hair — black. Yes." Another tick. "Strong build but no surplus flesh on him." He examined my waistline for several seconds before he grudgingly accorded me a further tick. "Yes. Eyes —" He referred to the dossier. "Eyes — ginger!?" The tongue appeared again as he peered patiently up at me.

"Light brown," I snapped, but he ticked off the ginger.

"No scars on face or upper part of the body, but distinct tooth marks on right buttock."

"A dog bite as a child," I told him curtly. "I am sensitive about that scar. It has often humiliated me."

"I'm afraid I must witness it, citoyen," the Registrar said.

"But you know where it is — on my bottom."

"I have only your word for it, citoyen."

I took two steps backwards. "I'll be damned if I'll take down my breeches for you!"

"Then they will have to be taken down for you." He put out a hand to pick up a bell.

"Very well," I said. With ill grace I lowered my breeches, turned round abruptly, and presented him with my bare backside.

I heard him grunt as he leaned over his desk for a closer view.

"What happens if you get a woman bitten in a place like this, or worse?"

"She is sent to the infirmary and examined by a doctor. Thank you, citoyen, I've seen all of that side of you that I care to see."

I hiked up my breeches and faced him again.

"Now, then," he said, "I see that you claim some theatrical experience?"

"Blast you, man, I *am* an actor. I've been one all my life. I've never been anything else. It's because I'm one of the best in the world that I'm here now."

He interrupted me to take a sheet of paper from my dossier. He was one of those who read better with their spectacles on their forehead. " 'Took part in *Julie ou le Bon Père*. Secret Agent Jean-Claude Barrière of the Committee of General Security saw performance and stated worst he had ever seen. So-called actor was late for entrance causing embarrassment to fellow members of the company and amusement to the audience. Was unable to remember his words and fainted before the curtain fell. In the opinion of agent Barrière this man had never been on the stage before.' "

I clutched my head, lifting my hair in exasperation. I tried to speak quietly, appealing to him. "Now listen, you're a man of the world, I can see that. You've probably had more women than I have. That's the first time I have ever been off, or forgotten my lines. I had been making love; I had indulged myself too dearly; I sapped my strength; my body was beaten, my legs wouldn't carry me; I collapsed; I —"

He closed the dossier, folding his hands. "And you say that you are not the ci-devant Philippe-Jean-Baptiste-Raoul Vicomte de Lambrière?"

"I've said so fifty times and I'll say it another fifty."

"It would be strange if two different gentlemen received the same bite on the same buttock from the same dog."

"But it isn't two gentlemen, idiot: it is one gentleman — *myself*."

The dossier flicked open again. He pushed up his spectacles and peered at it. "There is a letter in the files of the Committee of General Security written by you to a lady in England to whom you were apparently betrothed. You signed it in the name of De Lambrière. There is also a letter from the lady herself claiming that you are the ci-devant Vicomte and offering to come over and prove it."

"Yes, yes, but she has a motive for all that. You see, the poor woman isn't right in the head. She just wants to have her revenge on me."

Up went the glasses and down went the eyes to the dossier. "It states here that the lady is personally acquainted with the Lieutenant of Police and she has always struck him as possessing considerable qualities and excellent sensibilities. He adds that he knows of few more reliable witnesses."

A second executioner's assistant came in to hand over his receipt, and when I looked up, the four prisoners from behind the partition had gone. I never heard them go. They must have trooped off without a murmur. Only the half-empty stew bowl was left.

I shook my head and tackled the Registrar again. "You've already admitted that you've got me down under two other names as well. I can't be three different people, can I?"

He glanced back at the racks of dossiers. It was like standing in a paper graveyard. Those shelves held the neatly filed premature ghosts of thousands of innocent people. The four behind the glass partition were buried in those racks long before they trooped out so quietly on their living feet. To me it was one of the most ghoulish rooms in a place that was full of ghoulish rooms.

"B," said the Registrar and stretched out an arm for a second file. "Mr. Anthony Buckland from the English Sandgate, near the town of Folkeston?"

"I am not Mr. Buckland and I've never been to Sandgate. I was obliged to adopt other identities when pressed."

"As Mr. Buckland you are of interest to the Committee of Public Safety."

"My name," I said slowly, "is Roberts. R-O-B-E-R-T-S. Roberts!"

"The agent Jacques-Phlipon of this committee states that it was his duty to trail Mr. Buckland of the Sandgate in England exclusively. We have here his full reports taken in gaming houses, cafés, and fashionable salons, as well as in the section commonly known as 'L'Étuve.' We have a record of Mr. Buckland's activities and conversations. The conversations, I must remind you, in certain cases were thought to be spoken in native English."

"But of course I speak perfect English: I was brought up there. I've already told them all that at the police office."

"And yet you are a Frenchman?"

"I was born here. I left when I was one year old. I also told them that."

The Registrar was clearly tiring of our interview. He sighed when he picked up my third dossier. "Citoyen, the man Roberts you claim to be is dead. It will be foolish of you to waste the time of the Tribunal with these concoctions."

"The man Roberts," I said doggedly, "is not dead. Otherwise how could he stand before you?"

"Citoyen!" There was a weary rebuke in his voice by now. "The agent Henri Pont, attached to the Tribunal in a special capacity, has obtained through the services of agents amongst the émigrés in England the following notable fact." He read out brusquely, " 'The man Roberts, sometime actor connected with the Little Apollo theatre of the English Somersetshire Department near Bristol, was in the English year 1789 drowned with his uncle in the river calling itself . . . calling itself —" The pronunciation of the word stumped him. The spectacles moved right to the top of his head.

"It calls itself the Wissey," I supplied, "and he wasn't my uncle."

"Ah, yes, the river of the Weezy in the Department of Norfolk."

"We weren't drowned. We did it on purpose. It suited us to appear dead. I have also explained all *that* to them, when I gave myself up voluntarily to the Committee of General Security."

He was an amiable man not easily put out of humour. I think he was seriously considering whether I might not be better suited to the prison infirmary. There were quite a few who became temporarily unhinged by their trials. He smiled at me. "The English miss has sworn on the Bible of her mother that you are not this acting Roberts."

"I tell you she's got good reason for that: it doesn't suit her to have been betrothed to a common actor. It pleases me to tell you that the committees are taking the evidence of one of the worst oppressors of the poor they're ever likely to meet. That woman's a born enemy of the people. She doesn't think they've a right to exist unless it's for her convenience. I've heard her myself refer to the sans-culotte as dirty rabble."

The Registrar raised reproachful eyes. "And you felt it an act of patriotism to betroth yourself to a lady of this kind?"

I stammered a bit at that. "Well, I severed the connection, didn't I?"

He referred to the dossier. "In the report of the Committee of General Security the lady claims to have had that honour herself." Then he told me gently, "I wonder that you trouble who it is that claims you. Does it matter so much? The Committee of Public Safety, the Tribunal, or the Committee of General Security? There are something like forty thousand revolutionary committees in France. We may content ourselves that one of them will get you. Does it matter which one it is, or what they call you?" He began to enter all my three names into his ledger and signed his own name to the hour and the date he had received me. "After all," he added, "our police are known to be exceptionally fine. There exists no more efficient body and our agents are second to none. It would be singular indeed if they failed to trace three gentlemen bearing the same marks of the same teeth of the same dog on the same buttock."

With that he rang a brass bell on his desk. A gaoler with a fluffy grey bitch at his heels answered it. "Escort, if you please," the Registrar instructed him. "The ci-devant Vicomte de Lambrière, and Mr. Anthony Buckland of the English Sandgate, and the late citoyen Roberts of France and Bristol to the Mousetrap."

The gaoler seemed quite undisturbed to be conducting a single personage. They are used to oddities in the Conciergerie.

The Registrar gave me a cheery flutter of his fingers in farewell.

The gaoler was amiable too. He told me that his bitch was called Fitchi. He also observed that it was hot and stood courteously aside whilst I preceded him through three more wicket gates. The prison became even gloomier from then on. Its close walls and passages seemed to snap off the daylight like snuffed-out candles behind us. The gaoler continued to chatter as if we were taking a social stroll in the Palais-Égalité. "We have had the ci-devant Queen in here since yesterday."

I made no comment. I am still a staunch Republican and have never been in favour of Royalty. But I was sorry for anyone who had been in this place since yesterday. It must already seem like an eternity to the poor woman.

I was destined for the Mousetrap because I could not afford to pay for my board, which would have made me a "pistolier" and entitled me to a cell on the ground floor or the first storey overlooking the men's court. The less fortunate class, the "pailleurs," were sometimes forty-five in a cell with ten straw beds between them. I was not even as lucky as that.

The Mousetrap was a hive of underground cells. A prison inspector who visited us the other day expressed himself incapable of describing it. He tottered out overcome by the stench. There is no air in these dungeons that has not already been breathed by hundreds of people. Add to that the heat of a fine August, the smell of mouldering straw, fetid clothing, human sweat, excrement, and frequently stale vomit and you have a moderately accurate picture of the charms of the Mousetrap.

Rats came up from the Seine by the sewers and pattered over the bodies of those fortunate enough to find room to lie down, and those forced to stand all night often fainted from fatigue and lack of air.

I managed to grab the gaoler's elbow and demand a lawyer. He reminded me that the old order of advocates had been suppressed, but if I made my request in the right quarter I should be allowed a "semi-official counsel for the defence," as they were newly named.

My fellow prisoners crowded round me in the exercise court. I was startled to find that some of them called themselves after the loving nicknames they had given their filthy cells. I was introduced to a "Monsieur le

Comte de Morgue," an "Abbé Chambre de Mouchards," a "Comte de Paradis," a "Monsieur de Tour Bonbec," and a "Vicomte Grand César." The more horrible the cell, the more jocular they seemed to become about it.

My colleagues were far from cheering over the services of "semi-official counsels."

"My dear fellow, it's a waste of time," said the Comte de Morgue. "It's true that the law still insists as a sop to revolutionary justice that a prisoner must be represented, but it's impossible to get hold of a good counsel."

Monsieur de Tour Bonbec chuckled happily. "Speeches for the defence are inclined to be a trifle timid as well as terse. Your counsel is far more worried about his own head than yours, and you can't blame him. After all, it's a recognised crime to defend the accused."

"But surely," I protested, "there must be some people who practised at the old bar with enough love of justice to —"

The Comte de Morgue interrupted me. "There certainly are and no more courageous men exist. But an advocate of the old régime has to present a Certificate of Patriotism to the Tribunal before he's allowed to officiate in court. If by any chance he hasn't got one, there can be some extremely awkward questions asked as to why not. To apply for one proves you haven't got one. You can see why they're never too willing to practise."

"Well, what about the new ones — the 'semi-official counsels' — aren't any of them any good?"

"They're all called 'semi-official counsels.' It's just a name. There's no such thing as the old-fashioned lawyer any more, and you don't have to have any training to defend. I could defend you and you could defend me and we'd still be called 'semi-official counsels.' "

"He wants to avoid Lafleurterie," laughed the Grand César, who was a boy of about seventeen.

"He certainly does," agreed the Comte de Morgue. "Lafleurterie was hired to defend some Carmelite Nuns we had in here. He scuttled down to their cells and demanded two hundred livres before he took on their defence. They had no money at all, of course, so we all put together for them."

"Then" — Monsieur de Tour Bonbec laughed again — "he stood up in court and told the jury that in his opinion no laws were severe enough to punish his guilty clients. He next asked permission to read them a thundering revolutionary lecture!"

"Very well," I agreed, "I won't ask for Lafleurterie. But who would you advise me to ask for?"

"No one," said Monsieur de Tour Bonbec. "Just sit down and take your medicine. You'll have to take it in any case."

"He'll have to have someone," said the Comte de Morgue. "He might just as well ask for the old school — and providing they can rake up a

Certificate of Patriotism between them, one of them might oblige."

"What I can't understand," said the Abbé Chambre de Mouchards, "is what makes him think he has a case."

"Well," I explained, "I'm not who they think I am. They've imprisoned me under a false name."

I might have made the wittiest remark ever to have been heard in half a century. Their arms wound round each other's necks in laughing.

"Tell him, tell him," gasped the Tour Bonbec, quite breathless from the humour of it all, "about the Public Prosecutor and the Duchesse de Biron!"

The Comte de Morgue was not quite so convulsed, but he was obviously vastly amused. "Well, you see, the Public Prosecutor ordered the Duchesse de Biron to be brought up to the Grande Chambre for her trial, and when they went to fetch her, they found there were two women of that name. So the Public Prosecutor said, "Good. Bring them both up!"

"And the pair of them went before the Tribunal," giggled the Tour Bonbec, "and were executed the same day on the same charge as the same person."

Great laughter greeted this. The Comte de Morgue added, "So it really doesn't matter what you like to call yourself. But we'll give you a list of the good advocates' names, if you like."

I was lucky. Out of a list of eleven, one of them consented to see me. His name was Lavaux and I was allowed to meet him in the "parloir," a bleak little reception room with uncheering railings round it.

I was marched in by a Tribunal gendarme and came face to face with a youngish and fresh-complexioned man. "We're privileged," he said: "more often than not I don't get an opportunity to see my clients before they're executed. Sometimes I get woken in the early hours and told to defend someone at ten o'clock."

"It's very good of you," I said, "to consider defending me. I gather it's almost as dangerous as being the accused."

He laughed. "Yes, you're right there. And I have to confess to you that I haven't a Certificate of Patriotism. But the Public Prosecutor has waived it aside. I really don't know why — perhaps he has an inclination towards justice — it's hard to believe. But on occasions I have had dealings with him which prove that he's not entirely without a conscience. I wouldn't put it more strongly than that."

"Then you think that I might have a chance?"

He gave me the impression that he thought I was making some kind of a joke. "No," he said, "I don't think you've got a *chance*, but I think we should do our best to try and disprove that dismal fact."

When I had told him my story he sat thinking. "So you claim to be an actor?"

"I *am* an actor."

"And you claim that you're neither the ci-devant Vicomte de Lambrière or Anthony Buckland from England?"

"I insist upon it."

"You took these names to suit yourself and through forces of circumstance you were obliged to act the parts of these two men in private life?"

"I was."

"Well," he said cheerfully, "even if we can't save you we must certainly try to see that you're executed in your right name." I thanked him for this courtesy and he began to take notes. "Now, from what you tell me, the Committee of General Security — which as you know has charge of police affairs now and in fact took over altogether from the police of the old régime — think you're the ci-devant Vicomte de Lambrière?"

"They seem convinced of it, and the Lieutenant of Police himself unfortunately knew me by that name."

"Then that makes you the Vicomte de Lambrière in the eyes of the Committee of General Security. Not a happy position in these days when one can be condemned to death for merely having a friend with a title, never mind possessing one."

"Quite," I said.

"The Committee of Public Safety, on the other hand, may not have been established very long, but in that short time it has achieved supreme power — *supreme* power. It looks after the affairs of the Revolutionary Tribunal and it has far greater authority than the Lieutenant of Police and his Committee of General Security. Now, these people, you tell me, think you're an English agent by the name of Anthony Buckland spying for Pitt's government?"

"So I'm led to understand."

"Both these committees will have had their agents on you, and while they're supposed to be working together I can tell you in private that the rivalry between them is acute. Their agents frequently spend more time watching each other than the victim. The Public Prosecutor is the servant of both of them: he certainly harries them into finding him victims, but he is subservient to them. He can't very well stand the same man up in the same court at the same time and accuse him of the crimes of two different people."

"According to my colleagues," I said drily, "he can."

Lavaux smiled. "Yes, it's been done, but not quite in that way. One person has been executed as two before now, and two people as one, but that's largely on paper, so to speak. Your case, I rather fancy, is somewhat different. We might find that the two committees are very anxious to prove themselves in the right. In which case they will both need to keep their man alive to prove it" — he smiled wryly — "at least for a while."

I jumped up. "Then you *do* think there's hope?"

His head shook. "No, there's not much. There might, of course, be a counter-revolution, but I doubt it. Our best hope is that officialdom is very jealous of its authority even in ordinary times. We can only pray that they'll neither of them want to be shown up for making a mistake. But it's time I need and I don't think they're going to give it to me."

He was right. Within half an hour of his leaving me I was called before the Tribunal.

My knees, attractive though they can be, are never my friends in moments of stress. They sounded to me like cymbals clashing together. My mouth was so dry that I might have been sucking fur and I felt giddy from fright. A janitor cleared my pockets of all personal possessions and I was marched up gloomy stairs and along a corridor that ended in the fateful Grande Chambre.

An appalling noise was coming from inside. It was all so swift that terrified though I was I can recall very little of it. I remember the judges taking their oaths and I remember the Public Prosecutor beginning to read the indictment against me. He had scarcely begun when an usher pushed himself forward with a note. The Public Prosecutor read it, conferred hastily with the judges, and then called out that the case of the ci-devant Vicomte de Lambrière had been temporarily adjourned. I was seized, bundled down the stone staircase, and pushed back in the Mousetrap. My colleagues were astounded to see me, but not as surprised as Lavaux when I saw him again in the parloir.

"I didn't even know you were being tried. They said they sent someone to my house but I was out looking for witnesses. Fortunately I went to the Tuileries and lodged a complaint with the Committee of Public Safety first. I gather they sent a note to the Public Prosecutor forbidding him to accuse you in the name of De Lambrière. They don't want the Committee of General Security decapitating their man."

"It doesn't make me feel any easier in my mind," I pointed out, "to know that both of them are so keen to behead me."

"No, but it might give us time. Nothing and no one is safe or sacred now, you know: even the committees must look to their laurels. It wouldn't do for either of them to have it known that they had wasted Republican time and money by having their agents trail the wrong man. I'll do my best to stimulate their confusion. I shall furnish them both with evidence that they are both right. In the meantime, I can't wish you a short stay in prison. Let's hope we can make it as long as we can."

With that piece of comfort he left, and I must say that however fearful the alternative may be, I shall never be thankful for prison life.

Chapter 2.

I HAVE always been fascinated, but never so much as now, by the infinitesimal splinters of chance that go to make up a person's fate. At which precise instant is that fate sealed and how far back do you have to go to pinpoint the vital step that took you to destruction?

A man who has been educated at great expense, say, to take a distinguished place in the world trips on a piece of orange peel and breaks his neck before he has fulfilled his promise. Whom should he blame and at which point? Should he — providing there's an after life that would permit him to brood upon the matter — consider only himself at fault for not looking where he was going? Or was his destiny settled earlier than that, at the moment when he chose to walk down that particular street? If so, he might owe his death to the friend he was meeting and who picked that particular rendezvous. In which case he could blame bad luck in making the acquaintance of that sinister individual.

Perhaps he should throw all the responsibility on the man who dropped the orange peel. In that event, was his end foretold when the fellow ate the orange or when he finished it? Was carelessness or hunger the cause? And what about the fruiterer who sold it to him? If there had been no oranges in stock, would the victim have been saved or would his killer have gone from shop to shop until he had managed to purchase the death weapon? It could even go back to the black hand that picked the fruit, or perhaps even the wind that scattered the seed in the beginning. Was it devil, or was it God?

Some of my more disagreeable friends suggest that in my case there's no need to look any further for the cause of my present predicament than my own character. I'm inclined to think that's unjust. After all, there have been thieves, liars, and murderers who have ended up on thrones before now. The fact that I have been all three with less success needn't necessarily account for my situation.

Nevertheless, there must have been some traceable moment when I took the one irrevocable step that brought me to this state of misery. It might have been when the crook of Manager Smith's umbrella first caught me round the neck. It might have been when the Puce's little thin fingers rifled my pocket, or when Nicholas Hawtrey lacked the courage to propose to Lizzie Weldon. It could have been when Marie-Clarice leaned out of her carriage and shouted the filthiest language at me that I had ever been privileged to hear. It could also have been when I first looked into the sleepy eyes of the Lieutenant of Police, but was it? I suspect that my orange peel was dropped much earlier than that. It was probably the moment when my father took off his false nose. My mother would never have fallen for him if he had remained in it — so I should never have been born. I have had occasion lately to wish that he had kept it on. He was an actor. How bad or how good I don't know. I never met him. All that was left of him which I could remember was a box in the attic. It had "John Charles Roberts" printed out on the lid in brass studs and contained a rotting periwig and three false noses.

My mother, Marie Lambrière, was a French laundress, and whether my father lured her to England with a promise of marriage I am not sure; he certainly never honoured it. She found herself with me in her arms at one year old in Liverpool and my father nowhere to be seen. She was not long finding a second Englishman, the Yorkshire farmer who married her for her cooking. Having done that, he told her he preferred "honest food" and refused to allow her to "mook anything oop" (obviously he found her sauces more appetising before they were married and perhaps it was the same with her lovemaking). I don't doubt he took advantage of her talents before the preacher made them his legal right; but afterwards he denounced them as "fancy French tricks" and "reet disgoosting." Apparently what was all right for an unmarried girl was not considered "nice" for a farmer's wife. He must have been an extraordinary man to prefer bad food and a cold woman just because he put a ring on her finger. My poor mother merely cooked with the confidence of any ordinary Frenchwoman and probably made love the same way, and she bitterly resented my stepfather's lack of appreciation. She worked up a steady hatred of him and I rather think slept off most of her chagrin in the company of the beastman. She used to come in with ominous bits of straw on her back and a somewhat smug smile on her face.

To annoy my stepfather she made a point of speaking nothing but French to me both in private and in public. Feeling ran high against the French in those days. The war had broken out the year after my mother's arrival in England. All friendly relations had been broken off by the two countries except between smugglers, and anyone coming "from over there" was an object of deep mistrust.

My stepfather was kept in a state of constant embarrassment by my mother's returning "Vive la France" to her neighbours' cold "Good morning." She was always known as Farmer Mason's French trollop, and I was her "Frenchy brat."

When I was ten I ran away. There was no real reason for it. No one was unkind to me. I was neither beaten nor starved. I was just ignored. Something I could never endure. So I rolled my belongings into a pack on my back and set off at six o'clock one very cold spring morning. It was eight before I had reached the grey huddle in the distance which called itself a town. In my spare pair of breeches on my back there was a whole round cheese and I took it out and munched it. It was an exciting moment striding out for freedom. The heather tufts, still brown from the winter, caught at my feet and a sweet wind skipped along beside me, tugging at my clothes like a mischievous puppy.

My real father's blood must have sung in me somewhere. The world of entertainment called me at once. My first job was as a tumbler in a circus wearing a false nose! I was not a noted success, but the engagement brought me to the attention of Sebastian Martyn of "Mr. Martyn's Celebrated Players." "Mr. Martyn's Inebriated Players" might have been a more accurate name for them. The leading lady and the leading gentleman frequently put back several pints of ale between them before a performance, and at the end of it they came very near to resembling the circus tumblers.

Mr. Martyn, who was happily out of touch with anything to do with real theatricals, minded nothing so long as his actors appeared. As we always played the yards of inns, he was often disappointed even in this modest wish. The leading lady was particularly difficult to dislodge from the taproom. Gin was her favourite tipple and it always reduced her to tears, which welled out of her great face like the overflow from a water butt. In view of this we tried to restrict her to tragedies. The audiences, who set up a fine odour of cow dung in hot weather, were delighted with her. They felt they were getting their money's worth when she sobbed throughout the piece. Hiccoughs invariably overtook her towards the end, but by then her admirers were always too much in sympathy to mind.

My debut was made in *The Sorrows of Mr. Jenkins*, or, *Should the Husband Tell*, although it was not strictly as one of the cast. We were playing in the courtyard of The Lion and Lamb in a busy market town. Halfway through the piece, the audience hanging over the inn gallery bombarded Mr. Martyn with rotting produce, but by the end they cheered him — entirely owing to me.

A sheep dog took exception to the comic. I was in private sympathy with the animal: the man was the worst comedian I had ever seen. The dog refused to allow him to make a re-entrance and pinned him up against the mounting block. I was sent to distract the dog and try and get it to return to its owner. Instead it sank its fangs into my bottom. The scar is angry to this day and is the one in which the French government are taking such an interest. But the audience literally rolled in their seats and I got the biggest ovation I have ever received.

Because of my public appeal I was promoted. A part was actually written for me in *The Unhappy Wife*, or, *Mrs. Dockery's Secret*. I was an angel the heavens would have failed to recognise. I was dressed in a torn sheet and enormous wings and my role required me to beckon Mrs. Dockery to her poignant end. Our rendering of the play was probably nothing like the original, but we had to do something to excuse our heroine's steady flow of gin-caused tears. My instructions were to retire backwards with an expression of "lofty piety," chanting, "Follow me, follow me, heaven is summoning you." Unfortunately Mrs. Dockery was no slimmer than she was sober. When she was stretched on her back in the death scene she was quite incapable of regaining her feet. While I was hovering above her, overacting grimly, she hissed, "Get me arse off the floor, yer gobby lout."

Owing to the fact that she was fourteen stone and I was an underdeveloped eleven-year-old, the odds were somewhat uneven and the end of the production was inclined to be drawn out. Heaven might have "summoned" her for ever if the male portion of the audience had not joined in. Strong country arms hauled up the sobbing, hiccoughing mass of flesh and bore her off between them like a slung ox.

Word soon went round that the angel had not the physique to manage Mrs. Dockery's ascent and the public poured in to see the fun. It brought me great personal acclaim. Mr. Martyn was most appreciative of my ability to make the audience feel personally involved in a production. The episode of the dog and the angel earned me his highest esteem short of payment.

From that day on, although I had only one line to say and that in English, my name always appeared in the programme with "French-speaking" in brackets beside it. Mr. Martyn was very conscious of effects. My stock rose even higher because of my improvement to the angel's wings. To these ungainly protrusions of greying cotton on painted frames I attached pieces of string. By putting my hands behind my back and using an even more "lofty expression" to cover the action, I was able to open and close them. The audience was greatly impressed. If my name was never billed, my effects were. *The Unhappy Wife*, or, *Mrs. Dockery's Secret* was announced after that as including "Angels with REAL LIVE WINGS."

I still got no salary, but I was allowed the food when the rest of the company had left the table, and I was promised a pint of ale on Saturdays. This last I rarely had more than the privilege of holding. Mr. Martyn, a puny, mild little man in most ways, became a positive tyrant if his pocket was touched. He was a deadly foe of waste. I've often gone to bed on half a cold potato because he thought I might leave a whole one uneaten. As for the pint of ale, I seldom got further than the first gulp. He would seize it from me and swallow the rest, reproachfully. "There may come a day you'll give a lot to have finished that ale, my lad. It never does to squander food nor drink."

When the Celebrated Players moved to Tunbridge Wells with a Spanish farce, I was still an angel, for Mr. Martyn had every intention of putting the "real live wings" into every production he undertook. It was difficult to fit me into those Bo-peep revels set in ancient Spain, but he worked me into the third act as a vision. It was my sixteenth performance and my "lofty piety" was growing more and more intense. I thought I was excellent. I didn't think it would be long before I found myself at the Lane.

My success made me more than unpopular with the rest of the company. All the lesser members of the Celebrated Players had to sleep where they could find room. Beds were only provided for the leads and there were often three of those tucked into one. I chose to be under the table in Tunbridge Wells because the rain was given to pouring through the roof of our lodgings. I used to make a tight cocoon of my angel's sheet and open my wings against draught. I should have been quite unable to unwind myself in time if the house had caught fire, never mind achieve any amorous tricks, but the comedian accused me of raping his wife, a leggy lady on whose elbows one could have cut a quill.

The leading lady, leading man, and the villain all swore they had seen me "roll on top of this beauty in a bestial fashion." In point of fact all I was doing was retrieving a mutton bone she had filched from me, but in my mummified state I was obliged to buffet her with my head and tail like a rocking chrysalis.

I think I was twelve at the time. My birthday is unknown to me, because Mother was in a wine haze for about a week before I was born and could never be sure on which day she produced me. But she was fairly certain of the year.

Mr. Martyn loyally supported me by saying that no one stark naked and burned up with unfulfilled desire would have troubled to turn over and rape the woman, let alone a child who would have had to struggle out of a shroud for the purpose. But I used the story to my own advantage. By putting up a deliberately weak denial, I managed to give people the idea that I had been justly accused. I allowed the pot boys and the stable lads to embellish the story, and spread the rumour myself that I wasn't safe with anything female from eight to eighty. It came to be true in a way later, but at that time my voice was scarcely broken. By carefully fostering this reputation for precocious sexual powers, I was able to steal scenes in which I should never have been noticed otherwise. I became the taproom's wonder boy, and the object of considerable interest on the stage.

I was also quite unbearable. My conceit was beyond imagination. I believed my own characterisation of myself. Convinced I was the ladies' dream and a menace to their menfolk, I used to strut about in my sheet and wings, masking people, cutting in on their lines, winking and bowing to the appreciative bumpkins who shouted lewd encouragements to me. What was worse, I also made myself believe that it was my acting that drew the applause. I'm sure I felt that there was nothing I could learn from Garrick himself. There was absolutely no one I admired as much as me.

Mr. Martyn, who put the French-speaking angel with live wings into any piece, however unlikely, never minded what I did as long as I could be responsible for keeping the audience from drifting away, or from having loud discussions amongst themselves, as they often did when a piece bored them.

It was just as well I left Mr. Martyn when I did. Had I remained I should have ruined for life all my chances of learning to act. Also, I think one of the Celebrated Players might have saved my present would-be executioners the trouble of putting an end to me.

Chapter 3.

THE REASON I came to deprive Mr. Martyn of the benefits of my genius was that it was one of my many duties to fetch the comedian a pint of ale from the inn each night. On a wet, black evening in mid-November my sheet-like draperies were hitched round my stomach and my wings were water-logged like full sails in a storm. I was about to go back to the barn where we were playing, carefully carrying the ale, when a voice bellowed at me, "Boy! Come here!"

I turned to peer into the darkness and from somewhere behind me a cold instrument hooked me round the neck and pulled me forward. I got quite an affection for that umbrella later. But I was terrified of it then. I had never seen such an apparatus in my life before. I was convinced it was some kind of deadly firearm.

I dodged the crook and stayed in the small circle of light shed by the inn lamp. I could still not see the owner of the voice.

"Boy!" it said, "what's your name?"

"Actor Roberts, sir," I answered nervously.

"Oh, it is, is it? Then if you call yourself an actor, what makes you turn your eyes up like a winded 'orse?"

"I am portraying an angel," I replied with dignity. "Mr. Martyn's very pleased with my expression. I'm *supposed* to keep looking towards heaven."

It was a deep voice and the most expressive I'd ever heard. "Mr. Martyn!" It scorched the name. "Mr. Martyn knows as much about acting as I do about the midwife business." Then the voice demanded, "What's that you've got there, boy?"

"Ale, sir," I told him, and held my hand over the top of the tankard to keep out the rain.

"Very well. I'll take a sip. It's not me favourite tipple, but I'll take a sip."

He moved into the light then, a great black figure dressed about ten years behind the fashions. He wore a morning frock under a large coat and a bob wig that hadn't been powdered for months. He was holding the programme of our wretched little Spanish frolic. His eyes were a strong grey and his eyebrows were dark above them. He bared his teeth when he breathed in. His sip drained the tankard. He put it into his pocket, looked me up and down, and tapped the programme.

"French-speaking, are you?"

"Yes, sir. Sir — you've put the tankard in your pocket."

"I won't say you'll do," he said. "On the other hand, it's too early to be sure you won't."

"The tankard, sir," I said, "it belongs to the inn, sir."

"When you learn to forget your face and make use of your stomach, when you stop turning up them horrible eyes and put your bones into it, you'll probably still be a disgrace to the boards, but I daresay you won't be worse than some."

I was about to fetch the landlord when he mentioned money.

"How much does old Martyn pay you?"

"Nothing."

"Then that's the first bit of sense he's ever shown. Well, there's the offer, boy, do you want with it — a shilling a month and your food."

"But what for?" I asked. "What would I have to do for it?"

"Do? Do what you're told, of course. But it's just as you like: go back to old Martyn and turn up your eyes. It's the best way to stay at the bottom I know."

Under the wig, which was by no means a fit, his hair was thick and strong. "Manager Smith, boy," he introduced himself. "Lambert Smith — ran the Yorkshire circuit under Tate Wilkinson — seen you three times and think you're worth saving. There's an honour for you! But do what you please." He turned to walk off, but I caught at his coat.

"Where shall I find you," I asked pompously, "if I can get out of my present commitments?"

He jerked his eyes towards my wet sheet and wings. "You can drop your present commitments in a puddle. Join me now or you don't join me at all," and he walked off sturdily into the night.

It was then that I found out that an umbrella was not a lethal weapon. Nevertheless I remained in considerable awe of the great black mushroom that kept the rain off his head and shoulders.

I was in a panic of indecision. A man who had run the Yorkshire circuit and bothered to see my performance three times! I tore off my wings and struggled out of my sheet. I wore the only suit I possessed underneath, so there wasn't any luggage trouble.

I followed him cautiously at first. I was nervous of catching him up, yet anxious not to let my first paid offer out of sight. I could hear his hard foot-steps ahead of me. There was a cluster of shops at the end of the town and he seemed to be making for them. He turned into a pawnbroker's. The rain racing down the windowpanes made the light of the one candle inside jiggle and dance. It was difficult to look in, but I saw him pass the tankard over the counter and pick up two coins in exchange. He came out whistling. I dodged quickly back into the darkness, but he didn't even trouble to look for me. I followed the sound of his whistling like an uncertain dog. At the crossroad he kicked open the door of an ancient posting house and went inside.

It was spitefully cold and I was drenched. I hung about for a quarter of an hour. But there was a strong smell of onions and roasting meat, and the firelight glinting beneath the door tempted me. I pushed it open and looked in. He was sitting in a settle, his frightening umbrella hooked over the back. He was staring steadily into a mug. I tiptoed across and sat opposite him. I didn't dare attract his attention. I sat with my hands pinned between my knees and tried to swallow quietly. It was several minutes before he spoke to me. Then he held up his mug. "Hot ale and ginger, boy! It's the finest thing out for preventing a stoppage of the bowels."

"I haven't got a stoppage, sir," I said.

"You haven't? Well, remember it if ever you're blocked. A good actor needs to keep his bowels open as well as his eyes and ears." Then he patted his stomach and told me mournfully, "I'm labouring under the stone. You won't have me with you for long." I wondered what kind of a stone it could be. I think I saw it as one off the roadside and I couldn't think of how he had come by it. He leaned forward so suddenly he made me jump. "No!" he said, as if I'd spent the last half-hour trying to persuade him. "You won't get *me* under the surgeon's knife. No, my boy, I'll bear with the stone for your sake."

"Thank you very much, sir," I said. Later I learned that nearly every form of nourishment other than beer, brandy, or wine "came hard" on the stone.

The pawned tankard paid for our dinner and a double bed. It was a luxury for me after a year with the Celebrated Players. Manager Smith lay propped up against the bolster, his arms folded. His face seemed to have no bones in it, yet there was some kind of power behind it which enabled him to hold any expression he cared to assume for any length of time. It was gloom at the moment. "The late Mrs. Lambert," he told me, "would have settled your eyes. Turn 'em up in front of the late Mrs. Lambert and you'd have been short of a backside. *There* was an actress for you!"

"Yes, sir."

He gave me a push out of bed. I was cold in my patched shirt and a little sulky when he shot a question at me. "What destroys an actor, boy? What destroys him most?"

"Mr. Martyn?" I ventured.

He laughed at that, but shook his head. "No, it's reading and learning without *looking*. An actor has to learn to *mark* people, boy. People and things."

He leaned out of bed and tugged the bell pull. The pot boy answered. He was loose-boned and gangling. "Two hot ales and ginger," ordered Manager Smith. "Now," he said to me, "who's your mother and who's your father?"

"Well, my father's name was Roberts. But my mother's —"

"Wrong," he said. "The theatre's your father and mother. Who's your wife going to be?"

"Well, I don't know yet, I —"

"Yes, you do. The theatre! Who's your mistress going to be?"

"The theatre?"

"Right. When this lad comes back with the ale I want you to study him. Mark everything you can about him."

When the pot boy came back with the order, I watched him carefully. After he went out, Manager Smith pointed to the tray and said, "Take that to the door and bring it in like he did."

I was so cold I was only thinking that the hot ale would be a good idea after all — stoppage or no stoppage. I carried the tray to the side of the bed. I was startled at the anger of Manager Smith. He bellowed at me, "Didn't I tell you to *mark* him? Didn't I tell you to look? You should've watched every inch of him — seen how he breathed. *Actor* Roberts indeed."

And he made me do it over and over again until the ale was cold.

When we were sipping it in bed at last he sighed. "*Actor!* You wasn't a pot boy, you looked more like a sickly stork." A fierce depression seemed to settle on him. Then he emerged from a silence to say, "I fear it's the second Mrs. Lambert for you, my boy."

"Is the second Mrs. Lambert alive?" I asked. I was so sleepy my eyes felt full of mud.

"She is," he snapped, "and she's not the second Mrs. Lambert yet. For your sake, she will be — but it's a rare sacrifice. A rare sacrifice!"

Chapter 4.

WHEN WE woke up he was still depressed. He ordered me to get dressed quickly and be ready to start.

"Where are we going, sir?" I asked.

"Never you mind," he snapped. "It's a rare sacrifice, a rare sacrifice." Then he added, "French-speaking, didn't you say you were?"

"Yes, sir."

"That might come in very handy," he told me.

I gathered that the "rare sacrifice" must live somewhere in the south, since that was the way we seemed to be heading. He told me he had "played out" the north and I could imagine that it was not always as an actor on the stage.

I began to realise the way in which he might have run the Yorkshire theatre circuit under poor Tate Wilkinson, and possibly the reason he was not running it still. His gold tortoise-shell watch had initials entwined on the case. But they bore no resemblance to an "L" and an "S." On the other hand, they bore a very readable likeness to a "T" and a "W."

I asked him about it. "Did Mr. Wilkinson give you his watch in return for your worth, sir?"

He turned his strong grey eyes upon me. "Nothing could have repaid me for my services to Tate, boy." With that explanation I had to be satisfied. But when we left the inn with another tankard and three pewter spoons, I began to wonder whether perhaps my new friend was not entirely honest.

It was not long before he left me in no doubt whatsoever.

For some time, tramping beside him, my spirits had been in tune with the ominous lights over the black lump of cloud ahead of us. It was an eerie, threatening sort of day and I felt afraid of the big man beside me. The road was lonely. We had only passed one carter and a postillion galloping to a stage.

Manager Smith said nothing to me by way of explanation, but he suddenly spoke out loud to himself. With his hands behind his back and his head held well down into the darkness of the day he seemed to be answering someone I couldn't see. "Yes, yes," he said, "disgraceful! I'm with you, sir. Disgraceful." His voice and whole manner were quite unrecognisable. He now had a precise little stammer and a fussy little twitch in the corner of his right eye. He kept winking it most evilly at me; he swallowed his words and then began them again in a kind of rumble. He seemed to have put twenty years on his age.

"Disgraceful," he said, "you take your life in your hands with these drivers today. Y–y–yes, yes indeed you do."

"Beg pardon, sir," I piped.

"Being a legal gentleman," he replied. "I shall have no difficulty obtaining retribution, and my clerk here will bear me good witness. Yes, a g–good witness. Aha! Yes, aha! Hum!"

I became convinced that I had thrown in my lot with a madman. His subsequent actions did nothing to calm me. He pitched me into the ditch, held me down, and then rolled me over and over in the mud like a housewife flouring a lump of beef. He plastered my hair with slime, slapped it all over my face, and made sure that my clothing had soaked it up. Then he helped me out, stood me still, and hacked at my breeches with a sharp-edged stone. As soon as he let go of me, I made for the open road, but his umbrella hooked me back by the leg.

"Stay where you are, boy," he thundered.

I stood. I watched him wallow in the ditch himself like a great crow taking a bath. After that we proceeded along the road in silence until he ordered me, "Limp."

I was so dazed and frightened I hobbled along peg-legged. It was better, I thought, to obey him in everything. Lunatics become more violent if crossed.

I think I was crying behind my mask of mud. The first person we saw I intended to rush at for help. In the meantime I must pretend that I saw nothing amiss. Lunatics are sensitive about their sanity.

"Boy!" he suddenly bellowed at me, "what's your name?"

"Ac–Actor Roberts, sir."

"Wrong. Ned Salmon, apprentice clerk."

"Yes, sir," I said brightly, "Ned Salmon."

"One of five, mother dead, father alive, brother ran away to sea at nine."

"Yes, sir."

"And who am I?"

"Manager Smith, sir, late of the Yorkshire theatre circuit?"

"Wrong. Benjamin Pollack. Legal gentleman of Cheapside. *Much* revered."

"Much revered, sir."

"And me father the same before me, *much* revered."

"Oh, yes, sir, *much*."

"Now, listen carefully, boy. Four miles down the road our post-chaise overturned. Thrown into the road and lucky to escape with our lives, we were. Every penny piece we had and every bit of baggage strewn from here to kingdom come. The postillions are collecting it up and following us up with it on their backs. Come near to breaking your leg, didn't you, boy! LIMP!"

I limped.

"Now, what's your name?"

"Act — Ned Salmon, sir."

"Right. And who am I?"

"A legal gentleman, sir, much revered like your father before you."

"Right. Well marked, boy, well marked."

He made me repeat everything over and over again and I was utterly relieved to see a squat little inn in the distance. I should demand protection of the landlord and refuse to leave until Manager Smith was well on his way.

"Ah!" he said suddenly in his own voice. "The Plough, if I'm not mistaken. A draughty hole and the beds are bad, but it's good enough if you don't intend to spend any money there."

Chapter 5.

JUST BEFORE we reached the Plough he gave me further instructions. "When I wink at you, boy, get up and go out. Pay no attention to what I say to you. Just walk ahead and wait for me in the next village you come to." Then he became the old-maidish Mr. Pollack again and stumped irately into the Plough.

I really couldn't get over his performance. He was a typical musty old legal gentleman in looks and speech and even smell, I thought. He fitted so well into the part that I could have sworn he managed to alter the shape of his bones. He nearly had me believing the accident that had taken place a mile or two up the road.

"Disgraceful!" he snorted. "Disgraceful! You take your life in your hands with the drivers these days!"

The landlord, his wife, and the few customers in the Plough were full of indignation on our behalf. It was all the fault, Mr. Pollack assured them, of the reckless young man who drove as if he wanted to get us to our own funerals before time.

"Not fit to transport the p–public. I k–kept on warning him. Young Salmon here will tell you the number of times I warned him."

Young Salmon agreed that his employer had spent the better part of the journey trying to persuade the wretch to spare our lives. Everyone else agreed that there was not a good word to be said for modern youth. Their love of speed and pleasure and their lack of respect for their elders had not only overturned our coach but was threatening the stability of the whole country.

"There's several sitting back up the road nursing their bumps and bruises," Mr. Pollack said, "just because one young fellow's dad didn't take a big enough stick to him when it would have done him some good. Young Salmon here will tell you they're lucky to be alive."

Young Salmon said that the other passengers were a pitiful sight with their bruises and bumps.

"I fancy you'll have them all here very shortly," Mr. Pollack told the landlord. "So I think we'll take our dinner while you've still enough food."

We had eaten five courses and drunk two bottles of the best French Burgundy wine when Mr. Pollack discovered that his purse had also been hurled into the ditch.

"I'm likely to find it empty," he grumbled, "if I don't offer 'em a reward to bring it back full." He borrowed a shilling off the landlord for me to go and bribe the mythical postillions who were supposed to be bringing our baggage on their backs. The shilling would persuade them not to tamper with the contents of the purse. "Be sure to look in it first, young Salmon," he ordered me, "before you hand out the reward." And he added, in case I'd forgotten my injury, "Go easy on that knee of yours." Then he winked at me.

I got up, limped out of sight, and trudged along the road towards the next village. The first thought that entered my mind was to run away from him. It was a great opportunity. I had enough money to rejoin Mr. Martyn or attach myself to another troupe. The only thing that kept me undecided was the wonderful performance he had given as Mr. Pollack. I couldn't fail to learn something from an actor as good as that. On the other hand, there was the disquieting thought that as he was not oversensitive to the more ordinary differences between right and wrong, the pair of us might see the inside of a gaol.

The day was getting darker and a fog was creeping up. The bare trees seemed to me to spread out their branches like galleons, and the fields looked flat and desolate. There was a penetrating chill in the air, and with evening coming I felt younger than my years and not very confident. The prospect of another comfortable bed such as we had shared the night before and another steaming remedy for a stoppage, sipped before a cosy fire, was alluring. It made the thought of escape and trying to find shelter in this sparsely populated countryside a much less attractive alternative. I kept telling myself that I ought to strike out through the woods and hide until I had seen him pass. But the fog hung between the trees like gloomy cobwebs and I could imagine the undergrowth filled with goblins.

I was still plodding along the road when he overtook me. He was riding a pony that he had borrowed from the landlord to go and see what had become of young Salmon. In spite of my qualms I was not sorry to see him. He was so big and cheerful. Now that he was not playing Mr. Pollack, the muddy stretch of the road seemed unfriendly no longer and the fog less menacing.

"Up you get, boy," he said.

I clambered up and he slid his hand behind him. "I'll trouble you for that shilling I gave you, boy."

I slipped the "postillion's reward" into his hand and off we jogged. At the first turning we came to, he left the main road.

"Doesn't do to stay in the same neighbourhood when you've taken people's hospitality," he explained.

"Sir," I ventured, "isn't it wrong to — to *take* hospitality?"

"An actor," he told me quietly, "gives a lot to the world, boy. He can laugh it out of its sorrows: he can brighten up its dull life. He shows folks things they'd never get a taste of without him. It doesn't hurt them to support him once in a while when he's inconvenienced. A *good* actor, that is." He added sternly, "No one owes anything to a bad one."

In case our reputation had travelled a stage or two before us, we kept well off the main posting route and concentrated on isolated inns. He was most incensed when I asked if we were going to play Mr. Pollack and young Salmon for our bed and board that night.

"Certainly not, boy. We'll pay like decent travellers. Have you forgotten the tankard and spoons I borrowed? Besides, it's unprofessional to use the same names twice."

I think he guessed from my silence that I was still a bit bothered by a certain little point connected with honesty. My mother had been a strong Roman Catholic. While she was obviously untroubled by such sins as love-making out of wedlock, she had always been very firm about other people's spoons. My ears had once been boxed for stealing a slice of beef from our own larder.

"Boy," said Manager Smith, "there come times in an actor's life when he hasn't got a stage under him. When that happens, there's only one good part left open to him. He has to play Lord Credit. There's many different characters you can fit into that name and it's all in a good cause if it helps to put a stage under him. That's if he's a good actor. A bad one does better to starve."

The tankard and the spoons paid for a reasonable bed in a tiny stone-walled inn miles from nowhere. I remember my glow of well-being that night. The supper of hare soup, followed by bread and cheese, was plain but good. We also had two boiling hot mugs of stoppage preventer. We sat sipping them in front of a fire that hissed from the damp moss on the logs. A whole cured pig hung down from a hook in the ceiling. I pushed my legs out, enjoying the warmth of the hot ale and ginger. The fog had closed in round the house like a blanket nailed over the windows, and I felt thankful I wasn't hiding in the tangle of a damp wood. It was pleasant to feel I had a protector in the big man beside me, even though his protection took a rather strange form. I was sure that evening I had made the right decision in staying with him — and even as things have now turned out, I've never regretted it.

The next day we sold the pony. He said that word might have gone round about our free lunch at the Plough and the pony would help people to recognise us. We had to let it go for a poor price because we couldn't afford to have too many questions asked. I dealt with my conscience by telling myself that it was all to put a stage under us.

The money would have kept us going for quite a while, but Manager Smith told me that on a long journey you had to look ahead. I was puzzled when he bought an empty leather trunk and new clothes. He chose sober clerical garments for himself, but for me there was the smartest suit I had ever seen. I was quite beside myself with excitement.

He told me solemnly, "An actor has a thousand souls, not one to call his own. So the sooner you get used to other people's, boy, the better."

He continued to give me a rigorous training in "marking" people. I was made to give him a character sketch of everyone we met. I had to watch out for gestures and mannerisms. He had me trying to copy every type of accent we ran into, and it soon stopped being work and became fun. I enjoyed taking people off — from old men to young girls — and I began to take a pride in observation. I loved to find some little peculiarity about them and try and surprise him with it. He was, however, never surprised, having noticed it himself first. But he was appreciative. "Well marked, boy, well marked."

As soon as we were in our new clothes, we booked inside seats on the coach to Huntingdon. From the first he had been very insistent upon my keeping up my mother's language and I now saw why. We put my French ancestry to immediate use for the purposes of defrauding the George. I was to be a French aristocrat travelling with my learned tutor, the Reverend Mr. Jabez Stock. We added a "de" to my mother's maiden name of Lambrière, and with the addition of my own Christian names I became the young Philippe-Jean-Baptiste-Raoul Vicomte de Lambrière.

Mr. Stock was worth looking at in his black gaiters and parson's hat. As for me, I was so busy admiring my new silver shoe buckles I tripped up and dirtied my new velvet coat.

We bowled into the courtyard of the George and took a small room that looked on to the open gallery.

It needed a porter and a squinting ostler to carry our trunk upstairs. It was filled with stones packed round with straw to stop them rattling about. It was not only the ostler's crossed eyes that made me take notice of him. He was practically incapable of taking his share of the trunk from laughing at Manager Smith's ears. Those protrusions were M.S.'s worst enemies, the only part of him he could never disguise. They certainly stuck out in a most original manner and I realised that it was to try and hide them that he wore a wig a size too large. This same wig became dislodged on the gallery stairs and the ostler had a good view of his peculiarity. I heard him giggling to the porter, "Look at un's yeres, will you! Look at un's yeres!"

I was so annoyed that I used my new authority as a young vicomte to complain to the landlord. It was appalling, I told him, that my much revered tutor should be held up to ridicule by a hoggish ostler. No such impertinence would ever be tolerated in France. (How much I had to learn!)

The landlord bent double in apologies. We shouldn't be troubled with the lout much longer. He was due to marry a girl in Surrey and was transferring to an inn down there which was welcome to him. Nevertheless, the ostler was severely told off, and ever afterwards I thought he crossed his eyes at me more than before.

I imagined that Manager Smith would be pleased at the way I had taken the initiative in my role, but he was angry. It was dangerous to have drawn attention to the ears. It was bad enough that the ostler had noticed them, never mind emphasising them to the landlord.

My "tutor" took his job seriously. An actor must learn to read and write, and I could do neither. I began, in return, to teach Manager Smith French. On his side he threw in all the knowledge he had accumulated through a lifetime of "markings." It was an extraordinary mixture; scraps of history, Latin, astrology, fencing, how to be a gentleman, mathematics, doctoring, geography — everything, in fact, from tips on farming to how to beat the law.

He had no real education himself and his information was acquired through the eye rather than through formal schooling; it had no depths of learning, but it certainly had depths of living. It was like being shown life through somebody else's spy glass.

In public he addressed me as Monsieur le Vicomte. He was wise to have started me off as a French Lord Credit. I wasn't yet fit to play an English one. My voice was still in the flat in-between stage. I was affected by my mother's tongue and still had traces of my Yorkshire accent. It took me many years of "marking" before I hit on the true note of the "gentleman born." The aristocrat has an odd voice — borrowed in many cases from the lower orders. They will both talk about a "corf" for a cough, and "orf" for off. The top and the bottom so often speak alike. Who was taking off whom I was never sure, but they had words in common which the more careful middle classes didn't dare use. It took me a long while to talk from the bottom and be accepted at the top. Their conspiracy of carelessness was so close that the smallest slip was a complete giveaway.

If we had had a choice we would have stayed longer at the George to continue my education, but we were forced to leave at rather short notice. The landlord told us that we were in for some excellent entertainment: Mr. Martyn's Celebrated Players were coming to render *The Unhappy Wife*, or, *Mrs. Dockery's Secret* in the courtyard.

The George never suspected when we went out for an afternoon "walk" and left our handsome trunk behind that we had no intention of coming back for it!

We bought a small valise to impress our next lucky hosts, and searched round for more stones and some bracken to wedge them. Then we walked to Bedford. On the road to St. Neots a thick ground mist was rising like a wandering shroud. Out of it came a figure on horseback and ordered us to halt. We were told to deliver our money and goods. I made a bolt for the bushes but was hooked back by Manager Smith's umbrella. "You've no need to hide your face, boy," he told me, "we're bigger rogues than he is."

He showed the highwayman our valise full of rubbish and told him how we'd tricked the George. He wished us luck and sent us on our way. But not before Manager Smith had touched him for half a crown.

In Bedford we were just in time to catch the *Civility* as she was leaving the Red Lion for London. There was only a single seat left, so I had to sit on Manager Smith's knee. The *Civility* was very fast, but her springs were good, and for once Manager Smith didn't suffer. Normally he was a shocking victim of travel sickness. I'm convinced it was self-induced. He began to go green even before the wheels started to turn. I think he'd have been sick in a funeral car! We intended to pass straight through London. Our money was low and we were "not far off our pocket seams," as M.S. preferred to put it, rather than admit anything so common as being short of cash. But he insisted on visiting Drury Lane. Garrick was leaving the stage at that time and selling his share in the Lane, and I might never get another chance to see him. There was such a demand for him to renew some of his best-loved roles that he made them his official farewell. He gave his Benedict from *Much Ado*, *The Alchemist*'s Abel Drugger, Horatio from *The Fair Penitent*, his Hamlet, his Lear, and his Richard III. Being so young, I glorified chiefly in his Abel Drugger, but now I realise that there never was, never will be, and never could be another Richard III.

I stood in great awe of his name, although I'd heard it savagely criticised. Popularity made him enemies amongst his inferiors.

Many of the older pompous school despised him for his modern technique. Declaimers like Quin must have shuddered at his naturalism. Some even accused him of filching Macklin's style of playing Shylock. But the cause of the spite was really his success. When you think that Covent Garden and the Lane got him closed down at Goodman's Fields because of the way he was drawing in the public, it puts Garrick in his rightful place and them in theirs. Such people as Mr. Martyn of the Celebrated Players, called him a "tailor's mistress." This was simply an insulting nickname for an actor who stole someone else's hard-earned scene. The "tailor" who had cut the cloth and sewed the seams got none of the rewards, whereas his "mistress" whom he had clothed got loud applause for her beautiful dress!

It was nonsense to say it of Garrick. I've heard since from people who played with him — always from good actors, never from bad — that he "gave" to every minor character who crossed his path, and I'm convinced that his genius lay in that. He got the best out of everyone else as well as himself. He had an almost psychic ability to judge the mood of a house. His critics said he read the daily papers to study the nation's pulse. If it was slow he'd play to rouse it, and if it was restless — he'd go out to calm it. Anything for popularity, they carped. I often wish envy was wittier. He was the only God for Manager Smith. "You may have your Colley, Youngs, your Barry's — whoever you like! That's the finest portrayer of naturalness, boy, you'll ever be likely to see. Watch him for half an hour and you'll save yourself a hundred years of markings."

When the diligence left the Blue Boar at Holborn, my head was still swimming with Garrick. I took no notice of the other passengers. I was being assured by a wet-eyed Garrick that my Richard III had surpassed his. He was having to calm the house so that I might make my modest speech. They were tearing up the pit benches. I think I was vaguely aware that some-one was staring at me in an unpleasant manner, but I couldn't be bothered to look round, for Garrick had his arm round me. It wasn't until we were coming into Guildford that the nasty coincidence occurred. Someone had "marked" *us*!

We had sold our clothes and were no longer a parson and a vicomte. But a voice suddenly roared above the clatter, "There un be: I know un be un's yeres."

Of all the bad luck in the world! Behind us sat that blessed squinting ostler from the George. He must have kept his crossed eyes fixed on those "yeres" all the way from the Blue Boar. He was travelling to Guildford to claim his bride, poor girl.

"There un be all right," he insisted, "and there be lad. Left a box of stones behind at George and never paid a farthing, they did."

Even the inside passengers were hanging out of the windows to see what the noise was about, and the coachman warned us not to frighten the horses. M.S. went red in the face with honest indignation. He could do this when-ever he liked. He said he held his breath and then forced it down to press on his heart. He attacked the ostler in a thick Yorkshire accent. "Ee, lad, thou must be daft! We never saw thee before, nor thou oos."

"I swear I seen ye," the ostler said.

Manager Smith turned astonished eyes on him. "Nay, doest?" he asked, pronouncing it "doost". "I reckon thee must be reet mad," pronouncing it "mud".

I joined in with the same accent, and the ostler's confidence was certainly shaken. Nevertheless, he wouldn't give up. "The George to Untingdon," he told us sullenly, "were tricked by an old devil of a parson and a French lad — *yon* Frenchy lad!"

Manager Smith gave me a poke in the ribs which nearly put me over the side. He laughed until real tears ran out of his eyes.

"Tom Baits from Wensleydale, a parson! And my son, Willie, 'ere, a Frenchy lad! Ee, I could bust ribs wi' laughin'. Parson! Tom Baits from Wensleydale — and Willie 'ere, French lad! Oh! Wait til 'is moother 'ears joke." "Willie 'ere" also rolled about with mirth, echoing, "Aye, wait til moother 'ears joke!"

But the ostler was one for sticking to a point. "I know un by un's yeres," he insisted, and pointed them out to the other passengers. M.S. stopped laughing. He leaned behind him and hauled the ostler on to his feet. He had colossal strength and the man was lifted out of his seat like a babe from his cradle.

"Sit down," the coachman ordered. "There's no standing allowed at the trot."

"I've 'ad enoof o' thee," Manager Smith informed the ostler. "One more word from thee and I'll trooble thee to get down at Guildford court 'ouse and accompany me inside."

The wretched boy shut up at that. But when we got out at Guildford he was still muttering, "I know un by un's *yeres*."

After that Manager Smith gave me a warning about the pitfalls of playing Lord Credit. Apart from his ears, the greatest dangers he had encountered were coincidences. They were something impossible to guard against. "There's so many in life, boy. You don't always believe 'em when other folks tell you, but they're there, all right. Round every corner and on your tail all the time."

"Then what do you do, sir, if you can't avoid them?"

"You think fast, boy, like I did in that coach. Tom Baits sprang to me mind pretty quick, but if I hadn't gone red in the face, quick wouldn't have been soon enough. A second's delay and you've got 'em suspicious. But going red and wrathful gives your brain time to turn round and flurries 'em. I must teach you that trick, boy. It'll give you a touch of wind at first, but it's worth it."

As two Yorkshire bumpkins we booked a bed and had a good meal at the Cock Inn. M.S. had a pint of hot ale and ginger on the house as a reward for making the postmaster laugh at our being so absurdly accused of defrauding the George at Huntingdon. In the general merriment he even made me try to take of the "Frenchy lad" I was supposed to have been. I made such a careful mess of the Vicomte de Lambrière that there was no fear of suspicion. The postmaster was most unsympathetic towards the fate of the George. It deserved the two rogues who tricked it out of its just dues. "They'll oblige *me* by trying to catch *me* out," he boasted.

We obliged him by going for a walk before breakfast the next morning and not returning. We left our valise behind.

At Chichester we were undecided as to whether to trick the Dolphin or the Anchor. They both had good reputations for food and comfort. We sampled the ales of both, making a great show of treating other people on the last of our money. It was in the Anchor that we overheard an unpleasant piece of news. It was concerned with an incident that caused a lot of talk in the town. A horseman had galloped round the corner so quickly that he had knocked a woman down. There was a penalty for taking a corner too quickly in some towns (how I wish it was the same in France!), and an irate crowd had marched him off to the courthouse. He was the postmaster of the Cock Inn at Guildford. In his defence he must have told his story of our obliging him. He was soon released and ten minutes later the town crier was out. "O yez! O yez! To all whom it may concern!" He gave a rather biased description of us, I thought, and warned all keepers of inns, pliers of trades, and honest citizens anxious to protect their property to beware of a pair of cutthroats living on their wits.

We buried our wits in a hayloft for two days. Manager Smith made forages for food and heard that our detractors were on the increase. A messenger must have ridden to London and the Bow-street runners were out after us. The law had a long way to leg it, of course, but, even so, the prospect of its catching up with us was not reassuring.

M.S. told me that the sooner we reached the shelter of the Rare Sacrifice, the better. He never felt happy to think of himself as being the cause of the runners taking exercise.

I was practically gnawing my nails with curiosity over the Rare Sacrifice. But every time I mentioned her, his whole face seemed to darken and he told me to keep my questions to myself. I would meet her only too soon and have too much of her.

We had been on the road the best part of a week, hiding by day and travelling at night, when he suddenly brought up the subject himself. "Well, there it is, boy, a widow lady of many years standing who still minds being single."

"Is she pretty, sir?"

He turned his great mobile face to me and forebore to comment. At the next stile, with the wind on the prowl in the cold darkness, he said, "She's got a pretty enough little business though, and that's what we've got our eye on, boy. Not her rosy cheeks."

"Are we going to swindle her out of it, sir?" I asked cheerfully. I was no longer shocked by such a prospect.

"I wouldn't say *that*, boy. Certainly I wouldn't. *Ease* her out of it, I should rather say, and all to her own advantage. I've got another bit of property in mind, much more in our line. She's always fancied me since she saw my Lord Abberville in *The Fashionable Lover*. Kept after me till her husband came round to tell me he'd cut me up like a sheep's carcass if I went on making sheep's eyes at her."

"You must have fancied *her* at one time then, sir."

"I fancied helping her lighten her purse. But the late Mrs. Lambert was alive at that time — playing Augusta Aubrey she was. But when she came to 'I have no friend or refuge in this world,' she took a running kick at me shins on the stage and shouted, 'And no more will you 'ave if you go on gawping at Bessie Maddock!"

"I'm sorry, sir," I said. But he heard me sniggering.

"It's all very well for you to smirk, but I've never been a one for the maritals. I was put off it early in life."

"Does Mrs. Maddock know you're willing to make her a rare sacrifice, sir?"

"She does, but I dressed it up better than that. I wrote to her from Huntingdon. Said I was still hankering after her and I was coming to claim my reward."

"Then perhaps you could claim it without marrying her, sir."

"Boy," he said sternly, "remind me to watch your morals."

"But, sir, there *are* ladies who give in without rings."

"Bessie Maddock," he said shortly, "wouldn't pare you a quarter of turnip free unless you put a ring on her finger — never mind giving in to the maritals."

"Is she expecting me too, sir?"

"She is. You're the nephew my dying sister laid in my arms as a naked babe, and made me promise to protect."

"Did your sister really die, sir?"

"I hadn't got one," he said.

I felt horribly guilty. I couldn't forget that first night we met when I failed to mark the pot boy correctly. M.S. had taken the decision there and then that it would only be the second Mrs. Lambert who could put a stage under me. Of course I hadn't realised the nature of the Rare Sacrifice. I'd no idea he was going to have to marry a cumbersome widow and reinvest her fortune in order to insure that I no longer turned my eyes up like a winded horse. It was a frightful responsibility. My knees nearly gave under it. "Sir," I said, "couldn't we take up another profession?"

He stopped. It was dark, but I knew that he was staring at me. I counted up to thirty-five before we moved again and during that time I learned never to raise such an unfortunate topic again. Whatever happened — and God knows plenty has — I never suggested that we should take up another profession.

When he walked on, I followed him.

"Boy," his voice boomed from the blackness, "do you know what I could have been?"

I said, "No, sir." I had gone past taking risks.

"I could have been the son of a well-to-do malster if my mother had seen fit to put up with his snoring." Apparently this gentleman's nocturnal trumpetings were so loud that Manager Smith's mother refused to marry him. She switched her affections to the owner of a travelling street theatre, and M.S. was born on the road.

His childhood did not sound inspiring. The Smith family ended up in a cellar in Holborn, and at eight years of age Manager Smith took to the gin house. "I practically lived there," he told me. "It was better than sitting in

corners watching them knock each other about, and better still than watching them making it up. It was shocking to see them at love. The three of us
shared the same bed, you see: and I tell you, it set me against it. I'd come
home as drunk as an owl — no more than a nipper though I was — drunk
as a lord, on a squib of gin. I used to sing and dance for it. Then I'd roll
home and kick them apart for a place in the bed and snore through the lot
myself. But I never got over being set against it." He sighed when he told
me, "The first Mrs. Lambert was always failing, so she wasn't a one to press.
But the second Mrs. Lambert is *not* failing. It's a rare sacrifice, boy, it is
indeed."

When we reached the King's Arms I thought we were in for another
spell of Lord Credit. But no! The licensee was the Rare Sacrifice herself —
Mrs. Bessie Edith Maddock. We were home! I was cheered by the sight
of the place. It was a small but new building with big windows. I hate old
houses. Anyone's welcome to the picturesque places where Queen Elizabeth
slept amongst pokey inglenooks and gloomy gables. Give me the straight,
clean, modern lines and room to move about.

M.S. could hardly bring himself to go in. He was so low in spirits I broke
down in tears. "Please, sir, there's no need to be at love with someone you
don't like for my sake. After all, we've managed so far."

He looked down kindly at me. "We managed to eat and we've managed
to drink — but would you say we've managed to *act*?"

"Well, we've played plenty of different parts," I said.

"That's not acting, that's *marking*. It serves its purpose: it's better than
getting no practice at all. But it's not acting, boy."

"Well, if you ran the Yorkshire theatre circuit under Mr. Wilkinson you
must have many friends in the theatrical world who could help us."

"Oh, I have, boy, I have. The trouble is they're all after me. I've played
with the great one himself."

"Garrick?" I squeaked.

He nodded. "I was in his company for six months. Played with him at
the Lane. He was good enough to tell me I was one of the finest portrayers
of characters he'd ever seen."

"Then why didn't you stay with him?"

He shook his head sadly. "A fine actor but a suspicious nature. He lost
his gold watch one day and —"

"Oh," I said hurriedly, "I understand."

"They were all alike," he sighed. "I've played with the lot — Macklin,
Spranger, Barry, Cibber — fine actors but suspicious natures."

"Yes," I said, "I see."

"There's only one thing to do," he said: "strike out on your own, go into
management. There's where the second Mrs. Lambert comes in."

"You mean she'll buy us a theatre? One of our own?"

"She will, boy. Not the best, not the worst. But she'll buy us a theatre. I'll soon shift her savings into me box."

M.S.'s "box" was any receptacle in which he hid his money. It could be a boot, a handkerchief, the folds of his umbrella, or a chamber pot under the bed. But it always received the dignity of being referred to as his "box."

"Supposing she says no, sir?" I asked. "Then we'd be stuck with the second Mrs. Lambert and no savings."

"A lady's property," he told me, "belongs to her rightful mate: and I shall be her rightful!"

I was still anxious to stop him marrying for my sake. "Still, sir," I pleaded, "if it means being 'at love' when you're so set against it —"

"Boy," he said, "you've got it in you somewhere. Lord knows how I spotted it with them horrible eyes turning up, but it's there, all right. I don't want you to waste it like I did. Lord Credit's all right in-between times when you're short of a meal, but I don't want you to go getting him into your blood, or you might not get him out — like I can't. I'm not going to have you playing gin houses to get a free meal. I'm going to put a *stage* under you."

It's sad looking back to think he was too late even at that time. Lord Credit was already in my blood.

He pushed the gate open and we walked up the path. Manager Smith said mournfully, "Remind me to teach you to pick a pocket. It's useful when you're resting."

Chapter 6.

THE KING'S ARMS was only a mile from the village. The taproom was full when we arrived. Over the sound of voices someone was singing.

I was cheered by this. Bessie Maddock must be a popular landlord, I thought, and to be popular she must surely be pleasant.

M.S. pushed me into a bright stone passage and told me to go into the taproom.

"Commend me to the second Mrs. Lambert, boy, and tell her if she spares you a few moments in the kitchen, she'll find a husband waiting for her. She'll be serving at the counter, no doubt." He put himself through a green painted door and left me no option but to beard the Rare Sacrifice.

I pushed my way through the inn parlour. It was kept very clean and modern. There were no fusty corners filled with Elizabethan horrors, such as littered my stepfather's house in Yorkshire.

The customers were pressed to the counter like flies on a cold lamb chop. I had to use my elbows. When I finally cleared myself a space, I felt my first signs of my manhood. Not amongst the highly advertised "beauties" of Mr. Martyn's Celebrated Players had I seen such a pair of eyes and breasts. She must have been rising sixteen, I suppose, and her bronze curls made a match with the copper measures hanging on the walls. I could see the rarity of her, but I was blessed if I could see what sacrifice M.S. was making in tipping that dainty dish onto his plate. He was certainly not lacking rivals by the look on her customers' faces. "Dirty old dog," I thought to myself, "making such a penance of her."

I chose the most refined accent in my repertoire. "If you could spare me a minute in the kitchen, miss, you'll find a husband waiting for you." Gaiety seemed to live in her eyes and she had a dimple in each bare shoulder. Her dress just showed the rise of her breasts, pushed up by her stays. I grew up in the seconds I stared at her.

"Bit short for me, aren't you, lad?" she laughed.

An old farmer cuffed me playfully. "There's others before you on the list, my lad: you take your turn at the bottom."

"Strikes me 'e's too anxious to take 'is turn on top," another one said.

"Aren't you the second Mrs. Lambert, miss?"

"She's not first yet, lad, never mind second," the farmer joked. I realised my mistake and ran out of the room with my cheeks on fire. I collided with what can only be described as a minor mountain. Then I was nearly suffocated. Two big arms hugged me so hard that my nose glanced aside off a corset bone. "The mite," someone cooed, "the blessed mite!"

The blessed mite struggled fiercely, being quite unable to breathe. When I emerged, my face was caught between two wash-tub hands and my chin pushed up. I looked into a big, round face with chapped cheeks. Two bun currant eyes were wet with emotion. "The likeness!" she said, "I see the likeness. You're Lambert's poor sister over again."

Considering that M.S. had no sister for her to have seen, I was puzzled by this at the time. Later I ceased to be surprised at the things people make themselves think. The Rare Sacrifice didn't want her customers to suppose that she was "taking up" with a man she knew little about. Doubtless he'd just given her the story of myself laid in his arms as a naked babe and here she was recognising the non-existent sister who had put me there.

Yes, I learned that later; you tell people lies that they want to believe and you'll have them swearing to you that you're telling the truth. I learned it to my bitter cost.

The rest of the Rare Sacrifice was no more inviting. She had cut herself into two cumbersome bundles by a tightly tied apron. Her breasts, like those of the girl at the counter, were also pressed up by the string of her bodice, but hers were as chapped as her cheeks. She must have been a martyr to a constant raw wind.

It's possible that she was no older than five and thirty, but she looked to me as if she must have been past that when God began the world. When I realised that this was the sacrifice M.S. was making for my sake, I broke into uncomplimentary tears.

I was promptly hugged to the apron again. It had a most unusual smell, which I've since traced to meat stew. She was a great one for plunging her fingers into a pot, was our sacrifice, and she wiped them off on her apron afterwards.

She wrenched my wet face round. "Look at it," she invited the company. "Overcome! Maybe it didn't think it was welcome. The very idea. Lambert Smith's own sister's orphan boy and it doesn't think it's welcome!"

Actually, "it" was unable to breathe again on account of the corsets. When she released me she dealt me a kindly blow on the back which knocked me against the counter. I remember M.S. saying, "The second Mrs. Lambert is *not* failing." There was certainly nothing frail about our sacrifice; but otherwise she seemed a homely, motherly soul and the most pliable of God's creatures.

She was really very good to us in those few weeks before the wedding. She was the most appetising cook and fed us royally. She turned over two of the best rooms to us and kept a fire burning in each when the nights were cool. She did everything to please us except that she dispensed with the services of the girl in the taproom. "Now I've a lad that's as good as my own, there's no need to keep that Jenny on," she told us, and her little eyes so tightly enclosed in their sockets became wet with content.

We sat in the kitchen by the glossy new range, each of us holding one of her hands. "My man," she breathed, "and my son. What more could a body want?"

I wanted the girl in the taproom, but didn't like to mention it.

It would certainly be very easy, I thought, for us to shift her savings into M.S.'s box. I even felt a flicker of my dying conscience. She seemed pathetically unprotected in the company of such tricksters as ourselves. She responded to any suggestion or hint without any opposition at all.

M.S. was so confident he began his spade-work on selling the inn two nights after we arrived. "After all, Mrs. Lambert —" he began.

"Oh, Lambert, you mustn't call me that yet," she giggled. "They say it's unlucky to say it too soon."

He must have squeezed her hand. She let out an "Ow!" and then he squeezed her whole person.

"What's unlucky about me finding you, and you finding me, and this sweet boy between us?" M.S. enquired.

She wept at her good fortune until we comforted her and then he tried again.

"It's a new life *together* we must aim for, Mrs. Lambert. I'll not start off in the bed you shared with Maddock."

"We could buy a new bed," she offered with what I thought were the first signs of intelligence.

"What about the walls?" he demanded. "I'll not start off between walls that saw the first love of you and Maddock. Haven't I been plagued by envy of Maddock all these long and weary years?"

His hand went to his heart so naturally I could almost believe that he had been envious. "My God, that old brute's a good actor," I thought. It never occurred to me that Bessie Maddock was a better one.

Nevertheless, it worried me sometimes. She really seemed too good-natured even for a simpleton. I caught her looking at him once. It's a subtle glance to describe. It wasn't so much hard as amused. In fact it was a mixture of both. I mentioned it to him. "Sir, you don't think the second Mrs. Lambert could be marking *you*, do you?"

He laughed at me. "Bessie! Bless you, boy! What do you think she's got in that head? I tell you it's steak and kidney pudding. You can see the steam rise off it when she's trying to think."

The steak and kidney pudding boiled over at the wedding breakfast. On a small glass of Malaga she confided to him, "I'm sure I take it kindly in you, Lambert, to marry a penniless widow."

He affected to be touched by what he imagined to be her modesty. He could bring tears to his own remarkably innocent-looking eyes whenever he wished. He could merely moisten or flood them at will. But he never permitted himself real tears. "Never allow your own feelings to show, boy," he warned me. "A good actor's concern is to portray only the character he's asked to interpret."

At the wedding breakfast he dabbed his wet cheeks and put an arm round his bride. "Mrs. Lambert," he sniffed, "when a lady's about to fill her husband's box it's very nice to make so light of it."

"But it's true, Lambert," she cooed. "I've made over the inn and every half-penny I've got to me half-brother living in Leeds. It seemed the right thing to do, now I've got you and this lad to see to me needs."

M.S. did not believe it at first. He laughed at her. "I like a lady that jokes, Mrs. Lambert. It brightens up the long winter evenings to have a lady that jokes."

Then I saw the same look in her eyes that I had noticed before — a glitter of harsh amusement. But she kept up the same cooing voice. "It's no joke, Mr. Smith, I can tell you. With two strong men like you to support me, I put me poor brother first. I made him over the inn and all me savings a week before we was wed. I've not a penny piece to me own name now."

She looked up into her husband's open mouth. "Of course, I daresay that brother Reggie won't see me in want, but he'll take a lot of asking. He's known to be mightily close."

M.S. was so dumfounded. Poor man, I thought I'd lose him to the stone. He had, of course, no earthly means of redress. He could have claimed every penny she had as her husband, but he couldn't touch what was no longer hers. We should be in the humiliating position of having to wheedle her into supplying our daily needs through the half-brother, who was doubtless aware of the whole situation.

The shock seemed to have sapped all Manager Smith's natural reserves. He slumped in the kitchen a beaten man. "You'll have to forgive me, boy," he said. "I fear I've harnessed your future to a dishonest woman."

"Oh, that's all right, sir." I tried to comfort him. "We must just think of some way to get our own back."

"What do you make of it, boy?" he bleated. "A lady that diddles her rightful out of his box. I should never have introduced you into her company. She'll set you a bad example."

I was rubbing his hands to try and bring some warmth back into them. "I told you she was marking you, sir. I never liked the way she didn't bother to smile when you weren't looking."

"Tricked!" he moaned, "tricked by a steak and kidney pudding! I shall never find it in me heart to trust anyone again, boy."

"But we can trick *her*," I tried to cheer him. "We're two against one, aren't we? If she wanted to get married so badly, she'll want to stay married for the look of the thing. She'll put up with a lot before she'll let the neighbours think she had to get the law on us. We could fiddle the takings and sell off the stock. We can take quite a few risks against her pride. She'll want to save her face at all costs."

"Ah! You're a comfort to me, boy, you are," he said.

I began to feel the blood coming back into his hands, and a bottle of Malaga between us in the kitchen soon restored his optimism.

Even so, I felt sorry for him that night. After all, I was responsible for the whole situation. If he hadn't been so anxious to put a stage under me he never would have had to follow that salacious old mountain up to bed.

She was determined that he follow her as quickly as possible. He made every excuse to stay downstairs. He pretended the stone was troubling him and sipped a hot ale and ginger so slowly that she snatched the mug out of his hand. Her cooing voice had disappeared with the last of the wedding guests, and there were certainly no signs of modesty. "Lambert Smith, I married to 'ave a man in me bed, not a barrel of hot ale."

I was surprised at her talking like that in front of me, but soon realised that for her I was no longer there. In future I was to be treated as if I had no more feelings than a lump of wood. I was to be a pair of hands and feet in her service and a mouth to feed as frugally as she could. M.S. was right when he told me that Bessie Maddock wouldn't pare you a quarter of turnip before she got a ring on her finger, never mind give you anything else. But he hadn't bargained for her giving us nothing afterwards.

In spite of being sympathetic towards him, I couldn't help laughing. There can have been few more reluctant lovers. His footsteps dragged pitifully after hers. I hid under the stairs so that he shouldn't see the grin on my face. Not only for his sake, either. He'd have given me a serious hiding if he'd caught me giggling at him.

I heard the stairs creaking beneath her weight. "Thought I wasn't on to the pair of you, didn't you?" she taunted him. "Well, more fool you. What did you think I'd got stuck in the place of me eyes?"

"For a lady that's tricked her rightful," he answered, "I find your remarks out of place."

She gave her unattractive laugh. "Oh, I'll not be the loser," she told him. "I'm not one for the widow's state. I like company of a night and there's plenty of good solid work in the daytime to make you and that lout worth the candle to me."

He managed a mournful dignity. "You won't bully me, Mrs. Lambert. I've laid down to sleep beside hogs in my time, and found them sweeter company than yours. The boy and I leave first thing in the morning."

"That you don't," she chuckled. "Unless you've changed your ways mightily since I last set eyes on you, I daresay the law's got an interest in you. I've a horn I keep handy to blow through the window should anyone break into the place. It'll fetch half the village up here in an instant, and they'll hold you down till the law gets fetched."

It was impossible to resist a peep at this tender little scene. I poked my head out from under the stairs and peered up.

Juliet had reached the landing and hung over the railings in a flannel garment that must have been the original tent the Assyrian packed up in the night. Her little eyes snapped venom in the light of her candle.

Romeo stood, belligerently, torn between the law and the balcony scene.

I don't know why — it was nerves, I suppose — but the irony of simple Bessie proving herself a match for him struck me as being unduly funny. I rolled over and laughed like a lunatic. I was to pay a high price in later life for laughing at a love scene. It's a pity I couldn't have learned my lesson then.

M.S. came thundering down the stairs. He wrenched me up by the collar and let me swing from his hand like a clock pendulum. He was the most extraordinarily powerful man. All his anger against Bessie Maddock he put into walloping me.

Juliet resented it also. She leaned over the balcony and rasped at him, "I'll thank you to save your strength, Mr. Smith."

With that the crude old hen flapped into her bedroom and M.S. put me on the ground. His eyes looked quite savage with indignation. "Would you enjoy playing opposite *that*?"

I pulled myself together immediately, shaken by his blows. "No, sir, I'm sure I'm very sorry for you. I only hope it won't come too hard on the stone."

To my great relief he laughed himself. "Bless you, lad, I've played more difficult roles than that and remembered me lines! A good actor has to take these things in his stride. It's not a part I like, but you get bad and good and you just have to play them to the best of your ability and hope to be cast better next time."

Then he patted me on the shoulder and took himself upstairs.

The law and Bessie Maddock had won.

Chapter 7.

LAST NIGHT I dreamed I was there again, back in my attic bedroom at the King's Arms. But the attic was full of people, so crowded that whichever way I tossed I hit a leg, a head, or an arm. The smell was appalling and in my dream I was wondering why I was plagued with such company. Bessie put me into the attic because it was the worst spot she could find for me, but at least I used to have it to myself. I could never remember its smelling before, either. I used to get the first scents of the May trees through that high window long before the lower ones were opened.

It took me some time to remember that I was in the Mousetrap and that the reason I found it difficult to breathe was because of the hideous over-crowding.

Our population varied in a macabre way in those cells. Your fellow in-mates could appear before the Tribunal at twelve and be condemned and executed on the same day by two o'clock; alternatively, they could linger for months and months apparently overlooked.

The man who repeatedly beat me to the toilet bucket was a witness whom the gendarmerie had brought up from Compiègne. He was imprisoned by mistake with the man he was supposed to testify against and was still there eleven weeks after his would-be victim was acquitted!

We prided ourselves that we were the worst off in the Mousetrap, but we had a serious rival to our claim in the people imprisoned in the Tour Bonbec. It was a matter of honour to prove that one was more wretchedly housed than anyone else and it often led to quarrels in the exercise court. We com-pared notes when we were let out for exercise. They didn't ring the courtyard bell until eight at night in the summer and they unlocked the doors at six in the morning, so we had plenty of time to compare notes.

We all but crippled each other in our rush to get out. As soon as we heard the gaoler's dogs sniffing at the doors and the bolts being pulled back, we burst out in a thrashing lump of humanity and made for the nearest glimpse of sky. Most of my cellmates made for the men's court because, of course, so many Parisians were old friends, but I found a smaller court. I chose it because it was less frequented and not because it was near the women's quarters.

Those women were lucky. They had a fountain and could wash their clothes. It might have been a country village square the way they scrubbed, although there was an agreement to do no laundry after midday. The poorer ones washed out their skirts whilst they stood in their petticoats, and put shawls round their shoulders whilst they cleaned their one bodice.

As for the rich, they might have been at home on their salon days. They would take two hours over their toilette. Then they would sail in with their favourite négligées, hair perfect, nails perfect, faces perfect. Towards the end even those had only rotting straw to sleep on, but they still changed their clothes every afternoon as if they were going to preside over their own drawing rooms. In the evenings they appeared dishabille.

I was amazed at their spirit, but then I remained in perpetual astonishment at the behavior of people in the Conciergerie. A doctor with whom I discussed it said he thought it was induced by shock, but agreed that it was sufficient to confound all psychologists.

It would be giving a false impression to pretend that everyone in those wretched holes was a frivolous wag on the eve of meeting his creator, but the attitude of the majority, no matter what their station, was most perplexing. Whether they belonged to the aristocracy or the professional classes, whether they were shopkeepers, skilled craftsmen, or came from the lowest peasantry, they seemed determined to band together in turning their remaining hours into a festival. When you think that they had probably spent the night with thirty-eight others half dead from lack of food and air, it's amazing that they found such courage. As far as accommodation went, the women were no better off. In one cell fifty-four were tucked in with only nineteen thin stray mattresses amongst them. They used to take turns standing up, and they slept in shifts.

I am not the only one who found this ghoulish sang-froid amazing. Prisoners fresh in from the provinces, and my poor witness friend who was still trying to prove he was not the man he came to testify against, were open-mouthed at it. It seemed to be confined to the political prisoners. Your ordinary thief and murderer were not nearly so carefree.

Certainly a lot of quiet praying went on, but it is fairly safe to say that the only time a real hush descended on the men's court was when the tip-staves shouted out the indictments. All singing and laughter stopped on the instant while we listened to the *Journal du Soir* to see if our names had been called out for preliminary examination. If you heard your name, you rushed to the Tour Bonbec staircase gates and received a slip of paper. You read through this quickly to see what they had charged you with and more often than not you could make neither head nor tail of it. But the next day you would mount the fatal staircase and face the great Tribunal.

The clerks were given to jokes while handing out indictments, not pleasant ones to my ears. "Well, now, citizens, here is a honour for you. It's not everyone has the privilege of studying his own death certificate."

They were usually answered in kind with verbal whip cracks, and someone was sure to see fit to sing a little verse or cut a little caper.

I simply could not understand such courage. Did they not wish to live? Had they given up caring? Were they so used to suffering that they were dulled towards further feeling? Or was it just bravado to make the next fellow think you minded less than he did?

They were not much different when they trooped back across the men's court from their examinations and told their anxious friends that they had just been sentenced to death. No amount of jostling from the gendarmes to get them to the greffe, where they would meet their executioners, would stop them from giving us the morbid details. The minute we saw the gendarmes we raced to find out how many of the day's batch were "moving out," as we politely termed it. The jurymen often look out of their refreshment-room windows to see the effects of their verdict, and it's said that the Public Prosecutor spied on us from the little window the ushers used for calling out the *Journal du Soir*.

The gendarmes could do what they liked, but try as they might they could not stop the chatter of the farewells. They rushed at people trying to tug them on, but they were pulled back by the rest of us. We always made a double escort for the condemned, and we impeded the gendarmes until all the last messages to be carried to families had been delivered, letters and souvenirs handed over, and any little favour that old friends or complete strangers could do one another had been done.

How the tales varied! Some would tell you that the judges were brutal, that the President silenced them whenever they went to open their mouths; others that they were gently handled and that they definitely saw judges in the passage with tears in their eyes. A few things seemed to tally. The President was fairly generally recorded as shouting down the accused, and I thought there must be some truth in the business of tears in the judges' eyes. So many people mentioned it. Perhaps these men disliked the parts they had to play. The condemned shared one emotion in common: absolute astonishment at having been convicted. None of them seemed to believe it possible.

Long after they had gone and the night bell was rung, you could hear the singing starting up again, even from the depths of the cells.

It should, I suppose, have been a tonic for the spirits, but I'm inclined to be depressed by people who make the best of impossible things. They can be unnerving companions. There was I with my stomach jumping about, like a frightened cat, and sweat rolling down behind my ears every time the names were called, while those creatures sang in chorus and laughed like lunatics at their own imbecile jokes.

I made no bones about my longing to live and I could not, as they could, give up all hope and shrug off my fate. My waking moments were bitter with remorse at the way in which I had abused my freedom when I had had it. One takes liberty for granted, and until it's gone one doesn't realise that one has been imprisoning oneself all the time.

I swore to God that if I ever got out of there I would ask nothing more from life than to be able to open a door and go through it; to breathe air that was not fouled by a single toilet bucket used by dozens of men.

Air! I don't suppose I ever thought of it before. I certainly went out of my way to avoid it. I never took a walk for the good of my health or went into the open for the sake of it. My liberty was spent more often in the breathless box of a woman's curtained bedroom. Even when I walked — or, to avoid an irate husband, sometimes sprinted home through a clear dawn — my head was so muzzy from wine I failed to fill my lungs properly.

There have been so many wasted nights as well. The summer ones with tender breezes, the frosty ones glowing under a hard moon — and what was I doing in them? More often than not I was taking some wretched man's place in his wife's bed or lying flat on my back under somebody else's table.

It was the smells of liberty which I found so precious in retrospect — from the subtle scent of a ground mist rising, to horse dung under a baking sun. I never realised that there were so many life-giving smells — cosy ones, adventurous ones, sleep-making ones, and stimulating ones. My only ambition now was to walk and walk and walk and *breathe*.

The few times I did take a walk I never stooped to sniff at a flower. There were moments when I ached for the feel of rain; I would never again swear at it for trickling down my neck. The last person in the world I should have suspected of becoming maudlin and sentimental over such ordinary pleasures was myself. Heavens above, I had even gone back to the memories of boyhood newt-catching and found tears on my face as a result.

Another point brought home to one in the Mousetrap was the little one bothered about other people. I don't think I ever gave more than a fleeting thought to anyone condemned before, except when I was playing Buckingham or some other death scene. I turned my humdrum imagination to the obvious loneliness of heart, the sense of desertion, the wild hopes of reprieve. I put what I thought to be the correct interpretation on the last waiting moments of someone about to be executed or hanged, but I saw now that I must have given some singularly poor performances. The true sensations are scarcely actable without going mad. Perhaps that is why these people here played the opposite of them with such grim success.

Certainly I never supposed that there would come a time when the condemned were no longer single criminals but cattle for slaughter en masse. How could anyone have guessed that in an age of reason and enlightenment upon which we never ceased to congratulate ourselves, our leaders would appear to be driven by a desire to annihilate half the nation? How could anyone have suspected that in this modern world with scientific achievement at its height, medical knowledge at its peak, and the arts at their most appreciated, politicians would develop a passion for human sacrifice?

As for freedom — this greater freedom on which we had spent so much blood, this fight to end all fights which we thought we had won — that seemed to have returned to the age-old business of having a friend or an enemy in high places. And as the first never remained the same for long, it didn't really matter which.

In these days an early death was as difficult for the innocent to avoid as the guilty. It knocked on your door at night, smiled at you through the eyes of so-called friends, or simply hacked you down in the street without excuse. Let us all go down on our knees and thank God for politicians. At the worst they will merely ruin us; at the best they will make us extinct. It's my belief that they will not be content until they've blasted the whole world into space. Even then amongst the smoking ruins I don't doubt they'll find a few maimed bodies still capable of voting for them. Then they will finish them off with schemes for their welfare again.

My fellow prisoners were given to playing macabre little games of trials and executions. Their pallet beds were dragged into rings for the jury; lots were drawn for the President and the Public Prosecutor. The greatest prize was to be the victim, of course.

What fun they had found in it defeated me. I live in enough dread of reality. It would be so appalling to be one of the few examples of degrading cowardice. Supposing one's legs went weak, or one developed a tell-tale twitch, or, more ignominious still, supposing one were sick?

There was, I believe, a Duc du Châtelet who died badly. He tried to kill himself with a piece of broken glass when he was condemned, and went to the guillotine already covered in blood. When he was weeping and banging his head against the wall, a pretty young prostitute called Églé tried to shame him into showing courage. "You ought to know, Monsieur le Duc, that people who have never had a name acquire one in here, and those who already have one should know how to bear it."

The fact that no one could get over the Duc's performance showed how unusual cowardly displays were considered, and did nothing to cheer me. It was precisely how I feared I might behave.

My colleagues' unpleasant little dramas also did nothing to calm my nerves. The old man who repeatedly beat me to the toilet bucket was chosen for President of the Revolutionary Tribunal. I imagined the real Monsieur Dumas looked no more forbidding. The Public Prosecutor put a stocking on his head and assumed an expression of leering ferocity. The accused sat cross-legged on the table pretending to shake to such an extent that the whole thing looked like giving way. The jury sat round on its sour pallet beds, scratching for fleas and using bad language.

The cry went up — *"Liberté! Égalité! Fraternité! Flapdoodlère!"* The accused says he has always been a staunch supporter of the last. His defence is that he has done everything in his power to live up to it. He has taken the greatest care to tread on the faces of the poor, raped only the prettiest daughters of the best patriots, snatched food from starving babies, hoarded bread in famines, and made sure to sell his country's military secrets to both Pitt and Coburg. He also takes a personal credit for having caused the violent storms that ruined the famous ill-fated harvests of '89. He cannot conceive what possible charges could have been laid against him in view of this excellent record.

His crime is made clear to him in flowery language. The Public Prosecutor flings his hands about in violent emphasis and the jury pretend to be overcome by the stench of his armpits. They roll about holding their noses, coughing and sneezing and gasping for air. The victim is accused of counter-revolutionary practices. Can he deny that on the first of Pluviose he combed his hair and cleaned his teeth? Both treacherous, aristocratic practices in a direct line with priestcraft and despotism?

The accused proves beyond doubt that he couldn't have done either, as he has no hair and no teeth, but he is still promptly sentenced to death. The execution now takes place. The "Sainte Guillotine" is represented by the table tipped down, and the accused has his hands tied behind his back. The jury double for parts as *les oboyeuses* and *les insulteuses*, cackling old women screaming every known obscenity, which the accused acknowledges with gracious bows and lewd gestures. Feet pound the floor for drums. The executioner forces the accused down on the board, and sometimes as a subtlety he is bound face upwards so that he may see the knife come down. The barkers and the insulters sing hymns to the "Sainte Guillotine."

The accused roars out a poignant little song:

"Quand ils m'auront guillotiné,
Je n'aurai plus besoin de nez."

It becomes a matter of honour as to who can drown whom in volume.

Then a knotted handkerchief comes down on his neck and the "crowd" yells with joy. His head is off. He lumbers round in circles croaking like a decapitated chicken. Someone removes a boot and it is held up as the head amongst further catcalls of delight.

For anyone who has remained a Republican as I have, the whole thing was distasteful. (The rowdiness and the absurdities made it hard sometimes not to be on the side of the authorities who had seen fit to exterminate this lot in reality.) It was only when one remembered that tomorrow or the next day or the day after, their horrible play-acting would come only too true and that they were already the paper ghosts of the Registrar's office, that one could go back to admiring them.

Victim after victim came up for "trial" always on the same ludicrous charges. One had been discovered in bed with the wives of two Jacobins; another one had stolen the shirt of a sans-culotte, and his defence that the sans-culotte could not have had a shirt to steal was argued by his "semi-official counsel" at fever pitch.

In all fairness, it has to be mentioned that some of the true charges were no less ridiculous.

There was a doctor amongst us whose crime was that a letter had been found in which he had addressed a patient as "Monsieur" and signed himself, "Your humble and obedient servant." This apparently constituted an act of enmity towards the people and because of its bourgeois hypocrisy was a counter-revolutionary activity!

Even when the last of our mock victims had been decapitated and they were all lying in a happy heap with their clothes pulled over their heads to represent headless corpses, we were not free of them. The "ghosts" had the privilege of trying to terrorise their accusers. There was a brute in here named Lapagne who used to be Mayor of Ingouville at Havre. Apparently he had a bad record of atrocities and in the old days was some sort of high-way robber before mayoral duties gave him greater scope. He was sentenced to have his bones cracked on the wheel under the old régime. An influential person managed to save him, and Lapagne showed his gratitude by sending his former benefactor to the guillotine. Quite a common way of giving thanks these days. One of our inmates was a townsman of Lapagne's and had not forgotten his period of office.

Eerie in his sheet, he loomed over Lapagne chanting his crimes in an awesome voice and beckoning him to follow the "wraith" to hell. Lapagne's conscience or his stupefied brain made an idiot of him and he got up to obey! Round and round they went, with everyone flattening themselves against walls to give room. Lapagne, gibbering with fear, stumbled after the "ghost" until howls of laughter brought him to his senses. I think the man was really half asleep still and imagined he was having a nightmare.

These light reliefs of prison life are not exactly what one might call a comfort to those of us who take our impending deaths at all seriously.

I never thought that to dream of Bessie Maddock would be a pleasure in comparison with the realities of one's wakeful life. I tried to forget the Mousetrap and go back to my once despised attic in the King's Arms, but my companions kicked and cuffed me awake. I was pummelled to my feet before I realised that a gendarme was standing in the doorway.

It was early; even the prison water carrier was not about. Fear streaked down my body. I recognised the uniform of the gendarme. I closed my eyes, hoping the light of his candle had tricked me. But it had not. When I looked again he was still in the dreaded blue coat with the yellow belt over his shoulder, and his hat was a tufted bicorne. He belonged to one of the two companies attached for special duties to the Revolutionary Tribunal. And that could mean only one thing. They were going to bring me up for trial again.

I was a horrible sight. Sleep had puffed my eyes up, I had a beard that could hardly have suited me, and my hair itched with dirt. My clothes left a trail of straw ends.

When I reached the gendarme I asked, "Is it the Tribunal sending for me?" but he merely jerked his chin to tell me to follow him. "I shall know soon enough," I thought, "if we turn up the stairs by the chapel." There was none of your head held high, your little songs or merry capers about me. To make matters worse, I wished urgently to relieve myself. Suppose they would not give me time to do so? The shame of solemnly wetting those formidable gradins in front of the Tribunal! Still, it might allay a charge of aristocratic practices. On the other hand, it might come under the heading of fouling Republican property.

Of what were they going to accuse me this time and in which name, and where was Lavaux? I tried to argue myself out of my pessimism. "How about those wet-eyed judges? The ones who can hardly bring themselves to sentence people? The Naulins, the Harnis, the Maires, and the Scellières? Aren't they notorious for showing compassion?" I argued back, "Yes, but they might not be on duty and I might be one of the few who don't move them to tears. They can't weep for all three of me."

There was no doubt that things had altered since the first days of the Tribunal. I had picked a bad time. Trials used to spin out for days and days and the defence met with as much respect as the prosecution. There were few condemnations, plenty of transportation sentences, and many acquittals. Too many, I suppose, for the Public Prosecutor. I had heard that the juries were accused of leniency and had now been hand-picked by the Public Prosecutor himself.

It was a pretty foregone conclusion now that once you left your cell for the Grande Chambre — once you climbed into those damnable stands — you could be sure in next to no time that you would be coming down the steps of the Tour Bonbec with a death sentence, and the laughter of the jurymen already in the refreshment room ringing in your ears.

I was so busy arguing with myself I forgot to notice that we had passed the chapel stairs. We were not making for the Grande Chambre. We must be going to the parloir. Perhaps Lavaux was waiting to see me after all. But when we went through it I realised we were heading for the clerk's office. The thought brought me to a standstill. Good God! They were going to despatch me at once! They had tired of wrangling over my identity. They were even going to dispense with the doubtful mechanism of the Tribunal. I should simply be seated on the bench in the back office where I had seen the man plodding through his bowl of stew, and from the bench I should leave for the scaffold, with no time to relieve myself. Worse still, I should probably be hanged from the nearest iron bar holding the street lamps. I had seen many a dismal body slowly circling round at the end of a rope attached to one of these. I already shuddered when I saw some poor wretch being dragged off to the ugly death with the mob screaming, *"À la lanterne! À la lanterne!"*

The gendarme turned angrily to hurry me on. I followed and went through the door he opened for me. It was the clerk's office, lit by a lamp and several candles. Through the glass partition I could see the dismal little room and the deadly bench.

"The ci-devant Vicomte de Lambrière," the gendarme announced.

"Ah!" said a brusque voice. "Come in, come in."

I went in. A bright fire was burning in the room, and a round table put up for the occasion supported a bottle of wine, three glasses, and a mass of documents. A clerk sat at one end of the table. The man who had spoken to me was about forty-seven, I should think. He wore glasses and was neatly dressed.

"I am Maire Savary," he introduced himself. "I am a judge at the Revolutionary Tribunal —"

One of the wet-eyed judges! I searched his face for signs of moist compassion — but I saw none.

Neither, however, did he look the ruffian I had also heard him described. The tales about judges contradicted themselves, like everything else one heard in this place. For every two who had seen him bowed in regret over a condemnation, there were three to swear that the same man behaved like a barbarian. Personally, I thought a lot of their brutality was affected by these men to impress their colleagues. Left to themselves, without the suspicious eyes of the party on them, they became less violent. Judge Maire seemed a normal enough, if brusque, human being.

"This is my assistant clerk, Raymond Josse," he informed me. "We have a few questions to ask you. I'm afraid it's not a very congenial hour, but we can none of us choose when to work these days."

I had been warned about these midnight interrogations — questions fired at one repeatedly and out of order so that one was fighting confusion as well as fright. The bright lights, the lack of sleep, the words put into one's mouth all went to fuddle one's brain so that one sounded bigoted, obstinate, and an undoubted enemy of the people. On the surface one's interrogators were doing no more than giving one a reasonable chance to defend oneself, but a notable proportion of victims broke down under the strain and made false confessions.

Judge Maire Savary leant amiably across the table. "I have told you who I am, so perhaps you will be good enough to tell me who you are?"

"My name is Roberts and I'm an actor."

The judge frowned. "The one thing that the Committees of Public Safety and General Security appear to have in common in regard to your case is that they are both convinced that you are most certainly *not* an actor called Roberts."

I said wearily, "I made everything clear when I gave myself up to the Committee of General Security."

"Yes. But unfortunately the Lieutenant of Police did not believe you. He was also uncertain as to the reason you gave yourself up."

"Yes, I expect so. That was the one thing I couldn't explain to him."

"Are you going to explain it to me?"

"No."

Judge Maire Savary sighed and picked up the dossier that I had seen the Registrar checking. He passed it to the clerk. "Would you agree that this is an accurate description of this man?"

The clerk looked me up and down and nodded. "There is just one mark of identification not perhaps quite evident —"

Judge Maire Savary jumped up. "Yes, yes — the scar! Now then, citoyen, perhaps you'll be good enough to step over to the fire and —"

"I'm not taking my breeches down again."

"The whole thing can't take more than a moment."

"I'm keeping my breeches on."

The clerk looked pained. "The Judge ordered the fire to be lit on purpose, citoyen, so that you should not be chilled."

"Very good of him, but he needn't have bothered. I'm warm enough providing I stay in my breeches."

Maire Savary sat down again. "Look, my good man, I know it's undignified, but for your own sake try and help us. God knows, we're doing our best for you."

I allowed myself no visible reaction to this unlikely piece of news. There was only one rule for your protection in this sort of thing: hide your own feelings and try to guess theirs.

The clerk sat with pen poised. The Judge turned to him, spreading his hands out. "Don't put anything down yet, Josse. Let's — let's try and have an informal talk first."

The Judge filled a glass with wine and pushed it towards me. He seemed to have a little difficulty in starting the informal talk. One could almost see his forming and rejecting opening gambits. Finally he said, "It would be foolish to ask if you're comfortable here, but have you any serious complaints?"

"It's a little overcrowded perhaps," I suggested.

He looked genuinely concerned. "Yes, it's terrible. Terrible. But, you know, we aren't blind to it. We have plans for putting it right. We're going to try and separate all the ordinary criminals and see that you political prisoners have the place to yourselves."

"We shall miss the occasional murderer," I said politely. "They tell such good stories at night."

He ignored me. "We're going to replace all the old mattresses as well. But these things take time, you know. Take time!" His features had little to make his face live in your memory, but the eyes — if you looked long enough at them — were by no means uninteresting. They had a quiet, gloomy depth to them. A tired depth that, oddly enough, suggested no hint of weariness, but a struggling, fighting strength. I picked myself up immediately; there must be no question of my admiring him; he was there to kill me, and if he said he was not, he was lying. He was part of the tricks and the traps. He leaned towards me again.

"What I really meant to ask you was: would you be averse to shortening your stay here?" When I raised my eyebrows at him, he laughed. "I don't mean by the usual, somewhat abrupt means — and believe me, there are those of us who deplore such methods. I was referring to freedom. Do you understand me? Freedom."

I remained silent. It was a trap question. He wanted me to say that there was no such thing; that he and his leaders had abused it, had lost the meaning of it. I should have taken a sip of wine to steady my nerves if I hadn't suspected that they might have put something in it to make me talk.

He hit the table so hard with his fist that the clerk's pen leapt off it and the wine would have leapt from my glass had I not been holding it.

"I'm trying to tell you," he shouted, "that I prefer men alive to men dead, and I'm doing all I can to keep you alive!"

I put down my glass. "Why?" I asked.

My question seemed to flurry him. He made no straight reply. He got up and walked to the fireplace, kicking a log with his boot. "I suppose," he said bitterly, "you thought we should torture you? Beat and bully the answers we want from you?"

"I read in *L'Ami du peuple*," I told him, "that the editor suggests the guillotine is too easy a death. He puts forward boiling oil in the ear, slit noses, and nails torn off as an addition."

Judge Maire spat into the fire. "I don't read citoyen Marat's violent scribblings. That's not our way of working: we don't employ bestial methods. Those were for the old régime. It's to do away with the rack and the wheel and the thumb screw that we made our stand. What do you think we fought for? To keep on the old conditions? To see people like yourself as helpless in our hands as you would have been in the hands of the people we suffered under ourselves? Do you really think that our whole administration, our organisation, our hard-won success is only to turn the clock backward and not forward? Do you think we should have suffered so much and shed so much blood for the sole purpose of replacing tyrants with tyrants?"

"It may surprise you to know," I told him, "that I am a loyal Republican."

"It would not surprise me at all." He leaned over and filled his glass with wine — the first time he had done so. "You're a sensible man. I can see that and any sensible man could have no other choice."

A moth flew at the lamp beside him, battering itself to its own destruction. He squashed it and told me, "Well, you can see that you're not going to be tortured, we aren't going to bully you, we do only what I'm doing now: question man to man."

"Your man-to-man questioning on the Tribunal seems to get you the results you want without torture," I was idiot enough to answer.

He turned to me. I expected another crash on the table from his fist. So did the clerk. He seized his pen and rescued his wine glass. I took his hint and rescued mine.

Maire Savary spoke quietly. "I am completely neutral in this affair. I represent neither of the committees. I am interested solely in seeing justice done to you."

My expression must have shown that I found this fact hard to attribute to a judge of the Revolutionary Tribunal.

He walked slowly round the table towards me. "Presumably," he said, "you know that the Revolutionary Tribunal was formed to judge all people who, it considers, are obstructing the advancement of the Republic? But once the Republic is no longer in danger, once it's established, there will be no need for the Tribunal. It will be disbanded and we judges will be able to get back to our normal duties. The Tribunal is only an emergency court. It would be terrible to think of it as permanent. Terrible."

I said nothing. I was in danger of liking the man. But he had not dragged me out to discuss the future of the Tribunal. There was nothing to do but wait until he disclosed his real reason.

"I mentioned the word 'freedom' to you just now," he said. "You may take it from me that in your case there's a possibility of that. I suspect your lawyer of playing rather an adroit game. I admire him for it, but then I admire anyone willing to risk his neck in the defence of a prisoner these days. Every time the Lieutenant of Police provides evidence on behalf of the Committee of General Security that you are the ci-devant Vicomte de Lambrière, Lavaux supplies the Committee of Public Safety with proof that you are Anthony Buckland from England. In the opposite case he reverses the order. He is presumably playing for time."

"He knows who I really am and that circumstances forced me to adopt both those names."

"Possibly, but he is never going to be able to prove it. Each committee is naturally anxious to justify its own time and expenditure. No public body can afford to have it established in these days that they have been guilty of wasting national funds by sending their agents on a wild-goose chase. Neither will gladly relinquish its claim on you. That is the reason you're alive at this moment. Your lawyer is making good use of the rivalry between them, but he cannot expect to keep that up for ever."

"There'll come a time," put in the clerk, whom I suspected of having my welfare less tenderly at heart than the Judge, "when everyone will lose patience and execute you in all three names. The Public Prosecutor is already asking for a quick decision."

The Judge gave him a severe glance. "Speak when you are asked, please, Josse, and write only when I tell you." To me he said gently, "The Public Prosecutor is dependent on the committees for his own orders, but that doesn't mean that their individual members are safe from his enmity. You'd be very ill-advised to allow Lavaux to bargain for your true identity too long."

"What should I have to do in return for freedom?"

He sat again. "One can promise nothing, of course, but I think you should sign a confession for one or the other of them. It's not of the slightest interest to me which name you choose. I am only giving you friendly and informal advice. But I think that whichever committee you decide to support will be inclined towards leniency as a reward — if only to score off the other. In any event, I think it's a chance worth taking. I would go so far as to say that it is your only chance."

I looked carefully at him. He seemed sincere enough. But it could have been the trap that he had been setting for me throughout the interview. It was an impossible risk to take. Even if it were true that the committee for whom I signed would be willing to release me, what was to stop the other one from promptly rearresting me? Nothing at all, as far as I could see.

I knew too much about the horrors of trying to hide in present-day Paris.

Those nights of fear are still fresh in my mind. They were filled with the steady tramp of members of the Revolutionary Tribunal and their escorting guards. Behind locked doors and shuttered windows half the city lay wakeful and listening. Only the clatter of a sabre, the rattle of pike staves, or the shouts of the officer of the section could be heard. Even those who had nothing to fear lay uneasily in their beds, for you did not have to be guilty to be denounced. Any enemy or so-called friend could have sent your name to one of the committees. Anyone bearing you a private grudge or envying you a woman could see to it that yours was one of the doors to receive that dreaded knock of a "domiciliary visit." You lay waiting for it, your heart pumping and your mouth drying every time the footsteps marching up your street seemed to hesitate in front of your door. You lay tensed to aching point, waiting for the knocker to fall and the order to open in the name of the law. When they passed, you started to breathe again, or perhaps you lit a candle or put out a shaky hand for water, or perhaps you flung yourself down in the bed again immediately. That clanking! Were they coming back again? Were those your gates being opened?

Finally, you might fall asleep from nervous exhaustion. You would have reassured yourself by then; they had passed your house two or three times by now; they could not be looking for you; so you closed your eyes and tried to ease the tautness out of your limbs. Yes, they would have come by now if they were looking for you. It could not be your turn yet. So you dozed, still tight-muscled, with uneasy dreams. And then, just when you had told yourself a dozen times not to be foolish, that you had nothing to worry about, there it was! — a sharp thunder that burst into your dreams. Someone was knocking on the door.

You sat bolt upright. It need not be them. It might be a neighbour wanting help. It might be a friend sending a last-minute message. But it wasn't. It was the commissaries of the section to whom you had been denounced. You listened while a frightened porter threw the gates open. It was commissaries with their guard of pikemen making for your own front door. There was nothing you could do about it. If you pretended not to hear, they would break their way in.

You were wise to say goodbye to those you loved and not to fill them with false hopes of seeing you again. Accusations and death were synonymous.

There was no point in hiding. You just lay there, ice cold in the warmth of your own bed. In the short distance between the landing and your door, your brain buzzed. They could not accuse you of anything. You had done nothing. You have forgotten what goes to make a counter-revolutionary. Nothing!! But somehow and in some way you have sinned against the party. Your door burst open. The room was filled with uniforms and pikes. The warrant was read to you. You were told not to move and in the next minute you were tipped out of your own bed. You were told to say nothing and you were asked a dozen questions. Someone lit your lamps, someone stripped your bed. Your chest of drawers, your closets — anything that might have held papers was searched and sealed. Your dog might bark and your wife might scream. Nothing would make any difference. Sometimes your coat was thrown round you, sometimes it was not. Out you went, pushed through your own doorway, half thrown down your own stairs, booted up your own passage and into the night. You might not be the only one in your street, either. There could be several figures struggling in doorways, putting up the same resistance as yourself, shouting the same futile defences. It mattered not at all that you might have been one of the party's chief supporters; if the party had decided that you were against it, you were wiser to go along with no argument.

That was the Paris into which I should have been released by one committee only to have been rearrested by the other.

It would be safer to put my faith in Lavaux. Let him continue to incite the committees against one another so that they would both fight to keep me alive in order to prove themselves right!

I said to the Judge, "I should prefer to leave the case in the hands of my lawyer."

The Judge turned to the clerk. "Record that the accused was obstinate, un-co-operative, and often facetious at the expense of the Republic. No force was used to persuade him to confess."

Then he went to the door and called to the guard.

I said, "I suppose it's pointless to mention it, but I have a friend in the Mousetrap. He was brought up from Compiègne to testify against a prisoner. His name is Nicholas Prudhomme, and although he was only a witness, he's still here."

"It should have been brought to our attention."

"It was, but nobody took any notice."

"Josse," said the Judge, "make a note to look into the witness from Compiègne."

The Mousetrap seemed even less bearable after the clean company of the Judge, the homely spitting of the fire, and the glasses of wine. It seemed an age since I had been jerked out of my dream about Bessie Maddock. My floor space had been taken, so I was forced to stand up against the wall to finish my night's sleep. I kept thinking of the Judge and those strong, truthful eyes. But it was nonsense: of course it was a trick, and a clumsy one.

Incidentally, it's of no public interest, I know, but it was not pointless to mention the case of my witness friend from Compiègne. He was released within twenty-four hours.

Chapter 8.

BESSIE MADDOCK! What I wouldn't give to see that uncharitable old hulk again. It would mean I was free and back in England. If only I could see her once more with her great face bent over her own porridge and a jerk of her thumb to show that mine was in the barn with the dog's. All I had to do was to walk down the granite steps into the yard, into air that gripped your ears in a frozen bite — but air! Smelling of mists and clean bracken and leaf mould and slate roofs that had rolled off the rain in the night, and stone walls and old wooden gates and all the things I never knew had smells before.

I was up early the morning after the wedding. I couldn't contain my curiosity as to how M.S. had weathered the bridal night.

He had been up early, too. He was morosely at work in the kitchen preparing the bride's breakfast. She intended to have it in bed.

"Did you sleep well, sir?" I asked him.

He clouted me over the ear. When he came down again with the tray I was contrite. He had such a beaten, depressed look on his face.

"Sir," I said, "we must clear out of here. That half-brother's in the game with her. They've got some arrangement, you can be sure of it. He'll give her what she wants, but we'll be dependent on her."

"In time, boy," he sighed, "we might get the better of her."

"In time! How much time? She'll make us work like galley slaves, and if we refuse, she'll blow her horn and get the law on us. We must get away tonight — She snores, I expect?"

"She does, with a whistle to follow."

"Then wait until she is in full trumpet and creep out. She won't hear you. We'll be too far away in the morning for her to blow her horn and get the neighbours, and we can always change our names again."

"Boy," he said, "if I can support it — you can. I told you it would be a sacrifice. I knew what I was coming to. I'm willing to bear it to put a stage under you. I'll grant you I didn't know she'd trick me out of my rights. That's been a blow to me, that *has* been a blow."

"But we'll never get a stage under us here," I complained, "and with the half-brother in charge of the money, we won't get one anywhere else."

"There's just a chance," he told me, "just a chance . . ."

I was right about the half-brother in Leeds. He doled out the money to Bessie and not a half-penny came our way.

We snatched every spare half-hour we could to continue my "marking sessions." There was plenty to study in the characters who came into the taproom at night. He also made a rule that I must keep up my French. He said that only daily use of the language would stop me from forgetting it. I spoke French to him for three hours every day, and always in front of the Rare Sacrifice. It annoyed her as much as it had annoyed my stepfather when my mother and I prattled away together. M.S. was getting a good working grip of the language himself.

I wasn't allowed to sit down at the table with them, and when the inn was closed, she found so many extra jobs for me that I used to collapse worn-out in my attic bed.

M.S. was also at her beck and call. If he complained, she just shrugged her shoulders. "It's Reggie's money now. He gives me what he thinks and I can't make him give any more."

We knew perfectly well that for her own private needs Reggie gave her as much as she wanted. But we soon discovered we had one hold over her. She was a fiend for keeping up appearances; she minded what the neighbours thought of her. In front of people she liked to look a loving wife and have M.S. appear a doting husband. She even gave the impression of spoiling me.

"I can't refuse that boy of Lambert's anything," she'd giggle behind the taproom counter with all her great chins tucking down into one.

I quickly took advantage of her. I waited until she'd made this monstrous remark in the taproom and then asked for what I wanted in front of her customers.

"Mother," I'd say, smiling at her, "could you let me have the key to the larder? I'm hungry again."

She had to say yes, but, my God, the look I got from those little currant eyes. We helped ourselves liberally, but she was after us as soon as she could, and she paid us out by locking everything edible away for days.

I tried the same trick with money, but that never worked. "Try your sly ways on me again in company," she spat at me in private, "and they'll be the last you'll try under my roof." She was always holding over my head the threat that the half-brother from Leeds thought me an unnecessary expense.

"Stick it out, boy. Stick it out," M.S. told me. "It's only a means to an end. If we don't get what we're after, we'll have put up with her all these months for nothing."

I saw the sense of that, but I simply could not see how he was going to wring a theatre out of that ungracious mound of flesh. However, he was making quiet plans. Based on a sound knowledge of her character, he was moving forwards.

One snowy morning in February he walked out of the house. His footsteps were deeply imprinted on the fluffy white path. I sat at my attic window mourning his departure and staring at the black marks. They seemed my only link with him and I remember my dejection when the falling flakes filled them up. I can still see those great dark holes his boots made, and only now do I realise that I was looking at the marks that helped to take us nearer our unfortunate future.

It was not pleasant to be left alone with the Rare Sacrifice. Without M.S.'s protection I was completely in the hands of the unsavoury old lump. The freshness of her complexion was misleading. There was nothing fresh about her person.

There were moments when I gave way to fear. M.S. might be tricking me as well as the Rare Sacrifice. He might have walked out on both of us. I admit I shed a few tears at night. I had come to depend on him so completely, there seemed no future for me that was not connected with him. Perhaps I was not consciously aware of it, but his conviction that I was worthy of having a stage put under me gave me my only purpose in life. It made me feel that everything I did had a meaning and that I was not just a bony oaf growing up towards nothing. Everything we did was a preparation for what I was to become. I felt that no hour went by, even if it was only turning the spit for the Rare Sacrifice or pumping water in the yard when the ice in the spout had to be chipped away first, that was not being used for our eventual benefit. All the time I was working I was rehearsing, or perfecting in my head, the piece he had set me to learn: the "marking" of a type I had been told to study. It gave me a great sympathy for people who don't know what they're going to do in life. How aimless and empty their existence must be. I felt that I had been born for a reason — a pleasant sensation that has since left me.

Also, of course, I looked forward to the day when I could repay M.S. for all he had done for me. When Garrick was in tears at the strength of my Hamlet, M.S. would receive all the credit from me. There would be a handsome town house and an estate in the country, not to mention the tenancy of the Lane, and if our well-buttered existence should bore us — there would be this new horse-racing to remind us that life could still be precarious. I was even going to allow Bessie Maddock a small pittance for life. After all, she would have been instrumental in getting us our first theatre, and one mustn't be ungracious when one's great.

But with the snow pressing its way through my skylight, with the sky the colour of dirty putty and the inn cold and dreary in the early dusk, my hopes began to fade. Perhaps he would never come back. There was still sufficient conscience left in me to remember that he had a side to him of which some persons might not approve. The Guildford town crier had described him as a "rogue, a rascal, and a cunning thief." Perhaps people like that deserted even their closest friends. Perhaps the constant marital ceremonies demanded by the Rare Sacrifice had come "hard on his stone," and he was willing to abandon me for the chance of escape. He might even have lost faith in me and decided that it wasn't worth putting a stage under me.

He had refused point blank to tell me where he was going. If I knew nothing, he said, I could tell nothing. With his interest and encouragement withdrawn, I felt far more on my own in the world than ever I had when I set off across the Yorkshire moors with no idea of where I would sleep that night.

The Rare Sacrifice told her customers that he had gone off to visit an ailing relative.

"Such a good soul is my Lambert," she sighed to the locals. "He'd not hear a call for help from the other end of the world but he wouldn't go to answer it."

To me she hissed spitefully, "If we don't see the face of that villain again, you can take to the road yourself."

I contemplated leaving her there and then. If he had deserted me, there was no point in staying at the beck and call of the Rare Sacrifice. But I kept letting day after day go past in the hope of getting news of him. I would wait until the thaw set in — after all, the roads might be blocked; I would give the thaw a week and then if there was no sign of him I would pack up and walk out. But I found myself desperately hoping that the bad weather would last, so that I could give him more time.

Then, one morning three weeks later, when there were still four-foot drifts in the hedgerows, I looked out of my window and there they were again — the footsteps — deep in the snow marching back up the path. I went through the trap in the attic so fast I nearly broke my neck down the ladder. He was in the kitchen in front of the range taking his boots off. I leapt into his arms like a child. Questions popped out of me like a bubbling cauldron, but he would answer none of them. He merely smiled and patted my shoulder.

It was such a good feeling — security rushing back like a lost dog bounding home. While I was cooking him breakfast I felt a sense of relief I find hard to describe. He had not tried to spare himself at my expense. He had not lost faith in me. It was still worth putting a stage under me. I was someone growing up for a reason again.

The Rare Sacrifice came down in her night gown to see what the noise was about. There must have been creases in her pillow case, for they were imprinted on her cheek. She stood with her hands on her hips. Her eyes turned my stomach in early mornings. They had small gobs of green sleep in the corners. She snapped at me, "You'll kindly ask what kept Mr. Smith these last few weeks."

I turned to M.S. and asked innocently, "Where have you been, sir, please?" He stretched his great toes in his woollen stockings.

"Boy," he said, "inform the second Mrs. Lambert that I'm afraid for

what the neighbours will say." He turned earnestly to me. "It's not for
myself, boy: my skin's thick. It's a sensitive soul like my bride that I'm
worried about."

She forgot to talk through me, and shouted at him. "You've not gone and
got the law on you?"

"Mrs. Lambert," he said quietly, "the law's not got me yet. But it won't
be long," and he pushed towards her a copy of *The Gentleman's Magazine*
with a strip of paper to mark a place. It was a list of bankrupts, and as his
name wasn't on it, I understood it no better than she did.

"What's this got to do with you, Lambert Smith? Your dirty name isn't
down yet."

"Not yet," he said, smiling amiably. "But very shortly you'll find me
there. Then think what the neighbours will say. Bessie Maddock so full of
catching a man at her time of life she never stopped rubbing her cronies'
noses in it, and what has she caught? A debtor and a fraud. No one else
would've got himself tricked by a man that's not welcome with honest folk.
Bessie's grand husband in Newgate! Ah, come now, Mrs. Lambert, I've
heard you talk. You've told 'em I'm related to gentry, that I brought you
more money than this inn can turn over in fifteen years. You've put on so
many airs and graces you'll look undressed without them. You've looked
down your nose at your widow friends because you've found a man and
they haven't. You'll hear them laughing from Turnham Cress and back
again, I should say."

She looked so stricken I was sorry for her. I pushed a chair forward to
catch her from falling and fetched her a cup of hot soup from the stove.
She dashed it aside and it scalded my wrist. She was panting like a dog in
the bear ring. But she clung to her common sense. "How can you go bankrupt without one penny piece to your name? You old idiot, you have to
have something to lose, and you haven't as much as the cows in the barn:
at least they give milk for good value."

"Agreed," he said coolly, "that's what your friends will say. You'd have
done better to marry the cows in the barn: at least they can't turn round
and milk *you*!" He lit his pipe not bothering to look at her. "It's because
I've not a penny piece, Mrs. Lambert, that you'll find me on those lists next
month — and possibly in Newgate. It's never the rich men who go bankrupt. No, Mrs. Lambert, it's people like me, who've put their name to a
piece of property they've no money to buy."

"Property!" she croaked.

I sat down myself and gaped at him. Surely, I thought, he could never be
so silly as to imagine he could storm her into paying up for a theatre. She
was a fierce Anabaptist, was our Rare Sacrifice, and she thought everything
and everyone to do with the stage was poison to the soul. She'd put up with

the jeers of her neighbours before she'd help finance what she called "the devil's platform."

"What kind of property?" she screamed.

"An inn," he said mildly, "an inn on the outskirts of Bristol."

"I've a perfectly good inn of me own, Mr. Smith."

"I know, Mrs. Lambert, but I prefer the one I've signed me name to near Bristol."

He would give me no more information, either, other than to tell me that the property was a good investment and that it would "improve her money."

He gave her three weeks to make up her mind. Whenever she brought the subject up, which she did frequently, he said simply, "Yours is the choice, Mrs. Lambert: a husband in Newgate or a husband in Bristol."

She chose Bristol. The King's Arms was put up for sale, but as it had been made over to the half-brother in Leeds before Bessie's marriage, he got the money for it. As soon as he paid the sum required for the new property, we moved.

I still had no inkling of what M.S. was up to, and when we arrived in Bristol I really thought the old man had gone mad.

Chapter 9.

THE New Sun Inn was on the outskirts of Bristol. It was one of those black and white horrors I detest so much, and it had every inconvenience. Was there ever a more hideous period? Even I had to stoop in the taproom. I thought being "at love" must have affected Manager Smith's mind. I could see no excuse for exchanging the comfortable King's Arms for this Tudor hovel.

Then he took me round the back. Attached to the inn where the kitchen quarters seemed to have sunk lower than the main building was a derelict theatre. It had been a barn, I should think, at one time. Still sticking to one of the walls was an old playbill. It announced defiantly, "The world's finest seating accommodation! Tonight! Mrs. Floss in *The Drastic Cure*, or, *The Doctor's Mistake*, followed by a one-act farce in which Mrs. Floss will also oblige."

I thought it must have been twenty years since Mrs. Floss had obliged anybody but an undertaker.

"And what'll we do with that 'orror?" the second Mrs. Lambert enquired.

"Oh," said M.S. vaguely, "storage! Storage!"

But he pulled me inside and hopped about like a madman. He kissed his fingers to the murky interior. "I saw it advertised in the *Monitor*," he told me. "Went for a song, boy! It's a wonderful opportunity, quite wonderful. There's thousands of people living round here, boy. The poor like cheering up and the rich like a cry. What a position! They'll think it a lark to come out to this theatre. I tell you, we'll pull 'em away from the big ones. It'll be the smart thing to do to come out to the Little Apollo. We'll get all the fashionables in no time, and long before that we'll have got our regulars. Trust me, I've a good sense of smell."

So had I, and that theatre reeked. The "world's finest seating accommodation" appeared to be restricted to the rotting floor, and the decaying boxes were piled high in filth.

M.S. clambered up onto the stage and went stamping his feet all over it. "Can't you *feel* her?" His voice was exultant. "See, boy? Not a bad board amongst 'em. Steady as a rock, game to the end. Didn't I tell you her heart was beating? Some theatres are never a theatre whatever you do to 'em, and some can never die. She's alive, boy, she's alive."

I found myself the surprising ally of the Rare Sacrifice. I couldn't conceive that he could do any good with a rat hole like that. When the second Mrs. Lambert discovered his intentions, she addressed her husband for the last time during our first night at the New Sun Inn. She said, "Lambert Smith, you can take your snoring somewhere else. I'd rather share my bed with a horse thief."

I expected him to be elated at getting out of the dreaded "maritals." But, oddly enough, he was upset by her rejection of him as a lover. He couldn't bear failing in any part. "It's a long time since I've done a romantic," he confessed. "I daresay I was underrehearsed, but good God, boy, it comes hurtful to get the bird from a second-rate support like that."

Their lack of communication made business discussions difficult. They only spoke through me. I was left to persuade her to restore the Little Apollo. It took me the best part of a year until finally, coached by him, I made her see the trade that the inn might achieve by reviving the theatre. After that she gave in grudgingly.

She certainly helped him to keep his promise to put a stage under me. She made us sleep on it! We were only allowed at the inn to work our passage and to eat our meals in the scullery. She and the half-brother were so mean it was one long battle to equip the theatre. We did all the decorations ourselves, from the building work to the painting. Thanks to the tyrannical economies of the Rare Sacrifice, we could only get together a second-rate company. Some of them weren't fit to go into a Punch and Judy show. As I was young, there were not many parts for me at first, but I was tall for my age and well developed, so that I was able to double if the worst came to the worst. The worst came to the worst in a different way on our opening night. We opened with Cumberland's *The Fashionable Lover*. I thought it an ambitious choice on our low budget. The first scene called for "Hall in Lord Abberville's house with a staircase seen through an arch. Several domestics waiting in rich liveries. Flourish of French horns," etc. Needless to say, Mr. Cumberland's stage directions were severely modified. There was one domestic rather ordinarily clad and there was one flourish of a clarinet — both parts played by myself.

The second Mrs. Lambert was good enough to grace the theatre — the first time she had ever been in it. She sat in the ticket box. We went up at 5.15, and by 5.30 she was back in the inn with all the takings.

I was designed for the prompt-well after I had delivered the prologue "In the character of a printer's devil." I was nervous about the jibes against the press in this speech. I am never too happy saying, "If any critic pregnant with ill nature . . .", etc.!

Our preceding farce left the audience more than normally in the dark. The second Mrs. Lambert had cheesepared us on materials for mending the roof, and the place was a hell hole of scurrying draughts. One patron complained afterwards that he had caught a sciatica on our premises. Mrs. Lambert's thrift also played havoc with the lighting. She had allowed us only the poorest tallow, with the result that all the candles blew out in the upstage candelabra and most of the ones in the downstage one went out. I had to go up a ladder and relight the lot.

The Fashionable Lover started off very well, and the house, having been cheered by the lighting problems, was in a good mood. I gabbled the prologue and raced back to the prompt-well, where I noted that the floats were in danger of blowing out.

Our Lord Abberville would have done better to earn his living off the land, but he wasn't as bad as the maidservant who led him on. She dried up on her opening line. The wind made a helpful entrance at this point, and all four candelabras blew out, followed loyally by the floats. The maid lost her head. Apparently Lord Abberville had stumbled in the darkness and struck an unfortunate part of her. She yelled out, "Leave me alone, you filthy brute!"

I thought myself resourceful when I held up the two prompt candles. There was a delighted squeal from the audience. It was certainly a most effective piece of lighting. The maid had tripped over a stool and pulled her dress right off her shoulders. She was lying across Lord Abberville's lap, with two of the largest breasts exposed that I had ever seen. Lord Abberville also lost his head. He shouted at her, "If you think I'm after that glassblower's paradise, you've made a mistake, my girl."

We were astonished by our notices. One of our severest critics wrote, "No doubt the clergy and those who feel that the drama already sets a bad example to the younger generation will have something to say to the textual impertinences taken by Mr. Lambert Smith in Mr. Cumberland's comedy last night. The fact that it was an effective and well-planned theatrical device is not to be questioned. What is to be questioned is the effect it will have, not only upon the younger playgoing society, but upon the young dramatists about to prepare their pieces.

"It would be excusable if they supposed that the popular response to Mr. Smith's surprise last night shows the trend of public appreciation. The bookings, I am told, for the production have far exceeded all possible expectations. One is only left to hope that the younger dramatist in pursuit of success will realise that there are other forms of expression open to his talents in which to draw public acclaim and esteem."

Someone else said, "The Little Apollo reopened last night on a bawdy romp, while effective, overdid the lighting tricks."

Well, of course, you only need one or two of those and you're set fair. We were set extremely fair.

The second Mrs. Lambert doled us out pittances in salaries. M.S. received less than his juvenile lead. We had to clean up back and front ourselves when the last patrons had gone, and before we made our beds up on the stage, M.S. put me through a grueling series of performances. I was made to learn all the male parts in the play and run them through for him afterwards with my own embellishments, or what I thought were improvements on the actors' performances. As we changed the programme twice a week, I wasn't short of parts to study.

This wasn't so difficult when we had our original company, because they were all so bad it was easy to do better than they. But as we were doing such good business, even the second Mrs. Lambert saw the wisdom of getting a more superior company together. It made it doubly hard for me. The better the actor, the better the performance I had to give. Our newly acquired Mr. Bates was very nearly excellent. I was always getting into trouble through him. M.S. sitting quietly in the gallery would call out, "Learn what Mr. Bates can teach you, boy, before you try to better him."

I was in my late teens when our Mr. Bates was promoted to the Lane. We had done sufficiently well to be on speaking terms again with the second Mrs. Lambert. The inn was doing a flourishing trade, and she had given us a minute raise in salary. I think she realised she owed her prosperity to M.S.'s business acumen and secretly admired him for it.

I had a certain amount of personal success in *The Brothers* and was beginning to be aware of my effect on women. M.S. was under the impression that he was keeping me severely away from them. It was "too soon" for women; acting must come first, and women would dissipate my energies. He didn't know, of course, that I'd dissipated them with the young comedienne at the age of fifteen.

At twenty he let me play Sir Harry Wildair in *The Constant Lovers*. It was such a success we altered our plans and ran it for a week. It was on Friday afternoon that a rowdy party bought the prompt-side box. My God, if only the English county gentry took its theatre as seriously as the French! The French go to a play; the English go for the night out. The most poignant tragedy could turn into a regimental romp if there were enough young officers in a cheerful mood. I'm not saying that our experiences were typical of London theatre or bigger provincial towns, but with our position (and possibly with our reputation!) the theatre could turn into a rout. We had girls hooked off the stage from the boxes, intimate compliments showered on them, and the young bloods often joined in with the dialogue.

On that Friday I went up to the box, commanded the young men and women in it to keep quiet, and threatened to ask the constable to see that they behaved.

There was a knock on my dressing-room door after the performance. I thought it was my leading lady, who always blamed me for any outbreak that put her off. She had been the mistress of our Mr. Bates and she was angry at my taking his parts. I said with my usual off-stage charm, "Oh, come in and get it over with, you bitch."

In honour of the leading lady I hadn't even bothered to do up my breeches. I was also having trouble undoing my stock buckle and was swearing at it. Oh, the malevolence of inanimate objects! They can wage a definite war on you. I've had chairs and tables deliberately put out legs to trip me up. And as for stock buckles!

"My name is Eliza Weldon," a quiet voice said. "It was my cousin's party that caused the disturbance tonight."

I swivelled round and jumped up. A youngish woman was standing in the doorway. She was dressed with every aid to dullness. She was wearing a shade of cow dung, which with her rather sandy colouring, was not an ideal choice. Her face was big and pale, but there were beautiful bones in it. The skin was tight, as if she had smoothed it over the bones herself, knowing that they were her best point. There was surprising power in her round grey eyes, and about her whole person there was a calm that was attractive. She closed her eyes deliberately and I realised that it was a touch of delicacy to allow me to do up my breeches. Her voice was flat and condescending.

"I've come to apologise for the behaviour of my guests."

"They certainly added nothing to the night's entertainment," I admitted.

"I enjoyed the play," she told me, with a certain amount of genuine surprise, "and you must let me congratulate you on your own performance. You played Sir Harry so well I could have mistaken you for a natural gentleman." I replied that I thought Sir Harry's whole charm lay in the fact that he was so obviously not a gentleman of any sort, but she was not put out.

"You'll think it curious of me to visit you like this, but I've a favour to ask you." I pushed a chair forward and sat opposite her. I must have looked like a dog strangled in its collar with the stock I had been tugging at rumpled round my neck.

It was impossible to imagine the type of favour she was going to ask. Perhaps she wanted a private reading of my Sir Harry in her drawing room. I had been requested to do this sort of thing before. There was a queer rhythmic stiffness about her which appeared both in limbs and in expression and tone. In her movements and in her voice, I was reminded of the sharp tap of a music master's baton trying to keep a bad pupil in time.

"You've possibly noticed," she said, "that by no stretch of the imagination could I be called a beauty."

I should have liked to have said something comforting, but I was too startled to be gallant. By the time I had got over my surprise she was speaking again. "Also, I'm twenty-eight — which is old to be single." What in the world, I wondered, could the woman be going to ask of me? Surely she didn't intend to propose to me?

"What you probably haven't noticed," she said, "and why should you — because I dress quietly and my taste doesn't run to jewellery — is that I'm more than a little wealthy."

I sat back and stared at her, ready for the next confidence. With her turn of frankness it would probably be some intimate detail of personal health.

"My father," she said, "is Judge Weldon. He's an extremely rich man and I am his sole heir. He's devoted to me."

Some comment seemed necessary, as she had paused. "Well," I said, "that's nice, isn't it?"

"Yes," she said. "It means that I have as much money as I want while he's alive and even more when he's dead."

"You must allow me to congratulate you."

"Mr. Roberts, I'm not accustomed to talking to persons of your profession. You must try to make things easy for me. All I was trying to explain is that my father's more than able to pay for any favour you might do me."

"You haven't given me the chance," I pointed out, "to offer to do it for nothing — and you haven't told me what it is."

"You couldn't do it for nothing," she said: "there's cost to yourself involved."

"Please," I said, "I'm sweating with curiosity."

"You'll have to learn to avoid vulgarities — otherwise people will know you're an actor."

"Well, I am, aren't I?"

"Not if you do me this favour. Oh, you could regard it as another part, I suppose, but you mustn't look as if you're acting it."

"That," I said, "is considered bad acting."

"I've no intention of paying for bad acting," she snapped.

I leaned further back in my chair. Crossed my legs and folded my arms. It occurred to me that it hadn't once occurred to her that I might not be willing to act for her.

"That," she told me, "isn't a respectful attitude to adopt in front of a lady. There are certain things I see I shall have to teach you, or you'll be seen through at once."

My legs and arms remained folded and crossed. My face bore its difficult-leading-lady look. This was an expression in my eyes which had quelled many a fractious bitch who was trying to upstage me. I was taking a steadily mounting dislike to Miss Weldon.

She said, "Now, we've agreed that I'm plain." I did not contradict her. "My cousin has a friend. His name is Nicholas Hawtrey. He's attracted to my money, but not to my person." Silence from me put me quickly on his side. "Unfortunately, there's nothing to do — to spur him on, so to speak. He's taking his time about it. Too much time. I feel that if there was some-one else interested in me, it might make up his mind for him. He wouldn't like to see my money falling into other hands."

"Is getting married so important to you?" I asked.

She smiled at me. It was an unexpectedly pleasant smile. Not at all the kind I had suspected. I thought it might be pinched and humourless. But it was broad and rather puckish.

"Yes," she said, "it's more than so important to me. Imagine my friends! Most of them haven't a quarter of my money, but they get married. Men like them for themselves. One becomes an object of pity as well as fun if one has more money than anybody and one is still left on the shelf."

"I don't quite understand why you should be," I told her sincerely. "Even if we've agreed that you're not a Venus, you have a pleasant dignity, you have — "

"All I have to offer," she interrupted, "is strength of character, and men don't find that very alluring. You see, ever since I was in the nursery I've had my own way. I can't see other people's point of view at all. I don't doubt they exist, but not for me. That makes for a rather formidable wife, don't you think?"

"Your frankness," I said, "is alarming."

"I expect that's one of the things that puts Mr. Hawtrey off."

"Do you love him?" I enquired.

"No, but I don't actively dislike him."

"What a good thing."

She gave me a full glare from her powerful eyes. "I've told you, Mr. Roberts, there's no one interested in me except Mr. Hawtrey."

"I gather you're going to ask me to be a rival to him?"

"Yes, but not, of course, as yourself."

"Why not?"

"My dear Mr. Roberts, I could hardly appear in public with a common actor."

It was said so reasonably I could have struck her. Just as one was beginning to sympathise with her, she antagonised one. I thought Mr. Hawtrey showed great integrity by his delays. She would certainly make a formidable wife at any price.

"You'd have to play a part," she said. "It was my cousin's idea, really. He thought you played a gentleman so well on the stage this evening that — "

"That I might be able to play one off it?"

She missed all the sarcasm in my voice. She nodded. "There would be certain raw edges, of course, but we could soon smooth those out. You'd have to use another name and pretend that you were a private person of means, but I believe you've enough skill to go undetected."

It's very rarely that I'm short of a retort, but the woman annoyed me so much I could think of nothing to say.

"It would only be for one evening," she told me, in case a more lengthy performance should frighten me off. "We're giving a ball at my house on December sixth. I suggest you attend it as my escort."

"At the moment," I said, "I'm employed at this theatre. Any outside performance has to be discussed with my manager."

"Very well." Her poise was not even dented by the acidity of my tone. "I'm willing to come to terms with your manager whenever you wish."

Chapter 10.

MY MANAGER was far from receptive to the idea. He was interesting when he lost his temper, particularly as he never raised his voice; he whispered in a cautious gushing manner, like water trying to push its way through a blocked spout.

"Years!" he hissed, "years I've spent on you! I've trained you to be an actor, not a circus poodle to a love-sick harpy."

I held up my hand to halt him. "You're putting far more into this scene than is necessary," I said coldly. "I should never have entertained the idea myself if the theatre hadn't been short of money. We could make her pay well — I'm sure of that — and I thought the extra money would help, that's all."

In point of fact it wasn't all. I was rather amused by the whole idea. It would be interesting to play the lover of Eliza Weldon. Especially when one knew that she despised actors. It might be intriguing to see how she reacted to a first-class performance. There was just a possibility that I might make her forget for a few moments that I was acting. I hadn't forgiven her slighting references to "raw edges" and "being seen through." There was a definite challenge to my ability to charm Miss Weldon out of condescension. I might even leave her with a suspicion that her "false beau" could have been a more attractive catch than Mr. Hawtrey. It would have been an effective form of revenge upon someone who was so obviously unaware that "the lower orders" can have any feelings.

Manager Smith was still whispering at me. "December the sixth? You've forgotten, I suppose, that we're doing *The Ambitious Stepmother* on the sixth? Who do you suggest I get to play your part? That young drunk, Carpenter? Perhaps you think he can act? I'm not surprised if you do. You still come pretty near to turning up those horrible eyes of yours yourself."

I left the room with aggressive dignity. We were not on speaking terms until halfway through the second act that evening — and then we only exchanged one word: "fire!"

Our Mr. Carpenter, whose art, such as it was, could only be stimulated by copious draughts of rum, lost his bottle. He knew that he had deposited it somewhere handy in the wings, but could not remember where. He lit a candle to locate it and set fire to the corner of the prompt-side curtain. Mr. Carpenter made a sacrifice. He poured the contents of his bottle of rum onto the flames in an effort to put them out!

Most of the company leapt over the floats into the audience. Fortunately the audience flooded the stage in return. They tugged down the curtains and trampled the flames until a bucket gang was formed and the theatre was soaked out of danger. The damage to scenery was formidable, and we were obliged to cancel the next week's two productions.

Incredibly enough, the Rare Sacrifice refused to replace the curtains. She thought we had deliberately set fire to them to prize new ones out of her. She failed to see why we needed curtains at all. They didn't have them in Shakespeare's day, and as far as she knew, it had not affected the takings.

We travelled up to Leeds to try and persuade the half-brother to give us the money. We expected a mean, weazel-faced man, but he was the most deceptive barrel of goodwill I have ever seen; he looked like everybody's conception of John Bull himself. Several cosy flushed chins, a thrusting stomach, tight breeches, and a constant smile in his voice.

He lived in a seedy terrace house smelling of uncleaned bird cages. His wife was surprisingly young and good-looking in spite of the fact that she was producing his fifth child. She had glowing red hair and dark eyes. I took a liking to her and she to me. She answered my wink and was obviously pleased by my ill-disguised admiration. It was extraordinary to me that she could have saddled herself with John Bull. The whole house shouted of his meanness in its meagre furnishings and lack of warmth. Perhaps she too had been taken in by his joviality. He looked the spirit of generosity. He very rarely answered a question; he just laughed.

His phlegmy chuckle was his answer to our request for the new curtains. He laughed when we both offered to buy them out of our own salaries if he would pay us six weeks in advance. He kept shaking his great benign head and saying, "Gentlemen! Gentlemen! Me sister's quite right. If there was no curtains in Shakespeare's time, then there's no need for us to 'ave them."

There was so obviously nothing to be done with him that we left.

It was on the way home that M.S. recalled Eliza Weldon.

"How much did you say that love-sick harpy was willing to pay you?"

"She was going to discuss it with you."

"Then she'd better discuss it," he said. "We can't get along without curtains."

She made an appointment with us for five o'clock in the evening. She was insistent that we should go after dark. She pointed out with her delightful frankness that she could not risk her friends seeing her receiving such curious guests. The Weldon's mansion was vast, and comfortless. The butler led us through cold passages and delivered us at the door of an anteroom.

Miss Weldon was sitting by the fire, and with her was the cousin who had suggested that I might pass as a gentleman. He had one of those faces that are about as exciting as a glass of cold water. You could shut your eyes after studying him a full ten minutes and still not remember what he looked like. Miss Weldon was wearing heavy velvet of that mouldy shade of moss one finds on very old gravestones. Neither of them asked us to sit down. They were drinking Marsala, and of course did not offer it to us.

M.S. put on his undertaker's voice, which he sometimes used for tricking portly innkeepers. It was curious how successful this particular Lord Credit could be. He would look the host up and down over his glasses and mutter, "Oh dear, your sort's a *great* trial in our trade, a great trial! So difficult to fit and always go off in early life before you've shrunk to better measurement." It was extraordinary how it unmannered them. They were so anxious to get rid of us they practically assisted us to get away without paying.

He made a great play of clearing his throat to Miss Weldon and the water-faced cousin. "You'll excuse me, miss and sir, I'm sure, but I never care to discuss business with ladies and gentlemen who have been imbibing. You'll understand me when I say that on a Christian upbringing such as I have enjoyed you don't like to take advantage of people, their brain being clouded and yours being sharp, so to speak."

The water-faced cousin's mouth opened. Miss Weldon's mouth went tight with dislike. But she rang for the butler. At her orders he filled our glasses. Personally I thought I caught a gleam of congratulation in his eyes. It must have been the first time in his experience that such undistinguished guests had been offered any hospitality.

M.S. raised his glass. With an unctious smile and two fingers outstretched, he saluted us in turn and said, "To all!" pronouncing the "to" as "tew." I was angry with him. We were after a job and the way to get it was not to make fun of our would-be employers. But of course he always knew when he held the cards and it pleased him to make Miss Weldon feel that she was having to deal with even lower people than she feared.

He belched unforgivably after his first gulp and then gave a long-drawn-out "Ah!" of relief. After that he shot me a glance that I knew well. It meant that I was to say nothing unless he spoke. It was a sign from our early Lord Credit days.

The silence was appalling. Obviously neither Miss Weldon nor her water-faced cousin wished to be the first to bring up the difficult subject at hand. They were waiting for Manager Smith to speak, and he said nothing. I stared into my Marsala, and into the fire, and at the skirting boards, and at the canary in its cage by the window. The fire tried to help. Its homely crackles sounded like an earthquake. The canary tried to help. It sang gloriously and then broke off in the middle of a trill as if it felt suddenly self-conscious, and dived into its seed. The fire had given up, too. There was not one single living sound in the room. I am undoubtedly a sentimental hypocrite; much as I disliked Miss Weldon and Water Face, I would have done anything to break their embarrassment. I would have got up and sung a funny song. I would have asked them if they believed in God. I would have said that I thought royalty was out of date and we needed a republic. But M.S. gave me another of his looks and the paralysing silence continued.

Finally — and despite what has since happened, I have never ceased to admire her for it — Miss Weldon spoke. She turned to Manager Smith. She said, "If you are hoping to make me feel smaller than I felt when I originally agreed to this idea, you have no hope."

Water Face refilled his own and Miss Weldon's glass, but made no move in our direction.

M.S. recognised that he was not dealing with a "love-sick harpy." He dropped the unctious voice.

"You'll be receiving," he said crisply, "the services of one of this country's finest actors."

"Then why," she asked, "is he at the Little Apollo theatre?"

"Because he's young, madam, and I want his teeth cut on a hard-bone rattle, that's why. But I can tell you there's lively interest in him at the Lane. Mr. Kemble himself has an eye on him."

"My price," she said, "would remain the same if Mr. Kemble had his

whole heart set on him. He'll get his food and his wine on the evening concerned, I'll pay for his clothes, and I'll give him a guinea for his time."

"Then you won't get him," said M.S. "You'll provide his clothes and give
him *five* guineas for his performance."

Water Face gasped. "Good heavens alive, the fellow's only being asked
to act — after all, that's his business. He should be glad of the chance to
meet gentry. He won't get another invitation like this in a hurry."

"I'm in no hurry at all," I pointed out. "It's Miss Weldon who seems to
be in a rush."

She turned to Water Face doubtfully. "Edward, are you sure you think
Mr. Roberts can sustain the part of a gentleman for a *whole* evening?"

"Well, he was jolly good as one the other night."

"Yes, but he was only saying lines that he'd learned. It'll be quite different when he has to speak for himself."

"That," said Manager Smith, "is why we're obliged to ask five guineas.
The strain will be terrible for him, having to keep up with such well-man-
nered folks as yourselves, for instance."

Miss Weldon's dauntless eyes turned on him. "I am not well mannered,
Mr. — er — er — "

"Smith," he said helpfully, and spelt it for her. "S-M-I-T-H. Lambert
Smith."

"Mr. Smith, I have a reputation for being extremely rude which I take
care to preserve. It gets one out of boring small talk. But I *am* well bred,
which I'm sure you'll agree with me. Mr. Roberts is not. I should look very
foolish if that were discovered."

"Mr. Roberts is an actor, madam, and it's my dearest wish that one day
he'll be recognised as a great one."

"When you get your wish I will pay you five guineas. Until then I'll give
you one."

"Does he keep the clothes?"

"Yes."

"Clothes and four guineas, then."

"Clothes and one."

M.S. bowed first to her and then to Water Face. "With reluctance we feel
ourselves unable to help you, madam, but I'm sure we wish you the greatest
good fortune in your affairs of the heart. Perhaps one of those little love
spells you read about might prove efficacious." He signalled to me and we
made for the door.

"Just a minute," said Water Face, obviously afraid we might knock off
one or two knick-knacks on our way out. "Miss Weldon will ring for the
butler to show you the door."

"There's one point, Mr. Smith," said Miss Weldon, "you've overlooked.
I should be taking a risk. Mr. Roberts might give a poor performance and

give the game away: then I should be the dinner-table joke of the season. That's why I feel obliged to limit you to clothes and one guinea."

M.S. said coldly, "Mr. Roberts never gives a bad performance."

"But I shan't have a chance to judge it beforehand. We can't very well have a rehearsal. I imagine he can dance — and possibly very much better than I can — but I don't know how wine affects him."

"No . . . well, you wouldn't," Manager Smith agreed, "from that little drop."

Water Face said, "We're certainly not going to sit here while the fellow polishes off the whole decanter to find out."

It's curious how impressions of people can change. I would never have believed then that there could come a time when I actually liked Water Face.

M.S. made for the door again. Miss Weldon was the most sparing woman with gestures I had ever seen. Except to lift her glass up and down to her lips, she had hardly made a movement the whole time we were there. It was this extraordinary restraint that made for the calm that went a long way towards excusing her plainness. She was an essentially restful person, however jarring her forthrightness might be. Her eyes passed Manager Smith and came to me. "It's unfair at such short notice, but could you give us any kind of example of how I can expect you to behave on the sixth?"

"He hasn't decided on his character yet," said M.S. "An actor has to study a part."

"Oh, nonsense," said Water Face, "we can all do it. The other day I played charades. I was an old lady going to a shop. The word was 'misspent.' It was rather clever, really: I thought of it myself. I put a shawl round me and —" He was all set to totter along on an imaginary stick, but Miss Weldon stopped him.

"You were dreadful, Edward: you gave it away in the first three seconds, which is what I'm afraid Mr. Roberts might do."

I am not usually a quick thinker. It made me realise that in a way Miss Weldon was right about me. I was used to having my speaking and thinking done for me, not only by authors, but by M.S. Since a child I had relied on him to tell me whom I must represent and how I was to do it. He had planned and directed my every move. I was deeply unused to myself. If he suddenly told me in one of our Lord Credit ventures that I was a pot boy, an apprentice clerk, or a doctor's son, I became one quite efficiently, but "an actor has a thousand souls not one to call his own." I had very scant acquaintanceship with my own character. I doubt if I should have recognised my real self if we had met head on. However, on that occasion I thought individually and at once. Five guineas is twice the sum to the desperate. It would help to replace the curtains. I revived one of our early Lord Credits from the George at Huntingdon. It occurred to me that in order to escape detection as an ill-bred person it would be sensible to play a foreigner. Accent and faux pas would then be excused. I remembered Philippe-Jean-Baptiste-Raoul Vicomte de Lambrière! He had been a twelve-year-old boy when we diddled the George at Huntingdon, but there was nothing to have stopped him from growing up.

I crossed the room to Miss Weldon.

"I'll give you a taste, but if you like it, it will cost you clothes and five guineas."

"Very well," she said.

I was swiftly and thoroughly nervous. There was no point in looking at M.S. He might have shaken his head, and I was so trained in obedience to him I would have dropped the idea. With my back to him I told Miss Weldon and Water Face, "I am a French aristocrat. My name is Philippe de Lambrière. I am a vicomte. We are in France and this is my house. You are two of my English guests. My manager here is my tutor with whom I made the grand tour — the Reverend Mr. Jabez Stock." "Ready?" I enquired of Miss Weldon.

"Ready," she said, nodding.

I closed my eyes for a few seconds and then picked up the decanter of Marsala. I refilled Miss Weldon's glass, for which she gave me a small bow of thanks, showing no surprise. But Water Face gaped at me. I took it as a refusal and passed him to give Manager Smith a generous glassful. I was liberal towards my own as well. I chose only a lightly broken accent — not too heavily stressing the "r's" and paying special attention to the vowels about which foreigners are always so careful. I aimed at gaiety without effort, but also tried to give the impression that I was someone to whom serious things could matter. I felt the lack of rehearsal fearsomely and was afraid that I was giving no better performance than Water Face as Miss Spent. M.S. was instantly magnificent. The minute I referred to the Reverend Mr. Jabez Stock, his shoulders shrank and his knees sank down into invisible gaiters. He used his wuffling absent-minded voice, breaking off to chuckle at a joke he had neglected to tell, and leaving a sentence incomplete to tackle a new subject. Only his ears would have made him recognisable to those who knew him.

I jumped right into the middle of a conversation as if the discussion had been going some time.

"— it was something I always said to Monsieur Stock — so like a French town it felt to be quite at home there."

" 'I felt quite at home there,' " corrected M.S. "Or, 'one felt quite at home there.' "

I laughed. "Always the tutor, never the friend who forgets to teach you."

M.S. chuckled. "Dear me, dear me, yes — you had your first silver buckles and so proud of them — ah well, getting on, getting on, we all are, I suppose."

"You know it, Mademoiselle. Weldon? This St. Neots I speak of?"

She shook her head. "I'm afraid I'm very untravelled in my own country, but this is not the first time I have visited yours, Monsieur le Vicomte. My father is a great friend of the Lieutenant of Police in Paris and we've stayed with him." She gave her sudden broad smile which seemed so unsuited to her pale face. "As a matter of fact, he's making a return visit to my father's house in England at this moment. You will meet him if you come to my ball on December the sixth."

She could have said nothing more calculated to put me off and she knew it. But I forced myself to struggle on. "I was speaking of St. Neots, Miss Weldon."

"So you were. What took you to that part of the country?"

"The cathedrals," I answered. "Mr. Stock was showing me your beautiful cathedrals. We went to York and then we came down to see the lovely Ely."

"Yes, I envy you that," she said: "it's something I should like to do myself, a most interesting study. I long to see your wonderful Chartres."

"Ah!" I said, "we must make no comparison — but Chartres!" and I kissed my finger tips — a gesture I later pulled out of the part. It was grossly overdone.

"Stayed at Huntingdon," M.S. broke in. "The George — nice hotel, but we left very suddenly. Why was that, Philippe?"

It was one of the regular traps he sprang at me whenever we were playing Lord Credits to see if I was proof against embarrassment.

"We fell off with the management," I said.

" 'Out!' " snapped M.S. "Fell 'out' with the management," and he raised irritable eyebrows to heaven. "No one would think I had taught the boy English."

"Well, it was a long time ago," I laughed, "and I get not much practice."

I took the decanter to Miss Weldon again. She put three soft fingers over the top of her glass and smiled a refusal. Water Face was still gaping, so I passed him by and replenished M.S. By the time I had refilled my own glass, the Marsala was a dirty red-brown shadow on the bottom of the decanter. Miss Weldon asked sweetly, "Is this your own wine, Monsieur le Vicomte? I mean, did you grow it on the estate?"

"I am glad to say not, Miss Weldon, it is a particularly poor Marsala."

Then I sat beside her. "Mademoiselle must allow me to congratulate her on her gown." I ventured a finger to stroke the dull, close velvet. "Such an enchanting colour — the colour of the always green, which Miss Weldon will be for the rest of her life."

" 'Evergreen,' " corrected M.S.

Miss Weldon stood up with the easy grace of a nun rising from prayer. She was far more attractive in motion than she was in repose. "Your broken

English is effective, Mr. Roberts, and I must say that I should feel happier if you disguised yourself as a foreigner. There'll be less chance of your being detected as a common person. But, as you've just heard, my father's old friend from Paris will be there. What will you do if he speaks to you in French?"

"Answer him. My mother was a Frenchwoman, and I spoke it before English. But I think it would be better if I changed the character. I haven't been back to France since I was one and he might ask difficult questions."

"The boy can't take the risk of playing a Frenchy to a Frenchy," said M.S. "At least, not unless the money was put up to ten guineas."

"I could manage with the language," I insisted, "and I should keep out of his way as much as possible. But there's certainly a risk and it would be wiser to choose another character."

Miss Weldon sat down and looked thoughtful. She shook her head. "No, I like your vicomte. It would be more flattering to me to have a French aristocrat interested in me, and it would impress Mr. Hawtrey to know that I had someone so — so — young and charming and —" She broke off and flushed a little. I felt sure that she had been going to add "attractive," but she substituted "distinguished." "What part of France did you come from?"

"The slums of Paris."

"Oh, well, that of course we shall take care not to mention."

I shrugged my shoulders. "It must be your choice, Miss Weldon, you're taking the risk. I have nothing to lose by it," I added with that unhappy knack I have of making incorrect forecasts.

She turned to M.S. "Five pounds ten shillings, Mr. Smith."

"Ten."

"Six."

"Ten."

"Seven."

"Ten."

"Eight."

"Done," said M.S.

Chapter 11.

IT WAS just as well that we had been forced to cancel the two productions. We needed all our time to perfect Philippe-Jean-Baptiste-Raoul Vicomte de Lambrière. M.S. was far from complimentary about my performance in front of Miss Weldon. He said it had been like an actor trying to play an actor trying to play a Frenchman. "You're lucky she didn't come down in price from a guinea to ten shillings the way you rolled them 'orrible eyes up at 'er."

"It struck me," I said coolly, "that she was rather impressed. You'll notice she refused to allow me to change the character."

"She also put up a better performance than you did."

We rehearsed Philippe daily. We went very carefully into his background. M.S. pointed out that we could not be too circumspect with a Lieutenant of Police on the premises. I was not worried about my fluency in the French language, but my mother might have taught me the accent of her slummy neighbourhood, and I might have used words that would sound odd coming from a young aristocrat! To offset this I took lessons from a French master in Bristol. He quickly showed up my crudities and I was glad I had spent the money. I was soon confident that I could hold my own amongst my French betters.

Water Face gave me the name of a French tailor in London and a peruke maker. We even sent to France for newspapers, for I must be abreast of French thought — but not too much. It wouldn't be wise to hail from Paris, as that could be too easily checked. I was to come from the provinces. I was all for representing the liberal trends in France; apart from the fact that they were in tune with my own political opinions, I thought it would give me something to talk about. But M.S. considered it unsafe. Those first early stirrings of unrest which Tom Paine was already lauding in the *Chronicle* would be dangerous ground, said M.S. The movement had too many supporters in England who might like to question me on it. Philippe must represent la vieille France with a stolid inability to see further than his aristocratic nose. He must accept his own privileges as a divine right and see nothing alarming in the fermenting wrongs of his inferiors.

M.S. disapproved of my advanced ideas. His creed was fiercely traditional, a trait that I've often noticed with crooks. The King was the "Lord's anointed," good blood was good blood, and any reform (except prison reform, of course) was a sin against the Bible.

We decided to retain the broken accent. We concentrated on gestures with the hands. We took a refresher course in dancing, with M.S. partnering me as a simpering Miss Weldon. We studied somewhat bitterly the list of dos and don'ts that Miss Weldon had thoughtfully provided. It told me which knives and forks I was to use for each course; it pointed out that it was not done to comment, even in a complimentary fashion, on the food. But it was permissible to talk of the wine if I were asked my opinion as a vineyard owner. Cost must never be queried; only flattering remarks as to flavour were allowed. She was thoughtful enough to include the names of the wines we should be drinking so that I might be knowledgeable about them. I was not to fold my napkin after dinner but to leave it crumpled on my place. On no account was I to stack the plates or attempt to assist the footman removing them. I was to eat silently. I was not to mop my plate with bread. In brackets she informed me: ["The bourgeoisie adopt this custom in France, but not someone of your supposed pretensions to blood"].

I was not to remove my dancing pumps under the table even if they were drawing blood. I was not to blow my nose in public and I was to pay particular attention to stifling any tendency to belch after so much unaccustomed food. The list was interminable. She had forgotten nothing, down to the fact that I must not relieve myself in the garden, owing to the fact that it would be lantern-lit.

There was to be no coarse laughter or terms of speech, and I must not be in awe of her surroundings. "You must try to look used to graceful living and to the type of person you will be meeting. There will obviously be real titled persons present, and you must not show the honour you will naturally feel in being addressed by them as their equal."

Above all I must be attentive to her in front of Mr. Hawtrey; "I myself shall behave as if I found myself attracted to you. You must understand that this will only apply to you in your character as the Vicomte. When we are alone together — and this will be inevitable, for you will take me frequently into the garden as if you desired my private company — you will remember your place. There must be no attempt to play the Vicomte without spectators."

There was a small human touch that made me smile through my rage. "I should be grateful if you would compliment me as much as possible in front of my women friends. References to beauty or elegance would be a little difficult for them to swallow. Could you think of anything else that might make them believe that you could genuinely admire me? I shall not have many chances to triumph over them."

After such pathetic frankness, which was indeed one of the few appealing things about her, she antagonised me again by reminding me not to scratch, spit, or pick my nose even when I thought I was unobserved.

On the all-important night her carriage collected me at the theatre. Water Face was sitting in it presumably to make sure that I hadn't put my luxurious clothes on back to front and that I was not drunk. Manager Smith forebore to greet him. It really hurt him to see my talents wasted on such "an inglorious lot," as he called them.

"Nervous?" asked Water Face as the hedgerows unwound like black ribbons beside us. It was a grave-dark night and as cold.

"No," I answered.

"Good for you!" he was kind enough to say.

Turning a bitter eye towards him, I realised that he had actually meant to be kind. It occurred to me that Water Face had not come to criticise me but to give me support. His further remark convinced me.

"Thought it might be a bit of an ordeal. Thought if you came with some-one you knew it might make it easier, if you know what I mean."

I knew what he meant and was grateful to him. I happened to be ex-tremely nervous. It was absurd because I had played many Lord Credits before with far fewer rehearsals than this one, but I had never played them without Manager Smith.

"Thank you," I said to Water Face, and then, tempted towards friend-ship, I asked him, "This was *your* idea, wasn't it? I find that very curious. It doesn't sound like you. I could have believed it of Miss Weldon more easily than you." It obviously wasn't possible to tell him that it would have surprised me to find him with any ideas at all in his head, let alone an original one.

"Yes," he said. "Well, you see, I'm fond of Lizzie." He turned round to me as if he expected me to think this made him an eccentric. "We were brought up together. I'm rather the poor relation. I'm Lizzie's father's sister's son. Nobody approved of my mother's marriage, and when he left her, everyone said, 'I told you so.' " He looked at me as if I might find the phrase stimulatingly fresh. "My mother died and they took me in — but, don't you know, they took me in — sort of, well —"

"I can guess" — I nodded firmly — "exactly how they took you in."

"They were very kind," he said loyally. "I mean they paid for everything. But — well —" He shrugged in such an exaggerated manner that I knew he had been drinking, and when he next spoke I realised why. "It's silly really, I'm the same blood as them, but, well — I'm nervous about tonight as well. It's always been the same. Just because I haven't their money they think I don't know which fork to use either. My uncle tells me how to be-have before every affair like tonight. Silly, when they've brought me up, but it gets me so rattled I damn well do all the wrong things and that, of course, makes for an even longer lecture next time."

"You seem different," I said, "when you're away from Miss Weldon."

"Well, I'm very fond of Lizzie, but when you're the fool of the family and you're with one of the family, I suppose you feel the fool."

"Yes, I suppose so. Why don't you find something to do and leave them?"

"I'm supposed to be learning about the estate — to manage it for her when the old man dies. It's the least I can do after all they've done, and Lizzie's been particularly good to me. She's always been a terror for getting her own way — even when she was a child. She just sat and screamed until she got what she wanted. But she always screamed for two of it — so that I got one as well!"

"This idea of yours is more or less out of gratitude, then?"

"Yes. I'd like to see her hook this Hawtrey chap, although I think his father's the better man. Lizzie put the idea about you into my head and then sort of got me to suggest it. She's good at that. I tell you, there's no one to touch her for getting what she wants. She just goes on until people give in."

"What do her women friends think she lacks most?" I asked him. I was still trying to think of what compliments I could pay her.

"Well, they're a bit frightened of her, I think, so they make fun of her for being on the shelf, and for not being pretty and because she speaks her mind. They say she's too brainy to get a man, but, of course, they don't say it to her."

We were turning into the Weldons' drive. Water Face sighed as the black bulk of the house came into view with its lighted windows like square, orange eyes.

"Oh, well," he said, "it can't last for ever, can it?" and added, "I'm to take you to Lizzie first. The butler's been sent off duty in case he recognised you. The under-chappie's taken over."

"She thinks of everything," I said.

"She does," he sighed, "she does."

She was waiting for me in an anteroom. She was in green again! This time it was that unfortunate shade that people seem to insist is the colour of paint most suitable to orphanages. She did not greet me, and I was surprised to see that she was nervous. Her earrings trembled as she tried to keep her head erect. "You understand that no one other than our three selves and your manager knows who you really are? My father thinks we met on my last visit to London at the house of a friend."

"You put all that in your notes," I reminded her.

"I want to be sure that you won't drop your pose for a minute."

She spoke as if she were addressing troops on the eve of battle. In spite of her commanding tone, I was sorry for her. I knew what it was like to feel shaky with nerves. I bent forward to kiss her hand. She snatched it from me as if I'd been going to bite it.

"The salutation," I said bitterly, "would have come from the Vicomte, not the common actor!"

Reassured on this vital point, she graciously extended her hand.

Judge Weldon was what I expected him to be, about as warm as a clod of earth on a grave-digger's spade. He was a tall man and arrow thin. He had Lizzie's formidable grey eyes and her pale skin, but he seemed to have none of the occasional gleams of humour that could be seen round Lizzie's mouth. He studied me with deep prejudice. Far from being surprised that his uncharming daughter had collected such a personable young aristocrat, he seemed to resent it. It pierced my confidence at once. There's not much point in false modesty, so I'll admit that I looked very fetching in the finest clothes I had ever worn. Even Manager Smith had gloomily informed me that if I wasn't careful I should have female audiences more interested in my looks than in my talents. He hated a good-looking actor.

But neither Lizzie nor her father appeared to be the least impressed. I could read the father's thoughts as he looked me over coldly: "Young French fop after my daughter's money!" I could see why the poor girl lacked suitors. Even had she been able to attract them herself, Papa would have frightened them off.

I took Lizzie's arm when I led her into the ballroom. Her flesh trembled under my hand, and when I pressed her slightly to reassure her, she went as taut as a tow-rope.

I whispered to her, "In France, mademoiselle, we think it's a compliment that a man should want to get close to the woman who pleases him."

The Weldons' ballroom was uninviting. Heavy old-fashioned chairs lined the walls, and great carved mirrors reflected the dowagers shining with jewels. My quick eye told me that there wouldn't be too much temptation for me amongst the younger generation. There was one piece with fair hair I shouldn't have snubbed if she had offered to befriend me, but the rest were a plump line of good complexions and semi-precious stones. They handled their fans like butter churns. Their men deserved them. It was inevitable, I suppose, that the Weldons' friends would be unstimulating, but they must have combed Somerset for that selection of witless "well-breds."

The sole exceptions were Sir Gregory Hawtrey and the French Lieutenant of Police. They stood together at the end of the room. Sir Gregory was the father of the Nicholas I had been hired to fire into romantic action. I infinitely preferred him to his son. Had I been Lizzie I should have paid to have Nicholas fired into oblivion. I should have thought it would have been impossible for anyone to have been fond of him, but his father suffered from parental hallucinations. He thought young Hawtrey the world's finest specimen of manhood. It was pathetic to see pride leap into his eyes whenever the lout made a dull remark. His conversation was peppered with, "My boy, Nick." Sir Gregory was a finely built man — well boned and courteous — and his age compared favourably with his son's soggy youth. He was upright and spritely and he had no sign of the paunch that Nicholas was developing.

Louis Brissac, the Lieutenant of Police, had sleepy-lidded eyes in an expressionless baby-face, but I guessed that he was about the same age as Sir Gregory. He was tall and thin but powerfully built. One felt that, unlike Water Face, his lack of expression was studied. His voice was toneless and weary-sounding and he spoke slowly for a Frenchman. I sensed that he took a keen interest in me. Judge Weldon was not the only one who thought I was after his daughter's money. The heavy-lidded eyes took me in with professional care, but while I did not think he suspected me of being an impostor, I felt that he had no doubts that I was an adventurer.

Sir Gregory was attached to the Foreign Office, and it was a good thing I had taken pains with my French because he spoke it adequately himself. He warned the Lieutenant and myself, in what later proved to be rather an understatement, that from the way things were going he felt our country was "heading for a bit of trouble."

The Lieutenant was in favour of reform, and his politics were much nearer my own than the ones I had to profess to as De Lambrière. I should like to have talked at length to him but thought it safe to see as little of him as possible. Besides, I had to dance attendance on Lizzie.

Sir Gregory's "boy Nick" was not a gaper in the same sense that Water Face was. He was an aggressive starer. His pug-eyes clung to my face like a pair of barnacles. His obvious ill-will towards me did wonders for Lizzie. The pale face bloomed; the strong eyes were softened with excitement; the hand she frequently put on my arm to emphasise a point was warm and steady; and the earrings were shaking with genuinely gay laughter.

I was touched by such obvious signs of humanity. She could never have enjoyed herself so much in her life, and she certainly had her triumph over her women friends.

I was the undoubted king of the dung heap. I was little short of a sensation in that icy-cold ballroom which two fires failed to warm. Dowager after dowager found an excuse to present a daughter. The excuses were nearly all the same: their little Charlottes, Angelas, Katherines, and Amelias were all *so* interested in my country. They were all studying French, but of course they had *so* little practice, *would* I be so kind as to exchange a few words with them?

The ones who had crossed the Channel were the most persistent, and quite determined to air their knowledge. This was useful, as I had no recollection of my homeland at all. They twittered and squeaked and laughed at my flattest remarks and were all obviously bewildered as to what in the world I could see in poor Lizzie Weldon.

To compliment her wasn't as difficult as I thought. Firstly because of her pathetic radiance and secondly because it was not hard to compare her favourably with her rivals. Had she not been such a rude bitch, I should have preferred her company to any of those curl-bobbing squeakers.

"*Do* tell us, Monsieur le Vicomte," one of them chirruped, "are the women in Paris so very beautiful?"

"But more than beautiful," I told the flat-chested little brat. "They have much things more enticing. You find that over here as well," and I directed a warmly provocative glance straight into the eyes of Lizzie. "They have character. They set themselves out to please the male; they can talk to you and they have a mind of their own. They take as much trouble with their brains as with their bodies."

Perhaps it is the actor in me, but I have always despised people who are unable to control their expressions. That little collection failed completely. With the exception of Sir Gregory, who nodded agreement, and his "boy Nick," who continued to stare his unhealthy dislike of me, they all turned on poor Lizzie ill-concealed looks of pure astonishment. She retained her poise. She blushed, but with discretion; she did not turn the ungainly red-cabbage hue that any of her so-called friends would have turned.

Sir Gregory was not subtle. He left me in no doubt that his dearest hopes were centred upon the match with his son and Lizzie. This was not imme-diately easy to understand, but later, when I worked it out, I realised that it came out of his loyalty. He and the Judge had adjoining estates. They had known one another since boyhood, he had seen Lizzie grow up, and that was enough for Sir Gregory. Also, it occurred to me that much as he worshipped his "boy Nick," any man of that calibre could never completely trick himself. He must have had to deal very sternly with hurtful suspicions that his boy was a weakling. Perhaps he felt that his son needed the strength of a woman like Lizzie.

Water Face was in trouble with his uncle at nearly every step he took, but the poor lad was as proud of my performance as if he'd been giving it himself. My success was so obvious, as I was the centre of a clamorous circle of women, that it amused me to have him pull me aside and point it out to me.

"I say," he whispered, "you're doing quite well. Lizzie's pleased, I can see that, and Nicholas isn't pleased, I can see that too." He winked to push this naked truth home to me and added, "It's splendid. I'd have been taken in myself if I hadn't known."

I thanked him and slipped off with Lizzie into the great ugly conservatory, having first taken care that Nicholas was watching us. She snatched her arm out of mine the second we were out of sight and wound a lace shawl round her shoulders. Stupidly enough, I was taken off my guard. We had been getting on so well in the ballroom and throughout the lengthy supper that I had got used to her being pleasant to me. The sudden cold reminder of how far beneath her I was in real life made me so angry I hoped she'd get Nicholas. She sat as far from me as possible, and stared ahead of her in silence.

"I think," I suggested, "it would be more effective if you looked a little disarranged. A few hairs out of place or perhaps one earring missing. We don't want Nicholas to think you haven't appealed to me out here."

"I don't want *Mr.* Hawtrey to think I'm a harlot, either, and if you must address me, please do so in your character of a vicomte or not at all."

I sat back, and for the next ten minutes kept up a swift flow of French. I told her a little fairy story.

"Once upon a time," I cooed, "there was a woman. Not very young, not very pretty — but interesting. Strength of character can be alluring — pro-vided it's human. But the lady I refer to was not human. She thought she had only to nod her head to her so-called inferiors to make them content with their lot. Actors, of course, she particularly despised, and in sitting with one in a conservatory, no matter what favour he might be doing her and no matter how much more he would have preferred to be sitting with a prostitute, she felt herself contaminated. What she really needed was raping by the village half-wit, but what half-wit would be so silly? To whom, madam, do you think this pathetic lady has anything to offer? An actor, a half-wit, or the pop-eyed son of a besotted baronet?"

She was listening with great attention. When I'd finished my sadistic attack she stood up, removing one earring and untidying her hair a little. I thought that for a second the gleam of humour appeared at the sides of her mouth. But her voice was cold. "Thank you, Monsieur le Vicomte, it was a charming story, but I'd prefer you not to repeat it to any of my guests. Some of them speak French as well as I do."

Crushed, I held out my hand for the earring.

"You'd better give that to me. When you find you've lost it, I'll come out here and look for it. I'll return it to you so that Mr. Hawtrey catches me. That should kindle his imagination."

She handed me the earring without looking at me. But as we entered the ballroom she was smiling and intimate again. She listened attentively whenever I spoke, laughed flatteringly whenever I joked, and the hand was constantly on my arm. Then she gave a little cry. "Oh! Philippe, I've lost one of my earrings!"

We caused a little pother by searching round about us and then I said gaily, "Ah! The conservatory. Yes, I expect we shall find it there. . . ."

I returned it to her in front of young Nicholas, with the desired effect. He said he wanted a word with me. His aggressive eyes stuck out like brandy balls. He said, "Look here, I know you're a foreigner, but over here we don't compromise a single woman like that."

"But surely, monsieur, it's worse to compromise a married one?"

"I've never liked you Frenchies," he said, "and I can't see myself making an exception in your case."

"I'm stricken to hear such bad news," I replied.

"I don't like the way you behave with Miss Weldon."

"But Miss Weldon does — so it goes only to prove that you can't please everybody."

"Bear what I say in mind," he snapped, and walked off.

I promptly took Lizzie to the conservatory again. This time I made no attempt to talk. I sat staring ahead of me. It was just as well that I saw Nicholas in time. I leaned over and tugged Lizzie across the seat to me. I put my arms round her and kissed her lengthily on the mouth. I felt her gasp and the ripple of shock that ran through her body as she found out what kissing was like. I broke away only when Nicholas was standing over us. Lizzie collapsed against the white-washed wall, her hair genuinely disturbed. Nicholas Hawtrey shook his fist in my face. I jumped up threateningly. "How dare Monsieur interrupt us like this and frighten the lady."

"How dare you — how dare *you* treat her like this." He was so angry I thought the brandy balls would roll out of his face.

"Monsieur is not the husband of Miss Weldon?"

"You know damn well I'm not."

"And you are not her betrothed?"

"No, but I'm — I'm a very old friend and — and —"

"Only husbands have the right to interrupt lovemaking, and even they are often not welcome!"

He was thinking of challenging me but took my size into account. He turned and left us.

"That," I said, "has done more good than the rest of the evening put together."

I went to help Lizzie up, but she beat me away with frightened hands. She was still breathing fast and still trembling. It was the first time I had ever seen her lose her poise. She couldn't bring herself to look at me.

"You must go," she said. "You must make some excuse and leave at once."

"What about my salary?"

"My — my cousin will pay you outside."

I've never seen a woman so knocked out by a kiss. She seemed quite unable to pull herself together.

"Do you feel all right?"

"Yes, yes. Do as I say. My cousin will pay you at the door."

Water Face duly doled out my eight pounds ten, and that was the last I expected to see of either of them. But I was wrong. Water Face reappeared in my life exactly three days later.

Chapter 12.

WE WERE working on the damaged scenery at the Little Apollo when a message came that I had a visitor out front. I left M.S. to get on with the painting and found Water Face in the foyer.

He looked embarrassed. "Is there somewhere a little more private?"

"Yes," I said, "my dressing-room."

He was astonished at all the make-up on my table. "Do you really put all that stuff on your face?"

"Not all at once. What can I do for you?"

"Well," he said, "it's Lizzie."

"Safely betrothed to that endearing young man, I trust?"

"No, that's what I've come about. He was frightfully shocked at her. She thought at first it might have put him off, but he came round in the end."

"And proposed?"

"Not exactly, but he gave her to understand that he *might* be going to do so."

"An ardent soul, isn't he?"

Water Face was staring at me. "You know, I can hardly believe it's you after the way you played that Frenchy. It took everybody in."

"I'm only sorry it didn't have the desired effect on the reluctant lover."

"Well, he warned her you were only after her money —"

"That was true. We wanted the eight pounds badly!"

"And he told her you were the sort of man who couldn't be serious about anybody. He said he could see right through you."

"He was wrong there, wasn't he?"

"I mean he said you'd play up to any woman without being really interested in her. She wants to prove that you are. She wants you to play the Vicomte once more."

"Oh, good God!" I said. "I couldn't stand the strain."

"It would be much more money this time, but, of course, the same rules would apply: you'd still have to take no liberties in private. But she feels that if Nicholas saw that you were still courting her, it would convince him you were serious."

"I tell you I couldn't go through another evening at the Weldons' house."

"You wouldn't have to. We're going to take the waters in Bath. You'd be our guest and naturally you'd get all expenses, even medical ones."

I shot at him, "*Medical* ones! I'm as fit as a flea!"

He shook his head. "You won't be in Bath. They always find something wrong with you. It would only be for a week," he added encouragingly, "and Lizzie retires very early when she takes the waters. She doesn't like to waste the cure. There's plenty to do in the evenings. I daresay you and I could enjoy ourselves. Nicholas goes to bed early, too."

I thought of the seating that needed to be replaced, of the boxes that wanted repanelling, and of the new leading lady M.S. was so anxious to acquire. She was asking too much money and we couldn't afford her, but there was no doubt that she would be a draw. The curtains would not be ready for some time and it would be a good while before we could open again. I could easily fit in a week in Bath.

"Does Hawtrey know there's a possibility of my joining you?"

"No, Lizzie thought it better to surprise him."

"How much is she willing to pay?"

"Well, ten pounds, but then, of course, it'll cost her much more than that. There will be all your bills and you'll need several suits of clothing if you're going to look what you're supposed to be. She's going to order your clothes from the French tailor again. It takes too long to send to France. She had to write off for her own months ago."

I offered him a pinch of snuff. He accepted it. At least there was no nonsense about not being able to be at home with a common actor where Water Face was concerned.

"Well, I'll have a word with my manager," I said. "There's just one thing: I really couldn't struggle through another written lecture on how to behave. She must trust me this time or I won't take the part. She's seen my performance now."

"Yes, I'll tell her. But, of course, no one can really tell Lizzie anything."

"There's another thing. I'd like you to have a shot at getting her to understand that nothing in the world would persuade me to try and take liberties with her in private."

He nodded and, bending over my dressing-table, fingered my make-up pots. "I say — do you think I could try one of those things on my face?"

"You can try the lot." I sat him in front of the mirror and put a towel round him. In a short while I had made him up as a fairly convincing old man. He was as thrilled as a child at its first Christmas party. When I had cleaned him off, he looked round to make sure he could not be overheard.

"You know, it's an awful thing to admit, but I've always had a liking for this game. I rather think I'd have made a pretty good actor. I wish you could have seen me in that charade."

When he had gone, I tackled M.S. He struggled against the idea, but the money won.

"That plaguing half-brother's cutting us down again," he told me gloomily. "The second Mrs. Lambert heard from him this morning. It appears that he saw you wink at his wife."

"Well, she winked back."

"He saw that too! Very well, boy, off you go. But keep out of the gaming houses and don't go whoring."

Lizzie was certainly unsparing of money where her own ends were concerned. She had ordered me a handsome wardrobe. I had never possessed such fashionable garments in my life. But I became nervous again when it was time to leave. Water Face came to collect me. Lizzie had gone ahead with her maid, and was taking along an aunt as a chaperone. Nicholas was to meet her there. The plan was that I was supposed to have heard of her visit from mutual friends, and such was my eagerness to outdo Nicholas that I had promptly set out to join her without her knowledge. Lizzie was to be overcome with surprise at seeing me.

Apparently, however, it was nothing to the surprise I should receive on beholding Lizzie, Water Face informed me.

"You'll hardly know her!" he said. "She managed to get the French Queen's own dressmaker. She sent Lizzie about a dozen dressed-up dolls to choose from — you didn't have to choose the exact samples, you know: you could choose the style from one and the colour from another. But the sauce that woman had when it came to charging! They say she's so spoilt by the Queen she can ask what she likes."

Water Face was looking rather dashing himself. When I complimented him on his suit, he smiled. "Yes, well, that's what I mean about her. She didn't leave me out, either."

Not even Madame Rose Bertin could have turned Lizzie into a beauty, I suppose, but she had at least wooed her away from those fatal greens, and got her into an elegant deep blue. It suited her admirably. It accentuated the pale skin, making it live instead of die, as the browns and the grave-yard-moss colours had done. Moreover, the cut revealed the astonishing fact that she had quite a good figure. Furthermore, she had achieved a dignity that nearly passed for grace.

She did not overplay her surprise at seeing me. She was most convincing. She would have hated having to admit it, but she was an excellent actress. Poor Water Face nearly gave us all away. He professed such grotesque astonishment at meeting me again that I thought it would soon become clear even to Nicholas that we had only just parted. He was poignantly anxious to be praised. The second he got me alone he asked breathlessly, "Was I all right? Did I do it well? You'd know — I mean, it's your line of country."

"You gave," I told him solemnly, "a performance I should never have expected to see from any professional actor." The poor lad nearly wept for delight.

Lizzie, the aunt, Water Face, and the maid were all at the Bear. Nicholas was at the Hotel Angus, and I had lodgings near the pump room.

Whatever ailment had persuaded Nicholas to take the cure was made worse on sight of me. He stood in front of me for several seconds, forebore to comment, and went back to the Hotel Angus for the rest of the day.

The medical routine was a ramp. Two doctors and a nurse called on each of us the morning after our arrival. We were forbidden to start taking the waters until they had diagnosed our complaints. They gave us strong purges and left us twelve hours to let them work. The following morning they delivered their verdicts. Their fees were exorbitant and their theories absurd. Lizzie was suffering from nerves. Nerves! Lizzie! Without one in her body! Water Face was in danger of septic gout, and Nicholas suffered from chronic wind, which was probably true. They were a little stumped by me. I was so obviously glowing with health. But they found me an inflamed colon owing to my overspiced French food!

By arrangement with the doctors, chairmen called each morning to take us to the springs. There we bobbed about while music played upstairs.

Water Face and I certainly entertained ourselves in the evening when Lizzie had retired. We went to the assembly rooms and played faro and loo and then went on to the Subscription Balls. Seldom have I enjoyed myself more. There was one little piece with insolent eyes who did not need much persuading. It was difficult to shake her off in the daytime, but I had to remember that I was being paid to dance attendance on Lizzie Weldon.

She was playing beautifully. Her performance was so skilful that there were times when I was taken in by it. Her eyes softened on sight of me. She fussed over me as if I was an ailing child. Had I not known that she was not only acting but covering up a deep dislike of making herself pleasant to a common actor, I should have thought the woman was really in love with me. She even offered to repeat her ordeal in the conservatory. "If you think it necessary to compromise me again in front of Nicholas, I shall not object, providing, of course, it's in your character as the Vicomte."

I said that I thought we were doing quite nicely already, and there was no need for me to distress her with my physical attentions.

"I wasn't inviting them for their own sake," she snapped.

She showed a most convincing jealousy when we ran into Insolent Eyes. I had warned the girl that I shouldn't be able to acknowledge her in the daytime, but she danced straight up to me.

"Oh, Monsieur le Vicomte," she cooed, "it seems such a long time since we met, and yet it was only last night. *Do* introduce me to your mother." And she turned with an expectant smile to Lizzie.

For a second or two I was paralysed. Then I said coldly, "This lady is several years my junior."

Lizzie gave me a grateful smile, and I must say I admired her for her dignified handling of Insolent Eyes. She made the girl feel so small, she faded away.

It was a relief to me to reach the end of our week in Bath. In spite of the nights of pleasure spent with Insolent Eyes — and I did not renew them after the Lizzie incident — I was missing the theatre and M.S. *The Ambitious Stepmother* was well under my belt and I was yearning to get back.

It was a happy time for me when Lizzie came to me on Friday morning and told me, "Our little ruse has succeeded, Philippe. Nicholas Hawtrey has proposed."

Kissing her hand, I congratulated her.

"Thank you, Philippe," she said, "but I've turned him down."

Chapter 13.

I CLEARED off that afternoon. The look on Lizzie Weldon's face had frightened me. Surely, I thought, such a sensible woman couldn't be going to make a fool of herself. She couldn't have persuaded herself that Philippe de Lambrière really existed! But that is precisely what she had done.

We were playing *The Ambitious Stepmother* and rehearsing *The Discovery* when she called at the theatre with Water Face.

I was removing my make-up. There were great gobs of grease all over my face. She sat down on my only chair in the dressing-room and for once failed to keep her hands still in her lap. Water Face stood against the door. He was pink in the face and ill at ease. He lifted his shoulders helplessly at me as if he wished me to know that he disassociated himself from this visit.

Lizzie Weldon said, "I should be willing to pay you to act Philippe de Lambrière again."

"I can't," I told her, "I'm at work now."

"You're not on the stage the whole time."

"Yes, I am. I sleep on it."

She looked at me. The powerful eyes were hardly visible behind helpless tears. "My life isn't going to be bearable without Philippe de Lambrière."

My towel was halfway to my face; I lowered it to stare at her.

"Philippe de Lambrière doesn't exist."

"To me he does, and he could if you'd be willing to go on acting him."

"But I'm not."

"I love him, Mr. Roberts. I realise now that I've never loved another human being in the whole of my life. I'm fond of my father, I'm fond of my cousin, but I've never loved anyone. Philippe has made that different. It's a most distressing feeling, and I realise I haven't sympathised enough with people who have been through it before me."

Standing over her, I flung my hands out. "You know perfectly well that there's no Philippe — that there's only an actor you despise putting himself into a character for money."

"I've always seen only what I want to see — and I can only see Philippe. He is everything I admire in a man. Everything he does attracts me — the way he speaks, that funny half-smile, his mixed-up words, his laughter, his kindness — yes," she replied to my look, "Philippe's very kind. He knows how to make a plain woman feel beautiful. He can take years off a woman's

age. He can make her friends admire her instead of despise her, and —"
She stopped to twist her rings. "Well, I just don't intend to live without
him, Mr. Roberts, and that's all there is to it."

I slumped against my dressing-table. The grease was beginning to melt
on my face. I sent an appealing glance at Water Face. He shrugged again,
spreading his hands out.

"But, Miss Weldon, you'll *have* to live without him because he isn't
there. It's like falling in love with a character in a story: you can't make him
flesh and blood."

She looked up again. The tears were gone and some of the force had
crept back into her eyes. "I can if I pay you to play him always."

I flung down my make-up towel. "Miss Weldon, you're talking like a
madwoman."

"I admit that I have fallen in love with someone who doesn't exist, but
I have the money to pay you to *make* him exist. I call that a very sane
attitude."

The woman astounded me. I stammered at her, "Do you really think
I'd be willing to trip round you as a French vicomte for the rest of my days?"

"If you find keeping up the broken accent a strain, you could drop it
eventually. I don't object to your own. It's quite passable, and it would be
perfectly natural for a Frenchman living over here to speak better English
in time."

"But — but my dear lady, I have a career to think of. It happens to be
something *I* shouldn't care to live without."

"It wouldn't pay you as well as I should."

I said gently, "It must be hard for you to believe that money isn't everything, but in point of fact it isn't. The stage appeals to me for its own sake."

"But you'd be acting — you'd be acting all the time. If you didn't, I
shouldn't support you."

"Don't you think people might find it a little odd in years to come that
your aging vicomte was still paying court to you without success? Also, if
I have the luck I hope for in my career, someone might recognise me on the
stage and realise that we were one and the same person."

"You'd have to give all that up. We should have to be married. I'm really
very rich: you'd be making an excellent bargain for yourself. You'd have
opportunities you'd never have otherwise; living the life of a gentleman, for
instance — meeting people you'd never meet if you stuck to your own
kind. You would have a life of plenty and very little to do in return for it
except to pretend to be someone else."

I gaped at her.

"I love Philippe de Lambrière," she repeated.

It was still difficult for me to believe that I was hearing aright. She looked so utterly sensible and well controlled. It didn't seem possible that she could be sitting there demanding that I should renounce my own identity for life.

"After all," she added, "it shouldn't be difficult for you: you're half French in reality. I've sometimes wondered from your features whether you haven't some illegitimate good blood in your veins."

"My father was a strolling player and my mother was a laundress from the Parisian slums," I snapped at her. "I come straight from the sewers on both sides."

She lifted two deprecating hands and shook them as if the mention of my parentage had left a stench she wished to wave away. "All that belongs to Mr. Roberts and it's *he* who does not exist for me. There has never been any such person as far as I'm concerned. There never was and there never will be. Mr. Roberts is not just dead to me: he was never born." She made me feel like my own ghost standing there. I felt tempted to pinch myself to see if I was solid. "You will soon get used to thinking of yourself as Philippe de Lambrière, and in time I'm sure you'll be able to believe you've never been anyone else. Don't forget you'll be exchanging personalities for the better."

Again I could only stare at her. Then I made an effort and pulled myself together. "Miss Weldon, you frighten me. I put it as strongly as that. You seriously imagine that I would give up everything that's ever been dear to me — my manager, for instance, to whom I happen to be devoted — "

She interrupted. "I daresay we could find a place for him. If he's a good enough actor he could be your valet or something. Providing we could trust to his discretion, of course — or do you think he could learn to buttle? I should have to get rid of my present man. He saw you the night you drank all the Marsala."

I sat down for the simple reason that I was losing the power to stand up. "You really think," I gasped, "you really think I could ask the man who's done so much for me to dedicate his life to cleaning my boots and ironing my breeches while I sell myself to a woman in love with a myth?"

"A myth is only a myth when you can't make it a reality, Mr. Roberts," she pointed out.

I thumped my fist on the dressing-table. "Do you suppose — do you really *suppose* that I could ever bring myself to support such a life?"

She looked down at her hands. "I should be willing to excuse your physical attentions if — if you found them too distasteful."

"You combine modesty," I said, "and arrogance in the most confusing manner. But I can put you clear on one point. You are *not* in love with Philippe de Lambrière. You are in love with me and therefore you would insist upon my sleeping with you."

Water Face gasped in the background. "I say, don't you think I should wait outside?"

Miss Weldon snapped, "No, I do not, Edward. You will have to learn to excuse Mr. Roberts' crudities until he has learned to correct them himself." To me she said, "I think there will be no fear of my becoming enamoured of you for your own sake. I happen to dislike you personally very much indeed."

"No, you don't," I said. "Philippe's body is *my* body. It must be because *he hasn't any other*." My exasperation was so great that I was practically shouting at her. She opened her mouth to cut across me, but I gave her no chance. "Philippe's 'half-smile' is *my* half-smile. His 'voice' is *my* voice. That's one truth I'm not going to let you cheat yourself out of. There's no flesh and blood attached to him. What there is is attached to *me*. That's what you like about him."

She frowned as if genuinely puzzled. "But I should cross the street to avoid you as yourself. Quite apart from your profession, which naturally makes you an unsuitable companion for me, I find your own personality quite obnoxious. You're obviously conscious of what you suppose are good looks, but in point of fact, without Philippe's smile and his expressions" — she studied my face as if she were trying to find a trace of them — "without the way he lifts his eyebrows and uses his eyes, your face is vulgar and undistinguished."

"Other women don't find it so," I said, and was annoyed at myself for letting her see that she had offended me.

"Women of your own class might not know any better, but people like myself couldn't be expected to be attracted to you. It's not so much that your features are coarse in themselves: it's — well, it's just that you're a very objectionable person and I suppose it shows."

"I'm sorry to appear obstinate, Miss Weldon," I said, "but you see, money — even in the quantities you apparently possess it — can't create living material. There is *no* such person as Philippe de Lambrière and never will be. There's only me. *I'm* the one you dream about. *I'm* the one you take to bed in your thoughts at night." I looked closely at her to see if there was any reaction to this, but she continued to stare calmly at me. She was the most difficult person to fluster that I have ever met. "You'd rather die, wouldn't you," I asked her, "than agree that it's true?" It has to be admitted that she looked far from dying. She looked very much alive and thoroughly contemptuous of me. I fought on, determined to shock her. "But in point of fact that's what happens. When the curtains are tightly drawn round your bed at night and the candles are out, Philippe de Lambrière lies beside you. He might even take shape in your bolster. Oh, yes, you do — you cuddle that, and pretend it's your vicomte. But it isn't." I ended by shouting at her, "It represents me! I'm the hot, strong smell of man you're so sadly lacking!"

"Oh, I say!" said Water Face.

More unpleasant I couldn't have been, and possibly more inaccurate. It's very doubtful if at that time she would have imagined anything more sensual with her bolster than a polite tête-à-tête in the moonlight. However, I wished I hadn't kissed her at that damned ball. It must have gone a long way towards awakening her.

She stood up with the graceful movements that never failed to surprise me. "It's precisely because of that sort of thing that I prefer Philippe to your revolting self. He would *never* make a disgusting speech of that sort. But then, of course, he's a gentleman and you are not."

I cut back a profanity and once again thought quickly without the help of M.S. The obvious thing to do was to let her see a thoroughly unpleasant side to Philippe. I switched quickly to the vicomte. We talked French, and it was little short of sickening to see her admiration for me creep back into her eyes. Had I tried to kiss her there and then she would have let me. She prattled on happily in her reasonably good French as if we had never had our recent acid exchanges. It was an extraordinary performance on her part. Over again she made me feel utterly disembodied. I had never met a woman who could ignore reality so efficiently and believe in the life she had created in her own head. For her, I was Philippe de Lambrière, and she took it for granted that I was courting her. What she thought we were both doing in an actor's dressing-room I'm sure I don't know. But with her ability for flattening opposition to her fairy tale she was probably not even aware of her surroundings. A more charming scene with no rehearsals I have seldom played. I was so flummoxed I was hard hit to it to play Philippe at all, let alone his nasty side. She told me with endearing frankness that she had jilted Nicholas Hawtrey for my sake.

I sat down again. That woman had an unfortunate effect on me. She seemed to draw all the strength out of my knee-caps. It was her terrible combination of stilted sanity and lunacy which undermined me. She had told Mr. Roberts a short while ago that she was desperately in love with Philippe de Lambrière, but she was too modest to tell Philippe himself. I felt near to dizziness at such a fanatical determination to annihilate me and put the day-dream Philippe onto a material plane. I handled Philippe's nasty side with degrading lack of skill. A casual word picture of my lecherous life in France produced no expression on her face at all. I gave her to understand that I was by way of being a drunken sadist; that I had a series of resident mistresses at my château in the Auvergne; that in Paris my time was spent gambling and whoring in the Palais-Royal; and finally that I was liable to reduce us both to bankruptcy in the shortest possible time.

She came towards me and held out a hand. "It's flattering of you to pretend not to be good enough for me. But one must love people for their faults as well. I shall forget your past and look only to your future. That," she said firmly, "I'm quite confident will turn out as I wish it."

Then she reached the door. From it she said calmly, "Mr. Roberts, please never feel tempted to impress your own disgusting habits onto the character of Philippe again." With which she said, "Good afternoon" and left.

Water Face shrugged again and followed her.

I relaid the whole scene to M.S. He was far from sympathetic towards my embarrassment at being made to feel I did not exist.

"Serves you right for wasting time on a woman with love fever," he snapped. "She ought not to be seeking after the maritals at her time of life."

I felt myself oddly obliged to defend her. "She's not into the thirties yet," I pointed out.

"She's old enough to put on her cap and settle down."

What possessed me to go on arguing on her account I'll never know, but there were strange moments when her forthrightness made me admire her against my will. Of course, ten minutes in her company with her arrogance uppermost and her inability to accord feelings to anyone below her in class would have made me despise her again. But when she was absent I recalled only the calmly powerful eyes and the courage she showed in her convictions.

"The woman wants me but can't admit it," I told M.S. "It's rather a pathetic predicament."

"And I say it's disgraceful, chasing a boy like you. There's many a lady of her age content to take comfort from a parrot in a cage and a nice bit of gingerbread for tea. Now, I never want to hear her name again."

Neither did I, but my wish was not granted. Water Face called the following morning.

Chapter 14.

HE WAS not in good shape. "I'm so worried about all this," he confessed, "that I sat up with a couple of bottles of port trying to sort the thing out."

"There's nothing to sort out," I told him. "Your cousin must realise that for once in her life she's not going to get what she wants."

His head shook. "Unfortunately, I've made everything twenty times worse."

He looked so stricken I suggested we should adjourn to the inn. The Rare Sacrifice served us without giving a sign that she had ever seen me before. I was so used to being ignored by her that I didn't notice. We retired to a corner.

"How have you made things worse?" I asked him.

"You remember Nicholas Hawtrey?" he said.

"Vividly."

"Well, he's after you. He can't forgive you for doing him out of Lizzie's dowry. He's been all over the place looking for 'the Frenchy' who took her away from him. He wanted to call you out, and asked me to second him."

"I've no intention of crossing swords with anyone over Miss Weldon. I just want to forget the whole thing: De Lambrière was my least favourite part."

"I offered to fight him for you. I said it was all my fault and that I should be the one he called out."

"Noble if inaccurate. But as there's no such person as De Lambrière, he's not likely to be found, is he?"

"That's it. I told you I made things twenty times worse. My uncle's right. I certainly am the family fool."

"I suppose you told him I was an actor hired for the part?"

"Yes," he said unhappily. "You see, I thought I could turn the thing into a joke and get Nicholas to see the humour in it."

"I shouldn't think that's his forte."

"I explained that Lizzie wanted to — well, stimulate him into some sort of action. He refused to believe that Lizzie would be a party to such a thing."

"He doesn't know Lizzie, does he?"

The amusement in my voice pained Water Face. "Look here, Roberts, this is serious. I told him that if he didn't believe me I'd take him to the theatre and point you out. He saw you in *The Ambitious Stepmother*, and now he wants to kill you."

"Good God! I couldn't have been as bad as that!"

"Please!" he begged, "Nicholas means it. He was wild enough when he thought you were a vicomte, but now he realises that Lizzie's in love with a — with a —" Water Face was more considerate towards the feelings of his inferiors than Lizzie. I had to coax the words out for him.

"With a 'common actor'?"

"Well, yes."

I said, "He's got more sense than Lizzie. At least he realises it's me she's in love with: *she* doesn't."

"Oh, he knows it's you well enough. That's what's knocked his pride so hard. He's determined to get rid of you, but he won't challenge you now. You'll get no warning. He feels that he can't openly cross swords with you. He'd look such a fool if the story leaked out. His friends might find out that he'd lost Lizzie to — to —"

I didn't rescue him this time. I let him struggle. The poor lad tried to spare my feelings.

"Well, you see, De Lambrière was a gentleman even if he didn't exist, so to speak. I mean, it would be worse for Hawtrey if — if —"

I could bear it for him no longer. I said, "Quite."

He gave me such a grateful look at being spared embarrassment and blushed so youthfully that I asked him his age. He told me that he had just turned eighteen. It was easy then to understand how he could be so completely dominated by the determined Lizzie. From the superior height of two years' seniority, I looked down on him smugly. But his next remark touched me.

"Look here," he said, "I've come to offer you my sword. I'll take on Nicholas for you. I'm sure I'm a match for him."

He was big for his age, but shaken from his night of port he didn't look a match for a newborn lamb provided it was healthy. However, I thanked him and told him not to worry.

He refused to be calmed. "Look here, I've got a sabre that my uncle gave me — my mother's brother. He was a dragoon. I think you ought to have something handy."

"I'll be ready for him if he comes, but I think you'll find that even Hawtrey will stop short of bloody murder."

It has interested me since to note how consistently wrong I was in my predictions.

Chapter 15.

I KEPT the sabre in the dressing-room and forgot about the matter. We had an important interview in London. My reviews had been good and word of mouth was spreading. M.S. had got me an appointment with the new manager of Drury Lane. It was quite a feat on the part of M.S., for John Philip Kemble was making himself felt. His sister, Sarah Siddons, had overcome the nerves that had made her a failure in Garrick's final season and had flamed into glory with her Lady Macbeth. Kemble himself had a bee in his bonnet about revivals in historical dress. He was determined to do *Hamlet* and *Othello* as near to the original costumes as possible. It was an idea that had always held fascination for me as well.

M.S. felt that I was ripe for the Lane and was prepared to lease me out from the Little Apollo. He sent a collection of my reviews and a portrait of

me to Kemble, and on that we secured the interview. Our Mr. Bates had
returned to us for a season. We left him in charge of *The Country Wife*
at the Little Apollo and set off for London.

Kemble was a little disappointing to meet at first. I had the feeling that
his head might suddenly disappear like that of a tortoise and that one would
be left peering into a dark shell trying to find him. It was only afterwards
that one realised he was a man who preferred to think rather than speak
for the sake of it.

M.S. was magnificent. He was neither too eager nor too reticent about
me. He simply stated his faith in me. Kemble appeared not to be studying
me, but I realised that he was conducting a thorough examination. I learned
quickly to leave matters to him. One word too many from me and that head
would have disappeared. I gave three Shakespearean readings, to which he
merely nodded. Then he suddenly asked me if I had ever seen his sister
and if so what I thought of her. It was awkward because I had seen her
only in her nervous Garrick days and quite frankly thought her appalling —
an opinion that I must admit I saw no reason to alter. When I hesitated,
Kemble nodded again. Then he took a pinch of snuff and held out the box
to show me the hall-mark.

"They've put the King's head upside down," he remarked. They had,
too. After that he said, "You must look at my sister again. You'll find a
difference." Then he turned to M.S. "I'll send someone down to the Little
Apollo to see this boy. When I get the report I'll get in touch with you."
The head nodded our dismissal and we were on our way out.

It was on the evening of the day after our return that the trouble broke.
It was one of those wretched windy nights that made the Little Apollo such
a brute to play in. You not only had to pitch your voice against the howling
gale while you were on stage, but the draught numbed your feet afterwards
in the dressing-rooms. The Rare Sacrifice had clamped down on any more
repairs, and Lizzie's money had long since run out. Late rehearsals had
made it impossible for me to eat during the day, but there was time to
snatch some food before the curtain-raising farce. With my jacket over my
head I was about to bolt through the rain across the dark little alley that
divided the theatre from the inn when I heard, rather than saw, someone
step forward and then quickly back again. It occurred to me that my
shrouded head might have made my identification difficult and this could
have caused the indecision.

Recalling Water Face's warning, I went back for the sabre. I plunged
across the alley, splashing my breeches, but the only living thing I encountered was a soaked kitten belonging to the Rare Sacrifice. It skidded up to
me protesting at being shut out on such a night. I tried to pick it up, but it
suddenly danced sideways, its tail like a flue brush, and started spitting into
the shadows.

"Who's there?" I called out, but there was no answer. I bent down and seized the kitten. Its small fuzzy body felt like a handful of soap.

Dripping and still frightened, I handed it over the counter to the Rare Sacrifice. She was fond of her pets. To her songbird and her kitten she was the motherly soul she looked.

"He might have caught his death," she wheezed. Her giant bosom always made her breathing difficult. The pressure of those great breasts strapped so tightly to her lungs must have been considerable. By way of gratitude to me she said, "I shouldn't be surprised as how if you hadn't been brought up by that 'orrible Mr. Smith you wouldn't be better than what you are."

As I was unable to hear anything to the detriment of M.S., I was obliged to defend him. The Rare Sacrifice promptly returned to ignoring my existence.

On my way back to the theatre I was attacked by Nicholas Hawtrey. "Attacked" is really too complimentary a word for his intentions. His plan was to hack me down from behind and run away like a stone-throwing urchin. Doubtless he thought that would be a fair enough fight for an actor. But I heard the whip of his sword in the wind. I turned round on my heel like a ballet dancer on his points. I struck out in a defensive circular sweep. A short and curious cry was the result. It sounded more like a beast than a human.

It was still impossible to see him in that black and crashing rain, but a piece of flesh nicked from my left cheek told me he was still there. Blood thinned by rain spread over my chin and neck. The fact that he had hit my cheek warned me that in the dark we were probably both striking too high. I lowered my thrust. The result of that was another inhuman grunt. Then something struck my leg. It was Hawtrey's hand as he fell.

When I bent to find him, blood seemed to be everywhere. I called to him over the wind and I tried feeling him for injury, but all I got was the soft pumping of his blood falling over my hands. Even then I could not believe I'd brought him down for good. I was sure that I could have only nicked him in a fleshy part.

I stumbled to the stage door and snatched up a lantern. The memory of what I saw when I returned has lasted to this day. God knows I've become hardened to most forms of gore by now, but I'll never forget the sight of Hawtrey. My first wild cut had split his mouth right up his cheek. His tongue must have got it too, which accounted for his odd cries. He lay with his torn grin the width of his face and an ever-flowing red moustache on either side. For a moment or two I stood shaking my head. It was the silence and the dark, I think, which gave it that feeling of something that should never have happened. My sword must have gone through his ribs like a hot skewer through a piece of lard. The thought that this bleeding lump of flesh was my work at first refused to impress itself on my mind. All I felt was a sickly form of resentment at the horror he presented. Even the thought that it could have been my blood that was flowing over the cobblestones didn't pull me together. I just muttered stupidly, "He'll bleed to death if I don't get help." Then something cold took over and told me, "He's already dead. You killed him."

Then it began slowly to reach me. I had killed a human being. I had taken life from one of God's creatures however unpleasant. He might well have been intending to pass that compliment to me first, but I had succeeded and he had not. I simply stood there feeling a horrible pain for him.

It was the theatre that gave me the mental jolt I needed to stop me from staring at him foolishly. I remembered that I was due to go on in a quarter of an hour. Everything else was momentarily displaced from my mind. I had never been "off" in my life before. M.S. would not lightly forgive me.

I heaved up the body and dragged it across the lane. The theatre audience had already taken their seats, and apart from the few odd customers who would go to the inn, there would not be many people about on a night like that. The lane was little more than a mud track and it was quite hard going to drag Hawtrey across. I staggered to the ditch on the far side and pushed the body in it. The ditch was running freely from the rain and the body was half submerged. When I came back to the theatre I looked as if I had been rolling on the floor of a slaughter house. The doorman gave a shout of alarm, but I fobbed him off with a tale about having been run down by a carriage horse.

I have never made a quicker change than I did for that performance. The bloody clothes were stuffed in a cupboard on the right side of five minutes, but even so I was "off." They had given me my cue three times before I made my entrance. The thunder in the eyes of M.S. forewarned me that he would soon be whispering at me in that extraordinary manner of his when he really lost his temper. He was playing Sir Colin and he seemed doubly formidable in his red wig. He was the only member of the company who could manage a true Scot's accent. I did not look forward to telling him that I had just killed a man, but tell him I must. I think M.S. must be the only person in the world I should never attempt to deceive.

How I got my lines out that night I'll never know. Hawtrey's red grin and that body slowly stiffening in the cold ditch outside kept rearing up in front of me. I gave an appalling performance. The leading shrew I was playing opposite kept pinching me and spitting abuse into my ears whenever she was near enough.

"What are you trying to do, make 'em walk out, you bloody bastard?"

She was a moody cow at the best of times and spoke with a ghastly refinement on the stage which dropped like her sleazy petticoats when she got off. M.S. was longing to replace her, but we couldn't afford anyone better.

When the curtain came down she flew at me, thumping her fat fists against

my chest, screaming that I had given her nothing and ruined her performance and who the hell did I think I was just because Philip Kemble was
sending someone down to see me, and if I thought a bloody lout like me —
oh! It would have gone on half the night. I gripped her wrists and jerked
her away from me. I could still hear her cursing when I was trying to pull
myself together outside the door of M.S.'s dressing-room. I was right in
anticipating that he would whisper at me.

"And who in the name of all that's charitable do you think *you* were
working for tonight? Mr. Martyn's Celebrated Players?" His eyes seemed to
jig in the candles' flattened light. For a moment I thought he was going to
clout me. It wouldn't have been the first time. His great hand was raised like
a spade in the air as he walked slowly towards me.

"Everything!" he whispered, "everything you learned from Mr. Martyn!
We had the lot tonight! Them horrible eyes rolled up like a winded horse.
Smirking to get the ladies. You played on your face, boy. You think it's
good enough to spare you from acting. You think the ladies will jump at
both ends of you, don't you? No matter what you do in between —"

"M.S.," I said, "I've just killed Nicholas Hawtrey. His body is in the
ditch outside. I'll have to get to France."

He went back to his chair, sat on it, and remained silent until I had told
him my story.

Then he turned to his dressing-table and thumped a deliberate fist on it.
Even then he whispered, but there was no ferocity behind it.

"I should never have let you! I should never have let you play a prancing
cockerel to that woman."

"It wasn't your fault," I said: "we needed the money. God knows, we
might never have reopened if it hadn't been for what that Weldon woman
paid me."

His head shook deliberately as if he could make his brain work only by
throwing it from side to side.

"Lord Credit should have been buried. Buried and forgotten! Once we
got a stage under you we should never have revived him. Now we shall
probably be left with nothing else to play."

I felt immeasurably sorry for him. He sat there staring at the make-up
towel he had dropped on his foot. It is horrible to see someone's hopes
crumbling away.

"Kemble," he groaned, "just as Kemble was sending down someone to
see you. I'd have got you into the Lane this season."

I went up to him, but I knew him too well to think that I could help him.
M.S. was beyond comfort from somebody else. If he were in trouble he had
to put it right within himself. Not even anyone as close to him as myself
could help him from outside.

There was nothing to do but leave him there. I had to go out into the alley and see what could be done about clearing up the blood. There was so much and the sight of it brought back the black realisation of what I had done. I could not look in the direction of the ditch. I fetched pail after pail of water from the inn pump and sluiced down the yard. I kept trying to tell myself that Hawtrey deserved his death. The fool might have lived if he had not thought it beyond his dignity to fight me in the ordinary manner. But no, he despised my profession to such an extent that he couldn't risk his friends' finding out that he had been obliged to cross swords with a common actor. I was something to be hacked down from behind in the dark and left lying in the alley like a dead rat.

But it was not young Hawtrey or the memory of his red, wet grin that really gave me the bowel-loosening sensation at the pit of my stomach. It was the memory of his father's proud eyes whenever the plump oaf made the most ordinary of remarks at the Weldons' ball. Sir Gregory's clear face and his constant references to "my boy, Nick" forced me to lean up against the alley wall. I had deprived a father of his whole life's purpose. He would wake tomorrow without a son, without the being for whom he existed, and it was I who had sentenced him to a despairing old age. Leaning against the alley wall, not far off vomiting, I made a desperate attempt to dispel Sir Gregory's living ghost. But it haunted me far more than his son's. My brain seemed flattened by memories of him: the trustful strength of his eyes, that quick, intelligent smile, that trim, spare figure with its spring-like movements so much more youthful than the fat sloth of his son. "Oh, God!" I thought, "oh, God!" But how could I explain to that soldierly soul that his only son was a sickly little coward whose idea of a gentlemanly fight was to get a man in the back in a dark alleyway? My chances of his believing me felt about as good as my chances of getting to heaven at that moment.

Fortunately the audience rarely used the passage to get to the inn. They went on foot straight from the front entrance down the lane, and the carriage crowd never saw it at all. I had done my best with the alleyway. Any remaining blood would have to be attributed to my accident. Luckily the rain was still coming down hard.

Manager Smith was sitting where I left him, but now there was a prop basket and a spade beside him. His face still had a pallor to it, but he was no longer whispering.

"Boy," he said, "the first thing to do is to get rid of the body."

He handed me the spade and put the prop basket over his shoulder. I followed him into the darkness shielding the lantern as best I could. The rain had fined down to a chilling mist, but the wind had not slackened.

The body was not easy to find, and for a few moments of horror I thought that we were never going to be able to locate it. Then my lantern light caught the edge of a boot. We were just about to move him when we heard the sound of wheels. It was a carter making for the inn. I blew out the lamp and we pressed ourselves down in the watery ditch. My hand touched something soft and cold and flew off again like a beaten-up partridge. I had imagined I had caught hold of Hawtrey's soaked hair; but it must have been some sodden rag left by a tramp. The imaginary contact unnerved me so thoroughly I could hardly assist M.S.

"It's not safe to have the light on: we'll have to feel for him, boy."

M.S. went down on his knees and started groping about in the wet hedge-row. There were some nauseating sucking noises as M.S. prized the body up from the slime.

"Bring that basket nearer."

"Yes," I said, and dragged the prop basket closer.

M.S. grunted a little and then snapped, "Well, open the lid, you young fool."

As I felt for the straps, the soup I had drunk at the inn was sourly climbing up my throat. I flung the lid back and heard the water running off Hawtrey's soaked body. What an abysmal finale to Sir Gregory's cherished plans for "his boy, Nick." I wasn't sure that I hadn't heard somewhere that the mother had died giving birth to him. The soup rose again. I had a picture of the grieving Sir Gregory bending over his only consolation's cradle. A fine cradle we were providing him with at the end.

M.S. whispered fiercely at me. "What in the name of hell do you think you're doing, boy — rehearsing for Ariel? Give me a hand with him. Help get him in."

Like a fool I closed my eyes although the night was so dark I could scarcely see anyway. My hands shot forward as if they did not belong to me. I could hardly feel them grabbing at Hawtrey's stiffening limbs. I could still hear the incessant dripping from them, and a bellows-like breath broke out from him as we pummelled him down into the basket. M.S. wrestled with his carcass as if he were a cook trying to shape a bird that was too big for the oven. He told me to sit on the lid. In doing so, I lost my troublesome soup. I felt better after that.

It was hard going with the basket between us. The wind kept buffeting it as if trying to jostle it out of our hands. By the time we were a mile away from the theatre a prim moon pricked its way through the clouds. Thank God it was frequently covered again. The countryside was wild and the nearest village some way off, but there could always have been the odd poacher or even a couple of lovers to witness the sight of two men trudging over the black fields with an enormous basket and a spade between them.

M.S. was making for Berridge Wood. It clung to the side of a line of hills. It was tightly overgrown and few people entered it. There was even a legend that it was haunted. Some silly tale of the olden days when lovers had died on a pledge. I quickly clung to the olden days. The past has always had a soothing effect upon me. It gives me a sense of security to dwell on the homely fact that people have made love, been born, and died before me. It takes away the feeling that one might be an experiment.

I forced myself back to the "olden days": comforting, rollicking "olden days," when one only remembered the lack of stress and bustle, and forgot the lack of medicinal aid and the horrible conditions that must have prevailed.

"If it's not too much trouble to you," he said, "I'll ask you to attend."

We had arrived at the wood. The great prop hamper was on the ground. I didn't remember lowering my end of it.

"The lantern," said M.S. "God knows, I've told you ten times. Pass me the lantern."

I passed him the lantern and he exchanged the spade with me. We ploughed our way into the wood.

There is no way to account for it, but I felt drunk; just ordinarily, depressingly drunk. I could have burst into one of two things, tears or song. I tried to pull myself up. I said, "This isn't the way Sir Gregory would want you to follow his son to his last resting place. . . ."

But I could do nothing about it. I had had nothing to drink, but I was drunk.

The trees stood up like giant spikes, and the undergrowth clawed at our legs as we battled our way into the dimmest part of the wood.

We took it in turns to dig the grave. It was a heavy job. The hamper was large and we had to go deep. To my surprise I heard M.S. mutter a prayer as we lowered the prop basket into the ground. Again I tried to comfort myself that it was his own ridiculous pride in despising my profession which had put that young fool into his lonely pit. We trod the grasses carefully back into place and M.S. covered it with leaves and bracken. It was ice cold in the gloom.

We returned to the inn in silence, and M.S. put the spade back in the shed.

"Boy," he said when he saw my face, "you're a man now. Behave yourself." Then he gave me a full glass of brandy, which, oddly enough, dispelled all my drunken symptoms. I shot forward in my chair at a sudden sobering thought.

"His horse!" I said. "He couldn't have come on foot and he wouldn't have risked a carriage. If it's tethered near by or stabled somewhere, it'll prove he's been here."

M.S. went to look at the inn stables. The ostler had only two horses and their owners were both inside.

"Yes," M.S. said thoughtfully, "I think we'd better find that horse."

Chapter 16.

WE HAD a preliminary look for the animal, but it wasn't tethered anywhere near by. We were obliged to conduct our search with caution. Too many enquiries too soon would have looked suspicious. Over the next few days we made casual visits to all the taverns in the neighbourhood.

The amount of ale we had to drink gave me a liver like that of an ox, but M.S. had no trouble with his stone. We gossiped in all the taprooms trying to draw out information without seeming too curious.

It was at the Hare and Hounds that we got our reward. It was a posting house about half a mile from the theatre across a foot path in the direction of Berridge Wood.

The postmaster said, " 'Arse? Yes, somebody left an 'arse here. Oh, now, let's see, be about two to three days ago now, Willie, wouldn't un?"

Willie, an aging regular, scratched his nose. " 'Twould be more like to be four."

The postmaster argued in favour of three. Willie said he was sure it was four because it was the day old George Parkins took to his bed and he had been to see him and told him he was never likely to rise from it again. The postmaster declared that this piece of comfort was delivered to the lucky invalid three days ago and not four.

"Don't 'ee remember, Willie, you came in here straight after and told I as how un's face were the colour of tripe."

"You'm don't last long *that* colour," said Willie, and added, "But 'twould be more like to be four days gone, not three."

M.S. interrupted patiently. "Did the gentleman who left the horse leave his name as well?"

That got them off George Parkins.

"No," said the postmaster. "Young fellow he were and gentry, too. Would 'ee say un were on the stout side, Willie?"

Hoping to edge Willie out of a discussion on Hawtrey's girth, I asked, "Has anyone come for the horse since?"

Willie's head shook. "Well, I wouldn't like to swear un were *stout*. On the other hand, I wouldn't like to swear un were *thin!*"

"Has anyone fetched the horse since?" asked M.S.

"Un were on the stout side, Willie, un were on the stout *side*," the postmaster broke in reproachfully.

Willie's nose came in for further attention from his rheumaticky fingers. "Well, I wouldn't like to swear —"

I shouted, "Has anyone fetched the *horse*?"

M.S. put out a restraining hand. He was a model of discretion compared to me; his patience must have come from training so many bad actors.

The postmaster leaned on the counter to think. "Well, 'twere this way, you see, sir. This young gentleman — and he were on the stout side, Willie, he *were* on the stout."

My nerves had suffered so severely over the last few days that had Willie contradicted I think I would have leaned forward and wrung his old neck.

"Come in here," said the postmaster, "says he wants to stable his 'arse and he'll be back for his supper inside of the hour." It was interesting to note how little time young Hawtrey felt he needed to finish me off. "But that were three days ago now —"

"Four," put in Willie.

"Three days ago," repeated the postmaster, "and no sign of un since and not a penny paid."

"What did you do with the horse?" asked M.S.

"Well, I fed un up to two days gone. Said he were coming back inside the hour, you see, sir, and him being gentry like, I fed his 'arse up to two days gone."

"Said un were coming back inside the hour," Willie was good enough to remind us.

M.S. ordered two more hot ales and ginger, which was a mistake. It took the postmaster an age to get them. Willie kept dull eyes on us.

"They reckon that's what done for old Parkins," he told us. "It's the ginger sits on the liver and eats un away."

"Best thing out for a stoppage," M.S. answered cheerfully.

"Old Parkins didn't have no stoppage — other way round, more like."

The postmaster returned with our tankards. I snapped at him, "Well, what happened?"

M.S. frowned at me and the postmaster drew a long breath.

"Well, see, I fed this 'arse up to two days gone." I leaned against the counter and closed my eyes. They jerked open again when the postmaster added, "And then a lady comes arskin' questions with another young gentleman."

"What kind of a lady?" I barked.

The postmaster turned towards Willie.

"Oh, God," I thought, "oh, no!"

"Was she pretty?" I asked quickly.

They were both in agreement on that. Their heads swung in unison.

"Strong-looking lady, I'd put it, Willie."

Willie put it that way too.

"Gentry and a bit haughty like, if you know what I mean." I knew only too well. "Comes here arskin' your kind of questions and not one of 'em offers to pay for the feed I given that 'arse two days gone." That much I could also imagine as well. "I reckon that the lad was in service to her. It was 'come here, go there, do that' all the time." Had we needed anything more to help us identify poor bullied Water Face and the forceful Lizzie, that would have done it.

"Did they take the horse away?" M.S. enquired gently.

The postmaster held a conference of the eyes with Willie.

"Well, 'tweren't as though they could, you see, for un wasn't here be then."

"Who did fetch it?" I demanded, trying to keep calm.

For once I was grateful for a Willie interruption.

"Un sold un to gypsies," he said.

"Sold it?" repeated M.S.

The postmaster looked grieved. "Reckon I didn't see why I should go on feeding that 'arse with not a penny paid. Them gypsies is often in these parts — going north, they said they was. Gave a good price for it, too."

"So you think it's on its way north by now?"

"Yes, well, 'tweren't as if it were any good to me. 'Twouldn't serve my needs, I can tell you. 'Twere a bloody great huntin' kind of 'arse."

It was Willie who thought to enquire, "What be you two gentlemen askin' for, anyways? What be 'arse to you?"

"Oh," said M.S., "we just heard that a horse had been abandoned and we thought we might pick one up cheap. Pity we lost it to the gypsies."

We lowered our hot ales and ginger, thanked them both, and left.

Outside M.S. breathed, "That was a worse job than trying to rehearse young Carpenter for *Hamlet*."

"Thank God it's on its way up country," I said. "No one will recognise it there."

"Best thing that could happen," he agreed, and asked me, "I suppose you can trust that boy and that perishing woman not to make trouble?"

"I can certainly rely on Water Face. He's been on my side right from the beginning. As for Lizzie, I very much doubt if she'd do anything to risk the story's coming out."

Another of my fascinatingly wrong predictions!

Chapter 17.

WE SPENT several anxious days waiting for enquiries to be set on foot in our direction. I discovered M.S. breaking into the Rare Sacrifice's strongbox with a skewer and a chisel. He removed a considerable amount of money.

"After all, it's owing us, boy. An Egyptian slave gets more than the second Mrs. Lambert pays us, and when you think how the theatre's brought on the inn business for her, what I say is we're no more than robbing our rights!"

He had also contacted some of his crooked acquaintances and acquired two false passports. He had himself forged a very pleasant letter from John Philip Kemble recommending me to Dugazon of the Comédie Française.

"You never know when it might come in handy, boy, and we might have to leave in a hurry."

"*We* will do nothing of the sort," I said. "If I have to go I'll go alone. This theatre's your life. You've put years of work into it. You can't just back out and leave it."

"Boy," he said, "I've put years of work into you, too. If you think I'm going to leave you to go whoring your way round France with woman after woman under you and never a sign of a stage beneath you, you're misleading yourself."

Fortunately it looked as if neither of us would have to go, and M.S. returned the money to the Rare Sacrifice's strong-box. "I can get it out in a wink if need be," he said.

It was such an exacting time for us at the theatre that we gradually began to put the Hawtrey business out of our minds. We were having one of our greatest successes with *The Country Wife*. M.S. had used Garrick's version, and Kemble sent down a critic to report on my performance.

He was a small man with an intricate stubble over his chin which looked like ginger lacework. His name was Mitkins, and while he may not have been prepossessing, he was the most agreeable person I had met for a long time. He thought highly of my work and assured me that he would leave Kemble in no doubt of it.

We were drinking gin in M.S.'s dressing-room.

Mitkins was enjoying himself with M.S. "I know this old rogue," he said, winking at me. "I met him when he was with Garrick. There's no one to touch him for spotting the quality in an actor, but I can't seem to remember now why we always called you 'Magpie.' Why do you think that would have been, friend Lambert?"

"Friend Lambert" retained a church-like dignity, but I couldn't help wondering whether Mr. Mitkins had lost one or two personal possessions in common with Garrick.

M.S. led the conversation smoothly onto Garrick, and I assisted him by also enthusing over my hero. Mitkins admitted to having been against him in the first place.

"I used to think he had tricks, and I'd boast I could forecast the lot. I made a list of them and took it to the theatre. I wrote down every trick I thought he'd use and sat waiting to tick them off as they came up. But they didn't. I never caught him out in a single one."

The prompt-boy put his head round the door. "There's a Miss Weldon to see Mr. Roberts."

I jumped, but M.S. gave no outward sign of alarm. "Tell her Mr. Roberts isn't receiving, lad."

The prompt-boy retired.

Mitkins said to me, "I noticed your effect on the ladies. That can be useful, very useful. There's many a management will pay for that talent."

"Not the sort of management I want for him," snapped M.S. "I've trained the boy to be an actor, not a lump of sugar for a lot of young harlots to sit up and beg for. An actor wants to forget his own face and his own voice."

Mitkins returned to his sport. "I'm sorry, Magpie. Didn't mean to offend you. Just thought the boy had the right looks as well."

"The only right looks belong to the part."

Mitkins clicked his fingers. "I just wish I could remember why we always called you 'Magpie'!"

The prompt-boy reappeared. "The lady says it's important, sir. A friend of hers has been missing some days and she thinks Mr. Roberts might know where the gentleman is."

M.S. stood up. "I'll see the lady," he said. He left the room without looking at me.

I could barely pour Mitkins out another drink. He chuckled happily. "Poor old Magpie! But learn all you can from him, my lad, he's one of the best actors going. Only don't let him teach you his other tricks. I swear the whole company had hardly a watch left between them at the end of the season."

"He gets lost in his work," I said lamely, my ears straining for any sound outside. "He's not always responsible."

"He was responsible right enough," Mitkins said, laughing. "None of the rest of us could nick so much so fast. I'll always remember the hurt scene he put on for Garrick —"

"I insist upon seeing him!" cried Lizzie's carrying voice.

I poured most of Mitkins' third glass of gin on the floor.

"What's this?" he said. "Libation to the gods? Yes, I'll not forget that lightly." He proceeded to give a passable imitation of M.S. playing a hurt scene. Any other time I should have found it difficult not to laugh. But Lizzie's voice came between us again.

"If you stop me, I shall go straight to the courthouse and fetch the constable."

"What's all this about?" asked Mitkins.

"Oh, somebody lost a ring in front last night and she thinks we're hanging on to it."

"Well, if it's anything to do with old Magpie, she's right," Mitkins said, laughing.

I could have kicked myself for the stupid lie. Mitkins was still smiling at his reminiscences. "God love me, I'll never forget him with Garrick! He made himself strawberry red in the face and then washed it down with tears, like a February cloud-burst."

I could see it so clearly in spite of my distractions. The wind pressed down on his heart to get his colour up and those tears that I knew so well. How often he had told me that an actor must conserve his emotions. "It's a waste of energy to shed real tears, boy," he said.

Mitkins took him off again. " 'Mr. Garrick!' " he said. " 'As a Christian born and bred I cannot stand here and be insulted.' But he stood there, all right," added Mitkins, "stood there and wore Garrick out. The old rogue sobbed, 'If you're trying to say my work isn't good enough — well, say so, sir, say so! Let me have it straight through the heart. But don't pretend it's to do with a missing watch!' In no time at all," added Mitkins, "he had Garrick weeping and the whole lot of us begging his pardon and still not one of us able to tell the time!"

M.S. came back. My eyes questioned his, but he gave me no sign.

Mitkins twinkled at him. "Well, Magpie, what made the lady think her baubles might have got into *your* nest?"

M.S. ignored him. "I've sent her off," he said.

When we finally got rid of Mitkins I sprang on M.S. "What did she say? What did you say? How did you finally fob her off?"

"I don't know that I did, boy, but she went, and that bloodless cousin went with her. Whether they'll come back with the constable is a matter of 'wait and see.' " He was putting on his coat. "I'm just off across to the inn," he said. "I think I'll just lighten the second Mrs. Lambert's strong-box again in case of need. Also," he added, winding himself up in the giant muffler without which he never even crossed the alleyway, "I think we'd better give you a few rehearsals in picking pockets again. You'll be out of practice over the years and it's a useful trick if you find yourself short. Let's see what you can make of it now." He put a couple of coins in his pocket and stood close to me. "Come at me, boy," he said, "let's see you lighten me without me feeling you."

My skill was certainly dormant. It was a long time since he had put me through the pocket drill and even longer since I had worked a real case. Before the Little Apollo lulled us into a sense of security, M.S. used to make me flex the two first fingers on my right hand for an hour a day.

After a few months they were so supple that I could remove a full purse between them from a deep inside pocket without the victim's feeling the movement. But I was stiff now and made a clumsy job of relieving M.S. of his two coins. He shook his head reproachfully. "We shall have to work on that, my word we shall. You might as well walk up to the first prison you come to and knock on the door as play it like that." He transferred the coins to the inside pocket of my waistcoat. "Now, keep an eye on me," he instructed.

I kept both eyes on him and I couldn't have been standing much more than a foot away. I was nearly boss-eyes following the movements of his hands.

He tapped me lightly on the chest with the left one and laughed. "I said watch me, boy. Keep your eyes on me. I've warned you you're going to be robbed."

"I *am* watching you," I said.

"Then it must have been in your sleep," he snapped, and spread out his left palm. The two coins lay in it. I had not felt the smallest pressure of his fingers. I blew out my cheeks, depressed.

M.S. chuckled. "Never mind, boy, it'll come back to you, it'll come back." He was still chuckling when he turned from the door and rummaged in the pocket of his old-fashioned coat again. "By the way, boy, I was pleased with your performance tonight. I nearly liked it. It looks as if we might be shaking off Mr. Martyn's Celebrated Players at last. So I've got a small reward for you. Catch!"

He flung something at me which I caught. It was an obviously expensive gold watch. "M.S.," I said, "where in the world did you get it from?"

"Poor old Mitkins," he replied, and went out.

I was angry. "The old fool!" I thought, "not keeping his twitching fingers to himself. Mitkins will be so furious he won't recommend me to Kemble." The old man must be mad to jeopardise our chances like that. I thought that the only thing to do would be to send it back to Mitkins at once with a little note to the effect that I had lifted it off him myself in retaliation for his remarks about Manager Smith. On the other hand, that would show that M.S. had certainly taught me "his other tricks." Kemble perhaps preferred his company non-light-fingered. It was an exasperating situation, and I was surprised that M.S.'s professionalism had given way to his pride in getting his own back on Mitkins. Filling my glass with gin, I carried it down the passage to my own dressing-room, thoughtfully flexing the two first fingers on my free right hand. Perhaps it would be better to say nothing and stoutly deny any knowledge of the watch should Mitkins write and ask us. Again I was inwardly swearing at M.S.'s unaccountable folly. Later, of course, I realised that his action came from his preference for the bird in the hand. He had taken the opportunity of retaliating against Mitkins' handling of him because he was sure that we shouldn't be able to benefit from his recommendation to Kemble.

I opened my dressing-room door. Inside sat a calm-mouthed Lizzie and a sweating Water Face.

I sent a cool glance over Lizzie and smiled at Water Face.

"Hallo, Edward," I greeted him cheerfully.

He seemed grateful not to find me churlish. "Hallo, Roberts." Lizzie turned her whole body towards him. "Er — hallo — *Philippe*," he corrected himself with difficulty.

Hands on hips, I walked to Lizzie. "You're not *still* trying to keep that up? Do you think," I demanded, "that it's very complimentary to your beloved class — I mean do you think it's well bred, well born, or even faintly good manners for a maiden lady of your birth to pursue a man in quite such a relentless and undignified fashion?"

"I never recall giving you any undertaking that I should conduct a dignified campaign."

"You don't think your behaviour slightly reminiscent of a street woman's?"

Water Face sprang up. "Watch your language, Roberts."

"Sit down, fool," ordered Lizzie. "And his name is Philippe."

Water Face sat down. It was not going to be easy to shock Lizzie Weldon. But shocked out of her hopeless dream of turning me into a French aristocrat she must certainly be. If she thought actors low-born vulgarians, her fears must be quickly confirmed.

I presented my back to her and gulped down my gin. Then I proceeded to pull off my shirt. A squeak of protest from Water Face was obviously silenced by Lizzie's eyes. I belched freely and turned my bared chest to them. Water Face had fallen back on his exceptional talent for gaping. I managed to give him a secret wink that slowly closed his mouth. Mopping myself daintily under the armpits with a grease rag, I sat opposite them. Lizzie's big hands lay as still in her lap as if they had been two sleeping cats. She showed not the slightest sign of revulsion.

I pulled off a stocking, balanced one foot across my knee, and pretended to pick my feet.

Water Face shuddered as I'm certain he would never have done under true cannon fire, but Lizzie's eyelids hardly flickered.

"This woman," I thought, "must be beaten. This woman must not even for a few minutes be allowed to think she could win." I began to undo my breeches. Lizzie showed about as much emotion as a hippopotamus basking in a mud flat, but my heart, I must confess, was beginning to beat an apprehensive tattoo. Supposing she let me get out of the lot? I wouldn't put it past her to call my bluff and allow me to fetch up as naked as the day

I misguidedly left my mother's womb. Looking up, I saw that I had still not shaken her eerie poise. The cat-hands in her lap were still asleep. The only movement she had made was to close her eyes. The expression on her face was of pained boredom, rather as if she had been obliged to watch the rude gambols of an oversexed puppy until her butler removed it from her drawing-room carpet. I signed to Water Face that I had no real intention of exposing my whole body to the vicious dressing-room draughts. The poor boy's lower jaw looked as if it were about to come off its hooks.

I said coarsely to Lizzie, "No, I won't spoil you! You shall pant a little longer for a sight of a naked man." When she opened her eyes, I added, "I'm sorry if you find my manners distasteful, but we actors can't help it, you know."

She said, "I've no complaints against *your* manners, Mr. Roberts, they're exactly what I expected from *you*."

To my surprise, Water Face had the wits to realise my object and came to my aid. "He'll never be able to mend them, Lizzie. His habits would always disgrace you, and they'll get worse the older he grows. He'd never be able to keep up Philippe. He'd revert back to himself sooner or later and give us all away."

I belched agreement and climbed into a dressing-gown. I had had enough of those dressing-room draughts.

As far as Lizzie was concerned, Water Face need not have spoken. "I think not," she said. "If he did that he would give himself away too, and people might find out that he had something to do with the death of poor Nicholas."

Water Face's nerves collapsed in one of his squeaks. Mine remained calm, doubtless because of the amount of gin I had consumed with Mitkins.

"Is he dead?" I asked. She nodded. "Well," I said to her, "unlike you, I'm not a hypocrite, so I'm afraid I can't pretend to weep for him. How did he die?"

"Unlike you," she replied, "I'm not a liar, so I don't pretend to know. But I am aware that you've killed him somehow."

"Lizzie! Lizzie!" wailed Water Face. "You've no proof, you've no right to suspect poor Mr. Roberts."

"I not only suspect Mr. Roberts," she answered tartly, "I accuse him. Him and that rheumy old creature he calls his manager."

"I haven't seen Nicholas Hawtrey since the day I left Bath," I told her mildly. "Why should you imagine I should want to kill him?"

"I didn't say you *wanted* to. He was out to murder you and Edward warned you. He brought you a sabre to defend yourself with — if you remember."

It was my turn to gape at Water Face. Surely the boy couldn't have been so half-witted as to pass her on that information. He turned the same colour as M.S. pressing wind round his heart. "It was Lizzie's idea to warn you," he mumbled.

"And Lizzie's idea," she snapped, "to bring you the sabre. It belonged to my late uncle, Colonel Drew."

I might have known poor Water Face was not capable of showing such initiative on his own. I had a flicker of gratitude towards Lizzie for trying to prevent me from being hacked down in the dark. Then I cancelled it, remembering that it was only her precious non-existent Philippe that she would have wanted to save.

"I'm grateful to both of you," I said, "but in point of fact, Nicholas Hawtrey hasn't turned up yet."

"Rubbish!" said Lizzie, and stood up to her not inconsiderable height. "He rode off to look for you ten days ago. When Edward and I were making enquiries we found that he stabled his best mare at the Hare and Hounds about half a mile away from this theatre. What would he have been doing in this neighbourhood if he hadn't found you and got the worst of it?"

"It's possible that some other accident could have overtaken him."

"It's possible," she admitted, "but it hasn't."

"Perhaps he's still in hiding, waiting to get me," I suggested.

"If he is, it's as a ghost."

Water Face looked on the verge of collapse.

"Would you like some gin?" I asked him. I was beginning to regret having left the bottle in M.S.'s dressing-room. Lizzie answered for him. "Gentlemen do not drink spirits. Neither will you when you become Philippe de Lambrière. You'll have to learn to put the gutter behind you."

I seized on a hope. "I shouldn't dare play De Lambrière again," I said. "Everyone would suspect him of killing Hawtrey. Dozens of people know they were rivals. It wouldn't be safe."

"It would be safer than remaining Mr. Roberts. I'm the only one with any evidence against you and I certainly shouldn't give it against Philippe de Lambrière."

"But you would against Mr. Roberts?"

She nodded three times. She had gone back to wearing her dirty browns and grave-stone moss greens. They took all the lights from what could have been a pleasantly pale skin and they deadened the colour of her hair. Her Paris clothes were evidently not to be worn for anyone but Philippe.

Water Face said faintly, "You don't know my cousin, Roberts."

"Oh, I think I do by now," I breathed.

Suddenly she looked gentle and sedate again. "My friends are always asking me what's happened to Philippe. It's very embarrassing for me.

You made me shine in their eyes, and now that you've obviously grown tired of me, they're beginning to say they always said it wouldn't last."

"What have you told them about me?"

"I've said you've gone back to attend to your estates in France."

"That's stupid. You should have said you'd decided to turn me down."

"They wouldn't believe that," she said. Her frankness decided me to make one more attempt to reason with her.

"I apologise for my performance just now. It wasn't out of disrespect. I just wanted to make you see what you'd be taking on." I went so far as to drop a hand on her shoulder and turn her towards me. "You're a very rare woman in spite of your obsession. You *must* see that there can never be a real Philippe."

She laughed. Like her smile, it was unexpectedly pleasant. "Of course I do. I should qualify for Bedlam if I didn't. But I think it's very wise of me to make do with pretence. As you once pointed out, most people have to be content with living their fantasies in their own heads. They can't make theirs materialise, poor things — but I can." She held up a hand to stop an interruption. "Oh, all right. I don't deny it. Plenty of women have to get comfort from drawing the curtains round an imagined lover in bed at night. But then they've neither the money nor the courage to do something about making him come to life."

I turned for support to Water Face. His shoulders rose and dropped in a defeated shrug.

Lizzie continued. "I shall always be conscious of the fact that I'm hiring you to play a part, but if you play it well enough, there's nothing to stop me from enjoying it."

I asked softly, "Miss Weldon, how am I going to convince you that nothing on God's earth will persuade me to play that part?"

She smiled at me, and put on her gloves. The interview was evidently coming to an end. "I think that what's happened to poor Nicholas Hawtrey will persuade you," she said.

I made one last appeal to her. "I suppose you wouldn't consider having mercy on me?"

"I'm afraid not. I'm not used to putting others before myself. Oh, on the surface I'm most unselfish — my father's prop — Edward's advisor and friend. But I shouldn't hesitate to sacrifice either of them in my own interests."

"Yes," I said, "I see."

"There are plenty of people like me," she said lightly, as if to cheer me up. "The only difference is that they are not honest and I am."

"I certainly think you're the queen of them all," I assured her earnestly.

"We are as we are," she answered placidly. "But it's really only my frankness that makes me seem such a drag on you. Other women would work upon you just as ruthlessly and you wouldn't notice it. You'd think they were soft little helpless things."

"I doubt if I should ever think blackmail a soft little helpless thing," I said, smiling.

She sighed. "One has unfortunately to pick the most useful weapon within range." She jerked a finger at Water Face which lifted him off his chair like a puppet to her string. To me she added amiably, "After all, you won't be the first person to be playing a false part in private life. I can't think of anyone who isn't except myself. Take the great public figures who lead such impeccable lives on the surface: they'd probably fill the prisons if they were found out. Take my father! An eminent judge. He's so muddle-headed he's not fit to pronounce judgement upon whether an egg's correctly boiled. No, you won't be the only person playing a part and it will certainly be an improvement on the objectionable Mr. Roberts." Before I could defend Mr. Roberts, she asked politely, "Is it Friday?"

"Yes."

"Then I'll give you until Monday to make up your mind."

"Miss Weldon," I said as she reached the door, "there's just one thing I feel I should like to point out. If you get Mr. Roberts hanged for the murder of Nicholas Hawtrey, you'll have no chance of bringing Philippe de Lambrière to life at all, will you?"

"Mr. Roberts" — she smiled back at me — "there's just one thing I should like you to understand. If I can't have you as I want you, it would be much more convenient for me to have you out of the way altogether."

Chapter 18.

M.S. HAD recognised a serious threat in the Weldon woman long before I had done so myself. That was why he had taken the risk over Mitkins' watch. I was right in suspecting that he knew we should not be able to benefit from an enthusiastic report to Kemble.

"I saw the look in her eye, boy. She'll never let you be. I knew we should have to run for it."

While I was still taking Lizzie Weldon's dream-world infatuation lightly and belching to disillusion her, he was packing. He had crammed all our effects into his huge black trunk.

"With any luck," he said gloomily, "she'll lose your scent and stop sniffing after you. With even more luck, she might put you out of her head. When we come back I'll think of some tale to tell Kemble. In the meantime

Bates is in charge of the theatre. I've told him I'm taking you up to see Kemble and that we've business up north first."

"Why the north?"

"Because I don't want 'em following us south, boy, which is where we intend to fetch up. We shall have to hide out for a short while in France. It's a rare sacrifice for me, boy. They don't wash the dishes and live on muck. I shall go down with colic for sure. What do you expect," he added fiercely, "from a country that's not able to stay on the ground?"

M.S. had a quite unnatural hatred of balloonists. He said that men made quite enough trouble for each other on earth, and you could never tell what they would do if they took to the air. The fact that Montgolfier and the Duc de Chartres had achieved the feat of rising into the clouds attached to a balloon was enough, in his eyes, to condemn the entire French nation.

"Man wasn't meant to go flapping about in the sky," he complained. "Before you know where you are they'll be sailing over dropping cannon balls on decent folks' heads."

I thought this distinctly unlikely, but was not going to argue. A bee in M.S.'s bonnet was best left to buzz itself out. But I was not looking forward to our sojourn in France. I could see that he was going to develop into one of those English-pests-abroad, and unless he found everything in exact parallel to his home comforts, he was going to grumble ceaselessly. I prayed that Lizzie Weldon would give up her vain attempts to trap a shadow in the shortest possible time so that we could get back to M.S.'s plum-duff, hot ale and ginger, and John Philip Kemble.

M.S. had certainly laid a confusing trail. We left on the Saturday morning in full sight of the company dressed as ourselves with one small valise between us. Our huge black trunk was shortly to be transferred to a coach bound for Dover there to await the arrival of Mr. Anthony Buckland from Sandgate travelling with his valet, Mr. William Brown. It contained the French wardrobe I had acquired as Philippe de Lambrière.

The coach was uncomfortably crammed. I was pressed close to the dogged type of bumpkin I seem to attract. He asked me innumerable questions and appeared to find it hard to understand why his wife, who had been to the play the week before, should have taken a fancy to me.

Manager Smith was already showing symptoms of the colic he had every intention of contracting "on the other side." He was tenaciously clutching a large box containing the old-fashioned wigs from which he refused to be wooed away. He was also nose deep in *The Gentleman's Guide in His Tour through France*, which he had bought in an old book shop in Bristol. I pointed out to him that it was about twenty years old and possibly somewhat out of date as to practical details, but it was the Bible to him. One look at it showed me that the author was as dispeptic towards foreigners as Manager Smith himself. The preface stated that it was:

Wrote by an officer who lately travelled on a principle which he most sincerely recommends to his countrymen, viz: not to spend more money in the country of our natural enemy, than is requisite to support with decency the character of an Englishman.

I could imagine how popular we should be if an English-speaking Frenchman should happen to chance on that convivial little introduction.

M.S. read out from the book warnings ringing with hostility. We were not to collect crowds in the streets by throwing money out of our windows thereby "confirming Frenchmen in their unalterable opinions that the English are all immensely rich and consequently can afford to pay double what a Frenchman will pay for the same article." We were unsafe to dine apparently anywhere other than in a French officer's mess — these gentlemen being the only gentlemen with any pretentions towards honesty. As we were not soldiers, I thought we might encounter a certain difficulty here. M.S. read stolidly on, pink in the face from emotions he so rarely wasted.

Bank notes, he read, were not negotiable in France; it was extremely difficult to get them changed in any towns, and in some places absolutely impossible. If we drew on a banker abroad we might be charged seven or eight pounds discount. The wisest course was to draw on a French merchant wanting to have money transferred to England.

"M.S.," I said, "that was years ago. Things may have changed."

He ignored me and grew more and more irritated as he read that we must take over amongst our effects:

Two necessary articles called a knife and a fork which, if you neglected to take with you, you'll often run the hazard of losing your dinner, it being the custom of those very polite people (women as well as men) to lug out their great sharp pointed knives when going to their meals as there are seldom any laid on the table except when called for, and, when they appear (if they had any edge) an Englishman would suppose they were made to stick a roasting pig. And, as to their forks, which are made in the shape of spoons with three prongs, they are equally useless or unhandy.

To an Englishman it seems very strange to go into an inn and make a bargain for his bed, his supper, his horses and servants before he eats or sleeps. Yet this is common in France and for a stranger even necessary for, though you will meet with no kind of civil reception at the inns upon the road in France, as with us, at your entrance, you will meet with an exorbitant bill (without this precaution) at your departure. Therefore, when you come to an inn, where you intend to stay all night, or to dine, ask the price of your room and bed and order a supper or dinner at thirty, forty, fifty, or sixty sols per head. You will then be well served with, perhaps, many dishes, any one of which, had you ordered in particular, would have been charged treble.

"Barbarians!" snapped M.S.

"It might have changed," I repeated weakly, but he had turned over the pages to explode again into the author's warnings against the dangers of Southern France.

Having hinted at the affability of the ladies, I think it may be highly neces- sary to warn you to be extremely cautious in your amours (if any you propose). The air of the Southern parts of France is warm and impregnating, conse- quently, the women extremely amorous and the majority of them have it in their power to confer upon you a certain favour which, if it does not cost you your life, may stick by you all your days, it being reputed to be equally destruc- tive as that of the Neapolitans. The surgeons here make a very serious affair of such an accident and will run you up a bill of fifty guineas before you can look round you, so that a misfortune of this nature will throw your frugality out of the window and let your constitution go to wreck.

I shouted with laughter, but M.S. was so sure that the author had me in mind when he wrote these words that he lectured me for the next half- hour about keeping out of the way of whores and whoremongers, into which two classes he was convinced the entire French nation fell.

"Going to Vrance, then?" asked the dogged bumpkin with an expres- sion that struggled close to intelligence.

It's curious that it should have occurred neither to M.S. nor myself that it was not the height of caution to let our destination be known even to harmless-looking strangers, but M.S. was too full of emotion and I was too amused by his pig-headedness towards anything non-English to give our imprudence a thought. After M.S.'s laboriously complicated efforts to put anyone off our scent, it was ridiculous to give away our plans by care- less talk.

My suspicions weren't even aroused when we put up at the Blue Boar for the night and found the dogged bumpkin firmly planted in the taproom.

M.S. had gone out to buy some Daffy's Elixir and a bottle of Sir Walter Raleigh's Cordial to take against the colic awaiting him in France.

Clutching a pint of beer, the dogged bumpkin made straight for me.

"The wife took a fancy to thee," he said. "Came back talking o' no one but thee. Reckon I don't zee what her zees in thee. But then o' course, her zight be vailing."

I nodded graciously to this flattery and tried to shake him off, but he followed me sipping his beer.

"Wife's friend took a fancy to thee, too."

"Doubtless her sight be 'vailing' as well?" I suggested.

"No, but I've never reckoned her be too right in the head."

"Then that would account for it," I said.

I was used to certain sweltering looks from women which were not re- flected in the eyes of their husbands, so I thought his interest in my going to France came from a desire to get me out of the country.

"When be off to Vrance, then?" he asked.

"Oh," I said airily, "when we're ready."

M.S. came back clutching his colic remedies and we dined and forgot all about the dogged bumpkin. Evidently he didn't pay us the same compliment.

In the morning we left for the north. M.S. had arranged for us to stay with a number of his mole-like friends in various countries. A "mole" of M.S.'s acquaintance was an underhand as well as an underground contact involved in nearly every activity against the law. He could locate the "mole" in most towns, and they passed him on with messages of goodwill from one to the other. They were willing, in return for a fee, to hide thieves and murderers, dispose of stolen goods, procure bed companions of both sexes for illustrious customers, and spy for anyone in need of their services.

In Downham Market our mole on the surface was a second-hand clothes dealer. His shop smelt sour from soiled petticoats, musty shawls, and jackets reeking under the armpits. Breeches, hats, and carriage rugs rose to the ceiling in this moth's paradise. His service to us was to hide us until he could provide us with a new set of clothes apiece.

I shall not forget the shock of turning back on my heels to go into a tobacconist's and practically winging the dogged bumpkin. His narrow collie-dog's face broke into what was, in the circumstances, a praiseworthy smile. He was sufficiently well trained to make the best of being caught out clumsily trailing his quarry.

"Vancy zeeing thee," he chuckled. "Thee be lad the wife took zuch a vancy to when —"

Raising my hat, I said, "Yes, that's right." I then went on a tour of the taverns until I found M.S.

"There's no doubt about it," I told him. "That oaf is following us. But who the devil's paying him?"

M.S. was consuming a hot ale and ginger. His eyes slit thoughtfully. "There's only two it could be," he said. "It's either the Rare Sacrifice or the Weldon woman."

"What about Sir Gregory Hawtrey?" I suggested. "She may have tipped him off about Nicholas from spite."

He shook his head and blew in his tankard. He said that this helped the ginger to mix. "If it was Sir Gregory, he'd have come after us himself and the law with him. No, boy, it's someone who wants to know *where* we're going. What they want with us we'll find out later."

He swilled the hot ale and ginger angrily round in the tankard, gulped it down, and we set off to find the mole. When we unearthed him, we left our comfortable hotel to lodge amongst fetid underwear in the mole's garret.

The mole's stock was able to run to a good enough suit for Mr. William

Brown the valet, but it was not able to provide for Mr. Anthony Buckland, private gentleman of Sandgate.

We spent several hours sorting through the fruity piles, but when a pair of breeches might have got away with it, there was no suitable jacket to partner it, and no decent accessories at all.

The mole had one of those happy open faces with skin the texture of a bit of molten lava picked up by a tourist in Greece. "I'm afraid it's a case for a night tailor," he said, grinning.

I had no idea what he was talking about, but M.S. knew at once. He scowled. "If you think we're made of money," he snapped, "you've got brains to fit your face. We need what we've got for France."

The mole shrugged. "Suit yourselves," he said, and collapsed with laughter onto a pile of rotting shawls at the aptness of his choice of words.

M.S. turned to me. "We can't hang about to be tailored legitimate," he said. "Even with paying double it would take us past a week. They're slow enough in these country towns when you're not in a hurry, never mind when you are. Besides, we can't spare the money to buy the stuff new and we can't risk you being seen about in the town. Very well," he ordered the mole, "get a night tailor, but see it doesn't cost more than this," and he thumped Mitkins' watch on the counter.

The mole picked up the watch and promised us that the "measurer" would arrive as soon as it was dark.

"I'll come with you," M.S. said cheerfully. The amiable lack of trust which always existed between M.S. and his "friends" never failed to amuse me.

They left me in the attic with a piece of bread and cheese. The place was chilly and had such a variety of smells I was hard put to it to know which one I disliked most. Old clothes climbed into hillocks all round me. Un-shy rats were not put off by my presence and dexterously dragged fragments of cloth into their holes. Their irritation when they encountered difficulties was ludicrous. One well-scarred warrior would have sworn out loud if he'd been able to speak. He had pulled a pair of stays across the floor by the laces, backed into his hole, and got the bones wedged across the mouth of it. The more he tugged, the more the whalebones bent like an archer's bow and sprang forward, jerking him with them. That rat's private language must have bleached his whiskers at the roots. When I went to help him, he disappeared. I turned the corsets longways and stuffed one of the laces down the hole. I even went so far as to put a bit of my cheese on top of the corsets as a token of goodwill. In order not to frighten him, I took the most absurd length of time over every movement. I rather think I had my tongue between my lips. The rat was a good half-hour making up his mind whether my intentions were honourable or not. Then he crept out. I have admired rats ever since, and God knows, I've had enough opportunities to study them in human form. Never trust a helping hand: it can drop on you the hardest. Realise that your greatest friend can be your biggest enemy: he nearly always is. There's nothing quite so crippling as the well-meaning malice of a dear friend who has secretly never approved of you. If anyone does you a kindness, be careful not to believe it! Only your worst-known foe can be trusted. You are in no danger from him whatsoever, providing you don't let him out of your sight.

My rat moved his little pellet eyes between me and the cheese and corsets for several minutes. Then he came forward in a shy minuet. He ignored the cheese, ignored the corsets, selected a shred of some nasty child's underwear, and darted down his hole with it.

He was wrong in my case, of course. Mine was a genuine helping hand. But perhaps he felt they were so few and far between that the risk was too great to trust me. I could have benefited by being as suspicious myself in later life.

When the night tailor came in, I fell back on Water Face's most frequent expression. I gaped at him. Expecting to see a neat little fuss-pot, short-sighted from the strain of night work, I was introduced to a redheaded brute. If such a creature was possible, he reminded me of a blunt-nosed fox! He had crafty little eyes, wide-apart pointed ears, and ginger side-whiskers.

"This," said the mole, "is Mr. Templer. He's come to measure you."

Mr. Foxy Templer's method of doing so was original. He backed away from me, closed one eye, and snuffled. Then he walked round me twice. After that, he judged the breadth of my shoulders with his hands and did the same for my waist, hips, and thighs. It was only after that that he used his tape measure. Then he shook his head. "A difficult fit," he said, "oh, a difficult fit in the dark."

Both M.S. and the mole rounded on him at once.

"The boy's an easy fit," said M.S.

And from the mole, "You won't get your prices up that way, Templer. Mr. Smith's met a good few of your kind."

Some extraordinary arguments followed, during which I gathered that Mr. Foxy Templer was a burglar by trade. His manner of providing me with a suit of clothes would be to follow home someone as nearly resembling my proportions as possible. This might take him a matter of days. Having done this, he would try to break into the victim's home and remove as much useful clothing as he could find. But this, as he pointed out, took him off his real object, which was to remove "hardables as turns into money," i.e., silver, jewellery, etc. For this sacrifice — "After all, gentlemen, the danger's the same, an entry's an entry and you can 'ang just the same" — he charged a small percentage on top of his ordinary fee. Should he fail to find "a figure to match mine, or having done so, fail to follow him and effect his entry," he would be reduced to passing my measurements to various valets, butlers, chambermaids, and other domestics with no scruples about handing over the odd garment belonging to their masters. But a suit was "hard to put together" and it took more time.

I thought it would be quicker, simpler, and cheaper to risk being seen by the bumpkin who was trailing us and pay a daytime tailor to work overnight. I was howled down by M.S. and the mole, but louder still by Mr. Foxy Templer. It would be over a week before I could be fitted and three times the money, he assured me. M.S. and the mole were not embarrassed to point out in front of Mr. Foxy Templer that they had him under their control if he charged too much or took too long: his career could be affected by a word in the ear of the law. Foxy Templer agreed with startling amicability. He liked frankness in his clients, he said, and while he was one for standing up for his dues, he was not one for pushing the price above the point where it would be more economical to go to an honest tailor. They came to the following terms with Templer.

1. A half-share in Mitkins' watch.

2. Ten per cent extra for the possible loss of "hardables" and the danger of effecting an entry for goods other than convertible into money for himself.

3. Any "hardables" that he did manage to extract during his mission should belong to him exclusively.

4. He was to be reimbursed for any legitimate expenses he incurred en route.

He told me cheerfully that these were most likely to be met with in the taprooms. He found his most likely quarries in the inns and resting houses. He took up a pitch from which he could watch the coaches and stages roll up and where he could keep an eye on the private equipages. Then he marked down persons of quality, chose the best fit, and acquainted himself with their sleeping quarters. He explained that he infinitely preferred to lift the clothes of a hotel guest rather than those of a private householder. There was a bigger staff for suspicion to fall upon and access was much easier.

I gathered that the night tailors dressed many a person on the run in this manner, and that "night tailors" was a somewhat comprehensive term. It covered "night jewellers," "night bankers," and "night services" of many kinds in fact. There was always a Foxy Templer who would undertake to provide loose cash for the needy in return for a share in it.

I spent my time composing a letter to Lizzie Weldon. It occurred to me — and God knows it must have made me the biggest fool since Adam traded in the garden of Eden for one apple — that if I could give her a means of saving her face in front of her friends, she might stop chasing me. I wrote her a tender note from her heart-broken Philippe. Damn it! I didn't do it entirely for my own sake, either: I thought it might give the silly woman a modicum of consolation.

The night tailor kept us waiting three days. Mine was evidently an easy figure after all. Mr. Foxy Templer had found me a smartish suit that was a tolerable fit. The jacket caught me a little over the chest and the breeches were tight, but, I suppose, burglars cannot be choosers.

M.S. had his usual complicated plans for us. We paid Foxy Templer and the mole, who promised to despatch my letter to Lizzie, and we took to the road at midnight. It was as dark as a death mask and there was a cold drizzle falling.

We wore our own clothes but carried in our valise my stolen suit and the drab garments M.S. had chosen as correct wear for William Brown, valet to Mr. Anthony Buckland, private gentleman from Sandgate.

When I asked him where we were going, he said, "To the nearest river."

"To throw ourselves in?" I enquired politely.

"Yes," he said. "And keep that lantern shielded: we don't want anyone asking our business."

The nearest river, as I found out many years later in a French prison, was the unpretentious Wissey.

"There's not much of it," M.S. complained, flashing the lantern over its narrow flow. "But it's big enough to drown in." He jabbed the point of his umbrella into the muddy bank. A gluey white clay stuck to the end. "We could have got sucked down in this. It'll look as if I floundered in the dark." He turned to me and gave me a couple of bills and a letter. The letter was one from an admirer which I had received at the Little Apollo, and the bills were for theatre props mentioning the name of Manager Lambert Smith.

"Put them in your wallet," he ordered me. "It'll show folks who we were."

When I had done so, he said, "Now take off your coat and jacket, boy, and drop them on the bank there. The same with your shirt."

Unwillingly I stripped in the spiteful drizzle.

"Put your boots beside 'em," he told me. "Then give me your breeches and get into the clothes that Templer got you."

I obeyed him scowling until I saw that he was having to undress himself. He put on William Brown's shabby but respectable clothes and packed his own with my breeches into the valise. His own hat and one glove he threw into the river.

"There," he said. "If anyone comes across that he'll link it up with your pile on the bank. They'll think that poor old Manager Smith stumbled into the river in the dark and his young friend, Actor Roberts, who couldn't swim, tried to save him. The fact that we're never seen again will look as if I dragged you down with me. So that's the end of us, boy."

Prophetic words indeed!

Chapter 19.

My dearest little angel,

It is with the utter sadness that I write to you now. So much I hoped to be able to persuade you that my great devotion would be enough to make up for the lack of love you felt for me. But alas! you are a little angel of the strong will and you do not believe your poor heart-sore Philippe.

Even with this misery that drives me to make an end of myself, I cannot find to be angry with you. I understand that you have wishes to keep yourself for the poor lost Nicholas. Even when you so strike at my heart I can think nothing but tenderness for you. Should the poor lost one return and discover you the Vicomtess de Lambrière, how happy I should be, but how sad poor Nicholas! You see, my enchanting Eliza, how well your Philippe understands your noble nature.

For myself, my beloved, I shall return to France, my château and my vineyards, but I shall return with a heart full of emptiness because I have not brought back with me the only lady I shall ever love.

> *Your true and devoted,*
> Philippe-Jean-Baptiste-Raoul
> de Lambrière, Vicomte de Lambrière.

That was the letter I had written to Lizzie Weldon and which the mole had so loyally despatched to her. I had deliberately and somewhat vulgarly written my full title so that she could impress her friends.

I remember having chuckled out loud whilst writing it. It struck me as rather convincing with its poor English. It should give the love-sick idiot an excuse to show her friends why her vicomte had disappeared.

I did not chuckle at all when I was confronted with it four years later in the Conciergerie at half past one in the morning. My "little angel" had placed it in the hands of the Committee of General Security via the Lieutenant of Police.

A gendarme had just hauled me out of the Mousetrap with the information that I was wanted in the greffe. This was where I had been interviewed by the "wet-eyed" judge, Maire Savary. I had no doubt that I was in for one of those brightly lit interrogations that are so wearing to those who have suffered the rigours of the Mousetrap.

As I had refused to confess last time, I was frightened that they might be intending to use harsher methods of persuasion. One heard truly blood-chilling screams at night when the prison was quiet. One's colleagues' casual, "Some poor soul being tortured, I expect," was not something lightly to be forgotten.

I arrived at the greffe in my usual state of near-panic.

The Lieutenant of Police was waiting for me with two clerks from the Committee of General Security. He sat at the table, his soft baby-face looking even younger in the candlelight. With his chin on folded hands he contemplated me for some moments without expression. His opening remark was not comforting. "I cannot disguise from you, citoyen De Lambrière, that there is no prisoner for whom I feel more personal enmity than yourself."

I managed to stammer that I was distressed to hear this, as I harboured nothing but affection and admiration for him in return.

The sleepy-lidded eyes regarded me with something bordering on amusement. "That is very good of you. One is seldom complimented these days, so that even insincere flattery can be warming. You're aware, perhaps, that I've taken a personal interest in you ever since you came to France?"

"I know that you've been having me watched."

"Hardly an action of yours has escaped us. Unfortunately, the Committee of Public Safety has been unable to accept our findings. They do not agree with our conclusions and choose to think that the name of Buckland is your true one. It is this piece of obstinacy on their part which prevented your being executed in your rightful name of De Lambrière."

"Yes, I know. But my rightful name is Roberts."

He sighed impatiently. "We have agents amongst the émigrés in England, citoyen De Lambrière. They had very little difficulty in discovering that the actor you claim to be is dead."

"But I explained the reason for that when I gave myself up to you."

He ignored this remark. Instead he told me, "Everyone has to look to his laurels these days. I cannot afford to make mistakes. In your case I have made none and I do not intend to allow the Committee of Public Safety to prove that I have been incompetent."

I felt a ridiculous gratitude towards the Committee of Public Safety. I had forgotten for the moment that they were equally anxious to cut off my head in the name of Buckland.

One of the clerks looked up from his table like a nervous vole. I could almost see his whiskers twitching. "If they prove us wrong, it would bring our most trusted agents into disrepute."

His colleague was also a whisker twitcher. "We can't have the Committee of General Security accused of inefficiency. Heaven knows how many heads might fall!" He clapped a tiny paw over his mouth as if there was still time to smother his indiscretion.

The Lieutenant sent him one of the curiously blank glances that, while expressionless, could be so formidable. To me he said gently, "I should not like you to think that I have anything other than a very great admiration for the Committee of Public Safety. Better patriots are not likely to be found. But official bodies" — he spread out the hands that looked so hard in contrast to the soft flesh of his face — "do not always agree, and the Committee of Public Safety has some powerful members — the citoyens Danton, Robespierre, and Carnot amongst them — so you see, it's not only yourself whom your obstinacy could endanger, citoyen De Lambrière."

"You must pardon me," I said politely, "but I fail to see how confessing that I'm someone I'm not could assist me personally in any way at all."

The long, blank look seemed to start at the bottom of me and creep up. "Did the citoyen Maire Savary not suggest that a confession might be in your interests?"

"He did, but I think if you put yourself in my position you'd feel that it was a little risky to rely on anyone's suggestions in a place like this."

"It might be your only way of leaving it alive."

I tried to stare at him as forcefully as he was looking at me. "I imagine I shouldn't be given your word for it that I'd receive a safe pass out of the country in return for signing myself 'De Lambrière' on a confession drawn up by you?"

"You imagine correctly. But all sentences are not necessarily death sentences. There *have* been cases in which prisoners have been transported."

"I'm afraid, Lieutenant, that I don't put much faith in my chances of becoming one of these rarities. You said yourself that you felt more ill-disposed towards me than towards any other prisoner."

He nodded. "Yes, that's true. I don't think you've any conception of the trouble you have caused me."

I asked, hoping to endear myself to him, "Aren't I making the same amount for the Committee of Public Safety?"

"Possibly. But I doubt if that will be to your advantage."

"What would be to my advantage?"

The first vole eagerly pushed forward a piece of paper. The Lieutenant eyed it casually. "To sign a confession for me that you are the ci-devant Vicomte de Lambrière."

He must have thought me a lunatic to be trapped as easily as that. I should probably be executed within half an hour of signing without even getting the chance to give the Lieutenant a reproachful look.

I replied as I had done to Maire Savary. "I prefer my lawyer to handle my case."

The Lieutenant was playing with his pen on the table. Without looking at me, he flicked over the letter I had written to Lizzie Weldon. "If you're not De Lambrière, how do you account for this letter? Miss Weldon sent it to me when I wrote asking her to confirm your identity."

Lizzie must have read that letter often. It was limp from constant folding. It was a shock to see it again in such surroundings. "I wanted to help her save face. It was so that she could prove to her friends that there really was a Vicomte de Lambrière."

"I'm sure it was very useful," the Lieutenant said mildly. "It's certainly helped to convince me."

"I've already told you what really happened."

He clicked his fingers and the first vole handed him a second letter. "This is from Miss Weldon herself," said the Lieutenant in his slow and unemotional voice. "You might care to hear what she says." He waved a hand to dismiss the beginning of it. "The first part merely enquires after my own health and safety. This is the piece relating to yourself:

" 'I can understand poor Philippe wishing to save his own head, but that he should have told you such a story involving myself is inexcusable. I am sure you know me well enough to realise that I should never be likely to throw in my lot with a theatrical personage. Women of my breeding do not involve themselves with actors. I am convinced in my own mind that he is the Vicomte de Lambrière and cannot bring myself to think of him as anything else.

'The actor he refers to met with an unfortunate accident in Norfolk. He was drowned trying to rescue the manager of our Little Apollo theatre. This man's widow is still running the theatre. She told me that as the bodies were not recovered, she had her husband's hat and gloves, which were retrieved from the river, buried in the local churchyard. They were apparently very devoted and she grieves greatly for him, poor woman. So touched was I at the time by this tragedy that I also had the clothes of the actor Roberts interred at my own expense. Their headstones are side by side in the graveyard.' "

The Lieutenant sent his blank stare at me across the top of the letter. I could think of nothing to say. This last macabre touch on the part of Miss Weldon to destroy for ever the existence of the irksome Mr. Roberts and leave only Philippe de Lambrière alive was too much for me.

The Lieutenant continued to read:

" 'However badly he has behaved towards me, I should not like to think of misfortune overtaking Philippe. Is there not something you could do for him? Perhaps you could pretend to accept his story and release him on the strength of it?' "

The Lieutenant's glance this time was not blank. "I can*not* pretend to accept your story. Nor can I release you on the strength of it. You mustn't forget, citoyen, that I met you myself in Miss Weldon's house as the Vicomte de Lambrière. From the brief conversation we had together I also recall that you were very against reforms of any kind and had no sympathy with the lot of the peasant. In retrospect I should say that you showed marked counter-revolutionary sympathies and proved yourself a potential enemy of the people."

"I was playing a part," I said helplessly. "That was the character we had chosen."

"If that is the case, you were playing it with the skill of a professional actor, which my agents have since reported to me that you do not possess. You will not sign this confession?"

I shook a weary head.

He said angrily, "It is essential for me to prove myself right. If I fail, the consequences could be very serious for me."

I was so exasperated I almost shouted at him, "They could be just as serious for me."

"I have already suggested that if you sign, there might be a way of avoiding that."

"And I've already said that I don't think it's wise to adopt suggestions of people whose sole purpose is to execute me. After all, if it had been left to you I'd be dead now. You sent me up to the Tribunal as de Lambrière. It was only the interference of the Committee of Public Safety that saved me."

He turned to the senior vole. "Write down that the prisoner was aggressive and un-co-operative. No force was used upon him."

Chapter 20.

BACK IN the fetid atmosphere of the Mousetrap, I longed for the freedom of that wet night when we so unwisely left our clothes on the banks of the Wissey.

We had walked until daylight and finally made contact with the Dover coach. M.S. was rehearsing himself in the role of one of those familiar yet still respectful old retainers, and he coached me as a private gentleman from Sandgate.

Our trunk was duly waiting for us at Dover, and we boarded the packet as quickly as possible.

If M.S. suffered from travel sickness in a wheeled vehicle, it was nothing to what overtook him at sea. He was ill at the very sight of the boat. Long before we put out he was sitting on deck taking alternate nips of Daffy's Elixir and Sir Walter Raleigh's Cordial. With the result, of course, that before the coast line of France had come into view he was down with the colic and blaming the French.

He was greatly encouraged by two English farmers, who were also sea-sick and equally apprehensive of anything foreign. It made me wonder what had induced them to make the journey. Apparently they were going over to study French agricultural methods and did not expect to return from the venture alive. They sat passing the bottle of Daffy's Elixir amongst the three of them as if it had been a pleasant drink. It was hardly surprising that they had to make so many undignified dashes to the side of the boat.

Calais was a nightmare entirely owing to Manager Smith. He tottered into Meurice's Hotel holding his stomach and cursing the entire French nation. I had hoped that the farmers might take themselves to Dessein's or some other inn, but no, they were not willing to lose sight of their friend in affliction. Echoing his criticisms, they put up at Meurice's and sat by M.S.'s bedside loudly demanding an English cup of tea.

M.S. was so ill I was forced to send for a doctor. When he arrived he diagnosed M.S.'s complaint as nervous colic! He had not heard of Daffy's Elixir and after sniffing the empty bottle seemed to feel that his education in this respect had not been as neglected as M.S. appeared to think. He prescribed a perfectly efficient remedy, which M.S. refused to take.

M.S. and the farmers were served an excellent and very reasonably priced meal in their room by the bewildered Meurice. They had eaten every crumb, looked completely restored by it, and swore that they had been poisoned. I was damned if I was going to send for that unfortunate doctor again, so I retired to bed with the chambermaid by way of a peace offering to the French.

In the morning I discovered that the farmers had every intention of sticking closely by Manager Smith. We were all bound for Paris. We could none of us afford to take the Turgotine, which would have got us there in half the time. We were reduced to the public carrosse, and M.S. and I had to pay extra for the size of our trunk.

The carrosse was not comfortable and it was badly overcrowded. I recall my astonishment at the size of the postillion's boots. It seemed to me that a four-year-old child could have lodged in one of them. M.S. and the farmers were happily jammed together in a positive brotherhood of nausea.

I was watching the French countryside unfold like a patterned bale of cloth. It was, after all, my birthplace and I had a certain pride in it. My pride was not wholly borne out. The roads were wonderful. They made ours look like goat tracks, but the appalling contrast between the agricultural prosperity of the English countryside and this was lamentable at times. Certainly it varied, and there were stretches that made one feel better, but mostly it was mile upon mile of wretched poverty: hovel houses; villages piled like pig pens in muck; the peasants sombre-faced and undernourished. Now and again a derelict château loomed up. I raged against the owners, who were so obviously squandering the people's taxes at court, neglecting their country estates, and thereby leaving their tenant workers to starve. Also one saw a sight hardly possible even in dreams of the Far East: women and children yoked to the plough!

M.S. and I were on totally opposite sides of the fence in this. I am a decided democrat and a born Republican. I consider royalty in these modern days a drain on a nation's resources. I find it much more palatable to have a freely elected leader who has gained his position through his own abilities. M.S., on the other hand, will never hear a word against those who he is happily convinced are his "betters." No matter how dissolute the masters may be, M.S. is convinced that the peasants' miseries are no more than they deserve, and stem from ignorance and laziness. My argument that in France they are worn to the bone and crushed out of existence by taxes is met by his that they have probably never done an honest day's work in their lives.

It is not inhumanity that makes him so blind. It is obstinacy. He is a kindly man, and as he cannot alter the fact that people are ill-treated, he chooses to disbelieve it.

When we stopped to change horses, there was an example of inequality which should have impressed even M.S. It was in a dirty little village, the name of which I have completely forgotten. We climbed out of the carrosse to an inn that should have been forbidden as a chicken house. We were supposed to be partaking of refreshment. They offered us an unappetising form of black bread which was made from fern and rye. When we complained, they apologised and told us that the wheaten bread was reserved for the nobility and clergy!

Although I would never have admitted such a thing to M.S., my first sight of Paris was disappointing to me. It seemed huddled up compared to London. Naturally one had not the opportunity on that first introduction to admire the beauty of individual buildings, but there seemed a general lack of space and planning.

As for the traffic! Never, never in my life have I seen such confusion. Our carrosse was held up for no less than forty minutes while a carter and a young blood showing off with a brand-new cabriolet shouted abuse at one another.

I was bored and impatient until a girl joined in the argument. She leaned out of a yellow berline, on the doors of which were painted her family arms.

She used such language as one only associates with drunkards on Cheapside. She appeared to be an old friend of the cabriolet owner but entirely on the side of the carter.

I leaned out of the carrosse determined not to miss one foul word that escaped her gentle-looking mouth. The scene was made all the more pleasurable for me by the two liveried servants standing like ramrods at the back of her berline. Neither of them showed the smallest surprise that his young mistress could outswear a carter.

The cart and the cabriolet were by no means the only vehicles causing an obstruction. A coach and a post-chaise had collided head on and four chairmen had got into a tangle. I had plenty of time to observe the girl. Like a fool, I did not take note of the arms on the berline or I might have been able to find her more easily afterwards. I was more concerned with the line between her breasts, which was deepened by the pressure of the window from which she was leaning. Her long throat seemed to throb from the force, if not the filth, of her language. But her expression remained perfectly tranquil. She might have been saying nothing more innocuous than "good morning" to her Father Confessor. She was powdered very white, which suited her. When she turned her whole face towards me, it surprised me. It struck me as being too old for the rest of her. Her rouge stood out. She looked softly and prematurely tired beneath the eyes. The mouth, on closer inspection, was not gentle, either. It was heavy-lipped and unsubtle. She was dressed with that carefully adopted look of simplicity which costs so much. Her bodice was tight and her fichu flattered her. There was something fascinatingly vicious about her. Perhaps it was in the eyes, which belied the studied innocence of her ensemble.

There was nothing sophisticated in her reaction to my interest. She caught my grinning admiration and repaid it with crossed eyes and her tongue poked out.

I gave her a quelling stare that I reserve for critical friends in my dressing-room after I have given a bad performance. We might have progressed from there, but the traffic tangle suddenly sorted itself out. The cabriolet gave way to the cart, the post-chaise made room for the coach, and the four chairmen darted through the crowd and disappeared. Our carrosse started forward so suddenly that I found myself on the floor amongst a number of other passengers. When I regained my seat, the girl in her berline had been left far behind.

I was not nearly so heart-broken to say goodbye to the farmers. They shook hands with M.S. and myself as if we had been a couple of village pumps. M.S. was quite obviously going to miss them. He knew he lacked sympathy from me in his prejudices against France, and he begged them to visit us on their return from their agricultural studies.

He was so homesick I was really sorry for him. Even so, I was hard put to it not to smile as we trudged, with the porter shouldering our trunk, to our lodgings. Nothing Paris could provide was going to compensate M.S. for his own country's homely amenities. "Disease!" he muttered, "disease in every corner. You can see it. Boy, you'll have to get my body back to England. I'll never rest in *this* unholy ground."

He was lucky in our choice of lodgings. Our landlady was one after his own heart. She was an elderly, well-bred woman who told us, almost before extending a greeting, that she had seen better days. We might suppose her to be running the Hôtel de France in the rue Vivienne for her living, and in point of fact she could not deny this unhappy truth, but it was not what she had been born to expect. No, indeed not. Madame Angibault had been led to put her trust in her country's keeping its place in a normal civilisation; but what was it doing? It had started to demand equality for persons hitherto quite content with being peasants, and it reduced persons of note to running a Hôtel de France in the rue Vivienne for their living. Their *living*!

M.S. was so sympathetic towards her plight that I had the utmost difficulty in getting them both out of the foyer so that we could be shown our rooms.

I must say for Madame Angibault that she was not discriminating as to position. She was quite able to see that the valet Mr. William Brown possessed more gentlemanly qualities than his master, Mr. Buckland of Sandgate. I might have been a piece of her own nastily busy wallpaper for the amount of attention she paid to me when she ushered us into our living room. She spoke exclusively to M.S. He, the pretentious old devil, had not been able to resist stepping out of character. Gone was the familiar-from-years-of-devotion-but-still-respectful-old-retainer. In his place was something more in the nature of my erstwhile tutor, the Reverend Mr. Jabez Stock, who had undertaken the education of the young De Lambrière at the George in Huntingdon. The quiet, obviously good-blooded, intelligent Mr. Stock might, through force of unfortunate circumstances, have descended to the belittling position of servant-in-ordinary to a trumped-up piece of cheese like myself, but Madame Angibault, in her own reduced circumstances, would be the first to understand how this type of catastrophe could occur.

My God, that old man was a wonderful actor!

She sent down for a bottle of wine at her own expense and gave me a look that made my stolen breeches feel an even less good fit than the night tailor had feared.

They did not offer me a glass when the wine was sent up. They sat nose to nose on the seedy sofa toasting one another's misfortunes.

"What possessed you, Mr. Brown," she asked, "what possessed you to come to France at a time like this? Haven't you read about our troubles? Paris is *most* unsafe."

"We aren't interested in politics," I said.

She turned her head towards me but did not answer me. She spoke to M.S. "It doesn't matter whether you're interested or not. You'll get involved in them. You can't help it in modern France." She had strong little black eyes that vibrated fiercely in her face. "Oh, Mr. Brown," she said, "please don't believe the dreadful things you'll hear about our Queen." She did not know, of course, the staunch ally she had in Mr. Brown. For him, the "Lord's anointed" took precedence over everyone including the Lord. "It's that hairdresser," she added, filling M.S.'s glass without so much as an apologetic look in my direction. "The *Queen's* hairdresser, I mean. He does more damage than any of these horrible pamphleteers. She's such an unselfish soul. She wouldn't allow him to limit his attentions to her alone. She thought he would lose too much money if he gave up his other work in Paris. So she agreed to share him. He goes straight from her boudoir to dress the hair of any other woman who can afford it. You can imagine the tales he tells. People go to him just for the pleasure of gossip."

I have never seen M.S. so drawn to anyone as he was to Madame Angibault. I really believe that if I had not been a little peeved by their complete disinterest in me, there might have developed a lifelong liaison between them. They were made for one another. Their failures they could blame upon the community, their lost grandeurs they could concoct for themselves. They might have achieved a modicum of happiness together, consoling one another for the great days that had gone. She would have been no more genuine than he. She would have been acting, but unaware of it. He would have been acting, acting, acting. But how nice for him to have pulled off such an amiable part for the rest of his life!

He obviously wanted to be alone with the woman so that he could give her a picture of his background, which, owing to its inaccuracies, would have been embarrassing for me to overhear. He turned to me and gave me a look that indicated that he wanted me out of the way.

"As you're so busy, Brown," I said coldly, "I shall begin to unpack my belongings myself," and I stumped into the bedroom.

I heard him say to Madame Angibault, "He's not a bad boy, really. I knew him in better days, of course: in fact I brought him up. But now things are very different. He's very much the young gentleman and I'm — well, you can see what I've become."

"Oh, Mr. Brown," she twittered, "indeed I can. I knew the moment I set eyes on you that your positions should be reversed."

With my eye to the bedroom keyhole I saw the old rogue patting her hand. "The same with you, my dear lady, the same with you. The minute I saw you I thought, 'A great lady like that should never be in business.'"

"It's dreadful," she sighed, "it's a scandal that people like you and I who are used to positions of authority should come down to calling nobodies 'sir' and 'madame'!"

Disgusted, I walked to the window. There I received a shock. On the other side of the road, patiently watching the house, were the two farmers who had taken such a fancy to M.S. on the boat. I stepped back from the window at once. Memories of the dogged oaf who had followed us in Market Downham made me sure that these men were merely disguised as farmers and had been hired to follow us. I determined to find out. Marching through the salon without looking at M.S. or his conquest, I went into the street. I set off at a casual pace like a sightseer out to make a tour of the city. Long before I reached the rue St. Honoré I knew that one of the bumpkins was on my heels. I took him a good long walk. In the gardens of the Tuileries he was still keeping me in sight.

I went back to the rue Vivienne much quicker than I had left it. Outside Madame Angibault's, the other so-called farmer was still on guard.

I galloped up the stairs to our salon. Normally I should have been amused at the scene I interrupted. M.S. may not have been one for the "romantics," but he was playing his part exceedingly well. He was engaged in a long breath-stopping kiss with Madame Angibault. She was clutching him so firmly to her that when they sprang apart he got nicely caught up on her fichu pin.

"Excuse me," I said tartly, "but I require the services of my valet."

She went the colour of the wine they had polished off between them, and left the room, shaking herself like a sparrow after a dust bath.

"Young fool!" M.S. thundered at me. "Look what you've done with your airs and graces. We could have lived here a full year without a penny paid if you'd given me enough time to work on her."

"We can't live here another moment, thanks to you," I told him and marched him across to the window. I shot a finger through the lace curtains at the two "farmers" still so patiently keeping their watch. "You see them?" I asked him. "Your two fine friends? The ones you so kindly asked to look us up? They're not farmers at all. They've been paid to follow us over from England."

He was unnerved but determined not to show it. "Nonsense! You've got following on the brain. Why should they be after us?"

"Did I have following on the brain in Market Downham? Was that particular oaf after us or wasn't he? Well, if he wasn't, why did you make us hide out with the mole? Someone's been interested enough to pay these two to accompany us to Paris and I can guess who."

He looked defeated. "The Weldon woman wouldn't go to that much trouble to get you, boy."

"Not to get *me*. But she might to get her confounded Philippe. I tell you, M.S., we've got to shake them off."

He turned from the window nodding sadly. "It's a pity. Just as I was on the way to fixing us up with free lodgings. I told her I was a gentleman's son that had lost his way in life paying his father's gambling debts. I said I had chosen to work as a common servant rather than see my family name dishonoured. Very sympathetic she was."

"So I noticed. But you needn't be worried about the free lodging. I've no intention of paying her a sou after the way she treated me."

He followed me into the bedroom, where I was tossing out the clothes from our vast black trunk.

"You mustn't blame her for that, boy. I told her you were a young nobody risen from nowhere, resentful of someone like me with good blood."

"Thank you," I said.

There was a tap on the door and the concierge entered. She was carrying a white sheet of paper folded on an old brass tray.

The note brought us the compliments of the patronne and reminded us that it was the custom of the house to receive a week's rent in advance. I told the concierge to tell Madame Angibault that she would receive it at my convenience the next day.

Then I said to M.S., "We'll cram on every garment we can get into. The more we take away with us the less we shall have to buy. Your light of love can have the trunk in lieu of rent."

"But where will we go to, boy?" he asked.

"We'll find somewhere. There must be a place we can hide out in until those blessed agriculturists have given up the chase."

We took turns to stand watch at the window. One of the farmers left his post evidently for refreshment, but the other remained doggedly watching the house. The first one returned in due course to relieve the second. It was obviously their intention to mount an all-night guard.

M.S. recovered himself and took control. "Boy, send down to that woman and get three bottles of wine and a bottle of brandy. I'll go across to that fellow and pretend I've just spotted him through the window. I'll make out I've no suspicions, and ask him back. He'll jump at the chance of keeping an eye on us in our own home. If we can get him drunk enough we can slip out while he's sleeping it off."

"What about his partner?"

"With any luck he'll be on the day watch."

I sent down the order and watched M.S. crossing the street to the farmer. He clapped the man happily on the shoulder and after a few seconds' conversation they were on their way back to the Hôtel de France.

It could only be, I thought, that the farmers had been set on us by Lizzie. Pensively staring through Madame Angibault's lace curtains, more grey than white with the dust lodged in their pattern, I wondered what I had done to deserve Miss Weldon. Perhaps she was right when she said that it was merely her honesty that startled one. Women have chased men through the ages and intrigued to get them with equal vehemence, but their campaigns, being more subtle, were surely less repugnant to their quarries. Lizzie's form of attack was hardly calculated to endear her to her victim. I realised with an unpleasant stab of shame that I was frightened of Lizzie Weldon. I preferred her animosity towards Actor Roberts to her greedy passion for Philippe de Lambrière.

The wine and the brandy arrived on the brass tray with a small note to the effect that the patronne would prefer to be paid at her own convenience. She had added to the bill the bottle to which she was supposed to have treated M.S.

He came cheerfully into the salon, very much the cheerful valet in a position of easy privilege with his employer.

"Look who I've found outside, Mr. Buckland, sir. One of the gentlemen as travelled over with us from Dover."

I affected hearty surprise and shook the oaf by the hand. I told him it was always a pleasure to hear a fellow countryman's views of a foreign city and asked him what he thought of Paris. As I feared, he told me at great length. He had found it too hot, too crowded, and too French! We were on our third glass of wine before his arid observations ran out. Then I steered him on to agricultural topics. I asked him questions about the new trend towards turnip growing for winter stock and it was clear from his answers that I was right in suspecting that his knowledge of farming was negligible.

He was dressed in a thready-looking brown suit and had mean button eyes and a pointed snout. He reminded me of a bear that was shedding its coat.

It became pertinently obvious to me that we were not going to get this man easily drunk. We had finished a bottle of wine each and were well through the brandy. From the unclouded shine in the button eyes it was certain that his capacity was going to be Herculean. It was getting dusk, and it looked as though we might have our guest for the night.

I signalled M.S. to keep him talking, picked up the brandy bottle, and brought it heavily down on his head. He grunted and tipped forward as if in slow surprise. I gave him a second clout and he continued his gentle fall to the floor.

We left him where he fell and climbed into as many clothes as we could stuff under our greatcoats. We could not afford to be seen carrying out luggage. When we were dressed we looked mountainous enough to cause comment in any case.

We locked our victim in our apartment and walked with some difficulty and no grace at all down the musty staircase.

I had managed to cram on an extra pair of breeches, a waistcoat, and a jacket over my suit, not to mention four pairs of drawers, two shirts, and several pairs of stockings. My greatcoat had to be held together by hand, otherwise the buttons would have blown off like miniature cannons. The stress under the armpits was quite alarming. M.S. was dressed in much the same manner, but, being a bigger man than myself, looked even more mountainous.

There was a portrait of Madame Angibault in court dress at the foot of the stairs, but she herself was fortunately nowhere about.

The concierge looked at us with not more than mild interest. The French can be as tolerant as the English towards eccentrics, and if people like to dress up for the winter snows on the hottest night of the year, whose business is it but theirs?

Chapter 21.

WE CAUSED no excitement in the town, either. The heat seemed to be trapped in the narrow streets. I feared that the sweat gathering beneath my hidden layers would form into an underground lake and pour down my legs. I thought I should faint, but M.S., muffled to the eyebrows, plodded belligerently on.

In front of the great Bastille, which sprang up like a coarse growth against the night skyline, I approached a rough-looking character, and I told him as casually as possible that we wished to avoid unwelcome friends and wanted to lie low. His reply was to cross himself and hurry on. It wasn't until the beggar whom we next stopped made the same devout gesture that we realised that it was not directed against us personally. It was a protection against the shadow of the Bastille. I noticed that everyone scurried past it as if its horrors might take bodily shape and drag them down into its dungeons. It was certainly not a prepossessing edifice. Its slimy moat sucked down the glories of the summer night, and its gross shadow made black barnacles of the smaller buildings and cottages clinging to its walls.

The beggar's advice took us to the most fetid quarter of the town. This was, it seemed, the best place to go to if one wished to melt into obscurity. "Melt" was the correct word for us at the moment. The place was aptly nicknamed "L'Étuve," and one might just as well have been stepping into a stove, from the heat that seemed trapped in it. It was an ideal place in which to hide. The roads were solid with blocked traffic and what little space was left was filled with street vendors. Rag pickers jostled dog sellers offering mangy-looking puppies in baskets. Scissor grinders vied with butter merchants whose wares were running over their trays. Letter writers sat next to the ink sellers. Charcoal merchants and women selling strips of wallpaper lined the gutters. The sharp, parrot-like cry of the orange sellers — "Portugal! Portugal!" — rose above all the others. The population surged in between. Every unsavoury ragamuffin in the world appeared to have his home or his base in L'Étuve. There was no sign of hope. It was a place of ill health and extremes of heat and cold.

There were still remnants of affluence belonging to past decades. Some of the houses were tall and stately, their pride broken under warped wood-work and scaling paint. Here and there a wisp of curtain fluttered at a window, but more often there was nothing but blackness or rotten boards. The windows of L'Étuve reminded me unpleasantly of blinded beggars, some with their sightless eyes still glazed, some socketless, some with dirty patches across them, and all with their hands outstretched palm upwards. Every house in L'Étuve had outstretched hands.

I asked a mud carter where to find rooms. He was held up by a cumber-some vehicle I later learned went by the name of a "pot de chambre." I wasn't detaining him, but it didn't stop him from cursing me. His black cargo of mud in the cart behind formed a skin in the heat like that of milk coming off the boil. He knew of no rooms, he said. He collected mud for a living. He wasn't an authority on every rooming house in the place. He turned his flow of abuse onto two people clinging onto the back of the pot de chambre. His language reminded me of the tired-faced girl with the exciting body.

We asked a letter writer where to put up. He was unfortunately a wag — never a breed I have cared for. Would we like him to write round to every house in the neighbourhood and ask for accommodation? It would cer-tainly increase his trade. They would all have to write back through him, for there was hardly a soul who could sign his name. "You must understand that this is a very fashionable resort, monsieur, we are bound to be heavily booked."

I felt a tiny pull on my pocket. I shot an arm behind me and grabbed a hand. It was so small I nearly crushed it.

There was a sharp squeak of pain and I turned to find that I had a child dangling from the wrist. As it was bone thin, I let go immediately. I was afraid it might snap. She dropped down in the mud and I put a foot on her shoulder. M.S., who could never resist any child, even a thieving little grub like this, tried to push my foot off her.

"Look out, boy. She's only a ha'p'orth of skin and bone."

"She'll be a ha'p'orth of mince meat when I've finished with her," I promised.

But I removed my foot and pulled her up. She was shoeless, and the line of her spine was visible through her grey bodice as she tried to wriggle away from me. When she turned round, I saw shadowy patches under her eyes which I thought at first were dirt until I realised how neatly they matched. When I jerked her round to face me, she rolled back her lips in a silent jeer.

"Do you," I asked pleasantly, "know what happens to little girls who pick pockets?" For a moment I thought her Chinese. It was the hair that was cut like a boy's and the tilt of the narrow eyes. They were huge. They almost filled their slanting slots and left little room for the whites. Her mouth was working busily. I thought she was going to cry.

"Little girls who pick pockets," I told her, "end up in the Bastille. There's a dungeon so deep it goes halfway to the bottom of the earth and it's filled with great horned bats who eat little girls who pick pockets."

Her mouth was moving harder. She went up on her toes and spat at me. The little fiend had been working up her spittle and she gave it to me full in the face.

M.S. put the crook of his big umbrella round her neck and drew her towards him. He had an accent in French, but he used his words well.

"What do they call you, little girl?"

"Why have you so many clothes on?" she snapped. Her voice was as thin as her shoulders and the knobs that stood out at the sides of her throat. She repeated the question, suspicious and sharp. "Why are you wearing all those clothes?"

M.S. chuckled happily. "Ah! Ha!" he said, "there's a spry one. She's got some good markings in her."

I was often irritated by M.S.'s inability to see anything wrong in children or animals, however vicious. I saw his hand groping for his pocket. If he could have got through his layers he'd have given her a coin. I warned him, "You're not to take a fancy to this little brute. We've got enough to do looking after ourselves."

He chuckled again. "You weren't a much bigger little brute when I took a fancy to you."

Although we were talking in English, the child was quick to sense the sympathy in him. She gave him a smile and held out her skinny paw.

"The child's hungry," he said, trying to dig through his layers again.

I don't know what made me so antagonistic to that unfortunate snip of skin and bone. She must have been eight or nine, and normally the savage thinness of her arms and legs would have shocked me. But she thought me a fool for trying to frighten her with tales of great horned bats, and she let me see it. Imagine trying to scare a child who was used to the everyday horrors of L'Étuve with grim stories about the Bastille! Also, there was no need for my self-righteous attitude towards picking pockets, as I was so competent at the same game myself. But I took a dislike to that child on sight.

Her eyes were like poisonous berries when they turned on me. She put out her tongue at me, and in return I gave her my cross-eyed bedlam look. "That child," I told M.S., "hasn't got a decent thought in her head."

"Fit company for you, then," he snapped, and bent down to her kindly. "Now, then, little one, can you tell your old uncle where he could rest his old head for the night?"

She smiled at him, showing tiny sharp teeth. "*You* can spend the night at our house. But not *that* one!" She turned round and spat in my face again.

M.S. gave her a light cuff on the side of the head. "That'll do. That'll do. This young gentleman's my friend."

"You must be very rich gentlemen to have so many clothes to wear."

The thought evidently struck her as making it worth including me in her invitation. She said, "You can both come. But *I'm* not going to sleep with *him*. *He* can go in with my grandmother."

She started off through the close crowds like a tiddler darting through pond scum. We had difficulty in following her.

The brat's hospitality was reached through a tunnel in a sweating stone wall. When you looked back at the street outside, it was like viewing a little round scene through the wrong end of a telescope. A grey light crept through a narrow slit in the massive stonework. No. 15 rue Louis d'Or had seen the Middle Ages. All the walls were pitted and grimed; they were like discoloured bones that a dog has chewed and left in the garden all the winter. The stairs might have been created to ease the housing crush by breaking some of the tenants' necks.

Like an elephant testing false ground with its foot, M.S. prodded each step with his umbrella. The child went ahead of us and met an unshaven individual on the landing. This was the grandfather. There appeared to be no intermediate parents. I heard her gabble out her tale. ". . . so I said they could sleep here. You see, I was after the young one's pocket and he is the sort that would tell someone. They are very rich," she added brightly. "They have so many clothes they can wear them all at once."

"And where," demanded the grandfather, "do you think they will sleep?"

"The nice old one can come in with me, and the nasty young one can go in with you and your pig-mistress."

She was knocked out of his way for this, and we found ourselves facing her grandfather, whom I took to be an ancient with rabbit teeth. In point of fact he was not yet fifty, but years of L'Étuve had bitten into his face.

"What is the child telling me?" he asked.

"That we caught her trying to pick our pockets," I snapped, "and we shall give her up to the police unless you give us free accommodation."

Monsieur Lapin spread out his hands. "But we have nowhere! As you see, we have nowhere."

The child looked frightened. "Yes we have, Grandfather. We can squeeze them in."

M.S. put a hand on the child's head to reassure her. She thought it was mine and shook it off fiercely. When she realised to whom it belonged she seized it, gave it a quick kiss, and cuddled up against him.

"Mind her fleas," I said nastily.

The grandfather was reinforced by a plump female with dull bronze hair. It was easy to see what had drawn these two together. They both had protruding teeth. I should like to have heard the clash on the wedding night, but apparently there had been no such ceremony.

"This," said the child, "is the pig-lady who isn't married to my grandfather."

Madame Lapin lashed out at the brat. She dodged behind M.S., who received the blow in his stomach.

Madame Lapin was suspicious of us. "What have you got under your clothes?"

"Clothes," I replied.

"Have you stolen them?"

"Yes, but only from ourselves."

With the close conspiracy of the poor, they asked no more questions. But Monsieur Lapin warned us, "If you're here by tomorrow you'll have to make payments. We haven't the money to take guests who don't pay."

A knock on the door sent Monsieur Lapin running below. He admitted a woman and then gave two melancholy whistles up the stairs. Apparently he was a cobbler by trade, but to augment his income he acted as caretaker. He had a grim little cubby-hole on the ground level as a workshop, and from it he could pull open the door by a pair of old leather reins. The number of his whistles denoted which floor was to expect the caller. The undertaker on the second story received the most guests.

When Monsieur Lapin returned, we agreed on a price if we were forced to lengthen our stay with him. But to provide us with actual sleeping space was an even greater problem. M.S. was shorter than I but much heftier. The grandparents had nothing but a straw paillasse on the floor of an otherwise bare room up the stairs. But it was wider than the plank bed that the child slept on in an alcove at the foot of the landing.

"The old monsieur is too fat to share with Suzon," announced Madame Lapin. "The young one must go in with the child."

"I'm not tucking down with that flea-ridden brat," I said loudly. But it was nothing to the wail that she set up herself. She lay on the floor and went rigid with obstinacy. She rattled her fists on the boards beside her and screamed, "I want to sleep with the old one, the old one!" M.S. knelt down to pacify her, but her grandparents stepped over her body and led me to the alcove.

"There will be difficulty with the young monsieur's length," said Madame Lapin. "But perhaps Monsieur Pêche from upstairs can help."

It was certainly a problem. I was six feet, and the child's boards on their unsteady trestle bed would have finished under my knees.

The Lapins disappeared upstairs and came down again carrying a coffin. "Monsieur Pêche has been good enough to put old Jacques Banet on the floor tonight and this will help you to stretch out your legs."

"But he must have it by six in the morning," said Monsieur Lapin. "Old Jacques has to be in his grave sharp at eight."

I regarded the undertaker's helpful extension to my bed with distaste.

"Tomorrow, if you stay, we will find something else," Madame reassured me. "If you have money, perhaps Pêche will make you an end."

I'm afraid it cheered me to see poor M.S. wedged in with the Lapins on the straw paillasse. But it didn't compensate me for my own bed. The child's mattress was five lengths of sacking. The heat was so powerful it was almost audible in that windowless alcove.

The child was sitting hunched pixie fashion on the stairs. As far as I was concerned she could have stayed there, and the grandparents seemed to share my view. It was M.S. who got off his paillasse and tempted her to join me. She hung back on his hand with her thumb in her mouth and he was obliged to pick her up.

He put her down in the alcove and patted her head. "The boy won't hurt you, little one," he told her. "He can't help his nasty face. He was born with his same as you were born with yours. It's not nice to blame him for it."

The child giggled and knelt on the plank bed to put her arms round his neck.

"What is your name, my new uncle?" she asked. When he told her, she turned hostile eyes upon me. "Are you *that* one's uncle too?"

He nodded. She seemed to consider it a calamity for him. She gave him a gravely sympathetic look and used a cold little adult voice to me. "You will please to note that my new uncle the poor Monsieur Manager Smith is more my uncle than yours from now on." She had the most curious turn of old-fashioned phrasing. It must have come from being brought up by elderly people.

"You're welcome to each other," I told her. But I couldn't keep from smiling at her tone. Possibly there was no such thing as a true childhood in L'Étuve. Immediate introduction to hardship at birth must have aged all children beyond their years.

She appeared to be intending to retire naked. I can't say I blamed her. An orange would have felt bound to shed its peel in that inferno.

But M.S. was shocked. "Haven't you a nightgown, child?" he asked. She shook her head, and he wrapped a piece of sacking round her bare body.

"It's not nice to go to bed with a gentleman without any clothes on," he explained to her.

I grinned at him. "She won't agree with that when she gets a bit older."

He sent me a stern look. "You mind what you say in front of her, boy."

She was extremely loath to let him go.

"You come in here with me and make *him* sleep on the floor," she whimpered.

"He can't sleep on the floor, child, he'd have rats running over his face."

"I know," she said gleefully.

"I'm only across the way," he reminded her. "You've only to call out and I'll come to you."

She refused to let him kiss her good night. She was angry with him for abandoning her to me.

I was possessed by a ridiculous modesty. Considering the number of nights I had spent naked with women, it was a little foolish to feel compelled to keep on my drawers in front of an infant. But keep them on I did and was soon drenched with sweat. When I finally stretched my legs onto the container of the late Monsieur Banet, she rolled as far away from me as possible. I wasn't sorry to have a distance between us. Apart from the heat, there was the question of fleas. She began to scratch viciously.

"I'll catch those for you tomorrow," I promised her, "and if you get any more I shall call you 'the Puce.' That wouldn't sound very nice to your friends, would it?"

"I haven't any friends," she said, and her icy tone discouraged all further conversation.

I was suddenly sorry for this child for whom life had done so little. She would never have seen a tree in the country, never have felt a sea breeze. If she had a birthday, it was doubtful if the grandfather and his mistress would even have given her their best wishes. Christmas would have meant nothing but extra hardships. Snow would not be a plaything for the children of L'Étuve. It would be a battle to survive the icy blanket it laid across the roof tops and the cold that bit into the bones. There would be few signs of spring in L'Étuve, and summer would be nothing but a matter of the sun stoking up the thick air and hatching out flies. I became quite sentimental over the child whose small body relaxed beside me only when she was not forced to scratch. I was clumsy with children and could think of no way to end hostilities. In the darkness I put out a hand to pat her head. "Tomorrow I'll buy you a comb for your hair."

Somehow she managed to bite my fingers. I was so startled I boxed her ears.

After that we lay in what would have been chilly animosity had we not both been awash with sweat.

L'Étuve was not silent at night. There were noises that came from the heart of it as if the stove was burning up its victims in its pulverizing heat. It was the dogs fighting over the refuse, and sometimes it was men. It must have been about one in the morning when the child woke up and screamed. By the time I had struggled into wakefulness she was sitting up in bed sobbing to such an extent that I thought she'd shatter her brittle bones.

"What is it?" I asked. "What's the matter? Are you ill?"

"The bats," she screamed, "the great horned bats!"

I was trying to take her into my arms when the grandfather came in. She was thrashing about as if trying to ward off the horrific creatures of her dreams. Although she was sitting bolt upright I realised that she was still asleep and I groped for her little plunging fists. I had taken her in my arms and was trying to comfort her when the scene was lit up by a candle stump.

In the light I saw that her sacking had slipped.

M.S. towered over us in the nightcap he had made sure to stuff into his overcoat pocket.

"Boy!" he thundered, "I should have thought you'd know better than that!"

"Don't be an old fool," I snapped at him. "I never laid a finger on her. She's only had a nightmare, and I think it's my fault."

The grandfather was holding the candle up. He looked at me suspiciously. "That one has never had dreams before."

The child, quite naked, scrambled over my body and leapt into the arms of M.S.

"The bats!" she sobbed. "The bats in the dungeon — they are biting me, eating me up."

Even in the weak light from a quarter of a candle I could see what had added reality to her nightmare. There were great angry flea bites all over her. She squashed her nose against M.S.'s shoulder. "My new uncle, I'm frightened of bats."

M.S. jogged her like a baby and patted her bony back.

"It was only a dream, just a silly old dream. There aren't any bats and you're not in a dungeon."

Madame Lapin pushed into the alcove. "It will be the child's fault if something has happened. She has always been bad. Only the other day I caught her on the knee of Monsieur Lattre, offering to kiss him if he gave her a pear."

"Yes," sniffed the child, "but he gave me the pear and I *didn't* kiss him."

Madame Lapin snatched her out of M.S.'s arms, clouted her firmly over the head, and dumped her down beside me again. "Be silent, Suzon, you're disturbing the gentleman's sleep. And fancy making us light up a candle for nothing."

The child's nakedness didn't seem to worry her. L'Étuve had no time for niceties. They departed in a grave little procession leaving Suzon lying taut again beside me. I did my best to make amends.

"I shouldn't have told such a silly tale. I was just trying to frighten you into being good. There are no such things as bats that eat little girls, so don't cry any more."

"I'm not crying over the bats."

"What's the matter, then?"

"Tomorrow," she said, "my new uncle the poor Monsieur Manager Smith will be going away."

I was annoyed at the constant inclusion of the word "poor" in her references to him. I had a suspicion that it came from sympathy for his being connected with me. I was right.

"I call him 'poor' because he is your uncle, too," she said, "and a thing like that must be sad for him."

She was not easy to like. Nevertheless I was not very proud of myself for reducing that puny little chip of defiance to tears. She had resisted the horrors of L'Étuve in the daytime and it had taken me and my fairy stories to make a nightmare of her sleep.

It kept me awake for over an hour. I was unaccustomed to feeling remorse.

Chapter 22.

M.S. WOKE up with the colic. When indisposed he was always very dramatic. He spoke with resigned courage. "Boy, if you're not able to find me a drop of Daffy's Elixir, you may as well make arrangements for me with the gentleman upstairs."

When I tried to explain to him that it would be unfair to expect to find his favourite remedy in a foreign country, he rolled over clutching his stomach.

"They've more ways of killing you than death itself. Barbarians! Savages!"

His loud complaints gathered the Lapins and the child round his bed. Even Monsieur Pêche, the undertaker from upstairs, stopped his hammering to put his head round the door. Fortunately they were not able to understand the terms in which M.S. held them all responsible for not stocking Daffy's Elixir.

Monsieur Pêche adopted rather a professional attitude. "I hope it isn't serious: he will take a lot of wood."

At this the Puce let out a shriek of dismay. She was the only person I have ever seen who could sob with her mouth wide open.

"For heaven's sake, child," snapped Manager Smith.

The nearest form of medical aid seemed to be a midwife two streets away, but advice was plentiful. Finally M.S. decided that only a cup of tea would save him from contributing to Pêche's livelihood.

"Tea!" exclaimed Madame Lapin. "You'll have a fine affair to get hold of that. There are shortages of much more important things than tea."

"An apothecary would be most likely to stock it," the ever-helpful Pêche told me. "But not in this quarter, of course. There's no market for delicacies here."

I had no option but to go in search of it myself. I left the child clinging to M.S.'s hand begging him not to die. Madame Lapin was fanning his face, Monsieur Lapin was rubbing his feet, and Pêche was assuring him of his best attention should the worst occur. "I will see you well boxed, monsieur, though God knows that timber's in short enough supply. It's the demand for it that makes it so scarce. I have seen people looking much better than you who have gone off in a minute. Pouf! Like that!" He snapped his fingers. "But do not aggravate yourself: you'll only hasten the need if you worry. Take the word of old Jacques Pêche: he'll find you enough wood from somewhere."

The battle of Parisian street life was even fiercer that day. I swear that the French driver, no matter what his vehicle, has only one ambition: to stamp out the human race! I was spread-eagled against a corner stone whilst an irate horse reared its forelegs under my nose. Nobody came to my rescue. Perhaps it was quite a common sight to see a pedestrian in danger of being savaged to death. Thank God the streets weren't any wider; it would have been intolerable if they had any more space in which to create havoc.

It was difficult not to get sucked out of my way by the stream of the crowd. The hysteria prevailing in the streets — shouts, screams, flaying arms, and tearful faces — was apparently not entirely an everyday occurrence. Even the children looked distressed, as if they felt bound to reflect the expressions of their elders.

When I finally fell into the doorway of an apothecary, I asked if anything had happened. Happened! The man shot from behind his counter. He took me by the jacket and shook me. *Happened!* Had I not heard? Monsieur *Necker* had been dismissed! Sorry though I am for anyone finding himself suddenly unemployed, I couldn't imagine why this one man's misfortune should reduce a whole town to a wailing fury. French politics have always confused me and still do. French wine, French food, French women — yes! But French politics — no! I had vaguely heard of Monsieur Necker, a Swiss financier called in to steady France's rocking treasury, but I had no idea that he was so revered by the people. To them he was "the wizzard," the brilliant magician who would right all their wrongs.

"He was only recalled to office last August," the apothecary practically sobbed at me. "And now — now they have turned him out again. I tell you, monsieur, this is a black day for France."

I gathered that even Necker had failed to balance the nation's accounts. The wizzard had run out of magic. The apothecary was too busy pouring himself out a restoring glass of brandy to bother with my request for tea. His hand was shaking as much as his voice. "On les aura!" he shouted, "on les aura!"

It was the first time I had come across that sinister phrase, but I was to hear it several times that day alone. "We will get them. We will get them!" I pushed again into the turmoil outside.

Even I was affected by the sight of those crowds surging aimlessly up the streets as if the mere turning of a corner might bring some assurance of hope. It would have done Monsieur Necker good, I think, if he could have seen the look of utter loss on those thousands of faces because of his dismissal. Certainly many of them would have been hard put to it to explain why they had such faith in him, but they could have said what they hoped from him — bread. Hadn't he been called the "Saviour of France"? To those who have nothing else in the cupboard, even words can be food. It's distressing to be in a city on the day it has declared itself bankrupt of hope.

With the volatile French it's also unwise to be in the streets. The crowds had found arms from somewhere. Despair was giving way to rage. I decided to be extravagant. I took a chair.

It felt a little foolish in that growing upheaval to be searching for tea. There were some really quite ugly disturbances. My chairmen were stopped several times. I called out to the crowds that I was English, a fact usually received with mixed feelings. I explained that English blood could boil at French wrongs and that mine had been doing so for some time, and my sincerity must have reached them; they did not molest me. Their ugly expressions became quite amicable. They weren't even put out when I had to confess I was looking for tea. I told them that my "old English father" was suffering from colic and that this was the only beverage that soothed the pain. On hearing this, they insisted on helping me to find it. Trotting cheerfully beside me, about ten people led my chairmen to apothecary after apothecary. They would have broken up one shop for failing to stock tea if I hadn't intervened.

They were an intimidating sight, and I knew their momentary good nature was about as stable as a tennis ball balanced on a pin head. The smallest incident might change their mood and nothing I said could save me.

In spite of his having fought somewhat flamboyantly against the British, the name of General La Fayette was bound to appeal to someone with my instinctive revolutionary sympathies. I have to confess to a schoolboy's excitement on seeing this hero plunging about in the crowd on a large white horse. His popularity nearly unseated him. The thundering cheers made the horse rear dangerously. I stuck my head nervously out of the chair window. In spite of his equine gymnastics, I had a good view of him. He reminded me instantly of Pêche! The latter, although a plebeian born and bred, had the same gently aristocratic features, the same soft strength. Whilst La Fayette had the talent of mixing with his inferiors with no trace of condescension, Pêche, I was sure, had the opposite ability to mix with his superiors with no resentment. The physical likeness between them astonished me.

Even now my admiration of La Fayette has not been tempered. I am aware of the criticisms of him. Many people blame him, as the head of the National Guard, for causing hostility between this body and the people. They accuse him of employing the National Guard to repress revolutionary activities. But surely this is only one of the somersaults truth has taken since everything got out of hand. He employed the guard to suppress outbreaks that might have harmed the people themselves. He used it as a protective force. But when truth is upside down, logic does not know where to lodge. A burgher guard becomes a privileged troop, which, having something to lose, has something to gain; therefore it is resented by the people.

Smoke was rising all over Paris. A cheerful drummer kept pace with my chair. "They are firing the barriers," the drummer explained. "You know, where they take the douane on the food coming in. Every day the prices grow higher and higher. They say the Gobelins is burned right to the ground. Isn't that splendid?"

I believe they set fire to nineteen barriers that day.

We were soon brought to a halt by a boisterous procession. The people had raided the waxworks, and two busts were bobbing above their heads. I shouldn't have known who they were, but the drummer told me they were of Necker and the Duc d'Orléans.

The drummer seemed remarkably conversational, if breathless. In all that upheaval he treated me like a tourist he was trying to interest in the sights. "They are the work of the great Monsieur Curtius," he told me proudly. "You may see the whole of Versailles made of wax in his place. They say there's no finer work in the whole of the world."

Our ragged escort made my chairmen join the parade. We headed for the Place Louis XV, where the crowd was becoming wild. They screamed, "Vive Monsieur Necker. Vive Monsieur Orléans!"

I didn't see how the fight began. My chairmen dumped me down and fled. When I struggled out, my drummer was in the midst of it. A detachment of dragoons were hacking at the crowds, and the wax effigies were shattered to pieces. The destruction of the one of the Duc d'Orléans raised an even louder howl of fury than the loss of Necker's had done. Orléans was one of the idols of the moment. I heard fearful tales about him later. He was supposed to have paid hired assassins to create havoc and murder, and he was credited with quite a few scurrilous pamphlets.

I pushed my way out of the Place Louis XV. I'd no wish to be mowed down either by dragoons or the people in something that wasn't my quarrel.

But it wasn't easy to find anyone who wasn't quarrelsome. Paris was reaching fever point. There was another fracas in the garden of the Tuileries which didn't improve the people's temper. The Royal Germans under the Prince de Lambesc also tried to disperse the people. I don't think there were over-many casualties, but the rumour went flowing up and down the street that Lambesc himself had trampled an old man to death under his horse, and finished him off with a sabre thrust. Everyone had a different version. From three separate people I heard that it was an old woman, a pregnant woman, and a small crippled girl.

The French guards broke out of barracks and joined the people in attacking the Royal Germans. I thought the whole city would end up in flames.

In the midst of the chaos my shoulders were violently seized from behind. I spun round to find myself nose to nose with my drummer friend. It's funny how absurdities stay in one's mind. I shall remember that ruffian long after I've forgotten the rest of that day. Still blood-spattered from hurling himself at dragoons, he yelled at me, "There is a grocer called Monsieur Piebot! He sells tea in the rue Montmartre."

I could hardly make myself heard to thank him above the din. He put two great helpful hands in my back and pushed me through the crush in the direction of the rue Montmartre. Then he shrieked further instructions, waved a cheery farewell, and went off to do God knows what.

Monsieur Piebot was quite unruffled in his little black box of a shop. Let turmoil rage, but a man must continue his business. He told me I would be wise to stock up with tea. The general unrest would be sure to bring further shortages.

The cost of the tea made it impossible for me to take a chair back to L'Étuve. I was forced to elbow myself a path through the crush. Even so, the force of the bodies flowing in a certain direction drew me off my route. I was sucked towards the gates of the Palais-Royal. There we came into a head-on collision with a stream of even more emotional people battling to go in the opposite direction.

I noticed that a large proportion of the shouting masses were wearing leaves in their hats. Now and again shrill voices rose above the tumult. "To arms! To arms! The King will cut every throat in Paris." There were shouts of "The barracks! The arsenals! Break open the arsenals! Arborns une cocarde! On les aura!"

I seized a sweating, flour-stained baker by the shoulders and screamed into his ear, "What has happened? What is the trouble about?"

He bellowed back, "The King has decided to murder the people. There will be a massacre worse than St. Bartholomew. We must fight to save our wives and children." He then burst into tears, kissed me, and leapt into the crowds with the vigour of La Fayette's horse.

I followed him in much the same manner. It was impossible to walk normally. Without stopping to wonder whether my informant was right, I was ready to follow the hysterics and help to plunder the arsenals. I should have joined in the burning of the barriers and fired on anyone sent to keep order. Such were my Republican sentiments that I accepted without doubt the fact that the monarch was planning a massacre. I should probably have gone down with a bloody head and never lived to hear that my heroics had been wasted on the complete fabrication of an emotional agitator.

However, the day saw no heroics, wasted or otherwise, on the part of the Vicomte de Lambrière, Mr. Buckland, or Actor Roberts. If there is any justice in the present imprisonment of those three gentlemen, it is because not one of them was able to place his principles above his personal desires. Dearly as I should like to claim that I raised my hand on the side of the French people, all I did was to wave it violently above my head at a woman I had seen flattened against the railings. It was the girl I had seen in the yellow berline the first day we came into Paris.

It was a struggle to reach her. When I did I was thrown against her so hard that some of my tea spilt down her neck.

"You'll be crushed to death," I shrieked at her. "You shouldn't be out on a day like this."

In spite of the sweat that had clotted the powder on her face, and the dress that was torn to her petticoats, she had not lost her insolent poise. Suddenly the major portion of the crowd surged off. There was a welcome space about us and an even more welcome opportunity to breathe. She leaned against the railings, my tea leaves freckling the bottom of her throat and the pushed-up line of her breasts.

"Only a fool would stay *in* on a day like this!" she retorted. "My brother's gone down to the arsenals. Why haven't you? We need all the help we can get."

"I was on my way," I assured her, "until I saw you."

It was not a pretty face upon closer inspection, but then I am not an admirer of prettiness as such. The cherub kind of looks and the ninny curls which our ancestors seemed to have found so attractive have always struck me as vaguely nauseating. This was a jaded little face with clumsy features and a mouth that was too wide. It sounds horrific as it's written down, but her whole charm lay in her complexion, her movements, and the commanding assurance that all men worthy of their masculinity would find her irresistible in bed. There was also a hint of depravity which has always appealed

to me. It was her figure that gave her her assurance. Any man would have
wanted that.

Her voice was attractive, too. It had an odd little swing in it, as if she
were used to fierce arguments and was treating it as a pendulum, waiting to
strike. She said, "What in the name of God are you carrying?"

"Tea."

Her tongue came out to catch the sweat from her upper lip. "How charm-
ingly domesticated of you on such a glorious afternoon."

"An English friend of mine has a stomach-ache, and this is the only way
to soothe it."

She nodded gravely. "I have always admired the English constitution."

I laughed at her pun and said that I was delighted that she could find
something to compliment us upon.

"Individually," she said, "I find you boring, but your government is an
example to the world."

"Then you don't sympathise with our American rebels?"

"I sympathise with *all* rebels. How is it you speak such good French?"

"Because I'm half French."

"Then let's hope you're not as boring as a whole Englishman."

I suddenly caught sight of the tea leaves slowly infusing in the moisture on
her neck. Tiny brown stains were coursing down towards her breasts. She
laughed as I mopped her up, and rescued the leaf that she had pinned to
her fichu. "Did you hear him? Wasn't he wonderful? But the poor man
looked half starved. They say his father even refused to send him a bed. Can't
you imagine the kind of stuffy little bourgeois parent who would try and
stifle a genius like that?" I was taking too long to remove the tea leaves and
she picked up my hand and put it firmly to my side. "Monsieur Desmoulins
is a writer of genius. Anyone who heard him just now couldn't fail to be
moved by such words. He jumped up onto a table, fired his pistol into the
air, and you should have seen the brilliant way he grasped the people's
mood. He might have been an actor. Not even Talma could have held an
audience like that. He made every other speaker I've ever listened to sound
like wind instruments. He worked them up to fever pitch. He said that the
King was about to start a new St. Bartholomew and cut every living throat in
Paris. It's nonsense, of course, but what does it matter if it makes the people
take action? We've had enough useless words. It was theatre — inspired
theatre. He made us all wear leaves as cockades. Look at the trees: they're
as bare as if autumn had suddenly struck." She tore her own leaf in two
and stuck one half of it into my button hole. "On les aura!" she said, and
laughed. "On les aura!"

In those days I was still surprised to find someone of her kind on the side
of what M.S. would have called "the rabble." I had not yet had any experience of that extraordinary society so eager to join in the ringing of its own

death knell. Nor had I any time to comment on it at that moment. With the complete lack of coquettishness which I found so refreshing, she admitted her attraction towards me by demanding that I should buy her an iced drink in the Palais-Royal.

Even had that place a less notorious reputation for expense, I shouldn't have been able to oblige her. I hadn't a sou in my pocket.

"Any other time," I said quickly, "and perhaps you'd like to name it now: I'd be enchanted. But my poor friend is really in need of his tea."

She smiled with a winning understanding, but all the interest had died in her eyes. She had taken my refusal as a rejection of herself. I begged her to meet me at the Palais-Royal that evening. I promised myself to find money from somewhere even if I had to cut a throat for it. But she shook her head. "It's *now* that I want my thirst quenched, monsieur, *not* this evening." She turned and called loudly, "Côté!" A young and good-looking footman ran up to her. "I'm ready to go home now, Côté." She did not look at me again and she gave no sign that she had heard me shouting that I would go to the Palais-Royal in the hope of seeing her. The footman steered her through the crowds, and I realised that I still did not know her name.

On the way back to L'Étuve I was telling myself that my instinctive dislike of the well-born was rarely misplaced. However liberal-minded that girl might consider herself in thought, she was still a spoilt little aristocrat in action. Because a whim had not been granted, she was willing to sacrifice all the mutual attraction that undoubtedly existed between us. She was used, I thought bitterly, to having her orders carried out as quickly as the young footman had answered the summons of her clapped hands.

I told myself that I should have nothing in common with a woman like that and that I would make no effort to see her again. It was depressing to realise that in spite of my firm intentions I should undoubtedly go up to the Palais-Royal in the hope of finding her that very night.

Chapter 23.

IT WAS even more depressing to find that M.S. had long since recovered on a mug of spiced wine prepared by Pêche and that the thought of my tea nauseated him.

"I've missed an important appointment getting this stuff for you," I grumbled.

"Well, you've just come in time for another one. With all this rumpus going on, those farmers are likely to have been put off the scent. It's a good time to take our letter to Dugazon. We can't stay in this hole for ever, and it's time that you got back to work."

With that I was in full agreement. My years at the Little Apollo had made me feel lost when I was not actively employed on the stage. I felt aimless and irritable, and it was obvious that my ambitions were not likely to be furthered in L'Étuve.

Also, it was becoming very necessary to earn some money. The contents of the Rare Sacrifice's strong-box would not last for ever, and whilst the price required by the Lapins for an extension of our stay was moderate, it still had to be found. Also the age-old question of eating had to be taken into account.

We agreed that even if it was only possible to persuade Dugazon to give me a part far below the dignity of the erstwhile leading actor of the Little Apollo, it must be accepted. It would give us a foothold in the Comédie Française. Our eventual aim was for me to do well enough in France to enable us to get to America, where we hoped to start our own theatre again. The drama was making great strides in the New World, and once over there we would be safe from Lizzie Weldon's blackmail and the fear of being involved in young Hawtrey's death.

We set off for the Comédie Française and gave in the letter that Kemble was supposed to have written. It was addressed personally to Dugazon and praised me so effusively that we were granted an immediate interview in the Green Room.

Even so, our reception by the great comedian was far from cordial. Unlike the girl with the jaded little face, whom I was unable to get out of my mind, he did not admire the English constitution. He admired nothing about us except our breed of Blenheim spaniels! There was one curled on his lap which seemed to view us with the same distaste as its master. It jumped down to sniff at our ankles and retired growling into a corner. From this vantage point it kept up a scrutiny of us as baleful as Dugazon's.

In his thin, affected voice he told us straightaway that he had only consented to see us because he felt it his duty. The celebrated Monsieur Kemble had written so warmly of me that it would have been grossly impolite of him to have ignored a brother actor's appeal. Having received us, he felt no more should be required of him and he wished us a very good day.

It was not an encouraging start. If I had failed to notice that on his jacket he was wearing a wilting leaf, our encounter might have ended there. As it was, I felt in my pocket and produced the limp half of the leaf which the girl at the Palais-Royal had shared with me. Dugazon's expression of deadly disinterest changed to appreciation. It was not hard to guess where his sympathies lay. I determined at once to play on them. Not for the life of me could I remember the name of the young man who had so successfully appealed to the crowd, but I recalled what the girl had said of him. "Did you see him, monsieur?" I asked Dugazon.

He shook his head. "No, no — unfortunately, but I was told it was something one shouldn't have missed. You were there yourself?"

"From the start," I lied. "I've never been so moved. What theatre, monsieur! What inspired theatre! What timing! He was brilliant in grasping the mood of the crowd — brilliant in holding it. He made every other speaker I've ever listened to sound like a cracked wind instrument. What does it matter if his information was not entirely correct? As long as it makes people take action? We've had enough useless words."

Dugazon crossed to me. His arm went round my shoulder and he kissed both my cheeks. "I never thought," he said with a tinge of disappointment, "that I should ever hear an Englishman talking so sensibly."

I told him that I was only half English.

"Ah! That accounts for it. I didn't think such wisdom could be found in someone with nothing but Anglo Saxon blood."

He was a vehement, jumpy creature consumed by a gripping hatred of the bonds that tied the French theatre to the crown. He interrupted M.S. in an account of my glorious services to the English theatre to shout, "Enslavement! That's what it is. No better than enslavement. An actor can be imprisoned, if you please. Yes! Actually confined in the Fort L'Évêque if he annoys anyone at court, or even if he irritates an influential member of the public. We are the official servants of the crown — *servants*! We haven't the rights of the humblest peasant."

I was about to make a comment but was given no opportunity. Dugazon's voice squeaked with rage. "We are not even allowed a church burial. An actor's soul isn't good enough! I must assure you, *assure* you, Christian sepulture is not accorded our remains. But" — he threw the word out of his mouth like a cherry stone — "this fate is only reserved for the drama. The Académie Royale de Musique is exempt from it. Yes! One has only to dance in the ballet or sing a little song or play an off-stage devil in *Orpheus* — so long as one is attached to the opera house, one may be buried in consecrated ground! *Why*?" he asked furiously, and promptly answered himself. "Because Louis XIV used to dance in the ballet and from then on the medium was sacred. The Académie Royale de Musique are pensioners of the King and therefore privileged. But we — *we*, the *true* exponents of the drama — are not fit even to bury properly. *And*," he boomed, in that curiously powerful voice which, oddly, had little strength in it, "there are those in our profession who glory in it, who *love* their chains, who take pride in being slaves to the crown."

I was about to express myself genuinely shocked at such an attitude, but I left it too late.

"Another thing, monsieur. During a famine the theatres of Paris once tried to help. We performed for nothing and donated all proceeds to public funds for the relief of the public distress. The Comédie Française made ten thousand five hundred francs. But we were considered such dirt that the money could not be accepted from our filthy hands! The curés of the parish, on the instructions of the diocesan, were not allowed to take it from us!! It had to be given to them by the Lieutenant of Police so that it shouldn't be soiled by our touch! Well," he concluded abruptly, "we've had a most interesting discussion. Perhaps we can find a place for you in the company. I have been impressed by your conversation, monsieur. I shall require a short reading, of course, before I can confirm Monsieur Kemble's opinion. Dine with my sister and myself next Thursday. We live on the Quai Voltaire. On les aura, my friend!" he concluded, slapping my shoulder.

When he left the Green Room he was followed by his small Blenheim spaniel.

There was a week between us and the dinner with Dugazon, and as I pointed out to M.S., we were likely to get hungry waiting for it. There was no food to spare at No. 15 rue Louis d'Or. The Lapins appeared to live on cabbage soup, but the Puce was fed on scraps that the street vendors sold off cheaply at the end of the day.

It was a good moment to suggest to M.S. that Lord Credit might come in useful and that the best place to play him would be at the Palais-Royal that evening. "If I dress up as Mr. Buckland and mingle amongst the well-to-dos I ought to be able to pick a few pockets and keep us going until Dugazon puts me to work."

M.S. was not enthusiastic but saw the practicability of the plan. He agreed to accompany me as my valet, and on the way back to L'Étuve I could see his face settling into the respectfully devoted expression of William Brown.

One could smell L'Étuve long before one came upon it. Oddly enough, Necker's dismissal seemed to have been taken less hard in L'Étuve, possibly because a place so inured to chronic discontent is more difficult to rouse, or perhaps because it had never been able to believe in any kind of saviour for France. L'Étuve had the face of someone expecting nothing; it had never believed in the magic of Necker; it had never believed in magic.

The child was sitting on the doorstep of No. 15 rue Louis d'Or, hitting flies away with her hands. She jumped up when she saw us and hugged M.S. round the knees. "Where have you been?"

"To see Monsieur Dugazon."

"Will he give him work?" Only a slightly scornful flick of the eyes in my direction indicated that the "him" represented me.

"Well, he's going to give him a hearing next Thursday."

"Will he be good enough?"

"I hope so," said M.S.

"Have you discussed my possible salary with her as well?" I enquired acidly.

M.S. had the smile in his eyes which any annoyance on my part always provoked. But he answered seriously, "She agrees with me that it would be worth taking a reduction to get ourselves a foothold in the French theatre."

"I can't tell you how relieved I am that our plans should have her approval," I said.

I left her jumping round him trying to guess which hand held an orange he had produced from his pocket. He must have removed it from a stall in passing, but I had not seen him do it.

Upstairs I found it impossible to dress for Buckland in our fetid little alcove. I tapped on the door of the ever-obliging Pêche. Guessing rightly that he would approve of anyone's setting forth to lighten the purses of the rich, I made no attempt to deceive him as to my intentions.

"You could choose nowhere better than the Palais-Royal," he said. "It's the stalking ground of every fool with money." He stood patiently holding up a piece of a broken looking-glass so that I could see to tie my stock. With his free hand he lifted a bottle of wine to his mouth. It was surprising that he had escaped the floridness of the constant drinker, for his complexion was pale and clear. Again I was struck by his likeness to La Fayette.

Two whistles from old Lapin below warned Pêche that he had a customer. He passed me the fragment of looking-glass and pulled open the door to admit a plump young woman. She was carrying three bottles of wine. Pêche's face and his voice became professionally sympathetic. "I'm sorry to see it's your father, madame, but on the other hand I'm glad to see it's not the little one."

She handed the bottles of wine to him. "Yes, the baby is better. We think he will live. But my poor father's heart was not strong."

When she had gone, Pêche said, "The fever raging again. I shall be busier than ever this week."

I asked him, "How in the world could you tell it was the father and not the baby who had died?"

He laughed at my bewilderment. "Because she brought three bottles of wine. That's what I charge for the fully grown. I only charge one for a child."

"Don't you ever charge money?"

"Oh, yes. This is only on account. If one asked L'Étuve to find money on the spur of the moment, one would have bodies rotting all over the place. I deduct the price of the wine from the amount that is owing, of course, and although they may starve their living to do it, they nearly always pay for their dead in the end."

M.S. came in dressed in his valet's clothes. The ubiquitous child was swinging round on his hand.

"They won't allow you in the Palais-Royal, monsieur," Pêche told him bitterly. "Servants, liverymen, people in shirt sleeves, dogs, and poor students are forbidden. If you try to get in, the Swiss guards will beat you back. And you, monsieur," he said to me, "will not have a chance in those black stockings. They're the sign of the common man."

I told him that I had a white silk pair in my pocket and intended to change en route. To have walked through L'Étuve with its rivers of filth would have stamped me a common man no matter what coloured stockings I wore, and mud on the calves would have given me away, as the gentry so seldom went on foot.

"Watch out for the police," Pêche warned us. "They've spies everywhere. They can be dressed up to look as good a gentleman as you, or they may be waiters or serving in shops. It doesn't do to trust anyone's smile in your business."

"We're old hands at this game," M.S. assured him. "The law's never got hold of us yet."

Pêche was alarmed at this boast. "I know nothing of the way the law goes to its work in your country, monsieur, but it doesn't do to think one is too clever for the French. Our agents are the highest paid and the most efficient in the world. They can practically sleep between a husband and wife without being noticed. They're in the wine shops, the eating houses, even the churches and rich people's homes, and the Lieutenant himself is as clever as a circus monkey. There is an old saying that even if you lose the wax out of one of your ears, he can not only find it but put it back without your knowing."

It was not an old saying that cheered me. I dislike efficient police activities. I prefer a city to spend its money on theatres and pleasure gardens. But I was not unduly worried. I flattered myself that they would not put the wax back in *my* ear.

Although my dressing conditions could not have been worse, Mr. Anthony Buckland looked quite elegant when I had finished with him. The night tailor of Market Downham had chosen a good model. My suit was very much a gentleman's, and if I took shorter steps than usual, no one would know that it was because my breeches were too tight.

I caused quite a stir when I went outside. L'Étuve rarely saw a well-dressed man emerge from one of its own rat holes. Pêche accompanied us through the tunnel to the street, pushing back interested spectators.

"Come along, now. Stand back there. Let Monsieur pass. These are English gentlemen. Do you want them to think we've no manners in France?"

Not the slightest attention was paid to him, although he fended people off by swinging out with his empty wine bottle. They fingered my suit and snatched at my cane and argued the cost of my outfit.

Outside the house a cocoa seller was ringing his bell to induce custom. The child went on ahead of us to wheedle a free drink from him. His equipment struck me as extraordinary. He carried a metal tank on his back which had a pole at the bottom to dig into the ground. Pipes with spouts shaped like dolphins protruded over his shoulder and were used to pour the cocoa into the cups hanging from his apron. He was evidently an old friend of the child's.

He stared at me with a slow interest while she jigged up and down with excitement. "There you are! What did I tell you? I said they were rich. That is the nasty young one who calls me the flea and that is my new uncle, the nice one."

The cocoa seller inclined his head. "We're honoured to have such a fine gentleman choose to stay in our part of the town. It's not where they usually come."

"I like to see life as it's lived," I said, and realised that it was a remark that made no sense at all. I had taken a dislike to the fellow's eyes. They were darting and shrewd and they made me nervous. They spent quite a while dwelling on my incongruous black stockings.

His complexion was about as clear as his muddy beverage. But then, there were hardly any fair skins in L'Étuve. The man's breeches were in tatters round his knees, and he wore heavy sabots. He bowed from the head again as we left. The child was so awed by my splendour that she preceded us backwards for quite a few yards.

M.S. tried to remonstrate with her. "Now, now, dear, home you go! It's getting late and where we're going they don't allow little girls."

"Or dogs or persons in shirt sleeves," I quoted sourly. My republican sentiments had been fired by Pêche.

The child's bare feet were the colour of tar. I made a mental note to buy some water from the water seller, soap from the soap seller, and a rag from the rag picker. I would scrub her from head to bottom before I shared her bed again. She had pretty feet for her class, narrow and dainty, with the long second toe so often seen in Greek statues.

"Go home, dear," M.S. pleaded with her, but she simply spun round and danced ahead of us. Then she skipped back and hung on to M.S.'s hand. "Is his suit real silk?" she asked.

"Yes, dear. Now run along, there's a good girl, and Uncle will bring you an orange."

I don't believe in bribing children. I put out a hand, turned her round by the ear, and headed her with a biff on the bottom back towards L'Étuve. It had no effect. She trotted behind us, stopping when we turned our heads and then following us again.

I stepped into an unlit doorway to change my black stockings and could have clouted the child for the attention she drew to me.

Pêche's information had not been exaggerated. Admittance to the Palais-Royal was a matter of keeping up certain pretensions to position and wealth. Doubtless many of the worst possible scoundrels found their way in, but nobody minded provided that they conformed to the fashionable conventions.

The poor and the humbly employed were certainly barred; and waiting outside the gates for their masters were a host of liverymen and servants. M.S. had to take his place amongst them. The fact that I should be allowed inside and that he was forced to join the menials was too much for the child. She went dancing up to a Swiss guard, put out her tongue, and dodged his blow with skill.

"You let him in!" she squeaked fiercely. "He *isn't* a servant. He's the young Monsieur's uncle. It's just his top clothes that are not so good. Underneath he looks just as rich. I know, for I sleep with the young Monsieur."

I was infuriated by the distraction. I had hoped to get into the spirit of Buckland; a well-to-do, cultured young man of ideas, but with all the charming reticence of the Englishman. My French must be good but noticeable as a foreigner's.

The pestilential child was drawing attention to me again. A pickpocket likes to be as unobtrusive as possible. The last thing he wants is to be the centre of a scene that will enable about fifteen people to remember him, should he have to make a quick retreat.

I sidled up to the child and managed to hiss into her ear. "Do you want your neck wrung? Do you want a bone left in your body? If you don't hold your tongue I'll shake the life out of you."

This produced a long, ear-splitting howl of terror. I left M.S. to try and distract her with the pretty lights twinkling in the Palais-Royal gardens and pushed my way through the small crowd that had gathered. There were one or two ill-natured comments about the seduction of young French children by the English. There were even more about the rich preying on the poor. "Just because he has money to spare, he thinks he can buy the body of an innocent little child."

"That's the age such a morsel appeals to a man of his appetite."

"In the war," someone added, "they made the bones of our prisoners into soup."

I managed to pass the Swiss guards with a certain amount of dignity, but not without a few shouts of "rich English pig" following me.

This was a help, as a matter of fact. It drew the right kind of attention towards me. A "rich pig" is less likely to be suspected as a pickpocket. The shopkeepers nearest the gates immediately solicited my custom.

A tailor with a smile like a ravine was bowing at me before I had got my bearings. Whether he actually pushed or pulled me or mesmerised me into his shop, I don't know. But I was instantly inside it. He shook out a frock coat under my nose.

"The English are the most welcome of all our visitors, monsieur. A fine race! It would be a crime to return to your country without a waterproof frock coat. It it the very best quality taffeta, monsieur, gummed to keep out the wet."

I fingered it casually. "Does it really stand up to the rain?" I enquired.

"Well, perhaps not a deluge, monsieur, but it's certainly proof against showers." He was looking me up and down with interest. He offered me a pinch of snuff from a box that I took an interest in myself. It was gold.

I decided to dally until I could jostle him into the right position for relieving him of it. There should not be much difficulty under cover of trying on the frock coat. But he coughed politely and the ravine slashed his face again. "Monsieur will forgive me, but the English tailor is far behind the French. Monsieur's breeches, for instance! They might have been made for another gentleman. Now, if Monsieur would place himself in *my* hands . . ."

I said I would think about it and walked out of the shop. Mr. Buckland could not afford to have professionals spotting eccentricities in his attire. The tailor lost my custom but kept his snuff box.

Outside I found it difficult to concentrate on my work; the place was so fascinating I forgot to look for victims. Everything was done to tempt the wealthy and the foreign visitor. It was a paradise for lovers of good living like myself. The shops, stalls, arcades, and galleries were lit with coloured beacon lights. Everything that was new and interesting seemed to be on sale. The noise was formidable, but I was getting used to noise in Paris.

Above the light orchestras playing in the cafés political agitators were still working on the crowd's emotions. I stopped to listen to one of them, and was applauding vigorously when I became aware of a sickly perfume. A woman was standing beside me also clapping, her fan feathers bobbing in time.

"Fascinating, isn't it? How *do* they remember what they have to say? And they say it all so *angrily*. That's what makes it so entertaining. One wonders where they get the energy, when they claim to have so little to eat."

I noticed immediately that she had very white wrists with flesh humped up on them like that on a well-fed capon.

They were adorned by twin emerald bracelets.

I gave her a smile. She returned it, not into my face, but towards a part of me at which, to be quite frank, I have never had any woman stare so unguardedly before. At least, not at the first encounter.

She must have been good-looking once. The eyes were deep and black, and the mouth would have been rewarding many years ago. She was seriously overdressed where clothing was indispensable, but seriously underdressed in other parts. There was little one could say in her favour; also, she had an irritating habit of clouting one with her fan.

"You're a foreigner," she said archly, "and a handsome one, too. Would you like me to show you the sights?"

If the sights included any more of her than was already visible, my enthusiasm was far from aroused. But I had a duty towards those bracelets.

She told me that she was the Marquise de Flambelot, but that I was to call her "Fifine." She had a disconcerting wink that was one of the most lecherous

I have ever seen. I nicknamed her privately "Lecherina, Marquise du Lit."

She tucked her great mutton bone of an arm through mine and winked at me. "I expect you'd like to see the pamphlets?"

All I wanted to see was the back of Lecherina, but I allowed her to tug me along. She marched me into a printer's and showed me some of the pamphlets concerned. I had never read such indescribable filth.

"Oh, little boy, little boy!" she giggled happily. "You're going to grow up when you've read some of these."

What struck me most forcefully about them was that they were extremely well-written. They were certainly not the products of lewd little minds in dirty garrets, but the imaginative efforts of subtle brains. I knew enough about dramatic presentation to realise that some very fine professional writers must have been behind them.

Nevertheless, well-written or not, that literature left me a trifle queasy. Some of the sheets pilloried the King, but most of them were aimed at the Queen. Marie-Antoinette was graphically described in the act of practising every known perversion and some that were new to me. A roaring trade was done in these pamphlets. They must have been rolled off the blocks in their dozens. I couldn't help being surprised at the type of people buying them. They fell into the category of what M.S. would have called his "betters." Presumably they had not his respect for "the Lord's anointed."

I managed to drag Lecherina away without buying any and was wondering where to manoeuvre her so as to detach one of the bracelets. I steered her towards a café that looked less expensive than most, but she halted me with a clout from her fan.

"My husband has left me alone for two months," she simpered.

I thought this showed extraordinary good sense on the part of the Marquis, but was obliged to respond to that painful wink with an interested smile.

"Shall we take supper at my home, then?" she said.

Those wretched bracelets snapped at me in the light from the lamps. I realised that my best chance of relieving her of them would be to get her into a thickish crowd. I could then bump into her and do a neat job.

I carried out the first part of the operation with no difficulty. I had just loosened the clasp, preparatory to giving it a quick tug as soon as the right moment occurred, when I received a shock that deadened my skill. In the centre of the knot of people into whom I had pressed Lecherina so that I could pretend to protect her from their buffetings, was that girl!

She was dressed in lilac silk. Her eyes opened wide when they saw me. They opened wider still when they embraced my companion. Then they narrowed as if they understood, and recognised, my type.

I was enraged at being seen with such an obvious body buyer as Lecherina, but I could hardly rush up and explain that my sole object was to steal from her.

I tried to appeal to the girl with a look, but her smile showed that she obviously despised me. She wore a little bouquet of real flowers on her dress. In spite of the weariness in her face which one suspected was due to excesses, there was also touching freshness about her.

She elbowed her way towards us. To Lecherina she bowed. "Good evening, madame." Her voice, when not swearing, was low and seemed a little hoarse. I noticed again that her face was flat and the bones ran high under the eyes. The eyes themselves were honey-coloured in the lighting of the Palais-Royal. They looked sleepy and vaguely insulting.

Lecherina was far from pleased to see her. She snapped unwillingly, "Good evening, Marie-Clarice."

I stepped closer, hoping for a formal introduction. Lecherina tried to push me aside like a hippopotamus nosing its young out of danger. I had to supply my own name.

"I am Anthony Buckland," I said in French, and spelt it. "B–U–C–K–L–A–N–D." It was my fervent hope that she would respond with her own surname. I could not very well search the whole of Paris for a girl named Marie-Clarice.

Lecherina cut across us. "Oh, yes. This is an old friend of mine from England."

Marie-Clarice inclined her small head. "He looks a very young friend to me, Madame la Marquise," and she passed us without a further glance at me.

"Who was that?" I asked promptly. Lecherina sent heavy shoulders up to jewelled ears. "No one of any consequence." But her eyes were shooting venom. I turned to watch Marie-Clarice join a group of friends. I was absurdly clumsy. "What did you say her name was?"

Had I made some derogatory remark about the girl, or compared her unfavourably with Lecherina, I should have been supplied with her name at once. I was so busy inwardly swearing at myself for being such a half-wit that I forgot to complete my work on the bracelet.

Lecherina said possessively, "My carriage is outside, Anthony. I only live in the rue St. Honoré. Near the convent — do you know it?"

That brought me back to business. Much as I wanted those bracelets, nothing was going to induce me to roll about on top of that old tub. I should have to lead her on, I supposed, and then be suddenly struck with a malady that incapacitated me. But there were hazards. A woman's bedroom is not the best place from which to remove valuables. If there happens to be no one else present but yourself and the lady concerned, suspicion is liable to fall in one quarter only.

I was deep in these admittedly not very moral thoughts when I realised that we were outside the gates and she was shrieking for her carriage.

There was still a crowd on the fringe of the Palais-Royal — liverymen, chairmen waiting for fares, beggars, and the usual collection of gapers. M.S.

and the child were waiting by the railings. They pushed their way towards me, and I told M.S. that I was taking supper with Madame la Marquise. The child put out a disgusting paw and fingered Lecherina's dress. Her mouth made a small round of admiration. "Ooh!" she said.

Lecherina hit at her with her fan. "You've completely destroyed my dress."

The child slunk back sucking her fingers. It occurred to me that this was the second time I had encountered a female with histrionic abilities comparable to my own. Lizzie Weldon had proved herself a good actress, but this pestilential little flea bag was an even better one. Her tears literally slopped out of her eyes. M.S. looked on with professional pride at such an exhibition of false emotion, but I was bridling. The scene was not going well for me in any case, and the audience were as out of sympathy with me as they were with Lecherina.

Such boring old phrases as "A cat may look at a queen" and "Won't poison you, will she?" grew from ugly murmurs into the threat of a roar. The child played well to her house. She cringed forward, all remorse and dewy humility.

"Oh, madame, you must pardon me, but I have never seen anything as soft as this before. I just couldn't help touching it, madame, I couldn't help it. It's so beautiful."

The crowds were very touched.

"The poor little one, what does *she* know of beauty?"

I made a mental note to murder the child as soon as we were safely enclosed in our alcove again.

We were saved in a most unfortunate manner. Marie-Clarice appeared. I was examining the silk that the Puce's grimy fingers had touched in such reverence. The damage was certainly not severe. I was trying to reassure Lecherina when I smelt a perfume that had struck me once before. It was a lily-scented soap, and was coming from the skin of Marie-Clarice.

She ignored me and addressed Lecherina. "How *dreadful* for you, Madame la Marquise! It's hard to know how God could allow such a calamity to overtake one of our kind."

She said it with gushing sincerity. I didn't suspect her of sarcasm until she stroked the Puce's head. Her rings looked like a cluster of fireflies descending on that little pile of black hair. Then she gave the child a twelve-sol piece, which is sixpence in our money, and got into her carriage.

Lecherina's language nearly outdid Marie-Clarice's when I first saw her leaning out of the berline.

I was quick-witted for once. "Tell me that creature's name, madame, and I'll go round and demand an apology."

The unfresh old lump was about to give it to me, but interrupted herself with a distraught wail.

"My bracelet! My bracelet's fallen off."

I could cheerfully have wrung my own neck. I'd forgotten I'd loosened the clasp and the wretched thing could have dropped off anywhere. A search in the immediate vicinity proved useless.

"It'll be trodden on!" she wailed. "My beautiful bracelet!"

I offered to go back and help her look in the Palais-Royal gardens. There was a faint hope that I might spot it before her and save the day for myself. But it was more likely that someone else of my type had already pocketed it or that some honest half-wit had taken it to the office of the Lieutenant of Police.

There was no sign of it, and Lecherina became so hysterical that I gave her the slip in the crowd.

It was a gruesome walk back to L'Étuve. God knows when that neighbourhood put itself to bed; it was still a mass of fetid life. The cocoa seller had moved his pitch and he stopped ringing his bell and bowed to me as I passed.

"Monsieur's stockings!" he sighed, and shook his head.

I realised that I had not changed into my black ones, but the state of my white ones proved him more than observant, as it was hardly possible to tell the difference. It did just occur to me to wonder what in the name of all that was Christian it had to do with him, but that was all. No friendly instinct told me to beware of the cocoa seller.

I was scowling with ill humour when I reached No. 15 rue Louis d'Or. It was a dangerous procedure getting upstairs in the dark. I nearly broke my own neck at each step.

As though anticipating trade, Monsieur Pêche appeared at the top of the flight with a candle stump. He put his finger to his lips and gave the exaggerated "shush!" of a drunk. He was a comical sight in a nightcap and a nightshirt over his National Guard trousers. It would seem that Pêche had been torn between wine and a turn of duty for his section. The wine had won.

"Shush!" he warned again in a deafening crescendo. "The child and the old ones are asleep. Come into my room. I have some wine."

His breath would have led me to suppose that there couldn't be much of it left. I realised that he must have had another adult to bury.

This assumption was promptly born out by the open coffin in the middle of his floor and the two empty bottles standing beside it. Nicholas Hawtrey's was the only corpse I had ever seen and even that grizzly sight did not prepare me for Pêche's wax-faced specimen.

"I'll hammer her down in a minute," he promised me, "but take a look at her, monsieur." He held up his candle and I drew near to the coffin with repugnance. The inmate did not make what the Irish call a "good corpse." The face was an old, old woman's and not gently sunk into death. A hawk nose the colour of pumice-stone shot upwards leaving the cheeks beside it a leathery grey. Straggling curls, which should have been white, clung round the forehead.

"How old do you think she is?" asked Pêche.

"Sixty-five?" I suggested, thinking I had erred on the courteous side.

Pêche was delighted. He shook his head. "No, monsieur. Twenty-seven!"

I stepped back swiftly, wondering what foul disease could have aged the woman to such an extent.

Pêche must have guessed my suspicions. He laughed. "No, my friend, it isn't catching. At least not unless you stay with us long enough. Mademoiselle Péronne died of L'Étuve." Suddenly his fist hit the side of the coffin, jiggling the sticky curls round the face. "Despotism, priestcraft, and lifelong starvation! That's what killed Mademoiselle Péronne. And the first two must answer for the last."

Overemphatic people make me laugh as a rule. Especially if they happen to be dressed in a wobbling nightcap and a nightshirt over National Guard trousers. But there was suddenly nothing amusing about Pêche. The thin face that should have belonged to a dancer circling on his points was flushed with more than wine, and the eyes glittered like a fever case.

"The life span of a peasant, monsieur, even in the country where the air is fresh, is not much higher than twenty-eight. So, how long do you expect them to last in L'Étuve? That child whose bed you share — she has as much chance of living past thirty as this poor woman I'm going to hammer up."

In spite of the airless grip of the night, I shivered. It became the Puce and not Mademoiselle Péronne lying in Pêche's crude box. It was her little nose that achieved such ugly prominence in death, her tight skin that lay as crumpled and dirty as the rags that covered the corpse. She was old before her time and dead before she had lived. She would never have tasted white bread, never have had a whole cup of coffee, never have tasted meat. It was absurd of me to hold such persons as Lecherina Marquise du Lit responsible, but I did. That child's body was already being starved into a Mademoiselle Péronne while the Lecherinas could pay young men to fondle their aging flesh.

The contrast between the Palais-Royal and the rue Louis d'Or was nauseating. The night in L'Étuve was a close box of bad air pressing down on us. The stench of the gutters crept in through the cracks in the walls and under the doors. It was as if the fermenting dregs of L'Étuve were brewing like a compost heap.

I sat raging inanely against the injustice of a fate that could make such a difference between a scraggy child and that old hulk of lechery whose bracelet I failed to remove. I told Pêche my whole adventure with her and about her savage rage at the Puce's daring to touch her dress.

"My God," I said, "I'd like to strip her of everything she's got and give it to the child. I'd like to put the child in her place and bring her here. I'd revel in seeing the fat fall off her and the child filling out."

Pêche had passed me a bottle of wine and I was halfway through it.

He had sobered up somehow, and he laughed. "I think you're just angry because you missed the bracelet!"

"I'm nothing of the sort. I'm a democrat. I'm a Republican. I want freedom for everybody, I want to see these terrible things put right."

"Then you won't do it by making a fat woman thin to make a thin one fat. That is not democracy, that is revenge. We don't want revenge: we want our rights. You are a revolutionary, monsieur, and we don't want revolution. We want justice. We are entitled to it: why should we have to fight for it? We should be given it."

"One always has to fight for what one wants," I reminded him. "Nobody gives you anything. You always have to take it."

"We have taken a lot without too much bloodshed. By the way, do you like to be called Monsieur Buckland or Monsieur le Vicomte de Lambrière? Are you English or French at home — if you'll excuse such a name for this place?"

I lowered the bottle on its way to my lips. It was an appalling shock to hear him refer to Philippe. I knew perfectly well that I had breathed no word about him and I was quite sure M.S. would not have dreamed of doing so. How in the world Pêche could have known that I had used this name I couldn't begin to think. He just shrugged when I asked him. "In L'Étuve everyone knows everything. Someone told me and someone told him. These things spread as quickly as the plague. But you have not said which you prefer?"

"My name is Roberts," I said shortly, "and I'm half English and half French." I determined to tackle M.S. first thing in the morning. It was just possible that he had shared wine with Pêche and become indiscreet.

"Well, Monsieur Roberts," he asked gently, "how well acquainted are you with the affairs of your half-country?"

I confessed that the activities of the French government had me in the grip of a certain amount of perplexity. This proved a mistake. Pêche ran political classes for working people and he did not run them for nothing. He was a born declaimer. He addressed me as if I had been a backward two-year-old, which was doubtless the wisest tone to take with me.

"We have to remember," he said, "that for centuries the greatest enemies of the people, the nobility and the clergy, have been the only privileged parties especially in regard to taxation. But now at last our own deputies are representing us — the third estate, the common people, are using their tongues. But even then, Monsieur Roberts, they found themselves with non-equal powers. They were determined to right this, and by the persuasion of the excellent Monsieur le Comte de Mirabeau — a God amongst men — they adopted a policy of complete inertia. They refused to do anything until the nobility and clergy conceded their rights, which would not only give them equality but the power to outvote. They kept this up for seven weeks, and the whole of France was behind them — that is, the whole of real France, the people. The King and the court became afraid, and our fighters for freedom found the hall of Assembly locked against them. But they did not shed blood, Monsieur Roberts. They used their tongues and their wits and their powers of endurance. It was on this occasion that they repaired to a tennis court last June and took a glorious oath not to dissolve until their will was met. Having triumphed in this, France may well expect her highest hopes to be fulfilled. That, monsieur, is as simple a picture as I can give of the case, I think."

I thanked him and begged him to bang down the coffin lid. The sight of the late Mademoiselle Péronne was unnerving me. Pêche had a lampion glowing in the window. I don't recall ever having seen such things in England, and the French usually keep them for festive occasions. They soak thick wicks in turpentine and float them in bowls of tallow. They give a curious light. The one in Pêche's window sent oppressive shadows circling round the room and they tricked me into imagining that Mademoiselle Péronne was opening and closing her eyes. They also seemed to me to be stretching the grey mouth into ironic smiles, as if the unfortunate woman had gone past believing that wrongs could ever be put right.

Pêche picked up his own bottle of wine and lowered most of it. Then he obliged me by hammering down Mademoiselle Péronne's lid with a tinny thunder that made me feel as if the blows were striking my very nerves. He was forced to bellow above this dainty exhibition of his art. "You mustn't think we're not willing to fight, monsieur. If blood must flow, it will flow. The people of L'Étuve, for instance — they are like a lion that has not yet learned to jump its fences. But it has the strength. Make no mistake of it — the strength, and the claws, and the teeth! Its appetite will be tempted one day. The door of its cage will be thrown open and it will rush out with a roar that will deafen the world. You can hear its footfall now if you listen." He held the hammer high in the air. "Do you hear it? Padding round and round its prison softly now, softly and hopeless. But they will tease the poor brute through the bars once too often." He brought the hammer down on a final nail with a crash. "There," he said amicably, "I think that should keep the rats off Mademoiselle Péronne. It's not the dead who mind so much," he explained solemnly. "It is those who have loved them. The idea is not nice to them." With which he lay down beside the coffin and went straight to sleep with no further comment.

I crept out to my alcove and found the child sitting upon our plank bed sucking a musty orange by the light of a whole new candle. The latter was an unheard-of threat. "Have you come into a fortune?" I asked.

"Yes," she said, and added, "Monsieur Pêche has drunk three bodies this week and you have been drinking Mademoiselle Péronne with him. I can smell it."

I ignored the small nose wrinkled in disgust at my breath and remembered the money that Marie-Clarice had given her.

"So you spent what the kind lady gave you all at once," I said, and smiled.

"She was not a kind lady. She was just jealous of the old fat one you jumped round so much."

"I was *not* jumping round her. It's the polite thing for a gentleman to show a lady to her carriage," I replied with restraint, but I was pleased that Marie-Clarice should have shown so much interest in me.

The child giggled into her orange. "You would have had to show the fat one to the bed after the carriage. But the other one would have taken you there and then said no."

I sat down and eased off my shoes. "Why should you think that?" I asked tartly.

"Because it makes it much better for next time if you tease someone a little first. The old fat one would not dare to tease you. It is so hard for them even when they pay."

I was making a sharp mental note to have a word with the grandparents about the child's whole moral outlook when I noticed that she was hiding her left arm from me. Suspecting that she was clutching another rotten orange, I went to remove it from her.

She dipped away from me and knelt laughing at the end of the bed. Something caught the light in a thousand prongs. It was Lecherina's diamond and emerald bracelet hanging from her bone-thin wrist. The chief emotion I experienced was fury at the child's good luck in discovering the thing. It must have slipped off Lecherina's wrist when she hit out at the Puce.

"Where did you find it?" I snapped.

She looked pityingly at me. "I *didn't* find it. I stole it."

"*Stole* it?" I tried to sound reproving, but I fear that I only sounded envious. The fact that the little brute should have succeeded where I had failed was embittering, to say the least.

"It was easy," she boasted, flashing the bracelet. "I just gave it a little pull when I pretended to touch the fat one's dress. It came off so quickly she didn't feel it."

"Yes," I thought savagely. "Because I had already loosened the clasp for you, you little fiend." I put on a severe expression. "Suzon, it's very wrong to steal. You must have heard that from the priests."

"The *priests*!" No one could achieve more scorn in her voice than that child. "They steal all the time. They tell us they take our money for God, but the food that should be in our bellies goes into theirs."

I could hear Pêche in that speech. I held out my hand. "Give that bracelet to me, Suzon," I said calmly, "and I'll take it to the police tomorrow morning."

She collapsed forward onto her elbows, her small behind stuck in the air. The sacking that covered her slipped further and further towards her heels as her body jerked with laughter. "Give it to you! Oh, yes, I should think so! A fine chance the police would have of seeing it then."

I tweaked the sack over her bottom and glared down at the child in cool fury. "Are you suggesting that I should not hand it over to them?"

When she looked up at me, her blackberry eyes seemed crystallized behind the tears. She was laughing so much she could only nod at me. Then she hauled herself onto her knees and jangled the bracelet again. "Half of this will be kept for my dowry. With what is left over I shall buy myself an establishment. I shall have a room to sleep in by myself and a real pair of shoes and a black boy to follow me like you see in the streets behind great ladies. The rest is for the box of my new uncle, the poor Monsieur Manager Smith."

"M.S.!" I could scarcely believe it. "He knows about it? He didn't help you to get it, did he?"

"I don't need any help," she said scornfully. "But he was very pleased with me. He said one fool in the family was enough."

I lay down beside her defeated. Every attempt I made during the night to get the bracelet off that child failed. She must have slept as lightly as a mouse. She was awake the instant my hand crept towards her. In the darkness her quaintly old-fashioned phrasing came prim and menacing. "If you try for the bracelet again I shall call for help. I shall say that you were trying to do bad things to me. They do not like that in L'Étuve — not when it is just a child of the people and her despoiler is an aristocrat. Monsieur Pêche says that is one of the things that may cause blood to be spilled. So you had better be careful, Monsieur le Vicomte."

Chapter 24.

WHEN I woke up after my disturbed night, the child had gone. The orange peel, dried and curling, that littered our plank bed was the only reminder of her.

Monsieur Lapin was at his cobbling and Madame had gone to the market. M.S. was lying on the straw paillasse opposite our recess studying a tattered copy of *Le Barbier de Séville*.

"Ah! There you are, boy," he greeted me cheerily. "I want you to read Almaviva. I'll take Figaro and Bartholo, but you'll have to help me along with the French. Anyway, some kind of rehearsal is better than nothing. We can't have you rusty for Dugazon."

I stood over his great body. M.S. had the art of loosening his muscles.

When he was resting he could look as boneless as a cat stretched by a fireside.

"Have you told anyone about Philippe de Lambrière?" I demanded.

"Have you ever known me to give away a Lord Credit?"

"Then how do people know? Pêche asked me if I wanted to be addressed as Buckland or De Lambrière, and the child called me Monsieur le Vicomte!"

"I know," said M.S., "and it makes me uneasy, boy. It makes me very uneasy indeed. I've not told them, you've not told them — but somebody has. I've said til I'm blue in the face that we're actors, but I'm not getting anyone to believe me. That fellow Pêche just smiles at me, and so do the rest. Pray God you get past Dugazon, and when they see you with a good solid stage under you, there will be no more smiles at your expense. In any case, boy," he added importantly, "this is no place for us to live. If Dugazon found out that you and your manager were reduced to a stew pot, he'd think nothing of either of us."

"And how," I asked mildly, "will we find the money to move out?"

He said casually, "There'll be a bit falling into my hands pretty soon."

I shot at him, "Did you encourage that child to steal that bracelet?"

He looked reproachful. "Certainly not, boy. She'd got it before I even thought of it."

"But you agreed to let her contribute to your box?"

He looked uneasy. "Well, she offered, and we could do with it at the moment. It's not certain that Dugazon will take you up. It depends on your reading."

"I know that Suzon: she wouldn't contribute to your box for nothing. What did you offer her in return?"

His eyes searched the ceiling and his powerful-looking eyebrows climbed his forehead as if it was an effort for him to recall what insignificant return he had agreed to concede the Puce.

"Well," he said, "nothing much, boy. A home, perhaps, when we find somewhere better. This place is no good to her."

"A home?" I shouted. "A home with *us*?"

"When we get on our feet," he said, "we shall need someone to keep house for us. She's growing up and she can get double her money's worth in the market."

"Now, you listen to me," I said. "You can share a home with her if you want to, but you won't find me in it. We shouldn't have a thing left. The child's a born thief."

He put on his parson's look and studied me with his head on one side. "Of course, boy, I understand that for a lad of your upstanding ways, the child must seem very sinful."

"Two wrongs don't make a right," I snapped with deep originality. "And, anyway, who taught me? Do you think that either of us are very suitable moral guardians for the young?"

The old brute pressed the wind round his heart and brought tears to his eyes. "Boy, not for one minute do I forget what I led you into. That's why I've done all I could to get a legitimate stage under you. The only times I've asked you to play Lord Credit have been when there's nothing else for it. Did I ask you to do it at the Little Apollo? Did I press you to do anything but keep your nose on your work? Didn't I make a rare sacrifice for you? Me with such a distaste for the maritals? Was it my doing we had to leave the Little Apollo? Do I like being in France at the mercy of a nation with nothing better to do than try and float in the air at the end of balloons? Do I like my stomach topsy-turvy with the colic and not a drop of Daffy's Elixir to set me right?"

"You're overacting," I told him crisply, "and it doesn't alter the fact that you've agreed to accept some of this child's stolen money. What kind of an example is that for her?"

"I did it to stop her in the future, boy," he explained sententiously. "With that amount behind her she won't need to steal any more. I shall have enough to keep her out of trouble until she gets married, a good dowry will help there, and then —"

"And then you're both going to buy yourselves a black boy to follow you in the street and a pair of real shoes! You seem to have split it up very nicely between you. Damn it!" I said before I could stop myself. "It was I who loosened the clasp."

He kept a smile off his face, but I saw the effort it cost him. "Anything that's mine is yours as well, boy, you must know that. I shouldn't do you out of your share."

"I don't want a share. I wouldn't touch a penny of that filthy child's."

He rolled off the paillasse and stood up, stretching. "That's a pity, for she's arranged credit for us at Mr. Lattre's. He's just bought an eating house on the corner. She says it may take her a couple of days to get rid of the bracelet. She's got to make sure of the biggest price. She'll have to get the thing broken up, and there can't be an honest soul in this district. It'll take all her wits to see she's not robbed herself."

To disguise the fact that my hunger was forcing me to follow him to Lattre's, I said shortly, "This place must have baked your brains out. How can you trust her to come back with your share? How can you trust a child of nine with business of that sort in any case?"

"She's not nine," said M.S., "she's twelve and getting near thirteen. There are mothers of that age in these parts."

I came to a halt so suddenly that I collided with the cocoa seller. We cursed one another and I caught up M.S. "She *can't* be thirteen," I argued. "She's hardly the size of a shrimp."

"Its all that good food and fresh air she gets, boy. It's bound to make them big and bonny."

"But I can't share a bed with a girl of thirteen," I protested. "She sleeps without clothes. There's nothing between us but that bit of sacking, and when it gets too hot there's not even that."

M.S. stopped and turned heavy eyes on me. We had to spring apart to avoid a gush of rain water that the gutters had stored up during the night.

"Now look 'ere, boy, I've 'ad enough of this. Just because you bungled getting an old harlot's bracelet off her doesn't mean you can come all high-minded with Suzon and me. The only difference between you two is that she was a good thief last night and you were a bad one. And as for beds — you've shared enough with naked women. There's no need to look so shocked about lying beside one that's pure for a change."

"Pure!" I echoed him. "You think the little brute's pure, do you? You want to hear some of the things she was saying to me last night?"

His eyes narrowed. Never a good sign, it usually meant that he was going to find fault with every line I read however well I delivered it. "You're past understanding sometimes, boy. You took a spite to this child from the start. You're for ever growling at her — and then again you carry on as if you'd written the Ten Commandments yourself. One minute it's me leading her astray that's worrying you and the next she's so bad she's not fit to save. Now, which is it? Do you wish her well or ill? Do you really mind what's good for her, or is it that you like to blame somebody else for being no worse than you?"

Put like that, it was hard to answer. I felt distinctly foolish, for I knew I was being inconsistent. I was still thinking about it when we sat down in Lattre's filthy little eating house. My feelings were certainly muddled towards the Puce. I alternated between being sorry for her and exasperated with her; rather like a tiresome younger sister for whom at times one feels a grudging affection, but at others could happily strangle. I was aware without M.S.'s drawing it to my attention that my priggish attitude towards her morals was ludicrous in view of my own. But one does not like to dwell upon imperfections in one's own nature. Other people's deserve criticism, but one's own must be excused. Similarly, I didn't care to admit that part of my resentment towards the Puce was owing to her unreserved dislike of myself. I preferred to say that I didn't care what the stinking little flea bag thought of me. But in point of fact I was thoroughly incensed and a little bewildered that she should worship M.S. and consider me worthless. I could hardly explain to him that my conceit had been challenged, so I said lightly, "I just haven't your affection for every stray urchin you come across."

"More's the pity," said M.S., and ordered a bottle of Chablis at two francs, a riz de veau aux haricots at three francs, a riz de veau à la financière aux truffes at three francs ten sous, two punch au rhum at six francs, and some fromage de Chester at ten sous.

Monsieur Lattre, looking like a rotund grub in a dirty apron, took the order without demur. The child's credit was certainly good with him. I remembered nastily what Madame Lapin had said about her sitting on his knee to obtain a pear.

We sat waiting for our meal in a somewhat touchy silence, which always followed our disagreements. M.S.'s French was not good enough to understand much of the swiftly gabbled conversation behind us, but I was entertained. A solemn little quartet were discussing the Queen. It appeared that they suspected her son of not being her husband's child. The Dauphin seemed to have a remarkable choice of fathers. In the next five minutes' talk he became the son of the Comte d'Artois, the Prince de Ligne, a Baron de Besonval, a Swedish nobleman, and the Cardinal de Rohan. Even so, I wasn't really impressed until I heard that he was also the son of a Duchesse de Polignac! This woman was apparently the Queen's favourite lover, a fact that I was quite prepared to believe, but I thought it an interesting biological feat if they had managed to produce a dauphin between them. I turned round and said as much.

Four heads looked towards my table: four ordinary bourgeois citizens, probably clerks or shopkeepers. They seemed surprised at my ignorance. "The Duchesse," they told me, "is a man."

"Oh!" I said, "Well, that accounts for it."

"You must understand, monsieur, the Queen cannot be satisfied. There have been so many lovers the King has been forced to protest, so that now a lover must dress as a woman. Like that he can sleep in the Queen's bed and attend at her bath." I said I could see the convenience of that arrangement. The nearest man told me earnestly, "At the Petit Trianon there are looking-glasses all over the ceiling so that the Queen may watch herself making love. There is one room where the floor is pure gold. The legs of the bed are set in diamonds and one may not put a pin between the jewels round the walls."

"These jewels are all made into pictures, monsieur," the second man said.

"Yes — figures making love," said the third. "It is said they are attached to clockworks representing the natural movements and that the mechanism is very life-like."

Curious about my chuckles, M.S. wanted to know the reason for them. I was unwise enough to tell him and only narrowly avoided a fight. He wanted to get up and "flog the fellows" for such disrespect towards the "Lord's anointed." He even got as far as shaking his fist over their table before I persuaded him to come back. Fortunately, "the fellows" could not speak English and I told them that M.S. was under the impression that they had been making derogatory remarks about him. He mistook their placating bows for an apology and sat down still growling, "I should think so, too. Put 'em up against a wall and shoot 'em, that's what I say."

"Yes," I sighed, "I thought you might. I agree that it's fantastic that ridiculous stories like that should be taken seriously, but the Queen must have done something to deserve a reputation like this."

He would have laid into me if the punch aux rhum had not arrived. But he contented himself by saying that had I been alive at the time of Charles I, he was certain that I should have been a regicide.

The four behind us continued to spin the most unlikely tales about the Queen, which I forebore to translate to M.S. I was still amused rather than alarmed. It did not strike me as sinister that these absurd exaggerations were made by four perfectly sober men in all good faith. In point of fact it was one of the more terrifying symptoms of the disease of the moment: gullibility. Had I been thinking, I should have seen that the disease was already fatal. The temperature was still low and the fever not yet raging, but the sickness was in the blood. The cry of those four bourgeois men was not the bitter complaint of the abject poor, or the justifiable grievances of the wretched people whom the court and nobility had drained of strength; theirs was the voice of the middleman always the last to rebel, and here it was raised in venom against the very people who once would have secured its undying support. These people had thrived in the past on the reflected glories of the court and nobility. But now they had suddenly ceased to cringe to their own bread and butter. Centuries of unquestioning loyalty was already dead in the nonsense talked by those four men. They would never have repeated any form of scandal against their own royal family if they hadn't sensed that its cause was almost lost. Some inner tradesman's instinct had convinced them of the fall of the ancien régime before the Revolution struck at it. Had the militants but known it, they had already won their fight in the minds of those men and their like.

The Queen's eccentricities were dropped when two chairmen pushed into the eating house and greeted the men behind us as old friends. To mollify M.S., I promised to spend the entire afternoon play-reading with him, but for the evening I had my own plans. It occurred to me that if I was a success with Dugazon, my chances of being a success with Marie-Clarice would be small. If I appeared at the Comédie Française, she would see me sooner or later and that would be that. From what Dugazon had said about the social position of our kind, it was not very likely that she would accept an actor as a lover. My only chance was to tackle her while I could still masquerade as an English gentleman.

"I think," I told M.S., "I'll go up to the Palais-Royal this evening."

His punch aux rhum stayed on its way to his mouth. "What for?" he asked suspiciously. "Suzon's got the bracelet, hasn't she? We can manage quite well on that."

"I've already told you I don't like the idea of living off the child."

The punch aux rhum was swallowed before he said, "You're a bad actor, boy, at times. I know you: you're going to try and pick up with that young harlot again."

Before I could argue, one of the two chairmen tapped my shoulder. His physique was extraordinarily spare for his choice of profession. He looked like an excited weasel. "Monsieur," he said, "I am trained in a little English. I heard that you wish to visit the Palais-Royal. I and my friend will be happy to carry you."

I scowled at him. I hate fare cadgers. "Thank you, but I'm going to walk."

He was joined by his friend, also a small man with pale eyes that looked happily unclouded by any strenuous thoughts. "Monsieur cannot walk. Monsieur might as well roll in the mud."

Weasel broke into a high squeal of a laugh which made me jump. "Monsieur will not impress a lady dressed as a mud pie."

I complimented them on their "little English." It had enabled them to understand quite a bit of our conversation. Weasel told me that this was because their best trade was done with English visitors and sometimes Americans. Very generous the Americans were, very generous indeed! I took this to be a hint and disillusioned him. "I can't afford to take a chair, gentlemen. We're poor men, like yourselves."

Weasel's squeak-laugh caught me out again. "But of course, monsieur. We know this. That is why we offered. We are friends of the good Monsieur Pêche, and the little Suzon and her grandfather and his mistress. It's not often in L'Étuve that we have gentlemen like yourselves who are willing to rob your own kind. We shall be honoured to carry you for nothing."

I was decidedly flattered to be regarded as L'Étuve's personal Robin Hood. M.S. used the Puce's credit with Lattre to buy them a liqueur apiece and was good enough to stand Lattre one as well. We arranged a time for the chairmen to pick me up and went back to rehearse in No. 15 rue Louis d'Or.

It was far from a peaceful choice. We would have done better to stay in the eating house. Old Lapin's constant double whistles seemed endless that afternoon. He made them purposefully mournful out of respect for the little

stream of bereaved. Sprawled on the Lapins' paillasse, I found it hard to
concentrate on the lines I was reading. M.S.'s grip of the language was not
really good enough to be of much assistance to me in a French-speaking
part. This was yet another reason for our wishing to get ourselves over to
America. Nevertheless, he had an uncanny way of sensing that I was giving
a poor interpretation.

"Boy, boy!" thundered M.S. "You're back with Mr. Martyn's Celebrated
Players."

But I couldn't keep my eyes off the staircase. Five or six people climbed
wearily up towards Pêche. Only two appeared to be paying customers. The
rest carried the inevitable bottles of wine. It was poignant to see somebody
clutching a single bottle when one knew it meant the loss of a child.

M.S. got up and drew the sacking that acted as a curtain between the
Lapins' "apartment" and the landing at the top of the stairs which led into
my alcove. "For the love of God, take your mind off it, boy. People have
got to die sometime."

"Yes, but they've all chosen this afternoon."

"It's no worse than other days. There's a fever running up and down the
street as fast as a cat with a dog at its heels. The place is a death trap, so
what do you expect? Now, take that last speech again and remember it's
not supposed to be in *Mrs. Dockery's Secret*."

Even with the sacking drawn, the dismal footsteps were still audible as
they laboured up to Pêche. One could no longer see that an infant had died,
but one could hear the payment on account for a deceased adult — the
chink, chink, chink of three bottles of wine. Even now I cannot have a glass
of wine without thinking of Pêche's customers. But I notice that it does not
stop me from drinking it.

I was heartily pleased when it was time to dress up as Buckland and go
down to meet the grinning chairmen. M.S. refused to accompany me, saying
that he had something better to do than play valet to a young fool chasing a
little harlot.

I climbed into the chair and had the door respectfully closed for me by
the cocoa seller. I gave him a twelve-sol piece, which was sheer ostentation
on my part. He put the coin into his pouch, bought himself a cup of his
own cocoa, and toasted me with it.

The chairmen set off at a jogging run, and I leant back happily contem-
plating the possibility of seeing Marie-Clarice again. Modesty has never
been my most prominent virtue and it was totally absent in me then. The
possibility that I could fail to excite Marie-Clarice as she excited me was
not worth my consideration. Given the opportunity of subjecting her to
my full charms, I was unshakably confident of victory.

Chapter 25.

I WAS not given the opportunity of exposing her to my full charms. She was nowhere to be seen. I searched the whole place, looking into cafés and restaurants, pushing my way into gambling rooms and shops. Disgruntled, I filled in the time extracting a few trifles from the merry-making hordes. I collected a silver spy-glass on a chain, a worthless fob, and about fifteen francs. I drank the last in the Café de Valois, still hoping the girl would appear. Eventually I gave up and walked back to L'Étuve, carefully changing into my black stockings in a deserted courtyard.

The whole city had an unusual air of desertion. Apart from the sharp tread of a few foot patrols, there was hardly a sound to be heard. Several streets were barricaded, and there were lampions alight in many windows. Paris reminded me of a fierce dog supposedly asleep but with its fangs bared.

It was even more weird to see lampions alight in L'Étuve, where tallow was considered a treasure. In the grimy cleavages that dared to call themselves streets, there were curiously few people about, but voices buzzed behind the doorways.

In view of the fact that Suzon had probably sold the bracelet by now, I should not have been surprised to find the child feasting in a blaze of light with a black boy in attendance. But our alcove was in darkness, and I heard snivelling coming from it.

I groped in the corner where I kept my clothes. In the pocket of my spare breeches I found the candle I kept hidden and lit it.

It showed me the child lying flat on her back with tears rolling out of angry-looking eyes. When she saw who it was, she sat up and spat like an indignant tiger cub. "I hate you. I hate you. There is no one in the world I hate so much as you."

I knew that the child disliked me, but I was surprised by the loathing in her voice. Her fists were clenched and for a moment I thought she was going to hit me.

"I suppose that woman thinks you're a very fine gentleman. I suppose she thinks you have more presents to give her where that one came from. Oh, yes! A very rich gentleman she must think she has found!"

"What *are* you talking about?" I enquired.

"The lady who showed off to you by giving me money."

"You mean the lady called Marie-Clarice?"

She considered the name and then sniffed. "Is that what she's called? Well, I don't like it. It isn't a nice name at all. I should have thought," she went on, "that you would be content to pay for your own pleasures, but take it from the pockets of myself and my new uncle the poor Monsieur Manager Smith."

I suppressed a smile at the stilted hauteur of her tone.

She was instantly back to childish fury. Her fists hit the planks on either side of her. "All last night you were trying to get it from me. I felt your fingers time after time. If I hadn't kept awake you'd have taken it. But it was mine. It was *mine*. I stole it first. You've taken my dowry just because you wanted to go·whoring and give presents to ladies to show what a grand-seigneur you are! Oh! I hate you," she howled. "I would like to kill you!"

She made such a noise that I half expected our neighbours to invade the room, but there was a drone of voices from upstairs which made me suspect that one of Pêche's political classes for working people was in progress. The Lapins were probably in attendance. I realised that the Puce was for some reason convinced that I had deprived her of Lecherina's bracelet in order to win the favour of Marie-Clarice.

"I thought," I told her, "that you had taken that bracelet out today to sell it."

"I did. But you followed me and stole it from me."

"What makes you think that?"

"You are the only one who knew I had it, except my new uncle."

"Does he think I took it?"

"No. He says you would never do such a thing. But I know you better. You would."

"Didn't he tell you that I spent all day with him?"

"Yes, but he was just trying to protect you."

"What time did you lose it?"

"This afternoon. I had it bundled up in my skirt. I was taking it to some-one I knew who would buy it, but when I got to his shop it was gone and in its place were some pebbles."

I said, "Listen to me, Puce. You're right, I should have taken it if I could, but I couldn't. I didn't even know where you'd gone. I was with M.S. right up to the time I went to the Palais-Royal this evening, so how could I possibly have got it?" She sat with her lips pursed, studying me. "Didn't you feel anyone near it?"

She shook her head. "No, and that is one thing that makes me believe you. It has to be someone clever when you don't feel the touch." I ignored this jibe and she suddenly shot at me, "Did you tell anyone I'd taken this bracelet?"

"No, of course not."

"Have you been talking about it where people might hear?"

I tried hard to remember. "No, I don't think so." And then I recalled the two chairmen who had carried me for nothing to the Palais-Royal. That morning in Lattre's their "training in a little English" had enabled them to overhear us discussing Marie-Clarice, and they admitted that they knew I was a thief. They could also have overheard us discussing the bracelet and the child.

I confessed at once to the Puce that we'd been indiscreet and described the chairmen to her. She nodded eagerly. "Jacques and Louis! Yes, that would be quite likely. They ran into me with their chair this morning. Jacques kept dusting me down with his hands. Oh yes, that's when it happened. They kept up such questions — was I all right, was I hurt anywhere! It was only to take my mind off it while they took out the bracelet and put in the small stones."

"Have they always been in our business?"

She shrugged. "I don't know. But I do know that they aren't the kind to carry you for nothing. They just wanted you to think they were friendly. They heard you say I had gone out to sell it, and they must have come straight to look for me. I expect they are spies for the police."

I took one of her hands. "Puce, I'm sorry. I didn't mean you to lose your dowry. It was very careless of us to talk like that. One should never presume that people can't speak English. But I tell you what I'll do." I fished in my pocket and brought out the spy-glass and fob. "I got these in the Palais-Royal tonight. You can have them to sell. At least it'll buy you the shoes."

She took them and examined them with professional care. "That is kind of you. I should get about twenty francs for these. But I can't have the shoes. I must pay Monsieur Lattre for your breakfasts."

I was surprised at her bothering with debts and remarked on it.

"Oh, but I have to," she said, "or he wouldn't trust me again. You see, whenever I make a few stealings, he lets me have something to eat on credit. He knows that I'm honest. I always pay. This time I told him I expected such big money that he said all of us from this house could have what we liked. It would be a pity to spoil his trust in me."

"Yes, it would," I agreed, and asked, "What will you do about the bracelet? Will you tackle Louis and Jacques?"

She shook her head vehemently. "I can't be sure that they took it and it would only show them that I had."

"Is it true that you're nearly thirteen?" I asked irrelevantly.

She nodded. "Yes. And it is time I am married. I don't want to be left on the shelf like my pig-grandmother and have to put up with old men." She suddenly raised her eyes and stared at me. She put her head first to one side and then to the other. She studied me closely from both angles. "Yes,"

she said thoughtfully, "I shall have to get a husband soon or my friend
Marie Lebrun will be laughing at me."

"You told me you had no friends," I reminded her.

She blew out her lips. "Oh! It's not that I like her. It's just that she's
someone I know so well I shouldn't want her laughing at me. Marie Lebrun
has shoes, you see," she explained seriously, "not sabots, *shoes*. Some
gentleman gave them to her for — for — oh! If only I hadn't lost that
bracelet. What a show I could have made for her! What a difference it
would have made in our lives."

"The best thing we can do," I said, "is to forget all about that bracelet.
Fate has a funny way of working. Obviously it wasn't meant to have any
effect on our lives. We've heard the last of it and that's all there is to it."

My capacity for being wrong really rises to sublime heights at times. I
doubt if there have been many others whose every prophecy has been so
completely incorrect.

Certainly it was not until four years later that we found out what became
of the bracelet and then in circumstances that I could never have guessed
would have been possible. Nevertheless, I really must be stopped from
tempting the gods. They never refuse my bait.

Chapter 26.

IN THE piled-up filth and heat of the Mousetrap I was trying to cheer a man
whose uncle had just had his name called out in the *Journal du Soir*. The
fact that appeared to upset the young nephew most was that he had never
liked his uncle. I should have thought that this would have been a comfort,
but apparently not. "Such a hard man he was: we never got on. It's been
six years since we've spoken to one another, and just now he patted me on
the shoulder and said, 'Well, my boy, who would have thought we should
meet like this?' "

It did not strike me as a very moving reconciliation, but it had reduced
the nephew to crying against my chest. Certainly he had no choice in the
matter of locality. It was our turn to stand and we were flattened against the
slimy walls of the Mousetrap.

The nephew had taken a strong fancy to me, which I can't say was wholly
reciprocated. He was a harmless-enough-looking lad with hair that was
probably corn-coloured if it hadn't been caked with the filth of the Mousetrap. However, no amount of dodging him, even in the exercise yard, could
relieve me of his company.

The Mousetrap smelled like a communal grave of decaying bodies. It was as if the living had already taken on the scent of the dead. Breathing in the evil heat that practically scorched the inside of one's nose, I swore that there couldn't be a more disgusting hole in the world. Again I was wrong. There was the Tour Bonbec, to which I should shortly be transferred.

My friend's hair was not adding any freshness to the immediate neighbourhood, and I was twisting my neck trying to avoid direct contact with it whilst still murmuring my condolences. But as there were at least forty or fifty of us squeezed together that night, evasive movement was impossible.

I should like to say that I was relieved when a gendarme shouted my name into the darkness. But I was not. I preferred the Mousetrap to a visit to the greffe.

"The citoyen Buckland will come to the front, please."

I must say for those gendarmes that they seldom neglected to say "please." It was touching in its macabre way. But getting to the front was not easy. My friend gripped me round the waist and burst into a tempest of French emotion. "First the uncle I've never liked and now the friend I've come to love! What a day! What a day for me!"

"It's not been all that happy for uncle or me either," I snapped ungraciously.

I swear I took about three minutes fighting my way to the doorway. When I reached it, sweating and covered in straw ends, I said to the gendarme, "My name is not Buckland."

"Then why have you come?" he asked, and hauled me roughly into the passage.

I knew that as I had been summoned as Buckland, it must be the Committee of Public Safety who wanted to see me. I felt my usual absurd rush of affection for whichever committee had not sent for me. I was sure I should fare better at the hands of the Lieutenant and his Committee of General Security. And again, as usual, I wished to relieve myself.

I should never get used to these summons. One could never be sure whether it was to be another interminable interrogation when sheer weariness might trap one into condemning oneself, or whether it would be torture or straightforward death with no further questions.

My major horror was still that of torture. I wasn't at all sure how I would stand up to it. I had fearful visions of giving way and incriminating both M.S. and the Puce.

There was a faded-looking man waiting for me and the inevitable copying clerk. The faded-looking man stood up and extended a hand. "I am citoyen Aubaisson. I am one of the chief secretaries of the Committee of Public Safety." He had my dossier in front of him. It was as thick as a bad play. He said, "You come from Sandgate, citoyen Buckland?"

"No."

"You come from Sandgate," he repeated pleasantly, "and you came from Sandgate four years ago on what would have been the eighth of July 1789 under the old régime. You understand that under the Republic's new calendar it would have been Messidor."

"My name is Roberts and I come from Bristol," I said: "otherwise your information is faultless."

Citoyen Aubaisson went on. "Citoyen Buckland, you realise that as a great favour to yourself we have chosen the friendly approach? Perhaps you do not realise that we have an alternative."

I bowed. "I'm aware of that."

"Then please don't force us to regret our good manners. You and your accomplice," he continued, "who posed as your valet, Mr. William Brown, entered this country for the purpose of espionage."

"Wrong, citoyen!"

"You confined yourselves to the lowest quarter of Paris with the object of passing yourselves off as friends of the people in order to obtain their confidences, and relay information to your government."

"Wrong, citoyen!"

"Right, I'm afraid, citoyen." He tapped the dossier in front of him. "We have here a detailed account of practically every step you took since you entered France. The reports were compiled by the agents of the Lieutenant of Police." He leaned forward confidently. "Now, the Lieutenant of Police is an admirable fellow, most conscientious and extremely astute. We are not disputing the reports of his agents in any way." He gave me an easy smile and added, "But we are inclined perhaps to suspect his interests in your case."

"I should have thought they were quite clear," I answered. "He wants to cut off my head as the ci-devant Vicomte de Lambrière."

Aubaisson swayed gently forwards and backwards like a snake about to strike. "Yes. *Now.* But he has been having you trailed for the last four years. Why do you suppose that he never arrested you?"

"He had nothing to arrest me for."

Aubaisson's head shook. "Oh, I shouldn't say that. As I told you, he kept an extremely detailed account of your doings. For instance" — he flicked open my dossier and read aloud — " 'Mr. Buckland was observed to enter the quarter known as L'Étuve wearing rather more clothes than normal-blooded men are apt to consider necessary when the temperature is somewhat high.' "

"Quite."

"That was what would have been called the eleventh of July under the old régime."

"But Messidor now?"

"Exactly. You lodged at number fifteen rue Louis d'Or with a family named Dupont."

"I called them Lapin."

"The police were aware of that. You formed a friendship with their granddaughter, Suzon. You called her 'the Puce.' "

I was silent. My thighs were shaking.

"On the morning of the twelfth of July under the old régime you went in search of tea. You returned and in the evening you repaired to the Palais-Royal." He stopped suddenly and peered at the dossier like a bird about to pounce on a grub. "You changed from black stockings into white silk in the courtyard of the widow Vavasseur at fourteen minutes to ten o'clock on the evening of the twelfth. You proceeded with your accomplice Brown and the uninvited attendance of the child Suzon. She caused a disturbance at the entrance gates. That was at two and twenty minutes to eleven on the night of July twelfth, 1789, under the old régime. Your intentions were to remove valuables from persons in the Palais-Royal. This information was supplied by two chairmen in the pay of the Lieutenant of Police. You failed to remove a diamond and emerald bracelet belonging to the late Marquise de Flambelot."

"Late?" I interrupted.

"She has been executed as a counter-revolutionary."

I couldn't control a shiver at the thought of the guillotine slicing through poor Lecherina's thick neck.

Aubaisson returned to the dossier. "The child Suzon, being more skilful, succeeded in removing the bracelet. You were overheard discussing the affair in the eating house belonging to the late citoyen Lattre."

"Late?" I enquired again.

"He was a monopolist. He was found to be hoarding food. He has paid the price. It was the chairmen employed by the Lieutenant who retrieved the bracelet from the child and gave it to the police. The Lieutenant returned it to its owner. I think that was the last you heard of it?"

"The very last."

"There were other objects too, I believe, which were retrieved from you by agents and returned to their owners by the Lieutenant. He had plenty to arrest you for. Why do you suppose he didn't?"

"Perhaps he was giving me enough rope to hang myself."

Aubaisson smiled winningly at me. "That is his explanation, of course, but it isn't ours." He studied his neat little hands. "It's possibly a matter of some resentment to the Lieutenant that the police should have been taken over by the Committee of General Security. One mustn't forget that he served his apprenticeship and came to his peak under the old régime."

He waited for the words to sink in. They sank. I was beginning to see why the Lieutenant believed himself to be in a certain amount of danger from the Committee of Public Safety.

"The Lieutenant tells us," said Aubaisson, "that he sincerely believes you to be the ci-devant Vicomte de Lambrière."

"He certainly does. I was using that name when I met him in England."

Aubaisson nodded sagely. "The Lieutenant has visited England once or twice. He has friends over there, amongst them a certain Sir Gregory Hawtrey of the British Foreign Office. No doubt you and the Lieutenant had many opportunities for lengthy conversations."

"We spent under five minutes together. I saw to that."

"When you came over here he kept an official eye upon you but allowed you to remain free, and then of course, citoyen, you finally gave yourself up to the Committee of General Security. The Lieutenant tells us that he cannot supply a reason for this."

"He can't. I didn't give him one."

"Are you going to give us one?"

"No."

"Then could your reason have possibly been, citoyen, that you expected mercy from the Lieutenant of Police?"

I was astonished. "My God, no. He hates me more than any other man alive."

Aubaisson smiled again. It was not a smile that one could love. "The Lieutenant's excuse for not arresting you was that he believed you to be a royalist agent and that he wanted you to be free as long as possible in order that you should lead him to more active agents."

"It doesn't sound like an excuse. It sounds true. What other reason could he have had?"

Aubaisson stared at me for several seconds. Then he said, "He could have known all the time that you were Anthony Buckland and an agent for Pitt in England."

I was sufficiently startled to gasp. "But — what good in the world would that do him?"

Aubaisson kept his eyes on me. "On the surface the Lieutenant is a staunch patriot, none better. However, it has crossed the minds of one or two of our members that if the Lieutenant were in secret sympathy with the Royalists — after all, they were his first masters — and if he were also in secret sympathy with our outside enemies, it would be useful to him to pretend that he thought you were a French aristocrat rather than a British agent. By not arresting the ci-devant Vicomte de Lambrière on the excuse of wanting to be led to more active Royalist agents, he would also be leaving Mr. Buckland free to continue his espionage work for England. That could suit the Lieutenant admirably, providing, of course, that he *is* in secret sympathy with our enemies."

Any preference I had for the Committee of General Security left me swiftly. I could see how vital it was for the Lieutenant of Police to extract a confession from me in the name of De Lambrière and execute me at once. It was obviously essential for him to prove that he had never thought me Buckland. I certainly appreciated the "trouble" I had caused him and it put me in mortal fear of him. Unfortunately, there was no way in which I could assist him other than signing the confession he demanded and forfeiting my head. The question of my identity was more than a pretty squabble between two officious rival committees; it was a deadly duel with my head as the trophy!

I said to Aubaisson, "As far as I'm concerned, you've completely misjudged the Lieutenant of Police. There's never been any question of his thinking me a British agent for the simple reason that I've never been one. He's equally wrong in supposing I'm a French aristocrat. I'm an actor by the name of Roberts, and please don't tell me that he was drowned in the river Wissey in the English department of Norfolk."

Aubaisson bowed. "As you have saved me the trouble, I shall certainly not draw your attention to that well-proved fact again." He sighed and asked me, "Citoyen Buckland, are you aware that to be the bone of contention between two highly respected organisations of the Republic is an unenviable position?"

"It occurs to me daily."

"You must not be under the impression that only the Committee of General Security are empowered to employ police agents. Granted we have not been in operation as long as the police, but we were formed to keep watch on *all* public affairs, and our agents are very efficient."

"Yes?"

"Yes. We are, for instance, aware that you have a great affection for your accomplice, whom you call your valet, William Brown, and for Suzon Dupont, whom we have no doubt you made use of for the purpose of espionage."

"That's rubbish."

"That is not rubbish. That is obvious. These persons would appear to be in hiding at the moment" — my heart gave me an unpleasant kick — "and we suspect that your giving yourself up has something to do with this. We shall not be long finding your friends." I took the threat in silence, trying to look as if it had not affected me.

"Are we to presume," Aubaisson enquired, "that the welfare of the Lieutenant of Police means more to you than your own safety or that of your friends?"

The trap was being baited. I answered carefully. "I'm afraid I shouldn't feel anything personally if the Lieutenant of Police fell down dead tomorrow."

Aubaisson signalled to the clerk, who handed him a document that he laid in front of me. "Now, this is just a simple statement to the effect that you admit to being Anthony Buckland and that you entered this country for the purposes of espionage. If you sign it, it's possible your wish in connection with the Lieutenant of Police might well come true."

So that was it. I was to assist the Committee of Public Safety in bringing about the Lieutenant's downfall. Once having signed the confession, I should no doubt go the same way myself. Also if I signed a confession that I had been guilty of espionage, it would be as good as signing on behalf of the Puce and M.S. as well. I could not risk incriminating them and I trusted the Committee of Public Safety no more than the Committee of General Security. I said, "I am leaving my affairs in my lawyer's hands."

Aubaisson was still amiable. "I should advise you to return to your cell and think everything over, citoyen Buckland. Perhaps you will change your mind."

I think it was more than coincidence that I should have been moved from the Mousetrap. The cell in which I was to "think everything over" was twice as gruesome. I had been transferred to the dreaded Tour Bonbec. In this subterranean hole we slept in a circle with our feet to the middle. Our beds were coffin-shaped.

Chapter 27.

ON THE night that the Puce told me the bracelet had been stolen she smelt unforgivably of garlic. She was the essence of every French stew pot, but she seemed to have lost some of her rancour towards me. I think it was because of the trinkets I gave her from the Palais-Royal and my promise to buy her some shoes.

She was leaning against the wall with her arms crossed. She had started to eye me, in that shrewd French way she had, as if I had been something on sale in the market.

"It was never your face I disliked," she explained.

"I'm so glad," I said.

"No, it's really quite handsome. And your body is nice."

"Thank you."

She lay down on the bed. I moved quickly away: it was far too hot to remain close to her. I had often noticed the extraordinary fire given off by the flesh of young girls, but I had never encountered anything like the Puce's slender thighs. I could feel their warmth through my clothes. She said a trifle tartly, when I rolled away from her, "I support the heat better than you. Marie Lebrun says people in bed together should never be put off by the weather. Not if there is a true relationship together."

It was my turn to be tart. "We aren't exactly in bed together in the way I'm afraid Marie Lebrun means. She's no business to talk to a child like you about that kind of thing."

She uncrossed her arms and said coldly, "Marie Lebrun is only one month older than myself. It's just that she's big. She is big here, too." She patted her flat little chest. "She has la poitrine and I haven't. But you wait: when I am gonflée, people will stare at me like they stare at Marie. Oh, yes! You wait. It won't be long." Suddenly she leant forward, her eyes anxious. "Will you make me a promise?"

"What is it?"

"If you do I'll tell you something important."

"What do you want me to promise?"

She said with such solemnity that I nearly laughed, "Will you promise that you will *never* look at Marie Lebrun like other people do? You will save it for me?"

I straightened my face and said, "Certainly! Now, what should I know that's important?"

She pushed the sacking aside and wriggled close to me. "You know the cocoa seller?"

"The one with the pitch outside?"

"Yes. But he isn't a cocoa seller."

"What does he sell, then — beer?"

"No. He sells cocoa, but he isn't a cocoa seller." I waited as I always do when I am a little confused by a female's conversation. "This morning he gave me a sou."

"What does that prove, except that he's a kindly man?"

"I was to tell him which way you had gone."

I sat forward. "Why should that interest him?"

She shrugged. "I don't know. But Monsieur Pêche says you can never be sure when somebody's not an agent of the police."

"My God!" I said. "Thank you, Puce. Now I come to think of it, we're always running into him. He seems everywhere at once."

"Yes. Well, I asked him why he wanted to know, and he said it was none of my business but there would be many more sous for me if I always told him where you'd gone."

"Did you say you would?"

"Of course. But I shall tell him all wrong and take the money just the same. It will come in handy for America. After all," she added sagely, "it's going to cost money getting to this America. It's very kind of my new uncle to let me come, too. It's not as if he was a real uncle, so I feel I must pay something towards it. You see, the bracelet would have been plenty for all of us."

I smiled at her. She looked so forlorn as she remembered the collapse of her hopes. I patted her hand, and instead of removing it she pushed it further into mine. I had not the heart to say that nothing would induce me to let her accompany us to America. Our future was quite precarious enough without burdening ourselves with the responsibility of a child.

"Yes" — she nodded firmly — "every sou we can make is a help. I shall go out for the pockets myself again tomorrow. You see, with the bracelet I thought we could all three retire, but with that gone — well, my new uncle is out after the pockets this minute."

"He could have left it to me," I remarked. "The Palais-Royal is by far the best spot, and I can go there and he can't."

A touch of rancour returned to her voice, and her hand was withdrawn. "He says you're a fool when a woman's about. You would never have missed the bracelet if it hadn't been for the pretty lady who gave me the twelve-sol piece."

I smirked at her. "So you've come round to agreeing that she is pretty?"

She shook her head so hard that the greasy hair flew out like a blackbird shaking its feathers. "I *must* wash that head," I reminded myself. "I agree no such thing," she retorted. "I'm using the words of my new uncle the poor Monsieur Manager Smith."

"Well, thank you very much for warning me about the cocoa seller." I bent down and kissed her cheek. For an instant she stared at me. I half expected a shot of her well-aimed spittle. But instead her thin arms wound round my neck so hard that I nearly choked.

"Promise! Promise you will not look at Marie Lebrun?"

"I've already given you my word," I reminded her.

"Yes, but if I catch you — oh! If I catch you!" She broke off breathless at the mere possibility.

"Marie Lebrun," I assured her, "sounds the kind of girl I most dislike."

This was not accurate. I had a hard job not to ask where to find the little witch. But it satisfied the Puce. She released me and settled down to sleep like a puppy that has suddenly tired of a game.

In spite of the grip of the heat, there was energy in L'Étuve. One could feel it seeping through the cracks and under the boards of the ancient No. 15 rue Louis d'Or. Although there was hardly anyone on the streets, there was a curious sense of activity. In the little rat garrets and cellars, and in particular on the floor above us, people were talking, talking, talking. I could hear the fluctuating buzz of Pêche's political class upstairs. That subject so dear to the heart of the French was being discussed all over L'Étuve — La France, La France, La France.

I went in search of Pêche. It occurred to me that with his sensitive nose for police spies he might be able to tell me a little more about the cocoa seller.

When I put my head round his door, he was engrossed in his class, but he beckoned me inside. The room was full of people. Squatting on the floor were the Lapins, Monsieur and Madame Lattre, the German breeches maker who lived on the top floor of our house, the letter writer, and the wine seller. The latter had either done very good business or been very generous. There were empty bottles all over the place. Pêche waved to me. "Sit down, Monsieur Buckland, sit down — here!" He passed me a bottle. "Our good friend Monsieur Didot has made us a present."

The wine seller started to make a speech in response to the applause brought on by the mention of his gift, but was firmly stopped. I took my bottle and sat down beside Madame Lattre. The heat in the room was formidable. One could feel it attacking one physically. The smell of secrecy and mistrust of me was almost as strong as the wine. Only Pêche and the Lapins felt at ease with me. The eyes of the others kept seeking me out. I could see them turning towards me in the dim light like insects creeping out of dark corners.

Pêche was heady with something more than wine that night. I remembered the sense of expectancy I thought I had imagined as I walked back from the Palais-Royal. The barricaded streets, the lampions, the odd impression of suppressed excitement gripping the throat. It seemed to have reached its peak in the face of Pêche. I have often wondered since whether he really had suspected what was afoot or whether he was affected by the inexplicable promise in the air, but there was a look on his face I had never seen before: it was joy.

He explained to me, not without difficulty owing to the wine, "The liberation of the people is at hand, monsieur, and the people must be ready for it."

A cheer went round the tiny room and bottles were raised to the wine seller. He got up to continue his speech, but was forcibly restrained.

"Not only ready," Pêche roared, "but worthy. It's essential if the people are to rule for the people that they should be politically educated. Good citizenship is dependent upon political awareness. Politics and loyalty to party should come before religion, as man can do so much more for man than God."

"Monsieur Dansart," whispered the letter writer, "who also gives classes, says much the same thing."

I endeavoured to look comforted by this uniformity and poured wine down my throat. My attention, I'm afraid, was not on Pêche. I was reaching a point when all I could think of was police spies. For all I knew I might be in a roomful of them, and Pêche himself might be the most skilful. I put the thought out of my mind. Not Pêche! Not the reasonable, embittered

Pêche, whose sentiments were so close to my own. I tried to concentrate on what he was saying.

It was evident that his classes were necessary. With the exception of the letter writer, who had heard everything before from Monsieur Dansart and never ceased telling me so, the ignorance was alarming.

"It's this Monsieur Veto we've got to get rid of!" shouted Madame Lattre.

"Yes. He's the Queen's lover," agreed Madame Lapin. "Together they're starving the people, and the King approves of it."

I had heard the King and the Queen sneered at as Monsieur and Madame Veto before, but I had never heard them described as a ménage-à-trois.

Pêche showed admirable patience in trying to explain to them. "The Veto is not a living person at all. It's only a power possessed by the King to give him authority over the National Assembly. But it's a dangerous thing for us because he can use this power to block a law that the people wish to pass."

"You're wrong there, Jacques Pêche," called out Lattre. "I've a friend who is a deputy and he says this Monsieur Veto is alive."

"He's the Queen's lover," insisted Madame Lattre, "and much more important than the King. Even the nobles have to do what he tells them, and he holds up supplies of bread."

A voice from the side wall called out in agreement. "That's true: I have heard it myself. If a man has a piece of bread, Monsieur Veto can force him to throw it away untasted. Yes! Even if the fellow is starving."

"And he can sleep with anyone he likes," came another shout. "Yes! That is certain! Anyone's wife or anyone's daughters. He has only to say and they must go to him. It is worse than the days of the Parc aux Cerfs."

It was sad to hear them spilling out the fantastic tales that had been told to them. Sad and degrading. These people had genuine enough grievances without their feelings being worked upon by fools telling grotesque lies to bring them to fever point. But were these agitators perhaps such fools? Pêche battled on tirelessly, explaining point after point, trying to get them to see the true dangers, the real threats to their rights, the full justice of their long-neglected demands. But I doubt if he made as much impression on them as the dirt writers and the gutter preachers pandering to the pathetic ignorance in which they had been kept so long. It was easier for these people of L'Étuve, whose every thought had had to be concentrated on the everyday business of keeping alive, to believe in a flesh-and-blood Veto who held up bread; much easier than following Pêche's complicated explanations, however simple he strove to make them.

How long Pêche struggled I don't know. The wine and the heat sent me to sleep. From time to time I heard through my torpor the letter writer telling me that something or other was exactly what Monsieur Dansart had said, and I was vaguely aware that the wine seller had finally not been prevented from making his speech. After that I did not wake until I felt something trickling down my throat. I sat up spluttering and found that it was Pêche pouring wine into my mouth. He poured quite a bit of it down my neck, but I directed the bottle back to the right quarter. Everyone else had gone; the empty bottles had been neatly piled in the corner. It was only then that I took a look at Pêche. He appeared to be armed to the teeth. He had a musket pressed under his arm like a walking cane, and his hand clutched a pike. "You!" he said slowly. "It's because of my faith in you. You shall come to the fight with Jacques Pêche."

"What fight?" I sat up, decidedly giddy. There was no doubt that I had consumed a most unwise amount of wine.

"*What* fight?" Pêche reeled backwards, an expression of shocked reproach on his face. "How can you *ask* such a thing, Monsieur Buckland, how can you *ask*?" Then he sat down apparently unable to remember himself. His musket and pike clattered to the floor beside him. He put his knuckles to his forehead and tapped it. "To arms!" he muttered softly to himself. "On les aura! To arms!" He waited as if he expected the words to remind him of the mission for which he had obviously rehearsed them. "This is the hour! The hour to strike. Every citizen will show himself a true patriot, and no one who is not a patriot will be a true citizen." He waited again in the hope of recalling the reason for this moving little speech, but, failing to do so, went to sleep.

I was also confused as to what it was I had come up to ask Pêche. When I remembered I shook him awake. He scrambled up like a fish beating about on the bank. "To arms! To arms! On les aura!"

"Monsieur Pêche," I said, "do you think the cocoa seller's a police spy?"

He opened a new bottle of wine, drank half the contents, and passed the rest to me. He turned to me and had a little difficulty in focussing his gaze on my face. It seemed to be easier if he tipped his head back and kept one eye closed. "The cocoa seller?"

"The one with his pitch outside this house."

"Who would have believed it?" Pêche asked dreamily. "Such an honest face! Well!" he said with sudden energy, "I shall refuse to bury him. Yes! No arguments. This is the final word of Jacques Pêche. He may go down on his knees to me. He may offer to give his life for me — and I shall refuse to bury him."

"I haven't any proof," I said hastily.

"Of course you have," snapped Pêche. "You don't need any. There's hardly anyone who isn't a police spy. Are you one?"

I shook my head. "No, are you?"

He shook his head. "No. How nice. It's very comforting that we are neither of us police spies. We must be the only two who are not in L'Étuve."

"It gives us a lot in common," I said solemnly. He leaned over and kissed me on both cheeks. I returned the gesture and we would have gone to sleep again if an irate little trio had not appeared in the doorway. They were M.S., Monsieur Lapin, and Madame Lapin.

"Boy!" said M.S. "Too much drinking's not good for an actor's face."

I rose with acute difficulty, tottered towards him, and would have kissed him on both cheeks if I hadn't misjudged the distance and landed up on the floor. He lifted me up by my collar. "You're still dependent on face, my boy. You're not a good enough actor yet to lose your looks and have people still as interested in your performance."

The Lapins converged on Pêche. "Monsieur Pêche! You have taken too much."

"On a day like this? No one could take too much. It's the duty of every patriot to take too much." He tripped over his musket. M.S. picked it up and put it out of harm's way.

The Puce appeared in the doorway. She looked minute by the side of the pike I was holding. She pointed to me and complained to M.S. "I don't like him getting drunk with Monsieur Pêche. I think they are bad for each other."

I made an effort to call her a pompous little chit but was unable to get the words out.

Pêche staggered towards me and slid gently down my chest, trying to hold on with his chin. He was unconscious when I stretched him in the corner. The effort was too much for me also. I lay down beside him.

It seems to me, looking back, that my every movement in those days must have been planned by some evil spirit to provide the Revolutionary Tribunal with fuel for my indictment.

It's surely a common enough occurrence for two men to get dead drunk together. It doesn't usually have the far-reaching effects that it had for me — and even for poor Pêche himself. In spite of what was to happen, I can still only think of him as "poor Pêche."

How long we snored on the floor I don't know. The next thing I remember was that the sun was high. There was no sign of the Lapins, the Puce, or M.S., and there were horrible bells ringing somewhere — really unfriendly, loud bells.

I took a look out of the window but could see no one about in the streets. The noise had returned in full force, but it was in the distance — and I also thought I heard cannon fire. I had difficulty taming the floor; the wretched thing was uneven in any case, but at that moment it swelled up against the opposite wall and then rolled back like a wave to break right in my face. I lowered myself onto my hands and knees and tried to swim through it. I was on my stomach doing the breast stroke when Pêche rescued me.

"I do not see water," he said.

"Then you're a fool," I snapped. He was only disconcerted a matter of seconds. He threw up his hands and dived in for me. I don't know who got whom back to land. Pêche pulled the cork of another bottle and put an arm round my neck while I drank. I did the same for him. He returned the compliment for me and I for him. He eased a wary head towards the window. "Cannons!" he said, puzzled. "And tocsins!"

Pêche clutched his head and let out a gurgle that I mistook for the death rattle. "Monsieur! Monsieur! I recall everything now. We are storming the Bastille!"

But I was sober. I knew where I was. "Nonsense," I told him. "We've been here all the time."

Pêche lay back, gingerly holding his head on. "I've been dreaming," he said despondently. "What a cruel dream." He was snoring again immediately.

I was woken by Manager Smith. He was forcing a cupful of something bitter between my teeth. "Drink it up! Drink it at once."

I opened an eye and examined him. I didn't trust one, so I opened the other. He looked very strange indeed. His wig was more or less in half. His clothes were torn. He was covered in dust and wore only one shoe.

"Have you been fighting?" I asked.

"Fighting!" he roared. "Yes, I've been fighting. There's been nothing else to do this morning. We weren't all lucky enough to be dead drunk. Drink this, I tell you. Nothing else will save you except a good turn-out."

"What is it?"

"It's a purgative tisane, that's what it is, and it's taken me five hours to get it. I tell you the whole of the town has gone mad. They're not safe to live with, these Frenchies. I'm lucky my throat wasn't cut."

I drank the tisane. It was filthy.

"Thank you so much," I said.

"So I should think. You might get a stoppage on all that wine. I went up to the boulevard du Temple to buy this stuff — and my God, I was caught in the midst of it."

"In the midst of what?"

"The fighting. They've broken into that old castle place."

"What old castle place?"

"The prison. And they've murdered the governor — just dragged him out and did him to death. There's blood and bricks flying all over the city. I tell you I'm lucky to be alive, never mind getting home with a purgative. How you escaped all the noise beats me. I hope all that wine hasn't rotted your eardrums." He stamped out, swearing at the French.

I lay thinking a minute or two. Something Pêche had said was worrying me in view of what M.S. had said: "broken into that old castle place," — "murdered the governor" — "cannon and tocsins!"

I rolled over joyously and clouted Pêche. "Wake up, man! Wake up! We've attacked the Bastille!"

He eyed me sourly. "That's folly, monsieur, we've not stirred from this house."

M.S. came back and poured a bucket of water over the pair of us.

Chapter 28.

IT CERTAINLY seemed impossible that we could have missed such an assault, but missed it ignominiously we had. It was serious for Pêche. He should have been out leading his section. His pupils were far from admiring their political instructor's absence from the proceedings. Old Lapin said sourly, "A fine thing, I must say. So much talk about fighting for the people and he sleeps through their most glorious hour!"

Lattre nodded bitterly. "He tells us every man's blood must be ready to pour into the veins of France, and he sits filling his own up with wine."

The German breeches maker shook his fist. "The greatest blow is struck for freedom and where do you look for Jacques Pêche? Drunk on the floor with his aristocratic friends!"

This jibe was taken up quite unpleasantly. It was the first time L'Étuve had looked at me askance.

"Well, well," said the letter writer. "In the next lot of trouble we shall know where to look for the bravest of leaders."

Hardly able to hold our heads up for shame as well as from the after effects of the wine, Pêche and I made a sickly pilgrimage to the scene of the battle. I think both of us felt that until we had actually seen it we couldn't believe we had missed it. We were obliged to support each other most of the way. I couldn't have felt weaker if I'd been going down with the plague. I doubt if I should have got along without Pêche's arm and he would certainly have tripped without mine.

The Puce came with us some of the way. "You must have heard the tocsins," she told us: "people heard them from miles and miles away, and even quite old men joined in."

We were not helped by being hailed as heroes. Our tottering progress and our shaky arms round one another got us mistaken for wounded patriots. "Voilà! Les braves!" the cry went up, and to our alarm we found ourselves shouldered the rest of the way to the glorious battlefield. Emotion was thunder-loud that day; people were singing, dancing, laughing, and even praying in the streets. A woman seized my dangling foot and kissed it. "Soldier of heaven, think what we owe you!"

The more we tried to avoid attention, the more attention we attracted. We even went so far as to confess at the top of our voices that we had slept through this most heroic of all events, but the rumour flew round that we had played an even more distinguished part than most. "Vive les combattants!" "Vive les courageux." I was never more embarrassed in the whole of my life, especially as I had a stomach ache from that blessed tisane.

Pêche had his eyes closed, perhaps from emotion, but I suspected from sickness. The jolting was formidable.

Near the fortress we saw that we were not the only ones being carried shoulder high. Poor Pêche opened his eyes just in time to come face to face with a skull hoisted aloft for the crowds to see. It had been found in a dungeon of the Bastille. The sun seemed to polish the yellow skull, and beetles ran out of its eye sockets. Pêche quickly closed his own eyes again.

Round the fortress there was a seething mass of joy. Parents held children up to look, and voices were raised in the "Ça ira" and the "Carmagnole."

Our little band of admirers pressed their way forwards. "Make way for the heroes! To the front with the brave ones! Vive les coeurs forts!"

Ill though we were from excesses, both Pêche and I were moved beyond words. I cried aloud when I saw those battered walls. That dismal horror that had withstood the great Condé and brooded for centuries impenetrable over Paris had fallen to the people in a matter of hours. *Only four, I heard, had taken them.* Was there ever a victory like that? Four hours! To put an end to tyranny. My own "vives" nearly scored open my throat.

Fortunately, "heroes" were picked up and dropped very quickly in Paris. Our supporters suddenly shot us down to the ground and went off to cheer somebody else. I landed on my feet, but I rather feared Pêche had come down on his head. I completely lost sight of him in the crowd. I struggled towards the great ditch to gloat over the damage. I was swept forward with the people who were still bringing the prisoners out. I found myself inside the place. It didn't seem possible that such conditions could exist in modern times. Surely flesh couldn't subject brother flesh to such torments. I was truly powerless to picture the sufferings of the creatures confined in there. Even with the fresh air that the cannons had blown through the walls there was an acid foulness still lingering in the vaults. There seemed no end to the labyrinth of dungeons; their chill could have come from the Ice Age.

I saw men with iron clamps round their waists chained to the walls. I saw others pinned by the wrist or by the ankle, and I saw a decomposing body upright in a cage. A skeleton lay on a flinty protrusion, its right foot still chained to a cannon ball. Round it were the powdered piles of its lifetime excrement.

But it was the living prisoners who touched the heart. The crowd, exultant at having rescued them, made no allowance for their broken nerves, and from the darkness of years they plunged the poor devils straight into sunshine. They shrieked with pain and covered their eyes from the light. Liberty had come too late for most of them. I saw one old man jibbering with fright. He had been buried alive for forty years — forty years! And the tears rolled down his face, not for the joy of being released, but from fear of a world of sights and sounds that his dulled brain had completely forgotten. He begged them to put him back in his grave, but they led him out tottering forward to limp in a triumphal procession.

I stayed out until four in the morning. I could not bear to say goodbye to that day. About twelve people gave me accounts of it and none of them tallied. But what did seem certain was that the people had broken into Les Invalides, dragged off eighty cannons and something like forty thousand small arms, and had definitely taken the place in four hours. I went home more drunk with elation than wine.

I ran straight upstairs to see what had happened to Pêche. I stopped at the door when I heard him sobbing. I didn't go in. My comfort would only have rubbed in the shame. I too would have given my ears to have played something better than the part of a clown that day.

M.S. was in bed with the Lapins, but the Puce was waiting up for me.

"What a sorrow you will be to your wife," she sighed.

The sobbing of Pêche was unpleasantly audible. She followed my glance to the ceiling. "My grandfather's very angry with him."

"The poor man just got drunk," I said.

"Like you?"

"Like me!"

I sped out of my clothes and got into bed. She wriggled close and leaned over me.

"Get up, please, I wish you to kiss me."

I was in no mood for anything but quick oblivion. I leaned over and pecked the child's cheek.

She said coldly, "Properly, if you please — like lovers do in bed."

"You shouldn't know anything about that sort of thing."

"My friend Marie Lebrun has a lover. Ooh! How I hate her. Just because she's gonflée!" She stuck her small chest out. "I've rubbed it with a clove of garlic. They say it helps to make it grow."

So that was the reason for the smell of the stew pot.

"It'll stick out by itself in its own good time," I told her. "And I shouldn't see Marie Lebrun again: she's not good for you."

The Puce's black pupils dominated the whites of her eyes. "She calls me 'child' and 'little one' and 'poor little thing' just because I haven't been properly kissed."

"I've just kissed you," I reminded her.

"Yes, but that is my poor new uncle's kind. I know, because Marie Lebrun has described what the right one should be like."

"Well, that's all you're getting from me. You don't know what you're talking about — or shouldn't at your age."

"She's told me the things people do in their beds and I want you to do them all to me, please, so that I can go back and say 'pooh!' in her face."

I rolled over. With any luck we should get something from Dugazon. Enough at least to provide myself and M.S. with a decent bed each.

"I don't want to hear any more about it," I told the child. "Either from you or your disgusting little friend."

She was incensed at my turning away from her. "The English!" she sniffed. "Marie Lebrun says if it was left to the English, there wouldn't be many people on earth. They are too cold for the things of the bed." I was silent. "Anyway, I've already told her you've done them to me. I said 'Oh! *that*! We do that hundreds of times every night."

"I hope she was suitably impressed."

"But if you really kissed me, I could tell her what it's like." I was silent again. She gave a little grunt of rage. I think she would have liked to hit me.

"Well, is it all right for married people?"

"Yes."

"Why?"

"Because —" I could have swatted the child. It was a question to which I had never been able to give a satisfactory answer myself. "Because marriages are made in heaven and therefore God thinks it's all right."

I sensed her scorn so strongly I turned round to look at her. She was sitting with her nose wrinkled up. "He can't think much of you, then, can he?" I ignored her. "Can I tell her we're married?"

"No."

"Why?"

"Because we're not."

"Well, can I tell her we're going to get married?"

"For heaven's sake, go to sleep."

"Can I tell her that we are betrothed?"

"Oh, tell her what you like," I snapped, "as long as you let *me* go to sleep."

She hauled her sacking round her and settled down contentedly. "That's a promise, then? I can tell her we're betrothed? You won't say we're not if she asks you?"

"I've already promised not to look at the wretched girl. I can hardly talk to her with my eyes closed."

She made a little purring sound. "I shall tell everyone else as well — my new uncle, and grandpère, and Monsieur Pêche, and Monsieur Lattre. I shall tell the whole of L'Étuve we're betrothed."

Chapter 29.

WE WERE only a few days away from the appointment with Dugazon. M.S. was taking me through lines and rehearsing me as the perfect dinner guest. But my mind was not on it. I was thinking of Marie-Clarice. Should I have any luck with Dugazon and become an actor again, my chances of becoming the lover of an aristocrat were slight.

I decided to take Mr. Buckland to the Palais-Royal in search of the girl. M.S. was not to be hoodwinked. "You're not going up there picking pockets. You're going whoring." The Puce was staunchly on his side, as always.

I had only one advantage over their combined attack on me and it amused me to use it. When his French and her English failed them, there was only me to interpret. He had more French than she had English; she knew only a few words and there were times when they were quite unable to communicate with one another. It was then that I sat between them and passed on as much as I thought fit, or something that made no sense at all.

"Whoring" was not a word he knew in French and not one she recognised in English. But she knew by his expression that he was displeased with me. She sat on his knee and, in loyalty to him, scowled at me.

"What is my new uncle saying?"

"He says, 'Three blind mice, see how they run.' "

"That's stupid. No one would say such a thing. Why are you going to the Palais-Royal?"

"To get a few trinkets to put in your new uncle's box to help get us to America."

She peered into M.S.'s face. "That's not what he looks as if he thinks you're doing. Anyhow, we are better at that than you. You will be much more useful staying at home getting ready for Monsieur Dugazon."

M.S. dandled her on his knee as if she were a three-year-old. "This child's got more sense than you had at her age. You'd do well to listen to her, boy."

"I'm blessed if I can see," I retorted, "that it's any business of hers what I do in the Palais-Royal."

"I don't want everyone talking about the man I'm going to marry," she said. "I won't have Marie Lebrun thinking you're chasing any ladies but me."

"What's this? What's this?" M.S. enquired.

"Last night," she told him, "we agreed to get married."

"In order to get some sleep," I corrected her, "I said she could tell that to her friend Marie Lebrun, whom for some reason she wants to score off. Needless to say, there's nothing more to it than that." And I took myself off to dress as Buckland.

I had no immediate luck at the Palais-Royal. It was not until my third visit and the night before Dugazon's dinner that I finally ran into Marie-Clarice.

It was depressing searching for her night after night, and I was beginning to give up hope when a young drunk cannoned into me. I had been watching him for some time. He was fascinated by a chemical lighter he had just bought himself and was having difficulty in making it work. I too was fascinated by it, but my major consideration was whether it would be a good contribution to M.S.'s box. I edged my way towards the young man. I had managed to remove his watch and his purse when he turned round and fell against me. He was a small-boned, dark boy. He was drunk with a clumsy puppy dignity. When he bowed his apologies to me, he would have tipped right over if I hadn't caught him.

"My name is Vergny—Vicomte de Vergny—but please call me Blaise," he introduced himself. "Please forgive me, I ate something at dinner which didn't agree with me and it's left me a trifle giddy."

I acknowledged the excuse and presented myself as Anthony Buckland of Sandgate.

"Delighted!" he said. "Always pleased to make the acquaintance of a foreigner. Even if you don't like them, it broadens the mind. Come and join my party." With my eye still on the lighter, I followed him to the Café de Valois.

"You've chosen an interesting time to visit us," he said. "Glorious things are happening. Were you here for that little shake-up last week? They knocked down the Bastille, my dear boy, they knocked down the Bastille!"

"You were in favour of it?"

"In favour of it? All thinking men should be in favour of it."

I couldn't help concluding that he meant all fashionable men should take this attitude. He was obviously one of those bright young things so busily helping to capsise their own boat, not because they had any genuinely democratic feelings about it, but because it was the smart cause to adopt at the moment.

We pushed our way to a table where two girls and a man were playing dominoes. One of the girls was Marie-Clarice. She wore a dress that was shaded from pale lilac at the bodice to deep mauve at the hem. Pinned across the front of her stiffly set white hair there was an amethyst brooch in the shape of a lilac spray. She had on no other jewellery. She looked up and said brusquely, "Good evening, Mr. Buckland."

Blaise squeaked, "Oh, you know one another already?"

"Mr. Buckland is a friend of Madame de Flambelot." Her voice was disinterested but caustic.

Blaise turned to me with no attempt to hide his dismay. "You don't mean to say you hang round that old pot de chambre?"

"No," I said firmly, "I do not."

Marie-Clarice waved a hand. "Well, sit down. My brother's not the soul of tact even when he's sober."

"Your brother?"

"So my parents always led me to suppose. But of course one can never be sure. He doesn't take after anybody."

I sat down more heavily than I had intended. Her brother! And in my pocket I had his purse and his watch. Somehow I must get them back to him as soon as possible. But he sat on the opposite side of the table. He presented the other couple as Rosalie and Cyprien. Rosalie would have been interesting if she had not been up against Marie-Clarice.

"Did you have a nice cup of tea the other day, Mr. Buckland?" she asked sweetly.

"Thank you, yes. I got back in time to save my friend a lot of distress."

"She must have been very grateful."

"Yes," I said. "*He* was."

Blaise was still staring at me. "Surely you can do better than old Flambelot. Good heavens, she even gets down to paying dancing boys from the ballet."

"Blaise!" said Marie-Clarice. "Don't be so rude. For all you know, Monsieur Buckland might be one."

I eyed her steadily. "The first and last time I ever met Madame de Flambelot was when you saw us together."

Marie-Clarice bowed. "I'm sorry. She said you were her old friend from England, so I took it that you were her — old friend from England."

"My God!" said Blaise suddenly. "Where's my purse? My watch has gone, too. I've been robbed!"

I sat expressionless, angry that he had discovered his losses before I could make restitution.

"Have you had a good look?" asked Cyprien.

"Turn out your pockets," Rosalie suggested.

"You've dropped them, Blaise," said Marie-Clarice. "You're as drunk as a pig. Perhaps you've left them in a shop. Go back with him, Cyprien."

Cyprien stood up and Rosalie held out a hand to him. "Where did you go last, Blaise?"

"I was buying the lighter. I swear I had both of them then."

He was turning his pockets inside-out, which was unfortunate. There were so many witnesses to see that they were empty that it made it impossible for me to return the objects without people's suspecting either myself or a miracle. I should have to wait for an opportune moment to drop them on the floor and pretend to discover them underfoot.

"Go back to the lighter shop," urged Marie-Clarice. "If it's father's old watch you must find it, Blaise. It's been in the family for years."

Supported by Cyprien and Rosalie, Blaise left the café. I moved closer to Marie-Clarice. "What may I get you to drink?"

"Oh, I'll have a bavaroise." She flicked her fingers and gave the order to a waiter herself. "What about you?"

"I'll try the same."

"Let's hope you like it. It's sweet tea with sirop de capillaire and milk."

"It sounds disgusting."

"It is."

She looked past me, gently fanning herself.

"Your brother didn't tell me your name," I said.

"De Faille."

"You live in Paris, Madame de Faille?"

"Yes."

"I should consider it a great favour if you'd allow me to call on you."

"Would you?"

"I should be interested to meet your husband, too."

"You certainly would. He's dead."

"I'm sorry."

"I'm not. He was an exceptionally unpleasant man."

"Oh!"

Her eyes were everywhere but on my face. Half my success with women comes not from what I say to them but how I look at them. Short of craning my neck round to cut off her frequent little smiles at acquaintances, there was nothing I could do but talk. All my eye play — all the cool insolence I knew so well how to combine with impertinent warmth — was lost. All my wry smiles and my tricks with my eyebrows and the invitations I could convey by lingering looks at her mouth were wasted.

She certainly glanced at me when the waiter put down the bavaroise, but it wasn't for long enough. The eyebrows must be raised and lowered slowly. They cannot jerk up and down because time is short. A warm look at a woman — if it's to be inviting — has to be lingering. It cannot be a quick race round all her good points; the whole thing is a matter of timing. One can hardly send seductive signals flashing all over one's face in a matter of seconds. It is apt to make one appear somewhat unstable.

I decided to attack her outright. "Why do you mind so much that I should be seen with La Flambelot?"

That got her to look straight into my eyes, and having got it, I held my house.

"I?" she said. "I don't mind in the least. It's not my business."

"Then what makes you take such an interest in it?"

Our glances were sparking against one another's. She was angry. "It becomes my business when you force yourself upon me."

"I had an idea that you approved of my company. You were annoyed enough last week when I had to deprive you of it to take home the tea."

Her breath came out sharply. I added, before she could speak, "You went off in a childish fit of temper just because you couldn't have an iced drink with me. You've been thinking about me ever since and it infuriates you to imagine that someone who attracts you so much might have belonged to La Flambelot."

She put down her cup and stared at me, which was what I wanted. I was having plenty of time now to use my eyes and smile. Her voice was deliberately unemotional. "I expect La Flambelot is intrigued by such audacity, monsieur, but I'm afraid I find it utterly boring." I was going to speak, but she held up her fan. "Oh, don't think I blame you for going for old Flambelot. If that's the way one makes one's living, you couldn't have made a better choice. I know how generously she pays and I'm sure you must earn every sou of it. It must be hard work catering for that jaded appetite, although I believe you're not the only one at it." She was looking at me constantly now, and in spite of herself there was emotion in her voice. She was getting angrier and angrier. "I've always been greatly in favour of equality, and if women can sell themselves, why not men?"

"You don't sound as if you approve of it."

"I neither approve nor disapprove. You can hire yourself to a dozen Flambelots. I don't envy you your job, that's all."

I shook my head. "It isn't all. You think it's a terrible waste in my case."

"As I said before, gross conceit may tickle La Flambelot's palate but not mine."

"Well, let's hope the truth tickles it — because here it comes. I don't earn my living by making love to old women. I don't make love to women for money at all. La Flambelot attached herself to me and I was in the process of trying to shake her off when you saw us. I haven't seen her since, and if I did I should get out of her way if I had to sprint ten miles." She regarded me steadily. "I'm afraid you'll just have to take my word for it. I've many vices, as I fear you'll find out, but they don't include catering for any appetite but my own." I had put my hand over hers and she let it remain. "You can get out of your mind once and for all that I'm the sort of man who acts as hired escort to the old, the rich, and the plain."

Her hand moved under mine. She picked up one of my fingers and examined it. "I'll confess that I'm slightly relieved. It makes your interest in me a little more flattering."

I turned her hand over and held it. "You realise now, I hope, that I like my women young and pretty and that nothing would induce me to waste time or sympathy on the opposite?"

I felt the warm pressure of her fingers responding to mine as I lifted her hand to my lips. She leaned closer to me; the lily-scented soap clung to her flesh. Her breasts were soft and white half-moons above the line of her bodice. Her voice went deep. "I'm glad that you don't like your women old, and plain, and rich!" Then, looking past me, her expression slowly changed from a look of mild enquiry to steely disillusionment. It was then that I felt a peremptory tap on my shoulder. Turning round quiskly, I came face to face with Lizzie Weldon. Behind her, smiling that ever-healthy smile, was old Sir Gregory Hawtrey. Next to him was Louis Brissac, the baby-faced Lieutenant of Police.

Chapter 30.

THE SHOCK was so great that for a few seconds I felt paralysed. My brain simply refused to accept such bad luck. Lizzie Weldon in Paris! Out after midnight in that Mecca of the licentious! It couldn't be true. But it was, and because she was with Sir Gregory and the Lieutenant, I could not go on calling myself Buckland.

I was still holding Marie-Clarice's hand. It stiffened as she withdrew it from me. "Please don't let me detain you if you've come across some other *old* friend from England."

Lizzie was staring at her with open hostility. She took a step forward, about to speak, but I jumped up so quickly I almost knocked over the table. To have had her address me as De Lambrière in front of Marie-Clarice would have been fatal. I literally wedged myself between them and felt Marie-Clarice's eyes hard on my back. I squeaked like a schoolboy caught stealing jam. "Miss Weldon! I didn't expect to see you."

"How quaint of you," was all she said.

I thrust a hand at her, and while she was shaking it, I managed to propel her away from the table. Anything to get her out of the ear-shot of Marie-Clarice.

"Philippe," she said, "I've arranged a little supper party at my hotel. It's so much nicer than this vulgar, noisy place."

"It's charming of you, Miss Weldon, but I'm afraid I've got a prior —"

"Philippe," she repeated. "I've arranged a little supper party at my hotel." Then she tucked her arm through mine in an intimate manner and forced me towards Sir Gregory.

He sent out a hearty hand. "Ah! De Lambrière. Miss Weldon was certain we'd find you here."

"You remember Sir Gregory and Monsieur Brissac, don't you, Philippe? You met them at our house in England."

I gurgled something. I could still feel Marie-Clarice's eyes like twin daggers in-between my shoulder blades. I could almost hear her drawing all the wrong conclusions. The old and the rich and the plain!

I said, "I'm sorry I can't ask you all to join me, but I'm afraid it's not my party. I'm only a guest and I —"

Lizzie interrupted me. "We quite understand, Philippe, and I'm sure that your friends will excuse you."

The eyes of the baby-faced Lieutenant travelled lazily towards Marie-Clarice; once arrived, they were human enough to show a decided interest in her. I was not pleased to see that she was a born coquette. She returned Louis Brissac's approval with undisguised frankness.

It was as much to remove the Lieutenant as myself that I agreed to go with Lizzie Weldon. How Marie-Clarice could have found those heavy-lidded eyes and that soft face attractive was beyond me. I managed to dodge Lizzie and return to the table. "I shall have to ask you to excuse me, Madame de Faille."

She gave me a look that left me in no doubt that she despised me. "I quite understand. It's easy to see that you're not your own master."

I was about to reply, but Lizzie claimed me and led me away. When I looked back, Marie-Clarice had left the table.

I managed to whisper to Lizzie, "Nothing will induce me to come home to supper with you. If you insist, I shall tell Sir Gregory who I really am."

"I shouldn't do that," she whispered back: "he's come over to find the actor called Roberts who killed poor Nicholas."

I accepted her supper invitation and climbed into her carriage. Lizzie and I sat side by side and Sir Gregory and Louis Brissac faced us. The latter kept those sleepy eyes on me, and I had the feeling that he knew that I had resented his success with Marie-Clarice.

He said in that strangely slow voice, "You've chosen to return in troubled times, Monsieur le Vicomte. Are you over here for good?"

"I'm trying to trace my family," I told him. "I don't even know if I have any relatives left alive. I lost touch with them years ago."

"The black sheep of the family?" he enquired politely.

Lizzie said, "Philippe was brought to England when he was one year old. The Vicomtess de Lambrière was widowed in early youth and married again."

The Lieutenant seemed perfectly satisfied as to my identity, but I could see that he had not altered his opinion of me. He thought me a rogue and let me see it.

We were driving to the Hôtel de Muscovie in the faubourg Saint-Germain. The lights of Paris bit into the dark sky behind us, but I found nothing enchanting that night.

Certainly nothing in Lizzie's rooms found charm in my eyes. To be just, I didn't see the rest of the Hôtel de Muscovie. Perhaps it reserved especially dull apartments for English maiden ladies. It was furnished in sombre antique style. The salon was hung with gloomy tapestries, and marble busts of dead generals glared at us from pedestals. It was airless and smelt of the camphor bottle. There wasn't a lively colour or a modern touch anywhere. Lizzie's deaf aunt, presumably acting as chaperone, glowered from a chair in a corner.

In spite of the heat, we all sat round the fire. Lizzie was determined that the air was damp from the river and she didn't care how much she roasted us.

I spent the whole of that uncomfortable little supper party trying to make sure that there should be no doubt in the mind of Louis Brissac that I really was Philippe de Lambrière. I did not want him discovering that I was an actor called Roberts in case he passed this interesting piece of information on to old Sir Gregory Hawtrey. I accounted for my lack of knowledge about my family by saying that my remarried mother had died when I was still an infant. It was only from the kindly English couple who had brought me up that I learned that I was indisputably a French aristocrat. For that reason I was determined to discover and claim my inheritance should any be owing to me.

Lizzie was greatly pleased with this explanation, and made constant references to the tragedy of my dear mother the Vicomtesse. Needless to say, I have since regretted spending so much time convincing the Lieutenant of Police that I really was a French aristocrat!

The Lieutenant left early, but Sir Gregory, who was also lodged in the Hôtel de Muscovie, lingered.

As soon as Louis Brissac had gone, Lizzie turned to me. "Sir Gregory is over on a very sad mission, Philippe. You remember poor Nicholas? He was murdered last month and we've reason to believe that he was killed by an actor called Roberts from the Little Apollo theatre! I think you went there with us once. You should remember him."

For a moment or two I floundered; then I managed to say, "I'm very distressed to hear about your son, Sir Gregory."

"Can't think what my boy Nick was doing to know such a fellow. But his favourite mare was left in stables quite close to this man's theatre, and the wretch himself has disappeared, and his manager, or whatever they call him, has gone with him. Miss Weldon's quite right. It looks pretty conclusive."

"Oh, it was Miss Weldon who suspected the actor?" I looked straight at her, and she gave me a calm smile.

"Yes, I remembered poor Nicholas saying he had met the man. He was very interested in the play, you know. He wouldn't have been too proud to converse with the creature."

"What motive would an actor have for killing him?"

"Perhaps it was robbery," suggested Lizzie. "He might have waylaid poor Nicholas, and I do think disappearing like that was extremely suspicious."

"You've no idea," said Sir Gregory fondly, "how good this dear lady has been. She agreed with me that the man was most likely to have made for France, and she insisted upon accompanying me. She's so anxious to see my poor boy revenged."

"Yes," I said.

"They were deeply devoted, you know."

"Yes," I said.

"So it's only a matter of time until we find him," added Lizzie, "and I don't envy Mr. Roberts when he comes face to face with Sir Gregory."

"No one will envy him," Sir Gregory said. "I'm over here to find him and find him I will."

Lizzie said softly, "If he did come to France he'd have to try and earn his living. They told me at the Little Apollo that he speaks French like a native. So perhaps he's trying to get work on the stage over here."

"Yes. I shall comb all the theatres," Sir Gregory said, and added warmly, "I'm sparing nothing to revenge myself on this actor. He's young, I believe, and I am not, but I've been a good swordsman in my time. There were quite a few people nervous of me, and I'm taking fencing lessons again from a French fellow just in case I've lost my touch."

"Sir Gregory," Lizzie told me, "is practising five hours a day, though I'm quite sure he doesn't need it."

"Oh, yes, I do," he said modestly. "One must be au fait with the modern coups, and these young ones know all the tricks."

I asked him casually, "Have you reported this actor to the Lieutenant of Police, Sir Gregory?"

He leaned forward confidentially. "No, and I should be grateful, De Lambrière, if you would take care not to mention it to him either. You see, being a friend of Louis Brissac's and being connected with the British Foreign Office puts me in a very difficult position. After all, I'm over here to kill a man. You can't expect him, or indeed my own government, to take a sympathetic view of that. My visit must appear to be innocent. I can assure you that in reality I intend to leave this actor in more pieces than he could have left my poor boy, but I should not like the police to suspect me of that."

"I can assure you," I told him gravely, "that they'll get no information from me."

Lizzie Weldon was smiling at me. Dislike of her had always been near the surface as far as I was concerned, but previously I had never taken her seriously enough to do other than regard her as one of nature's more sombre jokes. Now, when I saw her making a fool of that man so sincere in his love for his footling son, I detested her. I should like him to have known the lengths this "dear lady" had gone to to get me, and that it was through her infatuation for me that he had lost the son to whom she was "so deeply devoted." I should like to have told him that it was because of Lizzie Weldon that his son was lying in a prop basket in a wood. I longed to shout "I killed him," but I hadn't the courage. So I sat listening to the old man extolling Nicholas' virtues.

When he got up he shook my hand. "Look here, De Lambrière, it's no secret to me that you and my Nicholas were rivals. But now that my poor lad's no longer in the running, I'd rather see you successful with Lizzie than anyone else."

I thanked him. I felt horrible looking into those clear, brave eyes.

"I must tell you," he added. "I'm worried. I don't think Paris is the place for Miss Weldon."

"I heartily agree," I said.

"The political unrest is nearing danger point. Your people, De Lambrière," he told me, with what later proved to be another of his charming understatements, "are on the verge of an outbreak."

"They've good cause for discontent," I said.

"Possibly, but there's no need to abuse law and order and humiliate foreigners. Our carriage was stopped on the way to the opera. Apparently they forced the place to close, and these miscreants insisted upon my getting out and bowing to them, and they forced Miss Weldon to smile. They wouldn't let us proceed until she had."

"I hope they thought it worth it," I said.

"They were drunk." Lizzie shuddered. "The women, too! How dared they attack their betters like that!"

"There's a certain feeling against the nobility," I said, "and not without cause."

Lizzie snapped, "People like that should be locked away for no greater crime than being people like that!"

"Hundreds of them have been," I told her. "Perhaps that's what still rankles with their friends outside."

"De Lambrière!" said Sir Gregory. "I hope you're not a democrat."

"Yes, sir," I said. "I am."

"But I distinctly remember your calling a very different tune when I met you in England."

"My views have changed since I returned to my own country."

"It's dangerous folly!" he barked, "and you're not the first of your class I've heard putting forward these theories. Sheer idiocy is talked about liberating the masses and passing on equality just as if it was as easy as handing down an old coat. I tell you I've heard the most alarming ideas in the salons of people who should know better. That kind of talk is about as safe as a powder-keg over a lighted candle. If the people find out that their masters themselves don't think they are fitted to rule, they'll get the bit between their teeth. A horse soon knows when you fear it and bolts."

"I shall do my best to persuade Miss Weldon to go home," I promised.

"Good fellow. It's one thing for a man and quite another for a couple of women."

"How long," I asked casually, "do you propose looking for your actor?"

"Oh, I shan't grudge time or money," he told me. "We've only been here three days. Of course, with all that disgraceful business over the Bastille it hasn't been easy to carry on a search —"

"I've never known such a shocking thing," said Lizzie. "They should hang everyone who had any part in it."

"I've already been to the Théâtre Royal and the Comédie Française," Sir Gregory continued. "I drew lucky there at once. The fellow in charge said a French-speaking Englishman had been in a couple of weeks ago asking for work. So it shouldn't take long: he's bound to go back."

"Did — did the fellow in charge say when he was expecting him?"

"No." Sir Gregory's friendly eye grew puzzled. "Of course, he wasn't a gentleman — these acting people never are — but he got quite disagreeable. He told me I was lucky to be visiting Paris at such a glorious time. He was referring to the capture of the Bastille, if you please! When I said I thought the whole affair was a disgrace to the nation, he suddenly jumped up and said we'd wasted enough of one another's time. Damn dog bit me in the ankle, too!"

I silently praised God for Dugazon's Republican sentiment and dislike of Englishmen.

Sir Gregory held out his friendly hand again. "Well, good night, De Lambrière. I'm going to bed. Want to keep as fit as I can for this job of mine."

When he had gone I said to Lizzie, "So you sent the so-called farmers after us."

Once or twice during our conversation the aunt in the corner grunted "Eh?" but most of the time she slept.

Lizzie nodded. "I set a man to watch the Little Apollo. He followed you up north, but when he lost you in Market Downham and reported you both drowned, I guessed it was a trick. I got two other men to wait at Dover. I knew you would be making for France."

"I see. You don't feel it a trifle unkind to let Sir Gregory come over here on a wild-goose chase?"

"What makes you think it is a wild-goose chase?"

She was wearing a fashionable colour, described, I believe, as "flea." It would have flattered Marie-Clarice. It made Lizzie Weldon look sallow.

"Presumably," I said, "you don't intend to let him kill me, or you'd have told him who I was at once."

"I felt I should give you a chance to choose."

"Between what?"

"Between coming back to England with me as Philippe de Lambrière or facing Sir Gregory as Mr. Roberts. I don't care what it costs me. My friends at home expected me to marry you. I told them that we were going to be married and therefore we must be married."

"Under a false name and a false personality?"

"Those are the only two things about you which strike me as real. But if you think that with so many French aristocrats pouring into England there's a risk of your being exposed, I'm quite willing to live in Italy."

"That's good of you."

"It'll be disagreeable to be set down amongst foreigners, but one can't have everything."

"I'm astonished to hear you admit that."

She stood up and crossed over to me, her arms folded, her powerful eyes looking down into mine. "And now, Philippe, I'm sorry to have to tell you that I didn't approve of your companion tonight."

"You didn't?"

"I realise it's difficult for a man of your class to tell the difference, but she isn't by our standards a gentlewoman."

"She's a countess."

"Foreign titles mean nothing. Who is she, Philippe?"

"My wife."

She fainted, so slowly that at first I didn't realise she was falling. She melted into a cloud of flea-coloured taffeta onto the carpet.

I was delighted. I could not conceive how it had not occurred to me before to tell Lizzie that I was already married. It was such an obvious solution. Had I thought of it in time we might still be at the Little Apollo theatre about to follow up Kemble's interest in me. Even Lizzie Weldon would stop short at wanting to marry a false vicomte who already had a wife. I could have wrung my own neck. It would have been so easy to have got the ingénue at the theatre to have pretended to be my wife. However, better late than never, as the old saying goes. She now thought that I had married during my brief sojourn in France and that would be the last I should hear of Lizzie Weldon.

Her aunt was still asleep in the corner, and I picked up Lizzie, dumped her on what must have been deliberately built as an uncomfortable sofa, crossed her hands on her breast, and walked out of the hotel.

Chapter 31.

M.S. was appalled by the situation. He dismissed my skilful routing of Lizzie Weldon and concentrated on old Sir Gregory Hawtrey. "You'll have to go to him and make a clean breast of it, boy, it's the only sensible thing to do. Tell him this Weldon creature's part in it: tell him it was all her fault."

"And get him to believe that a woman like her, whom he's known from her cradle, would have lost her senses over a common actor in preference to his son? You're worse than she is if you think I'd get him to believe that! Anyway, she'd deny it. She'd say she'd no idea I was an actor and that I'd palmed myself off on her as a vicomte to extract money from her. Then he'd be out to avenge her as well. One thing's certain: we'll have to keep clear of Dugazon until Hawtrey's given up the chase. He can't stay here for ever."

"It'll ruin your chances, boy. Dugazon won't give you another. I know these big men. If they do you a favour, they expect you to accept it. Excuses won't count."

"It'll ruin my chances much more to be hacked to bits by old Sir Gregory."

"I'd better write a note to Dugazon."

As usual, the child was sitting between us. She was leaning up against M.S. noisily sucking an orange. "Did you do any good in the Palais-Royal last night?" she asked.

"How could I?" I started. "Things were just going marvellously when this fool of a woman —" I broke off. The child was looking steadily at me with her blackberry eyes. "Oh, you mean did I *steal* anything? No," I lied, "I had no luck." It was my intention to return the watch and purse to Blaise.

"It's a pity my new uncle can't wear the grand clothes," she continued. "He would attend to business in the Palais-Royal and leave the ladies alone."

She anticipated my clout and dodged behind M.S.

I sat down and wrote Dugazon a note:

Dear Master,
   I beg you not to take as lack of courtesy or appreciation the fact that my manager and I are unable to accept your kind invitation to dine with you tomorrow. The illness of a relative in England calls me to a bedside I have not the heart to neglect.
   I beg you to receive me on my return.

The Puce trotted off with it to the Quai Voltaire. I was about to join M.S. on a pickpocketing foray when a note was delivered to me. It was brought by Louis, the weasel-faced chairman. It said simply, "It would be to your grave disadvantage not to attend me at the Hôtel de Muscovie immediately."

Louis could give no explanation as to how Lizzie Weldon had come by our address. He said merely that a man had stopped him and paid the price of the chair to have the note delivered. It was addressed to Monsieur le Vicomte de Lambrière."

"Boy," said M.S., "I'm coming with you. We must settle this lady once and for all."

Lizzie received us in an unbecoming morning cap. The aunt was awake. She sat beady-eyed in her corner like a malignant old parrot. Lizzie behaved as if M.S. were invisible. She spoke exclusively to me. "You lied to me about your wife. I have had the matter investigated by Louis Brissac. The woman you were with is a widow."

"Did you get her address?" I asked hopefully.

"Come to that," boomed M.S., "how did you get ours? Have you still got those plaguing spies on us?"

Lizzie ignored him. To me she said, "I merely asked Monsieur Brissac to locate you. I said that I was anxious to get in touch with you again."

"Wasn't he surprised to find that your Vicomte de Lambrière was lodging in the slums of L'Étuve?"

"Not in the least. He said that there are a number of impecunious aristocrats whose estates have long since been sold up earning their livings by trading on an old name and preying on rich women. He told me that he suspected you of being one of these from the first moment he met you at my house in England. Naturally, I disagreed with him."

M.S. and I exchanged glances. He took a step towards her. "Now look here, miss. I call it disgusting chasing a young boy. Someone like you should know better." I could see by his face that he was working up to a big speech. "You've no business to be thinking of being in love at your age. You should put on your cap and sit quiet. As I said to the boy, there's many a lady in your position takes comfort from a parrot in a cage and a nice bit of ginger-bread for tea."

Ignoring him entirely, she turned to me. "As long as Sir Gregory's in Paris, you won't be able to earn your living on the stage. It's too dangerous."

"Aren't you cutting off your nose to spite your face?" I asked with my usual flair for originality. "If Sir Gregory finds me, there'll be no Philippe."

She smiled pleasantly. "I told you once before that if I can't have you as De Lambrière I'd rather have you out of the way altogether."

"You'd rather have a dead De Lambrière than a living Roberts?"

"Without question. It's a point of pride. If De Lambrière died, it would prove to my friends that he'd been alive. I should take your body back to

England and find you a place in the family vaults. A great aunt of mine did
that once when the man she was betrothed to died."

"And you'd spend the rest of your life mourning me to the clucking
sympathy of friends."

"Certainly."

"You'd be willing to condone a murder to give birth to a myth?"

"That is correct."

I turned to M.S. "She means it. She really would prefer to have me dead
than go back to England without her Philippe."

M.S. played it differently. His voice became kind, if condescending. "Miss
Weldon, I've said some hard things to you, but I'm not sure we should hold
you responsible. It seems to me you're not right in the head. It happens to
ladies that's drawn towards love too late in life. You want a good dose of
salts and a hot ale and ginger: clearing the bowels can clear the brain."

Again she behaved as if she had not even seen him. She crossed to a
hideous sideboard and poured out a glass of wine. She handed it to me, and
I passed it to M.S. We took turns sipping it.

"The best way to avoid Sir Gregory as Roberts, Philippe, is to be in my
company as much as possible as De Lambrière. I'm sure you see the wisdom
of that. I shall be here for the next fortnight. If at the end of that time you
have not consented to marry me, I shall tell Sir Gregory that you're the
actor he's looking for. I shall naturally say that I've been your dupe all along
and he will believe everything I say and not a word that you say. You have
the choice of coming back to England with me in your own shoes or in the
excellent coffin I shall provide for you. Either way you will travel as
Philippe de Lambrière. Good morning."

Her back was turned when we left the room. She was asking the aunt
in solicitous terms if she would care for a cup of hot chocolate.

Out in the street we looked at one another. "I thought the idea was to
'settle her,' " I said nastily.

"I should never have let you have anything to do with her. I should have
kept you off Lord Credits for good and all."

"We needed the money," I reminded him. "We'd no idea it would turn
out like this."

We stopped to watch the Royal Bon Bons on manoeuvres in the Champ-
de-Mars. It was an amusing sight. I think it was supposed to be the young
Dauphin's own regiment. It consisted of toddlers in full military uniform
dragging one-pounders behind them. A large crowd was applauding the
exercise. Paris could still smile at children dressed as soldiers. It was surprising really how much Paris still found to smile at. It was a town of
absurdly changing moods. Every day there were ugly outbreaks. Apprehension in the assembly; chaos in the treasury; portable presses turning out
scandalous filth in the streets; souvenir hunters swarming over the ruins of

the Bastille; political meetings on every corner; hired assassins ready to pounce; burning barriers and overturned carriages in the Bois; threats in the air as heavy as thunder — and yet the crowd could still howl delightedly at the sight of a miniature Royal Regiment on parade.

M.S. and I walked gloomily back to L'Étuve. We were unnerved by the speed with which the police had run us to earth for Lizzie Weldon. I was only partly compensated by professional pride in having convinced Monsieur Brissac that I was a French aristocrat, however shady. There were countless De Lambrières in France and doubtless quite a few vicomtes. He must have failed to trace my particular estates and come to the conclusion that I belonged to a branch of one of those families that had lost their influence in past ages and still clung precariously to the fringe of society.

It would be pointless to try and leave Paris to avoid Lizzie Weldon. She had probably asked the Lieutenant to keep her informed of our movements. In order to escape, we should have to wait until her fortnight's stay was up, and during that time I should have to try and gain her confidence, and get her to remove her own spies.

In L'Étuve the mud was baked dust dry in the streets, and flung the heat of the day back into one's face. About twenty yards from No. 15 rue Louis d'Or we saw the cocoa seller. I marched straight up to him.

"I am the Vicomte de Lambrière," I told him. "I have just been to see an English lady in the Hôtel de Muscovie in the faubourg Saint-Germain. I was with her about half an hour. We discussed marriage. That would have taken us up to midday. And after that I spent ten minutes watching the Royal Bon Bons. It was an excellent display. I thought this information would save you a lot of trouble." I left him before he could think of a reply.

In the oven that was No. 15, the Puce was waiting for us on the stairs. It was the only cool place in the house. Flies buzzed round the orange she was sucking.

"You must have a friend in the orange business," I winced.

"Yes. It is Marie Lebrun. She gives me the ones that have gone bad at the end of the day."

She was waiting to tell us her news. It was scarcely comforting. She had delivered my note to Dugazon's sister, and the lady's reception of it had not been promising. She had only just returned from buying a capon in the market for our dinner. Her brother would neither be surprised nor pleased. He had never had any faith in the manners of Englishmen and he was not accustomed to having his appointments broken at the last moment. So much for the goodwill of Dugazon.

M.S. seemed to look on the child as a kind of partner. There was a peculiar adult bond between them. It made me feel an outsider and at the same time as if I was responsible for them as their joint bread-winning concern. Rather like a race horse on which two trainers have pinned all their hopes. He told her as fully as he was able exactly what took place with Lizzie Weldon. "So there you are, little one. Unless we get rid of her, we'll never get a stage under him. Years of training, years of marking, and an introduction to the Comédie Française all come to nothing because of a love-sick harpy with more money than is good for her."

The Puce spat out her orange pith. "She didn't believe he was married to the lady who wants to sleep with him?"

I was about to protest, but M.S. got in first. "No, girl, she found out he wasn't. More's the pity. That was about the first good idea he's had for months."

She sent me a slow and thoughtful look. "Of course, there is a way to make her believe it. He really *could* get married."

Chapter 32.

I CLICKED my tongue at the Puce. "My friend Madame de Faille is a widow, so perhaps she'll oblige."

The Puce climbed off M.S.'s lap and stalked out of our alcove with great dignity.

"Boy," said M.S., "you shouldn't upset her. At that age you take things hard. After all, she can't see inside you. You look wholesome enough from her angle."

"All that little baggage wants to do is score off some lecherous little orange seller."

"I'm not so sure. As I say, you're misleading from the outside. You be careful you don't go breaking her heart."

"I should think that would take a herculean effort."

I was dressing up in my Palais-Royal clothes.

"And where," asked M.S., "might you be going?"

"I'm going to visit Miss Eliza Weldon. I think she's right: the last place Sir Gregory will look for Actor Roberts is at the side of Lizzie Weldon. I shall cling to her like a barnacle."

"And how are we going to live while you're dancing attendance on her?"

I was tying my stock with extra care. "On Miss Eliza Weldon." It had occurred to me that with a little dexterity I might play Philippe de Lambrière by day for Lizzie and Anthony Buckland by night for Marie-Clarice.

I ran quite jauntily down the stairs. Outside, the heat and the smells struck me with the force of a prize-fighter.

A cry of "Portugal! Portugal!" drew my attention to a busty little piece with thick yellow hair. It was not until I saw the Puce in deep conversation with her that I realised that this must be Marie Lebrun. I presented myself at once.

The Puce put a proprietary hand in mine. She introduced us stiffly. "This is the gentleman, Marie, that I have consented to marry — Monsieur le Vicomte de Lambrière."

There was a look in the eyes of Marie which I should dearly have liked to challenge had I not given my promise to the Puce. I bowed coldly, and Marie's well-shaped head on its invitingly soft neck returned the compliment. It may have been poverty that had clad Marie Lebrun so scantily, but it suited her. Her blouse was tight across her breasts. Her ragged skirt with no petticoat beneath it showed the line of her thighs against the sunlight. Her arms and her legs were the colour of rich brown eggs.

Being under no obligation to disguise her interest in me, she was frank about it. She selected the best orange off her tray and held it out to me. The Puce snatched it and put it back.

"Tell Marie Lebrun that it's true that we're going to be married. She doesn't believe me when I say it."

I turned to the girl. "Why not?"

She certainly looked a good six years senior to the Puce. It was impossible to believe that she was only two months older. She put her head back and laughed until she shook. The Puce stood on tiptoe and spat at her. The laughter swiftly changed to a shower of abuse that would have done justice to Marie-Clarice. The Puce grabbed three oranges off the tray in succession and shied them at her friend's heaving bosom. Marie Lebrun sent up a howl of rage that collected at least sixteen people about us. It appeared to be her intention to strangle the Puce. She slipped the straps of her tray from her shoulders and sprang with her fingers outstretched. They were fighting like two little savages when a man caught Marie Lebrun from behind and I saw the white marks of his fingers on her brown flesh. "Cochon!" she screamed at the Puce. The oranges rolled into the feet of the crowd. "Putain!" yelled the Puce, who was still snatching up the fruits and hurling them at Marie. I got one in the ear and two in the stomach before I managed to pick up the wriggling and cursing Puce and carry her out of the fray.

"That was your fault," I said severely. "You began the whole thing."

"She laughed at me and you *did* like the look of her, I know you did."

"I didn't show it."

"No, but I heard you *thinking* it and so did she. Ooh! How I hate her, this Marie Lebrun."

"You won't get any more free oranges now, and serve you right."

She turned a surprised face towards me. "Oh, but we've had much worse fights than that. She cut open my eye once. See? — here's the scar!" She tapped her eyebrow. "And in return I bit her nose."

"Very pretty," I said. "Now, run off home, I've got an appointment."

"With the ugly lady who wants to marry you, or the one who just wants you to get into bed?"

She scuttled away at the sight of my raised hand, and I marched confidently towards the Hôtel de Muscovie.

Lizzie showed no surprise on seeing me, but she said sternly, "In future, please get here by ten o'clock. I like an escort when I'm shopping in this town of ruffians."

I ignored the order. "You've put an effective stop to my earning my living," I told her, "while Sir Gregory is combing the theatres."

"You will be well provided for once we're married."

"But until that happy hour I need food and drink like other people. I shall have to get a job as a house servant. I can act a good footman."

Even with the sun beating through the closed window she wore a light woollen shawl round her shoulders. She stood up. "You'll do no such thing. Supposing someone recognised you? You can't be seen escorting me one minute and opening doors like a lackey the next."

"Then what do you suggest?"

"That you come back to England with me at once."

"I can't."

"Why not?"

I helped myself to a glass of wine from the sideboard. "Because, my dear Miss Weldon, you've got the police interested in me. There's a cocoa seller following me all round the place."

"What cocoa seller?"

There was an unfortunate smell in the room, which had nothing to do with camphor. I soon recognised it as Lizzie's chosen brand of scent. Trust Lizzie, in a city that prided itself on delicious perfumes, to choose something reminiscent of cats.

"He's one of the Lieutenant's agents. You must have convinced him I'm up to no good."

"You're not seriously suggesting that you wouldn't be allowed to leave the country?"

"I shouldn't get past the first barrier. There's only one hope of getting me back to England."

"What's that?"

"You'll have to tell your Lieutenant of Police friend the truth. You'll have to admit that I'm only a common actor and that you're so enamoured of me that you're willing to pay me to play a vicomte."

"Never!" She stood in front of me. Even she was obliged to fan herself in the heat of that room, but she didn't remove the shawl. "Confess to someone who knows my father that I've taken an interest in an *actor*!"

"Well, then, don't *ever* go to the police about me again. And you had better tell Sir Gregory that you've had word from the Little Apollo that the actor he's looking for was drowned with his manager in Norfolk."

She sat down, batting colourless eyelashes at me. I was happy to see that my thrusts had gone home. I said comfortably, "In the meantime the only sensible thing to do is to play De Lambrière until Sir Gregory gives up his search, but I'm afraid I can't afford it."

"What do you mean?"

"I've no money and, thanks to you, no chance of earning any."

Her fingers ran up and down her closed fan. "I might see my way to making you a small allowance."

"You'll have to see your way to making me a thumping big one. Squiring a lady round Paris is a costly business — unless you want people to think that your intended is a penniless adventurer. Nothing excites suspicion so much in this place as having no money. My De Lambrière wardrobe was never very extensive, you know, and it's getting shabby. I can't wear my Buckland suit as a Frenchman and I think I ought to move out of the slums: that too is inclined to look a curious address for a landed gentleman. Then I shall need money for chairs and carriages — You didn't bring your own, did you?" She shook her head. "And there will be the everyday expenses of entertaining you, as well as my own living allowance."

She stood up and walked up and down between the window and the fire. The aunt's eyes followed her like the pendulum of a clock. I winked at the old harridan and for a moment I thought she was about to fly off her perch and peck me.

Lizzie came to a halt in front of me. "How long would this have to continue?"

"Until the police and Sir Gregory lose interest in me and let me go back to England."

"I told you I would only give you a fortnight to make up your mind."

From having wanted to get rid of her as quickly as possible, I had now changed to thinking that it might be in my interests to prolong her stay. I had decided to extract every penny I could from Lizzie Weldon. It would help towards our fares to America.

"I shall need a month," I told her.

"But I may tell my father and friends that we're going to be married?"

This request was beginning to have a familiar ring to me. "Yes," I told Lizzie. "By all means. But I should like you to realise that if you go on asking the police to check my movements, you'll make it quite impossible for me ever to return to England with you. Also, you mustn't set spies on me yourself. It will look as if you don't trust me, either."

"I've already dismissed the men I had following you. They went home last week."

"Good. Don't employ any more or you'll get me clapped in prison."

She asked a little pathetically, "But how am I going to trust you? How do I know that you won't try and escape if I've got no one keeping an eye on you?"

It was an excellent point, because of course she could not trust me. I had every intention of doing just what she feared. In a month I should be able to take enough money off her to get myself and M.S. across to America, which, with the police no longer reporting our movements to her, shouldn't be too difficult. In the meantime we should live comfortably and I could buy the Puce some shoes.

I shrugged. "My dear Miss Weldon, lack of confidence is a very bad basis for marriage. I'm afraid you'll have to get into the habit of considering me trustworthy for your own peace of mind."

The poor woman looked quite trapped. "You'll devote yourself exclusively to me? You won't leave my side?"

"Not in the daytime," I assured her. "I presume you don't want me with you at night?"

The colour leapt into her face, contrasting sadly with her flea-shaded dress. It was curious that Lizzie's features and eyes ought to have compared favourably with Marie-Clarice's. She had much better material on which to work, yet she managed to create a pease-pudding effect, whereas Marie-Clarice, with far less to start with, was — well, it's no good trying to understand those feminine riddles. Something to do with being French, I suppose.

Her neck had gone pink as well. I was interested to see that her unshakable calm had at last crumbled. "Philippe, it must be quite understood — really *quite* understood — that there's no advantage taken of me before marriage. I mean, a person of my breeding could never consent to — to — well, become your mistress."

I had to pounce on my pleased expression. I shot it off my face in favour of a hang-dog look. "It's rather a hard bargain," I told her glumly. "That sort of liberty gets taken regularly these days."

"Not amongst gentlefolk. You'll have to give me your word to guard my reputation."

"Very well," I said a shade too quickly. "I'll see to it that I'm never in your company after nine o'clock at night."

"What will you do when you've left me?"

"Oh, I shall buy books on form and etiquette and study them. I mustn't give away my low origin by letting you down in public." She nodded to the good sense in that. "Also," I added casually, making a rapid calculation of the places in which I was most likely to run into Marie-Clarice, "we'll have to be careful where we go. There are certain spots where I'm known as Buckland. We'll have to avoid the Palais-Royal."

"I wouldn't set foot in that abominable place. One doesn't wish to meet vulgar creatures such as you were with the other night."

"Quite," I said smugly. "We shouldn't go anywhere too fashionable in case I'm recognised. The Tuileries wouldn't be wise, but the Luxembourg Gardens should be safe. We must keep off the boulevards and we can't risk the opera or theatres."

"In that case," she observed sharply, "it's not going to cost you very much to entertain me."

One has to grant Lizzie Weldon that she was never astern for long. "I agree with you," I said: "it's going to take most of your allowance to keep up appearances myself."

"How much do you think you will need?"

I sat down with my head in my hands, trying to look as if I had not previously worked it all out. "There'll be clothes, lodgings, food, servants' wages —"

"Servants!"

"Do you want me to wait at my own table when we ask your friends to dine?" She was silent. "Then there'll be a certain amount of local transportation. It would be somewhat infra dig to be seen calling for you on foot. There'll be flowers and presents for you — I can't insult you by coming empty-handed — yes, I'm afraid it's going to come out rather costly." I gave her my "sincerity" smile. "Or would you prefer me to release you from our betrothal and go home without me?"

"I would not."

"Well, then, let's see . . . it's difficult to work out on the spur of the moment, but I should think five hundred francs would move me from L'Étuve."

"I should think twenty would do it, as you've nothing to move."

"But I must have something in hand — there's my clothes and new lodgings."

"You can present me with the account for your rent at the end of the week, and gentlemen are not expected to pay their tailors as if they were beggars at the kitchen door."

"But I haven't a sou."

"Then forty francs should seem a handsome sum to you until you present me with legitimate bills for the expenses you incur."

Some of my bounce was ebbing away. "What shall I do for ready money?"

"You'll have it given to you every morning according to your needs. Providing, of course, you can convince me of them." She went to her purse and counted out forty francs.

Chapter 33.

I WAS not quite so cock-a-hoop when I left her. But I cheered myself up. After all, I had a whole month to subject her to the melting tactics of my eyebrows and eye-play, my lingering looks and my smiles. If I couldn't get enough out of her for our fares to America in that time, I deserved to marry her.

On the way back to L'Étuve I stopped and bought the child a pair of shoes. They were a dainty green leather with a little steel buckle in the shape of a shell. I had to make a guess at the size, but they seemed to me slender and small enough.

She was sitting with M.S. on the step in the ancient passageway. She was seldom from his side. They reminded me of a picture I had seen of a shark and its pilot fish.

I intended the shoes as a farewell gift. There was no question in my mind of taking her with us when we moved. The sooner she forgot us, the better. Let her marry the first man who gave her a Marie Lebrun look when she was gonflée and pray God he didn't come from L'Étuve.

I dangled the shoes in front of her. "Look! If they don't fit we can go back and change them."

She jumped up, open-mouthed and silent. Then she snatched them out of my hand and ran up the street.

I told M.S. my plans. "Well, boy," he said, "let's hope you can handle her, but take care she doesn't handle you."

"The thing to do," I said, "is to get into new rooms at once. The boulevard du Temple's supposed to be the smartest place: we ought to try there before anywhere else."

We stacked up our few possessions, arranged with the Lapins to have them sent on later, and settled our account. I left enough money to buy extra food for the Puce and took care to entrust it to the grandfather and not his mistress. I put Blaise's watch and purse in my pocket. I intended to return them to him as soon as possible.

Outside No. 15 we found the Puce chattering excitedly to Marie Lebrun. There might never have been a cross word exchanged between them, never mind blows. The Puce had on the left shoe, and Marie Lebrun was trying to squeeze a much larger foot into the right one. There were squeals of delight and admiration. The Puce had gone up in the eyes of her friend.

She ran up to us. "Where are you going?"

M.S. patted her head. "We're going to find somewhere nice to live, dear, and when we do we'll send for you and you can come and look after us."

She sent a dubious glance in my direction. Women are apt to mistrust me. "How do I know you'll come back?"

"Because uncle has promised," he said reproachfully.

"But what time will you come?" she demanded.

"Well, we must find somewhere by six o'clock," said M.S., "or we'll have to come here for the night."

This seemed to satisfy her. She settled herself on the step with her shoes in her lap. "I shall sit here until you come back."

"You'll have a long wait," I said. "It's only just midday."

"I shall catch all my fleas while you're gone," she explained. "I don't want to take them to the new place and I'll only get more if I go back inside."

"You shouldn't let her think she can come with us," I told M.S. "Her grandfather wouldn't allow it."

"But my pig-grandmother will be so pleased to see me go she will make him say yes. Uncle!" she jumped up and clung to M.S. "You promise? You *will* come back for me? I shall wait here all night. I shall not go inside."

He patted her cheek. "Yes, I promise."

She sat down again with the shoes on her knees. M.S. waved cheerily to her, but I hadn't the heart to look back.

We found lodgings in the rue Matignon. It was a very pleasant street with elegant buildings and well-set-out gardens. Our house was older than most, but had pleasant green shutters and yellow sun blinds. It was owned by a Madame Brissot, who told the porter to show us the vacant rooms. It was quite exciting to look out on trees again; a soft wind would play in their leaves at night and bring us the smell of the grass after rain. I hadn't realised how much I had misssed air in L'Étuve.

The porter, whose name was Riche, opened the windows. "There are very fine views, monsieur," he said. "And we have nothing but excellent persons living near by."

The rooms were modern and nicely appointed. They were far from cheap, but that was Lizzie Weldon's business. The salon was a restful pale blue, and the wallpaper was sprigged with small flowers. The chandeliers shone and so did the furniture. The two bedrooms led off it at each end. No. 21 rue Matignon was a palace after L'Étuve.

I arranged for the porter's wife to feed us until we had made other arrangements. At half past five I locked M.S. into the small bedroom at the end. He rapped on the door, calling loudly, "Boy! Something's gone wrong with this plaguey lock."

"Nothing's gone wrong with it," I said. "It's working beautifully. You're going to stay behind it until I get your promise that you won't go and scrape up that child again."

"But, boy — !" he said. "I gave my word that we'd go back for her. She's waiting for us."

"That's your fault. I never wanted her in the first place. We'll have enough trouble looking after ourselves."

He rattled the handle fiercely and his great shoulder shivered the door in its frame. "But she'll sit there all night — it'll break her heart."

"You shouldn't have made such a ridiculous promise. We might have to run at any moment and then what in the world should we do with her?"

"She could always go back to the Lapins," he said, "and it would give her a nice little taste of life."

"No!" I said firmly. "You stay there till I get your promise. No supper, no breakfast, no lunch, and no tea!"

He was quiet for an hour and then called plaintively, "Boy, I've got nothing to put in me pipe. Just run down to the tobacconist and get me some."

"So that you can shout for help? No," I said, "not me."

He was a stubborn old devil. He stayed there the night. In the morning he was glum and sour-eyed. "Very well," he said. "I give you my promise, but you've come a long way from the lad I used to know."

I took him by the coat lapels. "Now, let's put an end to this new character of yours. I'm what you brought me up to be, no better and no worse. We've let people down before and we'll let them down again. We know what we are and we mustn't forget it. Let's not make the mistake of confusing ourselves."

He shook my hands off his coat. "I looked on that child as one of us. She was a good little marker right from the start."

"If you want to be kind to her, leave her where she is. She knows what she's in for there, and she's got used to it. Before you go offering a home to every stray kitten you come across, you ought to remember that you haven't got one yourself."

He gave me his word again that he would not fetch her. But he turned his back on me.

I spent an exceedingly pleasant day. In the Palais-Royal I went to the tailor who had begged me to put myself in his hands and bought the waterproof frock coat. I was fitted for two other suits, one in fawn velvet with silver froggings, the other in brocade with a red and gold stripe. I ordered a silversmith to start working on a cane head, and I acquired a gold and enamel snuff box from Boehmer and Bassange. From the same court jewellers I bought M.S. a tortoise-shell watch and an alarming set of coat buttons with horrid little pictures of Paris inside. I knew they would please him enormously. I spent an hour in the most fashionable print shop; then I bought six silver table knives in case we were asked out to dine. One thing had not changed since M.S.'s literary idol wrote his *Gentleman's Guide* to France: one was still expected to provide one's own knives and forks.

I was humming happily when I arrived at the Hôtel de Muscovie that evening clutching a small bouquet for Lizzie. I found old Sir Gregory Hawtrey with her.

"Ah!" he said, "just the fellow. Come and add your influence to mine. I'm trying to persuade Miss Weldon and her aunt to come home with me at once."

"Why deprive Paris of so much charm?" I enquired as I lowered my bouquet into Lizzie's lap and kissed her cold finger tips.

"My dear De Lambrière, you should know better than anyone the state your country's in. Taking that dashed dungeon place has given the people no end of encouragement. God knows what they'll get up to next."

"They're knocking it down," said Lizzie, "and selling the stones for souvenirs. I only hope the authorities have the good sense to rebuild it at once."

"There isn't any authority left," said Sir Gregory, "and certainly no good sense. I was at a meeting of the National Assembly this morning, and I tell you, there's considerable tension."

"There always is, but there's no need for Miss Weldon to bother her pretty little head," I assured him.

"I say that Paris is not safe for two English ladies alone: these people are bent on murder. That's why I want Miss Weldon and her aunt to leave. Do you realise that the King's own brother — your Comte d'Artois — and the Queen's friend, the Duchesse de Polignac, have already *fled*? Surely that shows you there's cause for alarm?"

"Have you," I asked him, "given up the search for that actor you suspect?"

"No," he said. "But I went to the Comédie Française again and that rude fellow I saw before showed me a letter from him. He's gone back to England because a relation is ill. I'm surprised he had sufficient decency to bother about the ailing. I shall go after him at once and I'm blessed if I can see what's to stop Miss Weldon from coming with me."

"I can," I thought. "Somebody's got to stay here and pay for that frock coat and all those little luxuries I've indulged in this morning. And somebody's got to pay our fares to America. Miss Weldon can go when it's convenient to *us* for a change."

"Lizzie," I suggested, "don't you think we ought to tell Sir Gregory the truth?"

She kept calm in spite of the fact that she obviously supposed that I was going to confess to being Roberts and therefore expose her to Sir Gregory. She said without emotion, "I don't think there's any need for that, Philippe."

I wanted to keep her on tenterhooks. "Surely," I argued, "it's better to make a clean breast of everything to Sir Gregory. After all, at the worst he can only run me through."

He put his clean, puzzled smile on me. "I've always had the highest regard for you, De Lambrière. I can't imagine myself wanting to challenge you."

"Oh, you might!" I said, "you might, when you hear what Lizzie and I have to tell you."

Lizzie was suffering, but she disguised it well. "I should advise you against it, Philippe."

"But, my dear, I was only going to tell Sir Gregory we were betrothed."

Out shot that poor man's generous hand at once. "De Lambrière, I congratulate you, and" — he paused a second — "let me add that if my boy were here he would wish you well too."

I could hardly take his hand.

"Will you be settling in France, Lizzie?" he asked.

"No," she said firmly. "We're living in England. As soon as Philippe can tidy up his affairs and estates."

"Splendid! Splendid! We should celebrate. Will you dine with me in the Palais-Royal this evening? We'll go to the Salon de Beauvilliers — we might make up a party of friends."

I said quickly, "Why don't you both come and dine with me?"

I wondered what Madame Riche would provide for us. I had no time to warn her. I muttered something about having to make allowances for our just having moved in and also wondered how to explain M.S. to old Hawtrey. I thought perhaps he had better play my valet again. Lizzie could hardly give him away.

When we arrived at No. 21 rue Matignon I was reassured to find that there was a good smell coming up from the kitchen. Madame Riche was an excellent cook. There was just time to signal M.S. and he grasped the situation at once. He became an obsequious manservant and I could see that Lizzie was greatly relieved. She approved of the rooms and all was going well until dinnertime.

It was when we were seated at the table that I got the shock. The Puce came in carrying a pot au feu. I could show no signs of surprise, of course, and M.S. made a face when I stared at him. He was trying to tell me it wasn't his fault.

Lizzie said. "Really, Philippe, how can you allow that little creature to wait with no shoes?"

As soon as I could I ran down to the kitchen. The child rounded on me at once. "Another time let me know when you're bringing home two guests for dinner. It's just as well I stole a few things on my way through L'Étuve or there wouldn't be enough to go round."

"Suzon," I said, "how did you get here?"

"Walked."

"I didn't imagine you swam. I mean, how did you know where to come?"

"I asked the cocoa seller," she replied.

Chapter 34.

LIZZIE SENT me a note in the morning. "Get rid of that disreputable old man and substitute a proper valet. Also dismiss that wretched little creature without any shoes. I prefer you to have mature and respectable women about your household. Also tidy up your affairs as soon as possible. I wish to leave France."

I replied in the same terse tone. "Wouldn't dream of getting rid of old man. Mother and father told me. As for creature without shoes, *can't* get rid of her. You try. Only way to leave France is for you to confess to Lieutenant of Police and vouch for me as an actor." I knew she would be weeks trying to conquer her pride enough to do this, and I should have plenty of time to melt her into supplying the fares to America. In the meantime I settled down to enjoy myself.

I quickly found out the fashionable round of a gentleman's life. One had one's coffee on waking, and one sent for the barber. When one was powdered and queued, one got dressed and sauntered out. It was wise to be seen in Didot's book shop studying a few classics, and after that one should drop in at a few well-chosen salons.

It was not enough to be accepted for good blood alone. It was preferable to be received by some celebrity or some personality in the news. Talent was exceedingly popular — a painter, distinguished writer, scientist, or inventor was essential to one's visiting list. One mustn't be caught dead with an actor, of course.

Conversational standards were undoubtedly high, particularly amongst the women. It wasn't sufficient to have a beautiful face and figure. The successful coquette must have brains as well. Without those she was in danger of committing one of the most unpardonable offences in France: becoming a bore.

Apart from the fact that the cult of collecting good minds was exacting, it made for enjoyment, and there was certainly none of the crushing dullness one met with in English drawing rooms — women simpering and relying on curls for effect and men talking of nothing but horses and blood sports. Politics and "schisms" are preferable to those I find. One never left those salons without feeling alive. There was always stimulation of some sort — whether from pleasure or annoyance.

If you could not boast of any particular talent or distinction, the best substitute to aim for was wit. If that was beyond you, you fell back on being caustic. A cynic could not be a bore. If you had no opinions, you stayed at home simply through not being invited out. To be democratic was also essential. You must deplore feudalism and mock tradition. You must sneer at everything including yourself, and it was absolutely inexcusable not to be angry about something. Complacency or content were social death knells. You could say anything however outrageous providing it wasn't reactionary. Above all, you must run down the Queen, the court, and the clergy.

Youth was in love with defiance. It was fashionable to be "against," and looking back, it seems incredible to have watched those young aristocratic idiots so persistently drawing up their own death warrants; screaming for a liberty they had always possessed and which they thought could be transferred to others like a scrap from their plates to a begging dog. Yes, to look back is appalling — intellectual depravity mixed with glorious progression of thought both marching ahead of wisdom.

The only slight irritation I felt in those happy days was the occasional sight of the cocoa seller. I questioned Lizzie about it. "You *have* called the police agents off me, haven't you?"

She said, "Oh yes, dearest Philippe. I trust you now." But she said it too meekly and it left me uneasy.

Every evening I dined dutifully with Lizzie, never failing to take her a little gift, tactfully leaving the bills under an ormolu horror on the hall table. The aunt dined early and there was never any trouble getting Lizzie to look into my eyes. My seductive machinery was working well. She showed signs of becoming exceedingly pliant. Smiles did wonders, hand-holding did even more, and my first kiss nearly got us halfway to America.

It was not a pleasant experience. She went rigid in my arms, nearly fainted, and then wept softly. When she finally wiped her eyes she whispered, "Philippe, you'd be happy with me, I promise you that. I love you as I've never loved anyone in my life before. I lie awake at night thinking of you. I shall do everything possible once we're married to see you don't regret your decision. There'll be no more adoring and willing wife, Philippe. I shall be quite different to what I am now when I've got what I wanted."

I was doubtful about this but I kissed her again, and when I left she pressed a hundred francs into my hand. "Buy something you want for yourself, Philippe, to remind you how much I love you."

I gave fifty to M.S. for his box and kept the rest for my nightly visits to the Palais-Royal in search of Marie-Clarice. I had tried asking for her address in the Café de Valois, but from the cold look on the waiter's face I gathered that it was not their practice to give information about their clientèle.

My only hope was to run into her accidentally. Night after night I sat waiting for her. I was seldom home before the diligences started rolling through the streets on their way to the outlying towns, but the Puce and M.S. always sat up for me.

I had to admit that the child looked after us expertly. Where she learned her housewifery I'm sure I don't know. She could have got no experience in L'Étuve. It must have been born in her with that instinct peculiar to the French. She had not forgiven me for leaving her behind. She knew about my locking M.S. in his room, and to show her disapproval of me she spoilt him atrociously. She filled his pipe, mended his clothes, cleaned his shoes, and was careful to see that all the best that was going in the food line came his way and not mine. I might not have been the provider at all. I was kept waiting while his soup was reheated, and anything I ordered was promptly cancelled in favour of something he preferred. She had the French house-wife's hard eye on the economic side, too. She was waiting with her hand out as soon as I got home from Lizzie. "My new uncle's box for America, if you please."

M.S. was teaching her to write and read English and she was doing well except for her accent. But her morals had not improved. "You should go further with this ugly lady if she pays a hundred francs for a kiss. You must stroke her and breathe hard — like this," and she gave an exhibition that fluttered the pages of the play M.S. was trying to read.

"Good God," I said, "she'd think I'd got a constriction of the lungs."

"That is how Marie Lebrun says men blow over her when they're after her body."

"Have I your permission, then," I asked, "to go after Miss Weldon's body?"

"Well, you must just make her think that you do, and then be too honour-able to take it. She'll pay you more for that."

"This child's outlook on life," I complained to M.S., "is outrageous. Can't you do something about it?"

He looked at me over the new spectacles I had bought him in the rue St. Honoré. "I don't think so, boy, she sees too much of you."

She had two dresses now and a good thick cloak. But she still refused to put on the shoes. "I might spoil them," she said. "My feet are still hard — but at night I put them in hot water. They'll soon be softer."

I could not help being touched by her awed excitement at having a room of her own. She spent every spare minute cleaning and polishing it. "As soon as my new uncle has taught me to write, I shall send a letter to Marie Lebrun and ask her to come and take chocolate with me. We will sit at my own little table and I'll show her all my things."

"But she won't be able to read what you've written," I protested.

She said gleefully, "The letter writer will have to do that. Then the whole of L'Étuve will know of my splendid circumstances."

She was rounding out considerably on her own good cooking at the rue Matignon. A few more hundred francs from Lizzie and she would be gonflée. As it was, the blue patches had gone from beneath her eyes, and her hair, although still short and boyish, was fluffy from contact with water and soap. I was surprised to observe that in her quaint almost Chinese way the Puce was about to be pretty.

The little fiend sensed that I had not been able to see Marie-Clarice. She smiled happily whenever I came in looking dejected. "Perhaps the lady who gave me the six-sol piece has run away," she said, "like the other aristocrats. They say there is going to be trouble. Lots of rich people are leaving France."

The suggestion shocked me. I hadn't thought of that as a solution.

M.S. never let me off without two hours' rehearsal a day. We ran through all our old Apollo productions as closely as we could from memory, and M.S. bought as many French-play copies as we could find, and we had of course his own volume of Shakespeare's works, which he would have held up to keep dry even if he himself had been drowning.

He trained the Puce to take small parts. He repeated her lines over to her again and again, but she wasn't above putting a spark into them that was all her own. M.S. was immensely pleased with her. "I won't say she's got what you had at her age, boy, but she's not without something."

I suspected that he was merely working up an excuse to take her to America with us and forebore to let him see that I was impressed. Nevertheless, I realised that the Puce was by no means without talent and she was a great comfort to M.S. While I was working on Lizzie Weldon, I think he spent most of the time talking theatre to her. He made a small cardboard stage with cut-out figures and spent hours explaining the technicalities. When I was not present they staged their own productions, each taking the lines of the cut-out figures. It gave him something to do, made him feel that he was still in touch, and for that I was immeasurably grateful to the child. On Lizzie's personal allowance to me I should think he must have taken her to see every play in Paris. I was glad of this because it was imperative that one of us should be keeping up with the new productions.

In their spare time they toddled to the market together, browsed round the book shops, and once they waited for hours in the rain to see the King and Queen dining in public. A less diverting form of entertainment I was unable to imagine. But M.S. was elated by the sight of the female half of the "Lord's anointed." "Boy! That's a glorious woman! There's one that's truly marked queen."

The Puce's only comment was, "She gobbles her food."

It was pleasant to get in at night and hear all their little daily doings. There was a cosy family atmosphere prevailing in No. 21 rue Matignon which I admit I enjoyed to the full. In some ways I thought it a pity that it could not last. But in others I was anxious to get over to America and try and retrieve my career again. The life of a gentleman, however tempting, could never be a permanency for me.

I foresaw that at the rate Lizzie Weldon was succumbing to my attentions the time for our departure was drawing quite close. She was besotted with me. In our drives out to St. Cloud and Vincennes it was a struggle to get her to take an interest in the countryside. She kept her eyes on me with a soaking adoration that left me damp from embarrassment. I felt wet all over from those dewy looks. She was either waiting for my next compliment or harping on the last in an effort to get me to assure her that it had been genuine. There were dangerous moments when I thought that the opposite of the Puce's forecast was going to be proved correct. Far from gaining me esteem and more money, my honourable restraint nearly earned me a conquest. The caressing of forbidden areas and the snorting over her to convey lust all but transported me into her bed. What is worse, I feared she would offer her favours for nothing. The more I said that I felt constrained to take no advantage of her, owing to my great respect for her, the more she wept at my nobility. There was hardly a dry spot between us.

But on one memorable Wednesday she mentioned the sum of a thousand francs. She was in a particularly mushy stage of her infatuation for me, and a little heavy breathing on my part stoked up her passion.

"Philippe," she said when recovery had made speech possible, "I'm so afraid sometimes that you'll hate me for — for — well, for giving you money."

"My dear, you must never think such a thing," I said hastily.

"But men don't like women doling their money out to them, do they? They prefer to be independent."

I was quick to seize on this. "Well," I said, "there's no doubt that it would be less humiliating to have a lump sum in hand — so that I didn't have to bother you for every sou. I should certainly feel more of a man like that, and I could always give you an account of how it's spent."

"Well, then, dearest Philippe, that's what we'll do. I'll give you a letter of credit for a thousand francs on my friend and banker Van de Niver."

"I'll get you a pen and paper," I said pleasantly, but she put out a hand to restrain me.

"Not now, dearest Philippe, another time will do." She went the colour of a peony, closed her eyes, and pushed her lips out. I gathered that she wished to be kissed again, and, closing my own eyes, I acquiesced. I should bring up the thousand-francs subject the following morning. But I had no chance.

That evening Marie-Clarice reappeared in the Palais-Royal. She was with a party of friends, and I went straight up to her. "You've no idea," I told her, "what a relief this is. I thought you'd joined the stream of émigrés who have left the country."

She said coldly, "As I've always been in strong sympathy with the cause of the people and done quite a bit in my own small way to further it, I'm hardly likely to desert when it looks like achieving success."

"Marie-Clarice," twittered the brunette I had seen her with before, "is a great friend of Camille Desmoulins."

"She likes all her politics pale, male, and underfed," complained Cyprien.

"She's desperately against the court," said the brunette. "Didn't you know that?"

"There hasn't been a court to be 'for' for years," Marie-Clarice corrected her. "There's only been a quite impossible clique, and there's no reason why Monsieur Buckland should be acquainted with me, Rosalie: we hardly know each other."

"To my infinite sorrow," I said gallantly.

"That's not how it struck me the last time. If you remember, you shed my company somewhat abruptly."

"It wasn't my choice."

"It was still rather pointed."

I sat down without invitation. Towards the end of the evening I managed to snatch a few words with her. "The woman you saw me with the other night followed me over from England. The sole reason I came here was to get away from her."

"I'm not interested where you go or who comes after you, Monsieur Buckland."

"That's not true and we both know it. Let me get to know you and prove that it isn't the old, the rich, and the plain who attract me. Or are you afraid of me?"

She accepted the challenge. "I'm not afraid of anyone, Monsieur Buckland. You may attend my toilette if you like. It takes place every morning at ten o'clock, but I should get there in good time. It's rather like a royal accouchement, I have so many visitors."

"Your address, madame?"

"Hôtel de Faille, rue du Bac."

The Hôtel de Faille was enormous. A great wall like a prison's ran round in front of it, and above it one could see the eaves of the granary on the topmost part of the house. There was some sort of haulage of fodder going on. A notice in exquisite lettering read, "Parlez au Suisse." It's curious that one got no sense of foreboding looking at those words.

There was nothing old-fashioned about the Hôtel de Faille. Anything antique was démodé, heirlooms were ridiculed, and traditions mocked. The attics were full, I was told, of priceless tapestries, and furniture going back to Louis XIII. What the late Comte de Faille would have thought, no one seemed to care. His tastes had been as effectively obliterated as his memory.

I was shown to an exquisite little anteroom. A maid handed me an odd-looking article. It was a toilet cloak to protect my clothing. It tied round the front like a child's bib.

At ten o'clock Marie-Clarice put her head round the door. Her hair was loose and a fine soft red. She wore a lilac-coloured négligée. "I've restricted the numbers to you today. I thought it would be easier to talk."

In her boudoir a chair was pulled up for me. She sat herself in front of a mirror and told me, "I'm expecting the Marquis."

"I thought you'd restricted the numbers to me."

She laughed. "Oh, he isn't a guest, he's an honour. You've no *idea* how difficult he is to get. I forget now who gave him the title — the Comte de Provence, I believe. It was to tell him apart from his brother, the 'chevalier,' but he's just a barber: he only *cuts*."

A small Gascon was shown in as if he were God. He was as neat as a little moorhen with about as much brain. I've never seen such arrogance! He deigned to say good morning to neither of us. It was the Queen's hair-dresser — Leonard! Marie-Clarice jumped up. "How *good* of you! How *good* of you to come!"

He deposited a large green umbrella in the corner of the room and advanced upon her. He ran strands of her hair through his fingers as if it might give him the pox. He wiped his hands on a silk scarf and muttered, "It is like hay, madame."

But what theatre when he set to work! If she moved when he wanted her still, he struck her head with his golden comb. There was silence until he wished to talk.

"I trust you've been well, madame?"

"Yes, thank you, Leonard."

"How was your coiffure last time?"

"The envy of all my friends."

"Of course."

More silence until he chose to speak.

His combs were laid round him like delicate instruments, and he had a deadly pair of crimping tongs.

"Things are dreadful," he sighed, "simply dreadful! There's nothing in the treasury, nothing in the King's privy purse. I always say they should never have let Necker go. You know, he spent some of his own money trying to put things right, and the Queen really *is* economising. She's had two dresses made over again. I ask you! The Queen of France! I was only saying to Madame Bertin —"

"That's the Queen's dressmaker," said Marie-Clarice: "she's mine as well." I gathered that this was a triumph equal to acquiring the services of this prissy little king of curls. He gave her a cold look for her interruption.

"I was saying, what a terrible pass things have come to."

"A worldly observation," I offered.

"Well, it's their own fault," said Marie-Clarice.

I asked, "Why is the Queen so unpopular?"

"Oh, chiefly because she's an Austrian, but also because she's a fool. She's alienated the old school to such an extent that they wouldn't fish her out of a pond if she fell in, and her new friends have got her a fearful reputation."

"It's always been a great sadness to me," Leonard breathed, "that Madame de Faille is not accepted at court."

"Why?" I asked Marie-Clarice.

"I was estranged from my husband before he died. Women separated from their husbands aren't allowed near the sacred person of the Queen. You may have lovers and giggle about them with her — everyone knows her unspeakable favourite, the Polignac woman, was practically sleeping upside down with that pox-ridden creole — but somebody separated, oh dear, no!"

Leonard's skill was undoubtedly considerable. He went up on his toes as he rolled a curl. "You know, they were saying that the Princesse de Lamballe was sleeping with Monsieur d'Artois?"

"How absurd, Leonard! That bowl of bread and milk couldn't sleep with a male moth in her room, never mind D'Artois."

I saw the purpose of the make-up cloak. Leonard brought out the powder shooter and the room hung in a busy white cloud. How he got any on her hair at all I don't know. "The Queen quite fell out with La Lamballe," he said. "The Duchesse de Polignac certainly won. They used to make faces about the Lamballe behind her back, and when she came into the toilette the Queen sighed and sighed and sighed, and Madame de Polignac nearly choked with laughter."

On and on and on it went: senseless chatter about nothing important and nearly every word of it barbed. Leonard made a record number of slanderous remarks between curling and powdering. When it was all over, Marie-Clarice served him with chocolate herself.

In the background the bed hung in a mist of embroidered muslin. Gilded flowers climbed up its posts, and it had not yet been made. I noticed the way she must slip out of her sheets, hardly disturbing them at all.

She let Leonard kiss her hand when he took his leave.

"What an appalling little man," I broke out when he'd gone.

"Yes, isn't he pitifully boring?"

"Then why do you let him talk?"

"Because if I didn't he'd tell my friends it was *I* who was boring."

"Would that matter?"

"Yes. I should lose all my friends."

"From the sound of them, that wouldn't be much of a loss."

"You're not, I hope, a prude?" she asked. She was swaying before me, her tongue on her lips. It was as pink-tipped as her small satin shoes. She did several little steps and smiled at me. "Are you fond of dancing? There's a masked ball at the opera house tomorrow."

"Even if I wasn't fond of dancing, I'd be there," I said.

She slipped off the shoes and walked back to the bed. She stretched her arms over her head. "I'm tired of all this, I'm having it changed. What colour curtains do you think would suit me best?"

"It depends on what you wear in bed."

"That depends on who's with me."

There was nothing coy about her, nothing mincing. She swung herself on to the bed and lay down. I advanced a little cautiously. I wasn't quite certain how far I might go.

She put a hand out and picked up a watch. "If you're bothered about how long we've known each other, it's just two hours and five minutes, counting the time you couldn't spare me the other night."

I leaned over her, enjoying the fresh smell of her flesh. She was still using the lily-scented soap. Then I caught sight of the watch she was holding and my knees gave. It was the one I'd removed from her brother's pocket, and beside it lay his purse.

I straightened up, my eyes still on them. They mesmerised me.

"What are you staring at?" she asked.

"I was just interested in that old watch. It's very fine."

"Yes. It belonged to my father. It's Blaise's now. He had it stolen the other night with his purse."

"But — how did he — how did he get them back?"

"The police brought them."

"The *police*!" I shouted.

She sat up, her hand to her throat. "Monsieur Buckland, do you usually scream at the top of your voice in a woman's bedroom? Blaise lives here with me, but he is away at the moment, so they brought them to me."

My voice became stuck in my throat. "I — I'm sorry," I stammered when I'd recovered it. "I — it's just — er — did the police say where they'd come across them?"

"No. They were rather funny about it. They said they didn't want to make an arrest. They wanted to keep their man in sight."

"What for?" I snapped.

"My dear Monsieur Buckland, I really don't know. But you could always find out by going to the police office."

I tried to pull myself together. "It's just that I admire their efficiency so much. They seem so clever that one wonders why, if they know who the thief is, they don't arrest him?"

"Would you prefer us to go down to the salon and have a really long discussion about it?" she enquired politely.

"No, no, of course not. It's just that I —"

"I'm not inflicting my company on you, am I?"

"No, I assure you."

She lay back expectantly, her eyes holding mine. I couldn't do much more than totter towards her. I had left that watch with the purse in the pocket of the suit I had worn from L'Étuve. They were in the closet at No. 21 rue Matignon. How and when could the police have extracted them? All the fire in my blood had died down. I had no more desire than a day-old chicken. The only physical action I felt capable of was running absurdly all the way home to make sure that I had really lost those two objects.

Marie-Clarice asked in a softly dangerous voice, "You're not regretting your decision to call on me, are you, Monsieur Buckland?"

I shook my head desperately, but could think of no excuse for my complete inability to take advantage of her charms. It would be useless to try and I knew it.

I said stupidly, "Wouldn't it ruin that elaborate toilet to go to bed so soon after you've got up?"

For a second or two her eyes went dead. Then she put out a hand and rang for her maid. "I am determined to take this as a compliment," she said. "I am obviously not old enough, not rich enough, and not plain enough for you."

Her voice was still soft and acutely polite. "I never," she added, "wish to set eyes on you again." And the flat of her hand flashed out and caught me smartly across the face.

Chapter 35.

I RAN nearly all the way back to the rue Matignon. Absurdly I looked in the pocket of my suit. But, needless to say, there was no sign of Blaise's watch and purse.

Neither M.S. nor the Puce had received any callers, but the porter remembered a gentleman who claimed to be a friend of mine asking to wait for me in my rooms. A description of him soon proved that it was no one I knew.

M.S. was worried about it. "Boy," he said, "I don't trust these police, they're a bad lot. The sooner we get to America, the better. Go and get that letter of credit from Lizzie Weldon, and I'll make arrangements to leave at once."

It seemed the most sensible thing to do. I set off for the Hôtel de Muscovie rehearsing an especially honey-tongued speech for Lizzie. I bought a large bouquet and a box of sweetmeats and wished that it was later in the day and cooler. The thought of making love to Lizzie on a stuffy morning was depressing. But it was essential for me to be at my most gallant. The eyebrows and the wry smiles must work overtime. I comforted myself with the fact that I had played against less appetising leading ladies before and given a creditable performance.

I presented myself jauntily at the Hôtel de Muscovie.

The concierge stopped me in the hall and handed me a letter. There was no point in my going up. The English ladies had left for England. I could scarcely credit my ears. I literally hacked the letter open. What could have happened? She had been swooning over me the day before. Perhaps her father had been taken ill, in which case this letter must contain the money to settle my debts and the note of credit to Van de Niver. It contained nothing of the sort. She had deserted me. My tailor, my shirtmaker, the print shop — no money for any of them, and No. 21 rue Matignon reduced to letting in unexcellent persons at last, and — no America. I couldn't remember having had such a low trick played on me before.

Her letter began with no form of greeting and had obviously been scratched off in the height of rage.

My informants have told me of your visit to that painted woman whom I forbade you to see. I am left in no doubt as to the purpose of your call. That you should dare to continue your association with a loose woman whilst privileged with the company of a person of breeding like myself is iniquitous. It is evident that I have been a prey to the most foolhardy dreams. Your behaviour with this woman of such obvious ill-repute convinces me that a man of your character could never play a gentleman for life. You are not a sufficiently good actor to sustain that part.

E.W.

Me! Jilted by Lizzie Weldon! I was obliged to sit down to recover from the shock, and the concierge went off for smelling salts. At any other time I should have been elated that Lizzie Weldon had finished with me at last. But that she had done so just before I could extract the money to get us to America seemed appalling bad luck. Also, she had obviously done the opposite of what I asked. She must still have had the Lieutenant of Police keeping an eye on me or she would not have found out about Marie-Clarice.

I hurried back to M.S. and the Puce with the news. I was incensed at their paradoxical annoyance at my failure to detain Lizzie Weldon in Paris. We all knew that we had wanted nothing more than to get rid of Lizzie and now that we had succeeded we were all blaming each other.

The Puce sobbed with such gusto that it was impossible at first to hear the rebukes of M.S. "My own little bedroom," she howled, "and my kitchen! All the things that I've polished and the flowers in the vases and the real knives and forks. We shall have to go back to L'Étuve and all because you couldn't keep out of the lady's bed."

"I did keep out of it," I yelled, "and it wasn't for lack of encouragement."

"You must have overplayed it, boy. That woman's been besotted with you for God knows how long — we've put the Channel between us and still she comes after you — and just when she's going to compensate us for some of the trouble she's caused us, you have to go and overact."

"I didn't overact," I shouted at him. "She was eating out of my hands, and the little speech I had planned for today aided by some tender gestures would have tucked the thousand francs in my pocket."

"Then what went wrong, boy?"

The Puce beat her fists on the table. "He can't keep his hands off any ladies." She wheeled round on me, her face a tragic wet sphere. "I told you to *pretend* to go too far with her, and then stop it halfway and say you were too honourable to go on. But you *didn't* stop it. You *weren't* too honourable. You went all the way and this poor English miss is a pious lady —"

I did some fist-thumping myself. "Damn and blast it, I haven't enjoyed simpering with her on musty old sofas just to get enough money to put in the box! What have you two contributed to it, I should like to know? You've been lounging about happy enough to spend my expenses, toddling off to watch royalty swilling soup in palaces, trotting off to theatres night after night, while I act the gallant lover at intolerable little supper parties."

M.S.'s fist came down on the table. "You can say what you like, boy, but the child's right. Lord knows you've tried hard enough to get rid of her — and failed! — so what happened just when we all wanted her to think well of you?"

I felt unable to tell them that she had caught me out with Marie-Clarice, so I sulked like a schoolboy. It would have been a slight compensation if fate had let me take advantage of my visit to Marie-Clarice, but to be accused of something I hadn't been able to achieve was insufferable.

It was not pleasant to see the child taking a watery farewell of the only brief taste of good living she had ever known. I think it was the luxury of privacy she was mourning most. I heard her saying farewell to her own little bedroom.

M.S. stumped about with his "betrayed" face on. "You'd think I'd deserve to keep a bit of comfort at my time of life. Brought up the boy, I did, coached and trained him. Showed him all the tricks and he can't even get a thousand francs out of a woman that's lost her senses for love of him. Wasted! Years of marking wasted!"

We waited until dark. Once again we were unable to leave with our heavy luggage because of non-payment of rent, so we stuffed ourselves into layers of clothes and crept out into the night. The Puce looked enormous in her two new dresses, her winter coat, and the two sets of underclothes with which I had provided her. She picked her way carefully in the new shoes and wept solidly all the way from the rue Matignon to L'Étuve. At intervals M.S. muttered darkly, "Broken her heart, you have. Look at the child."

Exasperated, I grumbled that I had always warned him that we should never have allowed the Puce to link her life with ours. She was bound to be subjected to midnight crises and we could never provide her with a permanent home.

Without regulating the flow of her tears, she said calmly, "Oh, that is all right. I shall learn to be braver when I get used to it." But her glance at me was still reproachful. She was convinced I had not resisted the temptation to ravish Lizzie Weldon.

Paris was in an ugly mood that night. Rioting gangs were roaming the streets. The temper of the people had not been sweetened by a severe grain shortage. Then, the fact that the King and Queen had given a banquet for the Flanders Regiment had for some obscure reason inflamed them further. Stones were being hurled through windows, private persons menaced in their carriages, and unfortunate government officials seized with shouts of "À la lanterne!" and hanged without further questions.

These "lanternes," or Parisian street lamps, made excellent impromptu gallows. The iron bars supporting the lights jutted out from the walls of houses and it was from these that the bodies dangled. I could never get the sight of their bloated and contused faces out of my mind. One form in particular plagued me in my dreams. It was the corpulent body of an elderly monk. His weight made the rope creak as he swung slowly round. Beneath his feet, which such a short time ago had been making such agonising attempts to reach the ground, a fiddler sat in the gutter and played a gay and lilting French tune.

Our peculiarities of dress made us dangerous targets that night. If I hadn't explained in a coarse accent that we had been thrown out of our lodgings because we couldn't pay the iniquitous rent required by our aristocratic landlords, we should have been in for some very rough handling. As it was, M.S. and I had to keep the Puce well sandwiched between us. If I hadn't seen how frequently she caught the eye of leering drunks and marauding ruffians, I don't suppose I should have realised what a startling difference taking a pride in herself in order to keep up with the rue Matignon had made to her. Even though she was grotesquely piled up with clothes, she was beginning to look quite attractive.

L'Étuve was a fermenting mob. God knows what the Royal Family could have done at that dinner for the Flanders Regiment, but it appeared to have acted like the candle under old Sir Gregory's powder keg.

Neither the cocoa seller nor the Lapins showed any surprise at seeing us. The cocoa seller called out to the child, "Couldn't you stay away from us, then?" And Madame Lapin said, "Didn't get rid of you for long, did we?"

"Now, now, Eloise," the grandfather protested. "This is the child's home, and if these gentlemen who have been so good to her want to stay here, I've nothing to say against it." But he looked far from pleased to have her on his hands again.

I saw the child's eyes wandering about. They seemed to shrink from the old familiar sights. It was the first time she had faced up to contrast. While L'Étuve was all she knew, it was bearable, but the rue Matignon had made the poor little creature vulnerable.

Being so used to ups and downs I wasn't affected at all. "Cheer up," I said, "it didn't kill you before, so it won't kill you now."

She shuddered. "Tomorrow I'll buy a cake of soap and I'll wash these filthy sackings out. We'll be covered in lice if I don't."

"There's no need to come back so grand," sneered Madame Lapin, "when you've only been away such a short time — more's the pity."

"I've been away all my *life*," snapped Suzon. "Oh! When you think of what I've come from — bed hangings and curtains to match, and my room was my own — a *whole* one to myself."

We were not short of food that night. I had sold three of the silver knives, and the Puce had stocked up. We had also bought candles, so the room was well lit.

The Puce could not stop talking about the rue Matignon. "People who wanted to come into my room had to *knock*," she said proudly, "and if I didn't want them to come in, I said no."

"Well, no one's sorrier you had to leave it than we are," snapped Madame Lapin. She dipped a whole slice of white bread in her gravy. "Wheaten bread! The last time I tasted it was the day I was married."

"You weren't married to my grandfather," the Puce pointed out.

"I did not say I was, pig-child."

"When you think," old Lapin interrupted, "that there are people who have this kind of bread every day and put out the crusts for the birds."

"We did! We did!" crowed the child. "We had small rolls in the morning and white bread all the time, and the pigeons took crumbs from my hands."

"Then it's sinful," said old Lapin, "it's sinful indeed that some should be able to live like that when others must keep body and soul together with cabbage water."

"It's that Pêche who fills you up with ideas like that," grumbled Madame Lapin. "That's him talking! Just give me the chance to be as sinful as that!"

"We ought," said old Lapin, "to ask in poor Jacques Pêche. You should share what you have with your neighbours."

I was sent up to fetch the undertaker. He was nailing down a customer. We had not met since our slight mishandling of the Bastille affair, and I thought he might resent me for it. People have a habit of blaming one for something they are ashamed of themselves. But he greeted me heartily enough: a great clout on the back with the hammer still in his hand and an "Ah! Monsieur le Vicomte or Monsieur Buckland — we haven't decided which yet, have we?"

"We decided to call me Roberts," I said.

"Well, monsieur, what do you think of the streets tonight? That shows people are thinking, doesn't it? Classes like mine are having effect. It's true that we don't approve of rioting, but at least it shows that inertia is dead."

"What's all the trouble about? We had quite a nasty time getting here."

"The King and Queen gave a banquet for the Flanders Regiment." He nailed up his customer as he spoke, and I winced at the blows. "A lot of foolish rumours are floating round about it: our people are still not considered adult enough to be allowed to hear the simple truth. Agitators must heap lies on to it and make a just grievance ridiculous. The King and the Queen tried to win the Flanders Regiment round to their side. They filled the soldiers with wine and the Queen showed off the little Dauphin to bring out their loyalty. Obviously they were trying to turn the regiment against the people. It shows that the monarchy has not yet conceded the claim of the people to share in ruling their own country. In the old days this would have gone unnoticed except by those few of us who were politically conscious. But now — thanks to classes like Dansart's and I like to think mine — the man in the street can recognise a move against his interests. Suddenly the man in the street is important. He takes a pride in his country's affairs. They have now become his affairs and he wants to discuss them. He no longer boasts that he knows someone at court. He boasts instead that he knows a deputy — a representative of his own kind. We have come a long way, a long way — and we will go further. Soon he will realise that to speak his mind there is no need to throw stones and attack innocent citizens. Then we shall have come as far as any human beings can wish to go."

Poor Pêche was no better at forecasting correctly than I was, but neither of us suspected it then. Even when I asked who was occupying the coffin he had just completed, we felt not the slightest tremor of a premonition.

"That," he said, "is a terrible thing. There is nothing so tragic as a mistake. I think you knew him. It's poor Paul Campon, the letter writer."

"Good heavens! He was young. What happened to him?"

"He was trying to calm a mob on the corner here when this news about the banquet for the Flanders Regiment broke through. They had been roused into bloodshed by ridiculous exaggeration. He was telling them what

we try to tell them: that wild rumours are not always true. He was hacked
down from behind with a pike. I can think of nothing so terrible that the
people should strike at their own kind."

He threw his hammer down on the coffin and put his arm through mine.
"Well, now, let's have a taste of this feast of yours. You can get tired of
living on wine."

When we came down, the Puce sang out, "Monsieur Pêche, we had sugar
on the table at every meal, and *whole* cups of coffee to ourselves every
time!"

Coffee was such a scarcity in L'Étuve that four or five people frequently
sipped from one cup and there were children who had never tasted sugar
at all.

"Monsieur Pêche," said old Lapin, "will not like to hear such talk. He
feels strongly about these wicked differences between the tables of the poor
and the rich."

The Lapins attacked their food as if they expected it to get away from
them. The news of our feast soon brought several of Pêche's pupils in to
have a look. We shared what we had with them and it was not long before
we had quite a crowd.

They were still inflamed by the royal banquet for the Flanders Regiment,
and I didn't care for the temper of our guests.

Pêche did his best to keep them down to facts. He agreed that the banquet
had been an insult to the people, and that the wine had been provided to get
the soldiery drunk enough to pledge their loyalty. He granted them that the
whole affair had ended up in a thoroughly anti-constitutional and pro-
monarchial manner, but he refused to accept the rumour that the Queen
enticed the soldiers by displaying a naked bosom.

"I tell you I have it for a fact from a friend who knows someone with a
relation who saw it happen," Lattre bellowed, a goose bone in one hand and
a chunk of white bread in the other. "The Austrian whore bared her breasts
to those men. She offered them her flesh to induce them to side with the
tyrants and cut every throat in Paris."

Pêche said patiently, "The Queen has enough real crimes for us to lay at
her door: we don't have to invent them. Stupid accusations like yours will
only get the true ones disbelieved. There was nothing immodest about her
dress. She merely presented her son in her arms to the regiment and asked
them to support him. That is quite bad enough. It's the spirit of the affair
that counts. It shows that the court doesn't believe there's a change taking
place. It shows that the King disregards the people even after they've dem-
onstrated their strength."

It was the Puce who began the fracas. It was an unpleasant taste of things
to come. She said impatiently, "Oh, what a place this is. You get peace in
the rue Matignon."

Madame Lapin, her cheeks full of food, gave her a savage push in the face. "Pig-child, to come back so grand. Oh, we are not fit to be seen with her now. The grand young lady who's used to having her own big bedroom! The little aristocrat who has never been hungry, so she throws out white bread for the pigeons!"

The child sprang and the woman rolled over her. I grabbed Madame Lapin by the leg and M.S. dived for the Puce.

"You leave her alone," I told the writhing, unsweet-smelling lump I held, "you've never even given her a kindly word, never mind anything else."

Madame Lapin shot at me, "You are the cause of it. You — no one else. You gave her the taste for fine living that makes her despise her own flesh and blood."

Even old Lapin sided against me. "It's true that the child has been spoilt. Someone has given her these bad ideas. She doesn't hear them in *this* house. *That* I can tell you."

"There's no change in her," roared M.S., "except what's been done by a bit of soap."

"Yes there is," shouted Lattre. "She isn't the girl that I knew before she went away."

"It's him!" screamed Madame Lapin, pointing a piece of bread at me. "I tell you it's that one. He pretends that he's on the side of the people, but look at his shirt. You will see that only the best silk from Lyons does him! And where does he get all the food that he's brought?"

"You didn't ask before you ate it, you old cow."

"Boy!" warned M.S. "Watch your tongue."

"That's right!" someone called out. "He buys geese and white bread."

"Monopolist!" shouted the German breeches maker, and Lattre's face was shoved under my nose. "You are the one who corrupted poor Pêche — forcing wine down his throat so that he couldn't bear arms."

The Puce tugged my shirt. "Come away, they'll hurt you. An actor should take care of his face."

She was too late. The breeches maker swung at me. I hit back, and then the whole lot leapt at me. M.S. plunged in at once. His great bulk brought three of them down.

The Puce kept up a high-pitched scream. Lattre knelt on me while the others pummelled my face and chest. M.S. tried to drag them off. It was Pêche's cold voice that saved me. It rose like a thin trumpet call over the storm. "Take your hands off him! This man is not an aristocrat, this man is a common thief, and robs only the rich. What offence is there in that?"

One by one they clambered off me. They sat looking owl-faced while Pêche's bombast rolled on. "*Citizens!* Let me see you worthy of that glorious status: you are truly *citizens* of France at last. Let me see you deserving your new inheritance. Are we not fighting for justice? Then we must administer it! Do we set on one man without proving his crimes? If so we are no better than our own persecutors. We are not fit to be ruled by gentle means! You take part in the affairs of your country now — is this how you'll be guiding her fate?"

"He's corrupted the child," Madame Lattre called out. "He's made her believe she should know better things."

Pêche answered, "It's L'Étuve that has corrupted her. It is want that has turned her against her own kind. Why should she *not* know better things? Is it because she's a daughter of the people that comfort and warmth should be strangers to her? You should honour this man! Does he keep what he gets to himself? Does he leave L'Étuve and desert his starving friends? Not he! He goes to better things himself, but he does not go without taking this child."

I felt the brat's black eye on me. I think it was the first time I had blushed in my life.

"He sees to it that at least one of our kind shall be fed," Pêche continued. "Has he the money to feed himself? No! He is as bereft as we are of the good things of life. So he *steals* them for her! He prizes them out of the jaws of the rich. He lives at the expense of our enemies and he shares their food with us. He has *stolen* this child a foretaste of her rights!"

I thought I was being attacked again, but this time it was clouts of friend-ship I was receiving.

"Vive Monsieur Buckland!"

"Vive Monsieur le Vicomte de Lambrière!"

"Vive the friend of the poor!"

Shakespeare was right about the spirit of a crowd. He never trusted it. He depicted it as wholly unstable with somersaulting loyalties that could change on a whim. And he was only observing the English crowd! He should have taken a look at the French!

From being ready to pull me to pieces a few minutes ago, these people were trying to find something to give me which would show me that they understood my worth. It was pathetic, as they had so little to give. Old Lattre came up to me. "Come to my eating house in the morning, monsieur, you can take your free pick of the food."

Even more, they would have happily died for me had the occasion de-manded it at that particular pitch of their emotion.

Pêche cleared the room. In spite of what happened later, I still remem-ber how I admired him then.

M.S. had an injured wrist. The Puce found a stocking and bound it for him. "Boy!" he said. "I've 'ad enough of these perishing Frenchies. The 'ole ruddy lot are up the pole."

"Look," I told him, "there's no need for you to stay here. I can't go back to England while old Hawtrey's still in search of me there. If he doesn't run me through he'll get me hanged. But there's nothing in the world to keep you from going home."

He drew back the wrist the Puce had just bandaged, brought it forward, and knocked me out cold.

Sometimes I think I'm not lucky.

When I came to I was lying on the plank bed. M.S. was sitting hunched in the corner overplaying his how-could-you-have-spoken-like-that-to-*me* face, and the Puce was cooling me with the painted fan I had bought her in the Palais-Royal.

As my eyes opened, M.S. made an affected exit.

"You have wounded my new uncle terribly," the Puce reproached me. "He is most angry at you for suggesting he would want to desert you."

"I seem to have difficulty in pleasing people," I observed with self-pity.

"We will never desert you," she told me. "We look on you as one of us, and when you and I are married, you'll become even more one of the family."

Chapter 36.

MY FIRST action after Lizzie's departure was to present myself to Dugazon. M.S. accompanied me and we found that we had chosen to call on the day Dugazon was resigning from the Comédie Française. My timing on the stage is excellent. My timing in life is impressively poor. We arrived in the middle of a real old-fashioned theatrical rumpus.

The Green Room was filled with irate actors and actresses. I had not seen the great Talma and Fleury before, but M.S. and the Puce had seen the former in *Charles IX*. The noise was being caused by an argument over this play of André Chénier's. We had no difficulty in gaining admittance, as everyone was too busy shouting to notice strangers. Dugazon seemed to be the centre of the trouble. He stood with calmly crossed arms and at the top of his voice was defending Talma against Fleury. Why this should have been necessary I don't know, since Talma was defending himself almost as loudly. I recalled M.S. having once said that he had rarely seen a finer piece of acting than Talma's, but in spite of his appreciation he had come back from the play in a fine fit of rage. Apparently the play had been fiercely anti-Royalist, and contained such a tirade against priestcraft that the court and clergy applied to the King to have the performance stopped. This promptly persuaded the public that they would be missing a masterpiece. The people clamoured for it, and the Commune supported them. Even the Mayor was drawn in, and that great natural comedian the Comte de Mirabeau descended on the theatre and demanded the production in the name of the provincial federalists. But most of the company, headed by Fleury, still proud to be considered the slaves of the crown, refused point-blank to produce it again. They threw out Talma, and Dugazon threatened resignation in protest. The public's answer was to insist, not only that the piece itself should be played, but also that no one but Talma should play in it. They tore up the pit benches and shied boots and bits of seating at the stage. Fleury, as a well-known Royalist, was the main target and was nearly knocked out. He accused Dugazon of agitating the audience and challenged him to a duel. "But, being actors," as somebody nastily remarked, "they didn't wish to hurt each other overmuch." Nevertheless, on the day I chose to call and see if anyone would like me to join the Comédie Française, the company was not in the happiest of humours. Everyone was threatening to resign, and there were furious bellows of "Can you discuss nothing without shouting?" Above the clamour Talma could be heard booming, "We will get nowhere by raising our voices!"

The Desmoiselles Contat and De Lange were sitting alongside one another on a sofa. De Lange was eating grapes and spitting out the pits. I had time to decide that she looked a better bedful than La Contat, who I felt might talk all through it. De Lange shook a long finger at Dugazon. "I should have thought, my *dearest* Dugazon, that someone who had had the privilege of teaching the Queen to act would have been more sensible of the honour of royal patronage."

"You flatter me too greatly, my sweet love, if you thought I ever managed to teach her to act," he purred.

His little red heels flashed over the floor as he paced up and down. His dog looked quite dizzy trying to follow him.

"She'd no business trying to act," stormed Talma. "Why couldn't she just play the part God gave her?"

Out of make-up Fleury was sallow, but his face was turning a steady red now. "You should be grateful she took an interest in our profession. I can think of no better advertisement for our art."

"Idiot!" screeched Dugazon. "She kept the court away from the real theatre, didn't she? If they could go and watch her frisking about on her own stage, why should they bother with ours?"

"I can remember," cooed La Contat, "when someone was terribly pleased to be chosen to coach her."

"I was not pleased," Dugazon shouted, "and I shall never cease being ashamed that I hadn't the courage to refuse. You can accuse me of *that* if you like, but not of being pleased. I should never have given the benefit of my hard-won experience to make sure of a smooth production on the stage of the Little Trianon. The despised professional shouldn't be expected to teach frivolous amateurs the tricks of the trade."

M.S. and I promptly took opposite sides. No one questioned our right. He plunged in with Fleury, La Contat, and De Lange, and I stood up for Dugazon and Talma.

"There's no better augmentation to a theatre's takings than a Queen in one of the boxes," M.S. remarked in his manager's voice.

"Not in these days," said Talma: "you're more likely to get the place torn up."

"Dugazon," sneered Fleury, "is trembling with excitement because some cheap little deputy from the Auvergne got up on his feet to clap for Talma."

Dugazon wheeled round on him. "The status of the whole theatre could be raised if more people like Monsieur Danton took an interest in it."

"Both Danton and Camille Desmoulins were a good two minutes applauding me," Talma claimed.

"That was not in appreciation of you," Fleury told him. "They were applauding their own political beliefs, and you were capering about supporting them like a monkey on a chain."

"Monsieur Talma gave the finest performance I have ever seen," I said pompously. I knew M.S. would not dare to point out that I hadn't witnessed it for fear of upsetting Dugazon.

I don't think Dugazon recognised me when I first came in: he was listening too hard to his own speech. But my support of Talma won me his arm round my shoulder. "My friend is right. Talma gave a blessed interpretation. He was jigging no one's politics."

La Contat narrowed her eyes and jerked her head in my direction. "Who is he?"

Dugazon informed her, "Monsieur Roberts is a protégé of the great English Kemble. He was recommended to me personally for his style."

"Oh, really," she said. "One must envy him. Style saves hard work, I always think."

Dugazon threw his arms out. "Well, there we are. If you continue to oppose this piece, I resign."

Fleury, La Contat, and De Lange called out, "We oppose it."

Dugazon clicked his fingers for his spaniel and marched from the room. It was not difficult to catch him up: he had remained outside the door to hear what was being said behind his back.

He told us that there was little he could do for us. Without him he obviously expected the whole company to collapse. But he gave us an introduction to the Messieurs Gaillaud and Dorfeuille, who ran the Théâtre des Variétés Amusantes in the rue de Richelieu near the Palais-Royal. "See what they can do for you," he said, "and keep them happy. I might be needing them myself soon."

It is curious that those fierce little Green Room differences never struck one as being so disastrous a sign of the times. In those days political feeling was as much a part of people as their livers and spleens, and one judged them according to individual symptoms. One practically asked after their politics as one might ask after their health. There were a whole series of personal warfares, but one never thought of them as anything more significant than petty squabbles. To me at that moment the Revolution was no more alarming than a fight between Dugazon and Fleury resulting in two tiny pricks in the sword arm.

It sounds absurd to say that one didn't notice the Revolution coming to a head. One noticed it daily — that is, one saw it manifesting itself daily, but one was still inclined (God help one!) to call it "unrest"! Had it been one of those sudden upheavals with the opposing parties properly lined up opposite each other firing at decent intervals, one could have said knowingly "Ah! Revolution!" and later one could have been excessively boring in pointing out the exact moment at which one had personally noticed it start. But our Revolution was not like that. Ours was in us, beside us, and round us. Those who were against it still referred to it as riots, and those who, like myself, were heartily in favour of it called it progress. It was a very long time before it sprang like Pêche's predicted lion. Certainly the lion had escaped at intervals, and when it did break out it clawed and it savaged and it killed. But it was also caught again and bolted back in its cage, and during these lulls we still referred to the riots as progress.

It isn't really so surprising that we managed to go about our own business. To begin with, it happened to everyone else but ourselves. It happened on the next corner, the next street, in the next section, and nearly always to somebody else's relatives and friends. We had a few casualties of our own, but we always thought of them as tragic mistakes such as the fate of the unfortunate letter writer. For the most part, people were still talking, talking, talking. Tongues and pens were still the major weapons.

I am not even sure of how soon I became aware that the pattern of our lives was changing for ever. I am not referring to the much-needed and long-overdue changes fought for so gallantly by the Third Estate deputies. People like myself called those triumphs, and those against them called them calamities. It would perhaps be more accurate to refer to symptoms. They were apparent to me first in L'Étuve. The close conspiracy of the poor was being severed by mistrust; conversation was becoming guarded. People thought before they spoke, not because they wished to think about what they were saying, but because of how other people might report them.

The Puce's pathetic boasts about the rue Matignon were becoming dangerous. Her pride in saying "I," "my," and "mine," small words that every human being should have a right to use without having them turned into death sentences, were being stored up against her.

Madame Lapin's hatred of the child was curiously enough less of a threat than the Puce's grandfather's idealism. While the woman was merely jealous and spiteful about her, old Lapin was genuinely worried about having a girl in the house with such aristocratic sympathies. Perhaps he saw further than most of us. He was constantly asking us to move again and find somewhere else to live. God knows we were anxious enough to do so.

M.S. and I went to the rue de Richelieu to present ourselves to the Messieurs Gaillard and Dorfeuille. We left the Puce sitting on the step with her fingers crossed. I don't think she could have uncrossed them until we came back.

Paris seemed hushed and empty when we started out, which was not surprising, since half the population had marched the day before to Versailles. I had heard that upwards of ten thousand women had set off, although I personally saw plenty of men amongst them, not a few of them dressed up in skirts.

Pêche had disapproved of it. "That is no way to get bread. What will happen? The King will receive the deputation. He will calm them with false promises. He will smooth away their fears and they will come back with their heads full of nonsense and their stomachs as empty as ever. They will have marched fifteen miles for nothing and spent a cold night in the wet."

Old Lapin was in favour of it. "It's a fine thing! The court will be set on by fishwives and market women! They will see that we're nothing to laugh at then! And the King won't fire his guns at women."

"More fool he!" commented Pêche.

At the theatre we handed in my introduction to the managers, and I was received by Monsieur Pierre Dorfeuille.

He read my introduction before taking much notice of me. "Dugazon says you were sent to him by the great English Kemble. Very well, we shall read something, shall we?" He gave me the script of a wretched little milk and water piece by Denon called *Julie ou le Bon Père*.

After the reading he was a little more friendly. He thought I might have an appeal for women after the style of the younger Molé. He gave me a script and told me to study the underlead. I wasn't any too pleased with my trial part. It was very youthful and eau-de-rose. But anything was worth a chance to start working again.

It was dark by the time we left the theatre. It was not easy to push our way through the crowds. The Versailles procession was pouring back into the town again. A soldier informed me, "The people are bringing the King into Paris. The kings have always lived here before the great Louis went to Versailles. It's the right place for them — where the people can keep an eye on them."

With my mistrust of French royalty I certainly agreed with him. The Royalists' vengeance would be appalling if they ever got the upper hand again. Crushing taxes would be nothing to what the people would suffer if the nobility and the clergy managed to seize back the power that was slowly being torn from their greedy hands.

"The National Assembly have come with them too," the soldier added. "In future we're going to be ruled from Paris. Now we shall find that everything will turn out all right."

As we rounded the corner we ran into a weird procession. We couldn't cut across it and could not turn round because of the mass of people pressing us from behind.

The procession seemed a mixture between a death march and a harvest festival. The people must have looted the royal stores at Versailles. They were flourishing loaves on their pikes and dragging cartloads of flour behind them. The King's calash, escorted by some ragged National Guards, was so hemmed in it could hardly keep its wheels turning. Women were sitting astride the accompanying cannons, and many more were riding on pillions with their arms round the waists of dragoons. It was the casualness of it which made it so sinister. Many of the dragoons smoked pipes as they rode like comfortable farmers clopping home after a day's work in the fields. They brought a farm smell with them, too. The air was fetid with the scent of clothes soaked in the sweat of a seven-hour walk and still damp from the merciless rain of the night before.

A ferocious-looking woman in a blue riding habit was cantering up and down the ranks cutting the air with her sabre. She was being cheered vociferously as the "Queen of the Amazons," and she was certainly shown more respect than the real Queen, whose carriage was being dragged along with about as much courtesy as a dead beetle caught by a swarm of ants.

It's inconceivable in retrospect, but even then it never occurred to me that I was taking part in a revolution. When to the fury of M.S. I stopped to cheer, I simply thought of it as high time that a French monarch came back to live in his own capital. No one at that moment suspected that the unfortunate man was being led to imprisonment and death. We cheered because we thought the people had achieved a great coup in bearing him with them so that they might keep an eye, not so much on him, but on his court and clergy. I think everyone believed that when the people's demands were satisfactorily met, there would be lasting peace and quiet. But it was certainly Pêche's lion that we saw padding home that night. It had tested its strength, sharpened its claws, and when it grew a little older, it would leap.

The crowd was so great that we had to walk several streets out of our way to get home. L'Étuve was in a ferment too. Madame Lattre was being hailed as "the angel of the rue Louis d'Or" for her part in the proceedings; apparently she had marched on Versailles with the Amazons! It was my private opinion that nothing would have induced the old duck to drag her thirteen stone on foot to Versailles if she hadn't got involved on her way to market and been unable to turn back. However, there she was being carried shoulder high by her admirers — bruised, exhausted, and panting with heroism. I never saw anything so funny as poor Pêche tottering under her weight. His little pale face peeping through her enormous thighs looked like a mushroom between two autumn marrows.

Accounts of the march on Versailles varied every few yards. I heard that the mob had broken into the palace and killed thirty-six guards. Later I think the number was whittled down to three, but facts flew as high as hats that night. I heard that the Queen came out on the balcony and that they cheered her for her bravery; and I heard that they had shot her because she spat on them. Madame Lattre swore that she had been dragged into the street, had her hair and her breasts cut off, and died shouting, "May God damn the people!"

A man who had squatted all night round one of the campfires in the courtyard told me that it was true that she had come out on the balcony and that her courage had brought forth long-absent cries of "Vive la Reine!" But he also said that she went "white to the lips" and that the people's cheers made her eyes "glisten with shame."

That was more or less the tone of the eyewitness accounts. Very few of them tallied, but many people obstinately believed that Marie-Antoinette was dead. Some had even "seen her body with a pike through the heart dragged between two cannons behind the royal calash." From what I gathered, the intention had certainly been to murder her, but the shouts of her bodyguard had saved her. You couldn't really make rhyme or reason out of the reports. They gained stature on every tongue. But the one that achieved the most persistence was that the King's own cousin, the Duc d'Orléans, and his own brother, the Comte de Provence, had helped to organise the proceedings. Most of the rioters had hardly set foot out of Paris before, and someone with inside knowledge was believed to have assisted the mob in the actual assault; otherwise how did the people know where to find the Queen's private apartments? The rumours were based on the fact that neither the Duc d'Orléans nor the Comte de Provence were in the palace at the time, and turned up rather carefully afterwards. The Duc was known to be hostile towards the King and court, and Provence could, I suppose, have wanted his brother out of the way for his own reasons. But I hardly think that either of them would have been mingling with the crowd like circus barkers calling out, "Walk up! Walk up! Sharp to the right for the Queen's private apartments!" I should have thought it more likely that a palace servant with democratic principles or a grudge could have acted as a perfectly efficient guide. However, I don't imagine we'll ever know the real ins and outs of it.

My hero, La Fayette, was knocked off his pedestal by that most deadly of all weapons—laughter. They were calling him "General Morphée." Although he was the head of the National Guard, he had slept through the entire eruption and turned up bung-eyed when it was almost over. The poor man seemed a natural target for nicknames. Mirabeau, suspecting him of wanting to set himself up as a dictator, called him "a young Cromwell," and I heard an acid Englishman refer to him as "Lady Godiva" because he rode a white horse and had been stripped of all respect! But that was the fate of our heroes: they were born swiftly and died even quicker.

Amongst our section only Pêche failed to be impressed by the people's achievement in breaking into Versailles. He was disgusted at the damage and the looting. "What kind of a triumph is that? We are respectable citizens claiming legitimate rights, not thieves. The people shouldn't have to break into the King's larder and steal for bread. Bread should be available to them."

I did a turn of duty under Madame Lattre and felt worse than if I'd marched on Versailles myself. The heat from her wobbling thighs was embarrassing, and I was grateful to be rescued by M.S. and the Puce. M.S. was angry with me for taking part in an anti-Royalist demonstration, and the Puce was outraged that I had hoisted Madame Lattre on my shoulders.

"Have you nothing better to do," she shouted, "than give donkey rides to fat ladies?"

"You should be ashamed, boy," barked M.S. "The 'Lord's anointed' dragged out of their own home by murdering ruffians, and all you can do is dance round the streets under one of the elephants that pulled them out."

I was sitting on the plank bed still panting from the load of Madame Lattre. The Puce had pulled my shoes off and was tugging at the white silk stockings I had not been able to change. "Look at you! Your only other pair have a mend in them, but they'll have to do. I don't want people to think I am marrying a man of the commonalty."

"I'm going to bed now," I told her. "I shan't need any stockings."

"That is not so," she contradicted me. "You have a visitor upstairs. Monsieur Pêche has kindly given his room for the interview. You cannot ask people to ours."

She managed to force me into my spare white stockings and I went up the stairs bewildered. A gay little priest was sitting in the window. He was the only hunchback I had ever seen who was not affected by his deformity. I recalled vaguely having seen him before. He was one of the priests in the L'Étuve section. He held out a miniature hand.

"I am the Abbé Servoise. I have come about Suzon Dupont."

I sat down on a coffin. "Why?" I asked.

"Her grandfather wanted me to ask a few questions. He seems a little confused as to who you really are."

"I've already told him I'm an out-of-work actor."

"Apparently you call yourself the Vicomte de Lambrière now and again?"

"Only when I'm forced to."

"He's had complaints from his neighbours that he's harbouring an aristocrat who has turned the girl's head."

As briefly as I could I explained my circumstances. The Abbé Servoise kept his peaceful eyes on me. "Are you trying to tell me that you're a thief, a fraud, and a liar, monsieur?"

"Certainly not," I said huffily. "I've been forced into playing these characters."

"I'm sorry to tell you that a thief, a fraud, and a liar are what you sound to me."

What I would have given to have had that little man as a witness against me a few years later!

"Do you think you're a fit husband for a girl as young and tender as Suzon Dupont?"

"Husband!" I said. "Tender!" I said.

"You're betrothed to her, aren't you?"

I laughed. "Oh, that was just a joke because I wanted to get to sleep. She was pestering me."

"It isn't a joke to Suzon. She's asked me to call the bans out. That's why her grandfather asked me to speak to you. He lives in perpetual fear that you might turn out to be a real vicomte and he couldn't risk his granddaughter's becoming an aristocrat."

That, I suppose, was the moment I should have realised that our reasonable demands for liberty and equality were already turning into a revolution that would rock the whole world. Only a year or so ago old Lapin would have gone down on his knees if he could have married his granddaughter off to a petit bourgeois three times her age. He would have crowed over his neighbours and boasted about it for ever afterwards. A title would have given him apoplexy from sheer joy. But now he was sending the priest round to make sure that I wasn't well born.

I told the little priest that there was no danger of my being discovered to be an aristocrat and that I had no intention of marrying the Puce. He quickly saw how the misunderstanding had come about and sent for the child.

The Puce was a fine example of rue Matignon dignity. That porter would have been proud of her. She wore the new clothes I had bought her and she had forced her feet into the shoes. She stood with her head and her eyes in the respectful attitude of an Oriental wife or a concubine.

"Suzon," said the Abbé. "Do you realise that this gentleman doesn't wish to make you his wife?"

"Yes, Monsieur l'Abbé."

"Then why did you tell me he did?"

"I didn't, Monsieur l'Abbé, I said *I* wanted to marry *him*."

"You can't force him to marry you, Suzon."

"Yes I can, Monsieur l'Abbé."

"How?"

"I know about the scar on his bottom, Monsieur l'Abbé, and if he ever finds his lady love again I will tell her where to find it. That will put her off. Also I know that he killed the Monsieur Nicholas of England. I have only to pay the new letter writer to write and tell the poor old Sir Gregory, to get him strung up on the Tyburn Hill near London."

The Abbé and I exchanged a look. "Suzon," he said, "it's a sin to use your knowledge about someone to do him harm. But you know that already. What happiness do you think you would find for yourself if you married Monsieur Roberts on those grounds?"

"If I marry him," she whispered, "it will be good for him. My new uncle says so. Between us we shall take some of the soap off his heels and he won't be able to slide off the stage so quickly into a lady's bed." She made a small bob as an indication that her side of the interview was over.

The Abbé turned to me. "I've known Suzon since she was an infant. I baptised her. I know that the grandparents have done even less for her spiritual welfare than her bodily. But I don't think I've actually heard her making blackmailing threats before. Someone must have set her an even worse example than she gets at home. I'm afraid I don't think she's improved since making your acquaintance, monsieur."

"I did my best to get rid of her," I snapped. "I can assure you it's not to my advantage to have a child hanging round my neck."

"Then I think you must be a little more efficient in loosening the ties. But be careful how you do it. While she was in L'Étuve she expected nothing, not even affection. But you precipitated her into a better existence, and that has obviously led her to expectations of love. You must be careful how you reject it or she might never have the courage to claim it again in the right quarter. You must make it quite clear to that child that she'd do better not to marry you. She can make up something to tell Marie Lebrun. Point out to her that she won't lose face. She'll be gaining it."

"Thank you very much," I said.

I sought out the Puce as soon as he had gone. She sat down and forced little pleats into her skirt by wetting her finger and thumb. "He's a funny one, that one, isn't he? He had such strange ideas."

"He's got one that is excellent. You're to tell that hated best friend of yours that you've decided I'm not good enough for you."

"She has told me that already. But it's only because she's so jealous."

"Puce," I told her, "you wouldn't be happy with me. I hate to feel tied to anyone."

She looked up in genuine surprise. "I didn't think you would feel tied if you had four wives."

"I'd pity any wife of mine, Puce, and I don't like feeling sorry for people.

It makes me bad-tempered and then I blame them. I'd rather save marriage for someone I don't like as much as you."

"Such as the Comtesse de Faille?"

I considered the matter carefully. "Yes," I answered, "such as the Comtess de Faille."

Chapter 37.

MONSIEUR DORFEUILLE disapproved of my reading of the sickly *Julie ou le Bon Père*. He said I had no sense of the dramatic. But I had a supporter in his partner, Monsieur Gaillard. He liked my natural approach. They argued in front of me without embarrassment.

"The boy *behaves*, he doesn't *act*," complained Dorfeuille.

"The essence of acting is to behave as if you are not acting," said Gaillard. "My God, Pierre, did Voltaire fight the bombastic school all those years for you to revive it? Besides, the boy's face will bring them in." To me he explained, "My colleague is a traditionalist sadly behind the times. He'd invite the gentry to sit on the stage if you gave him a chance, like they did in the old days. Think of it! There was no room for action and no room for scenery. It was more important that the nobility should get a good view, and the managements were afraid that the stage would look too empty with nothing but actors on it! That's how my friend Pierre feels. He likes everyone shouting at the tops of their voices and waving their arms about so that people will realise that he's employing actors!"

They finally agreed that I should be given a trial, but my salary was small even after M.S. had battled to have it raised.

It was enough to hire us two ill-furnished rooms in the street running at a right angle to the rue Louis d'Or. Pêche found them for us; they had been occupied by an old man he had recently boxed. They were at the top of a narrow building that had once known wealthy owners in the days when L'Étuve was the fashionable place to live. There were still traces of grandeur in the well-proportioned lower rooms. Ours must have been part of the granary and storage lofts. The rooms were divided by a thin wooden partition, and I should not have been surprised if the previous owner had died from draughts. In the summer it would be stifling to lie so closely under the decaying roof, but now there was an autumnal sting coming into the air at night. Nevertheless, No. 104 rue de Picardie was an improvement on No. 15 rue Louis d'Or. It was also an improvement on the Tour Bonbec.

There would be a little money for food left over at the end of the week, but there would be nothing saved for America.

The Puce announced her intention of accompanying us, and I appealed to the grandparents. "The priest himself said we'd be a bad influence on her."

"The priest doesn't have to feed her," snapped Madame Lapin.

"She'll be better off with us, boy," urged M.S.

"I don't want the child getting wrong ideas," said old Lapin. "Crumbling white bread for the pigeons! It isn't even right to store bread for oneself when others are dying from starvation."

Madame Lapin nagged at him. "Oh, let her go. She's not our sort any more. She's far too grand. Our place isn't good enough for her. She made the priest wait up in Pêche's room."

"I should like to make it clear," I said, "that she hasn't been invited to join us."

M.S. coughed. "Boy," he said, "we need someone to look after us, and she did very well last time."

The Puce pointed me out to her grandfather as if he had never seen me before. "That is the man I have chosen. Marie Lebrun says if you can't get the one you want, it proves that you're not a woman."

"But I am going to marry the Comtesse de Faille," I said. "I've already told you that."

"Yes, but you aren't married yet," she pointed out, "and we don't know that the lady will have you."

"You see!" said old Lapin. "The people he knows! Great ladies who live on our blood! Those aren't the people for you to know, child. Do you want to go with someone who makes love to our enemies?"

"The Comtesse de Faille," I said, "is more democratically minded than any of us, and I haven't yet succeeded in making love to her."

"She did give me a twelve-sol piece," the Puce remembered loyally.

"We don't want their gifts. Let them keep their soups and the remains of their meals and their gracious words. All we want from them is our rights, and what they don't give, we will take."

"He listens to Pêche too much," grumbled Madame Lapin. "Catch me saying I don't want a twelve-sol piece!"

Old Lapin took the Puce's shoulders and pulled her towards him. "Suzon, come with me, I want to talk to you."

He took the child upstairs to Pêche's room, and M.S. and I packed up our effects. I thought it a good idea to move to our new quarters while the child was still being lectured by old Lapin. "After all," I told M.S., "you can still see a lot of her. It's only one street away."

We were hardly settled in our draughty apartment before the Puce arrived with her new clothes over her arm and the shoes carefully wrapped in a piece of sacking. She looked round our lodgings despondently. "It's not what we're used to, is it? Still, many fine people come down in the world. The important thing is not to let your surroundings affect you. In ourselves we must let it be seen that we are people who should still be in the rue Matignon."

She turned the partitioned end of the room into private quarters for herself and was cleaning up ours before we had hung up our clothes.

"Your grandfather said you could come, then, did he, dearie?" asked M.S.

"No. He said if I came I was his granddaughter no more." She jerked her chin towards me. "I would be *his* woman and he would be responsible for me like the man who took Marie Lebrun to Dijon."

"You're not a woman yet, and furthermore your grandfather knows perfectly well I don't want you here."

"Exactly! He says that's just like an aristocrat. They have no sense of shame." She said it so smugly that I could see she enjoyed the myth of my being well born.

M.S. was stern with her for once. "It's never a good thing to believe your own lies, child. Keep them for other people. This boy's no more an aristocrat than you or I. Love him if you like, but love him for the good actor he really is, and not for any nonsense he isn't."

"The cocoa seller says you aren't actors. He says you just took the names of two actors who were drowned back in England. That's what he told my grandfather. He says you really are a vicomte and that you are working for the Royalists amongst the poor to put them against the Third Estate. He says it's a very clever game you're playing — pretending to be an actor who is pretending to be a vicomte!"

"Oh, let him think what he likes," I said. "It can't hurt me. Perhaps when he sees me at the theatre he'll change his mind."

My luck followed its usual sunny course. The day that the cocoa seller actually took himself to see my performance in the rue de Richelieu I convinced him once and for all that I had never set foot on the boards before.

I had been playing a series of flaccid parts that were so unrewarding I can scarcely recall them. Much as I admired Monsieur Voltaire for sweeping the gentry off the stage and giving the actors room to move about, I can't say I was impressed by his plays. To my mind they lacked stamina, and I can never forgive him for referring to Shakespeare as "an inspired barbarian." Shakespeare certainly suffered in the French translations. The man responsible for most of the butcheries seems to have been Jean François Ducis. He prided himself on refining the Elizabethan "barbarian" and reducing his poetry to nursery rhymes. But it was his textual impertinences that angered me most. Hamlet's feeling for Ophelia wasn't considered strong enough by Monsieur Ducis. His additions to the love scenes must have been as sickening to play as they were to read.

The joy of being at work again was soon tempered by the rottenness of the parts I was offered. Even Gaillard refused to accept me as a mature actor.

In spite of my experience at the Little Apollo I was not considered capable of carrying heavy leads.

Therése Lorraine, the girl with whom I went through my cheerless little love scenes, I cordially disliked. She was a poor and selfish actress and resented my popularity with audiences.

My management were pleased enough with me in their own way. But I was used more for my looks than for my talent, which annoyed me constantly, and I was for ever trying to bully Gaillard to give me something better. Dorfeuille had no use for me at all. He still complained that he couldn't see me acting. But I was bringing the women in and causing a certain amount of comment.

The rest of the company was undistinguished in most respects and resentful of a foreigner playing in their own tongue. I longed for the day when Dugazon and Talma transferred themselves to the Théâtre des Variétés Amusantes. But by the time they were in, I was out!

In spite of my weekly appeals, the management refused to increase my money. M.S. got a job as a Chinese bath attendant and the Puce became a scrubber at the Palais de Justice. Even so, we found it difficult to put up with the winter in L'Étuve. Extra blankets were beyond our resources and every week we combined our salaries and gave a small sum to the owner of No. 21 rue Matignon to settle our debts. This was a matter of self-protection rather than honour. M.S. insisted on the payments. "Sooner or later, boy, they'll see you on the stage. Then it won't be long before they'll see you in prison!"

I saw the sense in not taking a risk, but the payments made life very uncomfortable for us. The Puce took the money each week. She loved an excuse to return to the rue Matignon and always spent a good hour on her toilette. She was determined to convince the porter that we were "excellent persons" in spite of our lapses. It always amused me when she told me about these interviews. She was becoming a good little actress under M.S.'s tuition and I could see how well she would play her scenes with the porter.

She sat primly with her feet in the new shoes. It's surprising how long we continued to give them that title. They were still called the "new" shoes when they were three years older. She fanned herself as elegantly as Marie-Clarice. "I told this porter, Monsieur Riche, that it wouldn't be long before we were back in the rue Matignon. Of course I said that we were really used to better places than that, but we might see fit to take on the same rooms again."

"Well spoken, girl," said M.S. "It never does to be humble with people you might have to trick again."

"I also said to Monsieur Riche, 'We are not what you think, you know. Monsieur Smith is really a very great gentleman, too. He has suffered severe reversals in his circumstances through his father's terrible English debts. He works for his living because he is so honourable he wants to pay back every sou."

I was amused that M.S. should have told the Puce the same lordly tale he had thought up for Madame Angibault. It was a deep secret grievance to M.S. that he was not well connected. He and the Puce were certainly made for one another.

The fact that the Puce always managed to visit the porter when Madame Riche had gone to the market also amused me. But not for long.

"Do people always put their tongues down your throat when they kiss you?" she asked.

M.S. thumped down his book and I dropped the part I was studying. We both shouted at the Puce at once.

"Girl! What's this I hear?"

"Have you let that old wretch kiss you?"

She was mending a stocking and sewed on calmly. "I didn't *let* him. He didn't ask me. He just came up and kissed me when I wasn't looking. My arms were quite sore from pushing him off."

"In future I'll take the money round," I snapped. "It's disgraceful behaving like that with a married man. You're not fit to be trusted out of our sight."

"I'm to be trusted more than you," she flared at me. "The dog seller said he would give me a puppy if I would lie down in the straw with him when I was nine. But it was a poor little puppy: I could see it would die. So I said no, and I said no to Monsieur Riche as well."

"You must have given him the idea you were willing," I said coldly.

She had enough hair to fling back scornfully now. It was down to her shoulders.

"Of course I gave him the *idea*. You don't think I can save for America from the money you give me to keep house, do you? We should be here for the rest of our lives."

M.S. took her mending away and stood her in front of him. "Now, see here, girl. There's ways of getting money and that isn't one of them — not while you're with us, anyway. Don't you let me hear of you taking so much as a sou from that man again."

"But, my new uncle, ladies pretend to make love on the stage. They get money for that, don't they? Mademoiselle Lorraine makes love to *him* every night." Again her chin jerked scornfully in my direction. "Well, I pretend to make love to the porter and he gives me back a few francs every week."

None of our lecturing and moralising could persuade her of the difference. "It's not as if I really let him do it. I just make him think that the next time he can. I am just acting the part of a girl who will give in in the end — like Mademoiselle Lorraine with *him* each night."

What shocked me most was the fact that she had reached the age when a man of the porter's years should want her. While M.S. grossly overplayed the part of an indignant parent and pointed out to her the advantages of

young girls keeping their virginity as long as possible, I studied her thoughtfully.

I realised with astonishment that she was "gonflée." Her figure had not the
excitement of Marie-Clarice's, but it would have been good enough to stop
me in my path if I had been seeing her for the first time. I might even have
made the same efforts as the porter. Her face had lost some of its sallowness.
Better food and the air of the rue Matignon had given her a complexion that
paid an interesting compliment to her tilting black eyes. They took command
of her face. The nose and the mouth played lesser roles. If the hair had not
grown, she might still have looked like a coolie child from Cochin China, but
as it was, she had a precocious womanliness that I was surprised not to have
noticed before.

I suppose it was because I continued to think of her as a nuisance. Her
insistence upon marrying me I simply accepted as a piece of childish nonsense. She would soon tire of that, and her presence in the house was an
indisputable advantage. M.S. would have missed her badly and she was a
help in a hundred small ways. I treated her possessive attitude towards myself
as a joke and took care that she should be left in no doubt of it. The little
hunchback priest would find no way to blame me for encouraging her. But
it was disturbing to hear about the porter. I should like to have gone round
and throttled him.

M.S. sent her off to her room in tears, but not until she had insisted that
at her worst she was a saint compared to me. As soon as she had gone he
rounded on me and accused me of setting her a bad example. "What can you
expect when you put a harpy to bed every night as soon as the curtain comes
down?"

This was in the nature of a slight exaggeration, and M.S. always referred
to the partners in my affairs as "harpies" whether they charged me or not.

I was certainly not short of offers. Many a scented note found its way
round to my dressing-room. Some of them turned out to be from middle-aged
old trollops anxious to cling to the stormy days of their youth, but many
were from younger women.

One of the ironies which appealed to me was that a fair amount of garments cast off by the wealthy were given to the theatres and used in productions, so that one could find oneself not only standing in some unfortunate
husband's shoes, as a figure of speech, but actually in one of his suits!

It didn't surprise me, therefore, when the doorman brought me a message
that a lady waiting in a carriage outside would like to speak to me. I was
still annoyed at M.S.'s accusing me of leading the Puce into bad ways and I
was still bothered about the porter. I had given a rather rough performance
and was glad that M.S. had not been in that night.

It is always a good thing to keep a lady in a carriage waiting, so I took time in removing my make-up. I put on my waterproof frock coat and my most disinterested expression and went outside.

A torchman was waiting to guide me. I have a special "carriage-assignation" technique. To go boldly up to the windows is a mistake — not unlike jumping into a scene unrehearsed. There's not time to decide upon tactics. If you're immediately confronted with a face like a cracked soup plate, great gallantry is necessary to extricate oneself. On the other hand, if it's a pleasant surprise, nonchalance and a touch of insolence are more profitable.

In any case the occupant nearly always disappears coyly behind the curtains. The only guidance you get is from the voice. So you stand temptingly out of sight yourself and then saunter past, taking a casual pinch of snuff as if you were out for the evening air. This inevitably produces a voice. If it is a mature cooing, you are in for the soup plate; if it's a crisp little whisper, the pleasant surprise.

On the night I am recalling I received an *un*pleasant surprise. I had sauntered expertly, refrained from sneezing at snuff I don't normally take, and was standing provocatively out of sight. I was waiting for the traditional "Monsieur?" that would give me my voice clue.

It certainly did produce a voice, but it was one that could have belonged to either the cooing or the crisp school. It was obviously disguised. Also it said only two words: "Drive on!"

I was left gaping after the carriage lights with the mud spray from the wheels in my face.

Chapter 38.

PRECISELY THE same incident happened three nights running. The carriage curtains were always drawn, and it was never possible to discover the practical joker's identity. The second time she arrived I sent a messenger to tell the torchman that I was engaged. But curiosity overcame me and I went out. I was intrigued to know who was exciting my interest only to flick it back in my face with the mud from the wheels.

On the third occasion the carriage door opened very slowly. There was silence inside. My instinct was to jump straight in and take the occupant by the throat. But it occurred to me that it might be unwise. To walk into any trap would be folly enough, but to walk into a mobile one that could transport me where it wished was lunacy. The police might still have retained their interest in me, or even Lizzie Weldon and old Sir Gregory Hawtrey.

I went up to the door, tried to look as if I were about to get in, and then slammed it to with all the power in my arm. "Drive on!" I called at the top of my voice. The carriage remained stationary. The coachman was taking orders from no one but his mistress. The door opened very slowly again. I peered into the close black box of the interior. There was nothing to be seen, but there was a faint smell of lily-scented soap.

I climbed in and shut the door. She called out softly, "Drive on." The carriage rolled forward. I sat in silence, my arms folded. I could feel the vibration of her laughter beside me.

After a while she said, "It *is* Monsieur Buckland from Sandgate, isn't it? I really felt I must make quite sure."

"You mean you felt you must pay me out."

She chuckled. "You're not going to tell me you're really an actor?"

"What makes you suspect that I'm not?"

"Your performance, of course."

I stiffened. I could take criticism only from M.S. "I'm sorry you didn't find me up to standard," I said.

"Well, I suppose you weren't *too* bad considering you were up against professionals. Who are you hiding from? That hideous woman from England?"

"To stand up on a stage, madame, in front of the general public hardly comes under the heading of hiding."

"I think it's an exceedingly clever way. No one would look for a gentleman there, and I don't suppose she's much of a theatre lover."

"Are you?"

"Oh, yes! *I* am. I should have been certain to find you if you'd been hiding from me." She laughed delightedly. "Monsieur Buckland, I really *do* admire you. How in the world did you get yourself taken on? I mean, how did you trick the management into thinking you could act?"

A quickening dislike of the girl diluted my pleasure at seeing her again. "I have had," I told her, "certain experience of amateur dramatics in England."

She mistook the acidity in my voice for an apology. She sent out a small hand to pull down my arm. "Monsieur Buckland, please don't think I'm shocked at you. When you know more about me you'll see that my politics make that impossible. I don't even think the stage a disgrace for professionals and I think what you're doing is the most glorious joke I've heard for a long time. I adore the original, and you must admit it's getting harder and harder to find. Nearly everything's been done before." She ran the hand down my arm until it got to my fingers. She felt them over rather like a child trying to discover the contents of a surprise parcel. "Don't worry. I shan't give your secret away — at least only to one or two friends I can trust. We'll fill up the theatre and clap so loudly the management will think you're a better actor than the real ones!"

Short of killing her rather slowly, I couldn't think of a suitable revenge. Besides, I hadn't yet decided whether to admit to my true status would be to my advantage. "Have you," she asked me, "got wooden fingers?"

I relaxed them a little and allowed them to rest more loosely in hers. "That's better," she said. "Blaise must be let into the secret, of course. He's giving a party tonight, I think, but we needn't stay long if we're not amused."

We went through the carriage-way of the Hôtel de Faille. I thought at first that Blaise must be holding a rout. The courtyard was as congested as the streets of L'Étuve. It was thick with carriages, cabriolets, and liverymen. Every guest brought a servant to feed as well as himself, and these with the De Failles' own staff were streaming out of the house with great silver-covered dishes and trays. "Oh, dinner's over," said Marie-Clarice. "They're already selling it off." The servants carrying the leftover food were beginning to bargain with eating-house keepers clustered round the gates. "They do rather well out of it. The eating-house people have stalls outside and resell all the food to the public."

The contrast between the appalling extravagance of the leftovers and the dèche noir of L'Étuve made my teeth clench, but I said nothing.

The young footman I had seen before pushed his way through the crowd to open our door for us. "You know Côté, don't you?" asked Marie-Clarice. "He's very democratic, aren't you, Côté? Together we're planning the fall of the court and clergy. Isn't there rather a crowd tonight, Côté?"

The footman pulled a face. "Just the usual, madame."

"And who's here?" she asked.

"Oh, everyone, madame. You can't tell them apart. Even the great ones look the same after too much food and wine."

"Isn't he miserable?" she asked of me. "He disapproves of all frivolity. Where are they all?"

"In the blue salon playing faro, madame, in the yellow salon playing blindman's buff, and elsewhere as well they are playing something, madame."

Marie-Clarice seemed delighted with him. "Have you ever heard such insolence? I am not sure that feudalism hasn't its points." She went up the wide polished staircase and I followed her. "We shall have peace in my own rooms," she told me.

Her woman took our coats and brought in some wine. After that she left us.

The decorations had changed in her rooms. "I have had the bedroom and the anteroom redone — twice, I think, since you saw them. I just don't seem to get settled with anything. I must show you my shower-bath. It's really refreshing."

I noticed with a certain amount of delight that she was nervous of me. I think she thought there might be a possibility that I should turn her down again. She was wondering if she had been unwise in risking humiliation a second time. There was a slight anxious rash at the base of her throat, and under the eyes she looked even more weary. She talked over-quickly and kept jumping up to show me different things.

I watched her growing cheap in her own estimation. I sat back enjoying it. I hadn't forgiven her for those remarks about my acting. It was very amusing to watch this sophisticated, civilised girl become gauche. It was the last time that she was ever transparent to me, but I could see her thoughts then as clearly as if an artist were sketching them. She was rejecting every method of approach she suggested to herself. I could see her think up a fresh one and then change her mind in the middle of a move. She was badly underrehearsed, poor girl. She was thinking it too late for subtleties, and regretting her first choice of being crude. She was hoping, of course, that I would make the running. But I intended to play that little pantomime out to the end. "Let her," I thought to myself, "take the initiative again." Bad actor though I might be in her eyes, I knew how to twist the scene round her little gullet. It wouldn't be long before I had her down on her knees in angry tears.

I sat back with my legs crossed and relished my wine. I noticed an electrical machine on her dresser. It seemed an odd ornament for a woman. I said, "I see you're interested in science. Isn't that a static machine?"

"Yes, but I have other interests." She smiled at me and waited to see if I would pick up my cue. When I didn't, she made a plunge for her bookcase. She slapped down book after book on the table. "Yes," she said, "I *am* interested in science, as no doubt you'll see by my reading matter."

I picked up *Lucious' Scientific Wonders of Our Age* and flicked through it. She sat opposite, chin in her hands. "Monsieur Buckland, what made you come home with me tonight?"

"A fellow interest in science," I said. I went on reading. It wasn't long before I became immersed.

A small hand came out with no hurry and steadily lowered my book. "Are you deformed, Monsieur Buckland?"

"I don't think so," I said.

"Am *I* deformed, Monsieur Buckland?"

"I don't think so," I said.

She leant over and gave a great yawn in my face. She had excellent teeth and nothing to complain of in tonsils. "I'm sure you won't mind if I retire," she said, "and should you come across a point of interest in that book which you feel it would be to our mutual advantage to share, please don't hesitate to let me know about it. I shall be delighted to correspond with you. I've several old uncles in the country with whom I do the same thing. I'm sure they'll welcome you in our little postal circle."

I stood up, bowed, sat down, and went on reading.

I heard fierce noises coming from her bedroom. She could not send for any of her women without admitting defeat and she was obviously ill at ease looking after herself. I heard drawers banging and cupboards bursting open. I heard some impressive language, too. Finally she appeared in a lavender négligée with some sort of yellow thing underneath. Her voice would have been sweet if she had been a female adder trying to flatter her mate. "Good night, my dear Monsieur Buckland. Please don't feel you have to hurry. Finish your chapter by all means."

"Well, thank you," I said. "Perhaps I could borrow the book?"

"Certainly, certainly, do!"

I tucked the volume under my arm, kissed her hand, and thanked her for a pleasant evening. I could feel the difficulty she had in not sinking her nails into my palm. Then I walked slowly to the door and went out.

I waited a moment outside. But there were no sounds of her running after me. She was letting me call my own bluff. I had rather an unpleasant thought. I was afraid she might have stolen the scene from me. It would be depressing if it ended up with me in tears on my knees and the situation wrapped round my own gullet.

Chapter 39.

I SHOULD have got clean out of that house if a giggling fugitive from blind-man's buff hadn't caught me by the waistcoat at the foot of the stairs. "Jules!" she squealed through her bandage. "Jules! I've got you at last!"

By the time I had disentangled myself, the young footman caught me up. "Madame de Faille has a message for you, Monsieur."

"Yes?" I said. "What is it?"

"Madame says you have the wrong book, monsieur. You need Volume One and you have Volume Two."

I looked carefully at the cover of my book. It said "Volume One" in clear gold letters. "My goodness," I said, "so I have. What a stupid mistake." And I went swiftly back upstairs.

My God! If only I had got out of that house! She was certainly in tears and on her knees. But not quite in the spirit of the part I had assigned her. That rôle should have been highlighted by humility and tender appeal. But she was playing every outraged Frenchwoman there has ever been, and playing it well. There was no sophistication left, no pretences at all; she was a savage picture of tragic sexual bewilderment. She literally hurled her books at me. I caught one an inch off my face and she threw another straight at me. The pages dropped round me like dying doves.

The whole room smelt of lily-scented soap. It must have been oozing out of her pores. "What is wrong with me?" she shouted. "*Tell* me! Tell me what's *wrong*?"

She reminded me so much of old Ducis' rewritten Ophelia that I leant against the door and laughed. It was a mistake. But I never have been able to contain myself when the French say "bah!" They seem to put so much heart into it, and she put more than most several times right into my face. "Bah! You bloodless English toad! Bah, you coward! Bah!" And she said it again.

A fresh outburst on my part made matters no better. "That's it, monsieur! Let us have laughter. Only the English could laugh at love."

I regret to say I could hardly see for the tears in my eyes. I came near to old-fashioned hysterics. I once had an attack at the Little Apollo when the old war-horse I was playing opposite had to stamp her foot and say, "Kiss me at your peril, fiend!"

I could feel the bare toes of Marie-Clarice against my stockings, her nails chipping away at my calves. I hauled her up by the wrists so that her knees came level with my thighs, dropped one arm, and scooped her tightly to me. The lemon thing was thin and I felt her warmth through it.

"Non!" she gasped, "non! non! Even if I have to join the widows begging for attention in the boulevard du Temple! I would sit on those benches asking strangers to love me before I'd give in to you."

"But no one," I pointed out to her, "has asked you to give in to anyone yet."

Before she could start off on the bah-ing again I had found her mouth. She responded by biting my lip. I felt it swell up in a stinging lump, and the blood from it slid round my teeth. I took a handful of her hair and gave her head a savage pull backwards. I kept it down while I swore quite amicably for several seconds into her face. Then I let her fall away from me. She picked herself up. The blood from my chin had smeared her make-up.

"If I am so repulsive to you, why did you let me think that I pleased you? Why did you go out of your way to excite me? Just for the pleasure of making me want you in order to turn me down? Is that how the English find pleasure, monsieur? Do they make up for their lack of powers in the bed by torturing somebody into desire? Is that what's so funny? Is that why you laugh?"

I was holding a handkerchief up to my bleeding lip. "Are you quite sure that the English lack powers in the bed?" I asked. I was enjoying the fact that I shouldn't have to keep my hands off her much longer. It was an exquisitely pleasurable postponement.

She spoke in her normal voice, but I could hear the effort it cost her. "You found me so irresistible last time in bed that you ran."

"I was running away from your brother's purse and watch," I explained to her. "It was I who stole them. I'm a pickpocket, amongst other things.

I was going to give them back, but it came as rather a shock to me that the police had done it for me."

I could see her suddenly wondering if she might have been trying to seduce a madman. Her hand fluttered for the bell. Then she withdrew it and obviously felt herself a victim of a not very high standard of wit.

"It's true," I told her gently. "I'm a professional thief," and I added tartly, "I am also a professional actor whatever you thought of me tonight."

She put her hand to her head. "Ah! So you not only despise my body, you despise my mind. You must if you think I'll believe that!"

On the rare occasions when I have ever told the truth I have always failed to be convincing. Lack of practice, I expect. I had managed to staunch my lip, so I folded my handkerchief carefully and put it in my pocket. Then I moved closer to her.

I really felt it incumbent upon me to uphold an Englishman's reputation, not only in bed, but out of it. She backed away from me, enjoying the pretence of her reluctance. I had not picked the easiest of opponents. I have never known a woman so ardent for love. It was a madness with her, not a desire. I felt that she would gladly have choked me, killed me, in fact, to be satisfied by me.

Again and again our bodies returned to each other fighting on when our strength had gone. We detested one another. I no longer sought to give her pleasure nor she me. There was only a driving desire to use the act of love to win the vicious battle over each other. We were not lovers but enemies. We had no morals and no codes. We tortured one another and gloried in it. We forced each other beyond endurance. I heard genuine fear in her voice of a weakness she felt she couldn't survive. I had no mercy. I hoped to prove it to her. I tore her hair, bruised her face, left marks on her breasts, and treated her as I had never treated any other woman before. I wouldn't have cared if she'd died under me. We had our moments of collapse, of course, but we rallied. We resembled two warriors on the battlefield of Cannae trampled and wounded but crawling towards each other to deliver the final death blow.

But finally I lay broken beside her, the marrow sucked from my bones. My hair was wet from sweat, and my teeth ached from the impact of hers. I felt myself incapable of further emotion except by the shedding of tears. For once *I* had met my match.

In the morning, Côté's expressionless face was a great source of irritation to me. I found it difficult to be matter-of-fact and dignified as I took my coat and hat from him. I had a swollen lip and an interesting collection of little claw marks round my neck and shoulders.

The Puce and M.S. had been waiting up all night for me. What an exasperating habit that is on the part of people who are fond of one. It is far more annoying, of course, when one finally turns up and confirms not only their worst but their most narrow-minded fears.

"Ah!" said M.S. "With the kind of woman you know those scratches will go septic. They'll get into your blood and you'll die."

The Puce had on her martyr look. Her let-us-be-good-to-sinners face. The merit of a truly understanding, misjudged, and unappreciated woman who is ten times the worth of the trollop who has supplanted her is to suffer without mentioning it. You won't hear a word in rebuke. The smile will be tender and forgiving. It is her lot in life to have chosen you and that is not her fault. But it is certainly yours.

I said with considerable dignity, when you remember that I could hardly stand, "I was set upon! In the streets! Canaille!"

The Puce played her Madonna smile. "It's the times. Nobody's safe after dark now. It's a terrible world!"

They were terrible lines, too, but I glowed towards her. For once she was taking my part against M.S. She was accepting my story. She had me believing in it myself. "Six men," I said, and changed it to seven in case the even number sounded too prompt. "They leapt on me from a dark courtyard. They would have strung me up on the nearest lantern if I hadn't put my head in their leader's belly."

"He must have had a hard stomach, boy, to cut your lip open!"

"He was corseted," I said firmly.

The Puce put compresses on my bruises and dabbed ether on my aching teeth. There was nothing I wouldn't have done for the dear child at that moment. I treated her to one of my "bravely suffering" smiles, where the eyes go liquid and the lips tremble. She gave me a stern look in return. "Were you *drinking* before these men set on you?"

"He wouldn't have had time for that as well, girl," snapped M.S.

"I think you're very cruel, Uncle. He couldn't have been so knocked about if he hadn't been attacked."

"He was attacked, all right," M.S. agreed. "And if you'll take my advice, boy, you'll avoid these — 'rough men' in the future. That management's only employing you for your face, and if you get it turned into a pease-pudding you won't last five minutes."

"But he couldn't help it," insisted the Puce.

I realised, of course, that I should probably pay for her generosity later. There would undoubtedly be instances of "Look how I stood up for you against my new uncle!"

She put me to bed and sat gently stroking my head while I dozed off my exhaustion. Now and again M.S.'s great bulk blocked the doorway in silent but very well-acted reproach. I lay holding the Puce's hand and promising myself that I had had my first and last encounter with Marie-Clarice. Piously

I told myself that someone of my sensitivity required more from a love affair than a test of physical endurance. I needed affection, compatibility, and mutual respect. I certainly had no use for a savage struggle in love. Marie-Clarice must satisfy her vicious demands elsewhere. In future I should make only for the tender and true. I kissed the Puce's hand and slept on my saintly resolve.

I woke up not much refreshed and thinking of Marie-Clarice. I continued to think of her throughout my performance, which delighted La Lorraine, if not the management. I dried up twice and was nearly off altogether once. When the curtain came down I was still thinking of Marie-Clarice. When I walked dutifully home to M.S. and the Puce my mind continued to be centred on her while I was indulging the Puce in her favourite pastime: recounting step by step my early days with M.S. She never tired of hearing these tales, and even M.S. forgot his annoyance and joined in.

For three nights running I presented myself at 104 rue de Picardie straight after the performance. M.S. smiled; the Puce beamed. But on the fourth night I presented myself at the Hôtel de Faille. Côté informed me that Madame was away. Panic seized me. Supposing that Marie-Clarice had reached the same decision as myself with the difference that she was capable of abiding by it? It was possible that she had other lovers from whom she could extract the same amount of pleasure, but for me there was only Marie-Clarice. Desire made a lunatic of me. Everything else paled in importance. I called repeatedly, hung about the house, sent flowers, wrote daily, and bribed Côté, all to no avail. Madame was away. I knew perfectly well that Madame was at home and that her sole object was to prove that her body was less impatient than mine.

My work was suffering noticeably. Dorfeuille told Gaillard that he was not surprised. Gaillard told me that he was painfully surprised. M.S. thundered at me. The Puce, with that ritual absorption which the French have for the state of their livers, insisted that my "foie" was out of order and made me a succession of disgusting tisanes. I swallowed everything. Even food I liked had no taste for me. The more I tried to discipline myself, the more feverishly determined I became to have Marie-Clarice again if only to get my revenge.

Finally I raided the theatre wardrobe. I dressed myself up as a shabby eating-house keeper and got into the Hôtel de Faille in the stream of silver platters being carried in and out when they were selling off the remains of the dinner. With my dirty appearance, a wig, rickety-looking spectacles on my nose, cheeks swollen out by wadding, and my voice disguised, I managed to delude even Côté. I created a scene over a capon for which I swore I was being charged too much, and while he went off to fetch reinforcements, I slipped into a great stone larder and hid behind barrels of flour. I stayed there until the early hours. The whole house had sunk into silence.

Then I removed my boots and went upstairs. There was no difficulty in recalling Madame's bedroom. Madame was in it, too. Nor did she hear me creeping across her luxurious carpet. I had pulled the bed curtains before she sat up demanding who was there. I told her in my own voice, "I shouldn't scream. It might be embarrassing afterwards."

There were a few seconds of silence and then her voice, as unperturbed as if I had made a commonplace remark to her at a clerical tea party. Not for one moment would she relinquish her claim to be a fashionable upholder of ennui. Not even when her lover snapped back her bed curtains in the middle of the night must she give way to plebeian surprise.

"Sit down," she invited me cordially. "I haven't seen you lately. What have you been doing with yourself?"

I sat down. "Well," I said, "there are so many interesting things to do in Paris one hardly notices the time passing. I have naturally looked at the Louvre, and the Palace of Versailles, and I've been to Notre-Dame and St. Sulpice. Such wonderful churches you have! St. Roch, St. Paul, St. Eustache."

She interrupted, "I'm glad you're interested in old churches; they're a passion with me. So much better, I think, than wasting one's time in the Palais-Royal, or wine shops or coffee houses."

I made my voice prim. "My dear Comtesse, the modern coffee house with its contemporary decorations and that incessant music jangling away in the background is no substitute for the cultural delights of a past age."

"Of course not," she cooed. "I always knew that in you I had met a brother antiquarian. Where else have you been of such old-world interest that you were not able to visit me?"

"Well . . ." I hesitated. I was beginning to run out of the information I had acquired from *The Gentleman's Guide in His Tour through France*, written by an officer some twenty years ago. It was still a Bible to M.S., and he quoted from it liberally whenever he wished to prove to me that the French were an evil-living race. He was also an inveterate sight-seer. But I recalled one place that had interested M.S. "I went," I said, "to the Convent of the Augustins Déchausse. On the left-hand side going into this convent, Madame de Pompadour is buried in a small chapel, lined throughout with the choicest marble that Italy could produce, which with many magnificent ornaments cost the King ten thousand pounds sterling, in honour of her memory."

"How exciting," yawned Marie-Clarice. "Did you have time to look in on that little exhibition of needlework by women of birth who have fallen on evil times?"

"Oh yes! I was enraptured by it."

"I'm so glad, because I organised it."

She put an arm past me and in the close heat the scent of lilies reached me. She groped for a candle and when she lit it she squeaked aloud. She had not expected to see a ruffianly-looking gargotier perched on the side of her bed. Her hand clapped over her mouth and her eyes looked wild. "You *are* you — I suppose?"

"Never more myself," I told her, and took her in my arms.

If the period in which I was denied Marie-Clarice had affected my work, it was nothing to what happened to it when I achieved fulfilment. My visits were no longer restricted to the nights. I felt at the end of a fortnight as if I were shakily emerging from a debilitating illness. Marie-Clarice was no more robust than I was, I'm pleased to say, but she at least could sleep in-between our bouts. I had to get up and endeavour to entertain the public. I failed.

Gaillard, determined to prove to Dorfeuille that he had not been mis-taken in my case, thought my weary performances were owing to lack of encouragement and promptly gave me the hefty lead in Diderot's *Le Fils Naturel*. Although I was already acquainted with it from Cumberland's translation, I had the utmost difficulty in learning the lines. My concentra-tion was appalling, and I was apt to drop off to sleep whilst trying to get a speech into my head. Even M.S. was unable to imagine the degree of merci-lessness to which Marie-Clarice and I subjected each other, and began to have genuine fears for my health.

If it hadn't been for his tireless coaching, I doubt if I should have mas-tered the part at all. Now and again I steeled myself to do without Marie-Clarice. I swore that I would avoid her at least until I had recovered my energies, but if I kept away, her carriage would appear in the rue de Richelieu, and if she kept away, I went to the Hôtel de Faille. Sometimes I walked half across Paris trying to forget her, but however much I despised myself, my feet always led me back to her bedside in the end.

I can seriously say that my chief memories of that completely exhausting fortnight are not pleasant. I felt a bloodless fatigue that stupefied my brain. Also, I broke a lifetime rule in an effort to put fire into my performance: I drank heavily before I went on the stage.

I did quite well on the first night of my big lead, but instead of going from strength to strength, I went to the Hôtel de Faille. On the third night I was practically asleep on my feet. I could hardly get my lines out, muffed my moves, and finally fainted at the feet of La Lorraine.

When I came to I was stretched on the dressing-room floor and no longer employed at the Théâtre des Variétés Amusantes. I was quite alone, but on my dressing-table there was a note of dismissal signed by Gaillard.

On my way home I stopped at a wine shop and drank two and a half bottles of Bordeaux. I knew perfectly well that I had no one to blame but myself. But I blamed everyone. M.S. because I had let him down so grossly. The Puce because I should have to continue to let her think I was ill, and

Marie-Clarice because in spite of what had happened I knew I should go back to her. I was melancholy on my first bottle, tearful on my second, and violent halfway through my third. I got up, shouldered my way out of the wine shop against the advice of the kindly patron who tried to persuade me to sleep it off on one of his benches, and made for No. 21 rue Matignon. I hammered on the door until I heard the bolts creaking back and the porter's sleepy footsteps plodding across the courtyard. When he pulled open the door I dragged him out. The candle fell out of his hand and his nightcap fell off his head. I was not too drunk to knock him down in one blow. Then I heaved him up and put him inside his own doorway. That, I thought, was as good a way as any of thanking Monsieur Riche for his attentions to the Puce.

I was dusting myself, delighted at having settled this score, when I realised that my action had been witnessed by the cocoa seller. He was hurrying round the corner as I looked up. He had also witnessed my disgraceful performance at the theatre.

Chapter 40.

IT WAS my intention to give the cocoa seller the same hiding as I had given the porter Riche. I was, of course, quite unable to recall the reason I had wanted to try and throttle the porter, but I knew why I disliked the cocoa seller. He had been following me. I made an effort to run after him, but I tripped over my own unsteady feet and must have hit my head on the corner stone at the end of the rue Matignon.

Paris was climbing out of its dawn mists when I opened my eyes. I could hear the rumbling of the early diligences making for the outlying districts. I could remember nothing about the night before except a feeling that I had done something that had made me unworthy of M.S. and the Puce. Also, my hair was full of blood.

I dragged myself up and fell into a wine shop. There I put down a bottle of Bordeaux and managed somehow to write a note telling M.S. that his faith in me was as misplaced as Monsieur Gaillard's and that he would do better to concentrate on grooming the Puce for the boards. I thanked him for all he had done for me, spotted the letter with drunken tears, and announced my intention of breaking our partnership for his own good. My words may have lacked clarity, but certainly not sincerity. My memory had revived sufficiently to remind me that I had proved myself a disgrace to my profession. It seemed more than M.S. should be asked to support. I knew I had not the will-power to leave alone a woman who was obviously too strong for me. I felt in the grip of a fatal disease from which I knew that I could not recover. M.S. must not be allowed to witness the gruesome end to all his hopes. I wept so heartily that my head started bleeding again, and I was obliged to rewrite the letter with the help of another bottle of wine and an honest-looking citizen who kindly offered to guide my skidding pen. He also agreed, in return for a small payment, to deliver the letter for me. For all I know, he was one of the myriad spies I seemed to attract to my person like flies round a rotting hunk of horseflesh. However, he did not default on his errand. M.S. received his letter.

I dragged my unsavoury-looking person to the Hôtel de Faille. It was necessary to lean against the door whilst hammering on it. It could have been no mean knock that I gave to my head. My senses felt as if they were rolling from ear to ear, and blood was positively belching out of my gashed skull. My eyes felt as if they were being pulled into the bridge of my nose. When the porter opened the door, I collapsed again.

After that I have only jumbled recollections: Côté's supercilious face, Marie-Clarice's voice giving quick instructions, hot water, crisp sheets, lily-scented soap. How long I lay before recovering I don't know. However rough Marie-Clarice may have been in bed, she was nothing but soft femininity out of it — the scented hand on the brow, the soothing voice, the tempting delicacies offered by spoon with whispered encouragements. She spent nearly all her time in my room. If my head was bearable she read to me or told me the latest scandals and political gossip. If my head was painful she sat writing endless letters to the friends in the country who formed her scientific postal circle. She had a series of varied interests; she held meetings to encourage the lower orders to put their faith in inoculation; she asked medical men to the house to discuss the possibilities of isolating syphilitic cases in the hospitals; she was the patroness of a home that cared for children when their mothers were at work, and she ran a committee whose job it was to look into the plight of the insane. As an atheist she invited high-ranking members of the clergy to argue with her. She discusssed music with musicians, painting with artists, writing with writers. If I were well enough, the meetings took place in my room. I was introduced as Anthony Buckland, an English guest who had had the misfortune to fall ill in her house. She attended political classes, political clubs, and wrote instructive pamphlets herself. She was a member of the Fraternal Society of Both the Sexes, organised distributions of food, and in her spare time visited the ailing relatives of her vast staff. Even so, her energies hadn't a sufficient outlet. She was forever redecorating her rooms, and furniture was constantly coming into the house and going out.

She was as solicitous over my welfare as a mother with a dying heir. It was hard to recognise her as my bedtime tormentor. But when my brain began to fall back into its right position again, I realised that my diet was being carefully watched. It became curiously strict. I was allowed a profusion of some things and a deficiency of others in a manner that made no sense to me. All Marie-Clarice would say was that it was either good for me or not good for me. It was the oysters that made me rebel. I had seen enough of that revolting fish in L'Étuve. The Puce, when she could afford nothing else, sat up and chewed them in bed at night. As they had probably been hawked on the trays all day, I hadn't the happiest memories of them. It was surely carrying her democratic principles too far for Marie-Clarice to import this peasant food into a wealthy house. She soon made the reason clear, however.

"But, my darling, they are the best things for love in the world. Just swallow them down, and you will soon feel strong enough for us to be together again."

So that was it! I was being dieted to restore my flagging powers as a lover. Everything I ate and drank was directed towards this noble purpose! Too much wine was bad, but a little was excellent. Red meat was helpful; ordinary fish was not. Bread, potatoes, and rich pastries were lowering to the vitality; spices were encouraging to it. But, above all, the humble oyster possessed all the qualities needed to restore waning talents. I must have swallowed dozens of the nauseating things. Their reputation was not undeserved.

It would be nonsense to say I was held captive by Marie-Clarice. I had two perfectly good feet that could have carried me out of the house. But they only seemed to carry me to and from her bed and mine. We slept off our own battles like stricken animals and it was still a matter of pride to be the first to recover and the last to give in.

When both of us were quite unable to bear the thought of one another's bodies again — rather as one dreads the surgeon reopening a wound — we took our places in the life of the Hôtel de Faille. Blaise came and went, bringing hordes of elegantly rowdy young friends, and showed no surprise at his sister's lover occupying the adjoining room to hers, nor indeed at what must have seemed our permanently dazed condition.

In my few moments of rationality I alternated between an almost panicky desire to escape Marie-Clarice, even if it meant summoning the strength to run ignominiously through the streets, and a fierce longing to lose myself in her again so that I could forget what I was doing to M.S.

It was at one of Blaise's bedlam-like faro parties that we had our first serious quarrel. I was slumped weakly in a chaise-longue that had been imported that day in place of one that no longer amused her. I had still not recovered sufficient concentration to wish to play. We had already had words because of the keen eye she kept on the amount of wine I was consuming. It was particularly annoying owing to the fact that she was far from restricting herself. Every now and then she jumped up from her table to whisper into my ear, "You can't love me to drink all that. You'll undo all the good I've done you. You'll just sleep like a hog in bed tonight."

I immediately took another glass and she flounced back to her game. There must have been about forty to fifty guests round the tables that night. The vast pier glasses that reflected the avid players seemed to multiply the noise as well.

It did not surprise me that the Puce got in. Côté was sufficiently aware of Marie-Clarice's democratic principles to know that he would not be thanked for keeping out a "person of the commonalty" who wished to see his mistress. The Puce's entrance was defiant. Knowing her so well, I could tell how nervous she felt inside the rue Matignon manner. She held her head so high she could scarcely achieve the object of her visit, which was to find me in the crowds. She was clutching the shawl over the green dress, and I could guess that the new shoes were on her feet. For all her painful dignity, she looked primly frightened in the lofty doorway. Nobody took any notice of her. I don't think anyone would have paid any attention to a headless horseman asking the way to his own grave.

I raised a hand and gave her a casual wave. She sped towards me like a little arrow. When she reached me I said, "The cocoa seller told you where I was!"

She nodded. "You're to come home at once. My new uncle is losing his patience. He has found you a job. It's not much, but it won't wait for you." She held out a hand to me as if I were a child she had found straying in the streets. "Come along, please."

I shook my head. "I meant what I said in that letter. I've been a nuisance to your new uncle long enough. I'll find my own work from now on."

"Then you'll go without. Uncle has been round the managements. They've all heard what happened at the Théâtre des Variétés Amusantes. Monsieur Dugazon has washed his hands of you. He told Uncle that the great English Kemble had no business to throw his rubbish across the Channel."

I had been aware, over the Puce's last speech, that we had the attention of Marie-Clarice. She joined us.

She was dressed in pale blue and wore less jewellery than usual. She always loaded herself on her visits to the staff's ailing relatives. She considered it hypocritical to "underdress" for the poor. However, Marie-Clarice's elaborate simplicity mercilessly put into shade the Puce's complicated little green dress.

"Who are you?" enquired Marie-Clarice coldly.

"Suzon Dupont. I've come to fetch him."

"Where to?"

"Home."

"Is home with you?"

"Yes."

"Are you his sister? He says he is English."

"I'm not his sister, I'm his mistress."

Engrossed the faro players might be, but they did not miss that word. It could have been spoken into a silence instead of a bubbling inferno of noise. They nearly all craned their necks in our direction.

"Oh, I don't think so," said Marie-Clarice. Some of her essential kindness reached her eyes when she smiled. "You look a little young and I don't think you would be able to — well, give him quite what he wants."

The Puce's big grape eyes blackened. "How long have *you* been sleeping with him?"

The faro players were quiet for that. The pier glasses reflected nothing but the backs of heads all turned to stare at us.

Marie-Clarice took a slow breath. "Not long," she said coolly. "How long have you?"

"Since I was a child," the Puce whispered.

"She means," I said, getting up from the sofa, "that once or twice when I was short of a bed her grandparents let me stretch my length beside her — without touching her, of course."

The faro players gathered round us.

"That's not what I mean," said the Puce. She stood squarely up to Marie-Clarice, her hands clasped like a child answering her catechism. "Has he or has he not, madame, the marks of a dog's teeth on his right buttock?"

The faro players became quite dense round us. Marie-Clarice closed her eyes. Her forehead wrinkled. She said as if she had been asked to answer some knotty mathematical problem, "Yes — yes — I think it *is* the right."

I jumped up. "Suzon, you've never seen any such thing. I told you about it when I was telling you stories about our early life." It must be admitted that I have seldom heard anything sound so lame myself.

"First your hands," said the Puce in her flinty rue Matignon voice, "caressing me from head to foot. Then your tongue in my ear, then your —"

I seized the child and shook her. "You get that from Marie Lebrun."

"Oh?" said Marie-Clarice. "Has someone else shared in these pleasures too?"

The Puce's head suddenly dropped forward. She sobbed with a child's fist crammed into one eye. "He's mine. I love him. He said he would marry me."

"Did you?" asked Marie-Clarice.

"It was only a joke and her own idea."

"It usually is the woman's idea and it's seldom that they consider it funny." She turned to the Puce. "Are you pregnant?"

The little brute nodded vigorously.

"If she is," I shouted, "it's not by me!"

"Is it his child?" asked Marie-Clarice.

M.S. would have been proud of the Puce. She was underplaying commendably, but the tragic betrayal in her eyes was most moving. "If you please, madame, I think so. There's never been anyone else and with him such a gentleman I thought he'd keep his promise."

There was nothing, of course, more likely to appeal to Marie-Clarice than an underprivileged unmarried mother. It was the sort of thing that unfurled a dozen banners in her heart. To me she said, with the kind of warmth that I imagine blows off a glacier, "It didn't occur to you, perhaps, that this child has suffered enough with the hopelessness of her life and the sordidness of her surroundings?"

There was an indignant squeak from the Puce. "I am from the rue Matignon. I'm used to my own room with bed curtains. I had cups of coffee all to myself and I threw away the food that was left on our plates because the next day we could afford to buy more."

Marie-Clarice ignored her and it occurred to me that the faro players were not on my side. Quite apart from my being considered the seducer of an "innocent child of the people," which those libertines possibly thought themselves genuine in objecting to, there was continued ill feeling against the English. There were rumours that it was gold from England which was paying the street rioters in Paris to spread violence. The reason for this was supposed to be that the English government resented the French monarchy's support of the American rebellion and were getting their own back on the court. The Revolution certainly had many supporters in England, including Thomas Paine of *The Chronicle*, who went so far as to become a French citizen.

There were ugly murmurs against me from the faro players. Marie-Clarice, foreseeing a fight, said firmly, "This is a private matter. Follow me, Monsieur Buckland."

Still sheltering the Puce in the crook of her arm, she pushed her way through to an ivory-coloured anteroom with gilt music notes embossed on its walls. Then she lowered the Puce tenderly on to a sofa — solicitous of the poor child's condition, no doubt — and faced me.

"When I think of the tortures you must have put this young thing through —" Her voice was temporarily lost in her sense of outrage, but it soon recovered. "The agonies you must have inflicted on her!"

I managed to interrupt, "I have not slept with that child in the way you think."

"In the way I *know*," she cooed viciously at me. "Well, there is only one thing to do and that is to make practical amends. When the baby's born I will see to its welfare. This girl will live here until her accouchement. After that I will see that she is sent to a convent to get a good education so that she doesn't have to marry the first ruffian who offers her a home for the child. She will learn things that will lift her above her present position." Marie-Clarice's organising abilities for the unfortunate were formidable. I could guess at the bewilderment of those whose lot she set out to improve. They were probably rehoused, remarried, and remade before they could defend themselves, when all they wanted was the voice of their representative to be given a fair hearing in their Parliament!

"A new life will be opened up for her," declared Marie-Clarice. She looked delicious in her powder-blue dress, vibrating with goodwill. "It will be like growing new eyes and ears. She'll understand painting and music, take an interest in science, and be able to converse with anybody. She doesn't know what's in store for her."

I thought from the Puce's expression that she had a very good idea. She was eying her would-be benefactress in alarm.

"If when she's completed her education," said Marie-Clarice, "she feels she'd rather make a fresh start without the encumbrance of the child, I'll continue to look after it, and see that it has the same chances as its mother."

Its "mother" was tiptoeing to the door behind Marie-Clarice's back.

"There's only one thing I ask of you in return," Marie-Clarice told me, "and that is that you give me your word that you won't try to see her again. Not for my sake, but for hers. If you persist in interfering with my plans for her I shall take her down to my château in the Auvergne until she's confined."

The Puce made a sprint for the door and got through it.

"What are you daring to smile at?" demanded Marie-Clarice. "Don't you think I'll have the courage to deny myself your attentions? Well, make no mistake about it. I'm willing to sacrifice them. When I come face to face with a wrong like this —"

"You won't come face to face with it again," I pointed out. "It's taken itself off."

She spun round. "Where's she gone?"

"Back to her hopeless position. I think she prefers it to the future you outlined."

"Nonsense! It's always the same with these poor souls: they're overcome by the thought of good fortune at first. I shall get her back, but promise me — promise me you'll leave her alone."

"I think I can promise you that. I've no intention of going back."

My intentions, of course, and what actually happens to me do not always coincide. The double doors broke open and M.S. stepped into the room. Behind his great shoulders peeped the handsome face of Côté — anxious for once. M.S. could be intimidating.

Marie-Clarice might not have existed. M.S. came straight up to me. "Boy," he said, "I've got an engagement for you. It's not much, but it's more than you deserve."

"Didn't you read my letter?" I asked.

"Who is this?" enquired Marie-Clarice.

Nobody told her.

"You start Monday," said M.S., "so you'd better come back and get your-self into shape. You need to be in good health for this job."

"Who is this man?" repeated Marie-Clarice.

"I told you in my letter that I was going to spare you any further dealings with me. It's for your sake, not mine."

"I brought you up to be an actor, boy, not a stallion."

Blaise came in to say mildly to his sister, "Where's that girl gone? She was pretty. Who's this?"

Nobody told him, either.

"Boy," said M.S., "I'll give you ten seconds to follow me out of this room."

"You can do what you like with your ten seconds. I'm not coming back."

He walked up to me and knocked me out. I suppose I must have made my exit over his shoulder, hardly a dignified sight.

The Puce was already back at No. 104 rue de Picardie. When I came staggering up the stairs, half carried by M.S., I recovered enough strength to get my hands round her neck. "You little — you! — serve you right to be educated! She'll get you: don't think she won't. Nothing stops the Comtesse de Faille when she's out to improve someone's lot in life."

"Leave her alone, boy, and get some rest," ordered M.S. "That woman must be a man eater. There's not enough left of you to interest a carrion crow."

"But this child told her— told them *all* — that she was pregnant by me."

"Well, if she's not, there can't be many others who can say the same!"

He pushed me on to the bed and pulled off my boots. The Puce assisted him. "I am pregnant by you," she informed me. "Marie Lebrun says you can get pregnant just by thinking about it."

They put me to bed for three days. It was absurd to say that I was a cap-tive there, either, but I suspected that something in the tisanes with which the Puce so constantly plied me assisted my sleepy state. That and my natural exhaustion made me a willing enough victim for the moment. It was almost a relief to be forcibly restrained from clashing with Marie-Clarice. Sometimes I decided that I must have her, but the tisanes made lead of my limbs as well as my wits, and I was overcome by a drowsiness that made me content to dream about her.

They got me up by Monday. They shaved me, bullied me into my clothes, nagged me incessantly, and marched me off to the theatre. The theatre! To have called it a flea pit would have been high praise for Le Petit Théâtre de la Cité. Most of its "artists" were tumblers and jugglers. The major turns consisted of lewd knock-about comics, whom I was employed to interrupt. My rôle was to keep rushing on the stage in an attempt to deliver a highly dramatic speech only to be tripped up by the jugglers, tossed about by the acrobats, and mistaken for the lover of the comedienne. I spent my time racing about with my hair wild and my breeches down. I suffered some severe knocks from the acrobats. I was hauled to the top of their high tableaux, only to be allowed to slip and be caught just as my head was about to hit the floor. It was on these occasions that, to the shrieks of the enchanted audiences, my breeches were always left in the hands of the highest balancer. Now and again I was allowed to claim full attention with a piece from some famous tragedy, or to give vent to a heart-rending declaration of passion. The climax to this was always winsome: I turned round with outflung arms and eyes closed in ecstasy expecting to embrace my returning love, only to find myself being hugged by a tame bear that had been led on for the purpose.

At the end of the first week I felt as if I had spent a whole month with Marie-Clarice. I told M.S. I should have to give it up, but when I sent in my notice, the management offered to double my salary.

In the following weeks I achieved a certain amount of success. Women liked to have their laughter mixed with something they could find attractive. Word was going round about me and I was bringing in a wealthier class altogether. If ever there was a king of the dung heap it was I. But the management felt they had got a good drawer in me and intimated that, providing I signed a lengthy enough contract with them, I could more or less dictate my own terms.

M.S. and the Puce begged me to stick to it. It was our only chance to get enough money to go to America. "After all, boy, there's nothing else for you. Dugazon's warned the managements against you, and this clowning's not going to improve their opinion of you. It's better to get what you can out of it, and move to fresh parts altogether. Tate Williamson talked to me of the John Street Theatre in New York. We could make for that and get you started again. I'll write another letter from Kemble."

It seemed good advice and I took it. To lessen the strain, M.S. gave up his rôle as a Chinese bath attendant and joined me. We shared the ardours and the humiliations between us. He shamed me. A ten times better actor than I would ever be, he did not feel his dignity outraged at having to somersault over the stage, fall into water butts, and be left running round in bandy-legged circles in nothing but a long vest. It's a true saying that only the best can be humble. While I moaned and felt myself mercilessly wasted, my superior gave the audience the benefit of his highest skill.

We did more harm to poor Shakespeare than old Ducis in his worst moment. I played Hamlet and M.S. Ophelia; he did Othello and I Desdemona. Our textual impertinences were something that can make me shudder even now in the Tour Bonbec. The tame bear was frequently Falstaff. I was pretentious enough to wish to weep when I got home, but M.S. only laughed at me. "An actor has a thousand souls, my boy, not one to call his own! If you want to say his lines right, you'll have to win the privilege again. Can't you learn a good lesson when you see one?"

We worked out an act together which consisted of my teaching him incorrect French so that every word he said had a double entendre. It was immensely popular and it was the lowest form of wit we could possibly have devised.

The Puce pounced on our earnings like a little magpie. It was her favourite pastime to count the contents of M.S.'s box. It was certainly better filled than ever before since our arrival in France.

We were achieving a seedy fame. It became the sophisticated thing to do to visit the vulgar Petit Théâtre de la Cité. Word got about that the two chief comedians were inordinately funny taking off real actors. Our audiences became better dressed and the price of the seats went up.

I wondered how long it would be before Marie-Clarice and her clique found me out. It was not long. A letter reached our dressing-room. It read:

Wonderful! How you've improved since the last time I saw you. I've seldom been so gloriously amused. Incidentally, I have forgiven you. I found out that the child was lying. I asked the Lieutenant of Police to trace you and make enquiries. Her grandfather denied vehemently that she had ever been intimate with you. He sounds a man after my own heart and disapproves of our kind. I apologise. Blaise is giving one of his little parties tonight. Won't you join us?

I knew that Blaise's little parties would apply to any night and for a week I stood out against them. Finally I gave in.

Whether because I was too physically worn out from being part of the tumbler's act, or whether it was naturally impossible to make continuous love on the scale to which Marie-Clarice and I had been accustomed, I don't know, but our relationship grew a little more gentle and therefore more affectionate. We even made excursions together to places of interest. We took drives into the country with myself dressed up as Anthony Buckland, and it was through Marie-Clarice that I met many interesting people whose ideas coincided with ours.

In return I introduced Marie-Clarice to Pêche. We attended his classes together. I must say for Marie-Clarice that she showed no signs of condescension towards Pêche's ragged pupils. She was as at home with the Lattres and the German breeches maker as she was with any of her own friends. But I could not persuade her of the tactlessness of dressing up for the occasion. She shone like a frozen pond in bright sunlight amongst the rags of L'Étuve. The diamonds in her ears alone would have kept half the people at Pêche's classes for about five years. But she clung to the idea that it would be affected to dress down to them. She wanted them to accept her for what she was. She had a horror of hypocrisy. They accepted her with confusion. They were suspicious but had not yet been able to shake off a vague sense of pleasure that a glittering comtesse should choose to sit on the floor with them.

Through his deputy friends Pêche got us into the Jacobin Club meetings. He could never suppress a hint of pride when he claimed Marie-Clarice as one of his own pupils. It elevated him in the eyes of some of his friends to have acquired such a convert. Those were the days, one must remember, before such a connection would have meant an immediate death sentence. The press was not then advocating the overthrow of Royalty. They were still only urging a federative union and national representation. Camille Desmoulins said that in his opinion there were hardly more than ten French journalists who were truly Republicans. The Revolution's most violent English supporter, Thomas Paine, was still looked upon as a visionary incendiary.

Robespierre, so soon to become a leader in what one can only describe as a kind of bloodthirsty nightmare, said of Paine at one of the meetings we attended, "This Englishman's fire is not calculated to illumine but to consume." Moderation had not yet become a capital offence. It was still safe in those days for Marie-Clarice to lean up against one of Pêche's coffins in her cerise taffeta and allow Madame Lattre and Madame Lapin to try on her jewellery.

She was exceedingly generous. The street vendors were round her carriage as soon as it drew up. She bought geese and fruit and loaded No. 15 with more food than it had seen since its days of being an affluent dwelling. Nothing she did was from a desire to win popularity. It was from sheer horror at the want she saw all around her. None of us could have guessed the price she was to pay for this overdone but genuine good-heartedness. The time of the "civic dinners," when everyone was compelled to bring what food he could afford to these street banquets, was still round the corner. It was impossible to do right at these functions. If one was generous and brought a lot of food and wine, one was immediately suspected of being an accapareur — for if one wasn't a monopolist and hoarding food to the public detriment, how was one able to supply so much? Death could follow such generosity very swiftly. On the other hand, to bring too little was just as dangerous. One was accused of defrauding one's brother citizens and death could follow just as fast.

Old Lapin was against Marie-Clarice from the start, but Pêche was unrestrictedly grateful. He thought it an illustration of how this policy of keeping violence at bay could be employed to give the aristocrat a personal and practical lesson in the needs of the proletariat.

The only two people in our section of L'Étuve who refused steadfastly to have anything to do with Marie-Clarice were M.S. and the Puce. M.S. would not even allow me to talk of her and walked out of the room if I mentioned her name. He could see in her nothing but a threat to my career. In that, of course, he proved right.

The Puce rejected every effort on the part of Marie-Clarice to befriend her. We offered to take her for drives and show her the country, and Marie-Clarice sent her clothes and other presents, but they were handed back to the porter at the Hôtel de Faille within an hour of reception. Whenever I returned from a visit to Marie-Clarice, she turned her back on me. "You've been with *her*. I can smell her on you."

But it was not long before I noticed the Puce herself smelling like one of the whores in the Palais-Royal. Our rooms were filled with a ferocious perfume that even gained ascendency over the Puce's good soups.

M.S. was unsympathetic about it. "Well, what do you expect, boy, she's trying to compete."

Her efforts to rival Marie-Clarice's gentle fragrance were indeed pathetic, but unfortunately it was not the only way she tried to compete.

M.S. and I had the latter end of the partition dividing us, so that we achieved an effect of private bedrooms. It was the night of June 20 — a date not likely to escape a Parisian citizen's mind. It held L'Étuve in a thick box-like heat and I was aware in my dreams that my room was filling up with an obnoxious scent. I then realised that there was a curiously warm sensation in my left ear. It felt like the tip of a small tongue. And it *was* the tip of a small tongue. By the time I was fully awake the Puce's fiery little body had slipped in beside me and her mouth was over mine in a passionate but inexpert kiss.

I struggled like an old maid under the mistletoe. By the time I had freed myself the noise had attracted M.S. He stood in the doorway in his nightshirt and the inevitable nightcap. I believe he would still have worn this if he'd been cast into a furnace. The light of his candle showed me the Puce's nakedness. I flicked the covers over her. She lay without moving, but her sobs were enough to wake Pêche's customers in the next street.

"Boy," said M.S. "What's this?"

"What it looks like," I said angrily, "except that it wasn't my idea. Aren't you ashamed of yourself?" I asked the Puce, "creeping into my bed with Marie Lebrun tricks?"

She shook her head fiercely into the pillow. "They are Marie-Clarice tricks, not Marie Lebrun's. She only told me what you do to make people come back and back to you like you keep on going to Marie-Clarice. Oh, I hate her. I hope she *dies*. If I could make her die I would."

M.S. marched off to the Puce's room and returned with her shift. "Get into this while we're not looking and get out of that boy's bed."

She slipped into the garment but refused to move. M.S. sat on the side of the bed. "Now, listen to me, girl. That's not the way to get him. A man likes his appetite tickled. He doesn't want his food rammed down his throat however tasty it might be. The best way to get a man to want you is to put yourself out of his reach."

She sat up with a totally drenched face. "But how am I to make him see I want to keep away from him if I can't get near enough to show him?"

It was a problem with which I could sympathise, but I was too shocked to be amused. They continued to discuss me as if I were not present. "But, Uncle, I love him. I could be as good in the bed as that woman."

"The best thing you can do," I told her, "is to take yourself back to number fifteen."

This produced further sobbing. "Uncle, you want me to marry him, don't you?"

M.S. said quietly, "Well, I think he's a fool to play about with that creature when he could have someone like you. But that's the way it is, girl, you can't make a fool see sense."

With this little homily he departed to his own room, but not before he had said to the Puce, "Any more of this sort of thing and you go back to your grandfather over my shoulder and you won't come back to us again."

He left me staring belligerently at the Puce. My temper was not helped by the fact that in the few moments before I had come to my senses I had been conscious of a quick desire for her.

"Realise once and for all," I said, "that you'll never appeal to me in the same way as Marie-Clarice, and it's lucky for you that you won't."

She pushed back the covers sulkily. Her long narrow feet glowed in the candlelight as she slipped reluctantly out of my bed. I thought she was going to pass me and go to her room, but she suddenly stopped and pitched herself against me. I almost lost my balance, and I couldn't get her arms from round my neck without bruising them. She was crying, but silently now. "Oh, please, what is wrong? I am gonflée now. I *saw* how you looked at Marie Lebrun that time. You *wanted* her. It's not nice for me that I love you so much. It keeps me from much better people." She sensed my quick smile and was enraged by it. "That's true. Monsieur Lattre told me last week that if anything happened to Madame he would know where to look."

"I'm sure of it, the lecherous old toad," I said.

I freed myself and sat her down. Stooping in front of her, I took her hands. "Puce, when you grow older you'll see the difference. You don't always have to be fond of the people you make love to. I promise you that I love you more than Marie-Clarice."

"That's no good to me if you see *her* all the time. I want you to risk your career every night for *me*. I should cook and sew for you as well as wear you out in the bed."

"Well, it's very kind of you," I said, "and I do appreciate it. But, you see, I shouldn't love you at all if you turned into someone like Marie-Clarice. I like you as you are and I don't want you spoilt."

"You *don't* like me as I am!" she wailed.

It seemed impossible to explain to her. She drew up my hands and kissed them both. I pulled them away. "Now, now, Puce, I'm not worth that. It hurts at the moment, I know, but you'll find it wears off. You'll meet someone you really do love and you'll soon see the difference. You'll laugh when I remind you that you once thought you loved me."

She stood up, put out a hand for the candle, and said in a whisper, "Goodbye."

Chapter 41.

I HAD expected the Puce to make a dramatic return to the Lapins in the morning, but her "goodbye" was evidently on the spiritual plane of our acquaintance rather than on the material. It was intended to show me that she would never force her unwelcome attentions on me again. She spoke to M.S. in a small bereaved voice, but to me she made it plain that as far as she was concerned, I no longer existed.

The poor child had timed her scene badly. It was the wrong day for the Puce to try and make her personality felt. A political earthquake was shaking Paris. Pêche came bounding up our stairs as if a rhino were charging him from behind. "They've gone! They've escaped! They got away in the night! This will mean bloodshed — the streets will pour!"

It was some time before we discovered that the Royal Family had escaped from the Tuileries. M.S., who could sympathise with anyone wishing to leave France, never mind the sorely humiliated "Lord's anointed," failed to grasp the gravity of the situation. But in running away from his capital and taking his heir with him, King Louis had made clear that he had no intention of supporting the constitutional rights of his people. It was obvious that for all his apparently good intentions of being in agreement with his subjects' desires for reforms, he was only waiting his time to repudiate them. Having done that, he would not hesitate to rally every foreign power to his side and return with an invading army into France.

Paris, always ready to boil over at a moment's notice, excelled itself on that day and for several after it. The turmoil was indescribable.

At Marie-Clarice's house I found some of the English members of the London Society for Constitutional Reform every bit as excited as the French. Thomas Paine had written an address to the "People of France" claiming that as their King had deserted them they would be justified in considering it a de facto abdication, and that they should declare themselves rid of his shameless rule at once. Marie-Clarice read it out for my benefit, and it was in her richly decorated salon, with Côté offering wine cups, that I saw on the head of an astonishingly bearded foreigner named Anacharsis Cloots my very first Phrygian cap.

The people, spurred on by the press, the clubs, and the constitutionalists, speedily announced themselves in favour of a Republican government. Excitement mounted with such ferocity that it seemed that the whole city must burst a communal blood vessel. In the Champ-de-Mars the mayor unfurled a red flag — which apparently typified the willingness of the people to shed their blood for freedom. Thousands of people tramped to the Champ-de-Mars to sign a petition to the assembly demanding the overthrow of the absent King. Marie-Clarice and I trudged along with them. To have tried to get a carriage through would have meant a ten-hour hold-up. Mayor Bailly unfolded his red flag amongst ear-splitting cheers, but then, as usual, rumour managed to make itself heard. My hero La Fayette appeared to have got hold of the idea that a certain brewer named Santerre was rallying the faubourgs to destroy not only the Tuileries but most of Paris. La Fayette promptly ordered the National Guard to disperse the people. They fired, and in the resulting horror, hundreds of people were killed and wounded. Rumour put it at four thousand, but that was rumour. Nevertheless, there seemed no end to the stream of dead and dying who were being shouldered away by their friends. Pêche's streets were certainly pouring out blood like cut veins. I had the utmost difficulty in dragging Marie-Clarice back alive to the Hôtel de Faille. We were too far off to see La Fayette's courageous but fruitless effort to put a halt to the carnage, for the moment he realised the effect of his ill-judged orders he jumped in front of one of the guns to try and stop the next volley. But it was too late. The crowd dispersed only to gather in greater numbers and surge round Paris looking for revenge. Anyone as well dressed as Marie-Clarice was in instant danger. I clawed at her hair, tore off her bodice, so that she looked as if she'd been a victim of the fray, and plastered her with blood from a poor wretch I found dead in the gutter. Like that, and in her camisole, I got her back safely to the Hôtel de Faille.

I don't think I shall ever get used to the mercurial temperament of a French crowd. From the gravity of the mass funerals, the mood soon changed to one of festivity. M.S. and I received a note from the theatre to say that our performances had been cancelled so that we could take part in a pageant with all the other entertainers of Paris.

The following evening most of the city was engaged in glorifying Voltaire.

As one of the first advocates of the revolution his sarcophagus was put on a pedestal amongst the ruins of the Bastille where he had once been imprisoned. M.S., who considered him a critic of Shakespeare, a cynic and a thorn in the side of the Lord's anointed, refused to take part in the operations.

Being more in tune with Voltaire's politics than his writing, I joined the hundreds of other actors, actresses, singers, and dancers who took part dressed as his characters. I was Orosmane, and I stood in an uncomfortably dramatic posture at the foot of Voltaire's statue with the Mahomets and widows of Malabar.

The various military bands could hardly be heard above the general noise made by the hymns of praise and the cheers. The ropes of the night lamps were wound round with oak leaves, flags and figures hung from windows, and it really seemed that in the joy of toasting the deceased Voltaire, Paris had forgotten her own dead of the day before. Twenty girls chosen for their beauty walked in front of the sarcophagus, which was drawn on a fabulously decorated car by twelve white horses.

Our job as actors was to fight our way back to our own theatres and take up our positions on stands that had been erected outside them. There we sang hymns composed by Méhul and Gossec and written by André Chénier, all of them lauding Voltaire. I don't know about the other actors concerned, but my services were considered voluntary contributions to the great writer's memory and were deducted from my salary at the end of the week!

Still made-up as Orosmane, I got home to find that M.S. had joined the Puce in not speaking to me. He was incensed at my part in the proceedings. The Puce wore her martyred look and M.S. his "betrayed friend." To annoy them I kept level with their conversation by quoting long passages from Voltaire's *La Pucelle d'Orléans*.

I took no more notice of the Puce's animosity than I took of her infatuation. I thought that they would both wear off. But I realised that a campaign was on foot. She was out to show me how desirable she could be to other men.

The next night when we got back from the theatre, there were signs that she had entertained a male guest. The rooms were cloudy with tobacco smoke and there was an empty wine bottle stowed in the cupboard.

Two nights later she was missing. Our suppers were ready on the stove, but there was no Puce. M.S. and I went out in search of her. The Lapins had not seen her, nor had the Lattres or Pêche.

It was no time for a young girl to be out in the streets. The King and Queen had been caught at Varennes. They were being escorted back to Paris. The town was in a torment of anticipation. Trumpets had sounded in every quarter announcing the intention of the National Assembly to put the King under arrest. He and his family were being escorted back to the capital, and round the Tuileries and the Champs-Élysées the crowds were a solid black force.

We searched every café and estaminet we had known the child to frequent before. We buffeted our way along the rue du Temple, but amongst the gingerbread sellers, the charlatans selling elixirs for eternal youth, the trained monkeys raising their caps, and the jugglers and clowns, there was no sign of the Puce. My mouth was dry from agitation. The mobsters were rolling round the streets determined on violence. One felt that if they couldn't lynch the Royal Family, anyone else might do. A young girl, perhaps, repulsing their drunken offers of friendship might well end up by being pulled apart. We realised that our search was absurd but couldn't bring ourselves to give it up. As long as we were looking for her we felt less fear.

When the Royal berline finally made its creeping progress towards the Tuileries, it was practically impossible to move. It was first sighted on the high ground beyond the Champs-Élysées, and a howl went up which should have been heard across the Channel.

When the berline crawled towards the Tuileries gardens, real trouble broke out. The mob dashed itself at the palace as if it had only one head and one limb. I have seldom seen such a massive assault. The National Guard was swept aside, broken through, and completely overpowered. How they ever got the King and his family safely into the palace I don't know. The mob were actually rioting on the steps of the Pavillon de l'Horloge.

M.S. had had his hat knocked off, and an ugly-looking deputy gripped his shoulder. "Put your hat on, don't you know the King is passing?"

"That," said M.S. "is a good reason to keep it off."

If I hadn't butted him suddenly in the stomach with my head so that he doubled up and I had a chance to pull him away in the crowd, he would have been attacked.

The recapture of the Royal Family did nothing to appease the furies. The fact that the King had solemnly sworn to uphold the constitution in the Champ-de-Mars and that the Queen had held up the Dauphin as a pledge, and the fact that they had then secretly attempted to leave the country, seemed to evoke a mass fury that had to find an outlet. The people formed themselves into destructive bands searching for any marks of Royalty. From small tobacconists to the more elegant shops carrying the Royal arms there was no mercy. Theatres and lottery offices fared the same. Any building carrying a Royal symbol was showered with stones and battered with pikes. Every Royal sign was either disfigured or torn down. Stuffed figures of the King and Marie-Antoinette were burned on bonfires to the tunes of the "Ça ira" and the "Carmagnole."

M.S. and I got drawn off our route like bits of driftwood in a gushing stream. We had to give up our search, and fight our way home.

It was on boulevard des Bains Chinois that we hit our next little bit of excitement. Everyone seemed to be kissing everyone else. In the centre of this affectionate foray was the postmaster of St.-Ménéhould, whose astuteness had caught the Royal Family. Crowned with a grotesque wreath of laurels, this man Drouet was the god of the moment. His adoring escort was marching him along the street forcing every woman he met to kiss him in gratitude. Men, too, were included in the compulsory honour. I kissed him, not only to get out of his way, but because I was delighted that the people had retrieved their King.

M.S., of course, saw only a brutally humiliated group of the "Lord's anointed" and he announced loudly that he would rather kiss a "goat's arse" than the cheeks of Drouet. Whether it was his choice of a comparison that tickled the eternally unpredictable crowd I don't know. But instead of lynching him they laughed at him. Their one object was to make him kiss their hero. Roaring gleefully "C'est un Anglais! C'est un Anglais!" they clamped his arms behind his back, seized his kicking legs, and carried him forward like a battering ram until he was level with Drouet's face. Drouet, who had no doubt also been rewarded in wine, danced back coyly saying that he preferred privacy when he kissed such a handsome lad. Shrieks of delight followed this and clapping broke out when he kissed M.S. tenderly on the lips and said that this was his favourite salute of the day. I dared not interfere, for any wrong move might have turned their goodwill into viciousness again. M.S. was carried like a battering ram all the way back to the rue de Picardie. There he was placed on his feet, kissed by Drouet again and by about a hundred women, and finally allowed to climb our stairs.

We were neither of us in the best mood to observe the Puce impertinently perched on the table swinging her legs and whistling the "Ça ira." We both flew at her.

"Where have you been?"

"What the hell do you mean by making us chase all over the town for you?"

"You're lucky you didn't get your silly little throat cut."

"You're lucky you didn't get worse with these loonies howling about."

"I have been," she said with dignity, "entertained by a gentleman."

"Who?"

"Where? You were nowhere round here."

"My friend is important and rich."

"Where did he take you?"

"How did you meet him?"

"What's his name?"

She was careful only to answer M.S. Her non-speaking policy was still in effect with me.

"He has been following me in the streets for a long time. He says my beauty made him dream at nights. He said I had everything to make a man go mad. He took me to his home, which was *much* grander than the Hôtel de Faille. The legs of his bed were solid gold and so was his chamber pot. He told me that he had never made love to anyone as good at it as me. He went down on his knees and thanked me afterwards."

M.S. took time off to choke, but my attention had wandered to her hair. It was spattered with sawdust and there was some on her shoulders and back. There was a carpenter on the floor below us and he stored his timber in a large recess on the landing.

"Well," I said, "I'm glad to hear it. At your age you should enjoy yourself."

M.S. blustered, "Enjoy herself! With some old tomcat who —"

I beckoned him outside. "That child," I said, "has slept with nothing more alarming than a few planks of timber. She's been hiding in old Moustier's cupboard. It's just to prove that I'm not the only pebble on her beach."

We imagined that she would be content with this little effort to show me what I was missing, but we were wrong. She launched into a campaign and a practical one at that. Having failed to convince us with her story, she was more than ever determined to prove that she could attract men. God knows, it wasn't difficult. The Puce no longer looked the "child" we continued to call her. She was still somewhat undersized — L'Étuve had left that mark on her for ever — but she was fully developed and in excellent proportions. There were times when I myself had to look sharply away when she came in with the breakfast with her hair loose and her breasts softly protruding under the second-hand robe de bain she had bought herself. Her eyes seemed to turn up ever more in the mornings and her lips looked warm.

She was frequently missing when we got back from the theatre. She was never in Moustier's cupboard, either. Sometimes there was physical evidence that she had received flesh-and-blood male guests.

"Nothing is taken from your suppers," she said when we remonstrated with her. "I feed my friends on my own money from the Palais de Justice."

Her conversation was loaded with masculine Christian names. What is more, their complimentary remarks had a more authentic sound to them than the praises of the gentleman with the gold chamber pot. If we questioned her, she simply said that she had been dancing in the boulevard du Temple with Jean, Pierre, Antoine, or Claude and added, "Why not? It's better than sitting about mending stockings until you two come home."

I must have looked at the Puce's face more thoroughly than at any other time. It was my boast that I could always tell when a girl lost her virginity. There is a certain difference of expression — a subtle alteration of character. But hard as I stared at her, I couldn't see that look on the Puce. She had changed, however, in other ways: her neatness was disappearing, and she was becoming as blown-looking as Marie Lebrun, with whom I was afraid she spent a good bit of her time. She often came back sick from too much wine, but none of M.S.'s reasonable little lectures had any effect on her. To me she was still speaking only when it was strictly necessary. We tried laughing her out of it, ignoring her, and moralising. Not even an appeal to her that she was lowering the prestige of her beloved rue Matignon had any results.

It was no time for a young girl to try and flaunt her attractions. The citizens of Paris were grossly overacting a kind of systematic depravity. It was a mixture, I think, of defiance and relief — defiance against everything they had once held sacred; relief from the overthrowing of an authority that had ground them down.

M.S.'s bigoted opinion that the Palais-Royal was nothing but a parade ground for whores was now coming true. They leaned out of the windows in the lateral galleries above the shops and shouted invitations to every male in sight. I was not cheered to observe Marie Lebrun amongst them. She had joined forces with a notorious prostitute who had turned herself into a kind of revolutionary angel. In the daytime Théroigne de Méricour strutted about waving a sabre and calling for the death of all aristocrats and modérés. At night she strolled in the Palais-Royal seeking her custom from young federalists, soldiers due for the frontiers, cordeliers, Jacobins, and people like Blaise de Vergny. She would probably have added myself to her list. She was an attractively dissipated creature. But this was the company Marie Lebrun was keeping, and so I was horribly afraid for our small Puce.

I have never seen so many drunks about. Girls lay up against walls deserted by men who were bored to find them too far gone for reciprocal intimacy. Boys of not more than fifteen rattled weapons and sang filthy songs into the faces of the elderly and timid. Revolting literature was sold on every corner, and erotic books advocated every type of lecherous indulgence. It was the birth convulsions of the age of reason. As such I think it was understandable. Loosened fetters lead to excesses, restrained youth must break out before it can be made to see the wisdom of settling down, hunger must gorge itself before it understands sufficiency.

People like Pêche never lost hope, and the assembly continued to debate a wise and justifiable constitution. Everyone had expectations that our troubles would subside. This was merely the early havoc to be expected after the overthrow of the chaos caused by an ancient and outmoded régime. There were even signs that the inexplicable mob were not wholly in favour of butchering their monarchy. The King — poor man, someone should have rehearsed him — had only to totter out and give a series of grunts to signify that he intended to support his people's aims, to be greeted with a roar of glass-cracking cheers. If he looked emotionally affected, which he frequently did, he could reduce the most savage amongst his audience to sentimental tears. I must say in the light of later events I can't blame him for suspecting them, but one wonders whether, if he had been a better actor, he might not have carried the day. Even the soldiers, some of whom were not over fourteen — the "gamins" of Paris — marched against the European legions who were gathered to invade France, carrying banners inscribed, "La Nation! La Loi et le Roi!" Old habits die slowly, and they still wanted to fight for King as well as country. One can't help feeling that the poor man had a good house to play upon. But he was up against considerable opposition. Every street-corner agitator was an actor too in his way. Political hysteria always encourages histrionic talent.

In view of the general collapse of law and order, we tried to restrain the Puce from staying out late at night. But she paid no attention to us. One morning we were woken up at two o'clock by a noise worse than any cat fight I've ever heart. Squeals of pain were intermingled with hoarse shrieks of "Cochon" and "Poule!" Finally we pulled open the door, to see the Puce struggling under the weight of Madame Lattre in the gutter. Blood and hair were flying about. The cocoa seller, assisted by a few interested spectators, was trying to disentangle them, but he was hampered by his gross equipment. He turned viciously upon me and I noticed that his eyes looked young in his grimy bearded face. "You took her away from her grandfather! You've warped her morals, why don't you take care of her?"

M.S. bent down and heaved up Madame Lattre as I had once lifted "Mrs. Dockery" when too much gin had made it impossible for her to make her own exit.

The Puce streaked upstairs like a shot kitten. When Madame Lattre had finished cursing her — which included us as bawdy-house keepers as well as the Puce as an open-legged strumpet — we discovered the cause of the trouble. Old Lattre had been missing and his wife had traced him to the Luxembourg Gardens. There, under a tree, she had found her portly husband in the company of the Puce. Madame Lattre's tale grew more alarming every time she repeated it.

I had gone upstairs, put the Puce over my knee, and given her a sound hiding before I reflected that Madame Lattre's first account — before she was encouraged to embellish it by sympathetic murmurs — was more likely to be accurate. In that she had simply found them "close together looking into each other's eyes." In view of the number of people walking about in the gardens, the later accounts of the Puce's being undressed and "stimulating" his desires seemed unlikely.

However, I was worried enough to ask Marie-Clarice for advice. I thought her experience might help me. We sat in her small yellow salon with the scent of the flowers reaching us through the windows. She was wearing my favourite lilac dress and the amethyst spray in her hair.

"How much do you mind about this child?" she asked me.

"Oh, a lot. I mean I feel the little brute belongs to us. We practically brought her up."

"You're not in love with her?"

"Great heavens no."

"She's quite attractive."

"I'm aware of that."

"Then why don't you accept her offers and put a stop to all the nonsense?"

"It wouldn't be fair. She deserves someone better."

"But you think you're good enough for me?"

I smiled at her. "Yes, I think I'm good enough for you."

I was always delighted by the way her laughter reached her eyes. "If you like, I'll have a talk with the girl. I'm used to this kind of thing."

"She wouldn't let you."

"I think I can lure her here." She went to the manly desk that stood in the corner. No dainty écritoire could have housed all Marie-Clarice's business-like correspondence. She read me out what she had written.

" 'Dear Mademoiselle Dupont,

I am quite aware that you dislike me, but I suggest that you pay me a visit just the same. Why not come and take chocolate with me at eleven o'clock tomorrow morning? I think I have something to say that might interest you.

Your friend,
Marie-Clarice de Faille.' "

"That ought to get her curious," she said.

She was right. Côté brought round the letter and delivered it personally to the Puce. She hid it from us, but we knew by the careful toilette she was making that she intended to keep the appointment. Gone was the Marie Lebrun clothes-off-the-shoulder look, the hair loose in the back of a sweaty neck, and the uncorseted hips swinging under a petticoatless skirt. Out went our Puce in the green dress, new shoes, and stays. M.S. and I sat back with our fingers crossed.

Marie-Clarice had sent Côté to escort her — I rather suspect to prevent her from changing her mind. I remembered thinking that they made a rather handsome pair. Côté was a good-looking boy when he took the insolent expression off his face which so tickled his mistress.

Marie-Clarice later confessed that she was nervous! She played her usual trick of dressing as if she were expecting a crowned head so as not to insult the Puce, and waited in the yellow salon.

Côté showed the child in, and Marie-Clarice noticed that he gave the Puce a kind of hope-you-get-the-better-of-her look, and that the Puce's glance back was friendly.

Marie-Clarice poured out the chocolate herself. "Now, then," she said, "I believe you're in love with Monsieur Roberts or Monsieur Buckland or the Vicomte de Lambrière or whatever you call him."

The Puce's eyes and voice were steady, but she obviously didn't trust her hands to pick up her chocolate cup. She turned a worried pink whilst staring at it.

Marie-Clarice took a quick sip of her own and sat back fanning herself. "Heavens! It's too hot for chocolate." She rang the bell and had it cleared. "The last time we met, Mademoiselle Dupont, you lied to me on a rather lurid scale. To me that proves you love him."

She thought she had won a point. The Puce was grateful to her for getting that much out of the way. "I imagine you don't hate me because of what I look like, or because of what I smell like?"

The Puce managed to say, "I think you're very pretty, Madame la Comtesse."

Marie-Clarice admitted to being mesmerised by the "new shoes." She had heard all about them from me. She said that they were displayed beneath the Puce's dress so proudly that tears came into her eyes. She knew that they were three years old. I think it might have been one of the first occasions upon which Marie-Clarice learned that there are other ways to help the poor than impulsive giving. She confessed that she longed to go out straightaway and order the child twenty pairs in the finest kid. But to have done so would have cast a slur on the old "new shoes" of which the Puce was so inordinately proud — the ones in which she had transferred herself from L'Étuve to the rue Matignon; the symbols of her dignity. Marie-Clarice restrained herself. I thought it an admirable self-victory.

"Why you hate me is because I'm the mistress of the man you love?"

"Yes, madame."

"You'd like to kill me, wouldn't you?"

"Yes, madame."

Marie-Clarice said that her heart first went out genuinely to the Puce when she found that the child was as forthright as herself. "Shall I tell you why that would be a waste of your time and why it would be much better to wait?"

"If you will be so good, madame."

"Because if you please one another in bed to the extent that I and your friend do, you destroy it. You can't help it. Such a thing is impossible to keep up. How old are you?"

"I am nearly fifteen, madame."

"You're small for your age! I must give you a mixture a nun made up for a small boy I adopted with rickets. It feeds the bones and restores the blood strength lost by lack of nourishment. I am nearly *twenty-four*. Don't you see that you have an advantage over me?"

"No, madame."

"Then you're a stupid child. Monsieur Roberts and I will get tired of one another. He will tire first because I find him outstandingly attractive. But you only have to wait. If you try and separate us at this moment you'll prolong our affair, you'll keep alive something that would have died a very normal death. You'll make us think it's worth it. And the way to draw him towards you, my poor infant, is *not* to let him find you in the arms of other men. The thing for you to do is to sit still and be the opposite of me."

The Puce stood up. "Madame, on the way here Monsieur Côté told me that he used to be your lover. Is that true?"

"Yes," said Marie-Clarice: "why? Are you shocked? Did you think that your friend Monsieur Roberts was the first man I had ever had? What is wrong with Côté? Do you despise him because he is a servant?"

Marie-Clarice said there was no venom in the Puce's voice when she answered. She felt it more in the nature of a return for her own frankness. "Côté hates you, madame. He told me he did when he brought me here. He hates all aristocrats, even when they're kind to him."

"Yes, that's what I like about him. As for his hating me, I'm not very surprised. One doesn't keep the same lover for ever — at least, not if you're someone like me. That's what I've been trying to tell you this morning."

It was Marie-Clarice who told me about the interview, and for a while it looked as if it might have had a good effect. The Puce lost her Marie Lebrun look. She still went out at night, but she allowed us to see her escorts and to know where she had been. She had two new admirers: Côté and the cocoa seller.

The young footman's attentions did not worry me. It was the cocoa seller's interest that kept me awake at night. I did not know that I had equal reasons to be afraid of them both.

Chapter 42.

IN THE Tour Bonbec I longed for things I had never appreciated before: snowflakes blown into one's face on the Yorkshire moors; the smell of a summer lawn freshly cut; a wild cherry echoing its foamy reflection in a stream; the colour of lichens on an old stone wall; that first kick in the air from winter frosts; the sudden appearance of bonfire smoke curling above cottage gardens — anything, I suppose, but the smell of one's self and one's neighbours in the Tour Bonbec. Compared to it, the Mousetrap was a comparatively pleasant memory. I could only surmise that our ventilation travelled through stale subterranean passages before it reached us. When we took our exercise in the men's court I spent my time swishing a stick through the air. If I listened carefully it reminded me of the sharp hiss of the wind on the Yorkshire moors.

It was while I was thus engaged that I heard my name called out again in the *Journal du Soir*. As it was De Lambrière and not Buckland, I thought that I was in for another wearisome interview with Louis Brissac. I was afraid that there would come a time when my bleary brain would come to believe facts that it would normally refute. I could see myself being worn away by the endless questions and finally confessing that I was both De Lambrière and Buckland. An old man in here broke down after hours of interrogation in the overlit greffe and admitted that he was his own son. As his head was not a matter of dispute between two rival committees, no one tried to preserve it and he died within an hour.

Louis Brissac was certainly waiting for me in the greffe, but beside him was a man whose name sent me cold in spite of the heat of the fire. I had heard far from pleasant accounts of the citoyen Bégnon, whose power in the Committee of Public Safety was well known. He was reputed to be so stern a patriot that he boasted of never having missed an execution. He attended the Place de la Révolution daily and applauded every head that fell off. It cheered me not at all to see that he was taking a personal interest in mine. He had one of the most repulsive faces I had ever seen and there was no difficulty at all in believing that he would crow with delight at the guillotine's bloody work. Although his expression made one shudder, his voice was a surprise; it was mild and pleasant.

He said softly, "Sit down, citoyen Buckland."

The Lieutenant promptly added, "Yes, please be seated, citoyen De Lambrière."

I sat. Bégnon and Brissac bowed to one another. Their voices were not friendly when they spoke.

"Please proceed with your questions to the accused, citoyen Bégnon."

"I'm content to follow you, citoyen Brissac."

The Lieutenant thereupon rang a bell, and when an usher came in, he snapped at him, "Bring in the witness."

I was no more than ordinarily curious about the unimpressive young man who then stepped into the room. Without his grotesque equipment, his dirt and his rags, I at first failed to recognise the cocoa seller. He had one of those faces that are easy to alter; there wasn't much there in the first place. He looked smaller without his encumbrances and he had presumably worn a wig before, because he was fair-haired now. It was not until I had the chance to study his undressed features without the trappings with which I had always associated them that I realised who he was.

The Lieutenant addressed him. "Citoyen Barrière, who is this man?"

"He is the ci-devant Philippe-Jean-Baptiste-Raoul Vicomte de Lambrière."

"This you discovered in your years of service as an agent in my employment both under the old régime and the glorious Republic?"

"Yes, citoyen, there is no doubt that he is this De Lambrière. He became betrothed to an English lady who visited him here. I observed them throughout this entire period. I have records of their private conversations. I paid servants at the Hôtel de Muscovie to report to me and I overheard them myself. The lady was in absolutely no two minds that he was the Vicomte de Lambrière, and he himself answered to that name."

"He tells us," said the Lieutenant, "that he was an actor."

The cocoa seller shook his head. "He was not and never could be an actor. It's true that I only saw him perform once on the stage, but a child in a nativity play could have done better. He forgot his words, fell over his feet, and finally became so confused by trying to compete with his superiors that he fainted on the stage. The Théâtre des Variétés Amusantes dismissed him at once."

"Thank you, citoyen Barrière. Now, as to the girl Dupont."

For the first time the cocoa seller showed emotion. He looked at me with such crippling hatred that I was heartily alarmed by it. "The girl Dupont," he said, "was born a child of the people, but he dazzled her with his title and his riches. He turned her against her own kind. He did it deliberately, but he had no real use for her. He was the lover of the ci-devant Comtesse de Faille while Suzon Dupont slaved for him in return for no money, never losing the hope that he would keep his promise and marry her. It did not matter to him that so unimportant a little creature as Suzon Dupont was breaking her heart for him. By spreading his poison through her heart and mind he hoped to find other recruits in L'Étuve to undermine the Revolution. That was the reason for his presence in L'Étuve."

"That is grossly incorrect," I interrupted.

"You, citoyen," the Lieutenant told me, "are not permitted to speak. Your lies no longer interest us."

"He was a Royalist agent," insisted the cocoa seller, "getting the people's confidence by pretending that he was Buckland, an Englishman of doubtful morals. In this way he won the sympathy of L'Étuve, which he used to undermine the Revolution. While he was supposed to be betrothed to the Englishwoman as his real self, the Vicomte de Lambrière, he was the lover of that notorious aristocrat the Comtesse de Faille. Under his assumed name of Buckland he introduced this woman into L'Étuve and passed her off as the so-called friend of the poor. If that is not the work of two Royalist agents trying to restore the old régime, I deserve to be dismissed from your service, citoyens. There is no greater enemy of the people than the ci-devant Vicomte de Lambrière."

When the cocoa seller was dismissed, it was Bégnon who rang the bell.

Another witness came in and this time I recognised him at once as my hysterical friend in the Mousetrap who had been so distressed at his uncle's execution. I should have guessed, of course, that I would not be free of spies in the Conciergerie. All the prisons were alive with these "moutons," as we called them. Their object was to pretend to share in our miseries and try and get us to denounce friends and relatives during unguarded conversations.

Bégnon addressed the young "nephew" who had attached himself so persistently to me.

"Citoyen Phlipon, who is this man?"

"He is the citoyen Englishman Anthony Buckland of Sandgate in England."

"This is what you discovered during investigations for the Committee of Public Safety?"

"Yes, citoyen."

"What were your conclusions?"

"That he was engaged in espionage for his own country. He came over with his manservant, who is his accomplice. His passport was in the name of Buckland."

"Did you later discover him to have changed his name?"

"Yes, citoyen."

"What did he call himself?"

"The Vicomte de Lambrière."

"For what purpose did you feel him to have done this?"

"He was masquerading as a Frenchman betrothed to an English lady named Eliza Weldon. This lady led the authorities to believe that he was her lover and that she had come over to France to find him. But this was not the case. You have only to look at her face to see that this would not be likely. She was obviously his accomplice. Her visit was purely to take back the information collected by the accused."

I sat back vulgarly blowing my cheeks out. The thought of Lizzie Weldon suspected of spying for Pitt was enjoyable even in those circumstances, but I was not so amused when the agent Phlipon continued. "She came over in the company of a member of the British Foreign Office. While this Sir Gregory Hawtrey was making a great play of searching the theatres in Paris for the actor Roberts — the very man the accused claims to be — the three of them were dining together in the accused's apartments in the rue Matignon."

I passed a hand over a sticky forehead. It sounded suspicious even to me.

"Buckland entertained Sir Gregory and the woman Weldon as the Vicomte de Lambrière, a name that he had only assumed and that was the woman's excuse for visiting him. It would be surprising if Sir Gregory was not aware of this." The agent Phlipon continued placidly. "The accused took the two names to extract information from different stratas of society. As the ci-devant Vicomte de Lambrière he lived the life of an ordinary French gentleman. I observed him closely during that period. He was received in good salons, he mixed with important people in politics and in the arts. His accomplice, the woman Weldon, was in Paris throughout, and he repaired to the Hôtel de Muscovie every evening to report to her. She effected her return to England with the information by pretending to fall out with him. She left him a letter, which I bribed the porter at the Hôtel de Muscovie to show me first."

"But in L'Étuve," prompted Bégnon, "when he wished to gain the confidence of poorer people, he still used his own name of Buckland?"

"That is so. But he played the double game of pretending it to be a false one. He represented himself and his male accomplice as being the actors we know to have drowned. In order to support his claims he let the people see him dress up as the gentleman he actually was — Anthony Buckland — and went out to pick the pockets of the rich. He was successful in duping the unfortunates of L'Étuve completely. He had the full confidence of the section leader, Pêche, whom he deliberately prevented from attending the storming of the Bastille."

"And the girl Dupont," asked Bégnon: "was she an accomplice of Buckland's?"

The agent Phlipon nodded. "She assisted him throughout — even to confirming, when the need arose, that he was the Vicomte de Lambrière."

"She was in love with the accused?"

"No. Her relations with him were entirely mercenary. She was employed to extract information for him. She let it be thought that she was in love with him to excuse her intimacy with him. But she was perfectly aware of the existence of the woman Weldon. She lived with Buckland and Smith at the expense of the woman Weldon at number twenty-one rue Matignon. The porter of these lodgings later attested at his trial that he was half strangled by the accused in an attempt to destroy the evidence of his association with Dupont."

It was hard for me to decide which of them had the better case against me. It was rather like attempting to claim sanity in a lunatic asylum. The more one tries to insist on the truth, the more mad one sounds.

The agent Phlipon continued. "Far from being in love with him, Dupont was so personally disinterested in him that she did not object when she discovered he was having an affair with the ci-devant Comtesse de Faille."

"Did not object!" I sat back, defeated.

"The accused," continued Phlipon, "made no secret of his true identity while he was lodging in the house of his mistress, the Comtesse de Faille. I have this on the evidence of her footman, Côté, whom I paid to give me information. He was known to the Comtesse and all her friends as Anthony Buckland. The girl Dupont and the man Smith visited him at the Hôtel de Faille. There was a moment when I was forced to the conclusion that the man Smith believed the accused to be neglecting his work of espionage in

favour of the attractions of the Comtesse de Faille. Côté reported that both
Dupont and Smith demanded that he should forsake this woman's bed and
return with them to continue his normal duties. The accused was reluctant
and the man Smith knocked him unconscious and carried him out over his
shoulder. I witnessed this myself. I was watching the house."

"They wanted me to go back to my work as an *actor*," I interrupted. I
was ignored.

"Also," said Phlipon, "this same Côté told me of how the accused used
to take Madame de Faille to the political classes of his section leader,
Jacques Pêche. She pretended to be in sympathy with the people and took
them large hampers of food to bribe them into giving her their confidence.
Citoyen Côté can vouch for this because he used to accompany his mistress
to L'Étuve. She and the accused so deceived the section leader, Jacques
Pêche, that he gave them introductions to persons of note and gave them
every facility of reporting information to the Royalists and the British
government."

I started to speak but was silenced by Bégnon. He said to Phlipon, "In
your opinion, then, citoyen, there is no truth in the accused's assertion that
he came over here as an actor escaping justice in his own country?"

The agent Phlipon laughed. "His efforts to prove that were pathetic,
citoyen. No respectable managements would employ him after his dismissal
from the Théâtre des Variétés Amusantes. To keep up the pretence of
being an actor, he went in for clowning at Le Petit Théâtre de la Cité. I am
a good and trusted agent, citoyen. I have no doubt from my own investigations that this man has never been a French aristocrat and that he has
always been a spy for the English Pitt."

He made a series of prim little bows before he went out and was good
enough to include me in them.

The Lieutenant and Bégnon exchanged cool glances.

Then Bégnon said to the guard, "Bring in the citoyen Dugazon."

My heart gave a happy little jerk. Lavaux had always hoped to get
Dugazon to testify in my favour. Surely here was someone who could not
fail to admit that I was the actor I claimed to be.

Dugazon came in with the inevitable Blenheim spaniel at his heels. I was
pleased to note that Chloe disliked the Committees of General Security and
Public Safety as much as I did myself. She snarled at both Brissac and
Bégnon with equal mistrust.

Dugazon did not look at me.

Bégnon asked him, "Is this man a member of your profession?"

"No."

I jumped up. "But, citoyen Dugazon, you *know* that I am. I brought you
a letter from John Philip Kemble."

Dugazon ignored me. His thin, affected voice was aimed at Bégnon. "I wrote as you requested, citoyen, to Kemble in England. He replied that he had never provided any actor with a letter of introduction to me and that if I had received one it must have been forged."

"I can explain that," I said. "It was a trick to get work. But Kemble must remember me. He sent down a critic to watch my performance."

Dugazon told Bégnon, "Kemble did recall an actor of the name the accused claims, but it only served to convince him that this man is an imposter. The actor from the Little Apollo Theatre whom he interviewed was drowned shortly afterwards trying to save his manager."

I sat down again clutching my head. Dugazon added, "I found work for the accused, but the management was obliged to dismiss him because his performances were so poor."

The Lieutenant leaned forward. "Citoyen Dugazon, you've doubtless heard that there has been a certain amount of criticism at the expense of the police. I happen to be aware that this man is the ci-devant Vicomte de Lambrière. I have been to a considerable amount of trouble and expense to prove this. I wish to justify myself. Have you ever known him by that name?"

"No, he used the false name of Roberts."

Bégnon leaned forward. "Citoyen Dugazon, the Committee of Public Safety has also spent time and money on this man — for which it must account. You will agree that no public body can afford in these days to fail the Revolution. Mistakes can be costly even in the highest quarters. We are convinced that we have not made any. This man is an English agent called Buckland. Are you in a position to confirm this for us?"

"No," said Dugazon. "He never called himself anything but Roberts as far as I was concerned. But we have the authority of Kemble that this was not his name. I can help you only by saying that I am confident that he was never a professional actor."

"We know that already," snapped the Lieutenant and Bégnon together.

I appealed to Dugazon. "For God's sake use your wits. I must be an actor and a thundering good one to have convinced one man that I'm a born Frenchman and another that I'm a born Englishman."

Dugazon answered drily, "Any trained spy could do that. The Committees of General Security and Public Safety are efficient bodies in whom the nation places great trust. It is unthinkable that after detailed observation either of them should have reached incorrect conclusions in your case."

"But don't you see that one of them *must* be wrong!" I shouted.

"Perhaps," said Dugazon, "but it would not be a convenient fact to admit. There are more important heads than yours at stake."

"Mine is the only one that interests me."

"Possibly, but you are alone in that preference." He took to the restless pacing that seemed indispensable to him. His little red heels caught the light, and the dog trailed dutifully after him. "As it is out of the question, citoyens, that either of your committees could be in the wrong, wouldn't it be possible for you to come to some agreement between yourselves?"

The Lieutenant told Dugazon, "If he would sign a confession to the effect that he is both de Lambrière *and* Buckland — a Royalist agent *and* a British agent — it might go a long way towards solving our difficulties."

"I'm not interested in your damn difficulties," I said. "I've admitted to the names and told you a dozen times how I came to use them, but I am not and never have been either a Royalist or a British agent."

The Lieutenant sighed. "So we come back to his story about being a dead actor again — and that is the one thing that we have jointly agreed that he is not."

Dugazon sent me an unpleasant glance. "Whoever he is, he came over from England. No good to France ever came out of *that* country. Can't he be executed on that evidence alone?"

Louis Brissac said wearily, "It's my business to prove that I am right to insist that citoyen Bégnon's Committee of Public Safety are in the wrong. Only this morning some of his fellow members — the citoyens Carnot, Billaud-Varenne, Robespierre, Couthon, Danton, Saint-Just — not names to be trifled with — told me that they would not give me much longer to prove my point."

"Similarly," said Bégnon, "these members of my own committee — certainly *not* names to be trifled with — gave *me* to understand that they would like me to hurry up and prove that we were right when we stopped the Lieutenant and his Committee of General Security from executing the accused in the name of de Lambrière."

Dugazon pondered this.

"It's also been hinted that these citoyens — decidedly not names to be trifled with — are not as friendly as it might seem on the surface. One doesn't know whether this case might not be seized upon by one faction to injure the other. Somebody else's mistakes might be very useful to them."

"Exactly," said the Lieutenant. "It's very important not to become a cat's-paw for anyone or anything these days."

Bégnon nodded agreement. Dugazon picked up his spaniel. "If I were you, citoyens, I should use every method available to you to get rid of the accused. Once you have done that, he will no longer be able to deny that he is either of your two prisoners. The longer you allow him to remain a threat, the more chances he will have of inspiring any private enemies you may have to use him as a weapon to bring you into disrepute. That is my advice to you, citoyens: get rid of him between you, at all costs — at *all* costs."

Chapter 43.

IT WAS my fault (of course!) that we did not finally leave for America. Our popularity at the appalling Petit Théâtre de la Cité had at last made the journey possible. But by the time we had collected enough money to go, I started to find excuses for staying in Paris. It was a reckless procrastination even from a financial point of view, for although the issue of assignats in place of the old type of money may have been an excellent idea, it was obvious to anyone with an eye to their savings that there would shortly be a serious depreciation in the value of property and funds. If we didn't leave for America soon, the worth of our money would be halved.

But I was still under the spell of Marie-Clarice.

On the abolition of titles of nobility, Marie-Clarice had dropped hers with a sincere lack of regret. She was actually proud of becoming plain citoyenne De Faille; she considered it an achievement and a distinction.

Not so brother Blaise. Like many of his contemporaries who had helped to capsise their own boat by inflaming the feelings of the suppressed, he was defiant at this attack on his own liberty. He felt it a lack of trust in the aristocracy that had already declared itself on the side of the people. In a way one could not help admiring him for it. Courage was needed to set oneself against public opinion in those days. But Blaise's method of demonstrating his defiance was sheer madness. Not only had titles been abolished, but all letters of nobility, armorial bearings, and personal liveries were forbidden. Blaise, in order to show that he considered these laws to be frivolous ones that would pass like an April storm, had painted a cloud over the arms on the doors of his berline. The arms were still perfectly visible behind the misty paint, and in lieu of a livery he dressed up his coachman and footmen as pierrots. He then set off to drive round Paris.

On the boulevard de la Madeleine his berline was overturned. The wretched servants were stripped of their fancy dress and driven naked along the streets until a commissary of police intervened. Blaise himself was half lynched. How he escaped the full punishment is hard to imagine. Two of his friends who played the same trick were killed. Blaise, with one arm pulled out of its socket and an injured eye that resulted in blindness, managed to keep ahead of the mob until the porter pulled him in at the Hôtel de Faille.

Marie-Clarice hid him in the granary. She went out to try and explain to the mob that it was merely a young man's idea of a joke, but was stoned and had to hide herself. She told Côté to call out the National Guard, but he refused. It was against his principles. He felt that Blaise deserved his fate. Being Marie-Clarice, she did not blame him and continued to employ him afterwards. Later one of her women smuggled a note to me.

I know you won't approve of this any more than I do. Blaise ought to be left to die up in the granary, but he's my only brother and I can't let him. It hurts me horribly to have to do anything against the Revolution: you know how I feel about it. But I shall have to get him out of the country. The people have quite rightly not forgiven him. They are watching the place all the time. Can you smuggle in some sort of disguise? Also, we need a doctor urgently: his wounds are quite beyond me.

In this M.S. helped me. As he considered Blaise one of his "betters," he approved of his stand against the "rabble." He was also under the impression that Blaise's action had something to do with striking a blow on behalf of the "Lord's anointed." I took care not to disillusion him. As the food was still being sold off at night at the Hôtel de Faille, it was easy to get a doctor to the boy disguised as a gargotier. My theatre wardrobe conveniently supplied the necessary costume.

M.S. also persuaded a drunken waterman who had greatly enjoyed our performance to visit the dressing-room and change clothes with me. We added to his headache in the morning by a punch on the chin and M.S. carried him out and laid him amongst other drunks in the boulevard du Temple.

I managed to get past the little group waiting for Blaise outside the Hôtel de Faille by saying I was related to one of the servants inside. No one suspected a waterman in a fair wig. Upstairs in the granary Blaise climbed into my disguise. His left eye was sightless, but his arm had healed.

He left the house with no difficulty. I sat in the granary waiting for Marie-Clarice to bring me fresh clothes. I waited quite a while — a day and a night. In between we found time for conversation.

"You must get out of France too," I told her. "They'll blame you as much as Blaise. It's not safe for you here any longer."

"Oh, everyone knows I'm with the people. One can't be blamed for one's idiot brother." She leaned over me. The lily-scented soap was a great comfort in the granary. We dared not go down into the house because of Côté. Marie-Clarice defended him. "He is a Republican like us. What in the world could I discharge him for? For being truer to our ideals than we've just shown ourselves?"

"Would you," I asked, my arms behind my head on the thick quilts she had brought me, "have still slept with me if I'd given Blaise away?"

"Certainly," she said firmly. "Principles come first, and if yours had forbidden you to help Blaise, I should have admired you for it. I should just have felt ashamed that mine were not as strong."

"The more I think of it," I told her, "the less safe I feel you're going to be. Can't you join in one of the émigré escape plans?"

"I suppose so. But I don't want to. What's happening now is all I've prayed for. I've certainly prayed for nothing else! It's bound to be difficult at first. If they really won't accept me I suppose I'll be forced to go, but I'm hoping they will. Besides" — the scent of lilies pressed closer round me — "I'm not quite ready to give *you* up. I promised your little friend I'd relinquish you in time, but I don't feel that the time is quite now."

Neither did I when she kissed me.

We never heard any more from Blaise, so we could only hope that he reached freedom. But to me it will always remain one of the curiosities of this spy-ridden Revolution that the one ill turn I really served it — by effecting the escape of one of its enemies — never appeared on any of my indictments. What happened to the cocoa seller? Where was that busy agent Phlipon? Where were the dozen and one other faceless bodies that must have been trailing me?

For the cocoa seller I can answer. He was clamped to the side of the Puce. But I had no time to worry about that.

While I was dallying in a hay loft, the rest of Paris was excessively active. There were proclamations pasted on the walls of all the sections urging the populace to maintain law and order but at the same time warning them that invasion was threatened!

Battalion after battalion marched off to defend the frontiers. I suppose it was owing to my sentimentality that many of the soldiers looked undersized. But perhaps it was just that Paris was formidably short of man power, and that recruitment was high among the very young. The gamins of Paris were needed badly now, to make up the revolutionary armies. Not much more than fourteen or fifteen, they were often uniformless, weaponless, and bewildered as they marched under their banners, which still proclaimed the legend "La Nation! La Loi et le Roi!"

When I was not bruising my bones with M.S. at the theatre by falling from acrobatic tableaux, I was trying to do my part in the defence of Paris. As a corporal under Pêche in the National Guard I drilled half the night.

The Duke of Brunswick's manifesto threatening the extinction of Paris if the Royal Family were harmed coupled with the fact that something like 150,000 supporters of the King were marching on the frontiers was good cause for alarm. Royalist forces in the departments were rallying. Every hand and every weapon was needed in Paris. Women and children packed the churches making lint and rolling bandages. Every male citizen with a second pair of shoes was compelled to give them to a soldier bound for the front, and house-to-house calls were made asking for any musket, pike, pistol, sword, couteau de chasse, or fowling-piece, no matter how old or rusty. Vaults were raided for the lead lining of coffins. These were turned into ammunition, and the remains of the corpses left wherever they happened to have been thrown. No one had a minute to spare for anything but defending the city. Even small children learned how to make cartridges.

I was so busy under Pêche I had no time even to visit Marie-Clarice. She would not have been able to receive me, either. She had upwards of two hundred women at work on lint in the Hôtel de Faille. When Pêche and I had finished our drilling and artillery practice we organised bands of twenty and thirty strong to scrape the walls of the cellars of every house in our section. Our work was turned into a lixivium from which we extracted saltpetre.

Even M.S., whose heart was undoubtedly with the forces marching against us, could not sit at home amongst all that activity. Every day he took his lunch in a parcel and joined the hundreds tramping up to Montmartre and Montrouge to construct field works.

After the first declaration of war against Emperor Leopold, it seemed to me that further declarations and retaliations were hurled at our heads like showers of apples.

I saw very little of the Puce. We were both engaged in war activities. But one morning she told me that the cocoa seller had proposed to her.

"Did you accept him?"

"No. I said I was betrothed to you. He told me to let you alone for my own good."

"That was wise of him."

"He thinks that you really are a vicomte and he says that the time is coming when all aristocrats will be slaughtered. If I don't leave you, he says, I will meet the same fate."

"Then you'd better take his advice."

She shook her head. "Citoyen Pêche says it would never come to that. The Montagne deputies may call for blood, but there are hundreds of sensible men in the Assembly whose aim is to build a new kind of world that everyone can enjoy."

I could hear Pêche's very tones in her voice. "Citoyen Côté also asked me to be his wife."

"You are doing well!"

"Yes. But I told him that it was the cocoa seller I loved."

I was cleaning my gun and not paying over-much attention to her rather complicated love life. "Why did you do that?"

"Because Pierre Côté is really in love with me. He says he would give his life for me. If he knew it was you I loved, he might want to kill you."

"Well, it's very nice of you to think of me, but doesn't the cocoa seller really love you?"

"Yes, but he hasn't offered his life like citoyen Côté. I wondered if he was just pretending to love me so as to find out all about you from me."

"Marriage would be rather a high price to pay for information, wouldn't it?"

She frowned. "Yes, but he's very devoted to duty."

"Send him along to me," I said. "I'll tell him anything he wants to know. Then you'll be sure he's marrying you for love."

It was about this time that M.S. counted the contents of his box and found that we had enough money for the three of us to reach America. My reasons for wanting to delay our trip were not entirely selfish. Much as I wished to put off the moment of saying goodbye to Marie-Clarice, I was also worried about leaving her behind. Jacobin newspapers were conducting a private war against aristocrats. They urged the people to destroy their domestic enemies before concentrating on outside opposition. The most vicious were *Le Père Duchesne*, run by Manuel and Hébert, *L'Ami du Peuple*, edited by Jean Paul Marat, Camille Desmoulins' *Discours de la Lanterne*, and Prudhomme's *Les Révolutions de Paris*. They all howled for the physical annihilation of nobility. And some of the more vitriolic pages were pasted on the walls. Frequently volunteers stood by to interpret their message to those who could not read. I took a knife and scraped several off the walls of the Hôtel de Faille. I didn't want attention drawn to the home of Marie-Clarice after Blaise's exhibition. These things were not lightly forgotten, and now and again crowds still gathered shouting for Blaise.

It was true that Pêche's sensible deputies with everyone's good at heart were still openly counselling moderation and issuing warnings against violence, but their opponents on the high seats on the left side of the Assembly — the Mountain — were loud in demanding extremes.

The ugly little deputy from Arcis-sur-Aube, whose unfortunate appearance was supposed to have come from a bull's objecting to his getting his childhood milk from its favourite cow and charging him to show its displeasure, was climbing steadily up the mountain. The eloquent voice of Georges Jacques Danton was very shortly to demand sixty thousand heads!

Marie-Clarice dismissed him as "one of those poor little advocates who hung about for years at the Palais de Justice in search of a brief. A little success has gone to his head. He'll soon get over the excitement of it all. He has a feeling of inferiority."

I noticed that quite a few little out-of-work advocates who had haunted the Palais de Justice failed to forgive their failure. The little advocate from Arras, for instance, was destined to make quite a pest of himself. But Marie-Clarice could always find an excuse for a revolutionary. I often wondered how she would have explained away the somewhat unlovable nature of our present Public Prosecutor. I found it hard to ascribe "feelings of inferiority" to the citizen Fouquier-Tinville. I had always heard that he came from a family that was quite well off and that he described himself as one of the

cleverest lawyers going. Doubtless, however, she would have found something to say in his favour.

Try as I might, it was impossible to make her realise she was in danger.
"*Me*! But they *know* how I feel about everything. They'd be losing their
greatest supporter if they threw me out."

She was quite impervious to the plight of the Royal Family. Heaven
knows, I was no supporter of the "Lord's anointed," but even I was apprehensive for them. Their position struck me as tragic, and the worst was not
even dreamed of yet.

"No harm will come to them," declared Marie-Clarice. "All they're being
asked to do is to take their positions seriously for a change. Hereditary
money and positions are iniquitous. Everyone should work for their living
in some way. You don't expect the unfortunate peasant to be delighted that
his grinding taxes should go towards supporting a corrupt court like Versailles, do you?"

Again and again our bodies returned to one another. She, I knew, was
doing everything in her power to prevent me from leaving her. She succeeded. I kept on putting off our departure, not only because I couldn't
resist her, but because I still hoped to persuade her to leave. When I became
really serious and told her that I had M.S. and the Puce to consider as well
as myself, she would say: "Just a few more days of you — on Tuesday
I'll decide."

I must say that when I realised that she had no intention of deserting her
beloved Revolution, I did put the Puce and M.S. first. I said goodbye to
Marie-Clarice and I had every intention of leaving for America. But it was
too late.

Sixty thousand Prussians were reputed to be marching on Luxembourg
and Longwy. Forty thousand Austrians were moving on the Prussians' right
flank and ten thousand Hessians on their left. The Royalist émigrants commanded by Condé were converging on strategic points.

Paris, which could be whipped to fever pitch by whispered rumours, excelled itself when faced with indisputable facts. Concluding — I am afraid
only too accurately — that their monarch and his wife, whilst proclaiming
themselves willing to accept the constitution, had been communing with its
enemies to achieve the exact contrary, the people rushed the palace. Their
intention was to murder their King and Queen on the spot.

If ever my Republican sentiments wavered, they wavered then. I felt that
Pêche was right when he once said that any people who could contemplate
such hideous atrocities in the name of freedom proved themselves unfit to
be ruled by gentle means.

To try and describe the tenth of August is absurd, really; one thought
nothing more revolting could possibly happen. One was wrong. One had
only to wait for September.

There was no doubt that it was organised. It was no more spontaneous than the September massacres, of which I have such personally horrifying memories. It must also have been financed. Marie-Clarice's "poor little advocate" from Arcis-sur-Aube was cowering in his house at the time, but afterwards he claimed to be the instigator. Similarly, Jean Paul Marat, who was found lying on his stomach in a cellar when Westermann, the Prussian officer who conducted operations, went to report to him, solemnly crowned himself with laurels and flourished a sabre he had never held.

Well, well, let us not be bitter: it never pays.

The mob broke into the Tuileries and the sheer damage to an unfeeling building was revolting enough. The ferocity towards human flesh was nauseating. Even Marie-Clarice could not have excused it. The Swiss Guard, who were doing no more than their paid duty in defending the Royal Family, were mercilessly hacked to pieces. Their heads were carried through the streets on pikes, their entrails were boiled over fires, and their ears, noses, and fingers were pinned to clothes as ornaments — even by women and children. Their arms and legs and their mutilated trunks were dragged on ropes through the streets. Dogs and sometimes cats followed these appetising remains to the resounding delight of the crowd. In front of the Tuileries millions of flies buzzed over the clotting blood.

I regret to say that I was in the arms of Marie-Clarice, so that my only first-hand experience was when a collection of ruffians pulled her porter out of his lodge and ran a pike through his heart. This, if you please, was because the notice above his lodge gates read "Parlez au Suisse." The lunatics did not realise that it was synonymous with the word "porter," and they murdered anything and everyone connected with the Swiss. Swiss-linen houses, Swiss bankers, Swiss watchmakers — all met with the same fate.

Later in the day Marie-Clarice and I walked up to the palace. It was one of those curious anomalies of the Revolution that spectators were quite often unmolested. We wandered undisturbed through what was still a battlefield. The King and Queen had put themselves under the protection of the Assembly in a reporter's box, but the people, deprived of further victims, were falling on each other.

The broken palace looked eerie in the dying light of what had been a wonderfully clear summer day. It looked as if it had been wrecked by a fire that left no marks of flames. It was gutted no less furiously. Exquisitely gilded and carved doors hung off hinges to show shattered rooms inside. Drunks rolled round the gardens dressed up in clerical garments they had stolen from the royal chapel, mimicking passages from the Mass. Others were prancing about in the building under court wigs and court dresses. Many a life was lost through quarrelling over the spoils. Small children dabbed themselves behind the ears with the caking blood of the Switzers for luck, whilst their mothers sat unemotionally fanning away the stench of piled-up bodies!

Some macabre instinct made me want to roam over the palace. I have always felt an empty room can speak more heavily of the personality of someone who has just left it than his actual presence. There is something about abandoned possessions that have been in everyday use which can give a truer picture of their owners than their owners themselves. Perhaps because they haven't the same power to deceive.

I felt quite uncannily conscious of the presence of departed Royalty. Their home — in pieces — was pathetic. Magnificent bed hangings had been shredded as souvenirs, tables and chairs had been broken up for sheer love of destruction, walls had been written on, urinated against, and worse, and from somewhere below there was a tuneless singsong chant. It was the drunks making free in the cellars.

The Queen's rooms had received particularly brutal attention. In the passageway there was one satin slipper. It looked forlornly desperate lying on its side. It may or may not have belonged to the Queen, but at the time I remember thinking that it was the nearest I should ever get to the person of Marie-Antoinette. I could hardly be blamed for not guessing that I should be imprisoned within a stone's throw of her.

Even Marie-Clarice was silent as we trudged over those savaged rooms. She did her best in defence of the Revolution. "I'm quite sure that our own nobility is behind all this. They want the whole thing to look bestial so that people will turn against the Republic."

When the drunks started to heave themselves out of the cellars, it was time to leave. Santerre stationed the National Guard round the palace, but, even so, people were still killing one another off for liquor or some other division of the spoils. And all that night there was the sound of their musketry fire.

Having seen how the mob could lose all sense of discrimination and turn on their own kind, I decided to put M.S. and the Puce before my own inclinations to stay with Marie-Clarice. But, as I've already said, I was too late.

Marie-Clarice's harmless little advocate from Arcis-sur-Aube demanded his sixty thousand heads. As a measure for preventing their escape, a commission was set up to arrest all suspicious-looking persons. The barriers were closed, and night and day guard-boats rowed along the river in search of anyone trying to get away. Those who remained were as good as sealed into the city. Unless we procured ourselves wings or one of M.S.'s detested balloons, it was impossible to leave Paris. To say that I felt guilty in trapping M.S. and the Puce would scarcely describe my feelings.

At the sessions of the convention, blood was the constant cry. Billaud-

Varenne said that the most dangerous enemy of the true Republican was the one who lived under his own roof. The only possible way for us to prevent the destruction of our social body was to destroy ruthlessly those amongst us who were not for us. We must make no exceptions for blood relatives, friends, spouses, or neighbours. Even our children must not be spared. Anyone who was not for the party must be sacrificed without hesitation on the altar of the country.

Domiciliary visits were ordered. House-to-house searches, midnight arrests with no questions asked — and the victims seldom seen again. Anyone not found at home on these visits was to be considered a suspicious person and arrested on sight. The citizens of Paris were told that it was their solemn duty to denounce anyone whom they suspected, and it was sometimes possible for one to be pardoned providing one denounced someone else.

I found that the cruelest disillusionment of all. This was the time when the close conspiracy of the poor was shattered for ever — when even L'Étuve, which had suffered so much in common, gratified its own personal spites. One was stupid, I suppose, not to have realised that envy is only a matter of comparison. People who have one crust are hated by people who have none, and hate in turn those who have two. I should not like to give the impression that there were no examples of courage. There were some that would have turned both St. George and his dragon a little pale. But in those early days personal grievances got the upper hand. I suppose it was too much of a temptation coupled with the fact that it was easy for a revengeful soul to fool himself that he was only complying with patriotic demands.

My perpetual fear was that someone would denounce Marie-Clarice. I spent as much time as I could with her, which, it has to be confessed, was hardly a penance. We were in one another's arms in the granary when we received a somewhat unexpected visit from M.S. We had imagined that we were safe from Côté, but apparently we weren't. It was he who told M.S. where to find us. He picked up my clothes and dropped them on me. He kept his face averted from Marie-Clarice's naked body, like a print of an old-time surgeon conducting a Cæsarean operation.

"Boy," he said, "come home quick, you're needed."

Something in his voice frightened me. This time he wasn't acting.

I got dressed and kissed Marie-Clarice goodbye.

M.S. was cruel enough to punish me by not telling me the trouble on our way home. I couldn't blame him. He was unable to forgive me for getting us caught in France because of Marie-Clarice.

Pêche was waiting in our rooms. "It's Suzon," he said. "She's been arrested."

I behaved little better than our local street half-wit who wandered about distributing invisible money as Louis le Grand. I sat down, stood up, opened my mouth, shut it, and sat down again. "The Puce! But it's ridiculous! What for?"

"She has been denounced," said Pêche, "for a counter-revolutionary spirit. She has boasted of living in the rue Matignon, she admitted throwing white bread to the pigeons, and she has considered herself too good for L'Étuve."

"But, Pêche," I said, "you know what that was! It was just a silly childish pride. It wasn't counter-revolutionary: it was just a young girl showing off new shoes."

"I understand," said Pêche, "but the authorities will not."

"Who in the world could have given her away?" said M.S. Some of his few real tears were coursing down his cheeks.

Pêche asked acidly, "Can't you guess? One is powerless, of course, to prove it, but I should imagine — Madame Lattre!"

Madame Lattre! Of course! In return for the Puce being found with her fat old husband in the Luxembourg Gardens!

"Unfortunately," added Pêche, "Madame Lattre has rather an excellent reputation as a patriot. She marched with the Amazons on Versailles."

Raised voices are so useless in a crisis, but I screamed at Pêche, "You must do something! You must get her released. You've known her for years. You can vouch for her."

"I have already vouched for her," said Pêche. "I went to the police office and lodged a formal complaint."

"What happened?"

Pêche smiled sadly. "My card of civisme was threatened. I was told that if I continued to support a counter-revolutionary, it would be replaced by a carte de sûreté, which means that you have to report to the section twice every ten days."

"But, Pêche," said M.S., "they can't lack proof of your civisme. God knows you don't need a certificate to prove it."

Pêche shrugged. "The members of the Revolutionary Committee seemed to think otherwise. It's a pity that Suzon stopped attending my classes. That's one of the things they held against her."

"She didn't want to go anywhere she might find that strumpet from the Hôtel de Faille," M.S. commented.

"There are other political meetings," said Pêche. "The women have plenty of clubs of their own. I warned her that it's practically compulsory to make a voluntary attendance. Never mind, we will see what happens when I lodge another formal complaint."

We were both too appalled to do anything but gape after him when he left the room. We had not even thanked him for his incredible courage.

"What prison is she in?" I asked M.S.

His huge hands flapped. "How do I know? They just took her away."

"But how? When? Couldn't you have stopped them?"

I had not yet had experience of a domiciliary visit. M.S.'s hands came uncomfortably close to my throat.

"No, I couldn't have stopped them. The first we knew of it was a great crash on the door. It must have been about — well, two o'clock in the morning. You were —" He refrained charitably from reminding me where I was. "Anyhow, all we heard was 'Ouvrez au nom de la loi!' The officers of the section were gathered outside. I went down to let them in and they pushed passed me. They looked into our rooms, and were on their way to hers. But she met them in the doorway. She thought something had happened to you. Some ruffians put a pike at her and told her not to move. Then another read out the warrant. They put seals on everything in her room and told me I'd find myself in gaol if I broke them."

"Was — was the Puce terribly frightened?"

"Yes, the poor child said all the wrong things. They asked her questions, wanted to know all she knew about the Rights of Man, and she got muddled up in her answers. When they took her off I lost my temper. I collared one fellow and kept him behind. I threatened to trample on his face if anything happened to her. He knew by my French I was foreign, so I said I was from America."

Our popularity at the theatre was the only reason that it was safe for M.S. to be about. I could pass myself off as a Frenchman, but an Englishman was safer in prison. Every outside disaster and every internal calamity were considered to be the direct work of Pitt. The government solemnly said so, and I think some of them genuinely believed it.

Marie-Clarice found out through the Lieutenant of Police that the Puce was in the Prison de l'Abbaye. M.S. and I thought it safer not to visit the child, as half the charges against her were through her associations with us. Marie-Clarice took food in a hamper and had to leave it with the turnkey. The Puce refused to see her. Marie-Clarice returned near tears. "Your little friend sent a message to say that she'd guessed who denounced her. She thinks I did it so that I could have you to myself."

A visit to the Lapins proved fruitless. Madame said it was the best place for a girl who would lie naked in the Luxembourg Gardens with another woman's husband. Old Lapin spoke as if he'd never heard of her.

Marie-Clarice visited her hero, Camille Desmoulins. "My dear Marie-Clarice," he told her, "I daren't interfere in a case like this. There seems to be quite a bit against the girl and you don't need much these days. It's getting like ancient Rome. According to Tacitus, a man could be guilty of lèse-majesté and State offences by his expression. If he frowned he was suspect, if he smiled he was suspect, if he wept for his dead he was suspect. If he was popular he was dangerous; if he was not, there was good reason. If he was rich he could corrupt the people with bribes; if he was poor he could not have been working hard enough. If he was cheerful he was pleased at the distressed state of his country, and if he was glum he approved of it! The whole lot carried a death sentence. Well, it's getting to be much the same here, and your girl is sure to be guilty of one of those crimes."

It was a speech on these lines which he was unwise enough to make in the Jacobin Club which cost him his own head, but it was no help to us.

I contacted Dugazon, who was aide-de-camp to the commander of the National Guard, but neither of them could do anything.

Marie-Clarice tried everyone she knew, and it was finally the cocoa seller who got me an introduction to the one-time advocate from Arras, through his secretary. As a police agent he could not intercede for the Puce himself, but he told me that if I presented myself amongst Robespierre's supplicants the secretary would arrange for me to be received.

I thought it best to present myself as an English actor so as to dispel the idea, once and for all, that the Puce was living with an aristocrat.

Personally I don't think Robespierre thought of nobility as a crime; it was just something to be cleared out of his way so that he could march ahead with his own ambitions. He had called himself "De Robespierre" when he first came to Paris, but quickly dropped the affectation when he saw how things were going. I am certain he was never genuinely in favour of a Republic. He was clearly aiming for a dictatorship for himself.

Early in the morning I took myself to the rue St.-Honoré and presented myself at No. 396. It was an undistinguished little house belonging to a carpenter with whom Robespierre lodged. There was a forbidding and extremely imperial-looking wooden eagle over his gate.

At the bottom of a timber yard I was shown into a room full of poor wretches clutching petitions. The cocoa seller must have described me well. The secretary picked me out at once. He was an intelligent lad with a wooden leg and he beckoned me to the head of the line. "Now is a good time to see him. He's at work on his sewage plans for Paris, like the one they had in Rome. He never can work it out. He's always glad to be interrupted."

He opened the door of Robespierre's cabinet and bowed me in. He knew his master well. Robespierre was always disposed to be more gracious to someone he thought might be important.

An astonishingly large Pyrenean dog uncurled itself to sniff at me. Robespierre told it to sit and it sat. He bent down and gave it a saucer of coffee before even looking at me.

Round his forehead there was a tightly knotted handkerchief. He suffered from headaches and this compression helped. That and the green preservers he wore to shield his weak eyes from the light did not enhance his appearance. Neither did the fact that he was pitted by the pox.

His room was pleasant enough. Whilst he lovingly fed his dog, I counted four cages of songbirds and three vases of flowers. His frills and ruffles seemed to me to be made of quite valuable lace. There was a lot of the petit-maître about the man, for all his reputed austerity.

When he pushed his glasses up on his forehead he reminded me of a vulture. His forehead and temples had a flattened look and his eyes were a curious fawn colour. The poor man was a shocking example of nerves. His whole face was taken over by a convulsive twitch, his fingers were for ever at his coat buttons, and any emotion seemed to bring on a kind of restriction in his chest.

"Why have you come to me?" he asked. "Why don't you go to the committee? I am not God."

I could see he didn't fully believe that statement. I began by describing myself as a common man who had had occasion to pass myself off as a French aristocrat. This probably did me harm in Robespierre's eyes. He was extremely proud, Marie-Clarice had told me, of his own acceptance in the aristocratic circles of Madame de St. Amaranthe's family. In fact it was his fury at their executions that helped to bring him down. "Citoyen," I pleaded with him, "Suzon Dupont can't possibly be accused of befriending a vicomte when the whole thing was a fraud."

I could see I did not have his attention. "Came from England, did you?" he asked. "Well, let me tell you something: you should be in prison yourself. All our miseries are the work of your Pitt and his associates. If blood flows, it's his doing. Do you know that your countrymen have put a price on my head and every one of my colleagues? It's their money that pays assassins roaming our streets. They want to destroy us eternally."

"But, citoyen," I said, "people like Thomas Paine and Horn and David Williams are more staunchly in favour of the Revolution than a lot of your own people."

"Hypocrites and traitors!" he shouted, and a hint of froth appeared at the sides of his mouth. "They're English agents paid by Pitt. If it weren't for the fact that I believe so strongly that the innocent must not be allowed to suffer for the guilty, I should put up every Englishman in France to public vengeance." He stood up so violently that he hit his head on one of his bird cages. "Do you know the ambition of your Duke of York? To succeed the Capets! Yes! Now that we have no king of our own, your Duke of York plans to step into his shoes!" Then he suddenly shot out a cold little hand to me. "Well, goodbye. I'm sorry I can't help your friend, but she should choose her own friends more wisely."

I went home convinced I had been talking to a madman.

"Oh dear," sighed Marie-Clarice. "I should have gone to see him. He's very susceptible to women. Well, I'll try and see Billaud-Varenne. I know someone who's sleeping with him."

It was she who suggested that I should try and get influential support through my own charms. "It's silly wasting time on the men when you're so good with women. Why don't you try the Roland woman, or Danton's wife? He's supposed to be devoted to her. If you got round her, she'd get round him. You try the women and I'll try the men."

Chapter 44.

ALL MARIE-CLARICE got from Billaud-Varenne was an offer to supplant the mistress who had introduced her to him.

M.S. and I could scarcely get ourselves to our scruffy little theatre, let alone fall about and embrace dancing bears. We could think of nothing else but the Puce locked up in the Abbaye.

We were at our kitchen table trying to work out the kind of letter which would entice Mesdames Danton, Maillard, Hébert, Barrére, etc., to give me an interview, when we heard the first cannon fire. We did not take much notice until we heard the tocsins.

The Abbé Servoise came hurrying in. The little hunchback could hardly speak from emotion. Having taken the civic oath, he was a non-juror and in no danger himself. But he had a horrible story to tell us. The refractory clergy who had refused to swear allegiance to their country before their faith had been arrested in the hundreds. The prisons were already overflowing from the arrests after August 10. Not only aristocrats and victims of personal spite, but anyone who could possibly be suspected of counter-revolutionary activities had been gaoled in those first days of bitter denunciations.

The Abbé Servoise had been transferred to the section Guillaume Tell, but he had heard about the Puce. What he had to tell us put a leaden lump of fear into my stomach.

"A hackney carriage was bringing twenty-four priests from the mairie to the Abbaye. The mob pulled them out and killed all except two. The people are breaking into all the prisons. I have some very old friends in the Abbaye. I'm going down to see what I can do for them. Perhaps you had better come with me. There might just be a chance of finding Suzon."

Until I die — and in fact even when I'm dead, if there's a life afterwards which will allow us to brood on such things — I shall never rid my mind of those seven days and nights of fear.

The National Guard and the gendarmes in charge of the prisoners, although they were heavily armed, surrendered to the people without orders from their officers. They just stepped aside and allowed the appalling mass murders to proceed.

There was no doubt that the murderers were unofficially paid and mustered. No civil or military authority seemed to consider it their duty to interfere with them. The most gruesome thing to my mind was the sight of these hired assassins being brought their lunches by their loving daughters and wives. They interrupted their atrocities, to which they solemnly referred as "leur ouvrage," as if it had been any normal job, to sit down and eat their meals amongst clotting blood and piles of mutilated bodies. They kept regular hours where their food was concerned.

The devastation at the Abbaye was indescribable. It was hardly possible to get near the place, much less make enquiries about a particular prisoner. Until three o'clock in the morning the butchering went on in the garden court. The screams of the wounded and dying hacked down by sabres and bludgeoned to death would have made me vomit if I hadn't been in such mortal terror for the Puce.

At the Conciergerie I saw La Belle Liègeoise, as Théroigne de Méricour was sometimes known, help to mutilate a girl of about the Puce's age. This poor little wretch's beauty had earned her the name of La Belle Bouquetière, and De Méricour shrieked that she would tolerate no rivals. She and her friends tore off the girl's clothes, nailed her hands to the door, sliced off both her breasts, and lit a slow fire under her while they chanted the "Ça ira" and the "Carmagnole."

There was nothing I could do except run away from her screams, but for ever after in my mind her face became the Puce's face.

M.S. and I separated and plunged on from prison to prison in the hopes of getting some news. He came head on to the procession drawing the entrails of the murdered Princess de Lamballe. A drummer named Mangin, of the section du Temple, wound his arms round M.S. and introduced himself as the hero of the day. Before M.S. could shake off the man, he had to listen to him boasting that he had cut out the heart of the Princess de Lamballe, broiled it, and eaten it "au carbonnade."

I had the utmost difficulty in refusing a cup of blood mixed with wine. It was offered to me as a test of my civisme. I had to lift the revolting mixture to my lips and pretend to take several gulps or I should have been killed where I stood.

When the political and clerical prisoners began to run out, the assassins, doubtless anxious not to lose their lucrative "ouvrage," set upon ordinary prisoners gaoled for debt and minor offences. Even lunatics were not spared. The huge asylum of Bicêtre had about two thousand inmates. Five days and nights were required for the business of butchering them. At the Salpêtrière the old women were killed instantly; the young ones were raped first and then slaughtered. Some of them were only eleven and twelve years old.

On behalf of the Puce I literally threw myself at the female relations of the people who suddenly seemed to have become important or influential. I knew that if we couldn't get the Puce released quickly, she would sooner or later end up as one of the mangled heaps one saw under shrouds of flies.

I made a mistake in trying to appeal to Robespierre's sister. Pêche told me that they were on very good terms and I hoped that she might influence him for me. But Pêche was not aware of the friction that had developed between them, and that Charlotte was hardly able to contact her brother herself.

She received me willingly enough in her little lodgings on the rue St.-Florentin, but it was chiefly to tell me her own troubles. She was flattered, too, to think that I should have chosen her instead of the women of the carpenter's family with whom Robespierre lived.

"I'm glad that *someone* realises the devotion that exists between Maximilien and me. He would certainly listen to me if he was given a chance. Do you know, monsieur" — she corrected herself quickly to "citoyen" — "that I stayed there first when I came from Arras? Naturally I thought I should be with my brother, but the Duplay woman and her daughters put me on a separate floor and would hardly let me speak to him. He thought it was I making trouble, and I had to come here. They are terrible women. Do you know, when I gave him two pots of conserve they sent them back saying they didn't want me poisoning him. My own brother! If he's left to himself he's so gentle and kind. He must be horrified at what is going on now. What was it you said you wanted me to do? — oh yes!" She wrote down the name of the Puce on a scrap of paper and tucked it behind a lead candlestick. "Well, if they ever allow me to see him again, I will tell him."

Gabrielle Danton seemed lost in the lavish apartment in the Cour du Commerce. She looked ill and depressed. She had not long given birth to a child and in point of fact the poor woman was actually dying. Her big-boned face seemed fleshless. I felt sorry for the erstwhile buxom daughter of the proprietor of the little Café du Parnasse. She sat in a high cotton cap and stared at me out of unhappy eyes. "I can feel for you, citoyen. I know what it's like to be anxious for someone you love. I will do what I can, but you see I hardly see Georges these days. Since he became Minister he sleeps and he eats — well, he *lives* in the clubs. He exists for nothing but work — work — work." She glanced at her extravagant furnishings as if they were enemies. "We used to be such a united family. Georges was so kind — you've no idea how considerate he was and how he spoilt the children. If he doesn't come home in the next few days I will send him a letter and beg for the life of your poor little friend. But I cannot say what good it will do."

Poor Gabrielle Danton! She was dead in a short time and three months later the husband she adored was passionately in love with a girl of fifteen.

I was at my wit's end when M.S. suggested that I should try the wife of the "thunder writer" in *Le Père Duchesne* and *Journal du Soir*. "He's got more influence than any of them, boy. He's just been put in charge of the King and Queen in the Temple. He's only just been married and Pêche says his wife used to be a nun. You should be able to get something from her."

The thought of visiting the household of "Père Duchesne" was far from reassuring. This was the man whose filthy pen was already accusing the convention of being slow in decapitating the "pig-capet," who called Marie-Antoinette an Austrian whore and threatened to chop her into sausage meat and saw off her head himself if no one else would do it. If the picture in his journal of the leering giant in a black carmagnole jacket waving an axe over the head of a prostrate member of the refractory clergy was a self-portrait, I didn't feel much confidence in getting help from Hébert.

Nor was I looking forward to trying my luck in charming the Puce's little life out of the ex-sister Goupil. The frontispiece of pamphlets showed "Mère Duchesne" as a savage pipe-smoking Amazon flourishing a sabre.

M.S. coached me tirelessly in the role of the most ruffianly shirtless one that ever gobbled a civic dinner. The importance attached to being a sans-culotte had reached hysterical proportions. A pupil of the painter David had presented the Jacobin Society with a picture of an undesirable-looking savage clad in tatters. He informed the impressed members that his immortal master David had discovered that the words "sans-culotte" were of divine origin. The portrait represented an Indian god called Camaltzequis, which (in whatever language he spoke) meant "without breeches!" Far from laughing at this absurdity, people took it seriously, and I hoped to be able to make the ex-nun Goupil think that I was Camaltzequis in person.

Pêche had found me a tattered old carmagnole and a pair of sabots. We studied *Le Père Duchesne* and I learned all Hébert's most sickening phrases and obscenities by heart. "If she's used to him, boy, you'll have to outswear him in every manner of talk or she'll think you're an aristocrat."

He poured so much Dutch courage down my throat that by the time I arrived in the rue St.-Antoine to visit the ex-sister Goupil I was decidedly unsteady. But, as M.S. said, she was probably used to nothing else.

I hauled myself up to the third floor of a house opposite the church of Petit Saint-Antoine and was told by the concierge that the citoyenne Hébert would not keep me waiting.

I was put into a little room whose peaceful atmosphere surprised me. It was not elegant, but it was cosily comfortable. Above the armoire there was an engraving of the *Last Supper*. Something was scribbled in the margin. It read, "The sans-culotte Jesus supping in the chateau of a ci-devant!"

A voice said, "I see you like my picture. I brought it with me from the convent. It's my husband's words in the corner. Don't you think they're apt?"

At first I thought I was being addressed by a pregnant mountain. The woman was extremely tall, and as she was six months with child, she seemed massive. But she had a gentle air and was plainly but prettily attired.

My appearance appeared to startle her. Perhaps her husband usually protected her from his followers. She was carrying some needlework and sat down in a rocker facing the window.

"Isn't it stuffy? Would you mind putting that window up a bit? It's dangerous for me to strain. I'm not young to be having my first baby."

I was still drunk and I asked her foolishly, "Where's your sabre?"

She laughed. "Oh, that! Well, you know, sometimes it's wise to give people what they expect, and that's what they expect me to look like. I've never been handsome, but I think I'm an improvement on those prints, don't you?"

I nodded.

"Yes — well now, who are you and what can I do for you?"

"I am Camultzequis," I told her with considerable difficulty; it is not the easiest word to pronounce even when one is sober.

She looked concerned. "Oh, dear, I'm afraid that must mean you're a heathen and I don't approve of that. Also you must be very unhappy to get so drunk. What's the matter?"

In the face of her gentleness and obvious good breeding I decided to drop my ruffian act and to save the profanities I had learnt for her husband if I ever met him. So I stammered out my plea for the Puce.

I tried to represent the Puce as the ideal female sans-culotte. "She's never been anything else but a born and bred child of the Revolution. It's for people like her it's being fought. They can't penalise her for enjoying the one time she had a taste of fresh air and clean linen. I daresay she did boast a little, but it's no more than a child showing off a new dress —"

"I think it's a very good thing to take pride in one's appearance. If I have a daughter I shall encourage it."

"Don't," I said bitterly, "it might land her in prison."

She looked round at me. "Are you in love with this girl?"

I did not hesitate to say yes. To have tried to give a realistic picture of my feelings for the Puce would have ruined the object of my visit. My hope of gaining assistance for the Puce depended largely on the ex-sister Goupil's opinion of me. She was obviously a depressingly sentimental soul, and this was probably one of her safeguards against the tedious business of facing facts. She must have used her sentimentality as a shield between herself and the Revolution. She must have deceived herself daily in connection with her own religion, her husband's activities, and what was happening round her.

For me to have confessed that I had only just discovered that the Puce's safety meant more to me than the safety of Marie-Clarice would have been fatal. If I had been as truthful as that, I should also have been obliged to add that I could not see myself forgoing the pleasures of Marie-Clarice. That would have shocked the ex-sister Goupil. She would have dismissed me and with me my hopes for the Puce. My true colours were no shades to hang out in front of Mère Duchesne. They would have punctured her unconsciously hypocritical shield. They would have caused her to suspect that in myself she was not face to face with her ideal sans-culotte. He should have been a murderous-looking individual in whom tenderness and chivalry shone like a torch. He should have had in him the makings of as perfect a husband as the ex-sister Goupil's own piece of bliss. He should have eyes for no one but the girl for whom he was pleading. His feelings for her should have been so extravagantly phrased that the touched heart of the ex-sister Goupil would shine through moist eyes. He should have said, "Citoyenne, don't judge me by my looks. I am a rough man, but, believe me, I love my Suzon — love her so much that I would give her more than my life. I would give her more precious things. I would give her my certificate of civisme, I would sacrifice my patriotism . . ." Here he should have thrown out his arms in a final gesture of despair.

This is exactly what I did, and I had not misjudged the ex-sister Goupil. Her eyes were wet when she said, "Well, then, we must see what we can do for you. You won't mind me preparing the supper?" She bustled up to the cupboard and brought out some thoroughly bourgeois crockery, and began to lay the table. I helped her remove the cloth. "I think there's nothing so wonderful in the world as marriage. I go down on my knees every night to thank God for the day I joined the Fraternal Society of Both the Sexes. It was there that I met my husband." She put a pot of conserve on the table. "Since then I just can't describe to you the bliss it has been."

It occurred to me with horror that the bliss must be expected home very shortly. "Then, citoyenne, you'll understand what I go through thinking about my Suzon. . . ."

She passed me a canister of coffee. "Put that at the end, please. He likes to make it fresh. Would you marry her if she were freed?"

Again I did not hesitate. "It is all I long for, citoyenne." It would have been a mistake to point out that I did not see myself as the marrying kind — for my own as well as the Puce's sake.

"You must keep up your religion," she told me, "and see that your Suzon keeps up hers. I know what you're thinking," she told me, "but I am still attached to Christianity. I think it's one of the most beautiful things about our Revolution. After all, our ideals are the very ones preached by our Lord himself."

"Yes, but his methods of achieving them were a little different," I managed to say.

"I see comparisons all the time between his teachings and our glorious fight. I am always pointing them out to my Jacobin friends. I can assure you that the sister Goupil in me is by no means dead."

The sister Goupil in her might not have been dead, but the Christian religion in France at that time was being surely but effectively stamped out. In this respect mockery was proving more effective than the rack and the thumbscrew. In the streets it was quite usual to meet gangs of youngsters, or drunks, or even quite respectable citizens going round "absolving" delighted bystanders of their sins.

I didn't notice my hostess's husband come in for the simple reason that her great bulk was blocking the doorway. But I saw her stoop a long way down to kiss something. She must have been three times his height. The first time I saw him was in the pier glass. He was a positive newt of a man, with pale eyes and pale skin. His small hands and feet gave him a whispy primness, and he was exceedingly elegantly dressed. Under his arm he carried a portfolio.

When one considers the true character of this monster, it is almost impossible to reconcile either his actual appearance or his primly happy little life at home. I could not take my eyes off that portfolio. After he had eaten his bourgeois little meal he would sit down and write some of the most lecherous, cruel, and coarse words that had ever disgraced a public journal. His pen alone would be responsible for hundreds of deaths, and it moved across the paper at the side of a wife who was "still attached to Christianity" and in an atmosphere of marital happiness and comfort which he would have condemned in others as counter-revolutionary.

The hypocrisy of the creature made me giddy, but it didn't take me long to realise that his greatest protection lay in the fact that the people imagined him to be what he claimed to be — a tobacco-spewing, wine-swilling, dirty-mouthed, mammoth-sized hog, smiling at every form of human depravity.

This was apparent from the first time he addressed me. His wife said laughingly, "This citoyen expected to find me like my picture in your paper. He asked me what I'd done with my sabre! I expect he thought you would look different too."

"Then I sincerely hope," said Hébert, "that he will disillusion nobody."

"He has a friend in prison and he wants to marry her." The ex-sister Goupil bent down and kissed him again. "I want others to share the same state of happiness as us, my love. I felt sure you'd use your influence to get her released."

He put his portfolio down on the table and patted his hair in the pier glass. "I'll look into the case and speak to Maillard, but I should like this citoyen to give me his faithful promise that he will say nothing of what he has seen or heard in this house."

When I promised, he nodded my dismissal and turned to his wife. "Now then, my love, let me hear how things have gone with you today."

Our agony was broken forty-eight hours later. When we got back from the theatre the Puce was waiting for us.

M.S. nearly winded the girl in his arms, but I felt oddly shy of her. It was as if I were seeing an entirely new Puce whom I had found in Madame Hébert's neat little salon. I looked sideways at her to see if I had been mistaken. But I had not. The Chinese eyes, the slender but well-proportioned figure, the dark, uncurling hair belonged to a woman now.

I said stiffly, "We're very glad to have you back. We've been a little anxious about you."

"A little anxious!" roared M.S. "We've been nearly off our heads." She was child enough to him, still. He was bouncing her on his knee. "Well, come on, boy, aren't you going to give her a kiss?"

I bent down and pecked her cheek. "This lad," said M.S., "has hardly closed his eyes since you went. Look at him, thirty years older! If it hadn't been for him, you'd have been there still."

"And if it hadn't been for him," she said coldly, "I wouldn't have been denounced in the first place."

M.S. slid her off his knee. "What are you talking about, girl? You don't suppose he gave you up, do you?"

"His woman denounced me to get me out of her way."

"Madame de Faille," I said angrily, "did everything she could to get you out — even to making herself pleasant to Billaud-Varenne, and God knows hardly anyone in Paris would care to do that."

"But she didn't succeed," said the Puce in her new grown-up voice, which was quite two tones deeper than her old childish squeak.

"Now, look here, girl," said M.S., "I don't like that strumpet any more than you. If it wasn't for her we'd be in America by now. But she didn't give you away. It was that old cow Lattre —"

"Whose husband," I reminded the Puce, "you entertained in the Luxembourg Gardens. She wanted to get her own back."

"She's boasted about it, girl, to Pêche. This lad's strumpet had nothing to do with it."

"Côté told me she's a terrible woman," said the Puce. "She puts love potions into men's food so that even when she's an old, old lady they'll still think her beautiful and won't leave her for anyone else."

"You're talking like a little idiot," I told her and banged the door, leaving the room.

I am ashamed to say that after I banged the door I stayed to listen outside. I wanted to know how fair M.S. would be to Marie-Clarice behind my back.

I need not have bothered. He was exemplary. He repeatedly told the Puce the efforts that Marie-Clarice had made on her behalf. "What would the boy want to lie to you for? Why should he make you think she'd tried to help you if she hadn't? He doesn't care if you like her or not."

"Oh, but I think he does," said the Puce. "You see, if I didn't like her, he might be afraid I'd denounce her."

Chapter 45.

I WENT straight round to the Hotel de Faille to tell Marie-Clarice the news about the Puce's release. If anything, the citoyenne De Faille wore even more rings than the ci-devant Comtesse. Her hands were on fire with diamonds.

I said, "Marie-Clarice, if anyone ever went out of his way to get himself executed it's you. People have been denounced as rich aristocrats just because they've been found to have clean linen in the house, and you cover yourself with jewels."

"I don't see why I should dress down to the Revolution: I approve of it."

"Well, it doesn't approve of you. You're denouncing yourself every time one of those rings catches the light."

"I don't go out very much.'

"You don't need to. There are enough people in the house to report that you're dressed up like a queen. I don't trust that insolent Côté, for one."

"Oh, he'd never harm me."

"I don't agree. Your family has looked after him ever since he was a child, and you've spoilt him ridiculously yourself. But the only way he could think of repaying you was to refuse to get a doctor when Blaise was hurt. He's an ungrateful, disloyal lout."

"He's in love with your little Chinoise. Could that be why you dislike him so much?"

"Of course not, but I certainly shouldn't choose him for her."

She was wearing the amethyst spray in her hair. It shot out mauve sparks as she raised her head and smiled at me. "Who would *you* choose for her? Yourself?"

"I've never flattered myself that I should make a good husband for anybody and I didn't come here to discuss my own marriage or anyone else's."

"What did you come to discuss?" She stood up and put herself into my arms.

We kissed, and when I released her I said, "You have to get away, Marie-Clarice. The Puce is a sans-culotte by birth and by environment, and you know the trouble we've had saving her from your beloved Revolution. You're a born aristocrat and there'd be no hope for you whatsoever."

"Would you be willing to marry me?"

"No."

"Why not?"

"Because I could never think of giving up the theatre."

"I shouldn't mind that."

"In time you would. You'd be amused at first but not for long. You'd resent the social stigma both for me and yourself. Our kind of love doesn't last. When it wore off you'd sleep with other people. That would annoy me and we should quarrel. We're neither of us made for marriage — at least not with each other."

Her arms went round my neck again. "Do you know what I think? I think your little Chinoise will get you in the end."

"Very probably. Now, Marie-Clarice, most of your friends have left. You've no family. There's no reason for you to remain here."

"There's you — and my beloved Revolution."

"I shall leave for America as soon as I'm able, and if you stay, your beloved Revolution will kill you."

Her nearness was upsetting me. I had come with the intention of persuading her to go and I did not want my desire for her to weaken my determination.

She used the low voice that always disturbed me. "When you go to America, will you be taking your little Chinoise?"

"Yes, I suppose so."

"Why do you 'suppose so'?"

"Because she's attached herself to us. She's been with us so long that we feel we're responsible for her. M.S. is training her to act. He's devoted to her."

"Aren't you?"

"I'm extremely fond of her."

"Fonder than you are of me?"

"In a different way."

"I don't think it's a different way."

"You must think what you like. Tomorrow I'm going to steal a disguise for you from the prop basket. You must try and get over the border."

"I thought I had made it clear that I am not quite ready to say goodbye to you yet."

"But *I* am ready to say goodbye to you." All my histrionic abilities were needed to make myself sound convincing. "I warn you, Marie-Clarice: after I bring the disguise, you won't see me again. I'm coming nowhere near you, so it will be pointless to stay behind for my sake."

"Are you frightened because I'm an aristocrat?"

"Yes, but solely on *your* account." I bent forward, kissed her quickly, and left the room.

I chose not to return home immediately. I wanted to think about Marie-Clarice. To have tried to use will power to put her out of my mind would have been useless; I wanted, before I carried out my threat of never seeing her again, to relive every moment I had ever spent with her.

I wandered in the Palais-Égalité. The change from its days as the Palais-Royal was very apparent. It was hardly recognisable as the decorous Mecca of good living in which I had first tried to contact Marie-Clarice. Gone were the days of "no servants, no dogs, and no poor students." Soldiers of the revolutionary army strolled up and down in their worsted epaulets in the company of what M.S. still referred to as "abandoned women." Less forsaken souls I've never seen. Every prostitute appeared to have about ten willing customers in her wake. The small and select cafés with their outrageously high-priced menus had given way to establishments offering beer, cheap wines, and brandy — a glass of the latter being called "du sacré chien tout pur."

From fourth-floor windows one could see an oiled paper lantern bearing the word "Bal." These balls were very different from the gallant step-outs at the Weldon's mansion and even from the gay days of the decadent ancien régime; it seemed to be taken for granted that a ball should end in a fight between the soldiery and the civilians over an abandoned woman.

An extraordinary modern jargon had sprung up in this society. If one was not acquainted with it, one was considered a fossil. Soldiers were called "epauletiers"; civilians were "pékins"; and the latter, if they were the chosen "mon homme" of an abandoned woman, had to compete for her against the "briquet," or infantry sword, or the "bancal," the curved sabre of the cavalry. But the "pékins" usually settled their differences in a quaint manner. It was called the "savatte" — a curious form of pugilistic combat in which each party used his boots to supplement his fists. Or else they employed "le bâton à deux bouts" — the "double stick," in the use of which they appeared most dextrous.

An abandoned woman fastened onto my arms, which frightened me considerably. I had no desire to be mistaken by an "épauletier" for a "pékin." But she insisted upon my having a glass of brandy and listening to her woes. It appeared, for some reason she was unable to make clear, that the journeyman butcher was the favourite "mon homme" amongst the abandoned women of the Palais-Égalité. But he was not a gentleman to be trusted. He was inclined to expect regular money from his lady, and if it was not forthcoming he was not beyond giving her a beating, which was courteously termed "une rencée," "une volée," or "une saboulade."

I left the Palais-Égalité having failed in my doleful decision to bury Marie-Clarice in a bog of sad-happy memories. I also left feeling a fossil. If this was modern youth, I failed to understand it.

When I reached No. 104 rue de Picardie I found M.S. rubbing himself with an unpleasant-smelling liniment. The Japanese acrobat had failed to catch him the night before, and M.S. had strained his shoulder.

The Puce turned to me without rancour. "You've been to see Madame de Faille, haven't you?"

"Considering her efforts on your behalf, the least I could do was to tell her that you're free."

M.S. stretched an arm behind him. He gave me a note. "This came for you."

It was from Marie-Clarice and it read:

I have just had an unpleasant ten minutes with Côté. I think you might be right about him. I rather think he was eavesdropping. He hinted that he knew I was trying to escape. It would not be safe for you to bring me a disguise. Côté would suspect you at once.

Marie-Clarice.

"It's from her," said the Puce. "It smells the same as she does." She screwed up her nose. "But it's better than Uncle's ointment."

We heard footsteps outside and Pêche came in. Pêche was even paler these days. He was working halfway round the clock with his political classes, and drilling with the National Guard as well as attending to his own trade. What spare time he had was spent at the Jacobin Club, where he often took me. When he slept I don't know, and there was a distinct falling off in the consumption of his "payments." Full wine bottles were stacked all round his room.

"Well, Suzon," he said to the Puce, "I hope this has taught you a lesson. It doesn't do to boast and it doesn't do to take other people's husbands. Madame Lattre would never have denounced you if you hadn't been found in the Luxembourg Gardens with her man."

"It was not Madame Lattre: it was Madame de Faille."

Pêche shook his head, and I could have kissed him. "Madame de Faille is a better Republican than you, my child. She's at one with the people. She fights for us. She would never give away a girl like you no matter what stupid things you may have said."

The Puce broke away from M.S.'s arms. "She's poisoned you like she's poisoned poor Côté and *him*." This was accompanied by the usual jerk of the chin in my direction. "She's such a grande dame she takes you all in."

Pêche frowned and I thought he looked nervous. "A grande dame is the last person to impress me, Suzon." He turned to M.S. and myself. "If you want to keep this girl out of trouble, you'd better set her to work for the return of her certificate of civisme. They're not easy to regain once you've lost them. She'd better be seen at civic dinners, and she ought to join one of the women's clubs. A person's civisme can be tested on things like that. She must also attend political classes. Not" — Pêche compared the backs of his own two hands as if it were suddenly vital to him that he should find out that they matched — "not mine, I think. It would look better if she went outside the section. Perhaps the corn market, or the section Guillaume Tell, or the Théâtre Français."

I came forward. "Why, Pêche?"

He turned to avoid my eyes. "Well, they — I — they know that I interceded for her. If she's seen at my classes it would not look so impressive."

"Have they been investigating you, Pêche?"

He shook his head, but I disbelieved him. "No, it's for her sake, not mine." He looked at me at last. "It would also be better if Madame de Faille did not come to my classes again."

He picked up his hat with its greasy cockade and left us.

"Well," said M.S., "something has turned him funny. He was all round your lady friend a short while back."

"Friendships are a trifle uncertain nowadays," I said bitterly, and went up to the Puce. I handed her Marie-Clarice's note. "Look for yourself. The next time I see Madame de Faille will be the last. She is going to escape."

The Puce jumped up. "You mustn't help her."

"I'm only going to provide a disguise."

The Puce tugged at my sleeve. "You're not to. She tells you herself that it's dangerous. You'll be arrested for helping her."

M.S. joined her standing over me. "Listen to what the child says, boy. If you've finished with that woman, stay finished with her. You saw the look on Pêche's face. He must have heard that she's suspect. He wants nothing more to do with her. Can't you take a warning from that?"

"If she's suspect, it's all the more reason for her friends to help her."

The Puce's arms went tightly round my neck. Her soft lips kissed my chin and my mouth. She was weeping now. "*Please* don't do it. Oh, I love you so much and I *hate* her for making you want to take risks for her. I wish someone would give her up and stop you."

"They'll be watching her, boy," M.S. warned me. "You'll just be in time to hand over your parcel to the officers of her section and accompany them to gaol. It looks to me as if Pêche is trying to push you into another section because he knows there's trouble coming. He likes you and he doesn't relish the job of having to arrest you. You can't afford to be seen helping aristocrats to escape."

"I don't intend to be seen."

The Puce pummelled me tearfully. "How do I know that you won't go with her? You could both escape and leave us behind."

"He wouldn't do that, girl," said Manager Smith.

"He would do anything for her. She can make him say and do just what she likes. It's not his fault he just can't say no to her. You, me, the theatre — there's nothing important, nothing except making love to that woman. It eats all his honour and strength away."

I said wearily, "Look, she's as anxious to get out as you are to get rid of

her. But she can't very well walk up to the barriers and say she's the ci-
devant Comtesse de Faille and that she has decided she'd like to visit England
for a change."

"It's just an excuse," sobbed the Puce. "When he gets there he'll find she
has made plans for him too — and he'll go with her." She flung herself into
M.S.'s arms, which made two of them smelling of liniment.

"She must have some sort of disguise," I insisted, "and there's no one in
the house she can trust."

That night I lay in bed behind my partition and tried to work out the best
way to get into the Hôtel de Faille without being recognised. It was evident
that I should need some disguise myself if Côté already suspected me of helping his mistress. He would probably send for the officers of the section the
moment I arrived. On the other hand, as my face was so familiar to him I
should need a really effective make-up. A beard and a wig, however, could
do wonders, especially if one lowered one's voice several octaves and took
to spectacles.

I was still pondering the problem when M.S. sat himself on the end of my
bed. "Boy, God knows why, when you've been so much trouble to me — but
I mind what happens to you. If you're still set on helping that harpy, I'll get
the disguise to her."

I sat up. "You'll do nothing of the sort. It would be just as dangerous for
you."

"I'm a better actor than you are, boy. I'll get in somehow and I won't be
recognized."

"M.S., it's kind of you, but I wouldn't hear of it."

"It's not fair to Suzon. She's a young woman now and she loves you."

"Then she ought to be glad that I'm going to get Marie-Clarice out of her
way."

"It's you she's afraid for, boy. That woman's done enough to us. If it
wasn't for her, we might be at work in the John Street Theatre by now."

As this happened to be the truth, I let him leave the room without
argument.

It was about an hour later when the Puce crept in. When I sat up she said
quickly, "No, no, I have not come to be like Marie Lebrun or that woman of
yours." She seated herself primly. "I've been thinking about things. This
woman has taken you away from me quite enough. She is *not* going to leave
me a widow before I am married. If you get the clothes, *I* will take them to
her. It would be easy for me: I could say I was visiting Côté. His civisme has
never been questioned."

"I know, Puce, but yours has. Nothing in the world would make me let
you take such a risk, but it's kind of you to offer."

She wriggled alongside me. Her hair was thick and heavy lying over her
shoulders and it moved as if it had a life of its own. She whispered, "Do you

know the best way for a girl to earn her certificate of civisme? It's to get pregnant and lay her sons on the altar of the country."

"I should think it's better to get married first, and earn your certificate by rolling bandages."

"Well, I don't mind getting married first. We've been betrothed such a very long time. Marie Lebrun is beginning to remark upon it."

"You've been betrothed to me" — I smiled — "but I haven't been betrothed to you."

"The man's opinion does not count in these matters. But in the clubs they tell you to get pregnant in any case. They say that to wait for marriage is a crime of lèse-nationalité. A sterile woman is only fit to keep house for a priest. They say we must all give a soldier a pledge of our loyalty, and the one who provides most boy babies to take the place of the men we have lost at the front will get a civic crown." Her small fist thumped the bed to emphasise this award to patriotic fervour. "People who do it before they're fourteen get their certificates at once and a medal."

"Well, you're nearly sixteen," I said, "so you've missed it in any case." I caught her fist and held it. "Who gave you these dainty pieces of advice — surely not Pêche?"

"No, Rose Lacombe. She is very important. She wears red trousers and a red cap and runs a political club in the St.-Eustache cemetery. But I do not wish you to meet her. She is very beautiful."

"She sounds it."

"You are laughing! But she is very well thought of. They let her impersonate Liberty."

"I can believe that."

"Monsieur Pêche says I must join her club. It would be good for my civisme, but how *can* I go there if I'm not going to be pregnant?" She said it in much the same tone as some women complain that they cannot attend a dinner party because they have nothing fit to wear.

I shouted with laughter. "You can always pretend that you're in the early stages."

"But this Rose Lacombe proposed that every woman should have a crown bestowed on her if she was pregnant four months from her last meeting." She moved closer to me. Then a finger came up and stroked my chin. "You remember the rich man I told you about with the golden chamber pot who fell in love with me? Well, I made it up."

"So I guessed."

"There's never been anyone."

"I'm glad, Puce."

"And — and in the Luxembourg Gardens, when old Lattre put his hand up my skirts, I hit him in the face. I won't let Côté touch me, either."

"Good."

"Or the cocoa seller."

"Better still."

"I never wanted anyone but you. So you see I *depend* on you for my certificate."

"I'll see you get one, but not à la Rose Lacombe."

I knew that behind her patriotic desire to feed the Republic with sons was the old bourgeois idea that if she were pregnant I should feel bound to behave honourably towards her; she still did not trust me where Marie-Clarice was concerned.

She said coldly, "If I was that woman you'd let me come into bed with you now, wouldn't you?"

"Yes, but you're not. So I won't."

She stood up, bitterly resentful that I was able to resist her.

When she left the room I lay chuckling in the darkness. It would be amusing one day to tell the Puce that it had not been easy to refuse her. M.S. was right. She was a woman now.

Chapter 46.

IT BECAME clear to me that M.S. and the Puce had entered into a pact never to let me out of their sight. Wherever I went, one of them accompanied me. They were determined that I should have no chance to take the disguise to Marie-Clarice. As I was equally determined not to involve either of them, it was put off from day to day until I became seriously alarmed.

I had managed to get Marie-Clarice's disguise together. I decided to settle for a wallpaper seller. These women usually sat in the streets with their samples pegged out round them, but sometimes they made door-to-door visits at various private houses. When they packed up for the day they had nothing heavier to carry than a few rolls of paper — which would be useful, as Marie-Clarice would have to travel on foot.

I thought up and then discarded various disguises for myself. A log seller seemed the safest choice. I could take in Marie-Clarice's disguise, leave it in the cellar, and no one would query the fact that my sack was now empty.

There are only certain hours when a log seller could legitimately call at a private house, and I never seemed to be free from M.S. and the Puce at the right time. Finally, in desperation, I crept out of bed in the early hours of the morning and got into my log seller's clothes. I was just stowing Marie-Clarice's disguise into my sack when I saw the Puce standing in the doorway. They had arranged to take watches between them. One or the other of them was always awake during the night in case I should try to do precisely what I was doing.

"Uncle," she called calmly, "he is going to her now."

M.S. was by her side in a matter of seconds. "Very well," he said amiably, "we're both ready."

I got up off my knees. "What do you mean, you're both ready?"

"We're coming with you," said M.S.

"Like this," said the Puce, "in our nightclothes."

"What do you want to do to me? Have me arrested on the spot?"

"We want you to stay at home, boy. But if you insist on going out, we're coming with you."

"It's much wiser to stay here," said Puce. "I'm afraid we might draw attention to you outside. We shall look very strange in our nightclothes."

I decided to call their bluff. Shouldering my sack, I pushed past them. Solemnly they turned and followed me down the stairs. The Puce was bare-footed, and her firm little breasts were pushing against the coarse cloth of her nightgown. Her hair reached her waist and she was wearing her most demure expression. M.S.'s huge frame was topped by his nightcap, and his nightshirt hardly covered his knees. I thought, "They won't do it. They'll never come out of the house."

They came out of the house. I broke into a run along the rue de Picardie. They broke into a run behind me. Thank God there was hardly anyone about except some men putting up the long wooden street tables for a civic dinner. But they called to each other to look at the strangely dressed couple pursuing a log seller, and very soon heads were poking out of windows.

"The old man has found him in bed with his daughter," one kindly soul shouted across the street.

We should soon have collected an interested crowd that would have fol-lowed us all the way to the Hôtel de Faille. It was hopeless. I had to turn back. To a fascinated workman banging the trestles together I said inanely, "I asked too high a price for my logs. They were after me."

"Monopolist!" he yelled at me. "Accapareur!"

I had to run back to the house. I was too angry to speak to M.S. and the Puce.

M.S. went quietly back to bed, but the Puce said sternly, "Now perhaps you see how we love you. We are willing to do anything to stop you risking your neck for that woman."

My opportunity to shake them off came on the day of the King's execu-tion. Paris had been buzzing with the trial of the King, but I think most of the city was utterly stunned when the news broke that he had been found guilty and condemned to death.

The day of his execution was the quietest I had ever experienced in France. Even L'Étuve was silent. One moment they were howling for blood and their monarch's head, and the next, when it was given to them, they were shocked into speechless grief. Fear prevented open protests, but the people had had a king for centuries and they could not bring themselves to believe that they were actually about to murder him. We all know that ruffians are given to sentiment, but I saw genuine tears on hundreds of faces that day. Shops were closed and few people had any heart for work. The crowds that took themselves up to the Place de la Révolution and lined the route along which he was to pass were orderly and quiet.

It was a dismal enough day in its own right. An icy cold mist hung over the city like a grey cloth, and the unnatural silence added to the chill of the atmosphere.

Côté arrived at our house before it was light. "I've come to take Suzon to the execution," he said, "but we must start now if we want a good place."

We were breakfasting and M.S. jumped up so angrily he knocked the candle out. "You'll do no such thing," he said. "I won't have the girl taken to see such a terrible sight. She'd never forget it as long as she lives. Can't you think of something better to show her than bloody murder?"

Côté's eyes narrowed in his smooth, round face. "It is a murderer who has been tried and found guilty, citoyen. He is paying the price of every criminal. Perhaps it's not easy for a foreigner to understand, especially one who comes from a country that enjoys being ruled by a despot — a country that has made war against our people's aims."

I didn't like the threat in his eyes or his voice. I said, "It may be justified, Côté, but it won't be a pleasant sight for a young girl."

"Mothers are taking their babies," said Côté. "Suzon has a carte-de-sûreté. One of the questions she'll be asked when she reports to the police office is whether she saw the pig-Capet die. Patriotism is very necessary if one wants to get back one's certificate of civisme. It's not safe to be without it, you know."

I did know. Also, I saw an excellent chance of getting both Côté and the Puce out of my way at the same time. It was extremely unlikely that they would get near the scaffold. It would be sure to be densely packed with Septembriseurs and wild fédérés from Marseilles paid by the Republic and stimulated with alcohol to roar abuse at the King. The most she would see would be the top of his carriage, or a glimpse of the poor man through his mounted guards.

I said, "I agree with Côté. It's something no true patriot should miss."

The Puce's voice was small. "I'll just go and put on my new shoes." It was quite a tribute to her ex-monarch, as they were now too small for her and pinched. But nothing would persuade her to part with them. They had taken her to the rue Matignon and I think she thought that one day they would take her back.

M.S. and I sat in one of our acid silences until they had gone. Then I said to him casually, "Are you coming?"

He stared at me. "You're not going to tell me you're going yourself?"

"Certainly," I said. "All France's troubles have sprung from the monarchy and I want to see it come to an end."

I knew I was safe enough there. A cannon in the back wouldn't have pushed M.S. out to see the "Lord's anointed" done to death.

When he left the room in disgust, I put on my log seller's disguise. It was not going to be easy to get to the Hôtel de Faille. All streets running to the boulevards were blocked by Santerre's troops, and cannons were dotted all over the place. Although my sack contained nothing but rolls of wallpaper, it was hard work pushing through the crowds.

On the corner of the rue Michaudière I got trapped outside the Bains Chinois. The procession was coming. My feelings were mixed, but my stomach turned. I was still in favour of a Republic, and I should have fought hard against a Royalist revival, but there was something about that mild, fat man going to his death on that freezing day that made one's heart feel as clammy as one's hands and feet. One couldn't help thinking that he was guilty of follies rather than crimes and that he was certainly largely paying for the sins of his ancestors. An old man and a woman were weeping audibly beside me. From the stench of the woman I suspected that she was a dame de la halle, one of the market women who had probably marched with the Amazons on Versailles, or helped to disembowel the Princess de Lamballe on September 2. But now she sobbed as heavily as if she had been attending her own child's funeral. Not a voice was raised along the congested route. No one shouted, no one booed, and no one shook a fist. There was nothing but a mournful resignation to the inevitable, which could hardly have pleased the authorities. Even the Republican party's generous distribution of money and liquor failed to make a brute of the average citizen on that day. He was too damped by the fact that he was responsible for killing his king.

Many hats, caps, and tricolour cockades were bravely doffed as the carriage ground past.

A vast number of National Guards and fédérés came first. Behind them marched the citizens of the faubourgs bristling with pikes and followed by two brigades of fieldpieces. I could scarcely see the top of the carriage myself. It was completely hidden by mounted gendarmes. Santerre and his escorting company were close behind.

Not until I had managed to cross the street and was on my way to the rue du Bac did I hear the hideous roar of cheers. The carriage must have reached the Place de la Révolution and its hosts of paid savages.

The porter's box at the Hôtel de Faille was empty. Presumably he had gone to the execution. I walked across the courtyard without being stopped and presented myself at the kitchen door. The house was severely depleted in staff, but a fat pantry lad told me that they had sufficient logs for their needs, and, like all good patriots, they would not rob the poor of one more piece of wood than they required. What did I think they were, monopolists? Hoarders of food and fuel? Unless I took myself off he would report me to his section leader, who would report me to mine, and I would see the inside of Sainte-Pélagie or the Abbaye. I maintained stoutly that the lady of the house had ordered my logs and that nothing was going to move me. I realised that the poor fellow was afraid I was an agent of the Revolutionary Tribunal, and so I played up to it.

"Show me the cellars then, citoyen. Let me see how much wood you have got stored. If there's nothing to hide, why don't you take me to them so that I can see for myself? It's not right to prevent an honest citizen from selling his goods. I demand to see your cellars."

It had the desired effect. Frightened to shaking point, he fetched the lady of the house.

She was wearing a pale-green dress. I had not seen her in that colour before. It suited her. She marched firmly up to me. "Now, what's this, citoyen? I've ordered no wood."

I turned to face her. "Why are you ashamed of your cellars, citoyenne? Is there something a good patriot shouldn't see?"

She said crisply, "We have nothing to hide. I will show you myself. Come this way." She snatched a candlestick from the huge dresser and passed in front of me. The pantry lad was more loyal than Côté. "Shall I come with you, Madame la —" He broke off in terror at having nearly pronounced her forbidden title.

"No, thank you, Pierre," she said. "This citizen mistrusts us and he can spend as much time as he likes looking for whatever it is he thinks he's going to find."

We proceeded in silence down the stone steps. She closed the thick wooden door behind her, put down the candle, and before I could lower my sack kissed me long and searchingly.

I felt my usual gripping want of her. But I was forced to free myself. "Marie-Clarice, there isn't much time."

"There's plenty. Pierre will expect me to try and seduce you."

"Well, he can go on expecting. Have you made any plans? Who are you going with? How will you get out?"

The candle lit only one corner of the great vaulted cellars. There were certainly very few logs. Marie-Clarice was no hoarder. She leant back against a wall thick with sooty cobwebs.

I opened the sack. "Here's your disguise. You must go into the streets and find yourself a pitch. Try the rue du Temple. Spread all these round you and keep calling out 'Tapissez vos chambres!' Do you think you can manage the accent? Try it."

The candlelight fingered her face. It seemed to ponder on the dark shadows under the eyes which I had always been pleased to note had seemed darker when I had made love to her.

"Do you know what used to amuse me when you were asleep and I was awake?" she asked. "The silly way your arms looked. They seemed so strong, and yet I've seen children sleeping like that. Your hair looked silly, too."

"Listen to me, Marie-Clarice. After you've spent a few hours on your pitch you roll up the wallpaper and wander off as if you want to find a new place. Where have you told your friends to meet you?"

"Oh, we've got some traitor bribed in a toll gate — and then there's a cart picking us up. It's going to be vile. I've always loathed travelling, especially when I leave behind people like you."

She came towards me, her arms out. "I'm glad you've come. I have a joke to tell you."

"Marie-Clarice, I must go now."

"Not till you've heard my joke."

The dust of ages and the dank smell of the cellars couldn't destroy the fragrance of her body. She kissed me full on the mouth again, her lips opened, and her breath was sweet.

"Tell me your joke," I said with the blood thumping hard in my wrists, "but it must be funny and it must be quick."

"Oh, but it's both." The tip of her tongue came slowly out to move over her smile. "I love you."

"That's nonsense," I said. "You've loved dozens of people and you've never found out what it means."

"And you have, I suppose? Do tell me who taught you — your little sainte nitouche?"

As this was a term largely aimed at prudish people who were forced into virtue, I was annoyed on behalf of the Puce. I was glad for any strong feeling that might help to destroy the mounting effect of Marie-Clarice.

I seized her shoulders. "This is no time for jokes. It's no time for you to do anything but get out of France, if it's not too late already. Pêche gave me a hint. He doesn't want to see you again, and that probably means that you're suspect. He believes in you, and if he is afraid to know you, you certainly are in danger."

She stood back looking at me. "Oh, very well," she snapped. "I didn't think my joke was funny either. Marie-Clarice de Faille! In love! At last!"

"The day you escape," I told her, "stand that big lamp with the gold shade in your window. Then I shall know that you've gone."

I picked up the candle and my empty sack and walked a trifle unsteadily up the stairs. I heard her behind me humming a tune. It was the "Ça ira."

In the kitchen we found Côté talking to the pantry boy. I quickly turned my face away. But Marie-Clarice appeared quite unperturbed. "Hallo, Côté. I thought you'd gone to the execution."

"I came back, citoyenne, because the girl I was with fainted and I had to take her home." He added with a curious bitterness, "You have dirt on your face, citoyenne."

I glanced quickly at her and saw that her face was almost as grimy as mine. On my way out I heard her say cheerfully, "Well, of course I have. I've been kissing the log seller. It's the best way to deal with troublemakers."

I hurried back, anxious about the Puce. In our apartments I found her on her bed with M.S. and Pêche in attendance.

M.S. was so worried about her he did not immediately notice my disguise. "She seemed so upset," he said, "that I sent for Monsieur Pêche to give me a hand with her. She was a terrible colour and was as sick as a dog."

Pêche was more observant. He walked up and studied me. "Why are you dressed as a log seller?"

"Oh, I've been up to my old tricks. One doesn't get value for one's assignats, so I thought I'd collect a few trinkets. It's easier in disguise."

I bent over the Puce. I felt immeasurably guilty for letting her go to the execution. "Puce, it's a merciful death in a way. The actual thing's over in a matter of seconds. It's too quick to have hurt him at all."

She stared at my dirty face and cap and turned away from me.

"It's never a pleasant sight," said Pêche. "I don't approve of young people going."

The Puce whispered, "He looked so lonely in such a great crowd. All the drunk people howled and spat mouthfuls of wine at him. It was so sad thinking that nobody liked him, that there wasn't anyone there to mind him. I did wish he could see just one friend. He looked so funny and fat, but he didn't seem frightened at all. He just didn't seem to know what he was supposed to do. If he took a step forward they bumped him back, and if he stood still they pushed him. He wanted to say goodbye to the people, but they wouldn't let him —"

"It's disgusting," said M.S. "They wouldn't even let him make a last speech. When he went to speak from the scaffold, that monster Santerre ordered the drums to roll and drown him. Old Lattre told me the brute is boasting about it."

"It wasn't Santerre," said Pêche. "He may be boasting, but the order didn't come from him. It came from the Chef-d'état Major, the ci-devant Comte d'Oyat. I know, for I heard him give the order. There's a spiteful turn of fate in that. He is a natural son of Louis XV, and therefore this

Capet's uncle. He has probably hated his nephew for years because his bastardy stopped him from being King."

On his way out he said to me, "You had better take care. I'm being questioned about you."

I took off my disguise and stowed it away under the bed. This was fortunate, because the Puce's faithful Côté called to enquire after her health.

I opened a bottle of wine and watched the man closely to see if there were any signs that he had recognised me in the kitchen at the Hôtel de Faille. I saw none. Thinking he would find it unnatural if I didn't enquire after Marie-Clarice, I asked cheerfully, "How is the citoyenne De Faille? I haven't seen her about for a long time."

He was unable to keep malice out of his voice. He hated me for supplanting him with Marie-Clarice and was anxious to let me know that she had been just as unfaithful to me. "I'm afraid she's forsaken you, citoyen. She made love to a log seller this afternoon."

I heard the Puce take a sharp breath and felt M.S.'s eyes roll accusingly towards me.

"Did you actually see them?" I asked.

Côté shrugged. "No, but she told me herself."

"What did she say?" asked the Puce's quiet voice.

"That she had been kissing this man — and from the state of her dress it was not only that. In fact she said it wasn't. He was a very different person from you, citoyen. He had none of your gentlemanly ways. I'm afraid you would hardly be flattered. But he must be the sort she prefers. Some women like it with peasants. She told me that she had never known such a lover before. He took her three times in succession, all in the dirt on the cellar floor! But then some women like it in dirt as well. Yes — I'm afraid that she's lost to you, citoyen, judging from all that she said."

I couldn't even get up and kick him. It wasn't possible to accuse him of lying and for all I knew he might not have been. Marie-Clarice would be quite capable of exaggerating her story if she thought it would lull his suspicions.

Needless to say, when he had gone there was a decidedly cool silence. The Puce said quietly, "I wish she was dead," and ran out of the house.

Once again the Puce refused to speak to me, and apart from our exchanges on the stage so did M.S. She spent most of her time with Côté, so God knows what else she heard about the log seller.

Every day I walked up the rue du Bac looking for the signal. At the end of the week when it had still not appeared I began to be alarmed. I didn't think there would be anything suspicious about my enquiring after her, since Côté had so clearly failed to connect me with the log merchant. So I called at the house.

Côté answered the door with a cold expression.

"Is the citoyenne De Faille at home?"

"No, citoyen, she is not."

"When will she be back?"

"Never, citoyen."

I affected considerable surprise. "She didn't tell me she was going away! Is she selling this house? Where's she gone — to her country estate?"

"She has gone to the Conciergerie, citoyen. She has been denounced."

Chapter 47.

ALL I could say was, "When, tell me — *when*?"

"The officers of the section came for her about three days ago, citoyen." With that Côté shut the door in my face.

I don't quite know how I got out of the place; the shock seemed to deaden my thinking powers. About three days ago! Just after the Puce had heard Côté's version of the log merchant's visit to Marie-Clarice; the day after the Puce had run out of the house crying "I wish she was dead."

I couldn't go home. I was dreading the questions I should have to ask, and I was even more dreading the answer I might get. I felt like stuffing my ears and covering my eyes so that I would never see or hear any signs of the Puce's guilt. I alternated between certainty and disbelief. It would be a severe coincidence if it were not something to do with the Puce. Surely the Puce, who had returned so upset from the King's execution, could never bring herself to condemn a woman she knew to the same fate. I was in such a state of emotional conflict that I sat for two hours in the gardens of the Palais-Égalité shaking as if I were suffering from quartan fever.

Then I went down to the Conciergerie. It would have struck me as even grimmer if I had known what a time I was to spend there myself. A gendarme took me in to the Registrar, who pulled down Marie-Clarice's file. "De Faille — De Faille — De Faille! Ah! Here we are, the ci-devant Comtesse de Faille. Denounced as an aristocrat pretending to be in favour of the Revolution."

"It — it — never says who actually made the denunciation, does it?"

"All denunciations are private, citoyen." He permitted himself a little joke. "Imagine what would happen to a man denouncing his wife. He would be at the mercy of his mother-in-law!"

"May I see the citoyenne De Faille?"

"She's not here now, citoyen."

"Not —"

He was a kindly little man. He reassured me at once. "No, no, citoyen, it's not what you're thinking. She's in the Hospital of the Revolutionary Tribunal. They might let you see her there."

"Yes, yes, thank you. I'll go there at once."

The overcrowding in the hospital was as bad as in the prisons, and the gaoler-concierge looked more of a villain to me than anyone in his care. It was this wretch Tarcilly who refused me any co-operation at all. I had to enquire at the Skin ward, the Equality ward, the Great ward, and the ward of the Republic, until a turnkey told me I was most likely to find Marie-Clarice in the Second Women's ward.

I could get no information about her. Three doctors were making their rounds and I had to wait until their visit was over. Then a turnkey to whom I had repeatedly appealed said, "Let me see, now: was it the Princess de Monaco you wanted to see? I'm afraid the poor lady's been executed. You see, she was deceiving us. She wanted to save her hair for her children, so she managed to arrange for an extra day in here and cut it off with a piece of glass. She was a very gracious, lovely lady."

"Yes, I'm sure, but it is the ci-devant Comtesse de Faille I should like to see."

"Oh, yes. Well, I'll have to enquire."

He returned to tell me I might have a few minutes with Marie-Clarice in the "office." I waited in this none too clean cubby hole.

When she came in, I jumped up. She appeared to me to be shining with health. But her hair was cut raggedly short to the ears. It made a stranger of her.

She laughed. "Hallo! This is brave of you. Your little Chinoise might get *you* next!"

"Marie-Clarice, we've no proof that it was the Puce."

"Well, I don't think we need any, do we?" She sat herself down on a small armchair. "My God, what must I look like! The executioner's assistant just dragged all my hair into the back of my neck and hacked through it. It was quite a change from Leonard!"

I asked her shakily, "You've been condemned?"

"My sweet love, of course I've been condemned. Everyone who gets tried gets condemned." She laughed again. "I wish to heaven you could have been at my trial. It was funnier than any farce. You should have heard my crimes. I have trodden on the face of the people, crushed the poor, starved the sick, and been a general drain on humanity ever since I was laid in my golden cradle."

"Didn't you have a lawyer? Didn't he point out how patriotic you've always been?"

"He might have done, poor man, but they convicted me before he was called. I was an obvious aristocrat befriending the people outwardly whilst

I plotted for the reinstatement of the King in private. Me! Working for that crowd at Versailles! Oh! I forgot to ask. How are you?"

Her gaiety exasperated me. "Never mind how I am. What's the matter with you? Are you ill? Why did they put you in here?"

"They didn't. I put myself. The Princess de Monaco gave me the tip. She didn't want the executioner touching her hair. Quite rightly, when you see what a mess he's made of mine. So she said she was pregnant. They bring you in here to examine you. Of course when they find you aren't that's that, and off you go to Sainte Guillotine — but it gave her enough time to chop off her locks herself. Then she wrote and told the Public Prosecutor what a naughty girl she'd been, holding him up like that, when she knew she wasn't pregnant, and he cut off her head."

"Are you pregnant, Marie-Clarice?"

"Certainly not. I believe I'm barren. But I howled that I was with child by my wood-seller lover. I said I had the seed of the people inside me and they would be decapitating a future Republican. I sent them to the house to ask Côté to tell them about the time he caught me with you. But he told them that I was too proud to acknowledge the existence of a man of the people with a glance, let alone sleep with one. I suppose he was trying to protect himself. Fortunately Pierre was frightened into truth. He testified to having seen my face begrimed from the log seller's kisses, and showed them my dress covered in dirt from his attentions on the cellar floor!" She laughed delightedly again.

"But what will happen when they examine you?"

"They have. Doctors Bayard and Théry swear I'm a liar, but Doctor Naury —" She gave me her quick gay smile. It looked a ghost on her face, framed by the unaccustomed short hair. "Well, I thought him very attractive and he returned the compliment. He says he's convinced that I am pregnant. I rather think he'd be willing to prove it in practice, but as I say, I'm afraid I'm barren. It was a great sadness to my late husband."

"Then what will happen to you?"

"Oh, well, obviously in time I shall be executed. One can't claim to be six months gone for ever and still be as flat as a board. But it's worth delaying it a bit, don't you think? I don't see why one should rush to the guillotine." She laughed again. "Couldn't you dress up as the log seller again and insist that you're the father of my unborn child?"

"I could and I would if it would be of any use."

"No, you'd better not. Your little Chinoise would undoubtedly give you up then."

The turnkey appeared. "It's time to go now, citoyen." And he added amiably, "I shouldn't be surprised if we didn't get some rain."

I tried to signal to Marie-Clarice that I would do everything in my power to help her, and then I left.

In the rue de Picardie I saw from the expression on M.S.'s face that he knew. "I'm sorry, boy," he said.

The Puce was sitting at the table. She had been crying and she could not look at me. I walked round to her. "You needn't have done it, Puce," I said gently. "I was telling the truth when I said I'd no intention of escaping with Marie-Clarice."

She jumped up, put herself into my arms, and wept quietly against me. "You were right all the time. She didn't denounce me. Old Lattre has told me it was his wife."

The Puce sensed my stiffness towards her. She looked up. The tears hovering in the corners of the turned-up eyes made her look more of a Chinoise than ever. She stood back from me. "Did you think I had given her away?"

"Who else had such a grudge against her?"

M.S. strode up to me. "Good heavens, boy, this child wouldn't do a thing like that. She's not a murderess."

The Puce put her hands to her face. "I didn't! I didn't! It was all my fault, but I didn't denounce her."

"Then who did?"

"Côté."

"Côté!"

"Yes. He has just been to tell me. He loves me. He thought it would make me pleased with him."

"But — but if he loves you, surely he wouldn't get her out of the way just so that you can have me?"

She sat down again, a weary head propped on her hand. "He doesn't know I love you. I've always been careful of that. He would get you arrested at once."

"Then why did he think you'd be pleased?"

"He thought that she was the one who denounced me. I told him she had and he wanted to get his revenge."

"Oh! God!" I said. "Oh! God!"

M.S. put a hand on my shoulder. "I never thought much of that woman, but seeing that Suzon is partially responsible, we ought to see what we can do for her."

I shrugged helplessly. "What can we do? It was difficult enough with the Puce. The Héberts aren't likely to speak up for a notorious aristocrat however democratic she may have been."

The first people who came to my mind, of course, were the Desmoulins, who had always been friends of Marie-Clarice.

Lucile Desmoulins was the prettiest thing I had seen for a long time, but she was very firm. "It wouldn't be fair to my husband. After all, Marie-

Clarice *is* an aristocrat. Whatever her feelings might have been, we can't alter that."

No, we couldn't alter that and we weren't going to try in case we got our fingers burned. It was the same everywhere. So many friendships had changed into fears.

We had another conference round our table.

"What about Danton's new wife?" asked M.S. "They say he worships the girl. Couldn't we get at him through her?"

"We could try. I wasn't very successful with the first Mrs. Danton."

"What about the 'friend of the people'?" M.S. enquired bitterly. "Hasn't he got a wife you could charm?"

"Is he married?" I asked the Puce.

"I don't know. I'll run across and ask Monsieur Pêche."

She came back panting. "Monsieur Pêche is so funny these days. I don't think he likes me any more."

"You didn't call him 'monsieur' to his face, did you?"

She snapped her fingers. "Oh, yes. It's supposed to be 'citoyen,' isn't it? I always forget."

"Well, don't. It's dangerous. It's that sort of thing that makes him think we're unsafe to know. What did he say?"

"Well, there isn't a Madame — I mean a *citoyenne* — Marat, but he has a 'free union' with a lady called citoyenne Evrard, who lives with him. Monsieur — I mean *citoyen* — Pêche says we should be proud of her. It was her money that helped him start *L'Ami du Peuple*."

"You didn't tell Pêche what we wanted, did you?"

"No — I just said we were having a little argument about the 'friend of the people.' You said he was married and I said he wasn't."

"Where does he live?"

"At the Hôtel de Cahors. He has an apartment there."

Dressed once again as "the honest log seller," I set off for the Hôtel de Cahors. It was a dull, solid-looking house with a shop on either side of the carriage arch. There was a well at the end of a small courtyard and stone steps leading to a brick platform. I knocked at the door of a surgeon-dentist before I found the "friend of the people's" iron bell pull. From his kitchen window came a cloud of steam and a smell of uninteresting cooking.

The door was pulled inward by one of the ugliest women I had ever seen. If this was the "friend of the people's" partner in his free union, I did not envy him. She was squat, fat, and had one bright glass eye.

"We have plenty of wood," she snapped.

"I'm not selling any. Are you the citoyenne Evrard?"

"No, I am the citoyenne Aubin. I am the portress here. What do you want?"

"Is the citoyenne Evrard in?"

"Which one? Citoyenne Catherine or citoyenne Simonne? Both of them live here."

"Um . . ." I couldn't very well ask which one of them was sleeping with the "friend of the people."

"Well, come in," she snapped. "I can't stand here all day. I've got to fold the papers."

The glass eye managed to flash even in that badly lit hall. Piled high on a bench there was a stack of copies of *L'Ami du Peuple*. The portress snatched one of them and began to fold it with a doubled fist. Then she shrieked into the depths, "Jeanette! Somebody wants something."

In answer to her call an untidy servant girl came in. "What is it, citoyenne Aubin?"

The glass-eyed one jerked a thumb over her shoulder at me and went on folding newspapers.

"We have plenty of wood," said the maid.

"I'm not trying to sell any, I want to see" — I took a chance — "I want to see the citoyenne *Catherine* Evrard."

Jeanette sloped off. She returned with a girl who was neither plain nor good-looking. She said, "Yes?"

I made my rough accent as sexually attractive as possible. "Am I talking to the lady who has the tremendous good fortune, although doubtless highly deserved, of being er — er — *connected* with the 'friend of the people'?"

She said, "No. I'll get her."

She came back with a hard-featured woman whose voice when she spoke was cultured and quiet. They both sat down and stared at me.

I addressed the hard-featured woman. "I hope you won't think badly of me, citoyenne, a humble person like myself. But my father was in the trade before me and we come from honest stock." I brought out my fullest bag of charms — eyes, smile, voice, and flattering looks. It was interesting to see them becoming slowly drawn towards this eloquent wood seller. "I've come to you, citoyenne," I said to the hard-faced one, "because of all people I thought you would understand love." They exchanged startled looks and the citoyenne Aubin stopped folding newspapers. "You feel more strongly for the 'friend of the people' than for anyone else in the world?" I suggested.

"I'm not alone in that," she said. "He's a God and it's right that he should be worshipped. Men as well as women kneel to my brother."

"Your *brother*?"

"Yes, I am Albertine Marat. Who did you think I was?"

"I thought you were citoyenne Simonne Evrard."

"It's *my* sister you want, then," said Catherine Evrard. "I'll fetch her."

She came back with a brown-haired, brown-eyed girl with a shiny forehead. "I am Simonne Evrard."

They were now all three seated and staring at me.

I was obliged to start all over again. I thought they looked the type of audience who might enjoy the old school of acting. I didn't think subtleties would pay. Probably in secret their hearts beat for Fleury and Mouet. I begged Simonne to imagine herself without the "friend of the people"; I implored her to think of what it was like for me to be without the woman I loved as much as she loved the "friend of the people." The woman who, as a result of our "free union," was carrying the child I hoped would be a son to lay on the altar of the country. I begged for the life of the unborn boy's mother. Finally I ended on both knees in front of them, head bowed, hands clasped, sobbing out my appeal to them to intercede with the "friend of the people." Dorfeuille would have been delighted with me.

I was right about their choice in performers. I was not the only one weeping. Even the citoyenne Aubin's one eye was streaming.

They conferred together and decided that I should be taken up to the great tribune, who apparently, to soothe an ever itching skin, spent most of his time sitting in warm water.

Clutching my cloth cap humbly in hand, I was led through a bedroom decorated with the most appalling tricoloured paper covered in revolutionary symbols. Outside a small door I was told to wait. Simonne Evrard went in and beckoned to me to stand outside the bathroom. I heard her regaling the soaking "friend of the people" with the petition of the emotional log seller. I could not see Marat. The bath was behind the open door. It was a minute compartment papered with long entwined columns on a white background that was yellowing from constant steam. On the wall opposite the bath there was a map of France. Next to that something ominous caught my attention. Two pistols were hanging on the wall and above them was a large inscription. It was the single word "death" in giant letters. It was an omen I remembered afterwards in the light of what happened to him in that very bathroom

I heard their murmuring turn to angry shouts. When Simonne came out, although the tears were not yet dry on her face from my performance, she looked severe.

"Citoyen," she said, "the friend of the people knows your woman. He's ready to believe that you, as a true man of the people, may have been taken in by her, because I have told him how impressed we were with you. But this woman De Faille is an aristocrat and she's probably carrying your child to prove her civisme. The friend of the people advises you for your own safety to pretend that you've never met her."

When I went out, a cocoa seller was moving down the street. I wasn't close enough to see whether it was ours and I was so distressed by the failure of my attempt that I don't think I cared.

Pêche was waiting for me when I got home. I admired him for it. The terrible mistrust that prevailed everywhere and that was to my mind the worst stain on the character of the Revolution was even affecting the iron-souled Pêche. He was afraid to be seen consorting with persons who had been under the eye of the police, like M.S. and myself, and with a girl who had been to prison, like the Puce. But his ideals were still alive and his hopes that "everything might still settle down" were not dead. His face looked thinner and his eyes seemed less bright, but he was indignant on behalf of Marie-Clarice.

"It is those people we want on our side. She was a true admirer of the Revolution. It is nonsense to say she was trying to deceive us. She was a patriot."

I told him about my attempt to soften the "friend of the people." He shook his head. "You will get nowhere with men like that. They have big names and fear makes them shout, but the people whose power you feel — the ones who really run the Revolution — are all on the committees. If you want influence, you want to win round one of the porteurs d'ordres of the Committee of Public Safety. Try Feneaux, or Longueville-Clémentière, Héron, Toutin, or Quesneau — those are the men with the real power!"

It was not my greatest wish to present myself to any agent of the Committee of Public Safety or the Committee of General Security, but I was stupidly convinced that the police, had they wanted me, would have picked me up before. I did not know then that the sole reason I was still at liberty was that the two most powerful committees in France would not allow me to be arrested until each had proved that I was not the person for whom the other one was looking!

Toutin was the only one who granted me an interview. I presented myself as the clownish actor Roberts from the Petit Théâtre de la Cité and pleaded with him to intervene for Marie-Clarice. He smiled gently and told me that no man's mistress was worth his neck. I would be wiser to forget her.

In desperation I decided to use every seductive trick I possessed on Madame Fouquier-Tinville. But she did not invite me over the doorstep. A sad, bitter woman of about thirty, with untidy hair, she laughed at me. "My dear citoyen, I haven't the right looks to influence my husband and neither have you. It has to be a very pretty woman indeed to do that." And her door closed firmly in my face.

The Puce enquired, "Am *I* pretty enough?"

"Yes," I said, "but you're not going near him. From the acidity in his wife's voice, I gather he's got somewhere more than a wry smile for the ladies."

"If that's all he's got," said the Puce, "it's not hard to smile back, and if he wants anything else, I shall let him think he can get it."

"And what happens when he comes for it?" asked M.S. "If he finds you've been leading him on for nothing, you might find yourself in prison again."

"I shall turn him over to the Comtesse — to the *citoyenne* — de Faille. She'll be sure to give it to him and then he'll forget all about me." She turned a blank stare in my direction.

As Paris was such a small city, I had caught sight of Fouquier-Tinville on several occasions. There was nothing particularly sinister about him. One saw a dozen of his kind in every bourgeois eating house. His face had a heavy look as if it were pressing down on his jaws, and he held his head low as if he were constantly weary. I had been told that he was overworking to such an extent that he had become a victim to nervous illusions. He imagined that the ghosts of those whom he had caused to be decapitated followed him at night in the streets. I doubt if he was short of spectral companions, as he was claiming thirty and forty heads a day and spent all his working hours trying to improve on his record. He even slept on the floor of his office so that he would be on hand first thing in the morning to go through the reports from the committees and study the dossiers. It was not easy to believe, as rumour had it, that he had confided to the woman in the tribunal refreshment room that his task distressed him and that he longed to exchange it for something more homely such as farming!

He was the last person I should have wished the Puce to seek out, but if he were as susceptible as his wife implied, it was just possible that the Puce might be successful.

"If he tries to flirt with you," I ordered, "use your well-worn armour of promising him 'more to come.' But don't give him *anything* at the time."

"And don't overact," said M.S. "You've a tendency that way, but it's never been known to help any performance."

She was away a long time, and M.S. and I were beginning to be seriously alarmed. Then she came back, her voice squeaky with excitement.

"He was so *gentlemanly*," she said. "And, Uncle, I know you'll be pleased with me. I didn't overact at all. I just went into his office and curtsied like this" — she gave a little demonstration bob — "and then I pretended I was so frightened of him I turned to run away, but before I got out of the door he came round his desk to me and told me not to be afraid, for he was just an ordinary man and he would never hurt anyone like me. He took me back by the hand and pulled out a chair and I made sure to sit with my side to the light."

"Why?" I asked.

"So that he could see my figure sticking out. Then I pretended I was too shy to say anything and he came round and put his hand on my shoulder and I began to cry very slowly — not too much, Uncle," she assured M.S.

"I didn't jerk or sob or anything — just as if I was in despair, like you taught me when we wanted free soup from old Monsieur Lattre."

"You didn't call *him* 'monsieur'?" I asked nervously.

She shook her head. "No. I said 'citoyen.' But I said I felt terrible calling such a great man 'citoyen,' and then he gave me a little lecture about the Revolution."

"Yes," I said. "He would after that."

"But he was pleased all the same. He kept chuckling and saying I was a silly child and he couldn't imagine what made me think he was such a great man. And then he asked me what I wanted, and I told him that a lady who had always been very kind to me had been wrongly imprisoned. He asked what my particular friend had done, because no one was in prison without very good reason. I said she was there because she slept with her footman." I exchanged anxious glances with Manager Smith. But the Puce went chattering on. "I said she thought it was her revolutionary duty to sleep with him to prove that she believed in equality and to try and get a son of the people to lay on the altar of the country, and when she didn't get one she slept with a log seller." Here a cold look was sent to me. "But when the footman found out about that he was so jealous he denounced her, and I thought it was wrong because at my club they told me if you didn't get a son you had to keep on trying — that's if you wanted a civic crown — and she didn't mind who it was so long as she conceived from a sans-culotte."

When the Puce took a breath I asked, "What did he say?"

"He said if I would meet him alone at the Tuileries on the terrace by the water he would do some thinking about it. So I said yes, and he met me. He didn't keep me waiting a second. He was wearing such a nice blue coat, but he kept his hat pulled very low. I don't think he wanted people to recognise him. He gave me his arm and held his umbrella over me all the way to La Rapée, where he gave me quite a nice little meal and some wine. He's a funny little man. He didn't say much and he didn't touch me at all. Not with his knees or anything. He just kept munching and staring past me as if he was dreaming of something. Then he said, 'Did you say your friend was enceinte?' and I said, 'Yes. By the log seller. One of the doctors at the prison is sure of it, but of course it's early days to tell, and the other two aren't quite sure. But even when it's born it might not be a boy, so she wants to be able to get out and try again.' He said she sounded a very enthusiastic Republican at heart. But of course her blood was still aristocratic and there was nothing he could do to alter that. Then he asked, 'Has she any money?' and when I said 'yes,' he said something strange — at least I thought it was strange. He said the prison doctors were so overworked that they might make mistakes and he thought my friend should go and see a private doctor he could personally recommend. But he was very expensive and my friend would need quite a lot of money, but this doctor looks after his patients well. His name is Belhomme and he lives at the top of the rue de Charonne in the faubourg Saint-Antoine. Isn't it funny advice? I mean, what can a doctor do?"

Chapter 48.

I FOUND out by calling at a pleasantly countrified-looking old house at the top of the rue de Charonne. It stood amongst decaying peasant cottages and it appeared to be a lunatic asylum. The first person I met was thin man with an exhausted face who took me by the arm and recited a lengthy passage from *Mérope*.

I was rescued by a fat woman who took his arm. "Now, now, citoyen De Lambour, you must save yourself for your evening's performance." She pushed him off still wildly declaiming and smiled at me. "That was the poor Abbé de Lambour. He thinks he is the great English Garrick or Lekain. Such a pity! He wears himself out, but he isn't dangerous. Anyone like that we keep in a special place at the end of the courtyard. I am the citoyenne Chabanne, assistant to Doctor Belhomme. I expect you would like to see him."

She marched ahead of me into the house and I followed her. In a wide passage we passed a long line of people waiting outside the dining-room doors. They were laughing and joking amongst themselves to such an extent that the place seemed as gay as a masked ball.

The citoyenne Chabanne smiled at me. "We are high up here, you know. It encourages appetites." She bowed to the waiting line as she passed. "Good day, citoyenne D'Orléans, good day, citoyenne De Penthière, good day, citoyen Talleyrand."

I was astonished to find myself saying "good day" to Mademoiselle de Lange from the Comédie Française.

She had not forgotten me. "You!" she said accusingly. "You have no right to be here. I remember an argument in the Green Room: you were with Dugazon. You were wholly on the side of the revolution!"

I said, "Yes, mademoiselle, but when the woman you love goes mad, you are bound to admit that she is no longer a reasonable mistress."

"Dugazon," she commented sourly, "has not yet realised that his love has gone mad." She lifted her pretty shoulders contemptuously. "It makes one despair of his own sanity. Oh, what we had to put up with! Our audiences consisted of 'knock hards' — I think that's what they called themselves —

doubtless *you* approved of them. They carried bludgeons which they referred to as 'constitutions.' I ask you! These are the people in whose favour you and Dugazon and Talma saw fit to argue. When we refused to sing the terrible songs they demanded, they swarmed onto the stage with their 'constitutions.' "

"I don't approve of that kind of person, mademoiselle," I managed to squeeze in. She ignored me.

"Our real trouble started in *Pamela*. Did you happen to see it? I was told it was one of the best things I had ever done." She gave me no chance to answer. "There were some lines in the play to which one of the ruffians took a political exception. He shouted that Fleury had no right to use them. Fleury stepped forward and told him, 'I assure you, monsieur, that I only speak the author's words.' He should have said 'citoyen,' but he said 'monsieur.' The ruffian left the theatre and came back with the officers of his section, and on the strength of Fleury's 'monsieur' we were all arrested and imprisoned in the Madelonettes. These are the kind of people you championed!"

She was prettier when she was scornful. Her eyes darkened.

"How did you get in here, then, mademoiselle? And what is the purpose of this place?"

"Oh, it's a kind of private prison, and you're safe enough as long as you can pay."

I left her to present myself to Doctor Belhomme.

He was an amiable little man and his study was very well furnished. He bounced up to greet me. "Ah! Sit down, monsieur, sit down." It seemed odd to hear him risking the use of this unpatriotic form of address when De Lange was in his care solely because Fleury had used it on the stage.

"You've come about a patient?" he enquired.

I sat down warily. The whole extraordinary establishment was quite beyond me. Mad priests convinced that they were great actors, and obviously sane duchesses and countesses waiting their turn for a meal, seemed a curious assortment to find in any Maison de Santé.

"I was advised," I said cautiously, "that you might look after a friend of mine — the ci-devant Comtesse Marie-Clarice de Faille."

He rustled amongst papers on his desk. "She's in bad health?"

"Well, yes — and she's also in the Conciergerie."

He looked up sympathetically. "Oh, dear. The conditions there aren't very inspiring, are they? And the air is so bad. The authorities do their best, you know, but it's really not easy." He pounced on a piece of paper. "Yes, here we are. Here is the order permitting me to take care of the Comtesse de Faille. It's signed by Monsieur Fouquier-Tinville himself." I stared stupidly at him. He filed the order and smiled above folded hands. "There are just one or two little details to be settled before admitting a patient. I'm not boasting when I say that we offer every amenity here. Our patients are not encouraged to leave the grounds, of course — for the good of their health.

But visitors are allowed at any time. Food and wines are permitted to be brought in from outside, although a small tax is charged upon departures from the Maison's ordinary diet. Patients who have come to me from some of the less — well, salubrious prisons — tell me they find my house a great relief. Of course, we're very crowded here as well. I've been forced to take on the adjoining house. Also the cost of living has gone up so formidably that we've been obliged to put up our fees." He leant back in his chair, coughed politely, and said, "What are the Comtesse de Faille's means?"

"Still adequate, I should say."

His lips pushed out. " 'Adequate,' " monsieur, is not a very enlightening word. My — er — medical services are in extraordinary demand. We could supply only a very small room for one thousand livres a month." He saw me gulp, and added, "Or she could rent a corner of a room at four hundred livres a month. Everything else is extra, of course — lighting, heating, food, drink — and the servants expect a little something. Then she will have to make voluntary contributions to the section's activities and, of course, there will be my own medical attentions . . . Shall we put it at six thousand livres paid in advance?"

When I gasped audibly he leaned towards me. "I have quite a remarkable reputation, you know, for — er — preserving health. I think I may say that I have possibly saved more lives than any other medical man in Paris. If your friend considers my fees too great in return for insuring that she lives — You *did* say she was in very bad health and that the end was near for her? Well, then, she must reject my offer to attend to her."

He escorted me to the door and at it said blithely, "Of course, no doctor is infallible. I do have my failures. It costs a lot of money to keep a patient alive these days." He turned a face full of genuine distress towards me. "Believe me, I take a real interest in my patients. I grow very fond of them. It grieves me to the soul when I can do nothing for them. The case of the Duchesse Beatrice de Choiseul became beyond my powers quite recently. She was an enchanting woman. I've not got over it yet."

"What happened to her," I asked with a rather dry mouth.

"She died. I told you that it costs a fantastic amount to keep patients alive. Her estate ran out and she was obliged to return to the Conciergerie. She was so pleasant about it, too. She quite understood my inability to help her any further. They are always sent to the scaffold within three days. An enchanting woman." There were sincere tears in his eyes.

"Very well," I said. "I'll warn my friend."

"Yes," he said dejectedly, "warn your friend."

I came out feeling distinctly unclear in the head. How this "amateur prison," which obviously kept a few of its original lunatics only as a cover, could exist amongst all the insane slaughter that had become part of daily lives I was completely unable to imagine. How the Public Prosecutor himself could not only be aware of it but personally countenance the removal of some of the most notorious aristocrats from their death cells was even more beyond belief.

However, I managed to achieve a short interview with Marie-Clarice in the parloir. I was still shocked by the sight of her short-clipped hair.

"Well," she said, "I can think of worse things to do with one's money. I can manage it for a bit anyway, and by that time let's hope things will settle down, as your friend Pêche says. Oh! And thank your little Chinoise for me. It was really very good of her to brave that man for me."

Three days later we went to see her at Belhomme's. She was vastly enjoying herself and she took us out on to the promenade, where poor De Lambour was still disclaiming long scenes from various tragedies.

"Did he remember to thank you for me?" she asked the Puce.

"Yes, madame."

"Well, he's yours now, and in gratitude to you for drinking soup with the Public Prosecutor, which must have been a very nasty experience, I promise never to lay another finger on him as long as Belhomme lets me live."

"Thank you, madame."

The Puce was excessively shy and quite overawed. The company flowing along that promenade would have inspired even the porter in the rue Matignon. But she managed to stammer to Marie-Clarice, "You do believe that it wasn't me who denounced you, don't you, madame?"

Marie-Clarice bent down and kissed her. "Yes, of course, but I did suspect you in the beginning. I ought to have thought of Côté at once." She smiled at us both. "I'm sorry I can't offer you anything to eat or drink, but it costs you a fortune to breathe in here. My 'corner of a room' really is a corner — up in the loft. Anything extra cripples one. There's a woman here called Breteuil who treats herself to cream and broth and a few mulled eggs and it costs her two thousand livres in twenty days! The ordinary food they provide is appalling. They feed thirty people on enough for eight."

"I could make you some broth, madame," offered the Puce.

"You could, chérie, but old Chabanne would stand at the door and tax me on it. No, I must curb my appetite. I don't want to see little Belhomme, handkerchief to eyes, waving me goodbye. Besides, it's so enjoyable here. It's really very gay with the music and dancing at nights."

We avoided the Abbé de Lambour, who was bearing down on us with another rendering of *Mérope*.

"That poor creature's rather a good advertisement for the lunatic side of the establishment, isn't he?"

"Have you found out what the Public Prosecutor's got to do with this?" I asked.

Marie-Clarice said, "No. Most people think he gets a good fat commission from Belhomme on every prisoner, but other people swear that's not true.

There's an advocate in here who knows him quite well. He says in spite of his wife's suspicions there aren't any women in his life. He has very little money and his only vice seems to be drinking too much in the buvette or a wine shop at the top of the Pont-Rouge. He seems to totter gloomily drunk from one to the other on occasions, but that doesn't sound like a man receiving vast sums of money. Another theory in here which I incline to is that it's a sop to his conscience to allow this — and other — Maisons de Santés to exist. He has a few nightmares about his activities, apparently, and he might sleep better if he thinks he's allowing this. Anyway, nobody knows for certain. Madame de Penthièvre thinks people make use of his name. Those vile porteurs d'ordres raking the prisons for committee victims aren't above suspicion. They could pick up hefty sums for favours like this and they can do what they like with Fouquier-Tinville. Madame de Saint-Aulaire told me that she got to see him through a creature called Vilain. She wanted her father removed from the Conciergerie. Vilain said if she produced six thousand livres he would take them to the Public Prosecutor and she'd get an immediate interview. Well, she did, and Fouquier-Tinville quietly wrote her out an order for her father to be brought to Belhomme's. But one thing she's quite certain of: Vilain never took that six thousand out of his pocket. He wasn't the sort to pass anything on. So there you are — who knows? You're very quiet, little Chinoise!" she said suddenly to the Puce.

It always amused me that Marie-Clarice should imagine that anyone else was able to talk while she was talking.

"For the moment you've saved my life, little Chinoise, which is nice of you, considering that I can imagine you would infinitely prefer to have me out of the way." The Puce coloured fiercely, evidently recalling her own words to that effect. "Never mind," said Marie-Clarice. "Jealousy is a disease."

"Yes, madame."

It seemed to be my lot in life to have women jerking contemptuous chins at me. Marie-Clarice pointed me out in this fashion to the Puce and added magnanimously, "Well, I meant what I said. You may have him in return for what you've done for me. I shall not try to take him away from you."

The Puce said humbly, "Thank you, madame," but as I had so recently made it clear to Marie-Clarice that I was not willing to offer myself to her as a permanency, I could not help smiling at her generous renunciation of me.

"Little Chinoise," said Marie-Clarice, "I told him that I thought you would be the one to marry him in the end."

"Thank you, madame."

"That is what you want, isn't it?"

"Yes, madame."

"Do you think you will be able to keep him faithful to you?"

"No, madame. But then I never think that bad people can become good all at once."

"Very sensible," said Marie-Clarice.

When we left Marie-Clarice, the road outside was thick with carriages. The inmates of Belhomme's were about to entertain their evening visitors. One carriage disgorged a crowd of musicians, and I recognised several actors who had come to give readings. Belhomme's Maison de Santé was certainly the most congenial of prisons.

The Puce took my hand and said confidently, "I think I shall trust Madame de Faille. I think she means it when she says I may have you."

"Haven't you both forgotten that I belong to myself?" I asked.

She flashed me a fiery glance from those dark slit eyes of hers. It was followed by the kind of look a mother gives a backward child. "I shall call our first daughter after her. Marie-Clarice is a pretty name. Our first son will be called Lambert for Uncle, and the second will be called Philippe after you."

"It's nice of you to remember me."

When we reached home, M.S. had distressing news for us. "Pêche has been arrested. I've only just heard. They took him away last night. No one knows for sure who denounced him, but everyone thinks it was old Lapin. He's always thought he'd make a better section leader."

"I'm sure it was Grandfather," said the Puce. "He's always resented poor Monsieur Pêche ever since he didn't go and fight at the Bastille."

M.S. and I found it even less easy to throw ourselves into our act that night. The tumblers had never seemed so inexpert, the dancing bears more grizzly, and our massacre of Shakespeare more villainous. The thought that Pêche would never live to see things "settle down" was hanging over both of us. Even the wine we drank at supper reminded us of Pêche. We tried to cheer ourselves by making plans for America, but we always came back to Pêche.

"Shall I go and see Monsieur Fouquier-Tinville again?" asked the Puce.

"What's the good? Pêche can't afford Belhomme's and we could never get that much money together."

"He must have friends," brooded M.S. "He knew dozens of people at the head of things."

"Friends," I said, "have a habit of disappearing these days."

"What about the Abbé Servoise?" suggested the Puce. "He has taken the civic oath to put the State before the Pope, so his civisme is good."

"A nice way for a man of God to behave," said M.S.

"Well, the Abbé says that it isn't a crime to take the oath. He says if nobody did, there wouldn't be any priests left to preach the faith at all."

The true Catholic Faith was still a short cut to the guillotine. Even the saints had been proletarianised and given symbols of everyday usage. St. Martin was a hand saw, St. Gregory a plough, St. Jerome a spade, and St. Matthew a pitchfork. Any little jokes on the changes, I might hastily add, were also a short cut to the guillotine. It was all as silly and as irrational as the names people were giving themselves. It was fashionable to be called after some ancient Greek or Roman hero. Old cobbler Lapin became Cincinnatus. Madame Lapin was Lucretia, and I heard that Côté went about calling himself Cato.

Perhaps I am wrong, but it seemed a little ludicrous for someone who had to be called Cincinnatus to go on his knees to someone who had to be called the Spade. However, it was possibly a step forward that we were allowed to go on our knees at all. Our churches, once ransacked and debased, now bore the following interesting placards: "LE PEUPLE FRANÇAIS RECONNAÎT L'EXISTENCE DE L'ÊTRE SUPREME, ET L'IMMORTALITÉ DE L'ÂME."

I don't doubt that God gave a sigh of relief, but it was confusing for the rest of us. Robespierre had decided that we should believe in the Life Eternal and the immortality of the soul, and should worship, not God, but the Supreme Being.

I think what really happened was that they were not doing well without religion. People like Cincinnatus, Lucretia, and even the abominable Cato were used to crossing themselves, lighting candles for the souls of their loved departed, and asking the Pitchfork for help in times of stress. Deprived of this comfort, they were bewildered. Also, having been told that no after life existed and that the all-seeing eye of the God of the priests who had refused to take the civic oath was moonshine, they failed to see why they should behave themselves in the present life. Something had to be done, and Robespierre did it. He gave them back immortality and he gave them the Supreme Being.

Having witnessed quite closely the immense ceremony in which he made his point, I have no doubt as to whom Robespierre believed to be the Supreme Being. Neither, unfortunately for him, had his colleagues seated on a rather unpleasantly green canvas mountain in the middle of the Champ-de-Mars.

The man's every gesture and every step made it quite impossible even for those of us who might have escaped from the Salpêtrière or Belhomme's original establishment not to realise that here was someone who fancied himself not only as an earthly dictator but as the Supreme Being as well.

It was a very impressive procession, with the members of the Convention marching in blue coats with their steel buttons gleaming and tri-coloured plumes nodding in their hats. The triumphal car, carrying the Goddess Ceres, played by the big-bosomed Clotilde of the opera house, was dragged by twelve white oxen. Impressive, too, were the nymphs in Roman costume; so were the hymns by Clerier and the music by Gossec; and so was Robespierre marching ahead like a proud little goose treading out to its doom.

Large statues representing Egotism, Discord, and Atheism had been erected, and after a long speech instructing us to worship the Supreme Being, Robespierre set fire to them. As they were filled with crackers and combustibles, there were considerable explosions. It may have been my imagination that Egotism went off with the loudest bang.

The procession included girls crowned in violets and boys in myrtle wreaths. They approached the mountain on which the crippled Couthon sat in his bath chair. Next to him the grim-faced Saint-Just was perched rather dangerously under a cedar tree.

As Robespierre began the ascent with a dangerous arrogance not likely to charm his jealous colleagues, I wondered stupidly who would look after his songbirds. Perhaps his sister would hang them round her dingy room in memory of the brother she had loved. I was perfectly certain, after that performance, I was watching the beginning of the end of Robespierre.

I had heard through Pêche that Robespierre's popularity amongst his colleagues was already on the wane. Unlike the public, they considered that the organisation of his corps of six thousand youths between the ages of fourteen and seventeen had a sinister side to it. These lads were of the age when their unformed minds were at the mercy of anyone who liked to influence them, and their commanding officer was hand-picked by Robespierre.

The public flocked to see them drilling in the uniform designed by David — brown frock coat, open-collared shirt, red trousers, and leather helmet. Robespierre claimed that the corps was intended as a model for the organisation of the army and as a school for officers. The public believed this, but one of Pêche's deputy friends told him that the youth army was viewed with deep suspicion in certain quarters, and that Robespierre was suspected of marshalling these pliable youngsters to augment his own ambitious schemes. It was certainly unwise of him to have put himself forward as the Supreme Being.

We were still discussing the best means of interceding for poor Pêche when I heard the patrol outside. I listened to the footsteps and the clinking sabres. For a few cold seconds I thought that they were stopping in front of our door. In the house, besides ourselves, there were only the carpenter Moustier and his ancient mother downstairs.

I heard shouts of instruction and orders barked out. There was no doubt that it was a revolutionary committee conducting one of its dreaded domiciliary visits. Yet another poor wretch had been denounced.

The patrol passed and we had scarcely breathed our relief when the footsteps returned. I crept to the window. The patrol had stopped outside our house. We heard the fatal knock.

There can have been no one alive in Paris, with the exception of the porteurs d'ordres, who did not go to bed praying that the night would pass without that knock. It echoed through our old house like a death drum and was followed by silence. A second knock seemed to climb the very stairs and tour the rooms. Then a loud voice called, "Ouvrez au nom de la loi!"

The Puce's hand went to her mouth. M.S. stood up slowly. I heard Moustier pulling back the bolts downstairs.

"Get the Puce out across the roof," I told M.S. "There's a ridge behind the chimneys next door. It's dangerous, but you'll have the strength to hang on to her."

"But, boy —" he began.

"Don't argue," I told him. "You look after the Puce: I can take care of myself."

The Puce sat herself firmly on a chair. "I will stay."

I picked her up bodily and passed her to M.S. M.S. was curiously expressionless when his real emotions were involved. But I knew that he was struggling to choose between us. Finally common sense and chivalry won. He carried the Puce through the doorway, and I was left to pray that they would reach the garret window in time.

Downstairs, I could hear the kindly Moustier raising his voice in warning. "I can't think who you want, citoyens. There's no one of that name in this house."

I ran to the chimney, put up my arm, and streaked my face and neck with dirt. Then I raced to the bed and dragged out the log seller's costume. It was the quickest change I have ever made in the whole of my career. The wig and the low cap hid a good portion of my face, but I was still fighting my way into the trousers, the ragged carmagnole, and the grimy necklet as the officers of the section climbed towards me. M.S.'s spectacles were left on the table. I put them on and had just time to splash wine into a glass and sit at the table when they pushed open the door.

It was going to be the hardest Lord Credit to sustain that I had ever played. The new section leader who had taken over from poor Pêche was old Lapin.

Chapter 49.

I JUMPED up from the table, spilling my wine. I made my eyes wild with fright and went stumbling backwards against the wall, where their torches could shine least on my face.

They advanced on me, and I shielded my face with my arm as if I thought they were going to strike me. "I've taken nothing, citoyens," I wailed. "I'm not a thief. That's my own wine — I brought it in."

There were about eight men behind old Lapin. They were all armed and clearly astonished to be confronted with an honest wood seller in the middle of his supper. But how long could I fool old Lapin? Certainly he would never recognise my voice; I knew too well how to imitate the street-vendor accents of L'Étuve. I blessed M.S. for his marking training. But while a carefully maintained expression and spectacles can help to disguise a face, they cannot change it. I should have to depend entirely upon performance and nerve. "I'm honest, citoyens," I whined. "Everything's just as they left it, you won't find a thing disturbed. What would you have done, citoyens? They owed me money. A man has to live, doesn't he?"

"Who owed you money?" snapped old Lapin. He was very authoritative in poor Pêche's shoes and, I thought, swaggering a little.

I swept my free arm round the room. My other arm was still warding off imaginary blows so as to cover my face more effectively. "The people who used to live here have gone," I told them.

"Where did they go?"

"I don't know. But this is a grander place than I've got — and do you wonder when they owe decent patriots money? I'm probably not the only one they owe. You can afford a good place if you don't pay hard-working patriots their just dues."

Old Lapin sat down at the table. He sighted my glass and poured himself some wine.

"Oh, God!" I thought, "he's going to stay."

"What's your name?"

"Jean Fleur," I said.

"When did you move in here?"

"Two days ago. I came for my money and found the place empty. So I thought, 'I'll eat all their stores and I'll drink all their —'" I clapped my hand over my mouth in abject terror. When I removed it I gabbled, "No, no, that's not true, citoyens, I haven't touched anything, I brought my own food and I brought my own —"

Old Lapin beckoned me, but I crept further away still cringing. "I just thought, 'I'll sleep in their beds and I'll have a bit of comfort.' My place isn't nearly as grand as this, but then I pay my dues like a good patriot —"

Old Lapin cut me short impatiently. "We're looking for the ci-devant Vicomte de Lambrière, who passes for an actor. Is that the man who owes you money?"

I nodded. Old Lapin exchanged an excited glance with the section officer nearest him. "That is the one who seduced and corrupted my granddaughter."

"Is that what he's been denounced for, citoyen?" I tried to snatch a glance at the warrant in his hand.

"No," said old Lapin. "He's denounced as a counter-revolutionary and for obstructing an officer of the Republic in the course of his duty."

The guards were sealing drawers, cupboards, and collecting papers. We had nothing of political importance, but all our play manuscripts and the rough sheets on which we worked out our acts were stuffed into a bag. So was our clock. I had often heard of knick-knacks disappearing on domiciliary visits. Several of those denounced had accused their guards. Theft could not be held against them because the object of their visit was to confiscate incriminating possessions. But the authorities disapproved of personal pilfering and quite a few guards were executed for conducting their duties in a manner likely to bring the character of the Revolution into disrepute.

"The late leader of this section denounced him at his trial yesterday," old Lapin told me. He seemed to be enjoying my wine; he was helping himself liberally. "The citoyen Pêche was accused of being drunk when he should have been helping to attack the Bastille. His defence was that the ci-devant Vicomte de Lambrière forcibly restrained him by intoxicating him so that he could not carry out his duty as a patriot."

"Oh," I said, "I see." And I did see, only too clearly. Poor Pêche! He had put all his faith into the new lies and the new promises. He had not recognised them as the old lies and the old promises. He must have gone to his death a desperately disillusioned man.

Old Lapin finished the last of my wine and stood up. "You've no idea where these people have gone?"

"No, citoyen. Have the girl and the old man been denounced as well?"

Old Lapin looked grimly pleased with himself. "Not yet, citoyen, not yet. But it won't be long. The girl's forfeited her citizenship by throwing in her lot with an aristocrat and the old man is spying for Pitt." He patted my shoulder. "You stay here, citoyen. Stay and eat what they should have paid you. But if they return, report to me at once."

"Yes, citoyen. You're sure that I shan't get into trouble for being here?"

"No, no. They owe it to you, citoyen. Stay and enjoy their wine." He seemed to have forgotten that he had left me none to enjoy. He ordered the patrol to leave the house, and I heard them move off in the street. I ran up the stairs to the garret window. I called softly through it and helped M.S. and the Puce back into the room. The Puce could say nothing. She clung to me.

"They were after me," I told her gently. "And we haven't much time." She stared at my dirty face and clothes. "Why have you —"

M.S. understood. "Well acted, boy," he breathed. "Do you think you've put them off?"

"Not for long. I doubt if I'd get away with it in broad daylight, and they're likely to call again. We'll have to move."

It was not easy to think of a hiding place. One could not trust friends or acquaintances any longer, and even if one had been able to, it would have been unfair to compromise them. The most suitable place I could think of was the cellars of the Hôtel de Faille. The house had been shut up after

Marie-Clarice's denunciation; the seals of the Revolutionary Committee were fixed to all its doors, but it might just be possible to hide for a few days in the cellars until we could plan our escape from the city.

M.S. tore his shirt into rags and we bundled it up the chimney and did the same with his breeches. We made him a cap out of the Puce's old skirt, and when we had finished with him, he looked a fairly convincing log merchant.

The Puce giggled happily climbing into his sack. She was never repressed for long. M.S. heaved her easily over his great shoulder. My sack was filled with blankets and provisions.

It was a nerve-racking walk along the streets. We passed a few early-morning workers before we reached the rue du Bac, but no one paid us undue attention.

In the courtyard of the Hôtel de Faille we groped our way down the cellar steps. The door was locked, but the combined shoulder weight of M.S. and myself soon forced it to give.

A sour-smelling atmosphere greeted us. We had enough food for three days. But I should have to make forays for water to the well in the courtyard.

It was in the early hours of the morning that we heard three sharp knocks on the door. We sat bone still, only our eyes conversing. We remained silent and rigid waiting for a repetition of the sounds. I would never have believed that I should come to fear, more than anything else in the world, the noise a human hand could make rapping on a piece of wood.

We sat waiting in silence for the knocks to be repeated. I knew that I should have to go to the well before it was too light; we could not spend the whole day without water. I picked up our milk can and pulled open the door. A sulky dawn was beginning to struggle across the sky. Paris woke up frowsily. It always reminded me of a sleepy coquette unwilling to get out of bed.

I was just about to climb into the courtyard when three homely objects caught my eye at the top of the steps. They were nothing more fearsome than three ordinary pewter mugs, but to me they were as gruesome as the sight of dead bodies in the damp of an early mist. They shone like wet bullets on the top of the steps. I climbed slowly up to them, knowing before I got there what they were likely to contain. I was right. They were full of cocoa.

Stepping over them, I managed to fill our can from the well. I left the mugs in their grim little line and blocked the door behind me.

To M.S. and the Puce I said as casually as possible, "The cocoa seller knows we're here. He's left three full mugs on the top of the steps, and I don't think it was done out of kindness."

"Why didn't he put the police or the committees on to us?" asked M.S. "It seems ridiculous just leaving cocoa."

"Perhaps it's his idea of a joke, and for all we know he *has* put the committees on to us. They'll probably arrive at any minute."

"It sounds more like some kind of a private warning," said the Puce. "Perhaps he has something to tell us. If he comes back, I will talk to him. He's always been a bit soft with me. I'll kiss him a little and make him think there's more to come and —"

I rounded on her. "You're far too generous with your 'more to comes.' You'll end up no better than Marie Lebrun."

We would have quarrelled had M.S. not interrupted. "The cocoa might just be his idea of playing cat and mouse. He's building up his scene, boy. He's writing himself in an extra part. If the guards aren't here within an hour, it means he hasn't informed on us yet. If he comes back alone, it might be wise to kill him."

"Yes," I said, "it might. On the other hand, if he has been to the committees, we don't want murder on our hands as well."

"If you let me see him," the Puce insisted, "I'm sure I could find out."

"In the meantime," said M.S., "let's see if it's possible to get into the house."

It was not possible. I found the staircase up from the kitchen, but the door through which I had gone before was not only bolted but barricaded with wood. I wondered whether it was the work of a domiciliary visit or whether Côté had been so determined that his mistress should not be revisited by her log seller that he had taken preventive steps himself. Either way we were confined to the cellar.

There was nothing to do but wait. M.S. rehearsed us in *Le Fils naturel*. We played Cumberland's translation and pretended that we were not listening for the sounds of a domiciliary visit outside on the cellar steps.

We were not aware of the actual time, our clock having gone to old Lapin's guards. But we got through *Le Fils naturel* and my favourite, *Le Barbier de Séville*. My enjoyment of it was, as usual, greatly enhanced by M.S.'s fierce disapproval of anything that sneered so wittily at the "Lord's anointed" and his own beloved betters. But he always lost himself in the part of Bartholo, and the Puce's Rosine was really good. I have always loved Almaviva, and in the heat of the action we forgot to keep our voices low. It was quite a while before we realised that there was an insistent hammering on the door.

Bartholo regained his senses first. He blew out the candles. Frozen in our attitudes and still absurdly waiting for our cues, we listened. The stillness outside was broken again by three sharp knocks. This was no domiciliary visit. Our friend was back. The Puce tried to run to him. I caught her and flung her across to M.S. He held her while I went as quietly as I could to the door.

"Citoyen De Lambrière," said the cocoa seller's voice, "I've not yet reported you. I should like to talk to you."

He was not a big man. I felt myself able to deal with him. I went outside. It was dark, but I could just make out his figure, grotesque in its cumbersome equipment. He was waiting for me on top of the steps. I was prepared for a trap, of course, but there seemed to be no one else about. I remained at the foot of the cellar steps. If I could lure him down, the scuffle would bring out M.S., and together we could silence him.

He repeated, "I've not yet reported you. But I have left a letter with my mother, and if I am not back within an hour she will take it to the office of the Commune. In which event you will all three be arrested at once." I said nothing, but decided against the scuffle. We might have known that the cocoa seller would have taken precautions. He said, "If Suzon Dupont stays with you, there will be nothing I can do to save her." He waited, and when I made no comment, he went on. "If you can't get her to leave you voluntarily, you must give yourself up. That's the only way she will be safe. It's only been with the utmost difficulty that I've persuaded her grandfather not to denounce her today. It's a crime against the Republic to be the mistress of an aristocrat."

There was no point in arguing either of those two points, so I asked, "Won't her grandfather denounce her in any case?"

"I could contrive that she escapes. I'm in a better position than anyone to help her. I could arrange to get her to Brussels."

"What about my other friend?"

Our voices seemed to be probing for one another up and down the dark expanse of the steps. "The old man can accompany her," the cocoa seller said. "She wouldn't be safe alone."

"Why couldn't you go with her yourself?"

"There are too many other agents watching me. All I can do is make the arrangements. The rest will be up to the old man and the girl themselves."

"What is my alternative?"

"You haven't one."

"What proof have I got that I can trust you?"

"I love Suzon. I am willing to save her."

He guessed what was passing through my mind. A quick call to M.S. would have finished him.

"My mother's letter," he reminded me, "contains your names, your descriptions, and your whereabouts."

The cocoa seller was right: I had no alternative. Even if I could trick the Puce into leaving me I should never get rid of M.S. I quickly closed the cellar door behind me, and he was good enough to hold out a hand to help me up the steps; I always have a little trouble with my knees in moments of stress.

It was only the futility of attempting to escape that prevented me from running away from the cocoa seller as we walked through the streets of a yawning Paris. He reminded me that if I delayed him in any way, his mother would put the worst construction on his absence and deliver her letter.

For a while we walked in silence. Then I asked him, "Do you happen to know if it's true that Jacques Pêche denounced me?"

He nodded. "Yes. I was at his trial. I was a witness against him. They accused him of counter-revolutionary activities through yourself and the ci-devant Comtesse de Faille. He knew that you were both Royalist agents and he allowed you to attend his classes. He encouraged the citizens of L'Étuve to take bribes of food from the ci-devant Comtesse de Faille, and he introduced you to important revolutionary officials to assist you in your work."

"There isn't one word of truth in any of that," I said.

The cocoa seller shrugged. "Isn't there? It has been my task to follow him for a long time. In my opinion he was as much a counter-revolutionary as yourself and the ci-devant Comtesse de Faille. The three of you worked together for the downfall of the Republic."

It was pointless to argue with him. "What was Pêche's defence?"

"He had none. Under questioning he broke down and confessed that he had always known that you were an aristocrat and a Royalist agent. He hoped to save his head by accusing you of forcibly preventing him from taking part in the glorious assault on the Bastille."

"But it didn't save his head!" I pointed out bitterly.

"Of course not." The cocoa seller turned to look at me. "He asked me to give you a message."

"What was it?"

"He said, 'There are still good men in this Revolution. Don't judge them by me. Things will settle down.' "

I said nothing. We had arrived at the offices of the Committee of General Security in the Hôtel de Brionne in the Petit Place du Carrousel. The cocoa seller explained that I had come to give myself up. The official was clearly unused to being confronted with citizens who gave themselves up. He went off to fetch a second official, who in turn fetched a third. A gendarme of the Revolutionary Tribunal sat staring at me as if I were some strange sea creature.

It was still very early in the morning. The committee members had sat late the night before and their officials were weary round the eyes.

"This citizen," I said, pointing to the cocoa seller, "is under the impression that my name is De Lambrière, but he's mistaken. It's Roberts. So I thought that the best thing to do would be to come to you myself. And I don't think," I added, "that we should detain this citizen any longer. He's in a hurry to get back to his mother."

After the cocoa seller left, the officials conferred with each other again and finally marched me off to the Committee of General Security's chief and most detested agent. I had heard through Pêche that this man, Louis Héron, was a Robespierre man and that he was employed by him privately to spy upon both the Committee of General Security and the Committee of Public Safety. It was Héron who had formed the all-powerful little band of porteurs d'ordres who rounded up victims for the guillotine on the flimsiest of pretexts, and who were themselves exempt from arrest in any circumstances whatsoever.

Pêche had also told me that much of Héron's bestial ferocity was owing to a persecution mania. He was convinced that everyone with whom he came into contact had a personal desire to destroy him. In view of his recent activities, he had probably justified his fears.

Sitting behind the table with his secretary, Pillé, he was little short of a human arsenal. I have never seen a man so covered in weapons. There were a couple of blunderbusses in his greatcoat, and besides these he carried a stiletto, a hunting knife, a poinard, and two pistols in his belt. On the table before him within easy reach were yet another pair of firearms. As further protection, two hefty men also armed to the teeth stood by his chair as a bodyguard.

The instant he was told that I had adopted the unusual procedure of handing myself over to revolutionary justice, he sprang up and retired behind his bodyguard. "Arrest him! Arrest him!" he shouted.

"There's no need to arrest me," I reminded him. "I'm here to give myself up."

"Search him!" screamed Héron. "He must be armed. He has come to kill me. No one but an assassin or a lunatic would give himself up."

The bodyguard lurched round the table and prodded me for weapons. Finding none, they turned somewhat nonplussed towards Héron.

He slid uneasily back into his chair. His secretary, Pillé, who had remained quite unruffled by his master's eccentric exhibition, sat exploring his teeth with his tongue.

"Who are you?" barked Héron. He kept his greatcoat round his shoulders, doubtless to insure that the extra blunderbusses were handy.

"I am an imposter," I told him. "I admit to being a fraud and an adventurer. As an actor in need of money I posed as a French aristocrat in order to prey on a rich Englishwoman."

"But why have you given yourself up?" asked Héron.

"My reasons are private. But I have sufficient faith in the justice of the Republic to feel that I am doing the wisest thing."

These remarks obviously convinced Héron that I was a dangerous lunatic.

He ordered Pillé, "Write down that the accused withheld information and was insolent at the expense of the Republic." Still intent upon his toothy excavations, Pillé started to scribble. "Add," Héron continued, "that no force was used. Also add that I gravely suspected the prisoner of having serious intentions against my life." Still unable to believe that I was making a voluntary appearance before him, Héron shouted at me, "Who denounced you? Don't tell me you're denouncing yourself?"

"I've come to claim justice," I repeated doggedly, "and giving oneself up voluntarily is not the same as denouncing oneself. But in point of fact a certain Jacques Pêche at his trial —"

Héron jumped up and, careful to keep the bodyguard between us, advanced on me. "You!" he said. "I know who you are. You are the ci-devant Vicomte de Lambrière."

"I've just explained that I am an —"

"Arrest him!" roared Héron. "Tell the Lieutenant of Police that I have captured the ci-devant Vicomte de Lambrière. Take him to the Conciergerie."

So that was how I arrived in my hackney carriage at the prison that had once housed Marie-Clarice. That was why I was obliged to show my undignified scar to the Registrar. That was how I met Lavaux and was tried before he could defend me. That was why Louis Brissac, on the strength of my giving myself up to the Committee of General Security, endeavoured to have me executed in the name of De Lambrière. That was why the Committee of Public Safety prevented him from doing so on the strength of their rival conviction that I was Anthony Buckland from Sandgate and an agent of the wicked English Pitt. That was why the two committees admitted their dissension in public and became determined to prove themselves right at my expense. That was when I ceased to wonder which infinitesimal splinter of chance had brought about my fate. My orange-peel destiny was no longer a mystery to me. It may well have been all the fault of my father's false nose in the first place, but it was my own two feet that took me into the Conciergerie. What is more, I was quite unable to imagine any way in which they could possibly take me out of it.

But I had forgotten M.S. and the manner in which he always affected my life.

Chapter 50.

WITH ASTONISHMENT I learned that my sacrifice had been for nothing. The Puce and M.S. had refused to escape. He wrote from the Collège des Écossais, a prison to which most Englishmen were sent:

Suzon and I did not feel inclined to desert you, so we were not able to take up the cocoa seller's offer to effect our escape. He denounced me and I was sent to this place. It is very nice and we spend most of our time playing cards or fives in the garden. Do not worry about Suzon. She is living with the cocoa seller and his old mother. You need not be afraid that she will misconduct herself. The cocoa seller says that she will be safer with him, as his civisme has never been questioned, and I have told her not to try to see you in case she makes the man jealous and puts herself in danger. Try to run through out loud as many Shakespearean parts as you can remember. I recommend Richard II, Richard III, and Buckingham in *Henry VIII*. This last you should understand well in your present position. You always needed more heart in the death speech. Then run through Almaviva and Sir Harry Wildair, as I do not wish you to lose your feeling for comedy.

There is a very nice type of person in here, Sir Robert Smith of Beer Church Hall in Essex, and one or two well-born army people. The Abbé Inez, who used to be the superior of this place before it was converted into a prison, is confined in his own apartments. He showed me a little relic of Mary Queen of Scots in a carved walnut shell. Most interesting.

I hope you are well. I have written to the Weldon woman, as it strikes me if she ever had any real affection for you she would not wish to see you harmed. I have suggested that if she wants to save you she should write to the Revolutionary Tribunal and tell them how she was instrumental in making you play the part of De Lambrière in the first place, and that in order to escape her you had to play Buckland. I am sure that when she realises you are in such straits she will remember that she is a gentlewoman.

> *Yours in haste,*
> Lambert Smith (Manager).

Poor M.S.! He never lost faith in his "betters" even when they were as fanatical as Lizzie Weldon. The thought of Lizzie bothering to save the head of someone who had obstructed her will and broken her lifetime record of getting what she wanted struck me as an excessively faded hope.

I was therefore nearly paralysed with surprise when about six weeks later I was told that my lawyer had brought a visitor to the parloir — and I discovered that it was Water Face!

Water Face in the Conciergerie! Water Face in the middle of a revolution! Water Face in France at all!

I sat straight down and outdid him in gasping.

He looked older than he should and it suited him. The lines on his face had given him some character at last. I didn't doubt that they had been put there by years of being at Lizzie's beck and call. He held out a limp hand. "Your — your manager fellow wrote to us."

I was quite unable to answer him. I was still so astounded to see him.

"I say," he said, shrugging at what I imagined to be the whole of France as well as the inside of the prison, "the French have got rather an upheaval on their hands, haven't they?"

Lavaux brought the conversation back to the matter at hand. "It was on my advice that Mr. Smith wrote. I thought that the lady you were betrothed to might like to prove that you were neither the Vicomte de Lambrière or Mr. Buckland, but just an actor she hired to play a part."

"You haven't met the lady in question," I said.

"She wrote to the Lieutenant of Police, who, I understand, is an old acquaintance of hers, and offered to come over as a witness," Lavaux said.

"I can believe that, but it would be as a witness against me."

"You can never be sure with Lizzie," sighed Water Face. "When her father died she offered to give me a private sum to start me off on an independent career. She said she didn't want me to feel beholden to her or her family. But I mean — I couldn't, could I? The family's done so much for me, and a woman needs a man to run an estate."

"Did the Lieutenant accept her offer to testify?"

"Yes. He made special arrangements for us both to come over." Water Face turned to me. "She said it would be to your advantage to see her. She's already been to your manager. He asked me to give you this letter."

I opened the envelope.

Dear Boy,

That woman's been to visit me. I always did say she wasn't quite right in the head. It seems to me you'd better take advantage of it. She has a good friend in the Lieutenant of Police. (Don't forget it was she that put him on our trail in the beginning.)

Now, I know how you feel about it, boy, but you'll feel worse without your head. So I beg you to talk to her and play the Frenchy for all you're worth. (Don't overact. She's not a fool.) But with any luck you could charm her into telling this Lieutenant that you aren't the right man after all. It's your only chance, boy, so play it well. Make her as many promises as you like: there's no need to keep any of them. She doesn't deserve to be treated honourably still chasing a boy after all this time.

She'd be quite willing to see you die, boy, if it would mean she could go home and tell her friends that she saw her Frenchy's head come off in the name of De Lambrière, so don't feel you've no right to cheat her.

Yours in haste,
Lambert Smith (Manager).

When Lizzie Weldon visited me, we shook hands and sat side by side on a wooden bench. Beyond the railings a gaoler kept his eye on us. "It's a long way to come to get your revenge, isn't it, Miss Weldon?" I asked pleasantly. "But perhaps you consider it worth it. After all, if you can get my head cut off as Philippe de Lambrière, it will prove once and for all to your friends that I really existed."

"Is that why you think I've come?"

"I didn't imagine that you were here to do me any good."

"Then you're mistaken. When I got your manager's letter it struck me that I had a chance of helping you."

I looked closely at her. The eyes were still powerful and the smile was still surprisingly puckish. "Do you mean to say that you're willing to go to the Lieutenant of Police and tell him that I am *not* Philippe de Lambrière?"

She shook her head. "That would be pointless. It's the last thing he wants to hear. He has allowed me to come over simply to help him prove that you are. You see, it appears that the Lieutenant is a little worried about his own head. I understand that the Committee of Public Safety is extraordinarily powerful. It's vital for him to have it firmly established that the Committee of General Security has made no mistakes under him. It could be very dangerous for him if he doesn't win this little dispute over your identity. If you were willing to help him, I think I could promise that he would be willing to help you."

"How would I have to help him?"

"By confessing in front of the Committee of Public Safety that you're Philippe de Lambrière."

"Whereupon he will cut off my head."

"I think I can guarantee that he would help you to escape instead."

"Miss Weldon, if the Lieutenant's worried about his own head, I can assure you that the last way to secure it more firmly to his shoulders would be to help spirit an enemy of the people out of the country."

"He isn't your gaoler, you know: that's someone else's worry. His responsibilities end with establishing your identity."

I shook my head slowly at her. "I'm afraid I don't trust either of you, Miss Weldon. I can see myself making the confession and not even living long enough to regret it."

She was quite prettily dressed, but she still smelt of camphor when she moved. "How do you think I should benefit by leading you into a deliberate trap?"

"You once told me that if you couldn't have me as you wanted me, you'd rather have me out of the way altogether."

She coloured heavily. "That was a long time ago, Mr. Roberts, and I'm very well aware that your present predicament is entirely due to me. My conscience demands that I should do everything I can for you, quite apart from my personal feelings."

"Your personal feelings," I pointed out, "have always centred on Philippe de Lambrière. It's Mr. Roberts I don't trust you with."

"It's true that I preferred you as Philippe de Lambrière. But I realise that that is stupid. I thought I could buy your services as I've had to buy everyone else's. No one does anything for me for nothing — why should they? I'm not very likable. Even my poor cousin Edward — I *have* tried to be kind to him, Mr. Roberts, I really have. My father reminded him that every step he took was at our expense, and I *did* try, I really did try, to make him feel that I need him for himself."

"Don't you?"

"Of course not. The poor boy's an idiot. I can run the estate ten times better at half the cost, but no one, Mr. Roberts, has ever bothered to go out of his way to make *me* feel that he needed me for myself."

I moved nearer to her on the bench, and the gendarme moved nearer the railings.

"Don't you think, Miss Weldon, that you might be making a fairly common mistake? So many people with a large amount of money have it in their head that no one can be fond of them for themselves. Are you sure you're not wrong?"

She said, "Don't be facetious, Mr. Roberts. In my case there's nothing to be fond of except my 'large amount of money.' When I first looked in my mirror and saw how I was going to grow up, I realised that I had only one safeguard — power."

"It can be uncomfortable for a woman."

"It is uncomfortable. It means that one despises everybody — there is no one to admire. Consequently you never care what other people think of you, because there's no one whose opinion matters to you. That's one of the loneliest situations in life. Perhaps that will help you to understand what you have meant to me. You're the only person I have ever been able to love. You're the only person I've ever wanted to love me."

"Aren't you still talking about Philippe de Lambrière?"

Her hands were at their old game of picking at her gloves, the only sign that her outward composure was not reflected in her mind. "He is part of the pattern I've been telling you about. In my position I couldn't look up to an actor. It's — well, it's impossible — especially one who has played a French vicomte to a plain, rich woman for money. I know that it sounds paradoxical, as it was my idea in the first place, but you were right when you said that it was you I loved. It is your face, isn't it? Not De Lambrière's?"

"I'm afraid so."

"It's your eyes, your hands, your voice. Certainly you change that for De Lambrière, but I'm not averse to your own."

"Thank you very much."

"You were right when you said that" — she looked into my eyes with that terrible frankness that must have made it so difficult for her to live with herself — "that I should weep into my bolster at nights longing for a man. Well, I'm perfectly aware now, Mr. Roberts, that the man is you and not Philippe de Lambrière." I was beginning to sweat a little. "At first I tried to tell myself that it was only when you were playing De Lambrière that I wanted you — that as yourself you could never appeal to me. It was my way, you see, of preserving my pride, and having my cake and eating it too. That is something that has always been supposed to be an impossibility. But I thought that I had enough money to make it come true. It wasn't that I believed De Lambrière really existed. I just thought I could *pay* him to. But when I heard of your danger, I asked myself some questions. One of them was, supposing there was a real Vicomte de Lambrière willing to marry me for my money: should I want him if he wasn't you? The answer was 'no.' So I realised that it was you I wanted."

I was not merely sweating, I was gently soaking my clothes right through. "But you could never bring yourself to marry an actor, Miss Weldon," I reminded her swiftly.

"I've already told you that I think you'll find it to your own advantage to prove that you are the Vicomte de Lambrière."

"And I've already told you that I can foresee a situation in which I carry out my part of the bargain and the Lieutenant doesn't carry out his."

She stood up. "I'm afraid you'll just have to try and trust us, Mr. Roberts. I give you my word that all your fears of my wanting Philippe to die so that my friends would never have a chance of finding out that he didn't exist are groundless. I also give you my word that if I can do the Lieutenant the favour of persuading you to confess in person before the Committee of Public Safety, he'll certainly do me a favour in return. I've always found him an honourable man."

I studied her face, but I could tell nothing from it. It was quite possible that she believed in the Lieutenant's promises, that she would be truly shocked and grieved when she found that she had been tricked. But her disillusionment could hardly help me.

I said, "The Committee of Public Safety has as many spies as the Lieutenant, Miss Weldon. There are dozens of them in here mixing with the prisoners. Even the Lieutenant of Police isn't going to find it very easy to spirit me out of here."

"So I understand. That's why he suggested that you should be transferred to an establishment run by a certain Dr. Belhomme."

Chapter 51.

I was transferred two days later. My first action was to write to M.S. and tell him to let the Puce know that she must not try to visit me. The cocoa seller would be sure to find out and he might denounce her out of revenge.

I could only hope that the Puce would by now have realised that she could trust me with Marie-Clarice and that she would be able to resist coming round to find out.

Marie-Clarice flung her arms about me. "Thank God for that old hag from England! I've been beside myself worrying about you, but I couldn't do anything to help you. My own money's running out. These brutes have confiscated nearly all I've got, otherwise I'd have sold everything up to save you."

I disentangled myself. "Marie-Clarice, what do you mean — your money's running out? If that happens —"

"Dr. Belhomme will have to part with me, but I assure you it will be reluctantly. He's very fond of me." With her arm through mine she marched me along the promenade to meet her friends. "Has that Englishwoman provided you with furniture? You won't get much here. I've sold all mine or I'd give you some."

We passed the Abbé, who still thought himself an actor. "There are two hundred of us in here," said Marie-Clarice, "as against a handful of genuine lunatics. But from the way our own people are behaving, you'll have difficulty in telling the difference. Do you know the sane idiots are actually making official complaints about the extortionate prices and the bad facilities! They'll get poor little Belhomme closed down. Wouldn't you think they'd be willing to put up with a few inconveniences in return for their lives? It makes me feel on the side of the Revolution all over again."

She introduced me to so many ci-devant counts, countesses, dukes, and duchesses that I felt quite dizzy.

Belhomme himself seemed genuinely glad to see me. "Ah, the gentleman who brought me the enchanting Comtesse de Faille. One good turn deserves another, eh? I hear some charming lady's sent you here. I was sorry not to be able to provide you with a private room, but for the price I'm afraid I can only allow you to share. By the way, she has sent you a bed."

Knowing what Lizzie must have paid for my floor space, I couldn't help sympathising with some of the complaints, but as Marie-Clarice reminded me, all we bought from Belhomme was our heads. We should expect everything else to be an extra on the bill.

That night at the common dinner table I counted eight apples amongst thirty-two people. But I felt it my duty to economise for Lizzie's sake. Food sent in from outside was heavily taxed at the door. In spite of the huge sums of money we were paying, we never got up from the common table other than hungry.

The congestion in my loft was nearly as acute as in the Mousetrap. Lizzie's bed was comfortable, but it was crammed in so tightly between two others that I had to scramble over them before I could get in.

My neighbours were both sans-culottes, and their names were Lefebvre and Ducassoy. They came from the Popincourt section, which had sent them as a test of Belhomme's patriotism. He could hardly refuse to take in two free patients "of the people" for fear of jeopardising his civisme. On the surface he had to look as if his Maison de Santé was not entirely reserved for the rich. They both complained fiercely that the facilities provided by Belhomme were appalling. To appease them, Belhomme himself had tried to raise funds amongst us to provide them with extras. Lefebvre was a cheerful, willing soul who was clearly enchanted to sit at the same common table as the Duchesse d'Orléans. He argued with his friend over my bed at night that what was good enough for the Duchesse should be good enough for them. But Ducassoy was a natural troublemaker. He said he had not come to prison to starve and he had every intention of denouncing Belhomme to the Popincourt section for making substantial differences in treatment between the sans-culottes and the rich. Nothing his friend or I could say would persuade him that the Duchesse d'Orléans and many others with names as famous were in exactly the same position as himself, owing to lack of funds.

I warned Belhomme that there was trouble afoot for him, but he shrugged it off. He felt that the Public Prosecutor understood his difficulties. In this he made a grave error, as I was to learn from Lizzie Weldon.

She visited me two days after I had been there. Marie-Clarice had jokingly threatened to ruin the interview, but when the time came she kept tactfully out of the way. I was hoping in any case that Lizzie would have failed to recognise her with the disfiguring short hair.

There was a small, tastefully furnished room in which one could receive visitors. The Doctor liked outsiders to feel that the rest of his establishment was equally well equipped.

Lizzie and I sat opposite one another. "It's good of you," I felt bound to say, "to pay for this."

"You agree with me that it would be the easiest thing in the world to leave here?"

"Yes. People don't, I suppose, because it's the safest place in Paris."

"Providing you can stay here. But I don't think it's going to last much longer. The Lieutenant of Police warned me that it has been reported to the Public Prosecutor as being run purely for the benefit of the aristos. He seems to think that it might be closed fairly shortly."

I was not sure how much of all this might be a threat from Lizzie and how much a genuine warning from the police. I should not have been surprised if either had been true. It was possible that the Public Prosecutor had some "leanings towards justice," as Lavaux had once hinted, and if he had no monetary interest in Belhomme's he would take very seriously the complaints of the two sans-culottes.

"Have you thought any more about escaping?" Lizzie asked.

"Have you broached the matter with the Lieutenant?"

"I've hinted at it. I think something could be arranged. I'm told that the gaolers are exceedingly lax, and our papers could be so arranged that we could get past the barriers."

"I don't think you ever quite explained to me what service I could do you in return for persuading the Lieutenant to be so helpful."

"I imagined you had guessed."

"Supposing I felt myself unable to — to meet your request?"

She stood up. "My resources aren't limitless. I couldn't afford to keep someone here for ever — especially someone who I felt was not willing to sacrifice anything for me in return."

"I see."

"Well, you must let me know what you've decided the next time I visit you. But I advise you not to wait too long."

My problem struck me as being insoluble. If Lizzie chose to cut off my "resources," I should have to leave Belhomme's in any case. On the other hand, I could see no means of escape with her which would also include M.S. and the Puce.

I was trying to come to some conclusion when Marie-Clarice sat herself beside me on the garden bench. It was a hard gold autumn day and the gardeners were raking up leaves. Belhomme's cat was rubbing against my knees. Marie-Clarice said, "I want to talk to you. Let's go behind those trees."

When I followed her she put her arms round my neck and kissed me in the style of our early days at the Hôtel de Faille. I'm afraid I was still not immune to her. Before I could speak she said, "Your little Chinoise shouldn't grudge me that. I'll be out of her way for good soon."

I asked quietly, "Why will you be out of her way for good?"

"Because poor little Belhomme, with *much* reluctance — he really is devoted to me — can't afford to keep me any more."

I gripped her arm. "You must have some money somewhere."

"I haven't. They've taken everything."

"Then talk to him, plead with him, sleep with him —"

"I've offered. He was really most gentlemanly about it. He said he couldn't dream of accepting such a favour from me when he couldn't do anything in return, so . . ." Her arms went round my neck again. "You don't think your little Chinoise should grudge me, do you? After all, she might have a lifetime of you and I've only got tonight."

I flung her arms off me and ran to Belhomme's study. He certainly did seem sincerely affected. "My dear Vicomte" — Belhomme always paid us the compliment of dropping out "ci-devants" — "if there was something I could do I would do it. I promise you that there's no lady I should like to help more. She's the most charming patient I've ever had — but there you are." His handkerchief came out to dry eyes that already looked pink from weeping.

"But for God's sake, man, you could give her a board to lie on, couldn't you? She can have my bed. I'll sleep on the stairs and I'll share my food with her."

He shook his head. "It would set a precedent, Monsieur le Vicomte. It wouldn't be fair to the others. I've had to make it an inflexible rule, and the same for everyone regardless of beauty or charm. Man or woman — they're all treated alike."

"But it's little short of murder."

He stood up. "I can only guarantee to prolong life in here, not to save it altogether."

"You'll prolong it just as long as they can pay."

"If I took people for nothing, Monsieur le Vicomte, we should soon be overrun and then it wouldn't be fair to the people who could pay."

"How much would it cost to keep Madame de Faille for another quarter if she shares food, drink, and lighting with me?"

"Well" — he executed a small sum on the back of an envelope — "if she moves from her present quarters to the attic — there won't be a bed, but perhaps you could —"

"She can have mine. How much?"

"It would have to be something like six hundred livres for lodging only."

"She was only paying four hundred before." He shrugged and his hand-kerchief worked on his eyes again. "Very well," I said. "Write to a Miss Eliza Weldon and tell her that you have underestimated the cost of keeping me here and that if she can't manage to send this extra money you'll be forced to send me back to the Conciergerie. Explain the rule to her — that once I'm back there I shall be executed without fail in three days. Tell her I'm too proud to ask for myself."

"And you'll contribute this money — the whole of it — to the upkeep of Madame de Faille?"

"It need never leave your hands."

"Very well. Where does this lady live?"

I gave him Lizzie's address.

"I shall give her three days in which to pay. If she fails, you'll either have to make other arrangements for Madame de Faille or you will have to accept the unhappy fact that I don't feel myself able to show favouritism amongst my patients."

Chapter 52.

TWO DAYS went by with no word from Lizzie. I was down to biting my
fingernails, but Marie-Clarice could laugh about it. "It's so unfair to make
that dowdy old hen pay up for me. Sometimes I don't think you know what
honour means." She leant over and patted my cheek. "Except where your
little Chinoise is concerned — we're very upright there, aren't we?"

We were sitting on a draughty staircase upon which Belhomme had not
thought it necessary to lay a carpet, as it was out of sight. "I'm still under
sentence of death, you know. You'll suffer from remorse for the rest of your
life. They tell me it's a very cruel disease, and there isn't any cure for it.
When my head's in the basket you'll wish you'd comforted me in my last
hours. As an old, old man you'll say to yourself, 'I could have made that
woman happy. I could have made it possible for her to leave the world
warm with love, but all I did was sit on a servant's staircase with my hands
gripped between my knees, and I sent her to her unknown grave without a
caress, without a —"

"Marie-Clarice —" I began. The setting October sun was finding strange
lights in her short boy's hair. "You promised the Puce that you would never
lay another finger on me as long as Belhomme let you live."

"But he *isn't* letting me live. If anyone does, it will be poor Miss Weldon."

"Marie-Clarice, you owe it to the Puce that you've lived as long as this.
It was she who got you moved here."

"I know, and I shall be eternally grateful to the child, providing there's
another life to be grateful in. But would she have to know anything? You
haven't got an agreement to confess to one another, have you? I do hope
not, it's such a bad beginning."

"I have no agreement with the Puce at all. It was you who offered to
relinquish me in her favour."

"Yes, but I imagine she wouldn't hold me to it in my last hours."

"We don't know yet if it is your last hours," I snapped.

Madame Chabanne interrupted us. She was out of breath and annoyed.
"I've been looking for you all over the place. For a minute I thought you'd
escaped and I summoned the gaolers, although much good they are. They're
not more than footmen in this place. Dr. Belhomme wants to see you,
Monsieur le Vicomte."

I fcrced myself not to run to his study. I knew by his smile that everything was all right. He said, "Well, Monsieur le Vicomte, your little ruse was effective. Miss Weldon has sent the money and I wish to be the first to tell you how delighted I am that we shall not have to lose the enchanting Madame de Faille." Again I felt that the tears in his eyes were genuine. He added after a homely sniff, "I have a visitor for you in the anteroom."

It was the Puce. It was the first time I had seen her since I gave myself up. For several minutes we stood in one another's arms. She smelt young and warm. "The cocoa seller tries to get into my bed every night because his mother is deaf."

Over her black head my mind went back to the day in the rue Louis d'Or when she tried to pick my pockets; a little, skinny, spitting fiend. It was not until I noticed that she had been crying that I came out of my dreaming.

"Puce, is the cocoa seller really upsetting you?"

"Oh, no," she said, "his mother is not as deaf as all that, so I shout. She always hears in time. It's Uncle I'm worried about. They're bringing him up for trial next week. They're going to say he's a spy, and the cocoa seller says there's no chance for him."

My heart turned one of those unpleasant somersaults. For a moment or two I was unable to think.

The Puce was still talking. ". . . and I went to the Public Prosecutor, but he wouldn't see me this time." She tugged at me. "Oh, what are we going to do? Can't we get money to bring him in here?"

Money to bring him to Belhomme's! The quick thought in my head made me sicken. The same trick would never work on Lizzie twice. I had to choose between money for Marie-Clarice or money for M.S.

I said, "Yes, Puce, we'll bring him here."

When she had gone I sat in the anteroom a full twenty minutes. I had never had to make a more ghastly choice in my life. I could go back to Marie-Clarice and tell her that Lizzie had refused the extra money, or I could tell her the truth.

My legs took me on several detours before I finally forced them to lead me back to the staircase. I came round a corner and saw her before she saw me. Her face was taut and her hands were gripped tightly in her lap. She looked younger than I had ever seen her, and she looked pathetically afraid. I stepped back out of sight. I wished at that moment that I had never been brought to Belhomme's myself — that the committees had decided to execute me in all three names. I should have preferred anything to having to walk up to that staircase and tell Marie-Clarice that she would have been saved if it had not been for M.S. I would have preferred to let her think that Lizzie had refused the extra money, but I was certain that Belhomme would tell her the truth in his own defence. There seemed nothing to do but be honest myself.

I gave the traditional cough so that she had a chance to shake off that lonely-looking fear, and then walked slowly round to face her. Her old gay smile was back and there was nothing in her eyes to show that she had been waiting to hear whether or not she had to die.

She said, "You look gloomy."

I sat down beside her.

"Didn't your lady friend think you were worth another six hundred livres?"

I said, "Yes, Marie-Clarice, she did."

Her eyes narrowed swiftly, and widened again. "Has Belhomme raised the price?"

I shook my head. "My manager's in trouble."

She was not quite able to control her quick intake of breath as she began to understand what had happened, but she spoke quietly enough. "They don't usually butcher Englishmen, do they?"

"They don't usually, but they're making an exception in his case. I rather think it might be to try and get him to identify me one way or the other at his trial, but I — I can't take the risk."

She stretched and yawned. "Of course you can't. What a pity I was always so rude to my husband's relations. They might have come to my rescue."

I turned sharply to her. "Write to them, ask them —!"

She laughed. "My dear, sweet love, I have. They said they were impoverished themselves, but I happen to know that my mother-in-law got out with all her jewellery. If I hadn't been so rude to her, she might have sold some of it."

I was grateful for anything to talk about. "Didn't you like her?"

"Oh yes. I liked her well enough. It was her son I didn't take to and she resented it. Have you told Belhomme yet?"

"No."

"Then I will." She jumped up and went singing towards the study. I stayed where I was. I seemed incapable of moving.

She was back within ten minutes. "I'm afraid it's upset him badly again. He's an absurdly sentimental little man." She sat down beside me, her skirts flaring up. Her hands took my face and turned it towards her. She kissed me and told me after it, "He wants me to go first thing tomorrow morning before everyone's up. It depresses the others so much to see someone going off. It's most considerate of him, really, because it's his best way of reminding them to pay their bills."

I managed to get out, "Marie-Clarice —"

But she cut me short. "So I think we can safely say now that these are my last hours — at least the last ones with you, which are the only ones I mind about."

Chapter 53.

SHE LEFT at six o'clock the following morning. I dreaded saying goodbye to her; if it had not been for Dr. Belhomme sobbing on the doorstep, I might have broken down myself. As it was, I took him by the throat and shook him off his feet. "Surely there's somewhere, just somewhere — For God's sake, she can sleep on top of my bed and I'll sleep underneath it."

"You torture me, Monsieur le Vicomte," he wept. "But there's nothing I can do about it."

"Of course there isn't," said Marie-Clarice. "He has the same rule for everyone. He can't be expected to break it." She opened her purse and tucked something into my hand. "That's for your little Chinoise. Tell her I'm sorry it isn't more grand, but I had to sell all the valuable ones."

When I opened my palm I saw a tiny ring of pale rubies set in the shape of a star. "Tell her it's to thank her for giving me some extra time with you." Then she kissed me as lightly as she kissed Belhomme, got into her hackney carriage, and was driven down the dismal street in which the workers were just beginning to emerge from their cottages.

I spent the day on my bed.

When M.S. arrived the following evening I was scarcely able to greet him cheerfully. I had decided that he should know nothing of how he had affected Marie-Clarice's fate. When he finally asked about her, I said, "She's no longer in here."

"She's not *dead*?"

"Tomorrow."

"Oh, I'm sorry, boy. What happened?"

"Her money ran out."

"Couldn't you have tried to get something more out of Miss Weldon?" I said, "No."

"How long do they give them when they take them from here?"

"Three days. She went yesterday."

"I'm sorry, boy."

"It's all right."

At three o'clock the next afternoon the Puce visited me. She put herself silently into my arms. We held one another until she whispered, "I watched her die."

"Why, Puce?"

"I thought — I thought — I didn't want her to be like the poor King and not see a friend. I got as close as I could, I was out there by five." She stopped and laid her forehead against my chest. I stroked her hair and waited. "Before they brought the first ones up they were working the puppet shows round the guillotine. Polichinelle was cutting off heads, and all the children were shouting and laughing."

"You shouldn't have gone," I said.

"No, I shouldn't! I shouldn't! It all went wrong." She shook so hard against me I couldn't keep her still. It would have been better if she could have cried. Anything but that terrible shivering in a small room with a fire giving out a strong heat.

I would dearly have liked not to question her further, but I thought it better that she should speak. "What went wrong, Puce?" I asked.

"It was the crowd. There were even more people than usual, and although I was so early I couldn't get to the front. You see, I had to be close to the scaffold so that I could make Madame de Faille know that a friend had come to be near to her at the end. But they wouldn't let me through. A big man lifted me up when the tumbrils were coming, and I saw Madame de Faille in the third one. I couldn't think what to do, so I said to this man, 'There's a lady I hate coming up to the guillotine. She has been wicked to me all my life and I must see her die. Please make a way to the front for me.' "

"Did he?"

"Yes. He held me in one arm and just hit his way through with the other one, pulling people back and knocking them aside, and he kept shouting, 'Make way for the little one! She has an enemy kneeling to Sainte Guillotine today.' It wasn't so bad until we got near the front, because no one could have heard in all that noise, but when we got close —" She halted again and the shivering started. "— when we got close I couldn't stop him from shouting. He kept roaring out, 'There's a little one here who hates somebody. Let her through to see them chop off the bitch's head.' Then it wasn't only he who was shouting it. Many others joined in, and I was pushed right up to the scaffold. Madame de Faille was just climbing the steps, and she turned to see what was happening in the crowd. My man carried me close to the edge and called out to the executioner, 'Citoyen Sanson, this little one wants you to give a certain lady an extra slice.' Everyone screamed, 'Which is it, little one, show us the one!' I tried everything I could. I tried to make her a sign to show her those terrible things weren't true, but as soon as I waved, they knew it was Madame de Faille and they all shouted and howled at her."

My throat felt cracked. I asked, "Do you think she saw you, Puce?"

"Of course. I was as close as anything in this big man's arms. She looked straight at me, and when she saw who it was she — she covered her face with her hands. She thought I had come because I was pleased she was going to die — and I hadn't, I *hadn't*, I'd come to be friends." At last she began to cry. "I kept blowing her kisses hoping she would look my way again. But she never did, and the crowd laughed and laughed because they thought I was doing it as a joke."

I said, "Puce, I think she guessed that something went wrong." But I knew there was no hope of any such thing. She could never have been expected to guess that such a savage scene could have come about by mistake. All I could think of was that bitter, bitter moment when Marie-Clarice covered her face to hide from the enmity of her little Chinoise.

I took out the ring from my pocket. I said, "Puce, she left you this. I don't think she would have done that if she thought you were the kind of person who would want to see her die."

It was a blessing that I could take her to M.S. The sight of him safely in Belhomme's was the best comfort she could have. She sat on his lap as she used to when she was a child, with her head against his great shoulder. When Madame Chabanne came to tell me Miss Weldon was waiting for me, I left M.S. trying to comfort the Puce.

Lizzie gave me her neatly gloved hand. "I thought that extra demand for your board was quite extortionate. I showed it to the Lieutenant of Police. He said it's not the first evidence he's had that this place is unscrupulously run for private gain, and he has passed it on to the Public Prosecutor. They are going to investigate it."

"Then it looks as if we might all be back in the Conciergerie — and Dr. Belhomme with us."

"There could be an exception in your case. Have you thought any more about the Lieutenant's offer of escape?"

"Has he offered again?"

"He's willing to assist us."

"In what way?"

"The idea is for me to withdraw your financial support here. That will mean that you will be automatically returned to the Conciergerie. You will then pretend to decide, in view of this, that there is no longer any point in maintaining that you are not the Vicomte de Lambrière. A carriage will be sent for you, but without the usual guards. It will take you to the Tuileries, where you will make your declaration in front of the Committee of Public Safety. This will clear the Lieutenant with the authorities who suspect him of counter-revolutionary sympathies. He will then order you to be taken to the Conciergerie, but by then your driver will have been changed. The new one will have instructions to take you to the barrier of St.-Denis, where I shall be waiting with Edward. As a witness from England I have a right to expect a safe passage out of the country. I shall be supplied with papers that will allow me through all the barriers on the road to Calais. So will Edward. Papers will also be provided for a police agent to travel with us as an escort. *That escort will be yourself.* Of course, the Lieutenant won't discover the deception until we're miles out of Paris! Then he will find that the daughter of his old friend Judge Weldon has abused his trust and managed to substitute the Vicomte de Lambrière for the police escort. The Lieutenant will start half-heartedly after us himself and give us a chance to board the boat I shall have hired at my own expense."

The part of the plan which impressed me most was the papers allowing three persons to travel to Calais. If, instead of Water Face and Lizzie Weldon, I could manage to substitute the Puce and M.S., it struck me as an interesting proposition. But it was not going to be easy to explain to Lizzie. I felt a twinge of conscience about trying to trick her, but I reminded myself that she was right when she said that my present position was owing to her. If she had not been so fanatically determined to get her own way, M.S. and I would not have been sitting in a French prison. My conscience, in any case, has always been the most amenable part of me, and its little kick was so faint I hardly felt it.

I said carefully, "Miss Weldon, I'm sure that you yourself believe the Lieutenant of Police intends to carry out his part of the bargain, and you probably think it very churlish of me not to trust him, but you haven't seen quite as much of revolutionary officialdom as I have."

"Surely you don't expect him to put his promise in writing?"

"No, I don't expect that, but do you think you could persuade him to let you bring these papers to show me first? A preliminary study of those would do a lot to reassure me that I wasn't going to walk into a trap."

She frowned. "Well, I'll ask him. After all, there wouldn't be anything in them to incriminate him. He owes Edward and myself a safe passage, as we've come over as witnesses on his behalf, and you would simply be mentioned as an unidentified police agent."

"Try and bring them tomorrow night," I suggested.

She opened her beaded reticule and fumbled in it. With the thief's close attention to detail, I took note of the fastenings and the exact depth to which her hand was plunged. I was out of practice as a pickpocket and I should need to be skilful when she brought the papers.

"There is just one small thing," she said. "You mustn't think that I mistrust you either. It's simply that once I've effected your escape I should like to feel that we could continue to — to be — friends in England. I should like you to sign this." She handed me a crisp sheet of paper. On it was written:

I, the undersigned, declare that it was by my hand that Nicholas Hawtrey,

son of Sir Gregory Hawtrey of Blaney Hall near Bristol, England, met his death
on the night of November 16, 1789.

I read it twice and said to her, "I imagined you'd given up blackmail,
Miss Weldon."

"It's more in the nature of a precaution, Mr. Roberts. You see, I am
going to quite a lot of trouble on your behalf. I'm even subjected to a certain
amount of danger. If the Committee of Public Safety found out that I had
contrived the escape of an aristocrat, the Lieutenant of Police would deny
all knowledge of it, and I should be held entirely responsible."

We smiled pleasantly at one another from the teeth outwards. I remember
thinking with one of those little flashes of warning that sometimes pass
through my head, 'I hope this woman isn't going to prove a better scoundrel
than I am.'

I said, "I hardly see how this document, signed or unsigned, could protect
you against the Committee of Public Safety."

"It certainly couldn't," she agreed heartily. "But you see, I can't disguise
from you that my feelings would be considerably hurt if, after all my trouble, you saw fit to — er — drop me as soon as you're safely in London."

"And if I did, I presume you would then hand over my signed statement
to the law?"

"Of course. But with great reluctance."

"Oh, I'm sure of that. It would be an action entirely foreign to your
delicate nature."

"How well you know me."

I stood up and bowed to her. "You bring the police passes tomorrow,
Miss Weldon, and I'll consider signing your confession."

She also stood up. "No, Mr. Roberts. You sign the confession and I'll
consider bringing the passes." She gave another outwardly warm smile. "It's
deplorable that we should have to go to such lengths with one another, but
I'm afraid that neither of us is entirely trustworthy."

I contemplated her gravely. If I refused to sign I should be jeopardising
the chances of escape for M.S. and the Puce. On the other hand, I did not
care to have a document of that kind in her possession. "I shouldn't be very
happy about it, Miss Weldon. You might get it stolen from you."

"I never get things stolen from me, Mr. Roberts."

I hoped to disprove that the following day. "You must understand that
from my point of view, Miss Weldon, I'd be taking a risk. I should prefer
to see your plans a little further advanced before I sign anything quite so
dangerous. Anything might happen: you could get held up on the road, we
could both get held up . . . Surely you appreciate my point?"

She nodded slowly. "Very well. You may sign it just before you sail. I
will call on you tomorrow. Tell Dr. Belhomme that I no longer feel inclined

to support you here, and he will undoubtedly arrange for the carriage to return you to the Conciergerie the day after. That is when the Lieutenant's part in the proceedings will come into effect."

We agreed that she should visit me at ten thirty the following evening. With any luck she would retire straight to bed after she had left me and not discover that the pass was missing until it was too late.

I hurried back to the Puce and M.S. "On Friday," I told them, "we are travelling to Calais under the protection of the Lieutenant of Police." I enjoyed their expressions. "Everything depends on speed and timing. It also depends on the Puce's being able to substitute a hackney carriage for the one that will be calling here at six in the morning to take us to the Conciergerie."

"The Conciergerie!" cried the Puce. "But why can't you stay here? What have you done?"

"Has the Weldon woman cut off our money, boy?" asked M.S.

"Yes, but it's done on purpose. It is part of her plan to rescue me. What she doesn't know yet is that I'm going to use it to transport the three of us to Calais. Puce, how much money does the cocoa seller keep in his house?"

"Oh, a lot. Police agents are very highly paid."

"We shall need as much of it as you can steal. At Calais we shall have to hire a private boat and it will cost us every penny of five pounds. Tomorrow night get the cocoa seller drunk and raid his funds. Then hire a hackney carriage and bring it here at half past five on Friday morning. The one to take us to the Conciergerie will not be expected before six, but I doubt if anyone will question its being early. You will be in it, Puce — as Miss Eliza Weldon. M.S. and I will get into it as ourselves and will then become, for the purposes of the passes provided, Water Face and an unnamed police escort. It should be some time before Miss Weldon and the Lieutenant discover that we haven't waited for them. They will have to confer with the Conciergerie, Belhomme, and each other, and as Miss Weldon and the Lieutenant are not innocent themselves, it should take them quite a while to decide how to proceed. That will give us a good start, and after that it depends on our own speed."

"But everyone will *know* I'm not an Englishwoman," squeaked the Puce.

"You can speak enough English to convince peasant barrier guards."

"Boy," said M.S., "I'm not happy about it. Are you sure that woman doesn't suspect you? She always struck me as a good marker."

"It frightens me too," said the Puce.

"Well, if either of you can think of something better, think of it," I snapped at them — and in the circumstances, it was a thousand pities that I didn't give them time to do so.

Chapter 54.

MISS WELDON had always been a punctual woman. At ten thirty exactly on the following evening she was waiting for me in the anteroom.

"Have you brought the passes?" I asked immediately.

"I have. But they're all written on one."

"Did the Lieutenant make any objection to your showing it to me beforehand?"

"Several. But I persuaded him that you naturally felt unable to accept his word."

"May I see the pass?"

"Certainly." Out of her reticule she produced a piece of thick white paper. It was signed by the Lieutenant of Police and it read:

To all whom it may concern at the barriers of St. Denis, Senlis, Roye, Péronne, Arras, Bethune, St. Omer, and others on the route to Calais, the Englishwoman, Eliza Weldon, the Englishman, Edward Small, and the police escort travelling with them have permission to pass.

I handed it back to her and watched where she replaced it in her reticule.

She sat with it on her lap. I settled down beside her. "Miss Weldon, you've really been very good to me. I hope you don't feel too badly about my not signing that confession just yet."

"In your place I should have done the same," she conceded.

I put my arms round her waist and kissed her. She made a modest struggle, during which I was careful to see that her reticule fell off her lap. I continued to kiss her and took advantage of her confusion afterwards to pick up the reticule, extract the pass, and stow it away in my pocket.

"I hope I've not offended you, Miss Weldon."

She said, "No one has kissed me since you last pretended to be Philippe for me in the Hôtel de Muscovie."

I felt a trifle ashamed of my trick. Her eyes shone quite pathetically. I told myself that it was her own fault for falling in love with a cheat, a fraud, and a liar.

"I will now see Dr. Belhomme," she told me. "I'm afraid it will mean an early start. He likes his patients to leave at six o'clock in the morning."

"I shall be extremely punctual," I assured her.

"Your carriage will call first at the offices of General Security, where you will tell the Lieutenant that you wish to confess. He will then accompany you to the Tuileries, where you will make your confession to the Committee of Public Safety. After that your driver and carriage will have been changed and I think you know the rest."

"I have the details firmly in my mind, Miss Weldon."

Belhomme called us in as soon as she had left. "The lady was not aware, of course, that in refusing to pay the extra six hundred livres you originally intended for Madame de Faille she was also withdrawing support for Mr. Smith." He coughed. "I remained discreet on that point."

"That was good of you," I said.

We then launched into the traditional battle for our lives which Belhomme expected. Not to have done so would have been extremely suspicious. I pleaded in a taut, urgent voice, and M.S. pressed wind round his heart and wept noisily. Finally we made ourselves so vulgar and unpleasant that any sentiment Belhomme felt concerning our departure vanished. This was what we wanted. We could not afford any watery farewells over the doorstep on Friday morning.

M.S. and I spent the night in gloomy apprehension. If the cocoa seller had spent all his money, it would be fatal; if he hadn't and the Puce failed to find it, it would be fatal; if our carriage was late and the official one was early, it would be fatal.

M.S. was far from comforting. "We haven't had enough time to rehearse, boy. I can't do with these quick productions. Something always goes wrong."

I did my best to reassure him, but was far from confident myself. "There's always an element of risk in these things," I said testily. "I had to do what I could with the cast and material I was offered. There was no time for a careful production."

"I don't like the timing of it, boy. One wrong move and we're all off."

It looked as if we were in for a smooth first act, at any rate. It was all extremely simple.

At half past five precisely a sleepy-looking Madame Chabanne shuffled in to tell us that the carriage was waiting for us. Needless to say, our few belongings were already packed.

The sans-culotte Ducassoy tried to cheer us by telling us that it wouldn't be long before every other rich pig in the establishment went the same way. He happened to know that the Maison Belhomme, as a private prison, would shortly be out of existence.

Madame Chabanne shuffled down with us. There was no one about except one yawning gaoler who offered to help carry our luggage. When we refused his kind offer, he did not even bother to accompany us into the street. He simply stood in the doorway, wished us well, and watched us climb into the carriage.

The Puce was tucked back in a corner. We sat beside her and I took her hand. I found it icy. "Have you told him where to go?"

"Yes."

"Did he ask any questions?"

"Yes. He wanted to know how he was to take us through the barrier and I said we had police passes. He just shrugged and said it was our business, but if we were stopped, he wanted to be paid for the whole journey."

The carriage jerked forward, but almost immediately came to a halt. The driver got down.

"Now what in the world can have happened?" I murmured.

The driver spat amiably into the road. I put my head out of the window and saw him peering underneath. "I thought I felt a bit of wheel trouble," he murmured. "Might have to stop off at a wheelwright."

M.S. sat back with his eyes closed. The Puce was moving her lips in prayer.

"In the name of God be quick with it, man," I ordered. "We want to get to Senlis before dark."

"You might get no further than a ditch, citoyen, if I'm too hasty," he answered. "These things need care."

"Oh, please God make him hurry! Make him hurry!" whimpered the Puce. I put an arm round her.

"It's all right, it's all right. We'll make him suspicious if we rush him too much."

The gaoler strolled across from the doorway of Belhomme's. "Hallo!" he called out cheerily. "Wheel trouble?"

The driver appeared not to have heard him. "Wheel trouble," he explained.

The gaoler grinned up at the window. "Well, I don't suppose you'll find these gentlemen worrying about the delay. They're not in a hurry to get to their destinations, are you, citoyens?"

At the risk of half suffocating the Puce I managed to shield her from his view.

The driver straightened up and scratched his head. "Can't *see* anything wrong."

The gaoler bent down to look. My stomach was behaving as it did when I was waiting to make my first entrance. The Puce's small hand was wet, and M.S. was sitting bolt upright beside me with both hands on the crook of his black umbrella. It was impossible to try and persuade the driver to hurry; it would have looked eccentric to be *anxious* to reach the Conciergerie.

Nevertheless, in a quarter of an hour's time, the official carriage would come up the hill to fetch us. Three people holding their breath in a confined space can make for a very unrestful atmosphere.

I let mine out when the gaoler said, "I should risk it. It looks all right."

The horse must have been on the side of escaping prisoners. It started forward by itself. The driver and the gaoler ran after it, shouting "Whoa!"

They stopped the animal, jolting the three of us painfully inside.

"Well," laughed the driver, "if he's willing, I am."

He climbed up again, cheered by the gaoler, and we started.

I turned my head and kissed the Puce's ear. The poor child was rigid with fright.

"Boy," said M.S., "it's started me colic."

"At the first stage," I promised him, "I'll get you a hot ale and ginger."

"What's the good of that?" he snapped. "That's only for when you're blocked."

I was so worn from anxiety myself that I was for once unsympathetic towards his internal problems. I lay back against the seat and closed my eyes. I wanted to calm myself for the ordeal of passing the first barrier.

The Puce's small voice enquired, "He's going a funny way out for Senlis, isn't he?"

I peered through the window. We were trotting towards the Isle de la Cité. I pulled down the window and called to the driver, "Citoyen, which way are you going?"

He called back, "The right way, citoyen."

"But we want to go to the barrier St. Denis."

"I know, citoyen."

I sat back and tried to crush the panic that was threatening to overtake me. The man might be intending to stop at a wheelwright after all. Or perhaps he was avoiding the heavier traffic. There was no point in worrying the others.

"He knows Paris better than we do," I told them. "He's probably got his favourite route."

Whether it was his favourite or not, I never had time to ask him. It became pertinently clear to me that he was making for the black bulk of the Palais de Justice. He was taking us to the *Conciergerie*!

I opened the door and said to M.S., "Throw the Puce down to me and then jump yourself."

But I was only halfway out myself when the driver shouted to the people in the streets, "These people are prisoners! Stop them!"

Three men promptly rushed at my door, and the carriage was soon brought to a halt by a crowd of angry men and women. I waved our pass through the window and managed to speak calmly. "If you can read, you'll see that I have the right to conduct these two respectable foreigners out of the country. I am authorised by the Lieutenant of Police."

But it was useless to try and make myself heard above the crowd, and we were escorted with shouts and waving fists into the Cour du Mai.

In other words, I had brought M.S. and the Puce from the comparative safety of Belhomme's and the cocoa seller's house to the Conciergerie, where in all likelihood they would be condemned to death. There was room for no other thought in my head. I said and did utterly useless things such as struggling with the turnkeys and begging them to let M.S. and the Puce go because I had tricked them into travelling with me. I was forcibly brought under control and marched behind the Puce and M.S. into the Registrar's office. The inevitable row of prisoners were sitting along the bench.

The Registrar looked up with interest. "These are the people the Lieutenant is waiting to see in the greffe?"

The turnkey who was holding my arms replied that we were. We were taken upstairs to the greffe. I had no chance to say a word to the Puce, but we found one another's eyes. Hers were dry, but mine were not. M.S. stumped solidly ahead, angrily refusing to be deprived of his umbrella.

In the greffe the Lieutenant sat with Lizzie and Water Face on one side of him and the cocoa seller, unfamiliar in ordinary clothes, on the other. We were lined up in front of the table.

The Lieutenant shook his head reproachfully at me. "Citoyen De Lambrière, I'm disappointed that you should have so little faith in our efficiency." He held out his hand. "Please give me the pass you stole from Miss Weldon."

I handed it to him and he put it in his pocket.

Lizzie was staring at the Puce, and the cocoa seller was staring at me. For a moment or two I pondered whether it would be worth pointing out to the Lieutenant that the cocoa seller had once offered the Puce and M.S. a chance of freedom, and then whether it would be worth while informing the cocoa seller of his superior's part in my attempted escape. But as they would both deny it flatly, I thought it better to remain silent on such a delicate subject as their own offences against the Republic.

The Lieutenant turned to the cocoa seller. "Citoyen Barrière, will you please relate the circumstances that caused you to report to us?"

The cocoa seller jerked his head towards the Puce. "The girl Dupont has been lodging with me as my housekeeper. I have shown her every evidence of kindness and affection. In return, she has done nothing but rebuff me. She has shut herself in her own room, and when forced to come out she never left my mother's side. She has always suffered from a dangerous passion for the accused ci-devant Vicomte de Lambrière. In my capacity as an agent I have been well aware that she has visited him at Dr. Belhomme's Maison de Santé. I knew that she had seen him on Thursday afternoon. On Thursday evening she was most unnaturally agreeable. My mother had been persuaded to retire early, and there was wine and an uncommonly good supper waiting on the table. The citoyenne Dupont was dressed in her prettiest clothes and gave me to understand that she at last appreciated my advances. It soon became clear to me that she intended to make me drunk. I wondered why. She filled my glass repeatedly. I was naturally unaffected, as the course of my duty lies largely in sitting in wine shops drinking wine with suspected persons. But I pretended to be overcome. She went to my room and I heard her opening the box in which I keep my assignats. When she emerged I was still lying with my head in my arms. She crept out of the house and I followed her. I am professionally skilled in such things, and it took me a very short time to discover that she had contacted a driver of a hackney carriage in the rue Louis d'Or. A few minutes with him and a threat of a domiciliary visit soon told me how she intended to use my money."

"So," completed the Lieutenant, "he reported the matter to the Committee of General Security and we were able to 'persuade' the driver to bring you all here."

I sent the Puce a smile. I felt indescribably tender towards her for having proved as ineffective as myself in the matter of our escape. Her eyes were not dry any longer, and there were two wet lines down either cheek.

"I should like to say," added the cocoa seller, "that the citoyenne Dupont should not be blamed. She has always been under the influence of the accused ci-devant Vicomte de Lambrière. Any misdemeanour she may have done should be laid at his door."

"That's perfectly true," I admitted. "In fact I did not fully let her into my plans. I forced her to take us into the carriage. She thought she was merely visiting me in it."

"Heroism doesn't suit you, citoyen De Lambrière," the Lieutenant growled. "So might we dispense with your attempts at it?" He turned to the Puce. "Give the citoyen Barrière back his money." The Puce stepped forward and handed him the purse. Then the Lieutenant ordered the turnkeys guarding M.S. and the Puce, "Take them downstairs to the Registrar's office."

The Puce struggled to reach me but was pulled back. "He isn't the Vicomte de Lambrière!" she shouted. "He's an actor called Roberts, I swear he is! This silly old woman just wanted to marry him! She was too proud to have a common man, so she made him take that name!"

The state of my nerves was not improved by the look the "silly old woman" directed towards the Puce.

"He certainly *is* an actor," said M.S., "and a good one — although I must say you'd never think it from the way he acted today. Screaming and shouting as if he'd spent all his life at the Petit Théâtre de la Cité, instead of being brought up by me on the stage of the Little Apollo and recommended in the great Kemble's own hand."

Lizzie Weldon interrupted. "The ci-devant Vicomte de Lambrière was a guest in my father's house. We were not in the habit of asking persons brought up on the stage of the Little Apollo theatre to dine."

"I met him there myself," said the Lieutenant, "and he didn't strike me as an actor. I'm sure I should have instantly detected a foreigner posing as one of my own countrymen."

"That only shows what a good actor he is!" shrieked the Puce.

"The girl's right," said M.S. "And the excellence of his performance is entirely due to me. Every move was rehearsed by myself. Boy!" he said suddenly: "let's show these folk we're actors, and kindly recall that you are no longer employed by Mr. Martyn's Celebrated Players."

The swiftness of our leap into a scene from *Le Barbier de Séville* so astonished the Lieutenant that he allowed us to proceed. We jumped quickly from that into our lowest comedy at the Petit Théâtre. The turnkeys were too startled to keep a hold on us, and I sailed into M.S.'s arms as a clumsy ballet dancer. This had always been one of our most popular turns at the Petit Théâtre. M.S. pirouetting about on his points was something to behold, and our vulgar asides when we failed to catch one another had the same effect on the turnkeys as on our audiences. They made no attempt to control their mirth, and I doubt if the greffe had ever housed such an extraordinary scene before. The Lieutenant would have laughed out loud himself if he had not caught the eye of Lizzie Weldon and the cocoa seller.

He signalled to the turnkeys, who took M.S. and the Puce out of the room. The Lieutenant dismissed the cocoa seller. I bowed to him on his way out. "Thank you at least for trying to save Suzon."

He replied, "The day that you are executed will be the happiest of my life."

I said to the Lieutenant, "Might I talk to you alone?"

He nodded. "Miss Weldon, perhaps you and your cousin would wait outside?"

Lizzie said, "I should prefer him not to see that girl again."

"As you wish," said the Lieutenant. It was obvious that he was frightened of her. If she chose to denounce him to the Committee of Public Safety, they would be only too pleased to give credence to her tale. He obviously wanted Lizzie out of Paris as quickly as possible. This desire was so strong that I could see how she had been able to persuade him to let her take me with her. I was doubtful that I should be able to prevail upon her to do the same again. Miss Weldon's glance, when it came my way, was very cold indeed. But she got up and, followed by Water Face, left the room.

The Lieutenant and I were alone. "You'd have done better to trust me." He smiled. "I intended to keep my bargain."

"Unfortunately, it didn't include my friends."

"I'm not in the position to order a general exodus from Paris," he told me acidly. "I took a big enough risk in helping Miss Weldon to get you out."

"Does it really mean so much to you to have my confession?"

"Yes, it does," he snapped. "I'm certainly not going to such lengths for love of you."

"I've often wondered why you didn't torture me. I'm afraid I shouldn't have stood up to it very well."

"It did occur to me," the Lieutenant admitted. "I didn't do it because the Committee of Public Safety would have said that I had got you to agree under duress, and would still have insisted that you were Buckland. You've got my head nearer the guillotine than it's ever been before, and I can't afford to be much closer."

"I don't understand why you didn't come to some agreement that I was *both* people. It's been done before, I'm told."

"You've been told rightly." He leaned towards me. "But the Committee of Public Safety don't *want* to come to an agreement with me, citoyen De Lambrière. I have many enemies on it, and only one friend. That one is powerful or I doubt that I should have lasted as long as I have, but he can't make up for those who want to get rid of me. You see, I have quite a bit against me. I've been thirty years in the police force — twenty-five of them under the old régime. That marks me down for counter-revolutionary sympathies, and I'm afraid there have been times when I've not concealed the fact that I deeply disapprove of our present methods. I can't afford a mistake, and you're the mistake the Committee of Public Safety are hoping I've made. That's why they've cherished you so lovingly — hoping to catch me out."

He looked wearier than when I last remembered him. His baby-face had aged.

"If they're so anxious to bring you down, they must have better excuses than me."

"I'm not uncareful" — he smiled at me wryly — "and I told you that in the Committee of Public Safety I have a single, powerful friend. But he has his own head to think of. He can't go too far in protecting me. No one's head is safe these days, not even the highest, and, don't forget, our agents are all spying on each other. I was under the impression that that odious little Héron was spying on the Committee of Public Safety for me, but I found out that he is also spying for them upon me and the Committee of General Security."

"Can you trust any of your agents?"

"Certainly not. The only consolation is that they can't trust any of theirs: it's not safe to take anyone's word —"

He opened a drawer in the desk and took out a bottle of cognac. He filled a glass and pushed it towards me. "The glass is for you. I've become used to drinking out of the bottle lately." He took a pull and choked a little. "I don't know how closely you've kept up with current affairs in Belhomme's, but did you read about the speech in the Jacobin Club by that raging lunatic Hébert?" I sipped my brandy and shook my head. "It was a criticism of our public services, mostly aimed at the inefficiency of the police. I was named in person. So you see why I was willing to help that Weldon woman when she told me she thought she could extract a confession from you." The fierceness of the way in which he referred to Lizzie made me smile. He saw my expression and explained, "It was Miss Weldon's father who claimed my affection. I have never been overenchanted with Eliza even as a child. She has no femininity. But she has the determination of ten men, which was why I believed her when she said she could persuade you. She has her own reasons, apparently, for taking such an interest in you."

"Do you still believe I'm the Vicomte de Lambrière?" I asked.

He took another great gulp of brandy. "No, of course not, but I'm hardly in the position to admit it now."

"Did you ever believe it?"

"Oh, yes. Your French was perfect and I saw very little of you at the Weldons' house. My chief emotion at that time was the fact that a man of your attractions should appear to be taking a sincere interest in Eliza Weldon."

"I did it too well," I admitted.

"Apparently. When you turned up in France and she followed you and reported you missing, I had you traced to L'Étuve and found you picking pockets in the name of Buckland."

"What did you think then?"

"That you were an adventurer. There are plenty of questionable French aristocrats trading on a good name. I warned her that you were no good and that she'd do well to be rid of you. It was I who persuaded her to leave you when I had you followed to Madame de Faille's. I hoped that might be the end of it from Eliza's point of view."

"So did I."

"That letter she sent me in which you said goodbye to her in England, signed yourself De Lambrière, and referred to your vineyards and estates convinced me that you were an adventurer but not an impostor. In fact it convinced me that you were an aristocrat fallen on hard times trying to resurrect past glories to impress a rich woman. I've seen many of those cases, too."

"I always wondered why you never arrested me. You knew I was a thief."

He passed a dead-looking hand over his forehead. "It was wiser to let you go free. I wanted to find out exactly what you were doing. The Committee of Public Safety had not been formed then, and I was my own master. You came at the beginning of all our troubles. I too began to think you were working against us politically. My service under the old régime did not stop me from feeling that the Revolution was necessary. I was in favour of it then. I left you free so that you might lead me to other enemies of the Republic."

"When did you suspect that I was who I claimed to be?"

"Too late. You were in the Conciergerie by then. You gave *yourself* up, if you remember. When I visited you and you told me your story, far from disbelieving it, I recognised it as the truth at once. Only Eliza Weldon could fall in love with an actor, not realise it, and insist upon his becoming someone who could save her face. But by then I was no longer my own master. The police force had been merged into the Committee of General Security, and the Committee of Public Safety had been formed. They have twenty times more power than we, and I was under suspicion and therefore in danger. Your case became their big chance against me."

"So you were willing to try and force me to confess to a false name and send me to my death?"

"Perfectly willing," he said in that soft voice that one sometimes had to strain to hear. "I'm fonder of my head than yours." He finished the remains of the brandy. "But I hinted on many occasions to you that in return for a confession I was willing to save you."

"I'm afraid I didn't feel like trusting you."

"Nor I you. If I'd been too plain with you, you might have tried to buy your freedom from the Committee of Public Safety — at my expense."

I stood up. "I realise," I told him, "that it was for your own sake that you agreed to let Miss Weldon help me. But you *could* have intended to extract my confession and fail to keep your side of the bargain. Apparently that wasn't the case, and I'm grateful to you."

"Don't be," he told me. "Nothing in God's name would have given me greater pleasure than to have you executed. There isn't a soul in the whole of Paris who has given me more trouble than you. It's not your fault that they've made your case a trap for me, but then neither is it mine. I should have kept no sort of bargain where you were concerned if I hadn't had to contend with Eliza Weldon. If I had failed, she would have gone straight to the Committee of Public Safety and denounced me. They would have been so delighted that they would have excused her her part in the proceedings. She knew that."

"Can you still keep a bargain?"

"What kind?"

"You've admitted that you can't force me to confess. Suppose I was even now willing to do it voluntarily?"

"In return for what?"

"In return for your arranging for my friends to escape."

"The old man and the girl downstairs?"

"The old man and the girl downstairs."

"You must think a lot of them."

"I do think a lot of them."

He stared at me lengthily. "Are you aware that you would have to take the consequences? I don't see how I could help you a second time."

"I'm aware of it."

The dead-looking hand supported his forehead again. "I'm not even sure that I see how to get *them* out."

"I can. You confiscated that pass from me just now."

"Well?"

"It's in your right-hand pocket."

"Well?"

"I'm an expert thief. Step up to me and I'll get it. Give me five minutes with my friend Manager Smith to say goodbye. He can go down again, wave it under the Registrar's nose, and in company with the girl leave as Mr. Edward Small and Miss Eliza Weldon. He's English, and she can speak enough to deceive a Frenchman. He can take the pass to the Committee of General Security while you are still here and ask for a police agent on your authority to take them safely to Calais."

"And what happens to the real Miss Weldon and Mr. Small?"

"They're waiting in the other room. By the time you and I have another long talk — What a pity we haven't any more brandy."

"We have," he said, opening another drawer.

"By the time you have discovered that you have been robbed, which won't be until you take the real Miss Weldon and Mr. Small down to the Registrar's and he queries their identities — because two people will have just gone out in the same names — my friends will be well on their way. Won't they?"

He stared at me again. "Yes, they will. Have I made it clear to you that you will have to stand by your sacrifice? I can see absolutely no way of getting you out again."

"You have made it very clear."

He got up, walked round the desk, and stood in front of me. I removed the pass from his right-hand pocket and held it up.

"My God!" he exclaimed. "I didn't feel it. Very well, I'll have your friend brought up to say goodbye. Then come back and we will drink our brandy before we discover that I have been robbed."

I was not sorry to be prevented from seeing the Puce. It would be difficult enough with M.S.

I was allowed to see him in the parloir. I handed him the pass. "Take this," I told him. "Go to the Registrar, tell him that you and the Puce are the witnesses brought here to identify the Vicomte de Lambrière this morning. Tell the Puce to speak English all the time: they won't know how bad she is. Take the pass to the Committee of General Security, and on the strength of the Lieutenant's signature you'll be given an escort and a carriage to Calais. Sell anything you've got and hire a boat at Calais."

I signalled the gaoler to show that I had finished my interview. M.S.'s great hand gripped my sleeve. "What about you, boy?"

"Miss Weldon is thinking up something for me," I said with that horrible tendency of mine towards unpleasant prophecies. "I'll see you both in Dover."

I could have wept at the nobility of that lie.

Chapter 55.

I WAS put into a single cell, where I had the whole day to go down on my knees and pray that M.S.'s acting ability would not forsake him.

He should make a very irate and authoritative Mr. Small, and his Lord Credit experience should enable him to hire a boat at Calais. If necessary, he would doubtless acquire a few possessions from the posting houses at which he stopped en route to assist him with the expenses.

I tried to concentrate on the gay and casual manner in which Marie-Clarice had accepted her fate. It was possible, I thought, that I should show no such sang-froid.

Two gaolers came for me about ten o'clock at night. As usual, they were polite. They discussed the unpleasantness of the weather as they marched me out to the waiting carriage, and one of them even offered to go back and borrow an umbrella to protect me from the rain.

The carriage rolled drearily behind an aging horse towards the Tuileries. The streets were wet, and I wondered how far M.S. and the Puce would have got on such roads.

The Committee of Public Safety operated in what used to be the Queen's apartments. The Pavillon de l'Égalité was still alight, housing such worthy bodies as the Committee of Assignats and Moneys, and the Examinations of the Accounts Concerning Bridges and High Roads. Everyone seemed to be working overtime. Our carriage passed innumerable guardhouses, finally rattled through great glass doors, and came to a halt.

One of my gaolers ceremoniously handed me down, and they both walked courteously behind me as I climbed up steps flanked by particularly elegant wrought-iron rails. I was in a mood to take note of details. I was in a mood to do nothing else. A dark, cold passage led off the landing, and it was along this that my gaolers pushed me.

We stopped at a door from behind which an incredible noise was coming. No one answered our knock, so we went in. My attention was first caught by Lizzie Weldon and Water Face. They were seated side by side at the end of a long line of people behind a well-lit table. My attention was next taken by the fact that the Lieutenant of Police was in an unamicable discussion with the odious Héron. Third, I noticed the extraordinary quality of the

Gobelins carpets. They were even better than the ones I had seen on the floors of the Hôtel de Faille.

The members of the committee were an ill-assorted collection of men. Barbers and philosophers could sit together behind this table having in common only the desire to destroy their fellow men. I was not cheered to see the shaggy-looking butcher Bégnon.

It was he who addressed me first. "Is it true that you robbed the Lieutenant of Police of a pass for the two English persons here present?"

"It is," I told him.

Héron, whose protective pistols were visible under his coat, shouted, "How is it possible that a man who is responsible for the protection of honest patriots can be robbed by his own prisoner in a small room?"

The Lieutenant rose to speak, but I answered for him. "If the citoyen Héron will step round here, I'll show him."

Héron came cautiously round the table.

"Nearer," I beckoned him, "nearer, citoyen."

The little coward turned to the committee. "If this prisoner strikes me —"

"I doubt that he would be so unwise," murmured Bégnon.

The room was so heavily lit it was positively throbbing with heat. Nevertheless, I thought that the sweat on Héron's forehead was excessive.

"Nearer," I coaxed.

He came within two feet of me and I stepped up to him. I removed with the greatest of ease the pistol at the back of his belt. When I flourished it at him, he screamed and half the committee jumped up. Some were on their way round the table when I handed the pistol back.

"Presumably, citoyen Héron," I said, "you felt nothing. Well, neither did the Lieutenant of Police."

"Which shows," said Bégnon, "that we are obviously dealing with a competent thief, amongst other things."

Héron retreated behind the table, and I caught the satisfied smile of the Lieutenant of Police. Looking straight at me, he said, "I have sent a man to apprehend the false Miss Weldon and the false Mr. Small, but unfortunately they had an excellent start and it's doubtful that they will be overtaken in time."

I thanked him with my eyes.

Bégnon said, "The Lieutenant tells us that you are anxious to make a confession as to your identity, over which there has been some dispute."

"Not as far as I was concerned," I answered truthfully.

The Lieutenant sat forward, no longer smiling.

"Who are you?" demanded Bégnon.

"I am the ci-devant Philippe-Jean-Baptiste Raoul Vicomte de Lambrière."

The Lieutenant sat back smiling again.

"What proof have you of that?" asked Bégnon.

"No more than you have that I'm not."

The Lieutenant cut across him. "I have my own recollections of meeting him under the name of De Lambrière in 1789, and two witnesses to prove it. Moreover, the lady concerned has a letter from him signed in that name."

The lady concerned stood up. "Without any doubt at all this is Philippe de Lambrière, to whom I was betrothed in England. My cousin will bear me out."

Water Face stood up to bear her out.

"You have," Bégnon reminded me, "been insisting that you're an actor called Roberts."

"He now realises," said the Lieutenant, "the folly of that. We have evidence from our agents amongst the émigrés that the actor he claims to be was drowned in 1789."

"That," agreed Bégnon, "seems to be the only positive evidence we have. That he is *certainly not* an actor called Roberts."

The Lieutenant leaned across to him. "Pardon me, citoyen, but what more positive evidence could we have than the word of the man himself? Now that he knows death is inescapable, he no longer feels the need to hide his true identity."

Bégnon lifted weary shoulders and turned to his fellow members of the Committee of Public Safety. "The Lieutenant would appear to have established his point, citoyens. The Committee of General Security are right, and we are at fault in staying the execution of this aristocrat for so long. He has deceived us into thinking him an English agent for the purposes of saving his own head. I suggest that we congratulate him and execute him concurrently."

A cheer followed this, and I think that the rest of the committee were as astonished as I was at the sudden outburst from the Lieutenant of Police. The cheers died down as his voice rose. "The accused has wasted public time and money. He has caused dissension between the servants of the Republic. He is on his own admission no better than a common pickpocket and thief. He has no right to expect the swift, humane death of the Revolution. It is our duty as patriots to see that this man who has cheated the guillotine so long should not receive its mercy. *He should be hanged!*"

There were only a few seconds of surprised hesitation before cries of "À la lanterne! À la lanterne!" filled the room.

My two amiable gaolers stepped forward and gripped my arms.

Bégnon appeared to argue for a moment with Héron, but was interrupted by an incident that completely addled my already impaired senses.

Lizzie Weldon went down on her knees before him. Her hands were clasped in a dramatic manner, and the anguish written all over her face might have been directed by old Ducis himself. Although I was scarcely able to take in anything other than the stark fact that I was not going to be allowed the quick stroke of what now seemed the friendly guillotine, I felt a rush of gratitude towards her. Even after tricking her that very morning she was willing to plead for my life.

It occurred to me that she must really love me. But the thought did not remain with me for long. She was only asking for my dead body. This much I discovered when the noise lessened, and I heard Bégnon explaining to his fellow committee members that the lady, in spite of my appalling treatment of her, still retained a surprising affection for me. She asked permission of the committee to receive my corpse and take it to England with her to be interred in her family vaults.

The committee, not surprisingly, thought the request a little eccentric. But I understood it; what better proof to her friends of her living vicomte than his dead body brought back to England? I supposed that I should not blame her for this rather macabre manner of saving her face. She had made a genuine effort to take back my living person and I had cheated her. Lizzie Weldon was not the woman to lose a chance of putting her own wrongs right. Doubtless I should receive the full honours of a funeral befitting an aristocratic victim of the brutal Revolution. Lizzie herself would go into permanent mourning and, for the first time in her life, become a romantic figure. She would be talked of throughout Somerset as the courageous woman who braved the terrors of modern France to save her lover, and who had brought back only the pathetic souvenir of his dead body in a coffin, upon which I could imagine his title would be written in very clear letters.

Had I not remembered that I should be playing the central part in the forthcoming death scene, I could have been moved myself by such a display of acting.

The Lieutenant saw no point in my waiting to see the outcome of the argument. He ordered my guards to take me away. To me he said, "You have been a source of continual irritation and danger to me."

I was still shocked and bewildered by the knowledge that he should have been the one to try and deprive me of a merciful end. I could only think that the man's personal enmity towards me was far more acute than I ever supposed. I realised that I had also done my best to trick him, but I thought it an understood point between us that we should strike when and how we could. One can feel a form of friendship towards one's enemies providing they are not as unpleasant as some of one's friends, and I had flattered myself that he had similar sentiments towards me. But there was nothing in his eyes to show that we had so recently connived together. Nothing to show me that he was grateful that I had at least adhered to my part of the bargain, although we were both aware that I had no alternative.

He said, "Nothing has ever given me greater satisfaction than the thought of the punishment you are about to undergo."

I was marched out to a guardroom and kept waiting two and a half hours. A clerk came in with a measuring tape. He took my width and my breadth. When I asked him why, he said, "Your coffin."

When he went out, there was no further conversation until the clock struck two. Then both my gaolers rose together and tied my hands behind my back. A gag was wound round my mouth. I could only imagine that the Lieutenant was avoiding a last-minute retraction of my confession on the gallows.

But there were not to be any gallows as I knew them. No humane cart whipped quickly from under one's feet so that the drop would be violent and the suffering swiftly terminated by a broken neck.

I was to die like any poor ruffian hanged without trial; a slow strangling from one of the brackets that pushed out the street lamps. I remembered the grisly bodies I had seen swinging from those iron arms; their tortured, swollen faces had always nauseated me. The memory of them now very nearly reduced me to a fainting fit.

A tumbril was waiting outside, and into this my two gaolers hoisted me. My wrists had been bound too tightly and my arms were going numb. The wooden seat was hardly big enough for the three of us, but I was glad of the tight support on either side. I think I should have toppled over without it.

The tumbril jerked over the cobblestones. Outside the Tuileries the rain was falling. It smelt cool and kindly in the slimy dark streets into which we were turning. I tried to force my thoughts towards heaven. But I had had too little experience of prayer and repentance. My mind would not leave the ghastly figures whose deaths had followed cries of "À la lanterne!" I vividly recalled their convulsive leaps like fish on the end of a line. As a small boy I had once impaled a wasp on a thorn and I remembered being sickened then by the sight of it thrashing out against its death. I had squashed it in a horror of remorse, but there would be no one to put a quick end to me; no merciful hands to give a pull at my feet. Perhaps it would be possible not to fight. Perhaps one could speed up the agonising procedure of dying. But I knew that I should jerk about as hideously and as uselessly as the old monk I had seen in the rue Michauderie.

I tried to pray for the Puce and M.S. But their faces became bloated and purple. Their tongues lapped out of their mouths and their figures became the heavy pendulous body of the monk circling about on its rope.

We turned into a cul-de-sac. The wet street was like a black river bed. The house-fronts ran with water as if they were shedding tears for me. Under the street lamp jutting out from the end wall, there was a group of about ten men. The rope was already hanging in place, a twisting, oily snake.

There was obviously to be no hope of their whipping the cart from under me. I was to die by my own weight alone.

I think that even the sight of the noose itself was not the shock to me that I experienced when I realised that Lizzie Weldon had actually come to see me die. Certainly she was having to be supported by Water Face on one side and the Lieutenant of Police on the other, but in the light of that grisly street lamp, hers was the only calm expression.

Water Face looked sick and the Lieutenant far from at ease. The Committee of Public Safety was also represented; Bégnon was not going to miss an execution no matter how it took place.

I managed to summon sufficient last-minute bravado to bow to Lizzie Weldon. It was clumsily executed, but while I was doing it I wished that she might for the rest of her life be plagued with the memory of my choking, plunging body at the end of that dripping rope. From the height of the noose I could see that I should dangle with my feet only about six inches from the bottom of the cart.

The gaolers knocked me down on the seat again and tied my legs together. Then two other men climbed into the cart and lifted me up. I thought I heard Lizzie Weldon cry out, but I was beyond everything then. I was suffering from a combination of a galloping and a freezing heart. Someone cuffed my head down and pushed it through the noose.

The words of the Lieutenant of Police seemed to shriek in my ears. "Nothing could give me greater satisfaction than the thought of the punishment you are about to undergo."

Wildly I tried to compel him to meet my eyes over the gag. It seemed inconceivable that I could have inspired such enmity in a man that he should deliberately order my agony to be as drawn out as possible. But this was what he was doing. His curt orders came through the rain. "Go slowly with him. I want this man to have time to know he's hanging."

They continued to hold me up while one of the men tightened the noose gently round my neck. Then, as carefully as if they thought I might come to pieces, they slowly lowered me until the noose was supporting the full weight of my body.

Then they jumped from the cart and there was an incredible creeping pain beneath the angle of my jaw.

I felt as if all the blood in my body was being forced out through my ears, my eyes, my nose and my mouth. . . .

Chapter 56.

THE MOST unbearable pain was in my spine. I had not expected that. It seemed an extra agony that no one should be asked to support. My throat, my head, my tongue, and even the backs of my eyes felt as if they were burning in oil. My limbs ached; each portion of them might have been broken by a bar, but my spine — my spine was unendurable. How much longer could it take to die? How long, how long?

I am not sure when it occurred to me that I was lying down. I went to sit up but struck my head. I went to turn over and found that I was wedged. I was still gagged and still bound. It was dark, but my eyes were open.

I then felt a panic I never wish to remember again. I was not dead but I was in my coffin. They had buried me alive.

I felt as if the narrow box was crushing in on me. I screamed inanely behind my gag. Without an inch of space on either side of me, I writhed and fought until I felt blood creeping over my face and limbs.

Exhausted from pain and fear, I must have fainted. I came to only to repeat my senseless battering and muffled screams for help. But my throat was too sore to keep up my cries, and my body too tender for further movement. After a while I realised that the coffin was moving. The jolting became insufferable to my wrenched spine. At first I thought that they must be carrying me to the cemetery, and I resumed the maniacal banging of my head against the coffin lid. To be hanged again would be preferable to being buried alive. I kicked with my bound feet and gashed open my tied hands. Somehow I must let them know that their victim was not dead. I suppose the effort must have made me faint again, because when I woke up, the jolting was over. My immediate thought was that they had failed to hear me and I was lying in a grave. Tears fell weakly out of my eyes, and I was conscious of the unpleasant smell of my own blood. Afterwards, of course, I thought myself ridiculous for not wondering how it was that I could breathe. But one is not always rational in one's coffin!

There was a light rap near my head. I should have guessed who it was at once: only Water Face would have knocked on a coffin!

He raised the lid and asked fatuously, "Mr. Roberts, are you all right?"

The rays from his lamp fell on my face. He gave a little cluck of alarm. "I say, Lizzie, he looks rather badly knocked about."

Lizzie's cool voice snapped at him, "Naturally. He's only just been hanged."

Water Face took the lid right off. The lamp showed me a beamed ceiling and white scrubbed walls. Water Face sawed away at my cords with a knife. "We had to keep you bound and gagged in case you made a noise or called out. You're supposed to be dead," he explained.

It was not easy to speak, but I managed to say, "Why aren't I?"

Lizzie advanced with her own lamp. On the table behind her a bowl of hot water steamed. There was a mean fire smoking in the grate, and in the corner there was a bed.

"Because the Lieutenant of Police arranged for you to be cut down in time."

"Why?"

"Because I threatened to expose him to the Committee of Public Safety. This whole idea was mine. Didn't you hear me pleading for your body?"

"We didn't want you to be guillotined," Water Face pointed out, "because we couldn't have taken you back without a head."

Lizzie's look crushed him, and they eased me painfully out of the coffin and supported me to a chair by the fire.

"The Lieutenant insisted that your sentence should be changed to hanging, and he deliberately made it look as if he wanted you to suffer as much as possible. That was the only way we could save you. But it was very unpleasant watching you." I forebore to say that it was very unpleasant being watched. "If anything had gone wrong," she added, "and the Lieutenant had misjudged the timing, our whole plan might have misfired. This was our only chance. We did not dare use the ruse of the police escort again because the Lieutenant thought it would be far too suspicious. As the Lieutenant had been tricked so often, the Committee of Public Safety would undoubtedly have suggested sending one of their own men with you. To transport you as a dead person seemed the only way to get you out of the country."

"I'm sure," I said bitterly, "that it gave the Lieutenant the utmost satisfaction to know that I was leaving it in a coffin."

"He suggested that it might be easier for us all if you were a real corpse, but I threatened him with the Committee of Public Safety again and he agreed to cut you down in time."

I leaned back in my chair and must have looked deadly pale, for Water Face brought me a large glass of brandy. I felt worse to begin with and then better.

"Where are we now?"

"We are in a posting house at a place called Roye."

"Where are we going?"

"Calais." Her lips tightened. "Thanks to those creatures for whom you were so anxious to give your life, things were made doubly difficult for us. They gave the same names as ourselves. Fortunately, the Lieutenant foresaw this and added a note to our present pass saying that the people who had travelled before us were frauds. I can't understand what you see in that old vulgarian or that girl who was so obviously born in the gutter."

"We have rather a lot in common," I reminded her. "I am a vulgarian and I was born in the gutter."

"Yes, but you've had opportunities to forget it meeting people like myself and my friends." I laughed, and my weakness brought tears to my eyes. She looked gravely at me. "I was afraid you would be bound to feel certain ill effects, no matter how quickly we cut you down. But by making them do it so slowly, the Lieutenant prevented them from breaking your neck. You were only a short while actually hanging. But it's bound to have jarred your system."

"Yes, it's bound to have been a bit of a shock to him," Water Face added solicitously.

Lizzie held out her hands for the basin and began to clean my wounds.

I held out my hand for more brandy. Water Face filled my glass. "How in the world did the Lieutenant of Police bring off something like that with Bégnon looking on?"

"Bégnon helped him. The two of them pronounced you dead as soon as possible. Everyone else took their word."

My brandy spluttered into my face. "*Bégnon* helped! But he's the Committee of Public Safety. He's a notorious brute. He wouldn't miss an execution if it killed him."

Lizzie looked up at me. "It might kill him if he didn't. I understand he's a very staunch revolutionary, but at heart he's a very nice man. Bégnon is very powerful on the Committee of Public Safety, and the Lieutenant was more nervous of him than anybody. Then he discovered that Bégnon had helped a friend of his to escape. He kept it secret and Bégnon was grateful. He realised he could trust the Lieutenant, and they became friends. It was useful for us because only Bégnon had the power to agree to your being hanged instead of guillotined and to my taking home your body."

Water Face pointed out to me again, "You couldn't have come without your head."

Lizzie's hot sponge was helpful over my sore arms and legs. She was not gentle, but she was efficient.

My brandy spluttered into my face again when I recalled that I had wished her to retain the picture of my dead body hanging from a rope for the rest of her life! I recovered myself enough to say, "I'm surprised that they took such a risk."

She shrugged. "They've taken many, I believe, and this was less dangerous than some. After all, they both witnessed your execution. The handful of people with them were ordinary simple folk. They also saw you hang. It wouldn't have occurred to them that you were being strung up in front of members of the Committee of Public Safety and the Committee of General Security for the sole purpose of saving your life."

It was a point I could appreciate.

"Monsieur Bégnon," said Lizzie, "will continue to keep up his brutal reputation and use it to save people he thinks worth saving, including his own head. I find it hard to believe amongst the appalling kind of person who has risen to power, but apparently there are quite a few of them with similar inclinations."

"It must have annoyed the Lieutenant to have to cut me down."

"Yes," she said simply, "it did."

"There's one thing," said Water Face, making his only pertinent observation of the evening: "you must remember you're supposed to be dead. If you make any noise in that coffin, people might think you're alive."

Lizzie was looking her best to me. In point of fact she was still wearing the shade of churchyard moss which I most disliked. But to me it began to glow softly and enticingly in the candlelight. Apart from her extraordinary efforts on my behalf, I was beginning to think she must have sterling qualities to be able to put up with Water Face.

I felt this even more strongly the following day. When I was in my coffin again, comforted by the fact that I now knew that there were air holes, I lay waiting for Water Face and the ostler to load me onto the coach. Water Face dropped his end of my coffin on the staircase. The pain from the jolt made me cry out.

Lizzie made an immediate covering scene for which I could admire her even from the depths of my unpleasant accommodation. She railed at Water Face for showing such disrespect for her dead love, and she tried to imitate my groan as if it had been she who had emitted it in the first place. But the ostler was convinced he had heard the corpse moan and nothing would induce him to touch the coffin again. The landlord himself had to be fetched, and while I was being carried out, I could hear by the tone of his voice that he was suspicious. Why had the lady been so anxious to have the coffin accommodated in the house? It was usual in such cases to leave it in the stables. Where did we say we had come from? Where did we say we were going? The citoyenne must excuse him, but the road to Calais could be a dangerous one. So many aristocrats tried to cheat the Revolution of their heads. A patriot could never be too careful.

Lizzie evidently discovered him with his ear to my coffin lid, for I heard her say coldly, "You are not likely to hear my dear one breathe, citoyen. If you could, I should be the happiest woman in the world."

The man grunted and I was finally loaded onto the coach. My worst bruises had been padded with two of Lizzie's petticoats, which made it a tight squeeze in my travelling compartment, but lessened the agony. At the posting house in Péronne, Lizzie was worried. "That wretched ostler guessed," she told me. "Even before we left the inn I saw him ride back in the direction of Paris. He's probably gone to report his suspicions. I'm not sure they haven't been warned to look out for something here too. I didn't see a rider pass us on the way, but he may have taken a short cut. They certainly seemed to be expecting a coffin, and they made a great fuss about my bringing it up to Edward's room. If I hadn't thought it was too much for you, I wouldn't have stopped."

"What excuse did you give this time for bringing me up?"

"I said it was my custom to keep an all-night vigil by your side and did they expect me to kneel in the courtyard?"

Her usually neat hair had escaped its dull style and made her look girlish. She had more colour in her face from anxiety. It suited her. Her pallor had always been an uncanny contrast to the strength in her eyes.

Water Face was sent downstairs for extra candles to lend authenticity to Lizzie's vigil. I locked the door behind him so that I should have time to get back in my coffin if we were disturbed. I half expected Lizzie to protest at being sealed in a room alone with a common actor. I was making no effort to play Philippe. But she seemed perfectly content with me pacing up and down in my breeches and open shirt. We might have been an ancient married couple entirely used to one another's ways.

I sat on the arm of her chair as she sipped a brandy. That was another surprise to me about Miss Weldon. Her dressing-case contained two crystal and enamel bottles and she never retired without her glass of "eau-de-vie."

"Miss Weldon," I told her, "you've been more than good to me in view of the fact that I tried to trick you."

She raised big, strong eyes to me, and I was astonished to see that she was fighting against crying. To my distress she lifted my hand to her lips and kissed it. She lost the battle against the tears, and I felt their wet warmth on my wrist.

"I know you think me old and plain and useless —"

"I could never think you useless," I told her. "I shouldn't be alive if it weren't for you."

She said, "I hate your gratitude. I should prefer to have done nothing for you and feel that you found me attractive." I was about to say something fatuous, but with that odd insight of hers and her inability to be divorced from common sense, she cut me short. "Shush! Speak lower. Don't forget you're supposed to be dead."

I was making efforts to release my trapped hand, which was still the recipient of her cold-lipped passion. It is, I suppose, impossible for some people to express their emotion physically. She was shaking with desire for me mentally, but in practice I was receiving a series of little toothy blows on the back of my hand which embarrassed me because I knew that she herself felt them inadequate. I felt she wanted desperately to become warm and loose and at ease when she was with me, but the more she tried, the more frozen she became. Her pathetic efforts to become a normal giving woman stood between us like a third and sneering personage. It robbed me of any of the artificial gallantries that are the accepted warfare between the sexes when one side is trying to retreat. Marie-Clarice would have fought straight back and undoubtedly won; the Puce would have retired wounded and furious to plan a thoroughly dishonourable counter-attack. Almost any woman I had ever met would have done something. But Lizzie Weldon did nothing but rub her angular jaw over the back of my hand until it became quite sore; and she wept and wept and wept.

I tried to rally in a different manner. "Miss Weldon," I told her, "I admire you very much. Your appalling frankness, your ruthlessness, your determination to have your own way, the lengths to which you're willing to go to get it, and the straightforward manner in which you do it — that has its own fascination. At least it's nothing one could ever despise. I'm sorry I wasn't able to support you in your make-believe."

She closed her eyes, which was unfortunate. When they were open, one realised that one was up against an adversary, and respect was forced out of one. But when they were closed, they looked lashless and reminiscent of a piece of egg shell. She should never have closed her eyes.

When she opened them it was to enquire, "What about that little peasant girl who looks Chinese? Are you in love with her?"

I hedged. "I'm always being asked that question."

"Then one can only think that your attitude towards her must inspire it."

I was at a loss to know how to answer. The memory of Marie-Clarice was still fresh in my mind, but if I had had to choose between her and the Puce as I had been forced to choose between her and M.S., I should have chosen the Puce without hesitation. Perhaps that was the answer.

I was saved from replying to Lizzie by Water Face. He knocked at the door, calling in a whisper that could have been heard at the next stage, "It's all right. Don't worry, it's only me."

Lizzie turned the key irritably, and Water Face burst into the room carrying the candles. I was pleased to see him. I was embarrassed by emotional scenes with Miss Weldon. He stood like the natural idiot he was with the door wide open behind him. "I say," he said, "these people really do suspect he's alive."

Lizzie Weldon spoke in weary exasperation. "You're liable to convince them, Edward, if you give them such a good view of Mr. Roberts taking time off from his coffin."

Water Face sprang to close the door. I couldn't help being amused by what the innkeepers must think of the large suppers we ordered for poor Water Face. It was our only way of getting extra food for me.

"I say," he said, in a loudly conspiratorial voice, "they must have been warned here. I heard them discussing it. That ostler fellow's really on his way back to Paris. He's going to go to the Committee of General Security."

"He won't have to go all that distance," said Lizzie. "He'll meet the Lieutenant of Police on the way."

"What?" I shouted, and immediately lowered my voice. "Why will he meet him halfway?"

"Because the Lieutenant is naturally coming after us."

"I see nothing natural in it," I snapped. "You told me he was behind all this."

"He was. But neither he nor Bégnon could risk being thought an accomplice. He let it be known that he thought I had tricked him. He told the other committee members that he was certain he had heard movements inside the coffin. He gave us as much start as he could and then came after us. It just depends on how quickly we can travel and how much he can loiter without looking suspicious."

My heart felt as if it was beating in my stomach. "What happens if we don't make enough speed and he overtakes us."

She answered calmly, "He'll do his best to avoid that. He has gone to so much trouble on our behalf now. But, of course, if he caught up with us, he would have to rearrest you. What else could the poor man do?"

Chapter 57.

WITH THIS comforting piece of news, I was forced to climb back into my coffin. Lizzie thought she heard the boards creak outside the door and was afraid that someone was trying to look through the keyhole. We had not liked to block it for fear of causing more suspicion. When the landlord knocked a minute or two later, I was firmly boarded down with candles all round me, and Lizzie was on her knees praying.

The landlord had supposedly come to say that Miss Weldon was expected to pay for the room she had booked for herself, even if she wished to spend all night praying in her cousin's.

Affronted dignity came naturally to Lizzie. She stood up to inform the man that such insolence in her own country would be met with a well-merited beating. Ladies of her standing were not accustomed to being interrupted in moments of private grief. Nor were they inclined to cheat common persons out of their dues. She ordered him to get her carriage ready. She would proceed at once to an inn where the host was better equipped to receive bereaved gentlefolk. She must have been one of the very few people in France at that moment who dared to address a patriot with such a lack of equality.

He argued volubly, bringing up the old grievance about the British having used the bones of French prisoners of war to make soup, and on the way out said ominously that it wouldn't surprise him to find that dead men could tell tales after all.

Lizzie whispered through my air holes, "He knows. I'm afraid we shall have to travel all night. Can you bear it?"

I gave the one light tap we had arranged to mean "yes." I should have preferred anything to the Lieutenant's catching up with us, however reluctantly.

As we continued our journey I felt that I should never get accustomed to that painful form of travel. I tried to keep my thoughts on the Puce and M.S. and the joy of seeing them again, but I was battered into thinking of nothing but my aches and pains.

When we next stopped, Lizzie told me that we couldn't risk taking the coffin upstairs again. I should have to spend the night in the stables. Water Face, on the pretext of being a mad Englishman needing fresh air, would try and slip out to me with something to eat and drink. I must on no account push up the lid until he knocked.

There are few less pleasant ways to spend the night hours of an icy winter than in an ill-fitting wooden box on the floor of a draughty French stable. The noises of the horses' munching and shifting foot were my only company.

Fortunately, the stable lads and the inn servants were far too superstitious to come anywhere near a dead body. I could have carolled with relief when I heard a quiet rap on the coffin lid. I was hungry and dry-lipped with thirst.

But Water Face had not come to bring me refreshment; Lizzie Weldon was with him. She was dressed and held a lamp. "Get up," she ordered, "quickly! You've no time for food."

I heaved myself up stiffly. "Why?"

"It's our driver," she said. "He's been listening to tales at the other inns. He had the impertinence to tell me that he wouldn't take the carriage out of the yard tomorrow unless I let him open the coffin."

"What in the world shall we do?" said Water Face.

"Leave him behind, of course," snapped Lizzie.

"But then — who will drive us?"

"Mr. Roberts. I don't trust you when we're going fast."

I had been bending and unbending my aching knees. I straightened them immediately. "What about the police pass? It's only made out for you, Edward, and a corpse. I haven't any coachman's clothes."

"You won't need any," she told me. "You can speak English better than Edward. You will take his place, and he will take yours."

"In the *coffin*?" Water Face almost screamed.

Lizzie said, "Edward, why don't you go and rouse the inn staff one by one? It would wake them more surely than shouting."

The poor man took an appealing step towards her. "But — but why can't we leave the coffin empty?"

"Because you have just heard Mr. Roberts say that he hasn't the clothes to pass as a coachman and also we haven't the man's papers. Mr. Roberts will have to represent you on the pass. We couldn't risk the coffin's being found empty. There's no reason why my cousin shouldn't be driving me, and Mr. Roberts can be just as English as he can be French."

Water Face continued to argue against his fate. "He may well be able to take my place, but how can I take his? I can't speak French well enough to pass for a French vicomte."

Lizzie reminded him acidly, "You're supposed to be a dead one, Edward. There'll be no need for you to talk at all. Now, harness the horses, get out the carriage as quickly as possible, load the coffin, and when it's in place, get in it. Mr. Roberts will see you're nailed down."

"It gets better when all your bones are broken." I grinned at Water Face. "Once they're jelly it doesn't hurt so much."

It might have been mid-summer from the way I was sweating. I had never harnessed a pair of horses so fast in my life. By the time I was taking the carriage out, three lights had been lit in the posting house and shouting was coming from inside. The horses were nervous in the dark, and we hadn't time to light the carriage lamps. Water Face guided me out. We stowed the empty coffin inside with Lizzie, and Water Face jumped aboard. By the time we were out in the street, the postmaster was running into the yard with a coat over his nightshirt. Other figures came tumbling out after him.

I went at full gallop for two miles out of Péronne down a dangerously slippery road. The wet wind was viciously cold against my overheated face, and I suffered acutely from the unaccustomed pull on my arms.

Under some overhanging trees I drew up. Water Face climbed meekly out of the carriage and we loaded the coffin onto the luggage space.

"Get into it now, Edward," Lizzie ordered calmly, "and please try to support the journey with as much courage and fortitude as Mr. Roberts has shown."

Poor Water Face climbed into the coffin, and I tucked his clothes under him so that they did not block his air holes. "It's all good practice for the real thing," I told him wickedly, and lightly tapped the lid down.

I lit the carriage lamps before climbing back into the driving seat. Rain began to fall, and it stung my eyes as we raced along. I thanked God a dozen times for the excellence of French roads. It wouldn't have been possible to keep up such speed in England. But I was determined to keep ahead of the Lieutenant of Police. However good his intentions might be of loitering to give us a chance, if he had anyone else with him he would be forced to show some semblance of urgency in his pursuit.

At the rate we were going, Lizzie could scarcely have been more comfortable than Water Face. The carriage was badly sprung, and she rattled about inside it like a pebble in a box. I had to grant her that she was an admirable sportswoman. When discomfort was inevitable, she accepted it stoically.

It was when we were thundering towards Arras that I saw the road barrier. Three scruffy-looking officials waved me to stop.

I reined in and climbed down. The man who seemed to be in charge looked the kind of villain M.S. considered all Frenchmen to be. He came at me aggressively, and I greeted him in the worst possible French accent. I told him that I was Edward Small of Bristol and that I had permission from the authorities to conduct my cousin and the body of her dead lover to Calais.

He regarded me with much the same expression as the one which the Rare Sacrifice used to regard M.S.

I struggled as if I were trying to make my French more lucid and showed him the pass. There was some doubt as to how well he could read. He frowned over it and consulted his colleagues.

It occurred to me that the rider who had been suspicious of us at Troyes and had confided his suspicions to Roye might well have reached Arras. I made a point of talking English to Lizzie through the window.

M.S.'s ideal Frenchman continued to scratch his head with much vigour. He shambled across to me belching and smelling of wine. Why had the lady been allowed to remove her lover? Wasn't French soil good enough to cover him? I explained that they had been betrothed and that the lady had bought the body from the Committee of Public Safety.

It was then that I made the unpleasant discovery that while M.S.'s ideal might look a mere narrow-headed oaf promoted to uniform, he was far from a fool. Also he had a good memory. He recalled that an English Miss Weldon and an English Mr. Small had passed that way before but without the encumbrance of a dead body.

I couldn't control a quick spasm of joy. Presumably, if they had not been detained at Arras, the Puce and M.S. would have got through the barriers at Calais and were possibly over the water by now.

Taking out the police pass, I drew the attention of M.S.'s ideal to the Lieutenant's note stating that we had been impersonated.

He read it and consulted his colleagues. It occurred to me that as the postmaster at Varennes had been responsible for arresting the flight of the King and Queen, it was possibly the ambition of every minor official to be equally astute on escapes.

I think, however, that we should not have had any further trouble if Water Face had not sneezed at that moment. I realised his difficulties. It was impossible for him to raise his hand to stifle it, but nevertheless one would have liked to strangle him. Both Lizzie and I sneezed to cover it together. This double effort was unfortunate, as the brain of M.S.'s ideal could be seen working behind the eyes so painfully close to the bridge of his nose.

He said, "I must ask you to open your coffin."

He little knew how accurate he was in describing it as mine.

Swift thinking not being my strongest point, I was proud of myself. "Certainly," I said, "on one condition: that you allow the lady and myself to retire to a safe distance."

I opened the carriage door, helped Lizzie down, and made a great play of muffling her face up in her cloak. Then I wound a handkerchief round my own nose and prepared to lead Lizzie off.

M.S.'s ideal pulled at my arm. "Why are such precautions necessary?"

I sounded nasal through my mask. "Because the dead gentleman died very recently of the plague."

They looked at one another and then at me. I sneezed behind my mask.

M.S.'s ideal stepped further away from me, the sneeze being a symptom of the plague. He ordered us abruptly into the carriage and told us that we might proceed. The barrier was taken down and I drove off.

I was still breathing with relief when he galloped past us. He was riding a great sturdy black mare. We had evidently failed to remove his suspicions. He had decided that the authorities at St.-Omer could risk the plague by opening the coffin, and was riding ahead to warn them. We were hastily trapped between the advancing Lieutenant and the guards waiting for us at the barrier of St.-Omer. There was no other road, and we could not desert the carriage and take to our feet. There seemed only one thing to do, and that was to try and bluff it out. It might be better to arrive after dark. Water Face would look more corpselike in artificial light. But to go too slowly would mean lessening the distance between ourselves and the Lieutenant. I stopped the carriage and climbed down. To Lizzie I said, "Try and look as if you're sickening. Keep on sneezing and behave as if you're ill."

Then I climbed up to the luggage space, rapped on the coffin, and asked Water Face the same fatuous question he had asked me. "Edward, are you all right? Would you like a glass of wine?"

Lizzie put her head out of the window. "Don't be ridiculous, Mr. Roberts. Supposing we were passed on the road? It would look most eccentric to be seen giving wine to a dead man."

I saw the point and shouted at Water Face, "If your coffin's opened, for God's sake look as dead as you can!"

Dusk had fallen two hours before we saw the lights of the road barrier guarding St.-Omer. To aid matters, the cold rain had turned to snow. It spun round our carriage lamps and hurled itself into my face — the snow I had so longed to see again in my cell at the Conciergerie. I thought of it piling up on Water Face's coffin and probably blocking his air holes. In defiance of Lizzie I climbed down to have a look. As I did so I saw snow-smeared lights bobbing towards us from the St.-Omer direction. Someone was riding out to meet us.

I pretended to examine a wheel. We were surrounded by five armed men. Amongst them was M.S.'s ideal. The first lantern carrier introduced himself courteously as Louis Charnier and told me to take down our coffin and open it unless we wished to be packed in with its doubtful occupant on the instant.

Inside the carriage Lizzie groaned and sneezed. I stepped up to Charnier. "Kindly be as quick as possible: my cousin has a high fever. I must get her to a doctor immediately. The citoyen De Lambrière, whose body we're carrying, died of the plague and I'm very afraid that my cousin has caught it."

The two men staring at Lizzie through the opposite window removed themselves quickly, but Charnier did not appear alarmed. "I have had the plague," he told me unctuously, "and they say that one does not contract it again." He was a big man, and the snow climbed into great white epaulets on his shoulders.

He signalled to the two men to take down the coffin. It was lowered into the dark slush the horses were making of the snow on the road. M.S.'s ideal was standing a good twenty feet away with a stringy-looking cravat held tightly over his nose.

Charnier knelt beside the coffin. He put all his strength under the blade with which he prized open the lid. It practically flew into his face. Our nails were little more than tapped into place.

The snow, as if morbidly curious, began piling into the coffin. Lizzie, as usual, was admirable. She was a grave loss to the theatre. She burst out of the carriage and lurched forward to kneel in the slush by the coffin. "Philippe!" she choked, "my Philippe!"

Charnier moved her gently aside, and I went forward to assist her. It was at that moment that Charnier lifted his lantern and the others gathered round at a respectful distance.

My heart gave a convulsive jerk. Water Face had no need to pretend to look dead. The snow had made a white line up his body and sat on his hair and face. His jaw had dropped stiffly onto his chest, his eyes were closed, and his skin was the colour of poor tallow. His whole body was lifeless and as wooden as his coffin.

Lizzie's shocked gasp was genuine. I myself had the utmost difficulty in not crying out. Charnier replaced the lid and gave the order to bang down the nails. Then he examined our pass, gave us the name of a good doctor in St.-Omer who had saved him from the plague, and gave us permission to proceed.

But we could scarcely draw up at any doctor's door and ask him to attend the occupant of a coffin. Speed was essential through St.-Omer. The town was shuttered and bleak-looking in the flying snow. The roads were dangerous now, but I knew that if by any chance Water Face had not actually died in that coffin, he would not survive it long.

The barrier at the other end of the town was not troublesome. The pass and the fact that we had been allowed into the town allayed all suspicion.

As soon as I felt it a safe distance I drew up on the dark road that led towards Calais. Lizzie, realising my intentions, jumped down to help me.

She was subdued but still practical. "He was never very strong as a child," she offered. "From what I saw at the barrier I'm afraid there's not much hope." And she added with a touch of irritation, "You supported it all right."

"I happened to be exceptionally strong as a child," I snapped at her.

I hacked at the cords holding the coffin and worked on the nails with the wrench we had brought. But the nails were far more heavily embedded than before. Lizzie stood by with the snow clinging to her. She shouted up at me, "Be quick. If the Lieutenant overtakes us alone it will be all right, but if he's got someone with him he'll have to arrest us."

I had snow in my ears, eyes, and nose. It fell in my mouth when I went to speak, slid down my neck, and made useless members of my hands.

At last the coffin lid lifted. I pushed it back and groped for Water Face. His body was frozen and stiff. I could hardly put it over my shoulder. Climbing down, I nearly dropped him, but I managed to get him onto the carriage seat. I noticed patches of hard blood on his blue hands. Poor Water Face had been knocking for help.

The lights were not good. One of them had blown out as we raced along. I pushed a hand under his jacket. His flesh was so cold it almost stung me. There seemed to be no sign of a living heart. I put a thumb on his eyelids and peered underneath them. His eyes were rolled up towards his forehead.

Lizzie climbed in beside me. She pulled a feather out of her bonnet. "We shall have to make up our minds, Mr. Roberts. If he's dead, we must put him back in the coffin. If he's still alive, we must get to Calais."

I took the feather and held it in front of his nose. It trembled so slightly I was a few seconds in making up my mind that it was not the shaking of my own hand.

I said, "Miss Weldon, rub his hands and feet as hard as you can. I'm going to close down the coffin. We shall have to risk its being found empty."

When I came back she said, "He moaned."

We both worked on his hands and feet. His jaw closed painfully and his eyes flickered open. Lizzie opened her dressing-case and took out the eau-de-vie. We poured as much as we could down his throat. He spluttered and retched, but made a feeble effort to sit himself up.

"Wrap him in the rug," I told Lizzie, "and if we're stopped, for God's sake try to hide him in it."

The horses upset by the snow were not easy to handle. I prayed that we could reach Calais without having to change at a stage.

I imagine that we had about seven leagues to travel, which, roughly calculated, meant about nineteen miles. It was snowing harder than ever and I couldn't keep up the pace. We stopped at a tiny village and I took out a tray of hot food to Water Face. He revived considerably after it.

Lizzie said, "We must stop on the outskirts of Calais, Mr. Roberts, and you must get back in the coffin. We shall never get through the barrier otherwise.

Edward will be well enough to drive us into the town. But go carefully, Edward. There will be no need to speed so close to our destination."

When the horses were refreshed I set off again. Within what I judged to be half a mile from Calais, I stopped and climbed down. Water Face was still weak but able to drive. Lizzie kept up a flow of cautions and was obviously more afraid of being driven by Water Face than of anything else we had had to endure on the journey.

He helped me back into the snow-soaked coffin with what I thought was a certain amount of satisfaction. I felt the cold sinking into my bones and wondered if I should arrive in as poor a condition as he had.

He was certainly no hand with the reins. The horses bolted with him at first and then, when he gained control of them, refused to move. I could feel us going backwards at one point. I could see why Lizzie had been so insistent that I should drive for the major proportion of the journey. Left to Water Face, we should probably have gone steadily backwards all the way to Paris, mowing down the Lieutenant en route.

At last we came to a grumbling stop. I heard shouts and voices and realised that we were at the Calais barrier. Apparently there were no difficulties, for we jerked forward almost immediately.

I can remember hearing no sweeter sound than the ringing of the bells of the Hôtel de Ville. When I first heard them in Calais I never imagined that the next time I listened to their delightful chimes would be from the inside of a coffin!

We rolled on and finally I felt myself being unloaded. We were in the courtyard of an inn.

The ostlers had small respect for the dead. I was dropped on the ground with no ceremony. Had I not by then learned to bite my lips during loading and unloading, I should have groaned aloud and given us away on the last stage of our journey.

I heard Lizzie making her usual request to have the coffin placed in her cousin's room so that she might keep her vigil in front of it. The usual offer to pay extra had its desired effect. I felt myself being heaved up again.

I was lowered fairly swiftly presumably in the foyer. The host informed Lizzie that persons claiming to be herself and her cousin had already spent the night with him, to his detriment.

My heart gave a kick of joy. M.S. and the Puce had reached Calais! I realised that we were at Meurice's Hotel. It was obvious that M.S. should choose to return to the place he knew.

Lizzie apparently showed her pass and set old Meurice clucking in sympathy. "You don't surprise me, citoyenne. These people were thieves as well as frauds. Not only did they order all my best dishes, but they left without paying their bill and took several of my most valued possessions with them.

When I tried to trace them in the town, I found that they had sold my things in return for a passage on an English boat."

From the depths of my cold, dark coffin, I smiled happily.

I was shouldered again. I gathered from the steep angle that I was being carried upstairs.

In Water Face's bedroom I was released and made straight for the fire like a frozen cat. Water Face, poor boy, retired straight to bed with a mugful of hot brandy.

Lizzie took her supper opposite me. "I should like to make it clear to you, Mr. Roberts, that I do not expect you to have anything to do with those appalling friends of yours in England, particularly the girl. If you make any effort to get in touch with them, I shall hand over your confession of murder to the nearest magistrate."

"I haven't signed it yet, Miss Weldon."

"You will," she assured me, "you will. My boat will leave on the first tide tomorrow morning, so I suggest we shut our eyes while we can."

I noticed that she did not shut hers at all. She kept them steadily fixed on me. She need not have deprived herself of much needed sleep. It would have been pointless of me to escape and try my own luck over to England. I should simply have laid myself open to immediate arrest. My only assured escape was in my coffin.

In the early hours Lizzie ordered breakfast, and after it I climbed into my unpleasant travelling compartment — I hoped for the last time.

The unfortunate Water Face woke up with a scarlet nose, running eyes, and a chill on his kidneys. "I say, I shan't be sorry to get home," he said lamely. "I've not enjoyed myself in France."

Lizzie and he nailed me in, and I was loaded on the carriage to take us to the quay. I was no longer concerned about the Lieutenant of Police; it would only be the worst luck in the world if he caught up with us now. But I was worried about the confession. I had no doubt that Lizzie Weldon would use it if the need arose. I had spent enough time in her company now to realise that she was every bit as great a scoundrel as myself. Perhaps I could delay signing it until we were well out in the Channel. She would never risk putting back herself and she could hardly have me thrown overboard. Once in England, it should not be difficult to escape her.

I was aware of my debt to Miss Weldon. No woman could have done more for me, but I looked on it as the paying of her own debt to me. Had she not driven me out of my own country in the first place, she never would have had to go to such trouble to get me back to it. However grateful I felt for the courage and ingenuity she had shown on my behalf, I didn't think it called for a life sentence of gratitude.

It was obviously my duty in the interests of M.S. and the Puce to trick her at the first opportunity.

Oh, those heaven-sent sounds of the sea! I could hear the bellowing of sailors, the waves harrying the jetty, and all the happy noises of a busy quay. I could hardly believe that I should once again be landing in Dover.

But I was being carried up the gangplank. I could hear the sailors swear as they were instructed to take their unwieldly burden down to the cabin. I was dropped once again without tenderness, and I could feel the roll of the ship through my coffin.

Then I heard Lizzie Weldon's voice. "Mr. Roberts, I think the time has come for you to sign that little piece of paper for me."

"I can't very well sign it in here," I complained.

"You will not be required to. But if you don't do it when you come out, you'll be taken ashore again."

I thought the threat more dramatic than practical. She and Water Face would have a hard time persuading me to get off the boat.

When they let me out I feigned dizziness. I staggered to a narrow little berth and collapsed on it. "It's the strain," I said. "Now it's all over, I feel as weak as a child."

"Then grow up again, Mr. Roberts," she advised. "Because it isn't all over. We shall not sail until you've signed."

I decided to call her bluff. "If we stay too long we shall miss the tide and get caught by the Lieutenant of Police."

"We shall not have to miss a tide to do that."

As she spoke a pair of feet climbed down the gangway into the cabin. They were followed by the knees, stomach, chest, and finally the face of the Lieutenant of Police.

Chapter 58.

THE LIEUTENANT'S appearance was evidently as great a surprise to Water Face as it was to me. We both gaped at him. Lizzie informed us, "I arranged not to sail until the Lieutenant overtook us in case Mr. Roberts became difficult about the little piece of paper I want him to sign. There were risks attached to it, of course, but my nature has never been shy of those. If the Lieutenant had not been allowed to follow us alone, or if we had been seriously held up, he would have been forced to arrest us all." She smiled amiably at me. "Now, then, Mr. Roberts, if you do not sign this paper, the Lieutenant will have you put ashore and we shall sail without you." She pushed the confession towards me.

I signed "Philippe Jean-Baptiste-Raoul Vicomte de Lambrière" with an angry flourish.

She put a stroke right through it. "I should prefer you to sign your real name, if you please."

I signed "Philippe Jean-Baptiste-Raoul *Roberts*."

She picked up the paper and tucked it far down the front of her dress between what I could only imagine were breasts and stays. "Now, I don't think even your skill will be able to remove it from there, Philippe, and if you try, I shall be very displeased. Edward, go up on deck and order the captain to get under way at once."

The Lieutenant of Police sat on the opposite berth grinning maliciously at me. "I had a most anxious journey," he told me, "wondering if you would be stopped at the barriers."

"We didn't enjoy it either," I snapped back at him.

Lizzie opened her dressing-case and got out the bottles of eau-de-vie. It was then that I became aware of the movements of the boat. I shouted in astonishment, "We're sailing!"

Lizzie said icily, "Naturally, Mr. Roberts. Did you expect us all to transfer to a balloon?"

I pointed, practically speechless, at the Lieutenant. "But — but *he's* still on board."

Lizzie poured out the brandy. "The Lieutenant is travelling with us."

I jumped to my feet, bumped my head, and sat down again. *"Travelling* with us!"

The Lieutenant said, "Come, come, Mr. Roberts, did you think you were the only person anxious to get out of France at this moment?"

Lizzie passed us both a drink. "It was as vital for the Lieutenant to have our plans go right as it was for us."

The Lieutenant raised his brandy to me. "Escape isn't easy, Mr. Roberts, especially for a person in my position. There's no one so closely watched as me. One has to wait for a good opportunity. You robbed me of the first one."

I managed to say to Lizzie, "Did you know I was not in any real danger from him all the time?"

The Lieutenant answered for her. "You were in acute danger," he said. "If anything had gone wrong, I should have been quite powerless to help you. I should have denied all knowledge of the trick. I warned Miss Weldon about that, and she agreed to take the risk. But I was every bit as anxious for you to succeed as you were yourselves. One doesn't often get the chance of pursuing people in the nature of duty right on board an English ship and then putting to sea whilst still interrogating them!"

"It must be a great relief for you, Lieutenant," Lizzie said kindly. "You were on the verge of arrest yourself, weren't you?"

He nodded. "So Bégnon told me. If I hadn't extracted Mr. Roberts' confession, I should have joined him in the Conciergerie."

"Well, now you must forget all your troubles. After all, you're not a stranger to England like most of the émigrés."

The Lieutenant smiled at me again. "Miss Weldon has offered me the hospitality of her home. I shall have the pleasure of attending your wedding."

I stood up again. "My wedding!"

Lizzie also smiled at me. "I wrote to Sir Gregory and told him to expect us. He has made all the arrangements."

I did not think it was my imagination that her hand stroked the piece of paper tucked down in her dress.

I spent the rest of the journey on deck. I could no longer endure the evil smile of the Lieutenant of Police, and his constant references to my coming marriage came near to wrecking my joy in seeing England again.

I leaned over the side of the ship, my eyes straining to catch the first sign of those white cliffs that have affected so many homecomers. My chief concern was how to rejoin M.S. and the Puce. When I told M.S. so gallantly that I would meet him in Dover, he had no reason to suppose that I was lying. He would be waiting for me there. My excitement at the thought of seeing his great black figure and crooked wig again was schoolboyish. Mine was not a solid world without M.S., and I was astonished at the strength of my longing to see the Puce again. There would be the same irritations, I supposed — the same reluctance on my part to be dominated, and the same tendency to quarrel with her. But there would be a pleasure I found hard to describe even to myself. It was nothing like the sensation I had experienced on seeing Marie-Clarice — and yet in a strange way it was the same.

When we put into harbour I was gripping the sides of the boat as I scanned the crowds. Surely they would be waiting! I looked and looked — but there was no sign of them. It was possible, I thought, that they had waited so long they had given up hope. But I felt, unreasonably, that people whom I loved and who loved me should have had second sight. They should have known *instinctively* that I was coming on this particular boat. I felt that they had betrayed the intimacy and the understanding between us. I became indignant to the point of fury.

Lizzie Weldon moved quietly to my side. The expression on her pale face was both sympathetic and reproachful. She said gently, "Mr. Roberts, I hope you are not expecting those friends of yours to meet you."

I defended them at once. "Of course not. How could they possibly know which boat I was coming on?"

She smiled. "Even if they did know, Mr. Roberts, I don't think they would have waited for you. Persons of that class are inclined to put their own fortunes first. I'm afraid you'll be very disappointed if you expect loyalty from them. They will have given you up by now and taken themselves off to find someone else to support them in a life of idleness. The old man has lived on you ever since you were a boy, and that girl is obviously willing to sell herself to any man ready to pay. I'm telling you this for your own good. You will miss them much less if you face the fact that they are utterly worthless. They will have abandoned you long ago, so there is no point in looking for them."

She left me before I could give the reply I had been rehearsing in my mind. I was obliged to swear softly at the sea gulls wheeling round the boat. By the time I actually set foot on English soil I was practically in a worse humour than I was at the moment when the gendarme turned the key of the Mousetrap behind me. The white cliffs of Dover were obscured by a nagging drizzle and Dover was a place of soggy gloom. In the congestion on the jetty there was still no sign of M.S. or the Puce, and I was in no mood for poor Sir Gregory.

He had not aged at all since I saw him last. He had the same youthful spring in his step, the same clean smile, and the same talent for understatement. "My dear De Lambrière! I don't mind telling you that I tried to persuade Eliza not to go to France in such restless times. I was afraid that something untoward would overtake you both. But here you are alive! Splendid! Splendid! Ah! Brissac!" He pumped the Lieutenant's delicate hand. "Now perhaps you see that I was right. Never let them get the bit between their teeth." He winked one bright and healthy eye at me. "I don't imagine, De Lambrière, that you will object to my giving your future bride a kiss?"

He was denied the pleasure. The drizzle turned to a heavy shower, and Lizzie threw her cloak over her head.

In that moment I saw a giant black mushroom open above the heads of the crowd. I ran towards it. They were both sheltering under it. The Puce looked unnaturally tall because she was perched on a pair of wooden pattens to keep her out of the puddles. Her hair hung glistening and heavy over her shoulders, and her black eyes glared furiously at me.

M.S.'s relief at seeing me again took the form of an ill-humour equal to my own. All the anxiety he felt on my behalf was put into a fierce whisper. "And where have *you* been, boy? We've come to meet boat after boat. I've caught a sciatica waiting about."

The Puce's new height made it easy for her to give me a quick kiss on the lips, but her voice was disapproving. "He is thinner. He has been sporting with the English Miss Weldon."

I snapped at her, "I made the journey in a coffin, and you can't sport in that."

M.S. said weightily, "It was very wrong of you to dilly-dally, boy. You must have known we'd be waiting for you, and Dover's no place to hang about in. There isn't an honest soul in it. We've had to move our lodgings twice and not a chance to walk out without paying."

"It was the cook in the last place," explained the Puce. "He tried to kiss me in the hall, and in my bosom I had some of his knives and forks."

"The girl's been a marvel," said M.S. proudly. "If it hadn't been for her we shouldn't have lasted out so long. But you shouldn't have kept us hanging about. You know better than anyone that you can't Lord Credit it in one place for too long. What *possessed* you to dilly-dally?"

I had intended that my voice should sound icily reproachful, but I only achieved a rather shrill pomposity. "I should like you to know that I had made a pact with the Lieutenant of Police to sacrifice my life for yours. I nearly died on your behalf."

M.S. might not have heard me. "Your fondness for comfort, boy, will get you into trouble one day," he snorted. "Travelling back in style with that woman as though you hadn't a need to hurry in the world. Playing the dandy at inns with rich old harpies at a time like this!"

"I travelled," I tried to tell him acidly, "in a —"

The Puce put a hand on my arm. She was wearing her leave-him-to-me-Uncle-I-understand-men expression. "It isn't that we *don't* believe you. I'm sure you would do something *very* brave for us — if you had the chance."

"I *did* have the chance," I shouted at her. "I was hanged for you!"

"Don't overact, boy," ordered M.S. "I tell you your dilly-dallying has put us in danger. The people of Dover are becoming too interested in us for our own good. We shall have to leave at once and get some sort of engagement. The little knick-knacks that the girl and I have been able to remove from our lodgings have all gone in keeping us alive while we waited for you. We might try our act from the Petit Théâtre de la Cité. It should go down well in certain places. With the money we make from that we can cross to Cork. From there we can get to America. We can't cross from Bristol. We might run into the Rare Sacrifice. So we'll get to Cork as quickly as we can. I have written a very good letter from Kemble to the manager of the John Street Theatre in New York — what's the matter?"

I shrugged. "Oh, nothing. It's just that part of the 'dilly-dallying' I did on your behalf has put me under contract to marry Miss Weldon."

The Puce stepped away from me. I pulled her back.

"*What* have you done, boy?" demanded M.S.

"Signed a confession that I killed Nicholas Hawtrey."

"Why?"

"Because if I hadn't I should have been left behind in Calais."

M.S. was good enough to say nothing more than "oh!" but the Puce threw herself into my arms. I held her warm, lithe body to me.

"I'm glad!" she said. "I'm glad he signed it! It's better for him to marry the terrible Miss Weldon than go back to France."

M.S. asked me, "Did you see where she put the confession?"

"In her bosom."

"Then fish it out."

The Puce looked up. "He is not to take anything out of Miss Weldon's bosom."

I said, "Even if I tried I couldn't manage that. She keeps one hand firmly clasped over it."

Water Face approached us. He coughed in embarrassment at the sight of the Puce in my arms. "Lizzie says . . ." His hesitation enabled me to imagine what Lizzie had really said, but he amended it to, "Lizzie says she's ready to start." Then he withdrew a tactful ten paces.

"Listen to me, boy," said M.S. "We'll wait for you in Cork, but we can't wait for ever. The Irish have suspicious natures too. If you're not an actor and a marker by now, it's through no fault of mine. God knows I've given you a good enough education. If you can't think of a way out of marrying Miss Weldon, you're a fool — and not worth the boards I was hoping to put under you!"

"He's not a fool!" the Puce said loyally. It was the first time she had ever openly supported me against M.S. I kissed her.

Sir Gregory blew his coaching horn.

"Boy," said M.S., "we'll wait for you in Cork."

He walked away from me in the falling rain without looking back as he had done so many years ago; but the Puce's little head kept turning as she stumbled along. She became smaller and smaller, and I could still see her looking round to get a last glimpse of me.

I walked back with Water Face to the coach containing Lizzie, Sir Gregory, and the Lieutenant of Police.

Lizzie and Sir Gregory were already inside. The Lieutenant was standing by the step. He made a clicking noise with his tongue as I came up. "Your future bride doesn't like to be kept waiting. I expect you will have to learn that."

I glared at him, and he added as he assisted me courteously into the carriage, "Do you remember my saying that nothing would give me greater pleasure than the thought of the punishment you were about to undergo?"

I was wedged between him and Lizzie, who put her cold, bony hand into mine. As we started off I wrenched my neck round to look back. M.S. and the Puce were nearly obscured by the giant umbrella. They were plodding steadily forward like a stalwart father and daughter determined to take the sea air no matter what the weather.

Sir Gregory said, "Well, de Lambrière, it's going to be my pleasure to give the bride away."

"I had hoped" — the Lieutenant smiled — "that it was going to be mine. There is no romance I have been more happy to see come to fruition."

I was too dignified to glare at him again. But it was a desolate feeling to know that only one's native dishonesty stood between marriage to Miss Weldon or hanging at Tyburn.

For the first five miles of that warming English countryside I had practically cried from the longing to see again, I stared blankly in front of me at Water Face. We must have travelled ten miles before it occurred to me that as an insurance against need, it might be wise to transfer the Lieutenant's watch and fob to my own pocket.

It could not have been until Canterbury that it also occurred to me to remove his papers. When your own name is a matter of interest to the law and you wish to leave the country quickly, you never know when someone else's identity might be useful.